THE WALKING DEAD

BOOK TEN

a continuing story of survival horror.

created by Robert Kirkman

image comics presents

The Walking Dead

book ten

ROBERT KIRKMAN
creator, writer

CHARLIE ADLARD
penciler, inker (chapter 19), cover

STEFANO GAUDIANO
inker (chapter 20)

CLIFF RATHBURN
gray tones

RUS WOOTON
letterer

SEAN MACKIEWICZ
editor

Original series covers by
CHARLIE ADLARD, CLIFF RATHBURN & DAVE STEWART

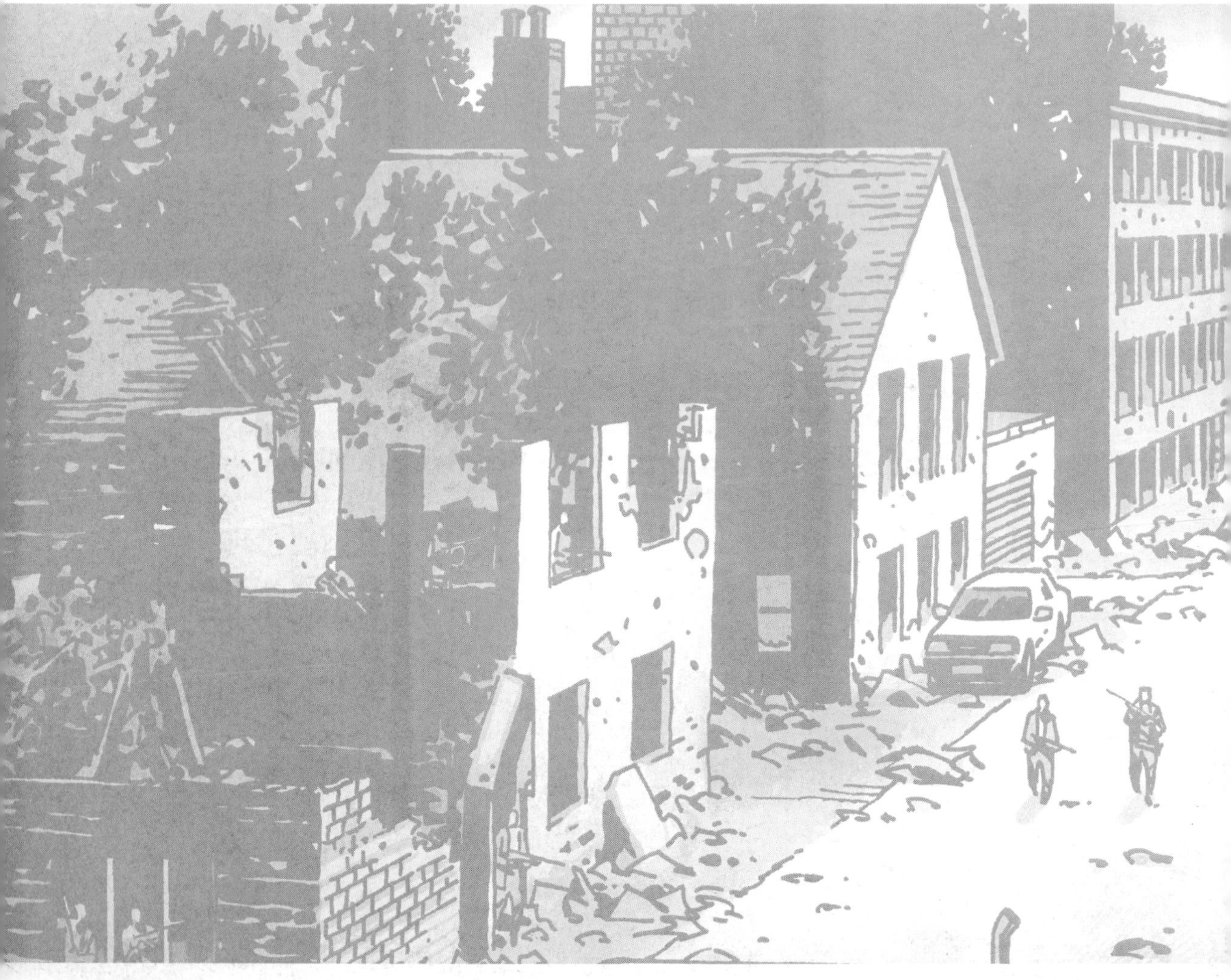

Robert Kirkman
chief executive officer

Sean Mackiewicz
editorial director

Shawn Kirkham
director of business development

www.skybound.com

Brian Huntington
online editorial director

June Alian
publicity director

Helen Leigh
assistant editor

Rachel Skidmore
office manager

Lizzy Iverson
administrative assistant

Dan Petersen
operations manager

Nick Palmer
operations coordinator

Robert Kirkman
chief operating officer

Erik Larsen
chief financial officer

Todd McFarlane
president

Marc Silvestri
chief executive officer

Jim Valentino
vice-president

Eric Stephenson
publisher

Ron Richards
director of business development

Jennifer de Guzman
director of trade book sales

Kat Salazar
director of pr & marketing

Jeremy Sullivan
director of digital sales

Emilio Bautista
sales assistant

Branwyn Bigglestone
senior accounts manager

Emily Miller
accounts manager

Jessica Ambriz
administrative assistant

Tyler Shainline
events coordinator

David Brothers
content manager

Jonathan Chan
production manager

Drew Gill
art director

Meredith Wallace
print manager

Monica Garcia
senior production artist

Jenna Savage
production artist

Addison Duke
production artist

Tricia Ramos
production assistant

www.imagecomics.com

Chapter Nineteen:
March To War

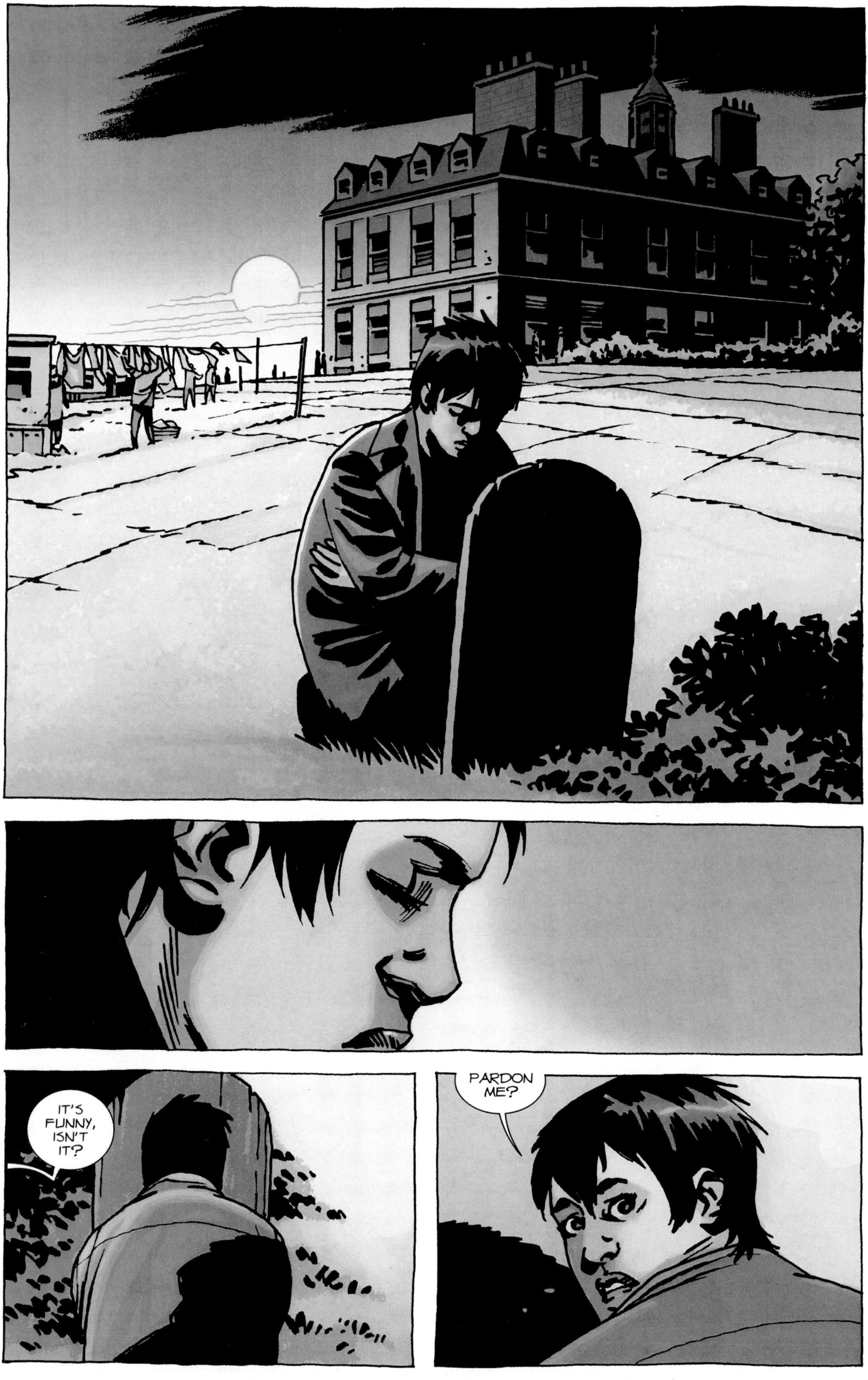
IT'S FUNNY, ISN'T IT?
PARDON ME?

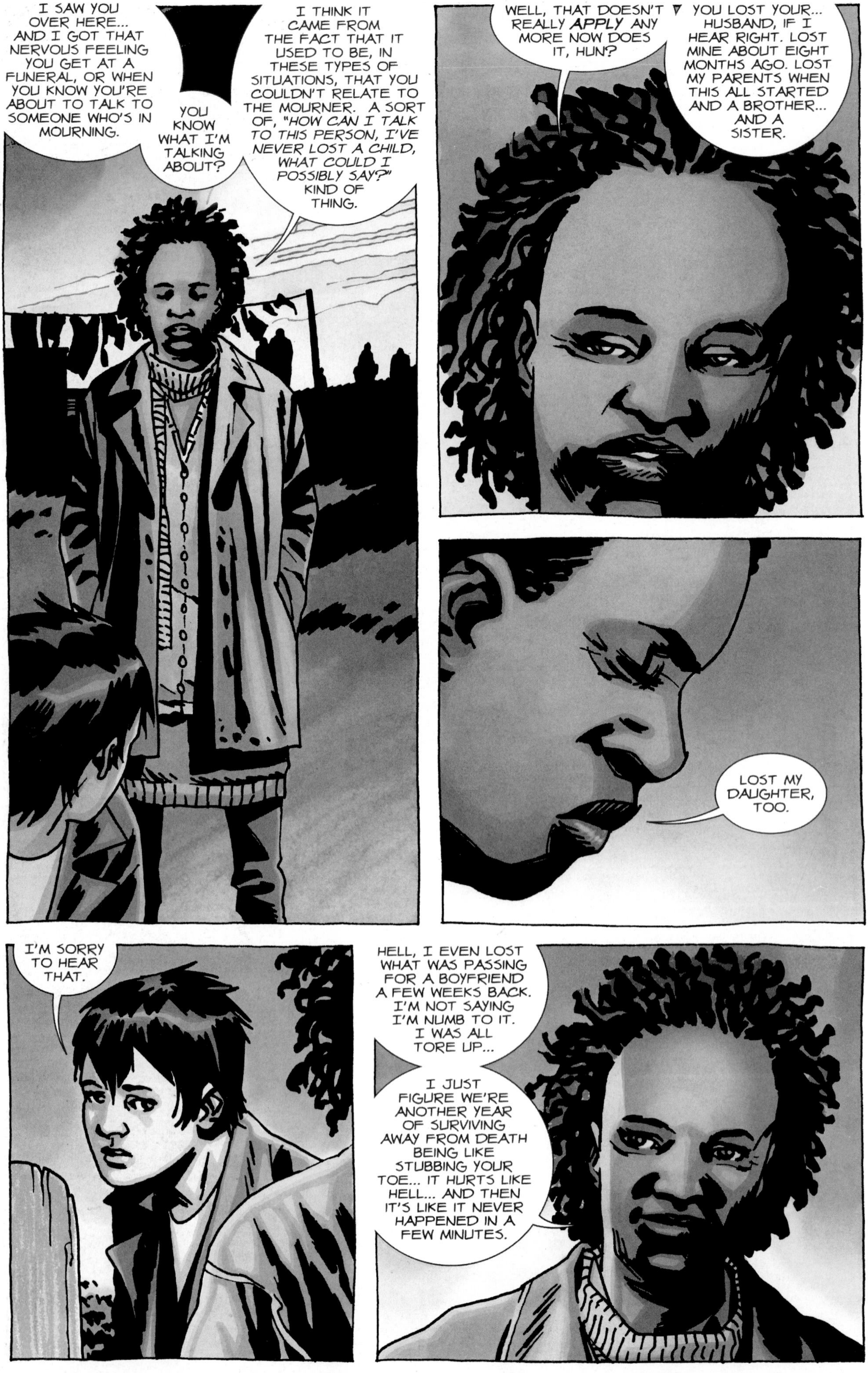
I SAW YOU OVER HERE... AND I GOT THAT NERVOUS FEELING YOU GET AT A FUNERAL, OR WHEN YOU KNOW YOU'RE ABOUT TO TALK TO SOMEONE WHO'S IN MOURNING.
YOU KNOW WHAT I'M TALKING ABOUT?
I THINK IT CAME FROM THE FACT THAT IT USED TO BE, IN THESE TYPES OF SITUATIONS, THAT YOU COULDN'T RELATE TO THE MOURNER. A SORT OF, "HOW CAN I TALK TO THIS PERSON, I'VE NEVER LOST A CHILD, WHAT COULD I POSSIBLY SAY?" KIND OF THING.
WELL, THAT DOESN'T REALLY APPLY ANY MORE NOW DOES IT, HUN?
YOU LOST YOUR... HUSBAND, IF I HEAR RIGHT. LOST MINE ABOUT EIGHT MONTHS AGO. LOST MY PARENTS WHEN THIS ALL STARTED AND A BROTHER... AND A SISTER.
LOST MY DAUGHTER, TOO.
I'M SORRY TO HEAR THAT.
HELL, I EVEN LOST WHAT WAS PASSING FOR A BOYFRIEND A FEW WEEKS BACK. I'M NOT SAYING I'M NUMB TO IT. I WAS ALL TORE UP...
I JUST FIGURE WE'RE ANOTHER YEAR OF SURVIVING AWAY FROM DEATH BEING LIKE STUBBING YOUR TOE... IT HURTS LIKE HELL... AND THEN IT'S LIKE IT NEVER HAPPENED IN A FEW MINUTES.

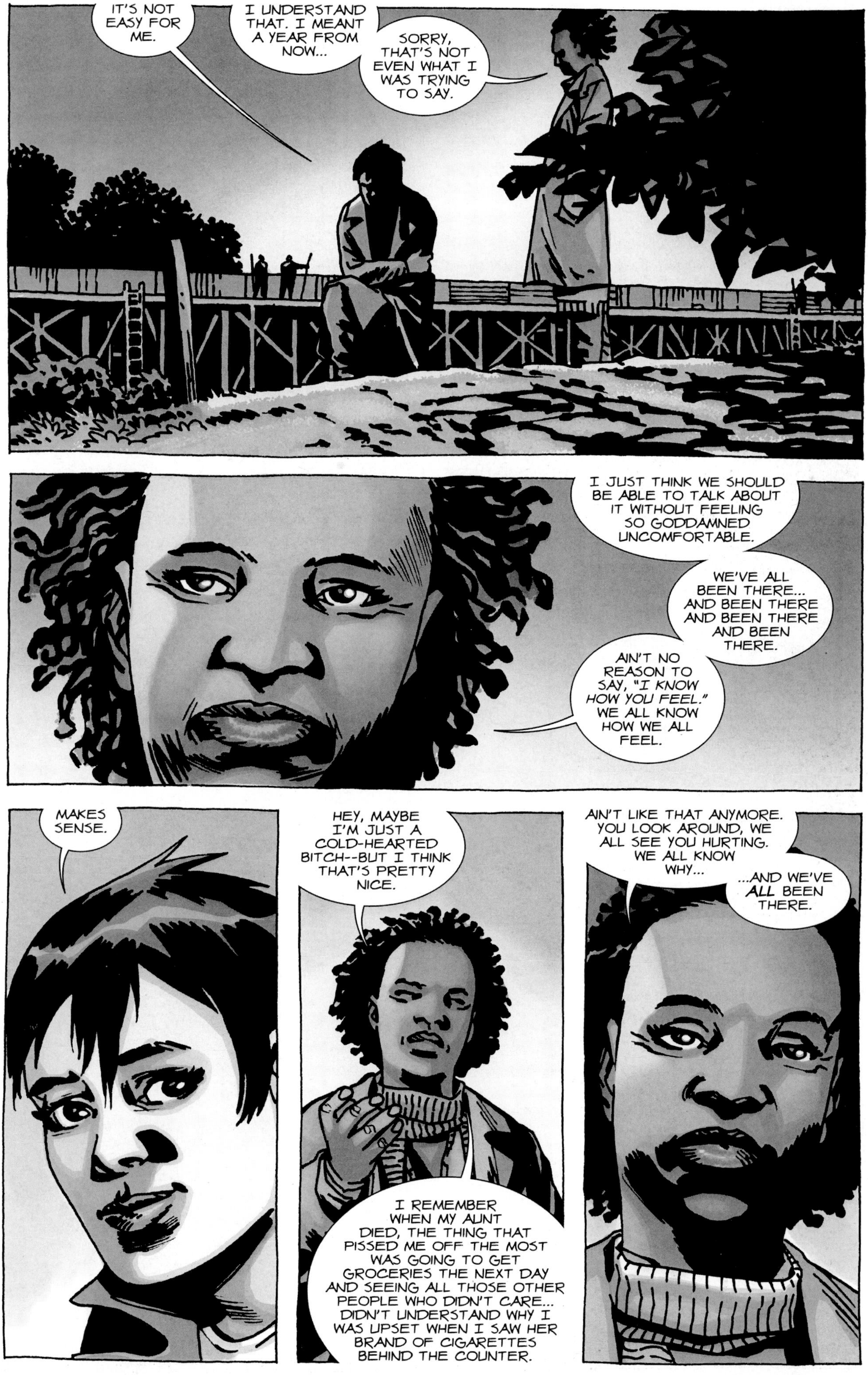
IT'S NOT EASY FOR ME.
I UNDERSTAND THAT. I MEANT A YEAR FROM NOW...
SORRY, THAT'S NOT EVEN WHAT I WAS TRYING TO SAY.
I JUST THINK WE SHOULD BE ABLE TO TALK ABOUT IT WITHOUT FEELING SO GODDAMNED UNCOMFORTABLE.
WE'VE ALL BEEN THERE... AND BEEN THERE AND BEEN THERE AND BEEN THERE.
AIN'T NO REASON TO SAY, "I KNOW HOW YOU FEEL." WE ALL KNOW HOW WE ALL FEEL.
MAKES SENSE.
HEY, MAYBE I'M JUST A COLD-HEARTED BITCH--BUT I THINK THAT'S PRETTY NICE.
I REMEMBER WHEN MY AUNT DIED, THE THING THAT PISSED ME OFF THE MOST WAS GOING TO GET GROCERIES THE NEXT DAY AND SEEING ALL THOSE OTHER PEOPLE WHO DIDN'T CARE... DIDN'T UNDERSTAND WHY I WAS UPSET WHEN I SAW HER BRAND OF CIGARETTES BEHIND THE COUNTER.
AIN'T LIKE THAT ANYMORE. YOU LOOK AROUND, WE ALL SEE YOU HURTING. WE ALL KNOW WHY...
...AND WE'VE ALL BEEN THERE.

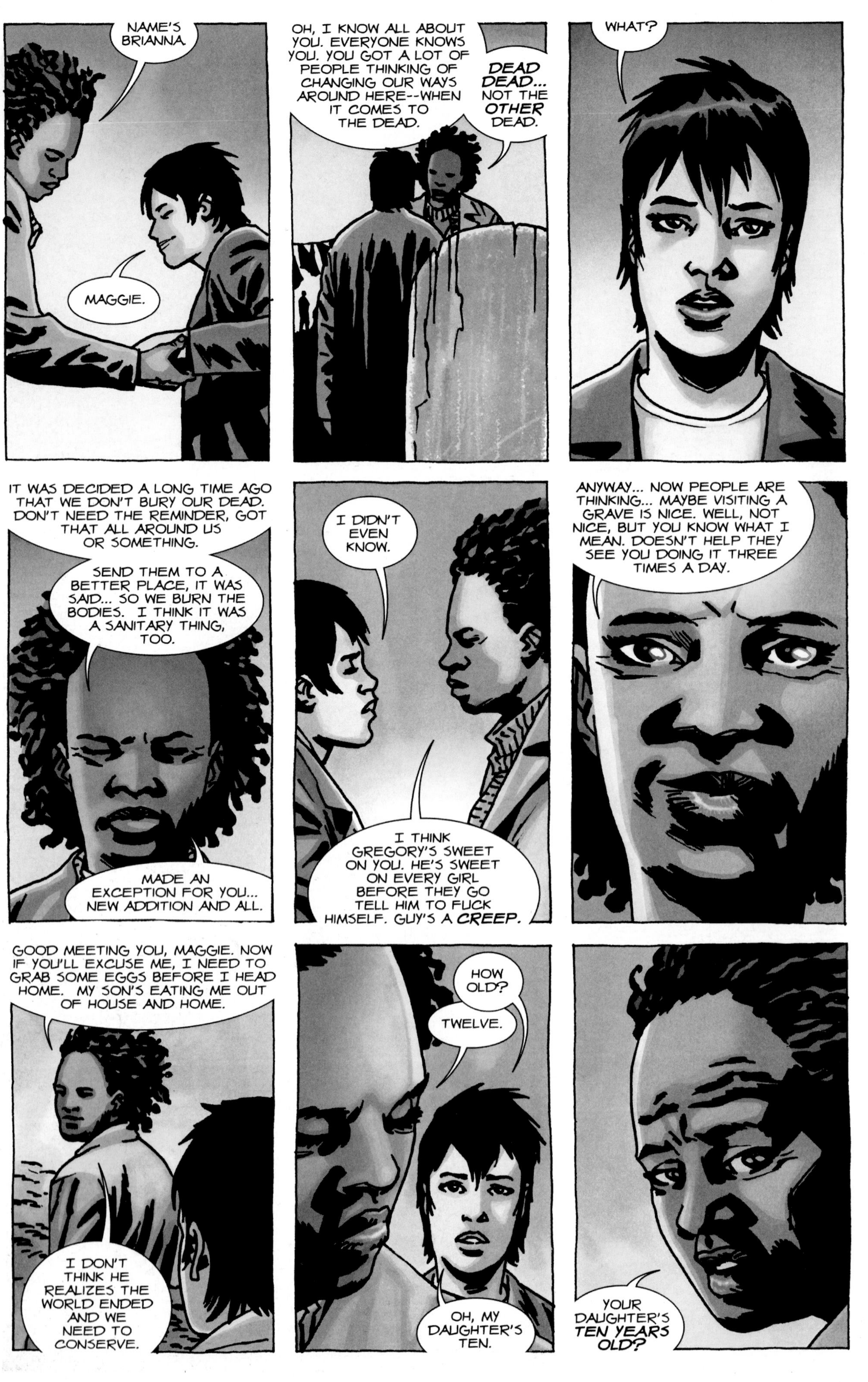
NAME'S BRIANNA.
MAGGIE.
OH, I KNOW ALL ABOUT YOU. EVERYONE KNOWS YOU. YOU GOT A LOT OF PEOPLE THINKING OF CHANGING OUR WAYS AROUND HERE--WHEN IT COMES TO THE DEAD.
DEAD DEAD... NOT THE OTHER DEAD.
WHAT?
IT WAS DECIDED A LONG TIME AGO THAT WE DON'T BURY OUR DEAD. DON'T NEED THE REMINDER, GOT THAT ALL AROUND US OR SOMETHING.
SEND THEM TO A BETTER PLACE, IT WAS SAID... SO WE BURN THE BODIES. I THINK IT WAS A SANITARY THING, TOO.
MADE AN EXCEPTION FOR YOU... NEW ADDITION AND ALL.
I DIDN'T EVEN KNOW.
I THINK GREGORY'S SWEET ON YOU. HE'S SWEET ON EVERY GIRL BEFORE THEY GO TELL HIM TO FUCK HIMSELF. GUY'S A CREEP.
ANYWAY... NOW PEOPLE ARE THINKING... MAYBE VISITING A GRAVE IS NICE. WELL, NOT NICE, BUT YOU KNOW WHAT I MEAN. DOESN'T HELP THEY SEE YOU DOING IT THREE TIMES A DAY.
GOOD MEETING YOU, MAGGIE. NOW IF YOU'LL EXCUSE ME, I NEED TO GRAB SOME EGGS BEFORE I HEAD HOME. MY SON'S EATING ME OUT OF HOUSE AND HOME.
I DON'T THINK HE REALIZES THE WORLD ENDED AND WE NEED TO CONSERVE.
HOW OLD?
TWELVE.
OH, MY DAUGHTER'S TEN.
YOUR DAUGHTER'S TEN YEARS OLD?

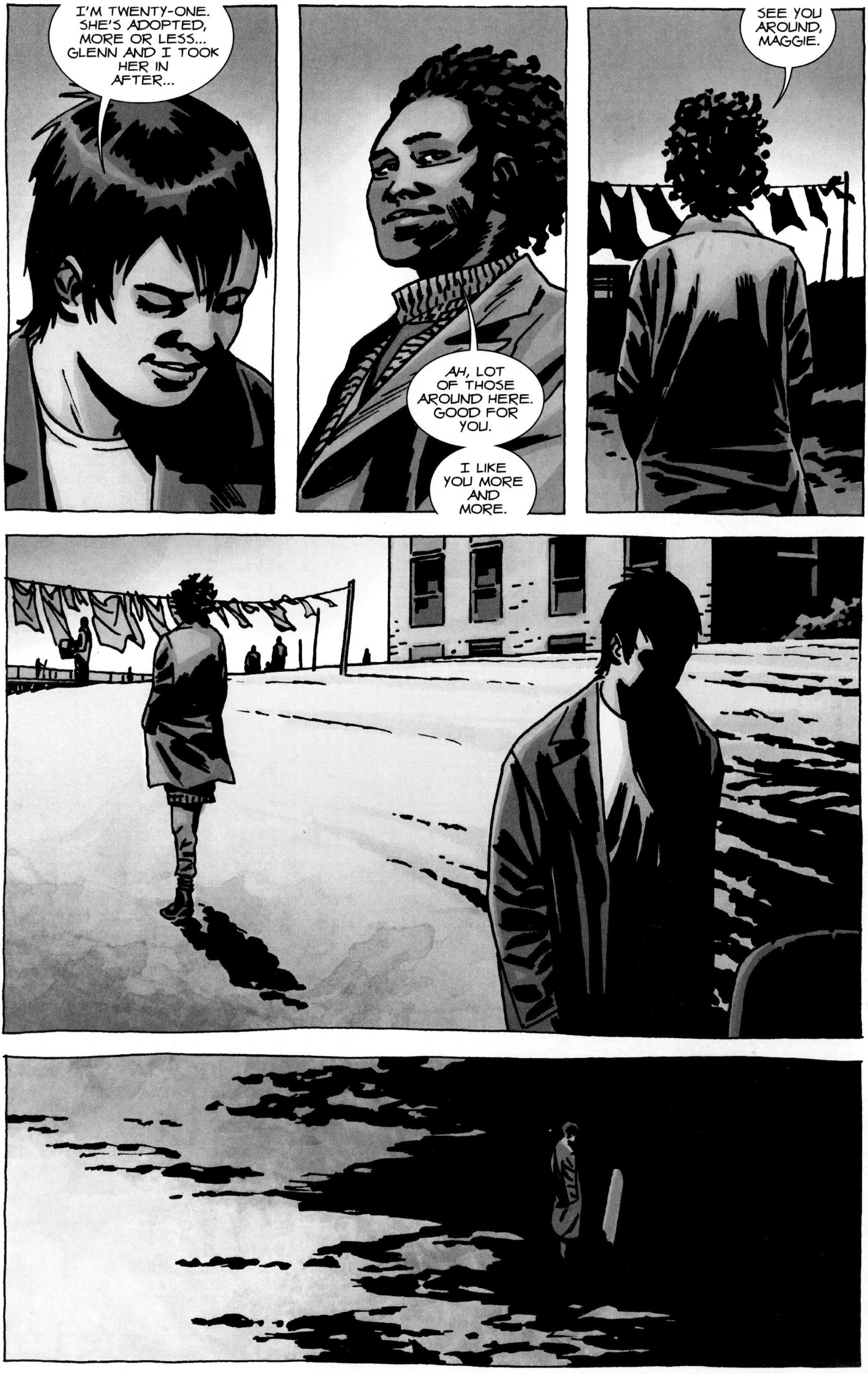
I'M TWENTY-ONE. SHE'S ADOPTED, MORE OR LESS... GLENN AND I TOOK HER IN AFTER...
AH, LOT OF THOSE AROUND HERE. GOOD FOR YOU.
I LIKE YOU MORE AND MORE.
SEE YOU AROUND, MAGGIE.

EVERYTHING LOOKS TO BE PROCEEDING EXACTLY HOW IT SHOULD BE.

NO NEWS IS GOOD NEWS. NATURE'S DOING ITS THING.

CONGRATULATIONS.

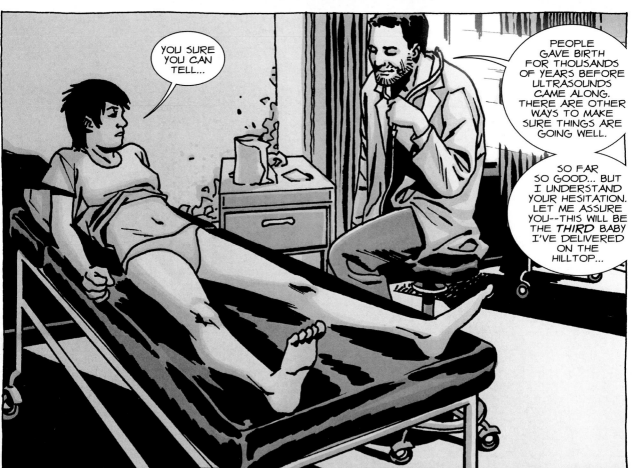

YOU SURE YOU CAN TELL...

PEOPLE GAVE BIRTH FOR THOUSANDS OF YEARS BEFORE ULTRASOUNDS CAME ALONG. THERE ARE OTHER WAYS TO MAKE SURE THINGS ARE GOING WELL.

SO FAR SO GOOD... BUT I UNDERSTAND YOUR HESITATION. LET ME ASSURE YOU--THIS WILL BE THE *THIRD* BABY I'VE DELIVERED ON THE HILLTOP...

WE KNOW WHAT WE'RE DOING.

I CAN VOUCH FOR THAT.

UH...

GREGORY, PLEASE.

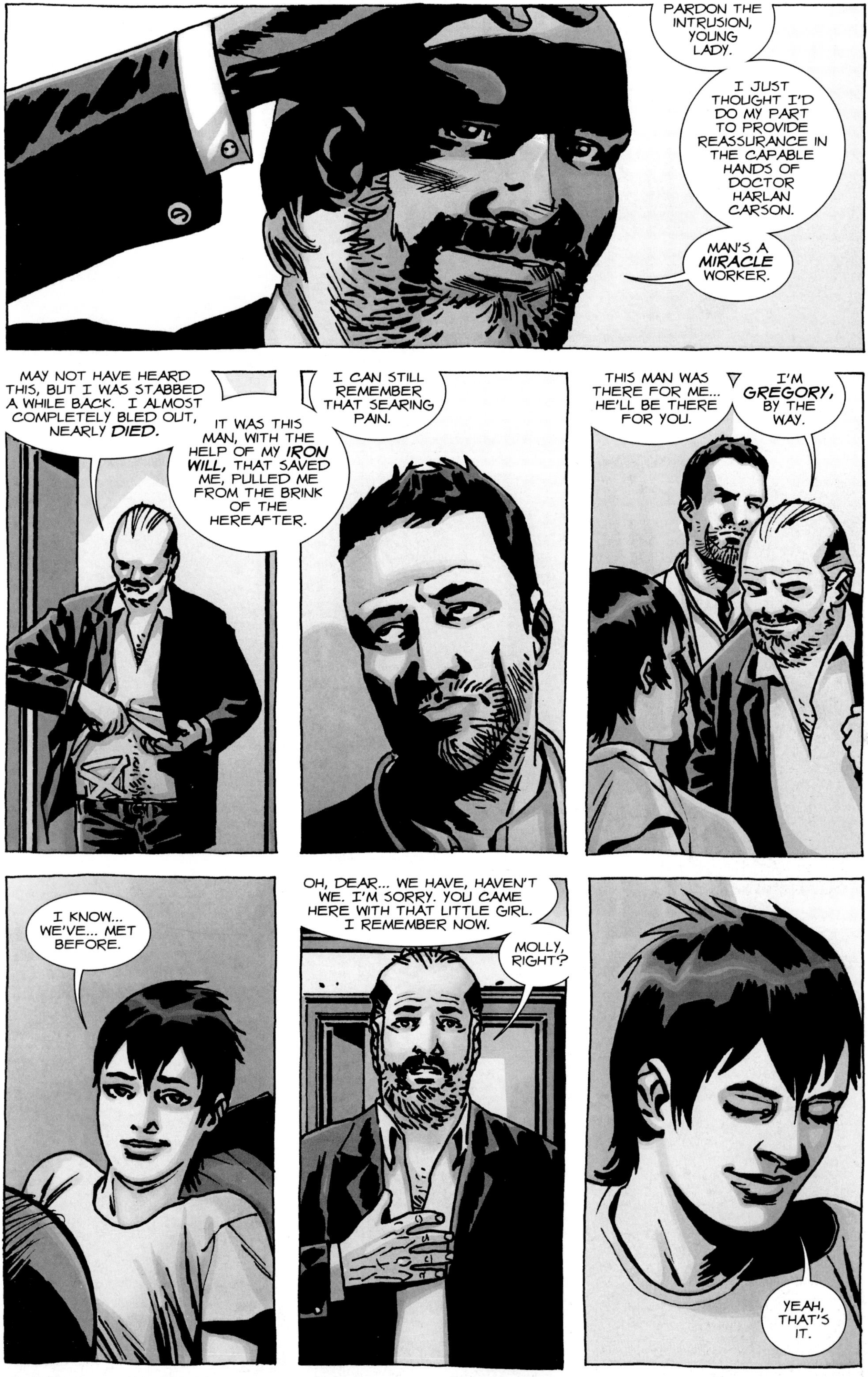
PARDON THE INTRUSION, YOUNG LADY.
I JUST THOUGHT I'D DO MY PART TO PROVIDE REASSURANCE IN THE CAPABLE HANDS OF DOCTOR HARLAN CARSON.
MAN'S A MIRACLE WORKER.
MAY NOT HAVE HEARD THIS, BUT I WAS STABBED A WHILE BACK. I ALMOST COMPLETELY BLED OUT, NEARLY DIED.
IT WAS THIS MAN, WITH THE HELP OF MY IRON WILL, THAT SAVED ME, PULLED ME FROM THE BRINK OF THE HEREAFTER.
I CAN STILL REMEMBER THAT SEARING PAIN.
THIS MAN WAS THERE FOR ME... HE'LL BE THERE FOR YOU.
I'M GREGORY, BY THE WAY.
I KNOW... WE'VE... MET BEFORE.
OH, DEAR... WE HAVE, HAVEN'T WE. I'M SORRY. YOU CAME HERE WITH THAT LITTLE GIRL. I REMEMBER NOW.
MOLLY, RIGHT?
YEAH, THAT'S IT.

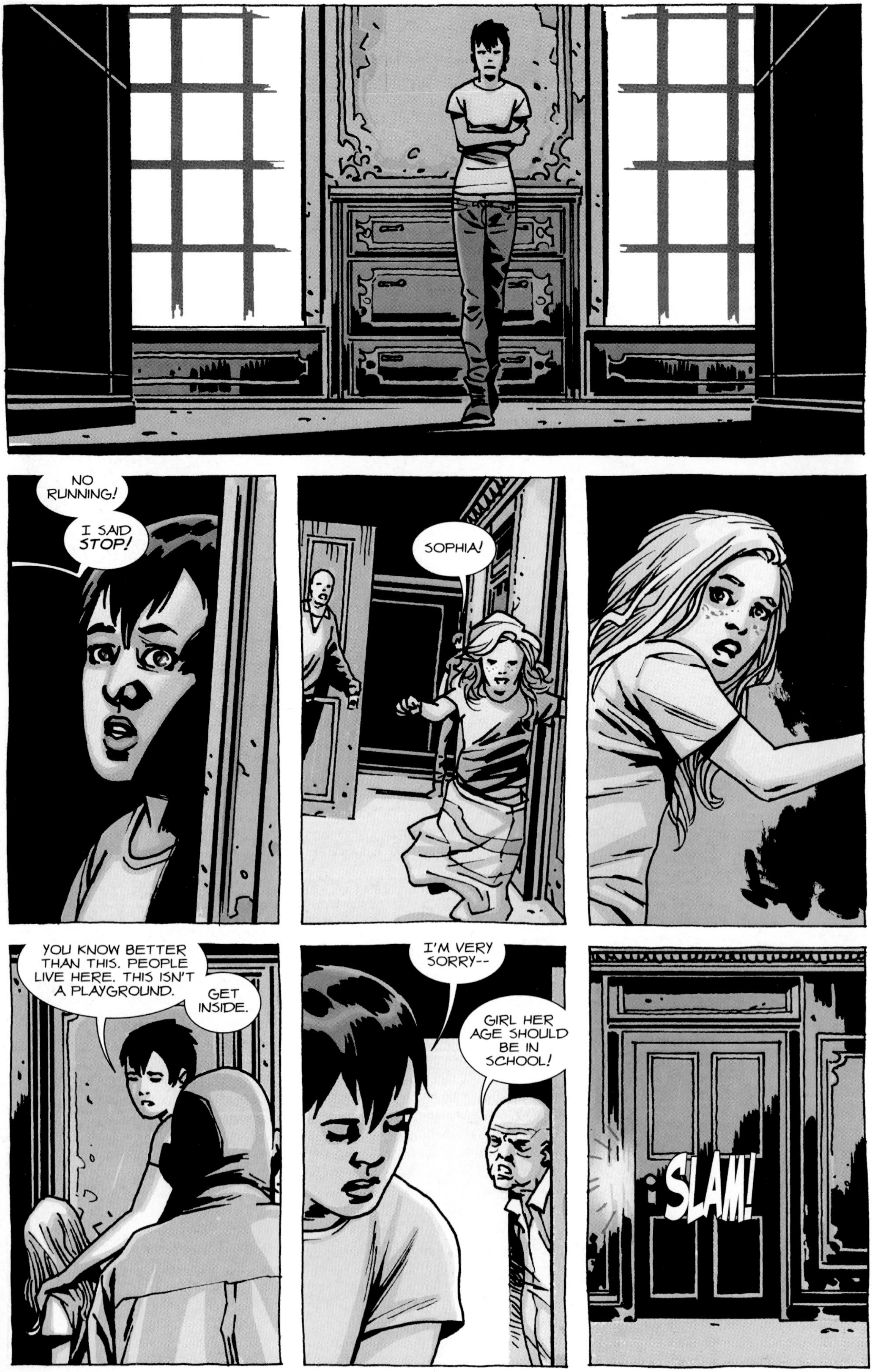
NO RUNNING!
I SAID STOP!
SOPHIA!
YOU KNOW BETTER THAN THIS. PEOPLE LIVE HERE. THIS ISN'T A PLAYGROUND.
GET INSIDE.
I'M VERY SORRY--
GIRL HER AGE SHOULD BE IN SCHOOL!
SLAM!

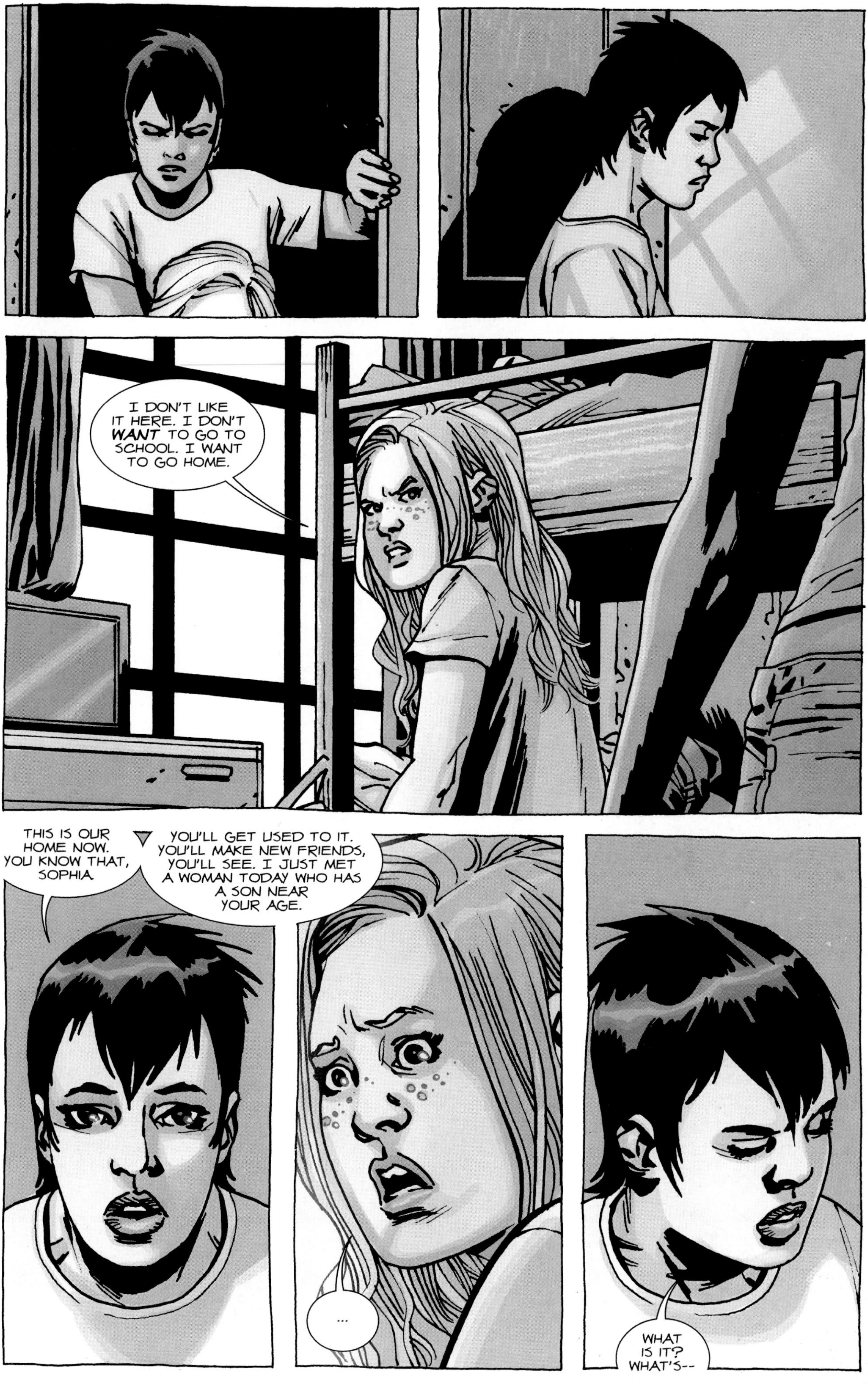
I DON'T LIKE IT HERE. I DON'T *WANT* TO GO TO SCHOOL. I WANT TO GO HOME.
THIS IS OUR HOME NOW. YOU KNOW THAT, SOPHIA.
YOU'LL GET USED TO IT. YOU'LL MAKE NEW FRIENDS, YOU'LL SEE. I JUST MET A WOMAN TODAY WHO HAS A SON NEAR YOUR AGE.
...
WHAT IS IT? WHAT'S--

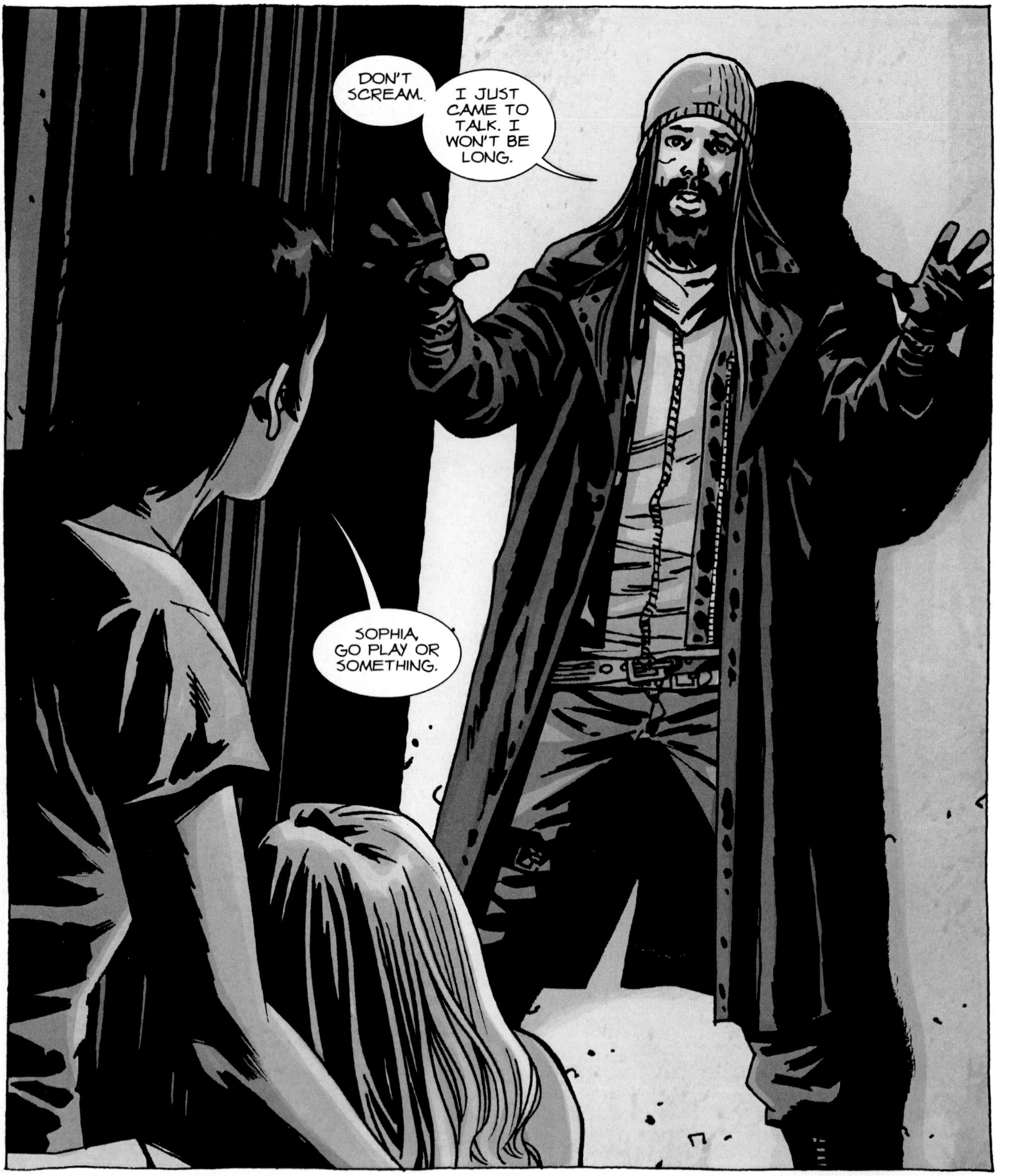
DON'T SCREAM.
I JUST CAME TO TALK. I WON'T BE LONG.
SOPHIA, GO PLAY OR SOMETHING.

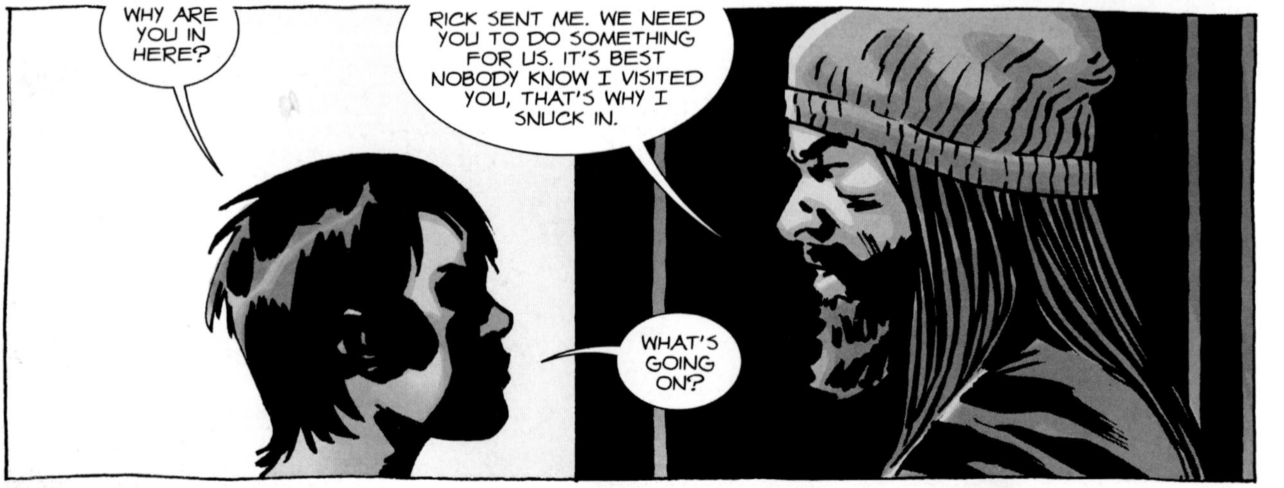
WHY ARE YOU IN HERE?
RICK SENT ME. WE NEED YOU TO DO SOMETHING FOR US. IT'S BEST NOBODY KNOW I VISITED YOU, THAT'S WHY I SNUCK IN.
WHAT'S GOING ON?

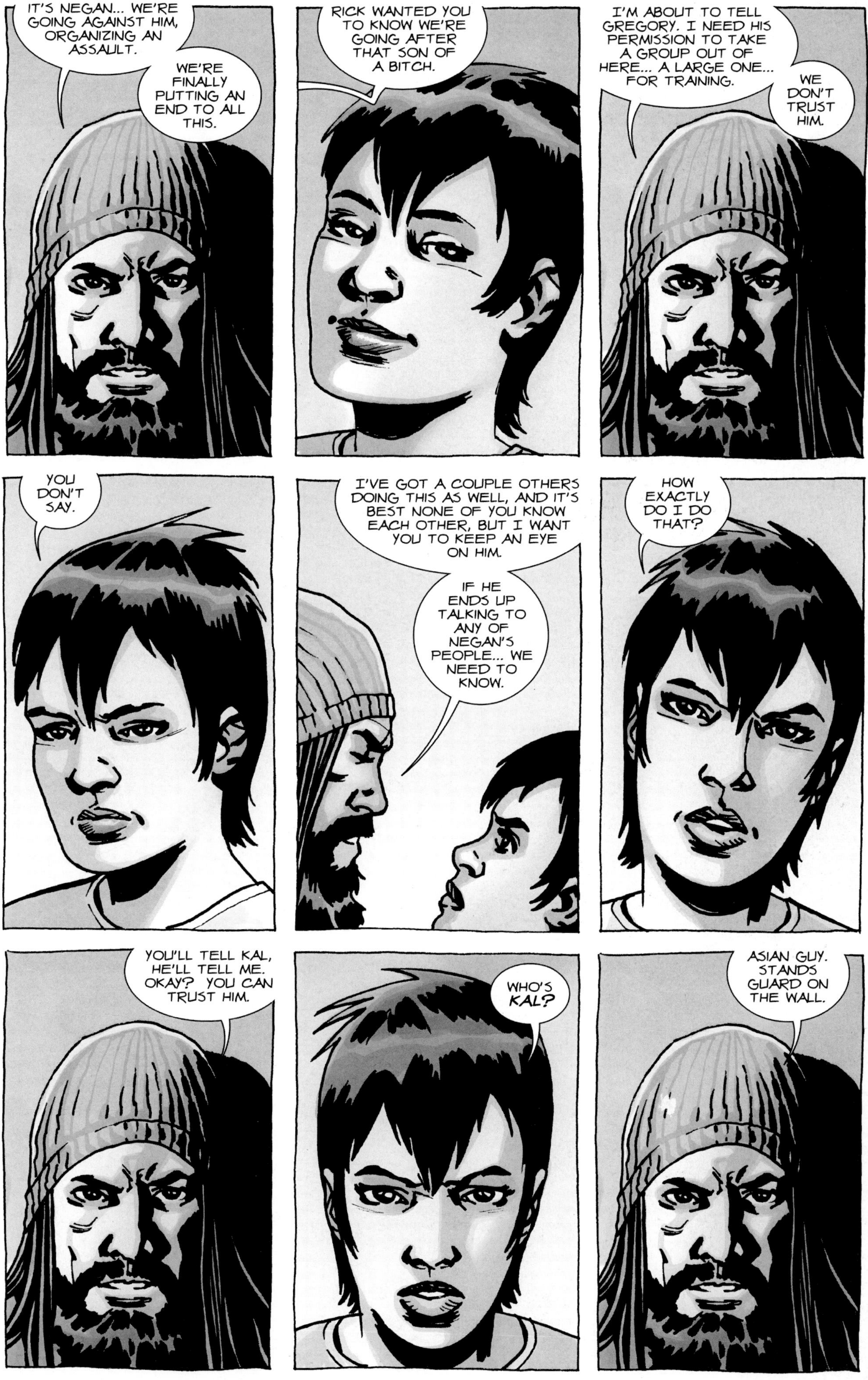
IT'S NEGAN... WE'RE GOING AGAINST HIM, ORGANIZING AN ASSAULT.
WE'RE FINALLY PUTTING AN END TO ALL THIS.
RICK WANTED YOU TO KNOW WE'RE GOING AFTER THAT SON OF A BITCH.
I'M ABOUT TO TELL GREGORY. I NEED HIS PERMISSION TO TAKE A GROUP OUT OF HERE... A LARGE ONE... FOR TRAINING.
WE DON'T TRUST HIM.
YOU DON'T SAY.
I'VE GOT A COUPLE OTHERS DOING THIS AS WELL, AND IT'S BEST NONE OF YOU KNOW EACH OTHER, BUT I WANT YOU TO KEEP AN EYE ON HIM.
IF HE ENDS UP TALKING TO ANY OF NEGAN'S PEOPLE... WE NEED TO KNOW.
HOW EXACTLY DO I DO THAT?
YOU'LL TELL KAL, HE'LL TELL ME. OKAY? YOU CAN TRUST HIM.
WHO'S KAL?
ASIAN GUY. STANDS GUARD ON THE WALL.

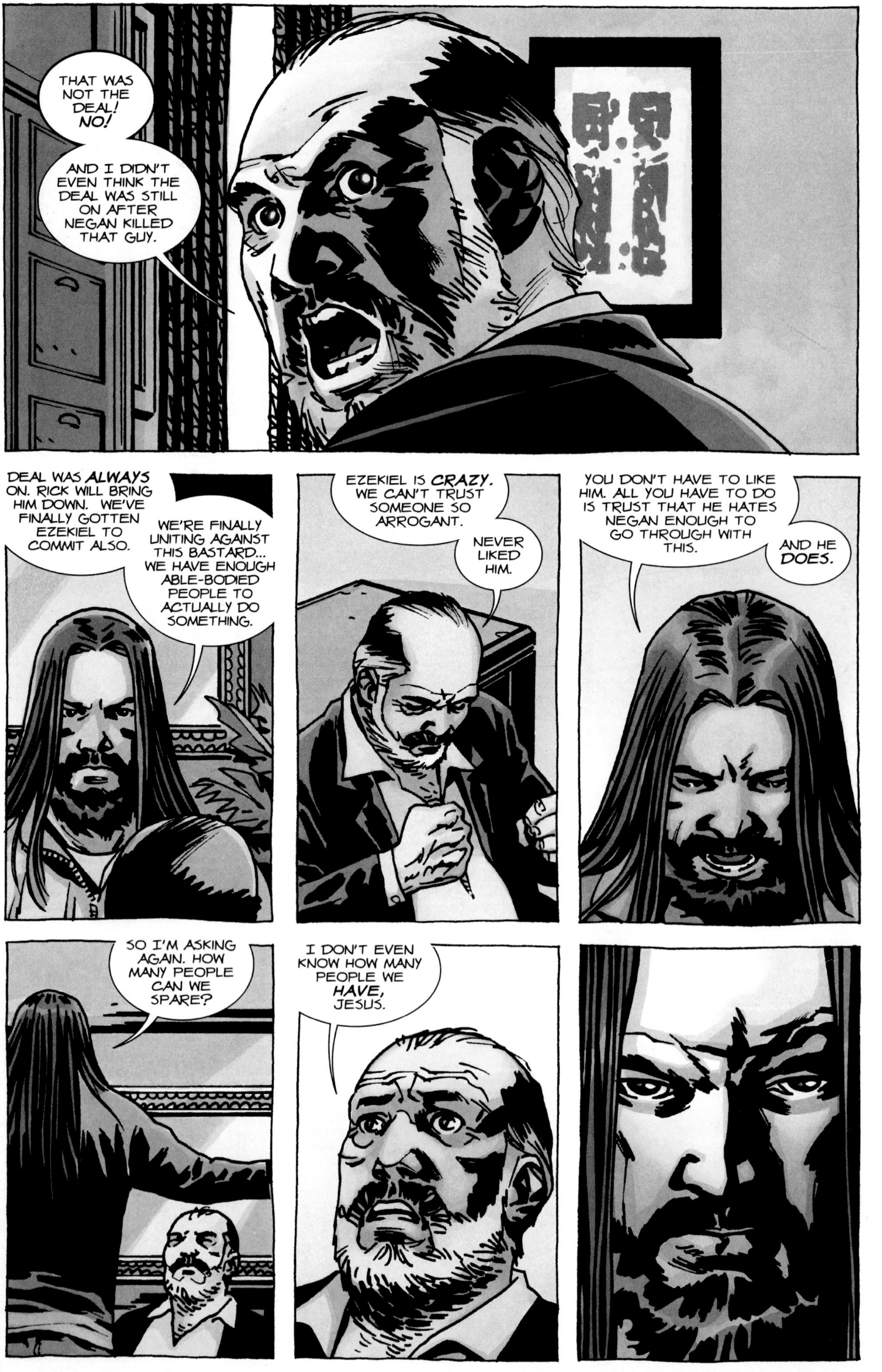
THAT WAS NOT THE DEAL! NO!
AND I DIDN'T EVEN THINK THE DEAL WAS STILL ON AFTER NEGAN KILLED THAT GUY.
DEAL WAS ALWAYS ON. RICK WILL BRING HIM DOWN. WE'VE FINALLY GOTTEN EZEKIEL TO COMMIT ALSO.
WE'RE FINALLY UNITING AGAINST THIS BASTARD... WE HAVE ENOUGH ABLE-BODIED PEOPLE TO ACTUALLY DO SOMETHING.
EZEKIEL IS CRAZY. WE CAN'T TRUST SOMEONE SO ARROGANT.
NEVER LIKED HIM.
YOU DON'T HAVE TO LIKE HIM. ALL YOU HAVE TO DO IS TRUST THAT HE HATES NEGAN ENOUGH TO GO THROUGH WITH THIS.
AND HE DOES.
SO I'M ASKING AGAIN. HOW MANY PEOPLE CAN WE SPARE?
I DON'T EVEN KNOW HOW MANY PEOPLE WE HAVE, JESUS.

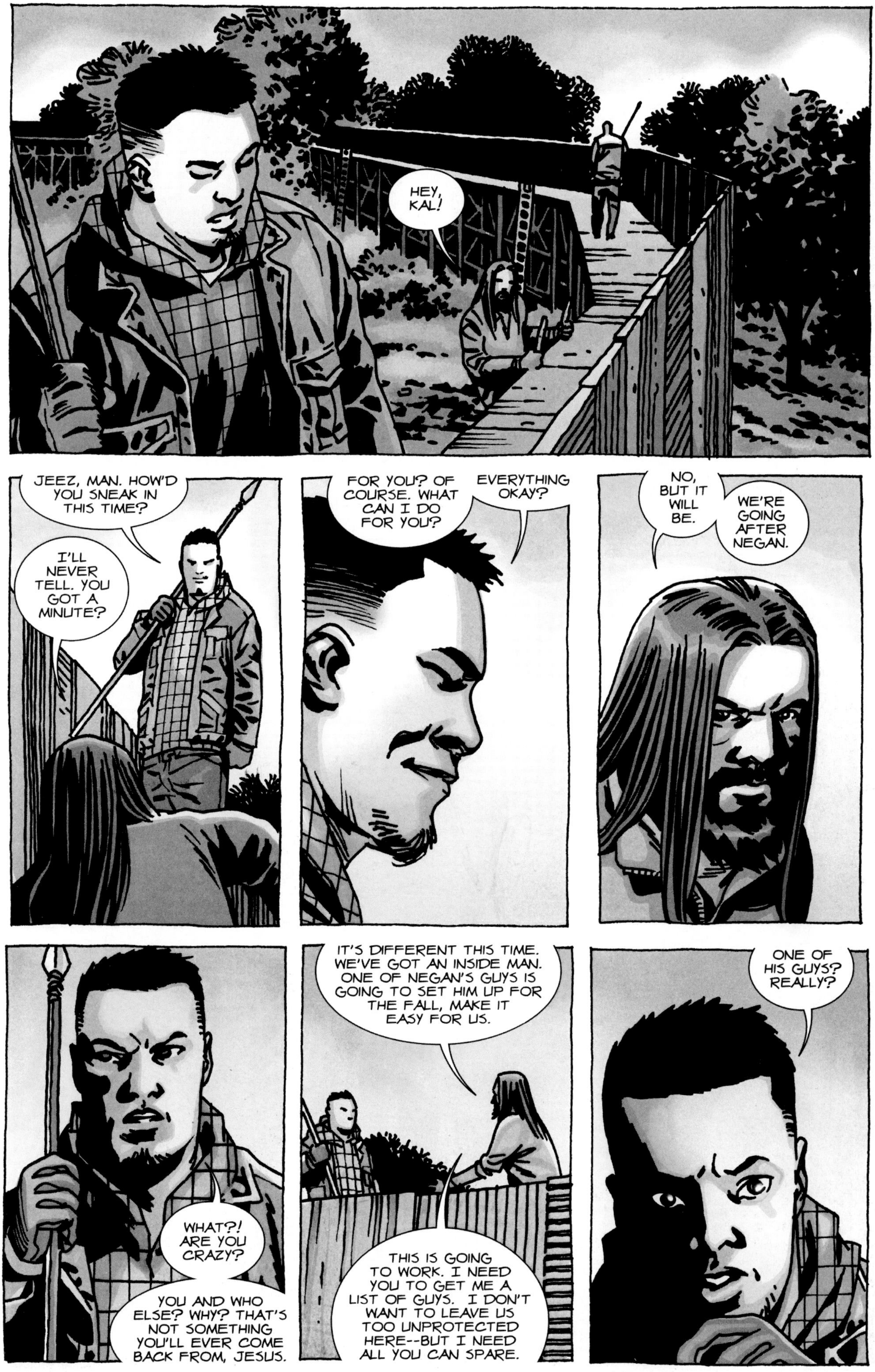
HEY, KAL!
JEEZ, MAN. HOW'D YOU SNEAK IN THIS TIME?
I'LL NEVER TELL. YOU GOT A MINUTE?
FOR YOU? OF COURSE. WHAT CAN I DO FOR YOU?
EVERYTHING OKAY?
NO, BUT IT WILL BE.
WE'RE GOING AFTER NEGAN.
WHAT?! ARE YOU CRAZY?
YOU AND WHO ELSE? WHY? THAT'S NOT SOMETHING YOU'LL EVER COME BACK FROM, JESUS.
IT'S DIFFERENT THIS TIME. WE'VE GOT AN INSIDE MAN. ONE OF NEGAN'S GUYS IS GOING TO SET HIM UP FOR THE FALL, MAKE IT EASY FOR US.
THIS IS GOING TO WORK. I NEED YOU TO GET ME A LIST OF GUYS. I DON'T WANT TO LEAVE US TOO UNPROTECTED HERE--BUT I NEED ALL YOU CAN SPARE.
ONE OF HIS GUYS? REALLY?

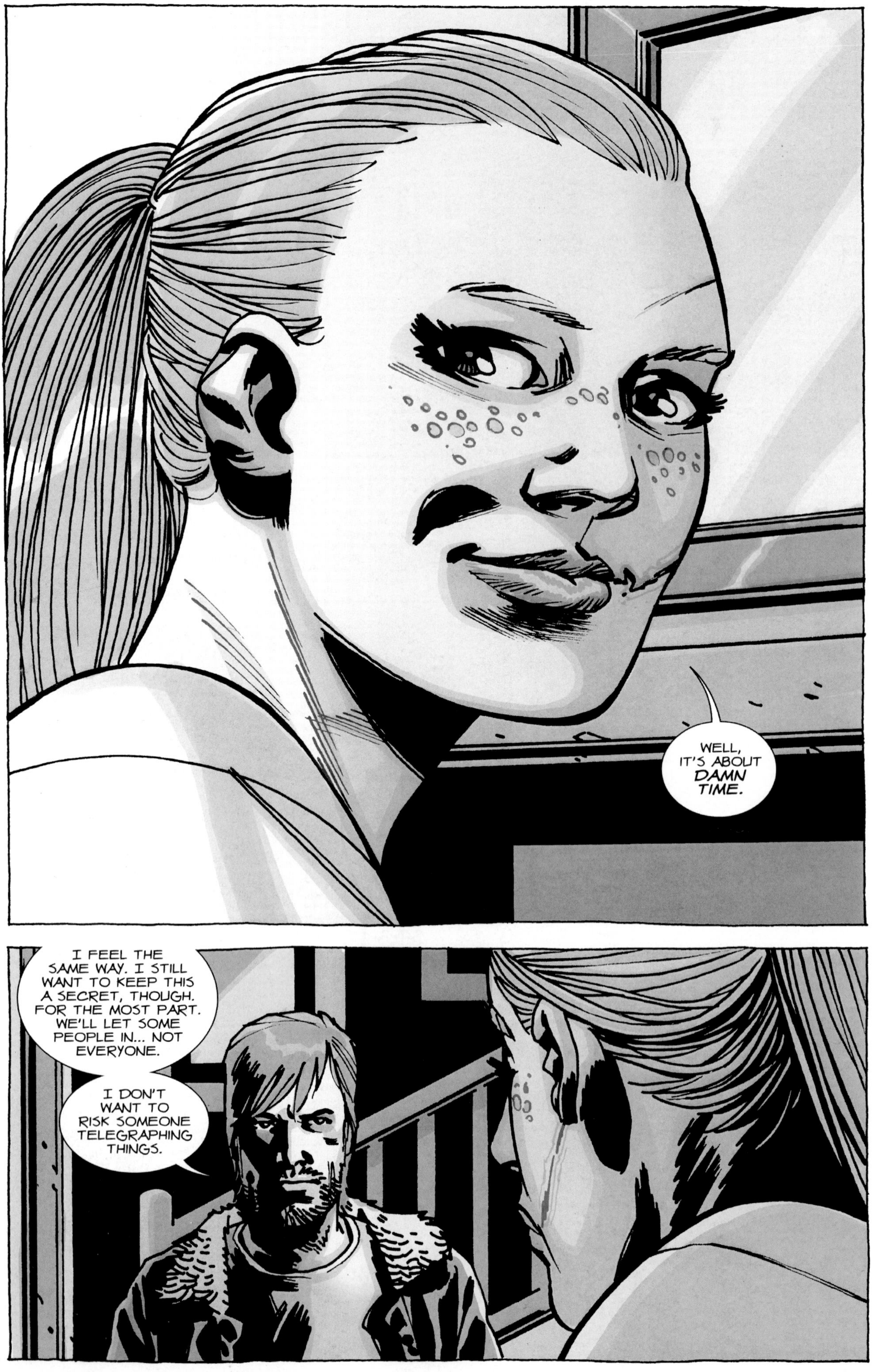
WELL, IT'S ABOUT *DAMN TIME.*
I FEEL THE SAME WAY. I STILL WANT TO KEEP THIS A SECRET, THOUGH. FOR THE MOST PART. WE'LL LET SOME PEOPLE IN... NOT EVERYONE.
I DON'T WANT TO RISK SOMEONE TELEGRAPHING THINGS.

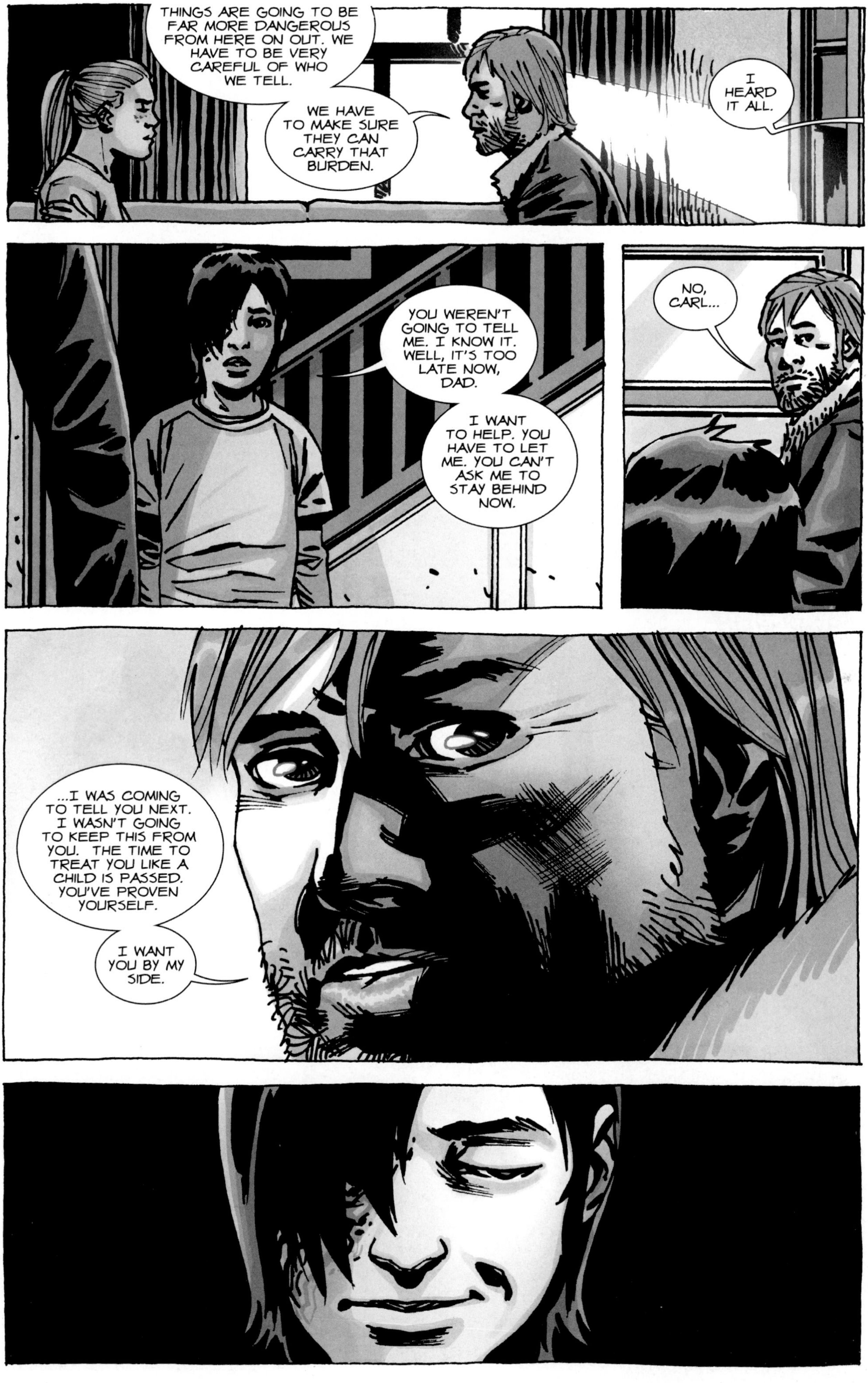
THINGS ARE GOING TO BE FAR MORE DANGEROUS FROM HERE ON OUT. WE HAVE TO BE VERY CAREFUL OF WHO WE TELL.
WE HAVE TO MAKE SURE THEY CAN CARRY THAT BURDEN.
I HEARD IT ALL.
YOU WEREN'T GOING TO TELL ME. I KNOW IT. WELL, IT'S TOO LATE NOW, DAD.
I WANT TO HELP. YOU HAVE TO LET ME. YOU CAN'T ASK ME TO STAY BEHIND NOW.
NO, CARL...
...I WAS COMING TO TELL YOU NEXT. I WASN'T GOING TO KEEP THIS FROM YOU. THE TIME TO TREAT YOU LIKE A CHILD IS PASSED. YOU'VE PROVEN YOURSELF.
I WANT YOU BY MY SIDE.

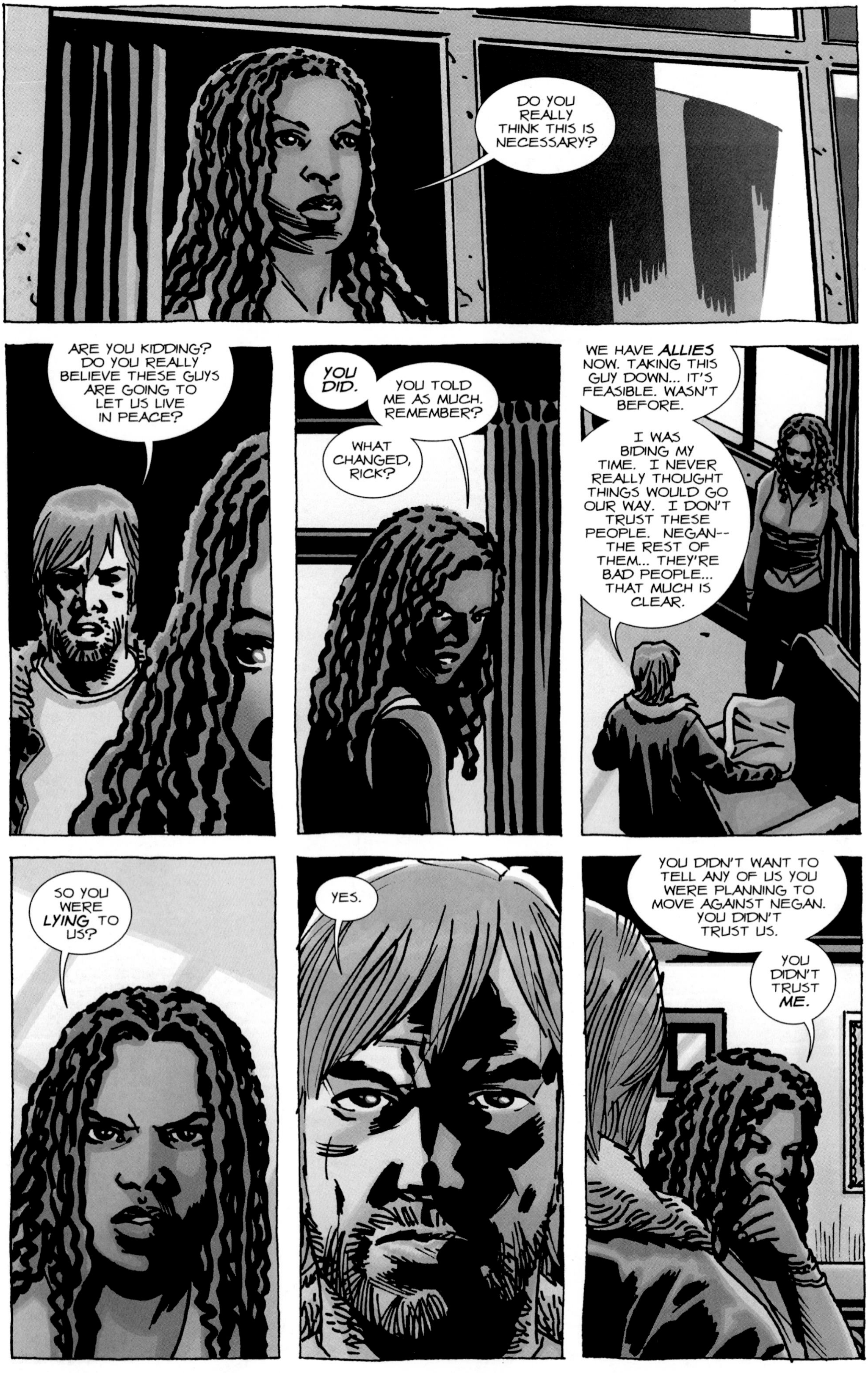
DO YOU REALLY THINK THIS IS NECESSARY?
ARE YOU KIDDING? DO YOU REALLY BELIEVE THESE GUYS ARE GOING TO LET US LIVE IN PEACE?
YOU DID.
YOU TOLD ME AS MUCH. REMEMBER?
WHAT CHANGED, RICK?
WE HAVE ALLIES NOW. TAKING THIS GUY DOWN... IT'S FEASIBLE. WASN'T BEFORE.
I WAS BIDING MY TIME. I NEVER REALLY THOUGHT THINGS WOULD GO OUR WAY. I DON'T TRUST THESE PEOPLE. NEGAN-- THE REST OF THEM... THEY'RE BAD PEOPLE... THAT MUCH IS CLEAR.
SO YOU WERE LYING TO US?
YES.
YOU DIDN'T WANT TO TELL ANY OF US YOU WERE PLANNING TO MOVE AGAINST NEGAN. YOU DIDN'T TRUST US.
YOU DIDN'T TRUST ME.

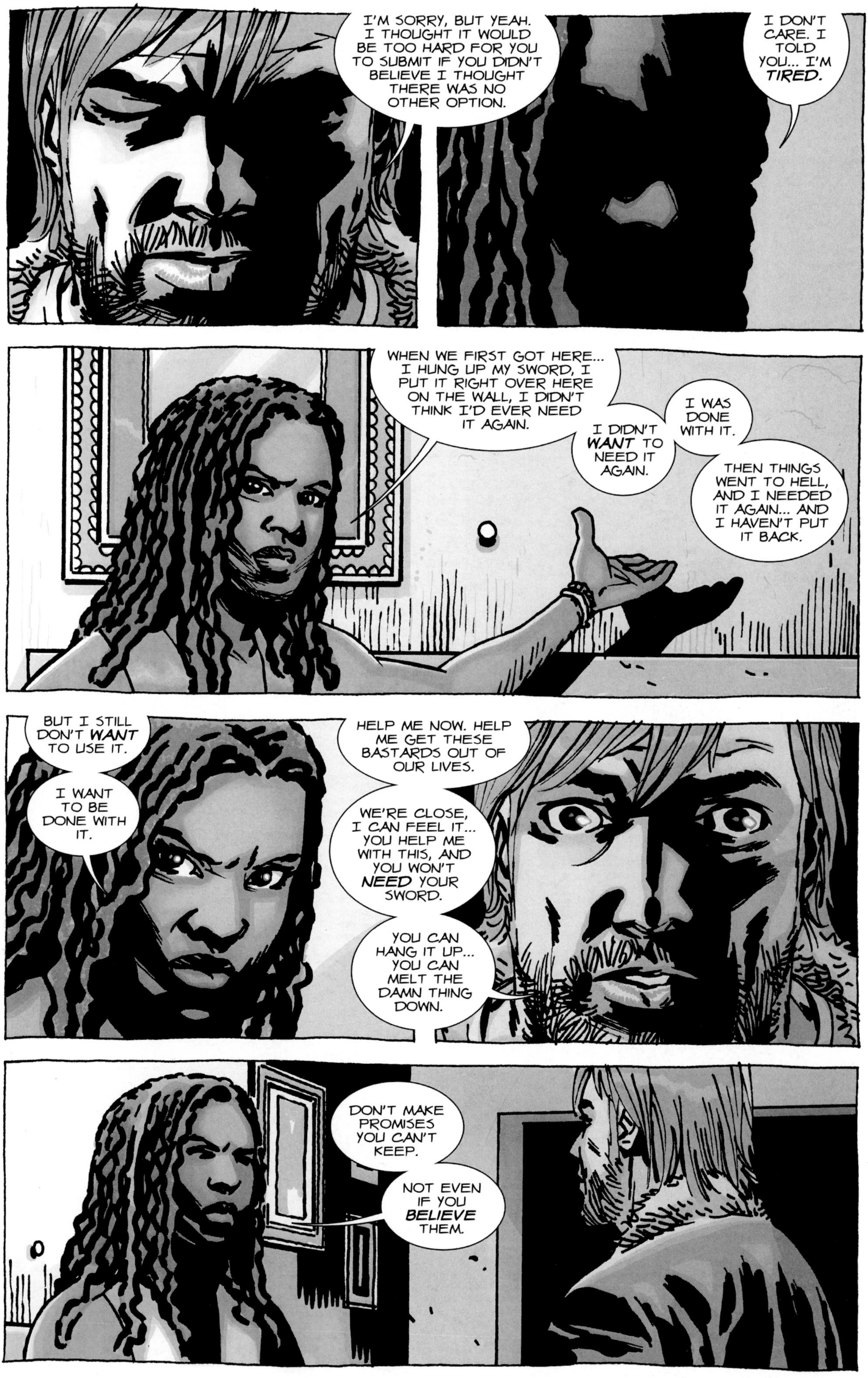

I'M SORRY, BUT YEAH. I THOUGHT IT WOULD BE TOO HARD FOR YOU TO SUBMIT IF YOU DIDN'T BELIEVE I THOUGHT THERE WAS NO OTHER OPTION.
I DON'T CARE. I TOLD YOU... I'M TIRED.
WHEN WE FIRST GOT HERE... I HUNG UP MY SWORD, I PUT IT RIGHT OVER HERE ON THE WALL, I DIDN'T THINK I'D EVER NEED IT AGAIN.
I DIDN'T WANT TO NEED IT AGAIN.
I WAS DONE WITH IT.
THEN THINGS WENT TO HELL, AND I NEEDED IT AGAIN... AND I HAVEN'T PUT IT BACK.
BUT I STILL DON'T WANT TO USE IT.
I WANT TO BE DONE WITH IT.
HELP ME NOW. HELP ME GET THESE BASTARDS OUT OF OUR LIVES.
WE'RE CLOSE, I CAN FEEL IT... YOU HELP ME WITH THIS, AND YOU WON'T NEED YOUR SWORD.
YOU CAN HANG IT UP... YOU CAN MELT THE DAMN THING DOWN.
DON'T MAKE PROMISES YOU CAN'T KEEP.
NOT EVEN IF YOU BELIEVE THEM.

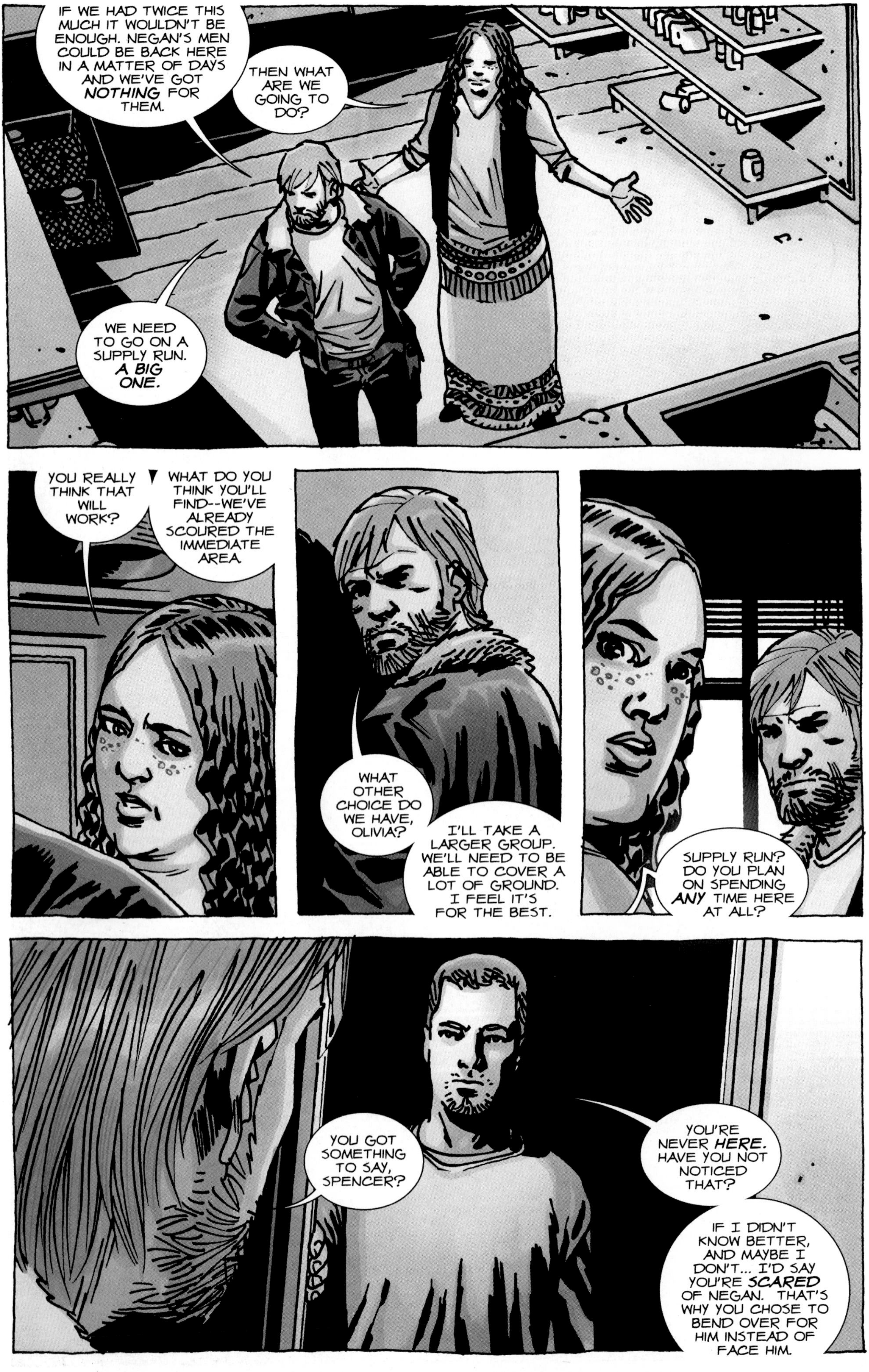

IF WE HAD TWICE THIS MUCH IT WOULDN'T BE ENOUGH. NEGAN'S MEN COULD BE BACK HERE IN A MATTER OF DAYS AND WE'VE GOT NOTHING FOR THEM.
THEN WHAT ARE WE GOING TO DO?
WE NEED TO GO ON A SUPPLY RUN. A BIG ONE.
YOU REALLY THINK THAT WILL WORK?
WHAT DO YOU THINK YOU'LL FIND--WE'VE ALREADY SCOURED THE IMMEDIATE AREA.
WHAT OTHER CHOICE DO WE HAVE, OLIVIA?
I'LL TAKE A LARGER GROUP. WE'LL NEED TO BE ABLE TO COVER A LOT OF GROUND. I FEEL IT'S FOR THE BEST.
SUPPLY RUN? DO YOU PLAN ON SPENDING ANY TIME HERE AT ALL?
YOU'RE NEVER HERE. HAVE YOU NOT NOTICED THAT?
YOU GOT SOMETHING TO SAY, SPENCER?
IF I DIDN'T KNOW BETTER, AND MAYBE I DON'T... I'D SAY YOU'RE SCARED OF NEGAN. THAT'S WHY YOU CHOSE TO BEND OVER FOR HIM INSTEAD OF FACE HIM.

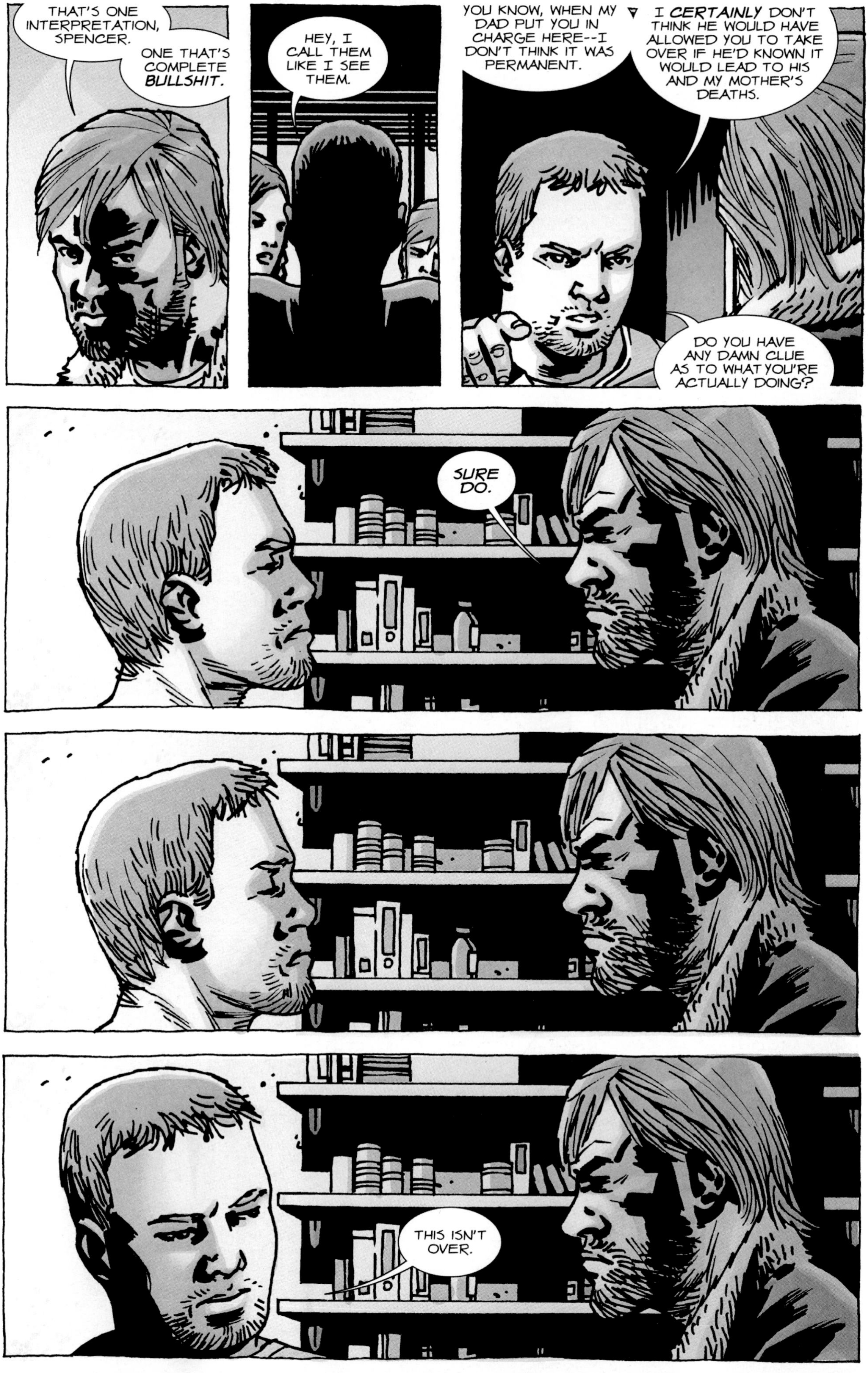
THAT'S ONE INTERPRETATION, SPENCER.
ONE THAT'S COMPLETE **BULLSHIT.**
HEY, I CALL THEM LIKE I SEE THEM.
YOU KNOW, WHEN MY DAD PUT YOU IN CHARGE HERE--I DON'T THINK IT WAS PERMANENT.
I **CERTAINLY** DON'T THINK HE WOULD HAVE ALLOWED YOU TO TAKE OVER IF HE'D KNOWN IT WOULD LEAD TO HIS AND MY MOTHER'S DEATHS.
DO YOU HAVE ANY DAMN CLUE AS TO WHAT YOU'RE ACTUALLY DOING?
SURE DO.
THIS ISN'T OVER.

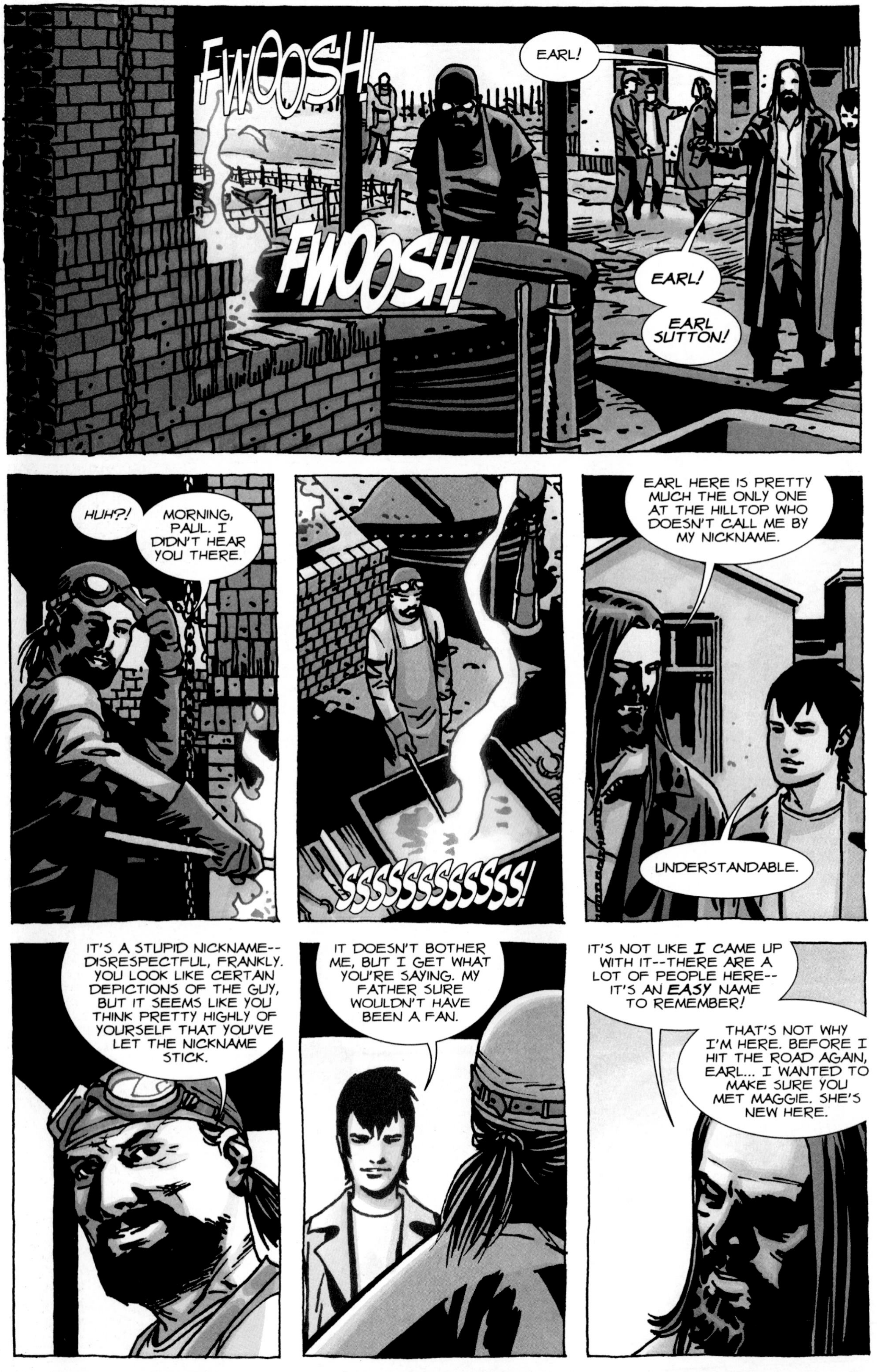
FWOOSH!
FWOOSH!
EARL!
EARL!
EARL SUTTON!
HUH?!
MORNING, PAUL. I DIDN'T HEAR YOU THERE.
SSSSSSSSSSSS!
EARL HERE IS PRETTY MUCH THE ONLY ONE AT THE HILLTOP WHO DOESN'T CALL ME BY MY NICKNAME.
UNDERSTANDABLE.
IT'S A STUPID NICKNAME-- DISRESPECTFUL, FRANKLY. YOU LOOK LIKE CERTAIN DEPICTIONS OF THE GUY, BUT IT SEEMS LIKE YOU THINK PRETTY HIGHLY OF YOURSELF THAT YOU'VE LET THE NICKNAME STICK.
IT DOESN'T BOTHER ME, BUT I GET WHAT YOU'RE SAYING. MY FATHER SURE WOULDN'T HAVE BEEN A FAN.
IT'S NOT LIKE *I* CAME UP WITH IT--THERE ARE A LOT OF PEOPLE HERE-- IT'S AN *EASY* NAME TO REMEMBER!
THAT'S NOT WHY I'M HERE. BEFORE I HIT THE ROAD AGAIN, EARL... I WANTED TO MAKE SURE YOU MET MAGGIE. SHE'S NEW HERE.

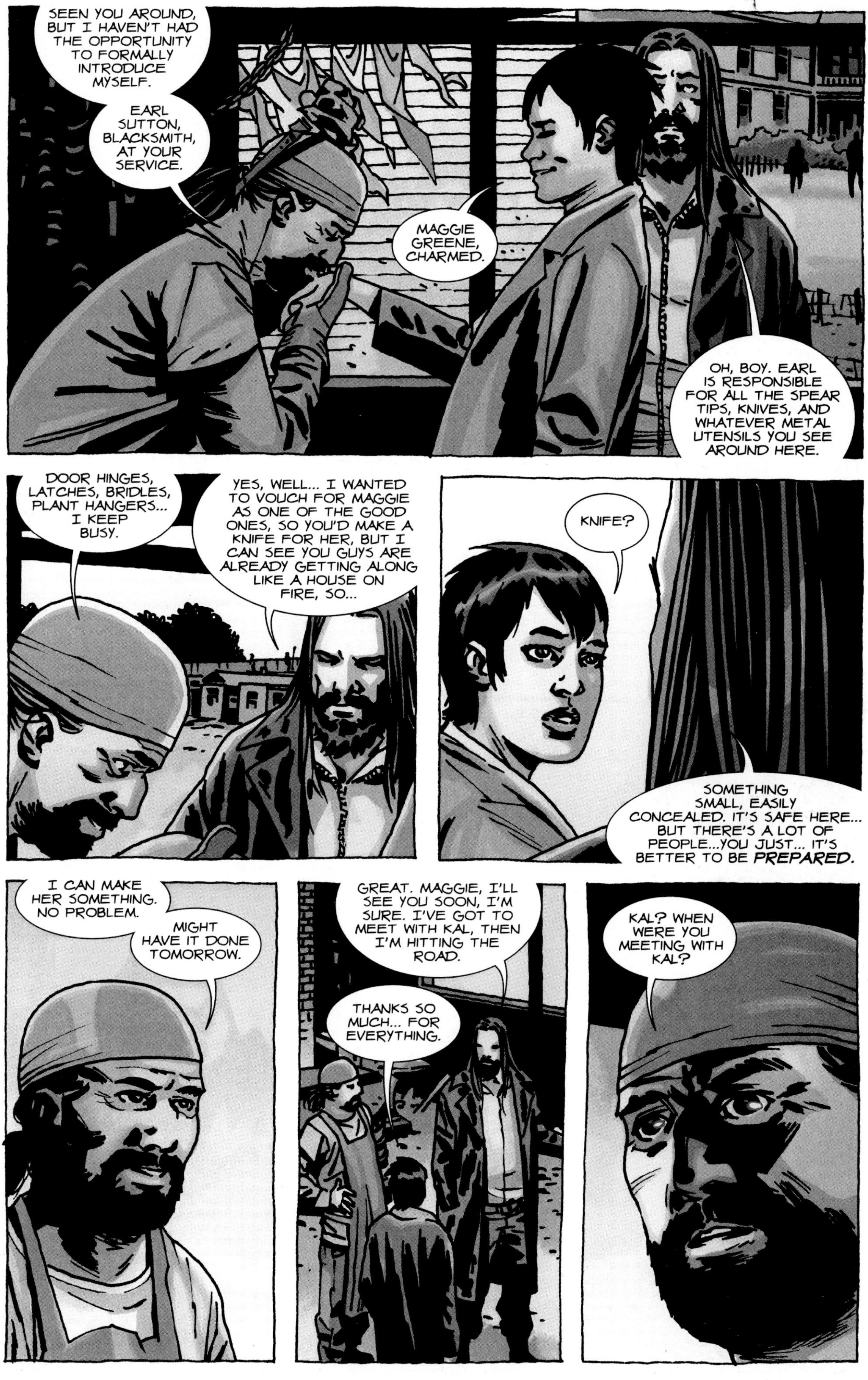

SEEN YOU AROUND, BUT I HAVEN'T HAD THE OPPORTUNITY TO FORMALLY INTRODUCE MYSELF.
EARL SUTTON, BLACKSMITH, AT YOUR SERVICE.
MAGGIE GREENE, CHARMED.
OH, BOY. EARL IS RESPONSIBLE FOR ALL THE SPEAR TIPS, KNIVES, AND WHATEVER METAL UTENSILS YOU SEE AROUND HERE.
DOOR HINGES, LATCHES, BRIDLES, PLANT HANGERS... I KEEP BUSY.
YES, WELL... I WANTED TO VOUCH FOR MAGGIE AS ONE OF THE GOOD ONES, SO YOU'D MAKE A KNIFE FOR HER, BUT I CAN SEE YOU GUYS ARE ALREADY GETTING ALONG LIKE A HOUSE ON FIRE, SO...
KNIFE?
SOMETHING SMALL, EASILY CONCEALED. IT'S SAFE HERE... BUT THERE'S A LOT OF PEOPLE...YOU JUST... IT'S BETTER TO BE PREPARED.
I CAN MAKE HER SOMETHING. NO PROBLEM.
MIGHT HAVE IT DONE TOMORROW.
GREAT. MAGGIE, I'LL SEE YOU SOON, I'M SURE. I'VE GOT TO MEET WITH KAL, THEN I'M HITTING THE ROAD.
THANKS SO MUCH... FOR EVERYTHING.
KAL? WHEN WERE YOU MEETING WITH KAL?

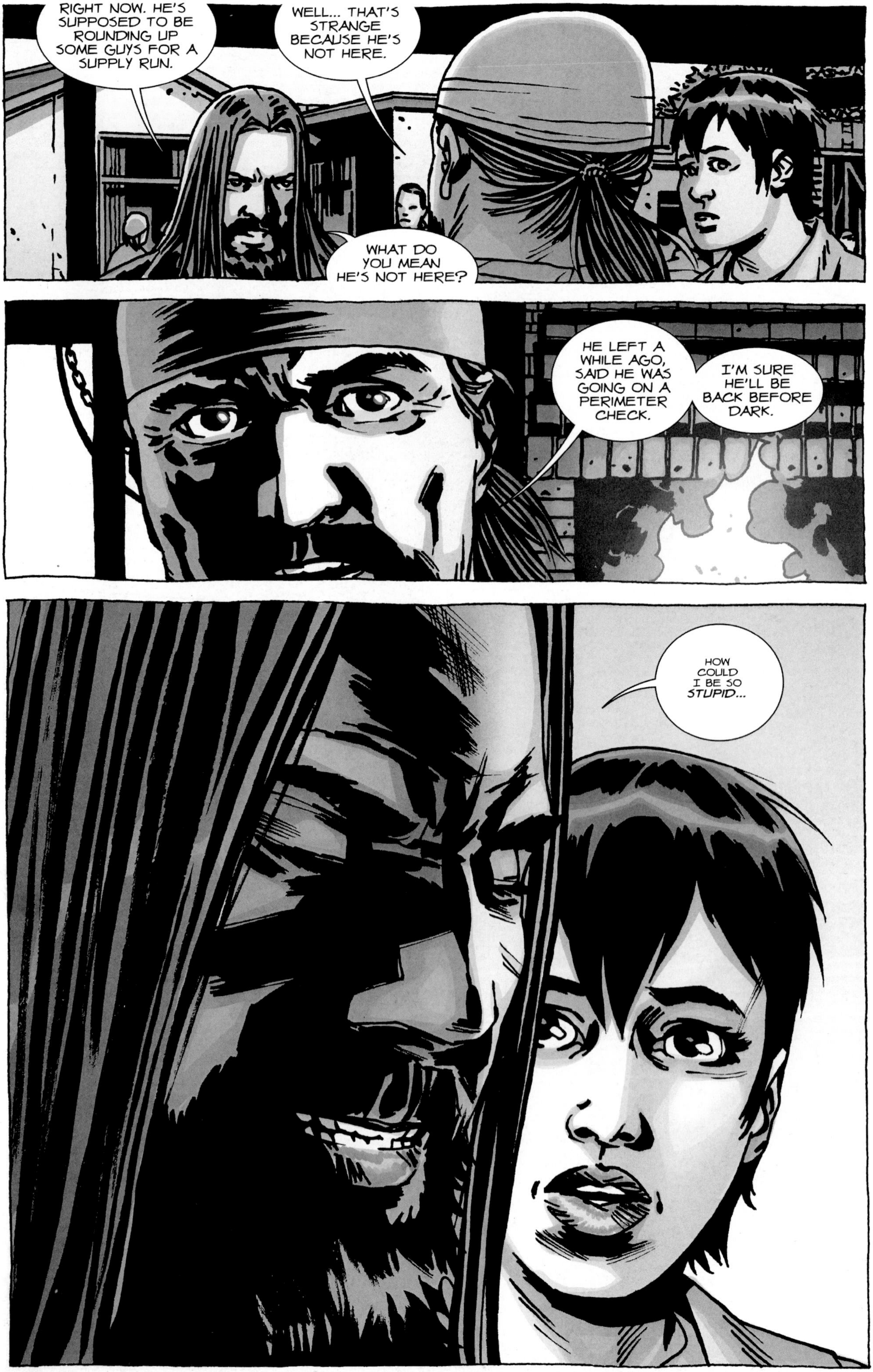
RIGHT NOW. HE'S SUPPOSED TO BE ROUNDING UP SOME GUYS FOR A SUPPLY RUN.
WELL... THAT'S STRANGE BECAUSE HE'S NOT HERE.
WHAT DO YOU MEAN HE'S NOT HERE?
HE LEFT A WHILE AGO, SAID HE WAS GOING ON A PERIMETER CHECK.
I'M SURE HE'LL BE BACK BEFORE DARK.
HOW COULD I BE SO *STUPID*...

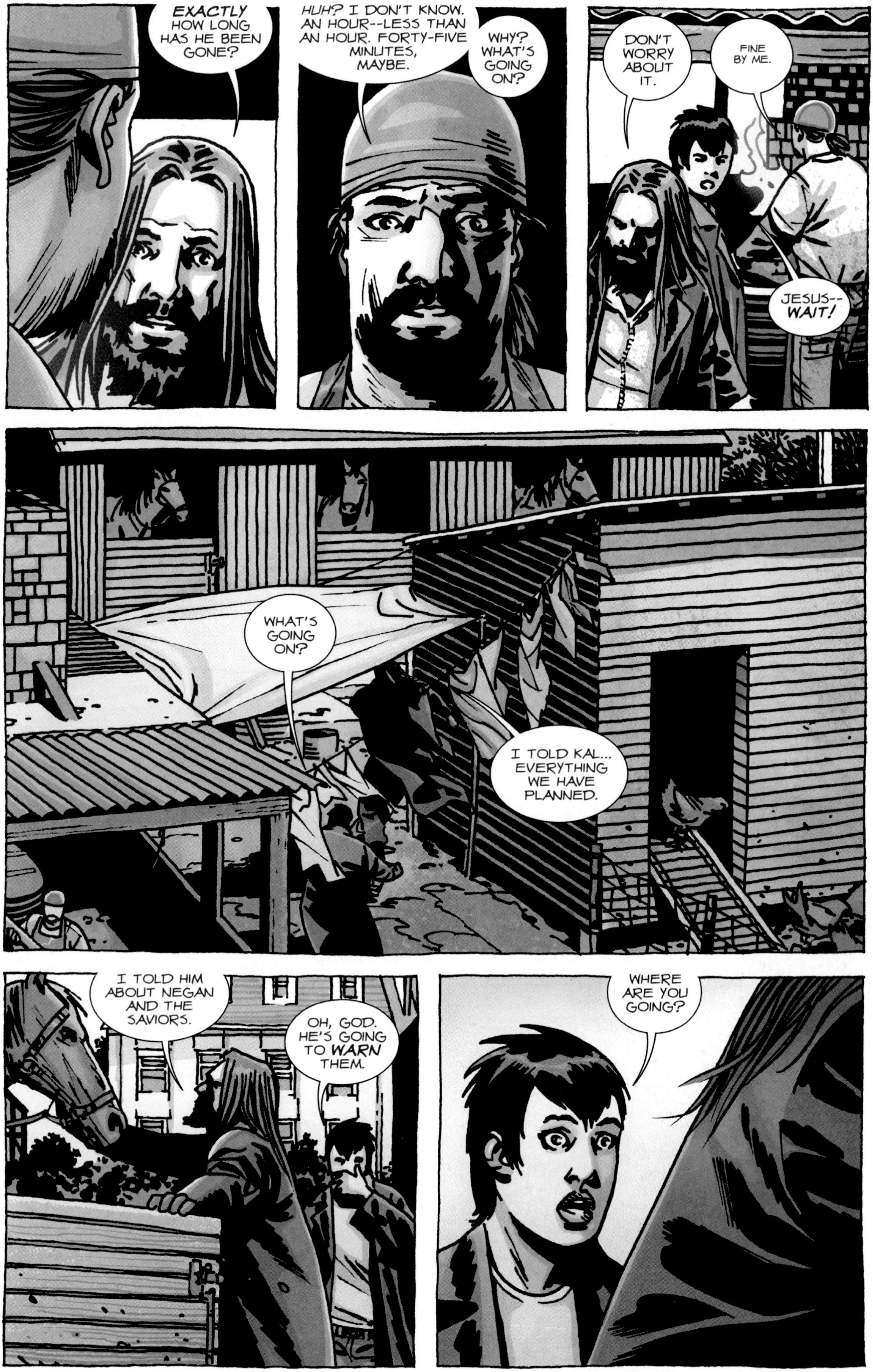
EXACTLY HOW LONG HAS HE BEEN GONE?
HUH? I DON'T KNOW. AN HOUR--LESS THAN AN HOUR. FORTY-FIVE MINUTES, MAYBE.
WHY? WHAT'S GOING ON?
DON'T WORRY ABOUT IT.
FINE BY ME.
JESUS-- WAIT!
WHAT'S GOING ON?
I TOLD KAL... EVERYTHING WE HAVE PLANNED.
I TOLD HIM ABOUT NEGAN AND THE SAVIORS.
OH, GOD. HE'S GOING TO WARN THEM.
WHERE ARE YOU GOING?

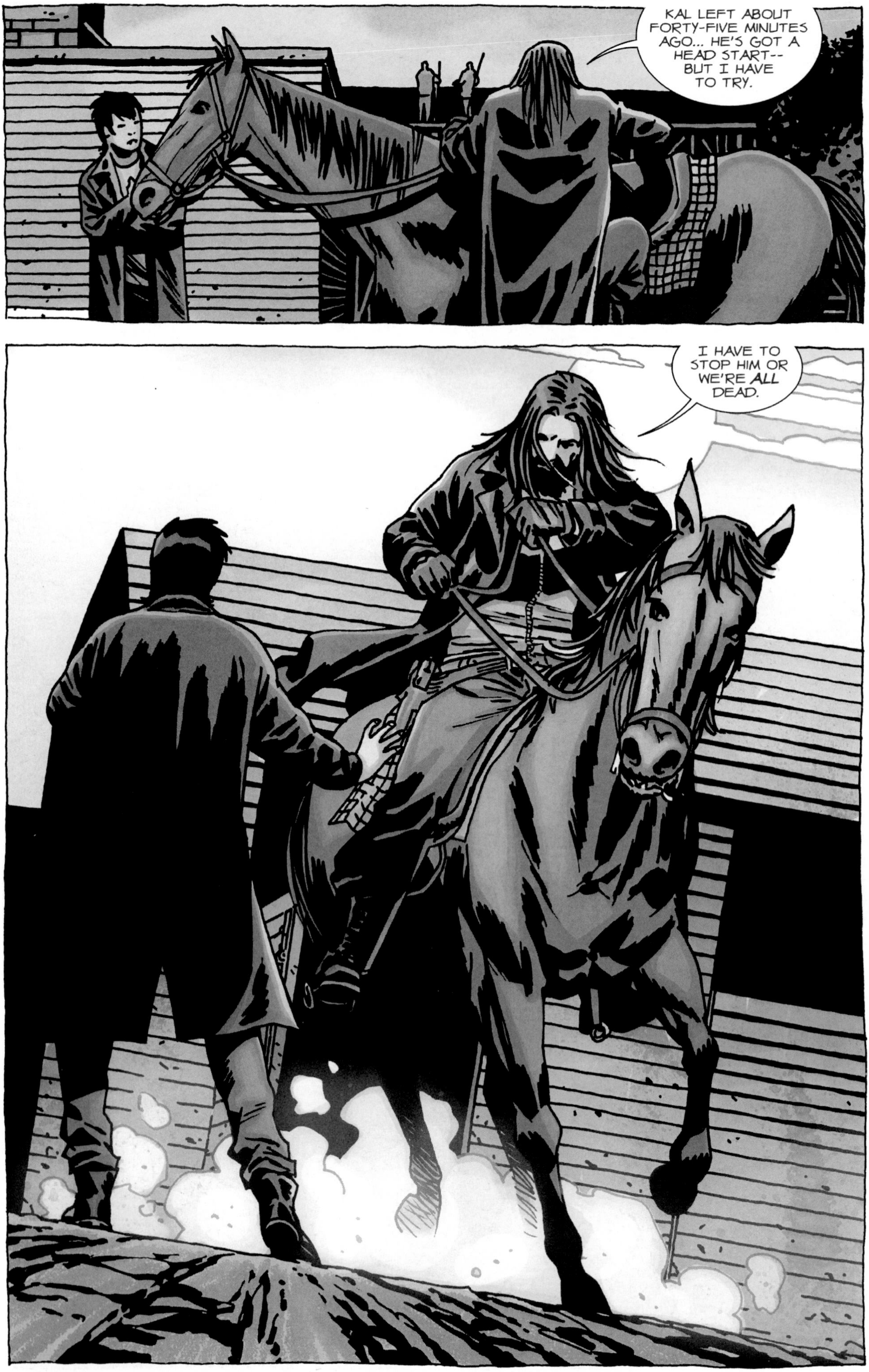
KAL LEFT ABOUT FORTY-FIVE MINUTES AGO... HE'S GOT A HEAD START-- BUT I HAVE TO TRY.
I HAVE TO STOP HIM OR WE'RE ALL DEAD.

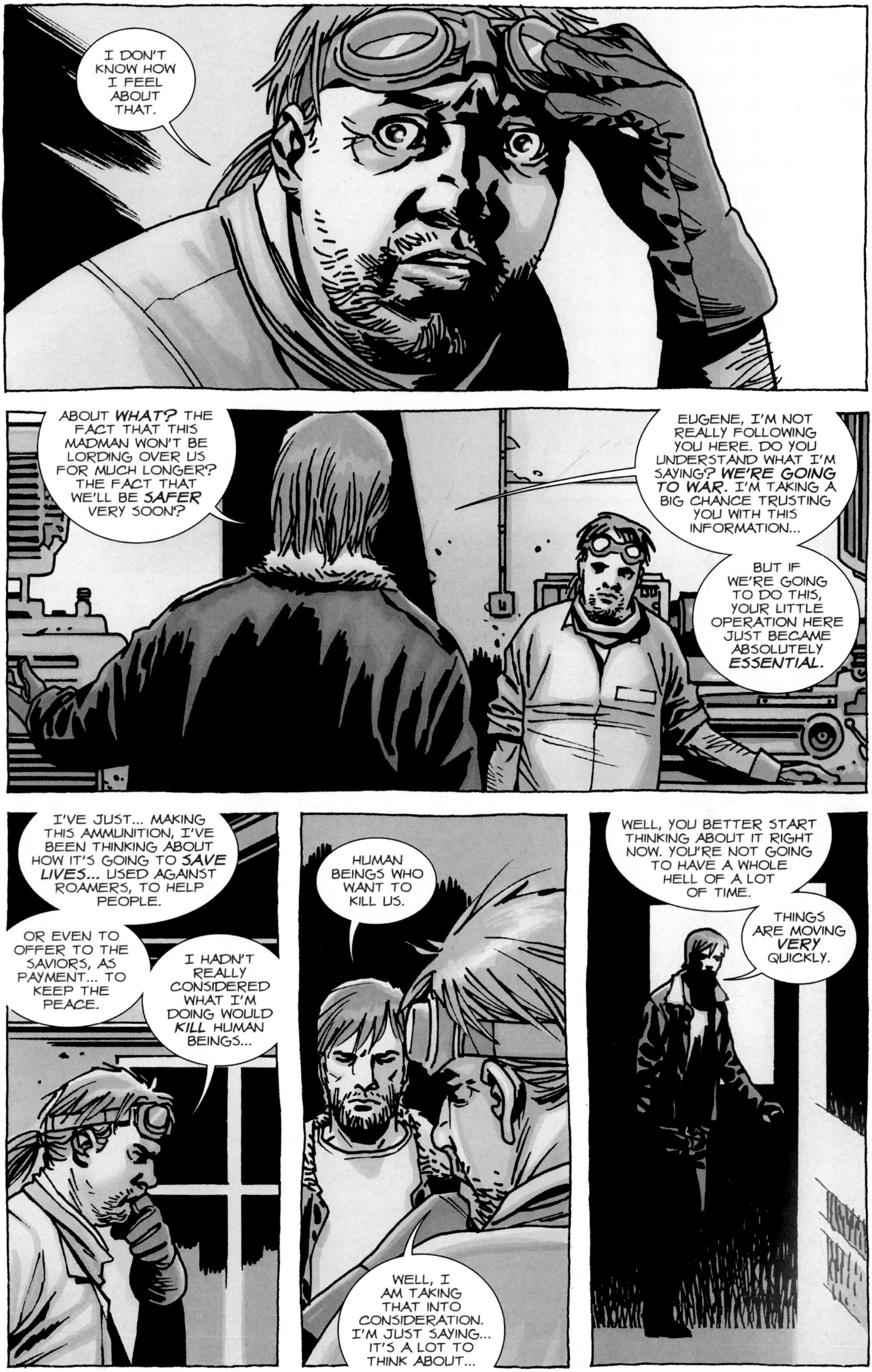
I DON'T KNOW HOW I FEEL ABOUT THAT.
ABOUT WHAT? THE FACT THAT THIS MADMAN WON'T BE LORDING OVER US FOR MUCH LONGER? THE FACT THAT WE'LL BE SAFER VERY SOON?
EUGENE, I'M NOT REALLY FOLLOWING YOU HERE. DO YOU UNDERSTAND WHAT I'M SAYING? WE'RE GOING TO WAR. I'M TAKING A BIG CHANCE TRUSTING YOU WITH THIS INFORMATION...
BUT IF WE'RE GOING TO DO THIS, YOUR LITTLE OPERATION HERE JUST BECAME ABSOLUTELY ESSENTIAL.
I'VE JUST... MAKING THIS AMMUNITION, I'VE BEEN THINKING ABOUT HOW IT'S GOING TO SAVE LIVES... USED AGAINST ROAMERS, TO HELP PEOPLE.
OR EVEN TO OFFER TO THE SAVIORS, AS PAYMENT... TO KEEP THE PEACE.
I HADN'T REALLY CONSIDERED WHAT I'M DOING WOULD KILL HUMAN BEINGS...
HUMAN BEINGS WHO WANT TO KILL US.
WELL, I AM TAKING THAT INTO CONSIDERATION. I'M JUST SAYING... IT'S A LOT TO THINK ABOUT...
WELL, YOU BETTER START THINKING ABOUT IT RIGHT NOW. YOU'RE NOT GOING TO HAVE A WHOLE HELL OF A LOT OF TIME.
THINGS ARE MOVING VERY QUICKLY.

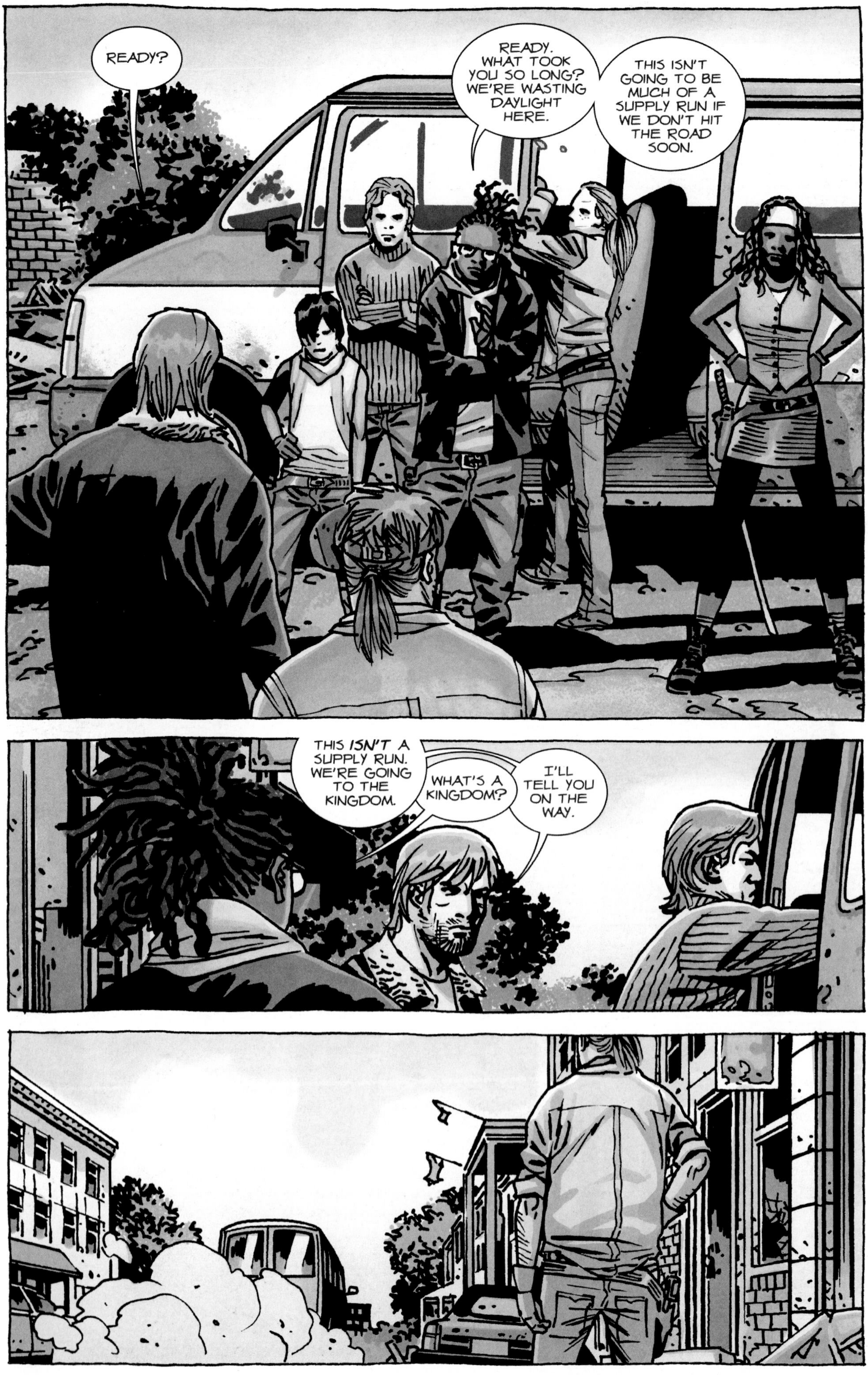
READY?
READY. WHAT TOOK YOU SO LONG? WE'RE WASTING DAYLIGHT HERE.
THIS ISN'T GOING TO BE MUCH OF A SUPPLY RUN IF WE DON'T HIT THE ROAD SOON.
THIS *ISN'T* A SUPPLY RUN. WE'RE GOING TO THE KINGDOM.
WHAT'S A KINGDOM?
I'LL TELL YOU ON THE WAY.

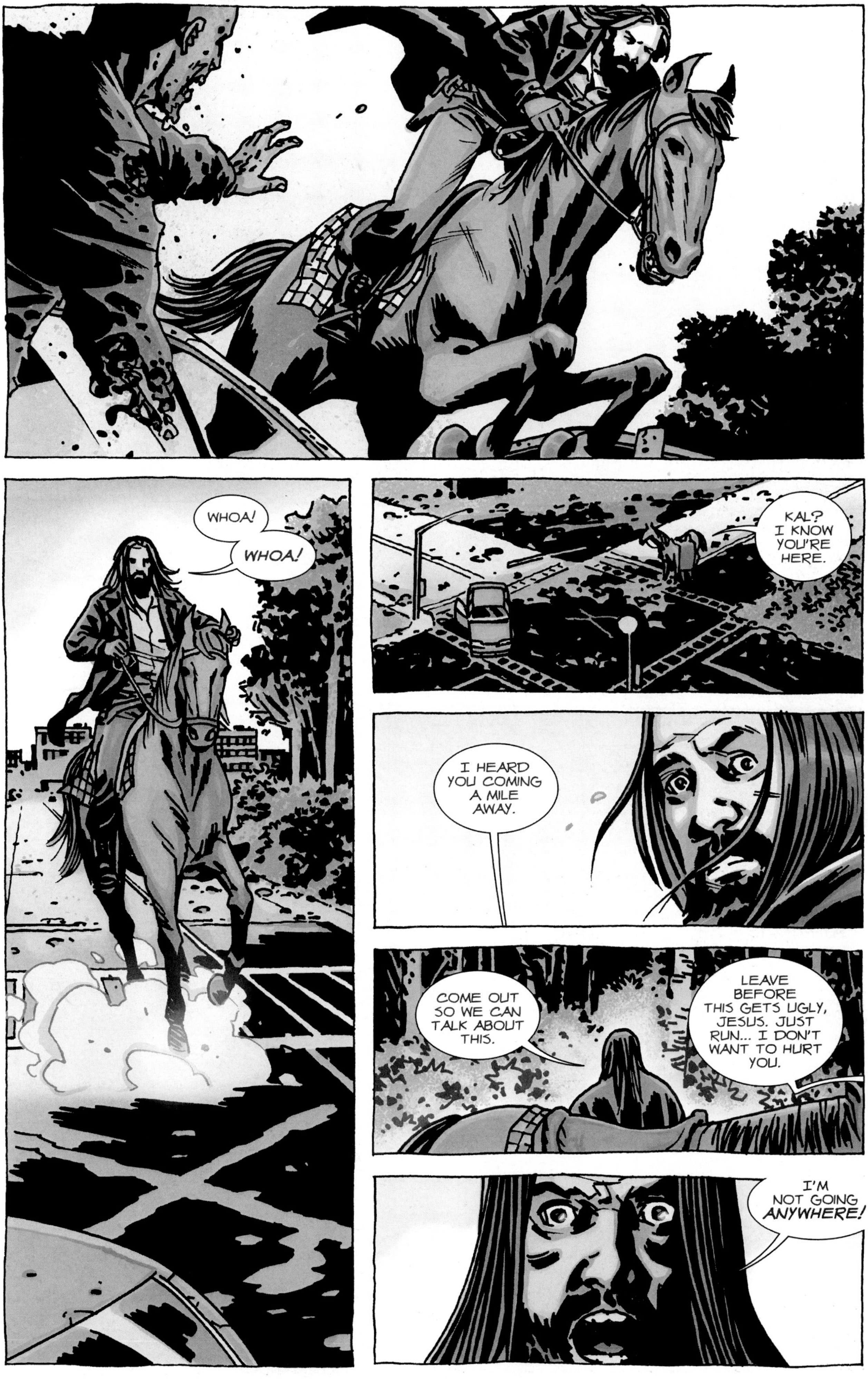
WHOA!
WHOA!
KAL? I KNOW YOU'RE HERE.
I HEARD YOU COMING A MILE AWAY.
COME OUT SO WE CAN TALK ABOUT THIS.
LEAVE BEFORE THIS GETS UGLY, JESUS. JUST RUN... I DON'T WANT TO HURT YOU.
I'M NOT GOING ANYWHERE!

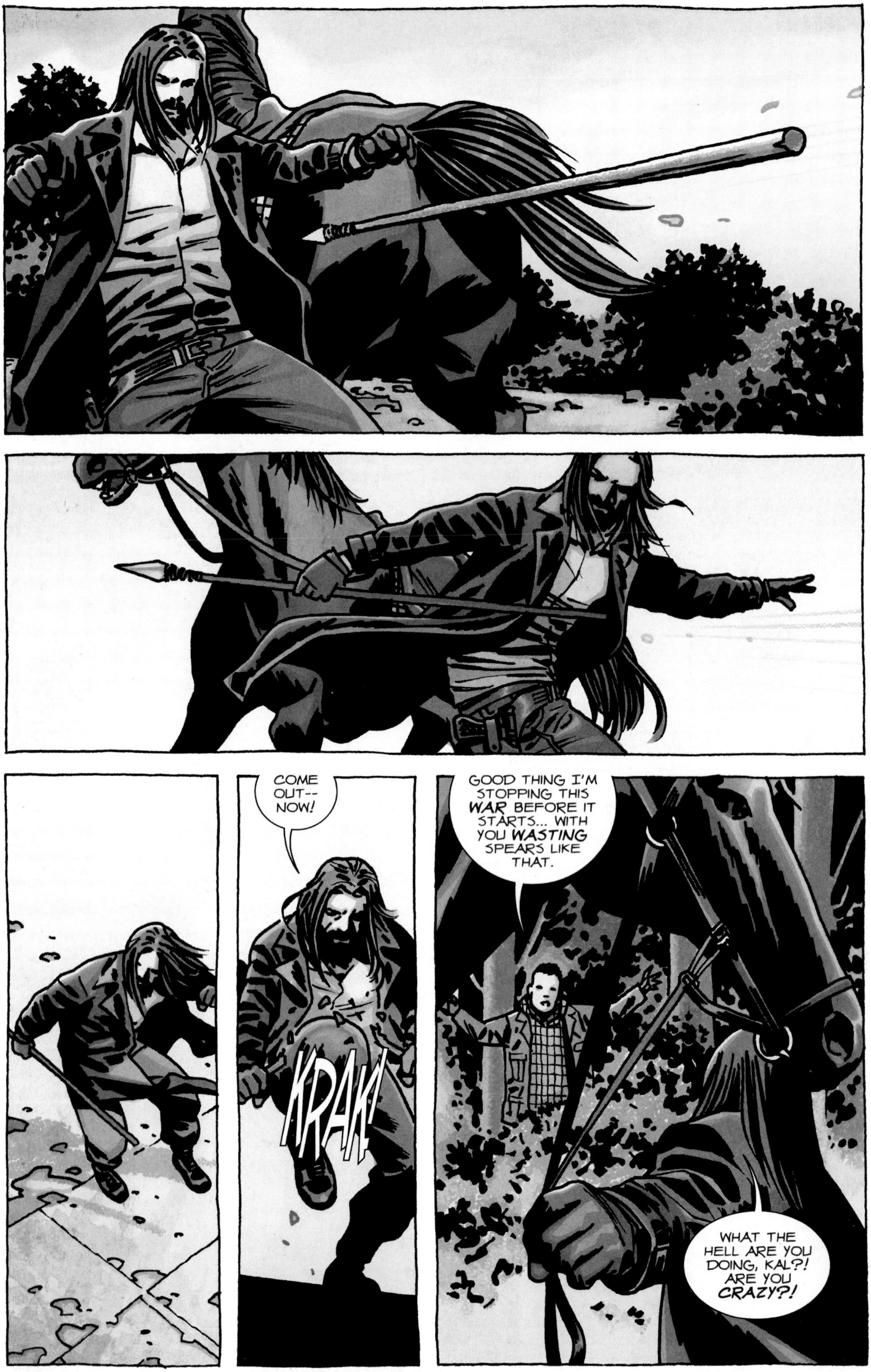
COME OUT-- NOW!
KRAK!
GOOD THING I'M STOPPING THIS WAR BEFORE IT STARTS... WITH YOU WASTING SPEARS LIKE THAT.
WHAT THE HELL ARE YOU DOING, KAL?! ARE YOU CRAZY?!

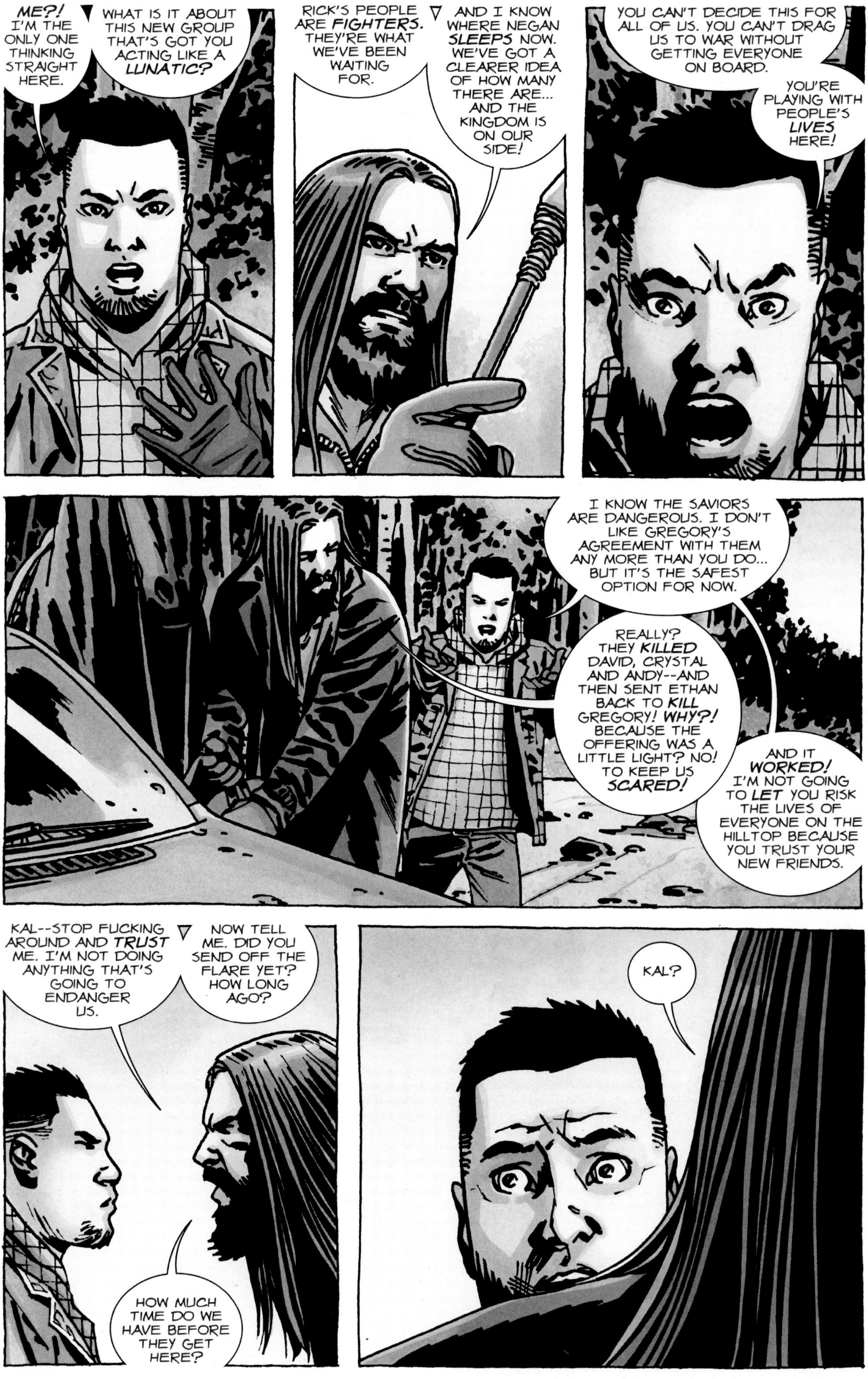
ME?! I'M THE ONLY ONE THINKING STRAIGHT HERE.
WHAT IS IT ABOUT THIS NEW GROUP THAT'S GOT YOU ACTING LIKE A LUNATIC?
RICK'S PEOPLE ARE FIGHTERS. THEY'RE WHAT WE'VE BEEN WAITING FOR.
AND I KNOW WHERE NEGAN SLEEPS NOW. WE'VE GOT A CLEARER IDEA OF HOW MANY THERE ARE... AND THE KINGDOM IS ON OUR SIDE!
YOU CAN'T DECIDE THIS FOR ALL OF US. YOU CAN'T DRAG US TO WAR WITHOUT GETTING EVERYONE ON BOARD.
YOU'RE PLAYING WITH PEOPLE'S LIVES HERE!
I KNOW THE SAVIORS ARE DANGEROUS. I DON'T LIKE GREGORY'S AGREEMENT WITH THEM ANY MORE THAN YOU DO... BUT IT'S THE SAFEST OPTION FOR NOW.
REALLY? THEY KILLED DAVID, CRYSTAL AND ANDY--AND THEN SENT ETHAN BACK TO KILL GREGORY! WHY?! BECAUSE THE OFFERING WAS A LITTLE LIGHT? NO! TO KEEP US SCARED!
AND IT WORKED! I'M NOT GOING TO LET YOU RISK THE LIVES OF EVERYONE ON THE HILLTOP BECAUSE YOU TRUST YOUR NEW FRIENDS.
KAL--STOP FUCKING AROUND AND TRUST ME. I'M NOT DOING ANYTHING THAT'S GOING TO ENDANGER US.
NOW TELL ME. DID YOU SEND OFF THE FLARE YET? HOW LONG AGO?
HOW MUCH TIME DO WE HAVE BEFORE THEY GET HERE?
KAL?

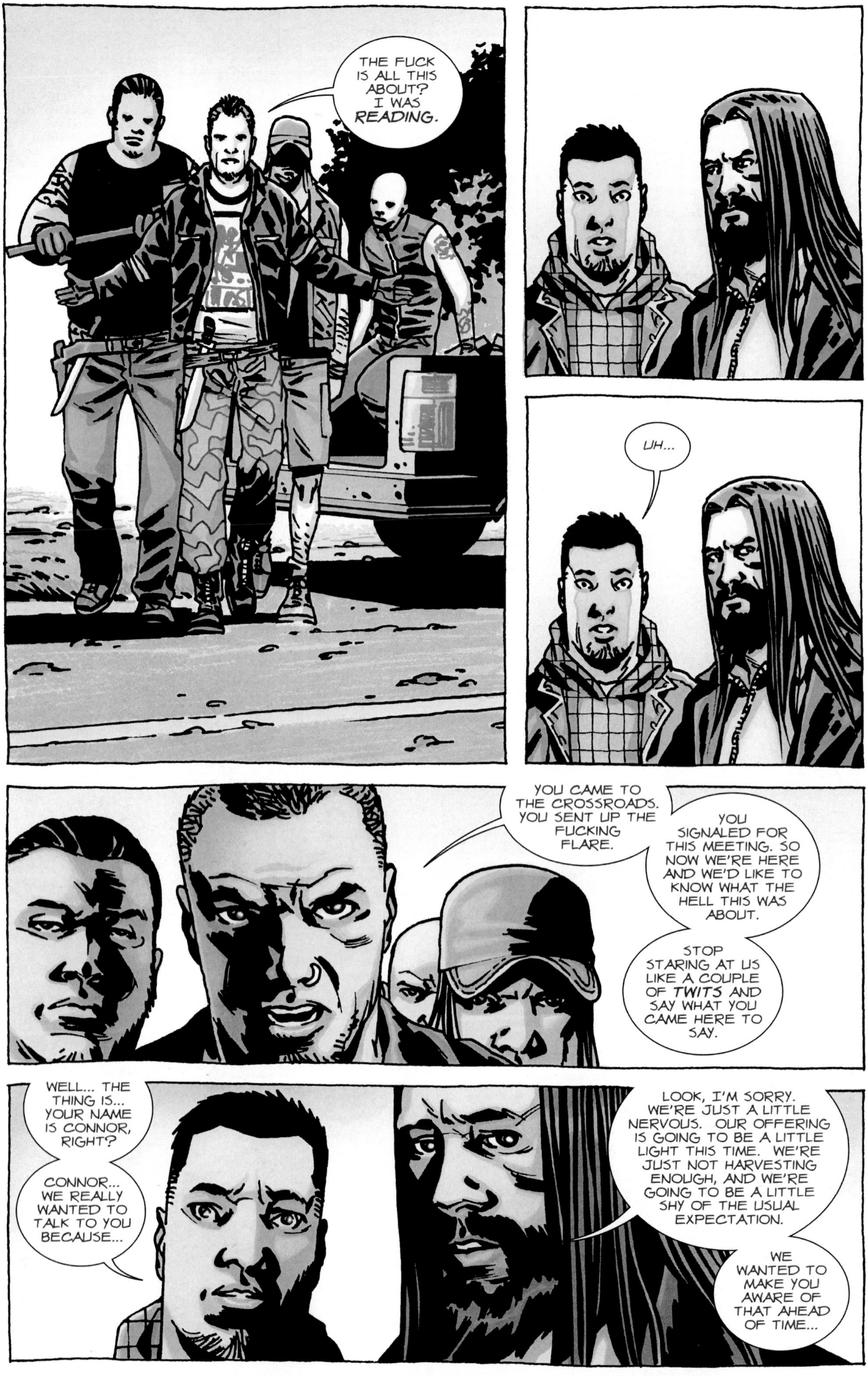
THE FUCK IS ALL THIS ABOUT? I WAS *READING*.
UH...
YOU CAME TO THE CROSSROADS. YOU SENT UP THE FUCKING FLARE.
YOU SIGNALED FOR THIS MEETING. SO NOW WE'RE HERE AND WE'D LIKE TO KNOW WHAT THE HELL THIS WAS ABOUT.
STOP STARING AT US LIKE A COUPLE OF *TWITS* AND SAY WHAT YOU CAME HERE TO SAY.
WELL... THE THING IS... YOUR NAME IS CONNOR, RIGHT?
CONNOR... WE REALLY WANTED TO TALK TO YOU BECAUSE...
LOOK, I'M SORRY. WE'RE JUST A LITTLE NERVOUS. OUR OFFERING IS GOING TO BE A LITTLE LIGHT THIS TIME. WE'RE JUST NOT HARVESTING ENOUGH, AND WE'RE GOING TO BE A LITTLE SHY OF THE USUAL EXPECTATION.
WE WANTED TO MAKE YOU AWARE OF THAT AHEAD OF TIME...

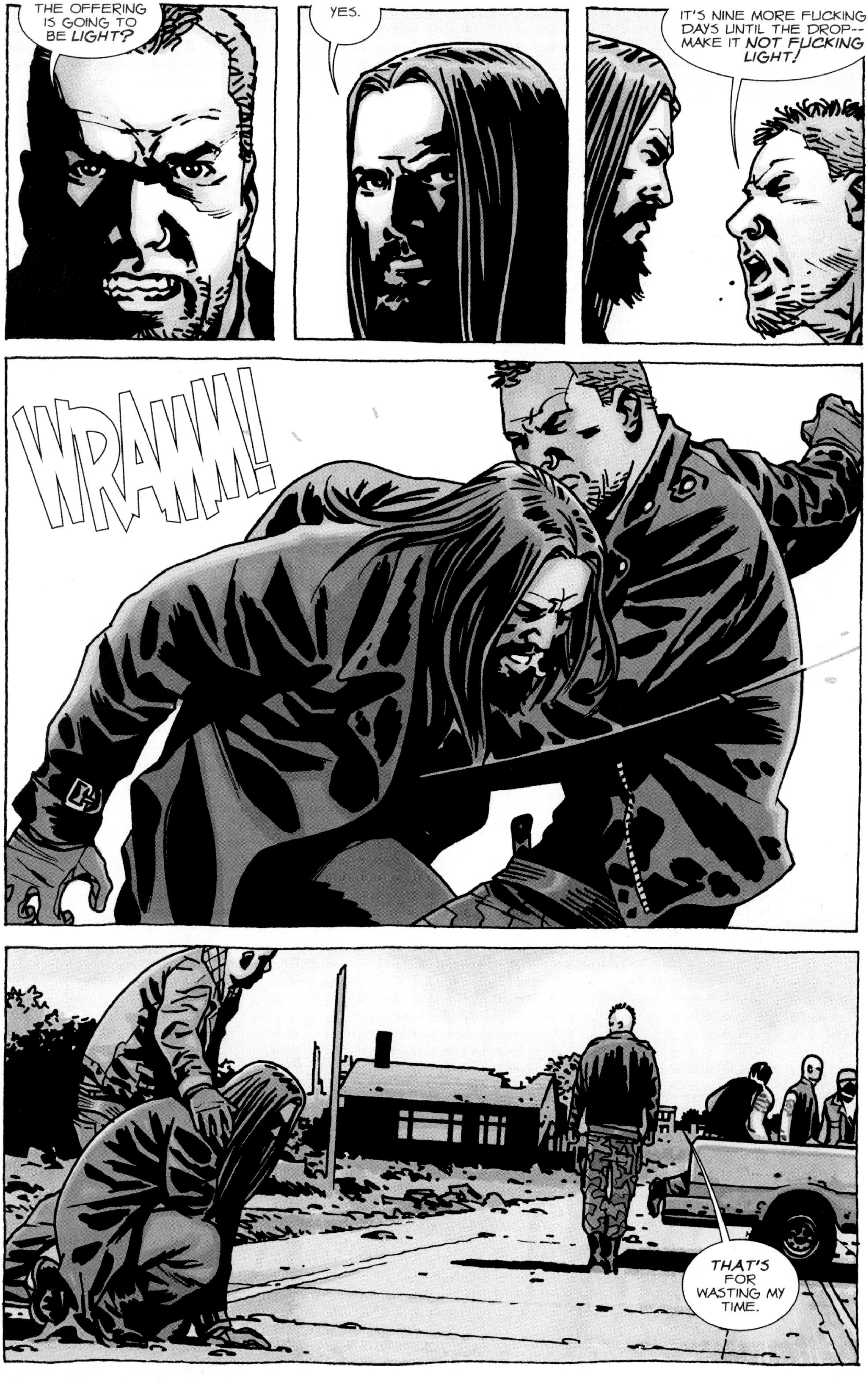
THE OFFERING IS GOING TO BE LIGHT?
YES.
IT'S NINE MORE FUCKING DAYS UNTIL THE DROP-- MAKE IT NOT FUCKING LIGHT!
WRAMM!
THAT'S FOR WASTING MY TIME.

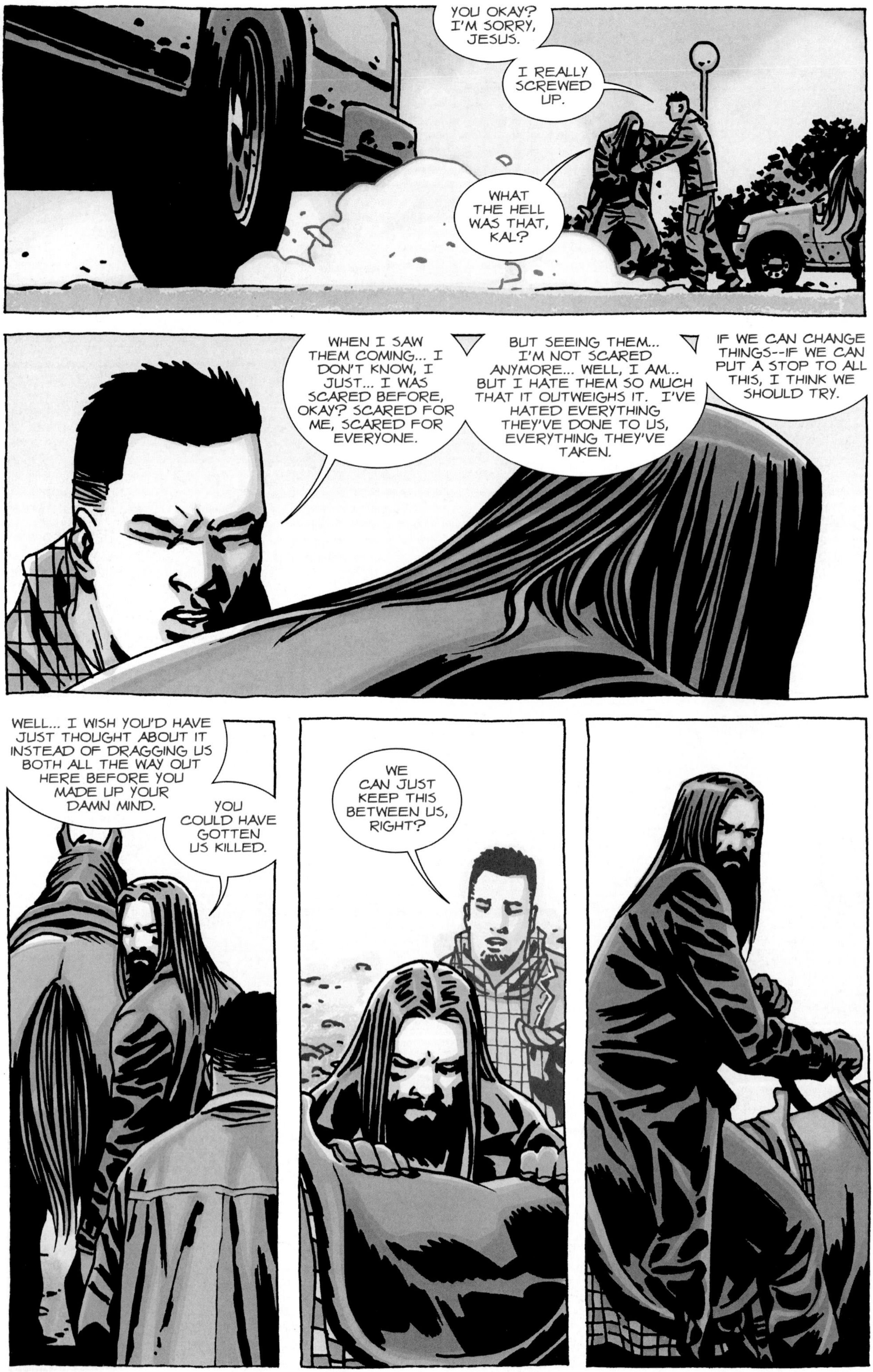

YOU OKAY? I'M SORRY, JESUS.
I REALLY SCREWED UP.
WHAT THE HELL WAS THAT, KAL?
WHEN I SAW THEM COMING... I DON'T KNOW, I JUST... I WAS SCARED BEFORE, OKAY? SCARED FOR ME, SCARED FOR EVERYONE.
BUT SEEING THEM... I'M NOT SCARED ANYMORE... WELL, I AM... BUT I HATE THEM SO MUCH THAT IT OUTWEIGHS IT. I'VE HATED EVERYTHING THEY'VE DONE TO US, EVERYTHING THEY'VE TAKEN.
IF WE CAN CHANGE THINGS--IF WE CAN PUT A STOP TO ALL THIS, I THINK WE SHOULD TRY.
WELL... I WISH YOU'D HAVE JUST THOUGHT ABOUT IT INSTEAD OF DRAGGING US BOTH ALL THE WAY OUT HERE BEFORE YOU MADE UP YOUR DAMN MIND.
YOU COULD HAVE GOTTEN US KILLED.
WE CAN JUST KEEP THIS BETWEEN US, RIGHT?

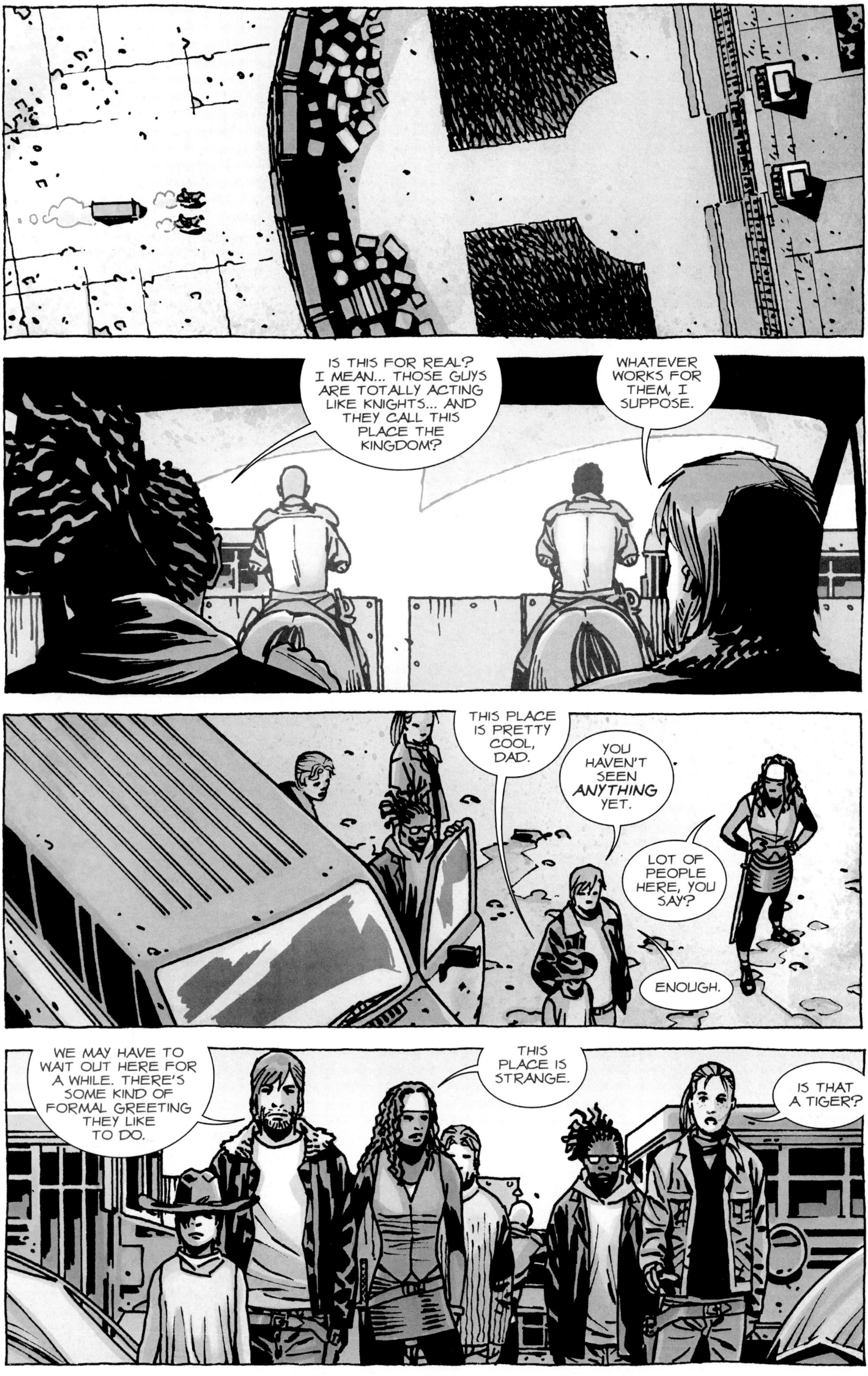
IS THIS FOR REAL? I MEAN... THOSE GUYS ARE TOTALLY ACTING LIKE KNIGHTS... AND THEY CALL THIS PLACE THE KINGDOM?
WHATEVER WORKS FOR THEM, I SUPPOSE.
THIS PLACE IS PRETTY COOL, DAD.
YOU HAVEN'T SEEN ANYTHING YET.
LOT OF PEOPLE HERE, YOU SAY?
ENOUGH.
WE MAY HAVE TO WAIT OUT HERE FOR A WHILE. THERE'S SOME KIND OF FORMAL GREETING THEY LIKE TO DO.
THIS PLACE IS STRANGE.
IS THAT A TIGER?

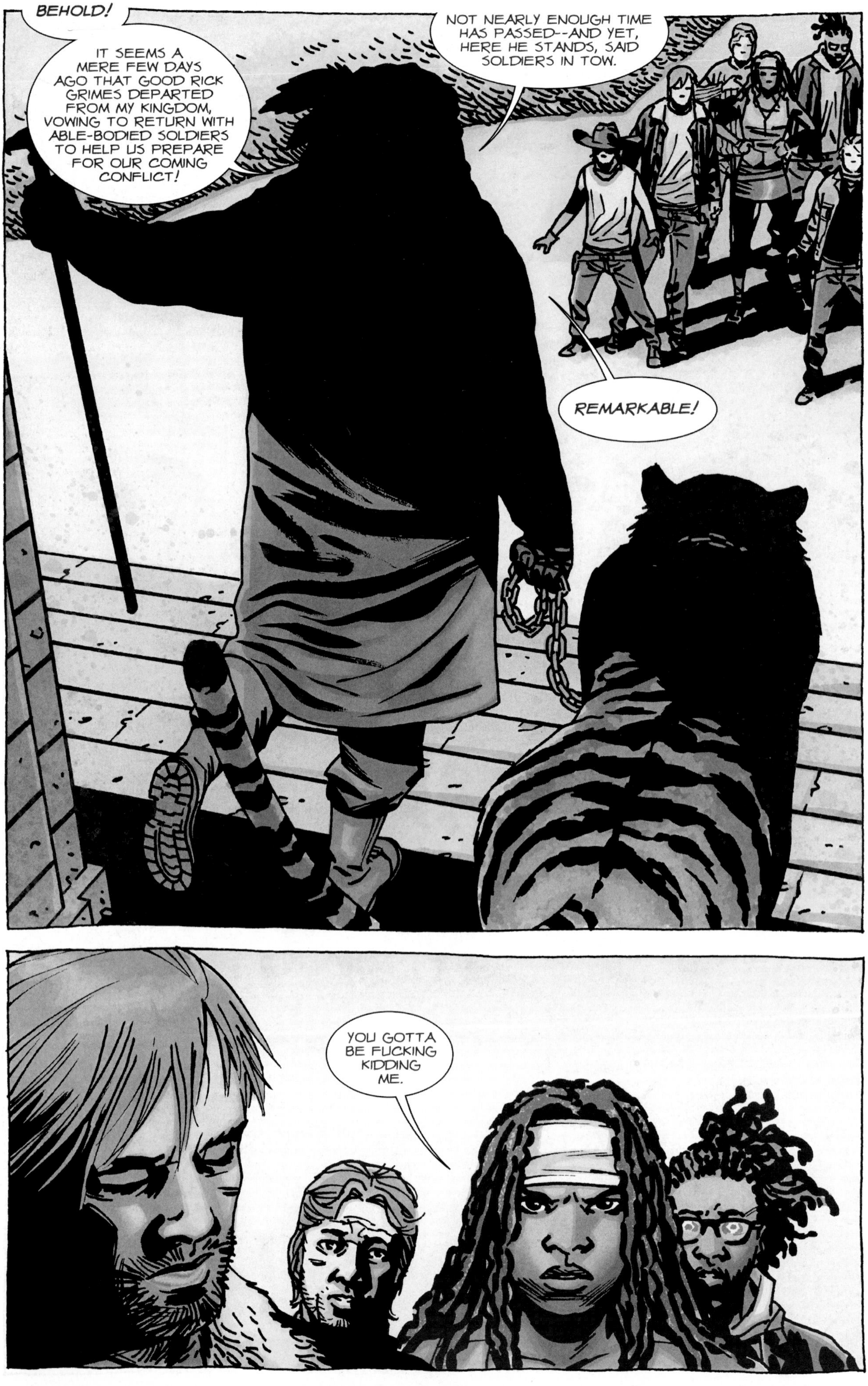
BEHOLD!
IT SEEMS A MERE FEW DAYS AGO THAT GOOD RICK GRIMES DEPARTED FROM MY KINGDOM, VOWING TO RETURN WITH ABLE-BODIED SOLDIERS TO HELP US PREPARE FOR OUR COMING CONFLICT!
NOT NEARLY ENOUGH TIME HAS PASSED--AND YET, HERE HE STANDS, SAID SOLDIERS IN TOW.
REMARKABLE!
YOU GOTTA BE FUCKING KIDDING ME.

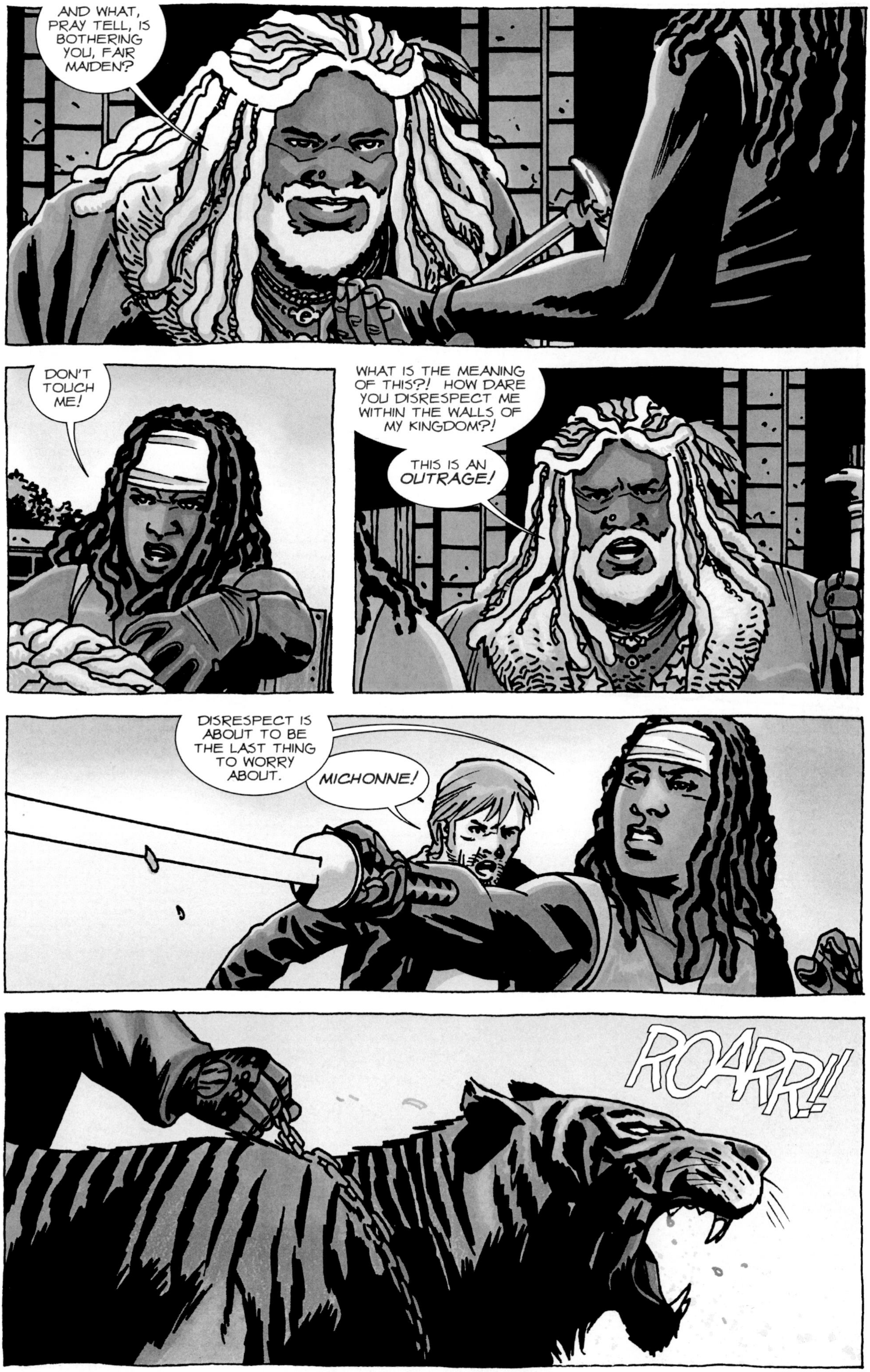
AND WHAT, PRAY TELL, IS BOTHERING YOU, FAIR MAIDEN?
DON'T TOUCH ME!
WHAT IS THE MEANING OF THIS?! HOW DARE YOU DISRESPECT ME WITHIN THE WALLS OF MY KINGDOM?!
THIS IS AN OUTRAGE!
DISRESPECT IS ABOUT TO BE THE LAST THING TO WORRY ABOUT.
MICHONNE!
ROARR!!

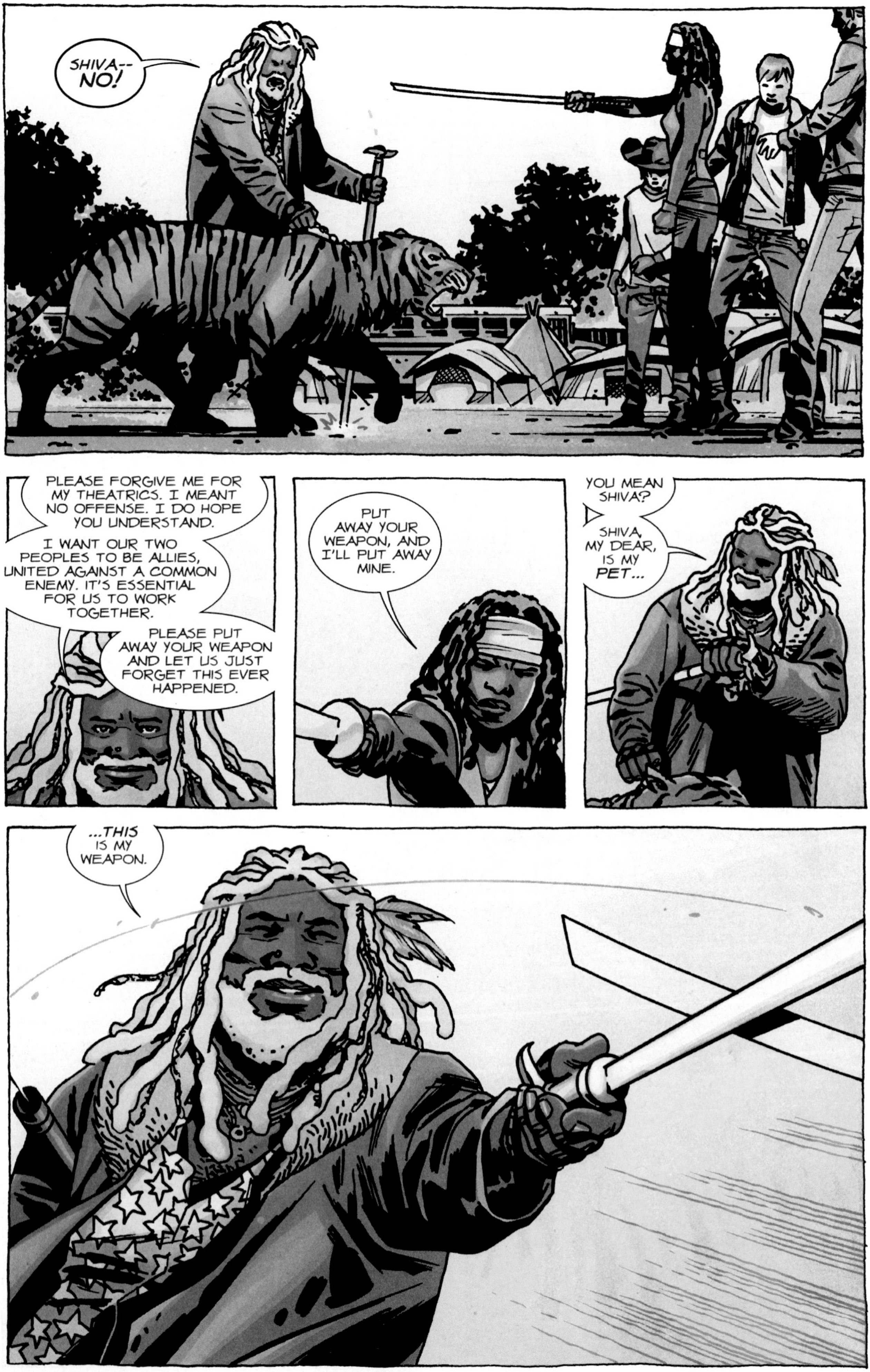
SHIVA-- NO!
PLEASE FORGIVE ME FOR MY THEATRICS. I MEANT NO OFFENSE. I DO HOPE YOU UNDERSTAND.
I WANT OUR TWO PEOPLES TO BE ALLIES, UNITED AGAINST A COMMON ENEMY. IT'S ESSENTIAL FOR US TO WORK TOGETHER.
PLEASE PUT AWAY YOUR WEAPON AND LET US JUST FORGET THIS EVER HAPPENED.
PUT AWAY YOUR WEAPON, AND I'LL PUT AWAY MINE.
YOU MEAN SHIVA?
SHIVA, MY DEAR, IS MY PET...
...THIS IS MY WEAPON.

THIS ISN'T--

IT'S OKAY. CALM YOURSELF.

I SIMPLY WANTED TO SEE IF *MINE* WAS BIGGER.

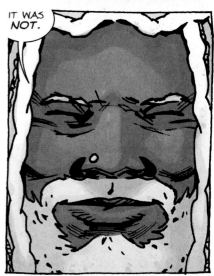

IT WAS *NOT*.

COME. MAKE YOURSELVES AT HOME.

YOU HAVE HAD A LONG JOURNEY. LET US PUT THIS NONSENSE BEHIND US AND *FEAST!*

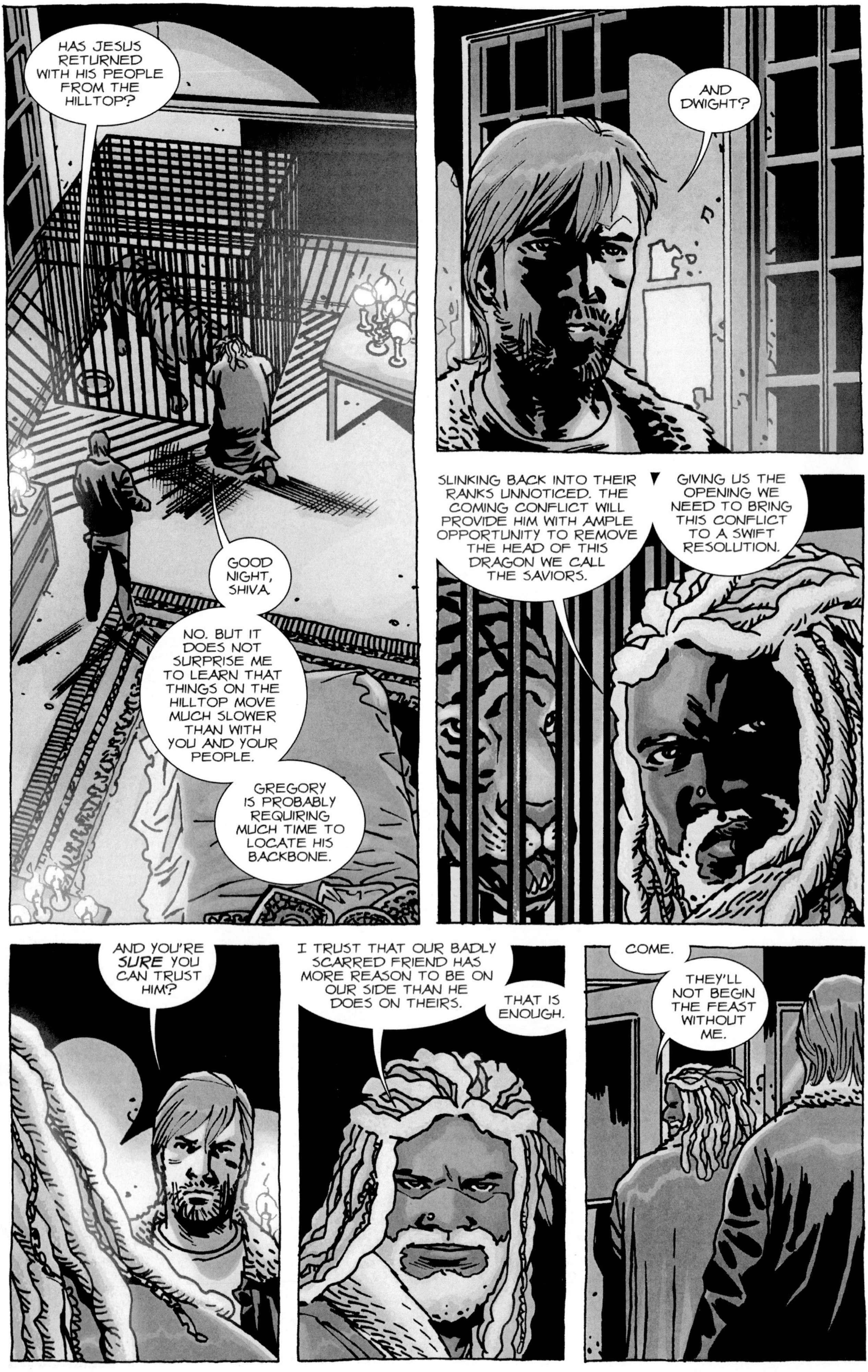
HAS JESUS RETURNED WITH HIS PEOPLE FROM THE HILLTOP?
GOOD NIGHT, SHIVA.
NO. BUT IT DOES NOT SURPRISE ME TO LEARN THAT THINGS ON THE HILLTOP MOVE MUCH SLOWER THAN WITH YOU AND YOUR PEOPLE.
GREGORY IS PROBABLY REQUIRING MUCH TIME TO LOCATE HIS BACKBONE.
AND DWIGHT?
SLINKING BACK INTO THEIR RANKS UNNOTICED. THE COMING CONFLICT WILL PROVIDE HIM WITH AMPLE OPPORTUNITY TO REMOVE THE HEAD OF THIS DRAGON WE CALL THE SAVIORS.
GIVING US THE OPENING WE NEED TO BRING THIS CONFLICT TO A SWIFT RESOLUTION.
AND YOU'RE *SURE* YOU CAN TRUST HIM?
I TRUST THAT OUR BADLY SCARRED FRIEND HAS MORE REASON TO BE ON OUR SIDE THAN HE DOES ON THEIRS.
THAT IS ENOUGH.
COME.
THEY'LL NOT BEGIN THE FEAST WITHOUT ME.

DINE! ENJOY THE BOAR WE'VE SLAUGHTERED IN YOUR HONOR!

EAT AND BE MERRY! FOR TOMORROW WE GO TO WAR!

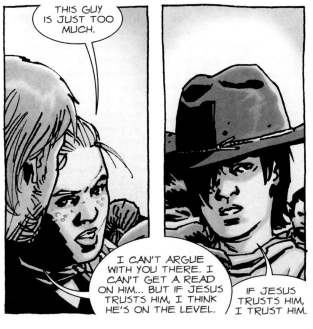

THIS GUY IS JUST TOO MUCH.

I CAN'T ARGUE WITH YOU THERE. I CAN'T GET A READ ON HIM... BUT IF JESUS TRUSTS HIM, I THINK HE'S ON THE LEVEL.

IF JESUS TRUSTS HIM, I TRUST HIM.

TO NEW FRIENDS-- AND THE END OF OLD ENEMIES.

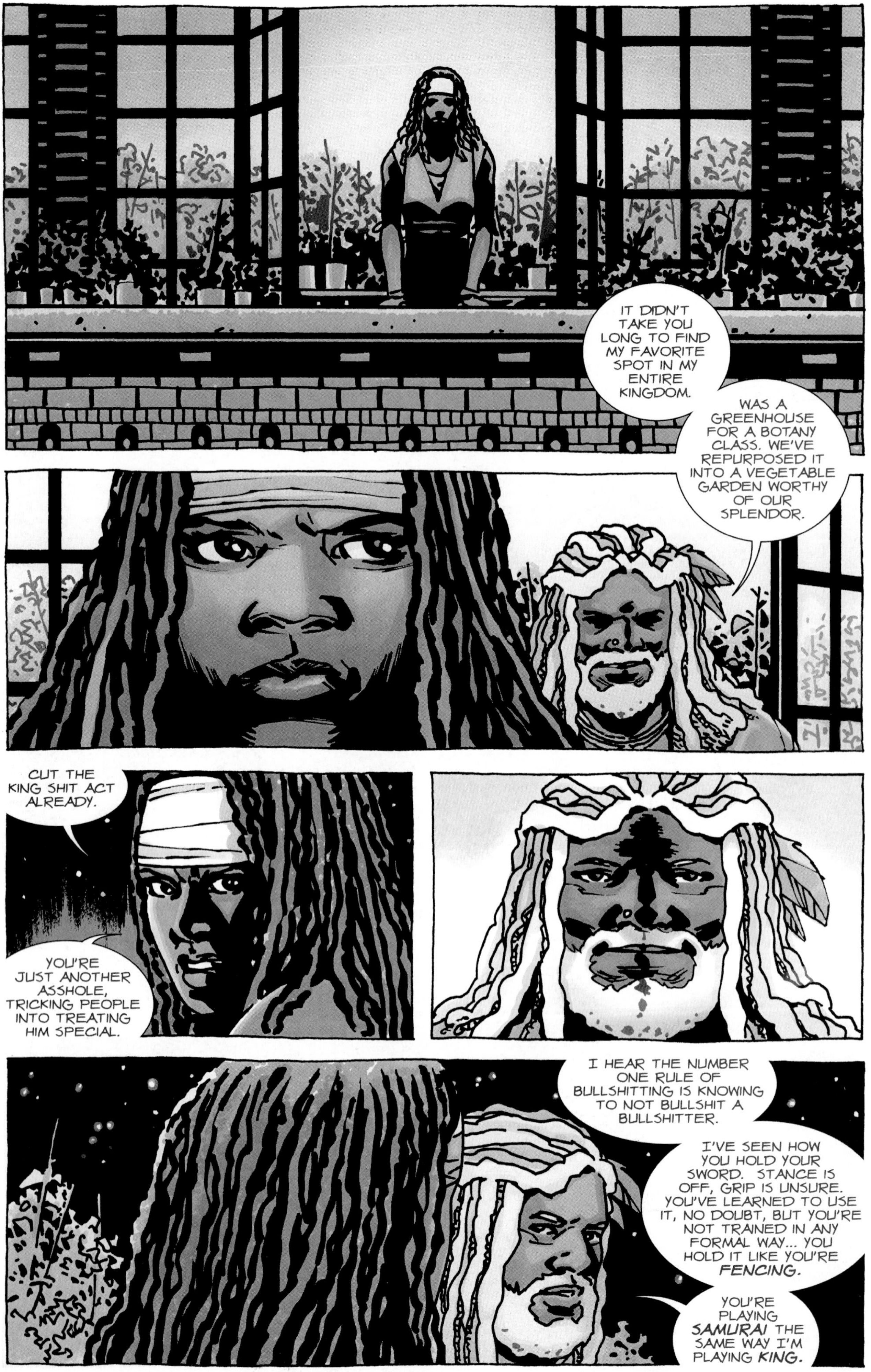

IT DIDN'T TAKE YOU LONG TO FIND MY FAVORITE SPOT IN MY ENTIRE KINGDOM.
WAS A GREENHOUSE FOR A BOTANY CLASS. WE'VE REPURPOSED IT INTO A VEGETABLE GARDEN WORTHY OF OUR SPLENDOR.
CUT THE KING SHIT ACT ALREADY.
YOU'RE JUST ANOTHER ASSHOLE, TRICKING PEOPLE INTO TREATING HIM SPECIAL.
I HEAR THE NUMBER ONE RULE OF BULLSHITTING IS KNOWING TO NOT BULLSHIT A BULLSHITTER.
I'VE SEEN HOW YOU HOLD YOUR SWORD. STANCE IS OFF, GRIP IS UNSURE. YOU'VE LEARNED TO USE IT, NO DOUBT, BUT YOU'RE NOT TRAINED IN ANY FORMAL WAY... YOU HOLD IT LIKE YOU'RE FENCING.
YOU'RE PLAYING SAMURAI THE SAME WAY I'M PLAYING KING.

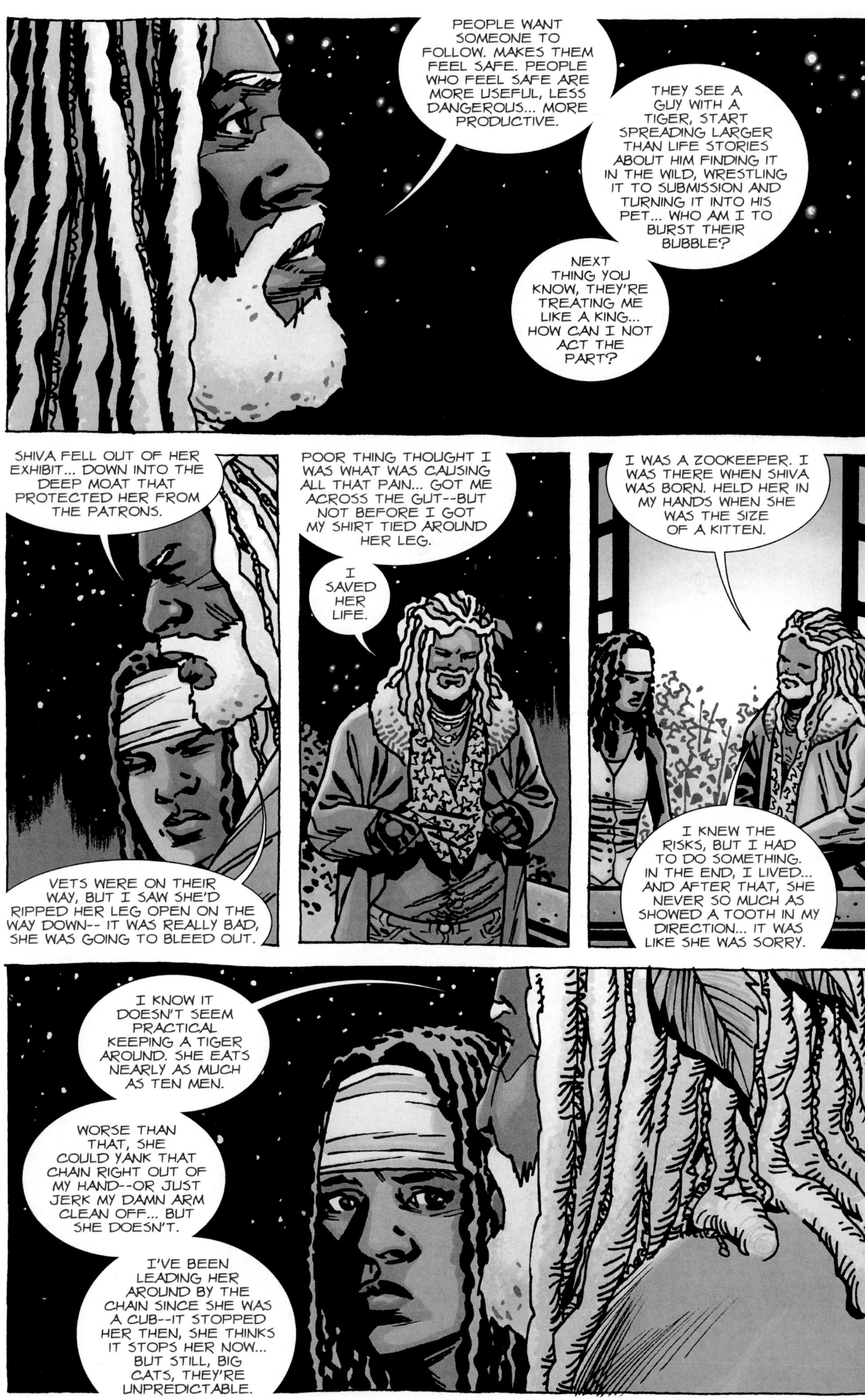
PEOPLE WANT SOMEONE TO FOLLOW. MAKES THEM FEEL SAFE. PEOPLE WHO FEEL SAFE ARE MORE USEFUL, LESS DANGEROUS... MORE PRODUCTIVE.
THEY SEE A GUY WITH A TIGER, START SPREADING LARGER THAN LIFE STORIES ABOUT HIM FINDING IT IN THE WILD, WRESTLING IT TO SUBMISSION AND TURNING IT INTO HIS PET... WHO AM I TO BURST THEIR BUBBLE?
NEXT THING YOU KNOW, THEY'RE TREATING ME LIKE A KING... HOW CAN I NOT ACT THE PART?
SHIVA FELL OUT OF HER EXHIBIT... DOWN INTO THE DEEP MOAT THAT PROTECTED HER FROM THE PATRONS.
VETS WERE ON THEIR WAY, BUT I SAW SHE'D RIPPED HER LEG OPEN ON THE WAY DOWN-- IT WAS REALLY BAD, SHE WAS GOING TO BLEED OUT.
POOR THING THOUGHT I WAS WHAT WAS CAUSING ALL THAT PAIN... GOT ME ACROSS THE GUT--BUT NOT BEFORE I GOT MY SHIRT TIED AROUND HER LEG.
I SAVED HER LIFE.
I WAS A ZOOKEEPER. I WAS THERE WHEN SHIVA WAS BORN. HELD HER IN MY HANDS WHEN SHE WAS THE SIZE OF A KITTEN.
I KNEW THE RISKS, BUT I HAD TO DO SOMETHING. IN THE END, I LIVED... AND AFTER THAT, SHE NEVER SO MUCH AS SHOWED A TOOTH IN MY DIRECTION... IT WAS LIKE SHE WAS SORRY.
I KNOW IT DOESN'T SEEM PRACTICAL KEEPING A TIGER AROUND. SHE EATS NEARLY AS MUCH AS TEN MEN.
WORSE THAN THAT, SHE COULD YANK THAT CHAIN RIGHT OUT OF MY HAND--OR JUST JERK MY DAMN ARM CLEAN OFF... BUT SHE DOESN'T.
I'VE BEEN LEADING HER AROUND BY THE CHAIN SINCE SHE WAS A CUB--IT STOPPED HER THEN, SHE THINKS IT STOPS HER NOW... BUT STILL, BIG CATS, THEY'RE UNPREDICTABLE.

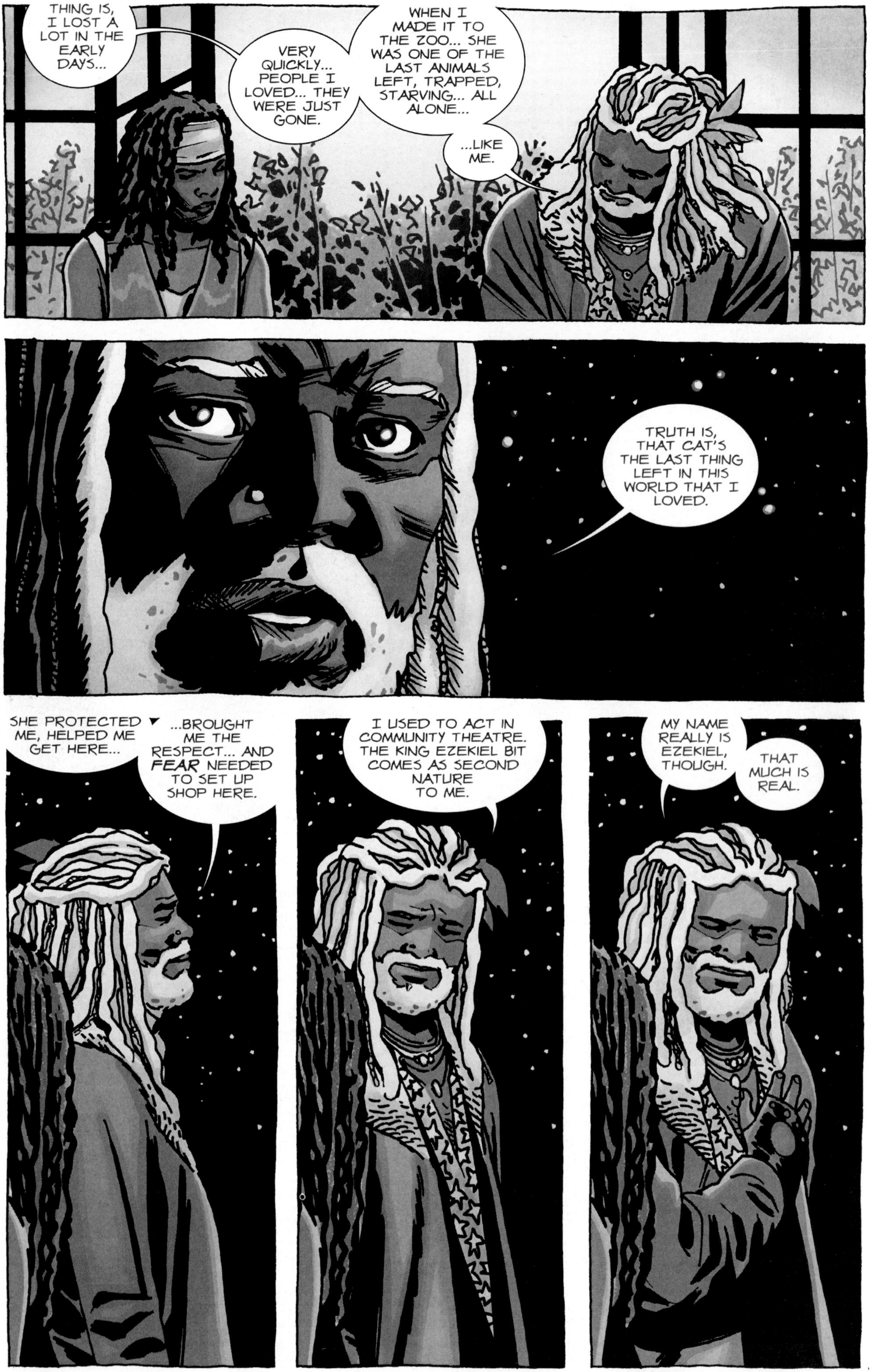
THING IS, I LOST A LOT IN THE EARLY DAYS...
VERY QUICKLY... PEOPLE I LOVED... THEY WERE JUST GONE.
WHEN I MADE IT TO THE ZOO... SHE WAS ONE OF THE LAST ANIMALS LEFT, TRAPPED, STARVING... ALL ALONE...
...LIKE ME.
TRUTH IS, THAT CAT'S THE LAST THING LEFT IN THIS WORLD THAT I LOVED.
SHE PROTECTED ME, HELPED ME GET HERE...
...BROUGHT ME THE RESPECT... AND FEAR NEEDED TO SET UP SHOP HERE.
I USED TO ACT IN COMMUNITY THEATRE. THE KING EZEKIEL BIT COMES AS SECOND NATURE TO ME.
MY NAME REALLY IS EZEKIEL, THOUGH.
THAT MUCH IS REAL.

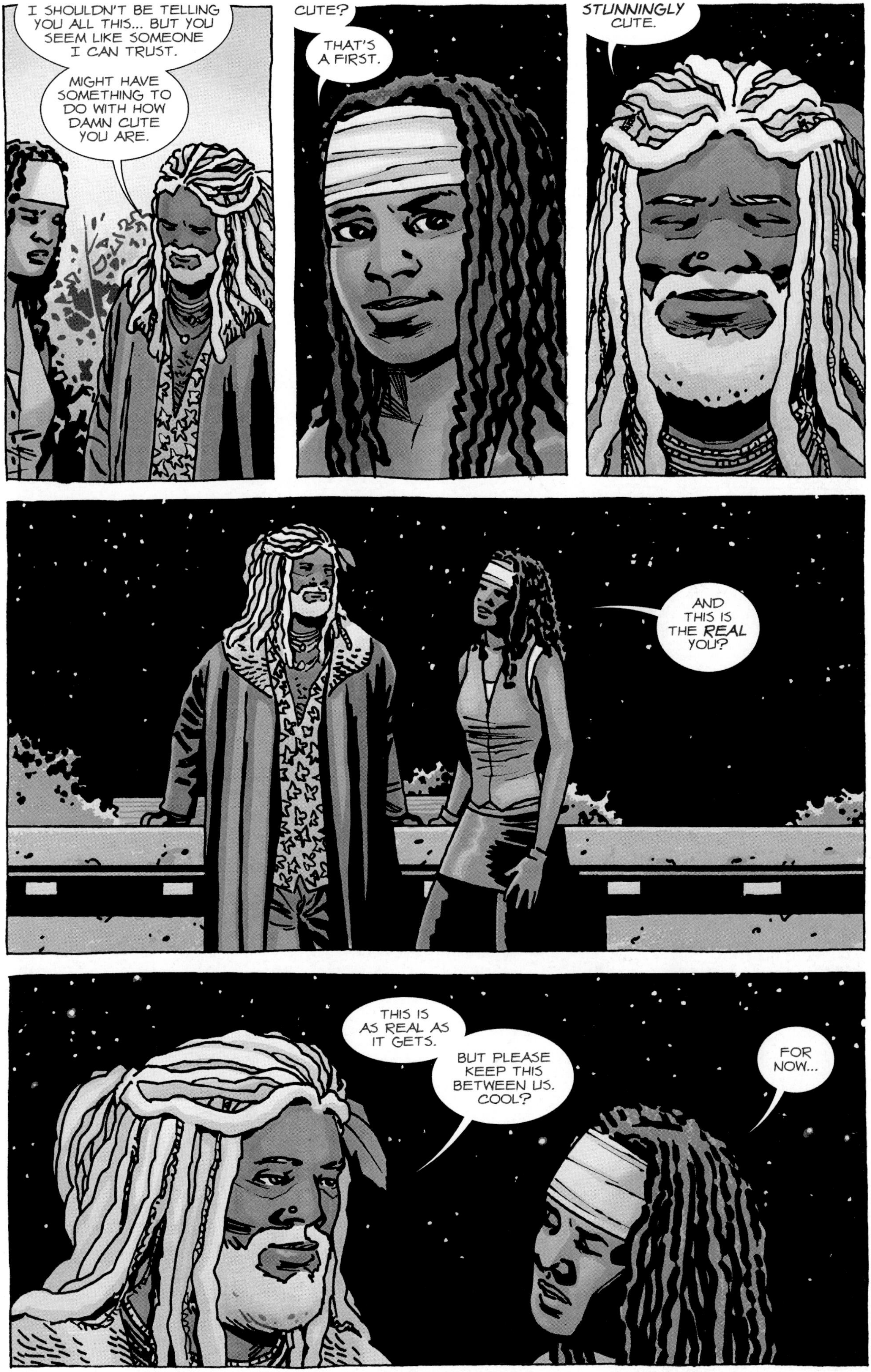
I SHOULDN'T BE TELLING YOU ALL THIS... BUT YOU SEEM LIKE SOMEONE I CAN TRUST.
MIGHT HAVE SOMETHING TO DO WITH HOW DAMN CUTE YOU ARE.
CUTE?
THAT'S A FIRST.
STUNNINGLY CUTE.
AND THIS IS THE REAL YOU?
THIS IS AS REAL AS IT GETS.
BUT PLEASE KEEP THIS BETWEEN US. COOL?
FOR NOW...

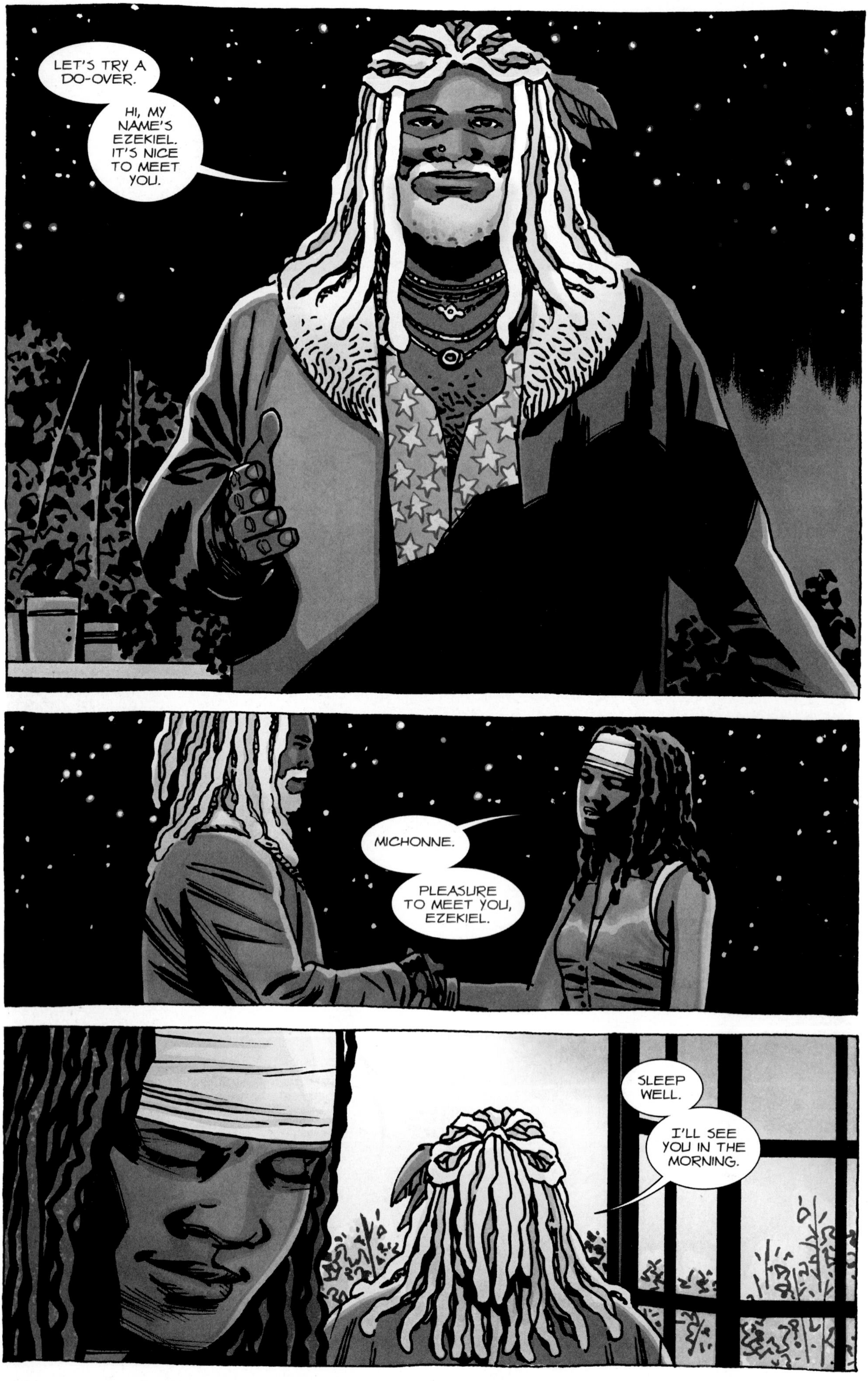
LET'S TRY A DO-OVER.
HI, MY NAME'S EZEKIEL. IT'S NICE TO MEET YOU.
MICHONNE.
PLEASURE TO MEET YOU, EZEKIEL.
SLEEP WELL.
I'LL SEE YOU IN THE MORNING.

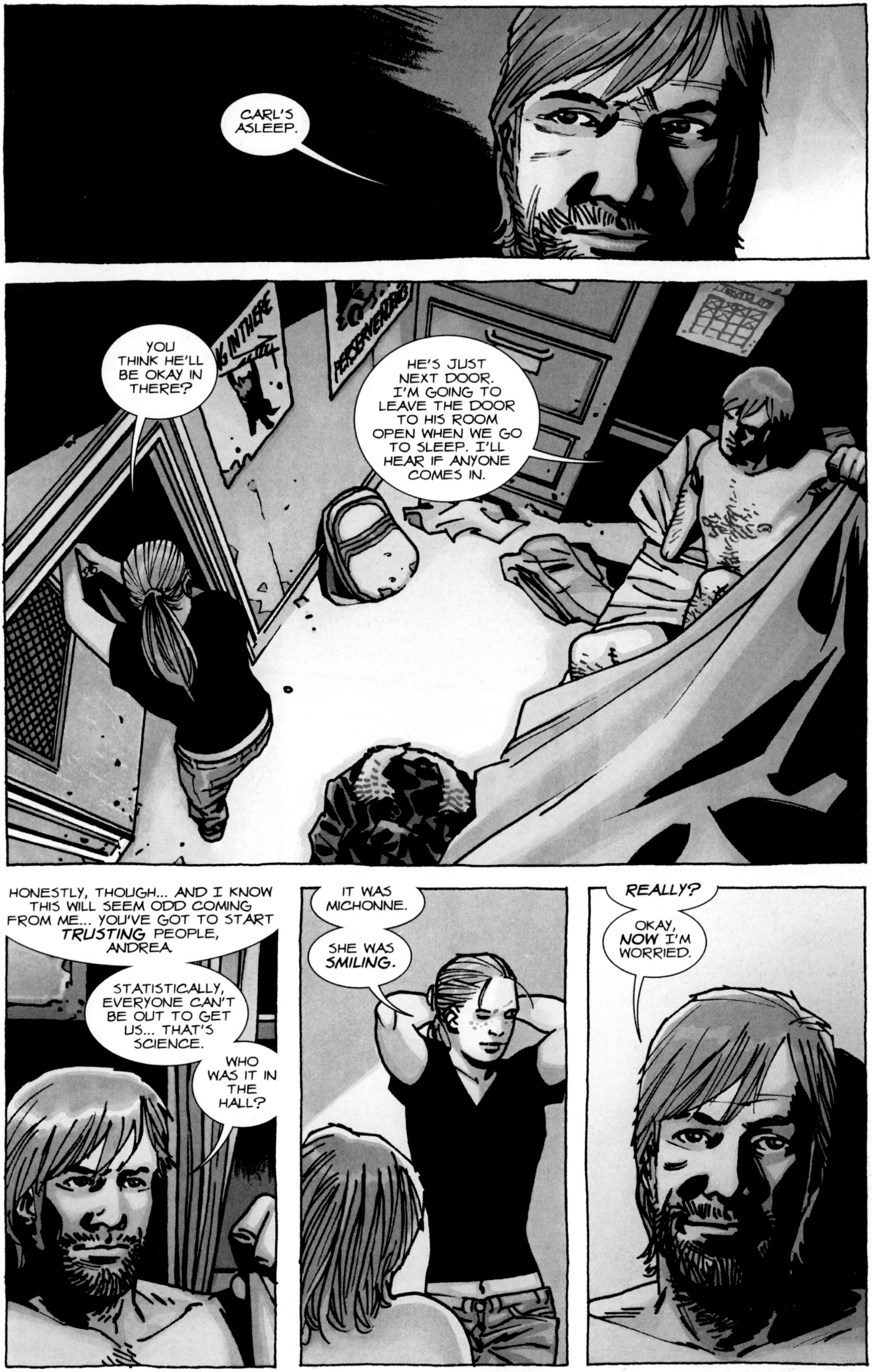
CARL'S ASLEEP.
YOU THINK HE'LL BE OKAY IN THERE?
HE'S JUST NEXT DOOR. I'M GOING TO LEAVE THE DOOR TO HIS ROOM OPEN WHEN WE GO TO SLEEP. I'LL HEAR IF ANYONE COMES IN.
HONESTLY, THOUGH... AND I KNOW THIS WILL SEEM ODD COMING FROM ME... YOU'VE GOT TO START TRUSTING PEOPLE, ANDREA.
STATISTICALLY, EVERYONE CAN'T BE OUT TO GET US... THAT'S SCIENCE.
WHO WAS IT IN THE HALL?
IT WAS MICHONNE.
SHE WAS SMILING.
REALLY?
OKAY, NOW I'M WORRIED.

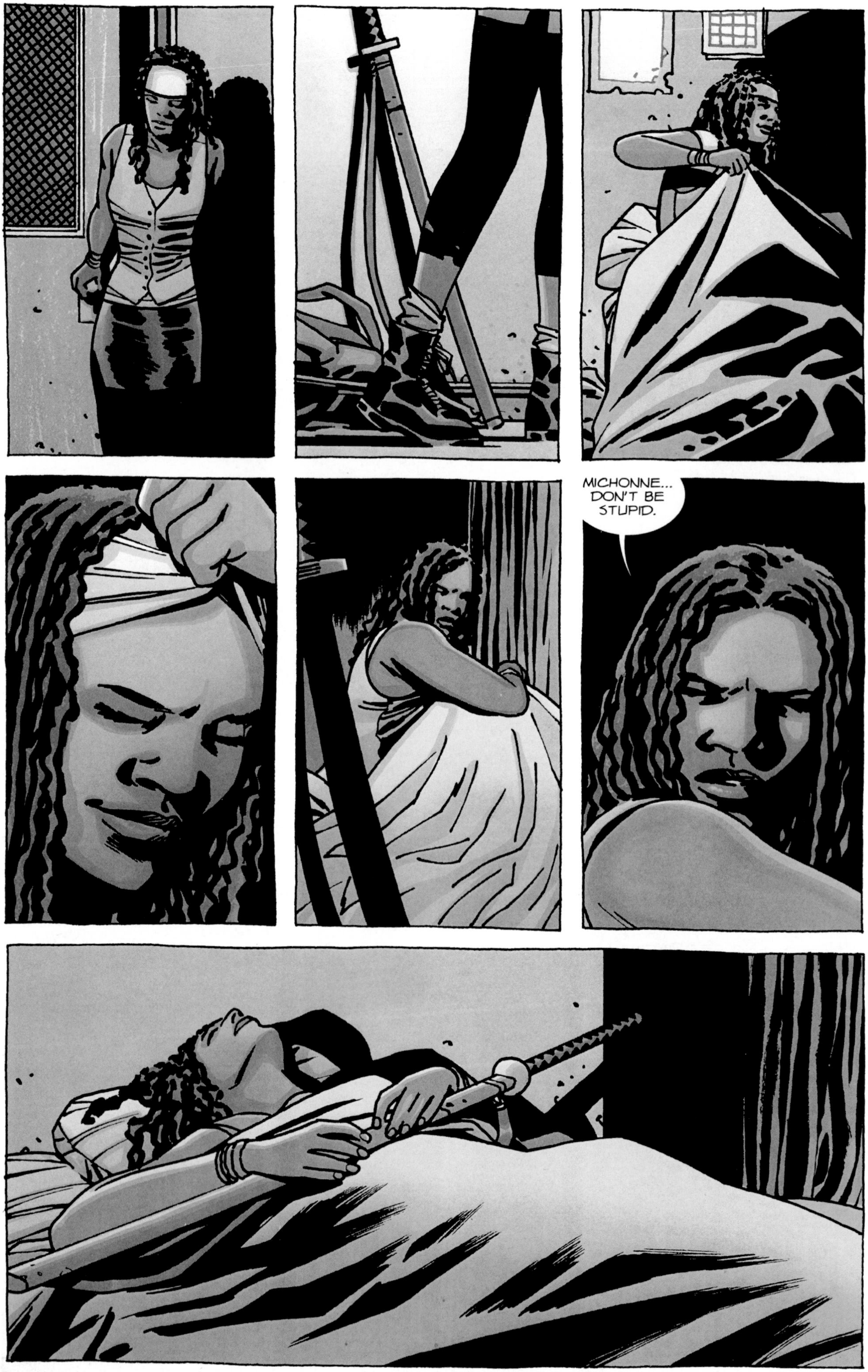
MICHONNE... DON'T BE STUPID.

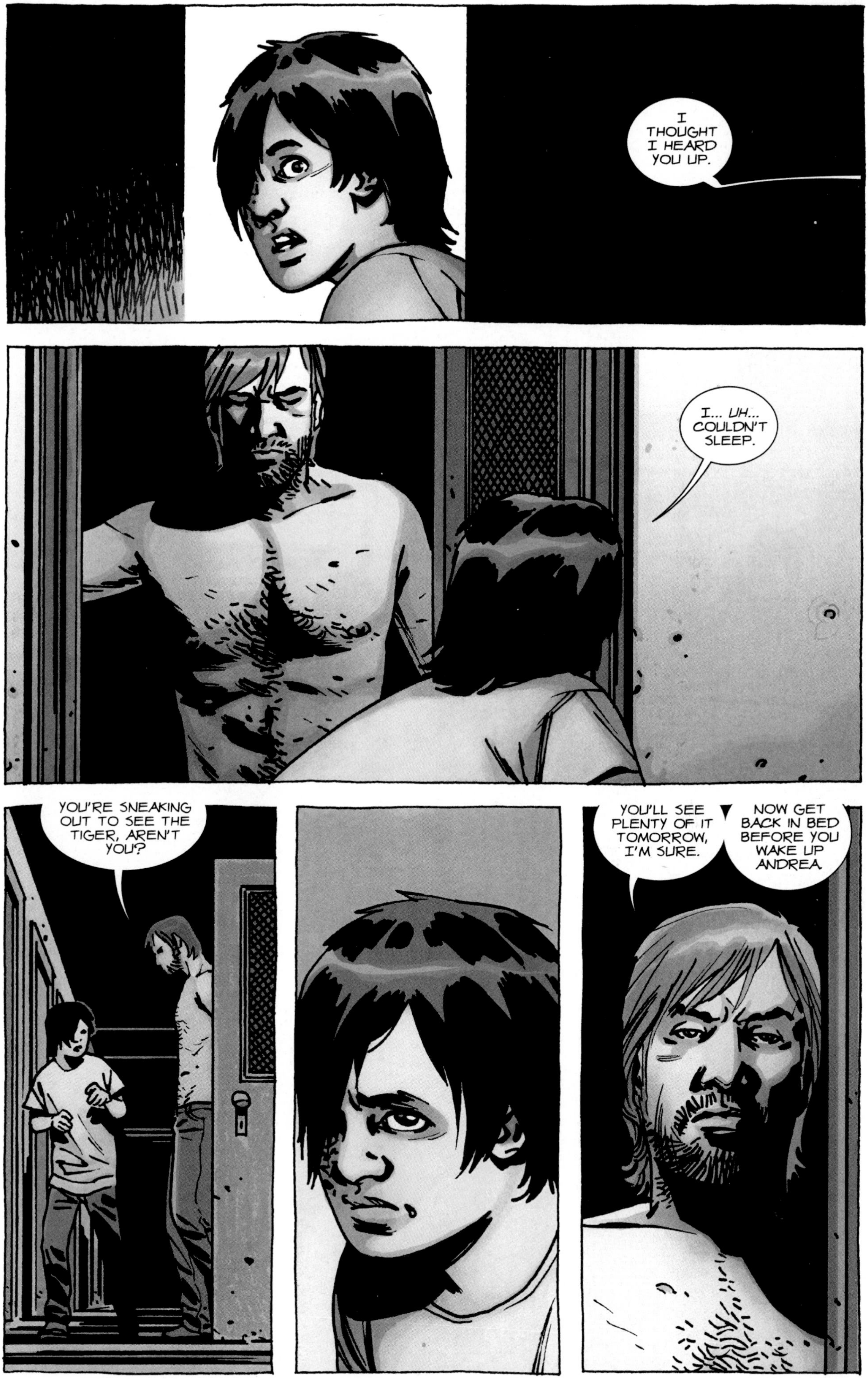
I THOUGHT I HEARD YOU UP.
I... UH... COULDN'T SLEEP.
YOU'RE SNEAKING OUT TO SEE THE TIGER, AREN'T YOU?
YOU'LL SEE PLENTY OF IT TOMORROW, I'M SURE.
NOW GET BACK IN BED BEFORE YOU WAKE UP ANDREA.

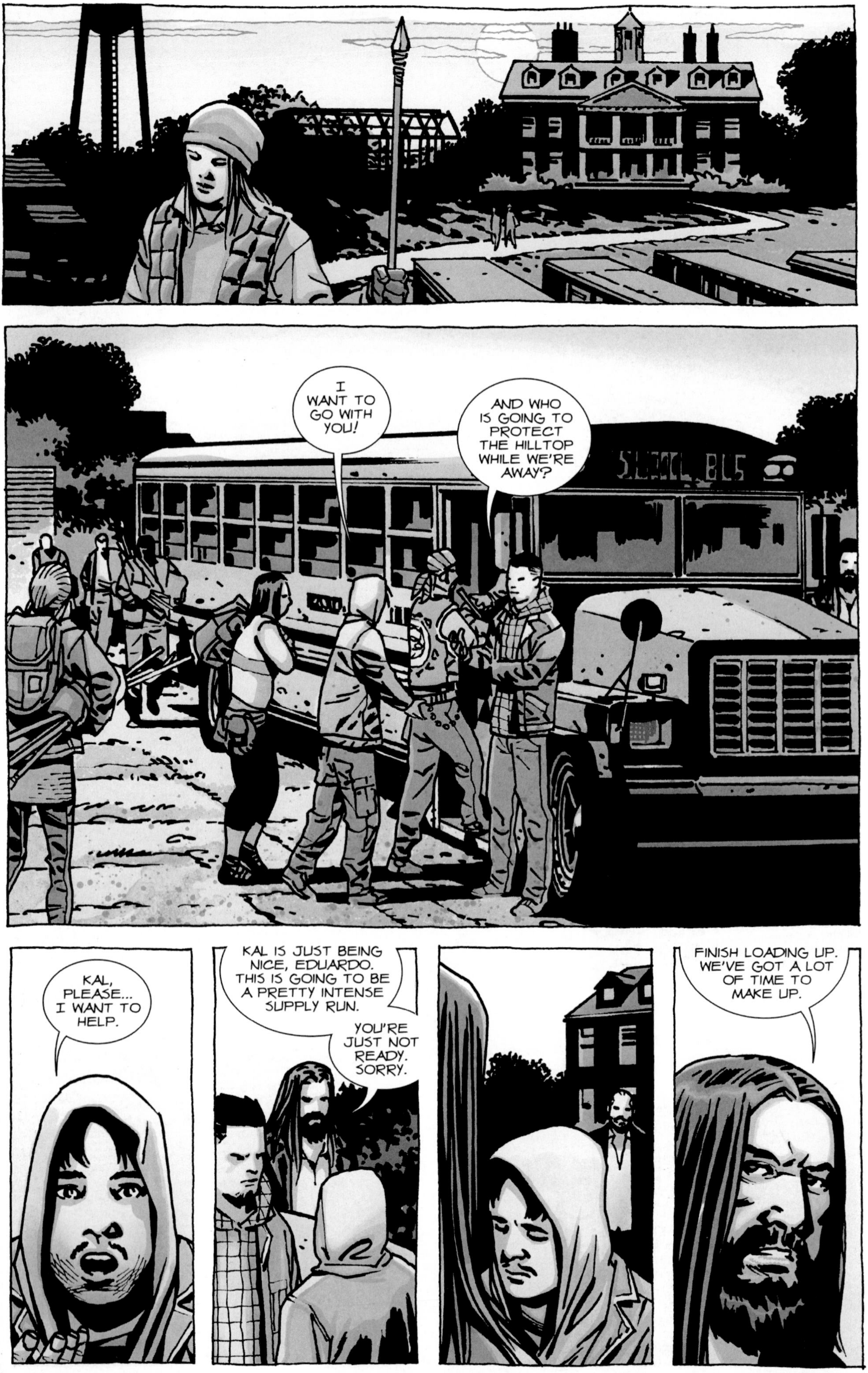
I WANT TO GO WITH YOU!
AND WHO IS GOING TO PROTECT THE HILLTOP WHILE WE'RE AWAY?
KAL, PLEASE... I WANT TO HELP.
KAL IS JUST BEING NICE, EDUARDO. THIS IS GOING TO BE A PRETTY INTENSE SUPPLY RUN.
YOU'RE JUST NOT READY. SORRY.
FINISH LOADING UP. WE'VE GOT A LOT OF TIME TO MAKE UP.

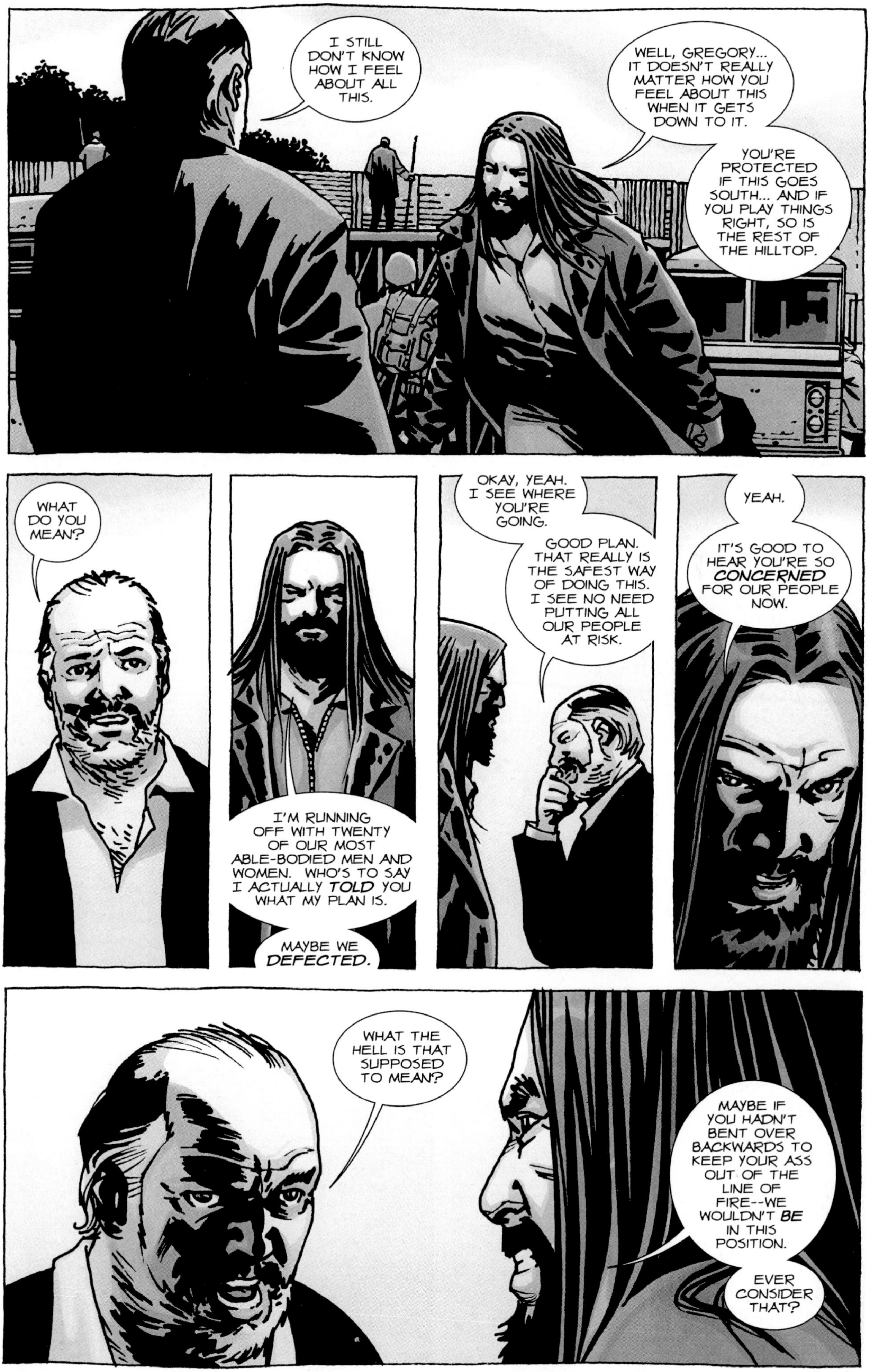
I STILL DON'T KNOW HOW I FEEL ABOUT ALL THIS.
WELL, GREGORY... IT DOESN'T REALLY MATTER HOW YOU FEEL ABOUT THIS WHEN IT GETS DOWN TO IT.
YOU'RE PROTECTED IF THIS GOES SOUTH... AND IF YOU PLAY THINGS RIGHT, SO IS THE REST OF THE HILLTOP.
WHAT DO YOU MEAN?
I'M RUNNING OFF WITH TWENTY OF OUR MOST ABLE-BODIED MEN AND WOMEN. WHO'S TO SAY I ACTUALLY TOLD YOU WHAT MY PLAN IS.
MAYBE WE DEFECTED.
OKAY, YEAH. I SEE WHERE YOU'RE GOING.
GOOD PLAN. THAT REALLY IS THE SAFEST WAY OF DOING THIS. I SEE NO NEED PUTTING ALL OUR PEOPLE AT RISK.
YEAH.
IT'S GOOD TO HEAR YOU'RE SO CONCERNED FOR OUR PEOPLE NOW.
WHAT THE HELL IS THAT SUPPOSED TO MEAN?
MAYBE IF YOU HADN'T BENT OVER BACKWARDS TO KEEP YOUR ASS OUT OF THE LINE OF FIRE--WE WOULDN'T BE IN THIS POSITION.
EVER CONSIDER THAT?

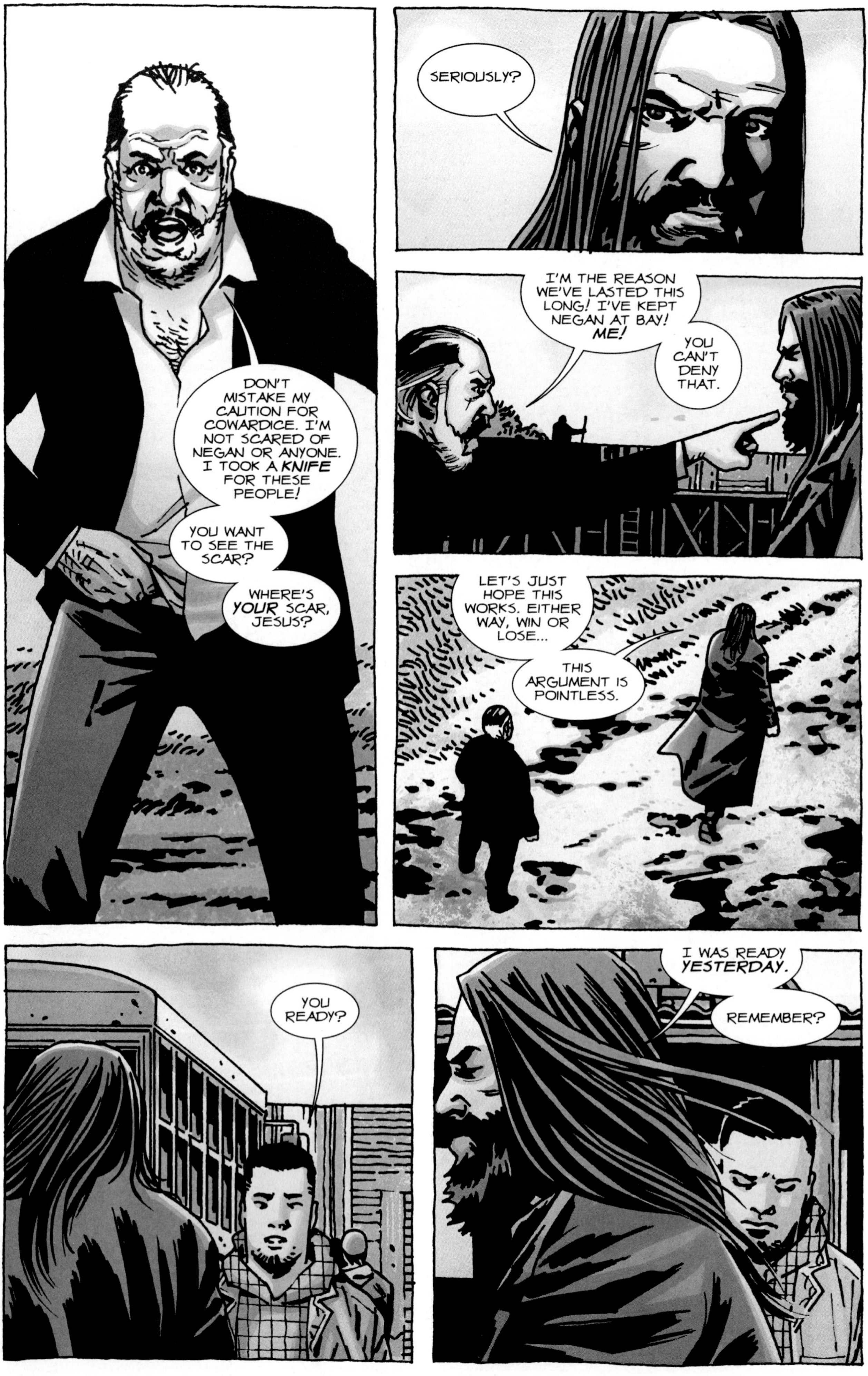
DON'T MISTAKE MY CAUTION FOR COWARDICE. I'M NOT SCARED OF NEGAN OR ANYONE. I TOOK A **KNIFE** FOR THESE PEOPLE!
YOU WANT TO SEE THE SCAR?
WHERE'S **YOUR** SCAR, JESUS?
SERIOUSLY?
I'M THE REASON WE'VE LASTED THIS LONG! I'VE KEPT NEGAN AT BAY! **ME!**
YOU CAN'T DENY THAT.
LET'S JUST HOPE THIS WORKS. EITHER WAY, WIN OR LOSE...
THIS ARGUMENT IS POINTLESS.
YOU READY?
I WAS READY **YESTERDAY.**
REMEMBER?

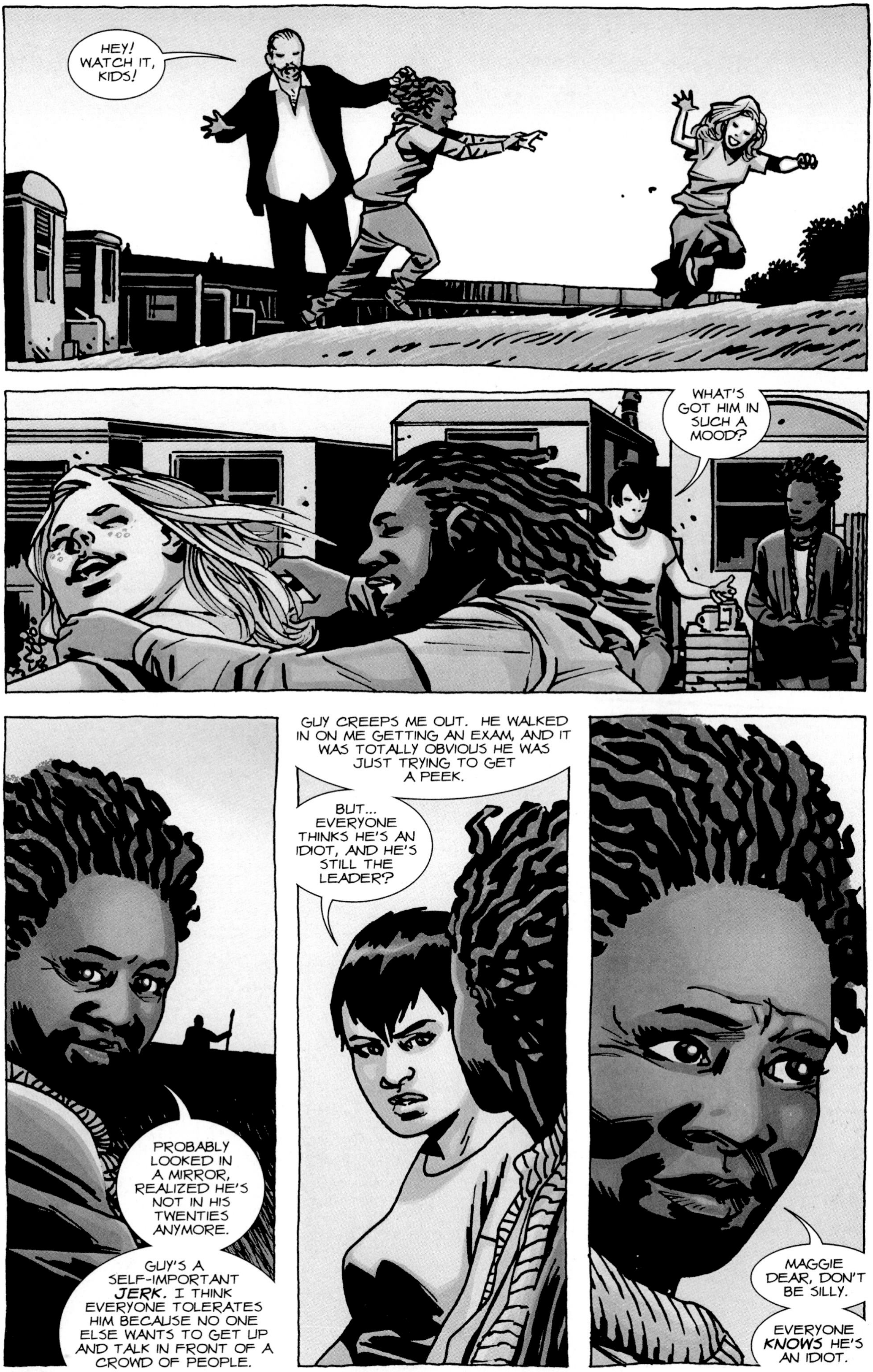
HEY! WATCH IT, KIDS!
WHAT'S GOT HIM IN SUCH A MOOD?
PROBABLY LOOKED IN A MIRROR, REALIZED HE'S NOT IN HIS TWENTIES ANYMORE.
GUY'S A SELF-IMPORTANT JERK. I THINK EVERYONE TOLERATES HIM BECAUSE NO ONE ELSE WANTS TO GET UP AND TALK IN FRONT OF A CROWD OF PEOPLE.
GUY CREEPS ME OUT. HE WALKED IN ON ME GETTING AN EXAM, AND IT WAS TOTALLY OBVIOUS HE WAS JUST TRYING TO GET A PEEK.
BUT... EVERYONE THINKS HE'S AN IDIOT, AND HE'S STILL THE LEADER?
MAGGIE DEAR, DON'T BE SILLY.
EVERYONE KNOWS HE'S AN IDIOT.

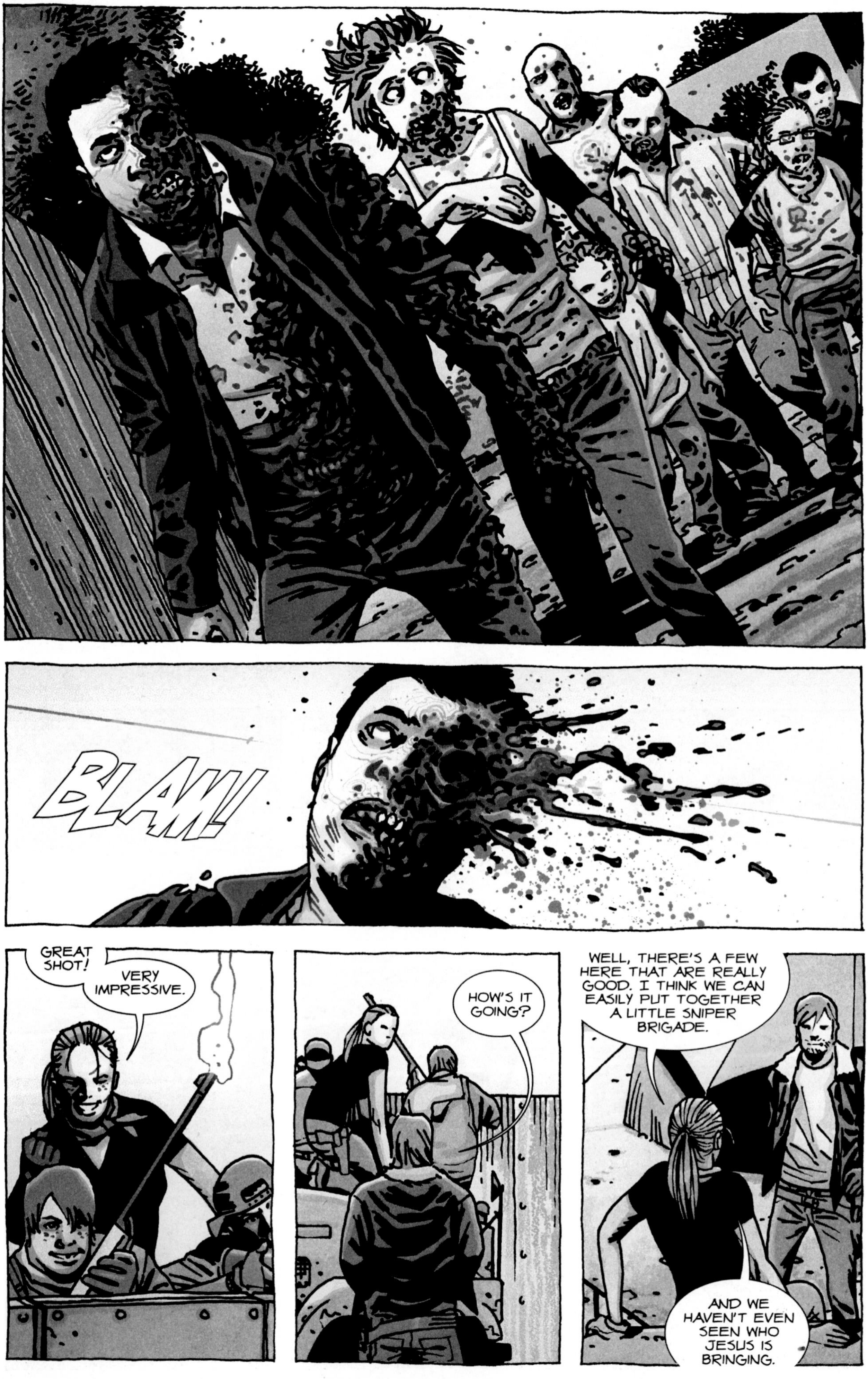
BLAM!
GREAT SHOT!
VERY IMPRESSIVE.
HOW'S IT GOING?
WELL, THERE'S A FEW HERE THAT ARE REALLY GOOD. I THINK WE CAN EASILY PUT TOGETHER A LITTLE SNIPER BRIGADE.
AND WE HAVEN'T EVEN SEEN WHO JESUS IS BRINGING.

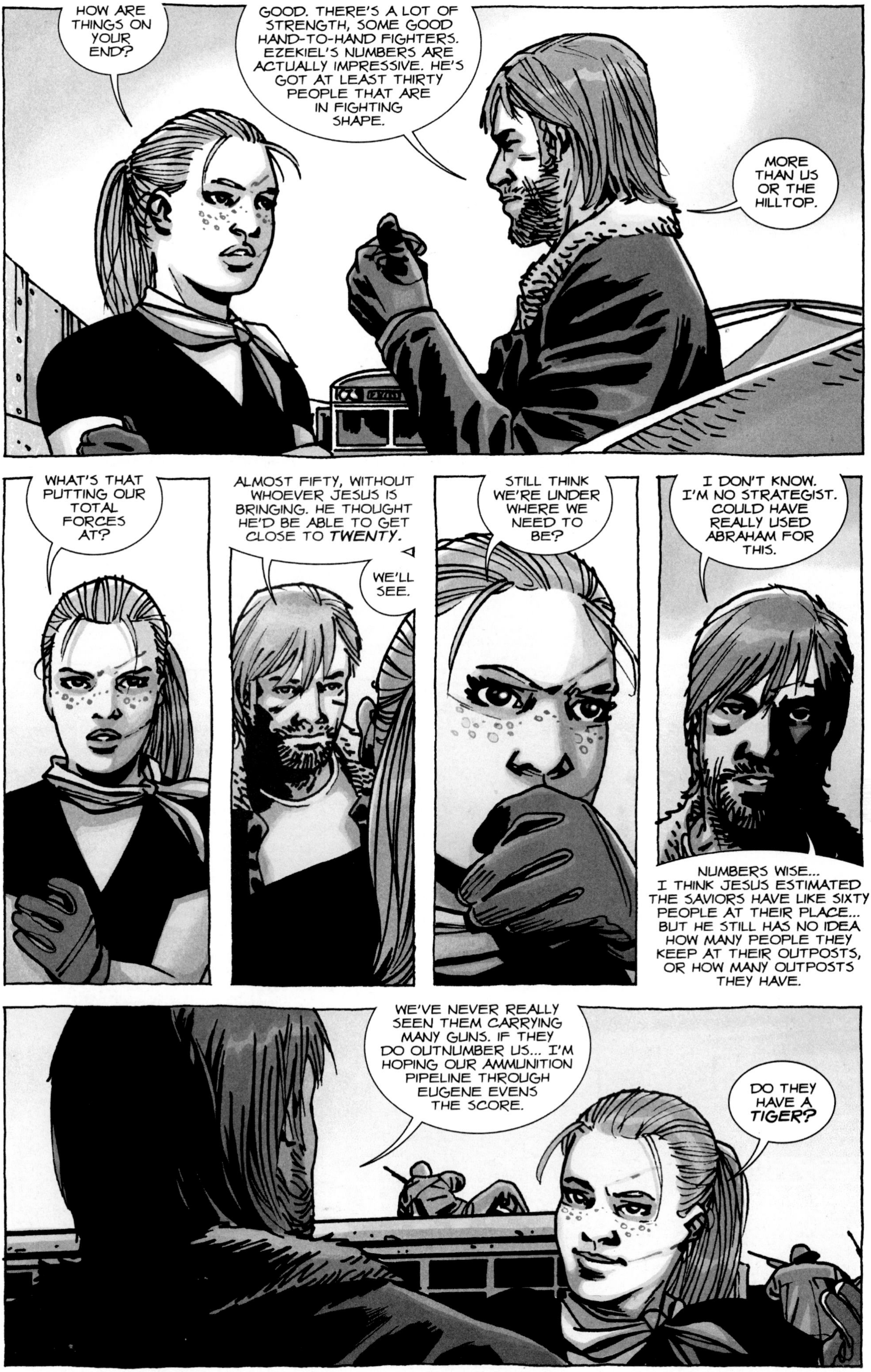
HOW ARE THINGS ON YOUR END?
GOOD. THERE'S A LOT OF STRENGTH, SOME GOOD HAND-TO-HAND FIGHTERS. EZEKIEL'S NUMBERS ARE ACTUALLY IMPRESSIVE. HE'S GOT AT LEAST THIRTY PEOPLE THAT ARE IN FIGHTING SHAPE.
MORE THAN US OR THE HILLTOP.
WHAT'S THAT PUTTING OUR TOTAL FORCES AT?
ALMOST FIFTY, WITHOUT WHOEVER JESUS IS BRINGING. HE THOUGHT HE'D BE ABLE TO GET CLOSE TO TWENTY.
WE'LL SEE.
STILL THINK WE'RE UNDER WHERE WE NEED TO BE?
I DON'T KNOW. I'M NO STRATEGIST. COULD HAVE REALLY USED ABRAHAM FOR THIS.
NUMBERS WISE... I THINK JESUS ESTIMATED THE SAVIORS HAVE LIKE SIXTY PEOPLE AT THEIR PLACE... BUT HE STILL HAS NO IDEA HOW MANY PEOPLE THEY KEEP AT THEIR OUTPOSTS, OR HOW MANY OUTPOSTS THEY HAVE.
WE'VE NEVER REALLY SEEN THEM CARRYING MANY GUNS. IF THEY DO OUTNUMBER US... I'M HOPING OUR AMMUNITION PIPELINE THROUGH EUGENE EVENS THE SCORE.
DO THEY HAVE A TIGER?

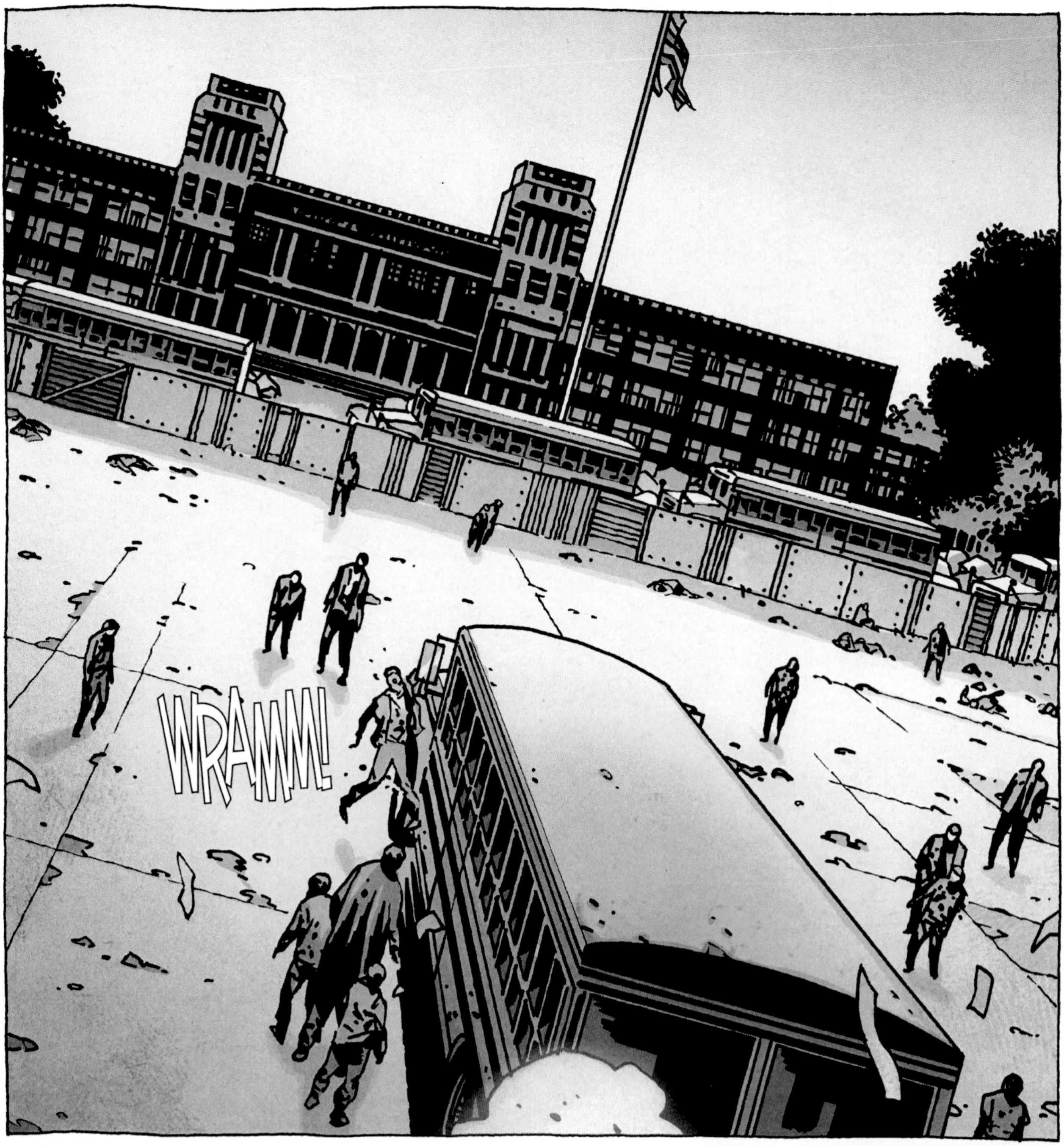
WRAMM!
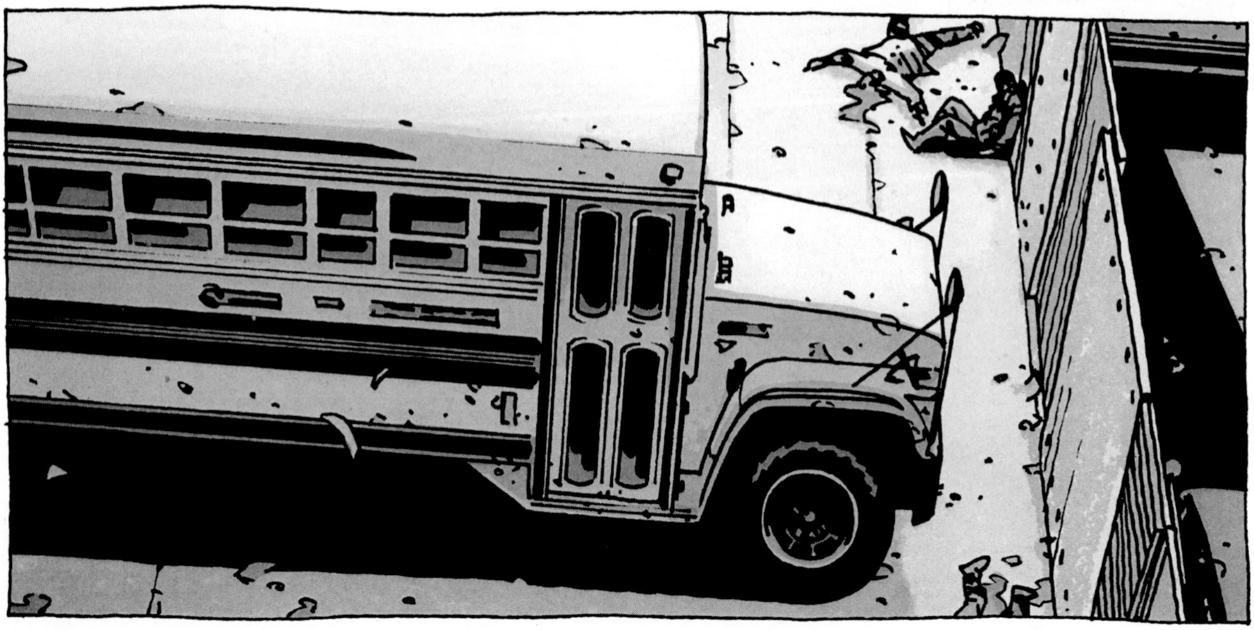

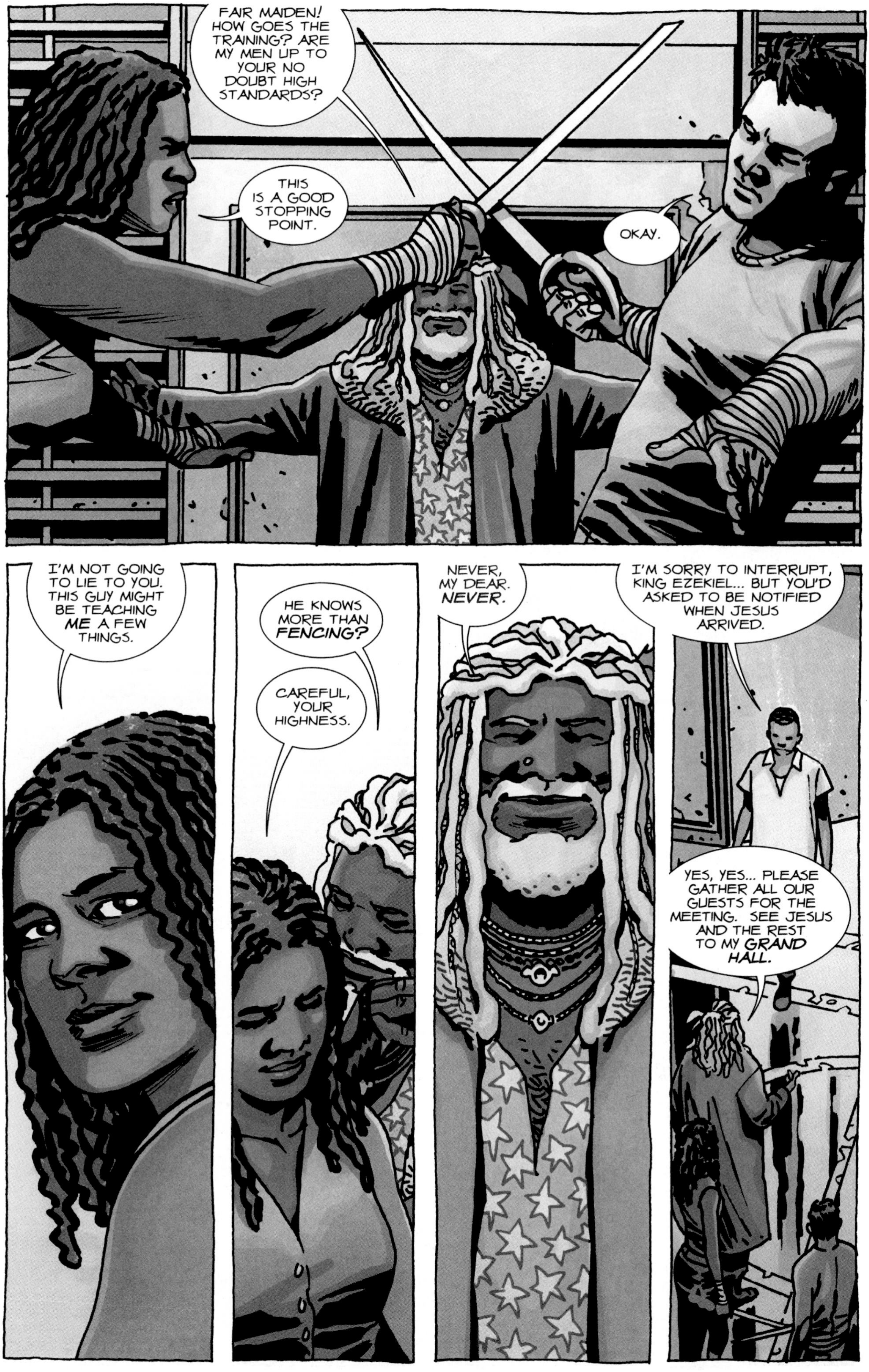
FAIR MAIDEN! HOW GOES THE TRAINING? ARE MY MEN UP TO YOUR NO DOUBT HIGH STANDARDS?
THIS IS A GOOD STOPPING POINT.
OKAY.
I'M NOT GOING TO LIE TO YOU. THIS GUY MIGHT BE TEACHING ME A FEW THINGS.
HE KNOWS MORE THAN FENCING?
CAREFUL, YOUR HIGHNESS.
NEVER, MY DEAR. NEVER.
I'M SORRY TO INTERRUPT, KING EZEKIEL... BUT YOU'D ASKED TO BE NOTIFIED WHEN JESUS ARRIVED.
YES, YES... PLEASE GATHER ALL OUR GUESTS FOR THE MEETING. SEE JESUS AND THE REST TO MY GRAND HALL.

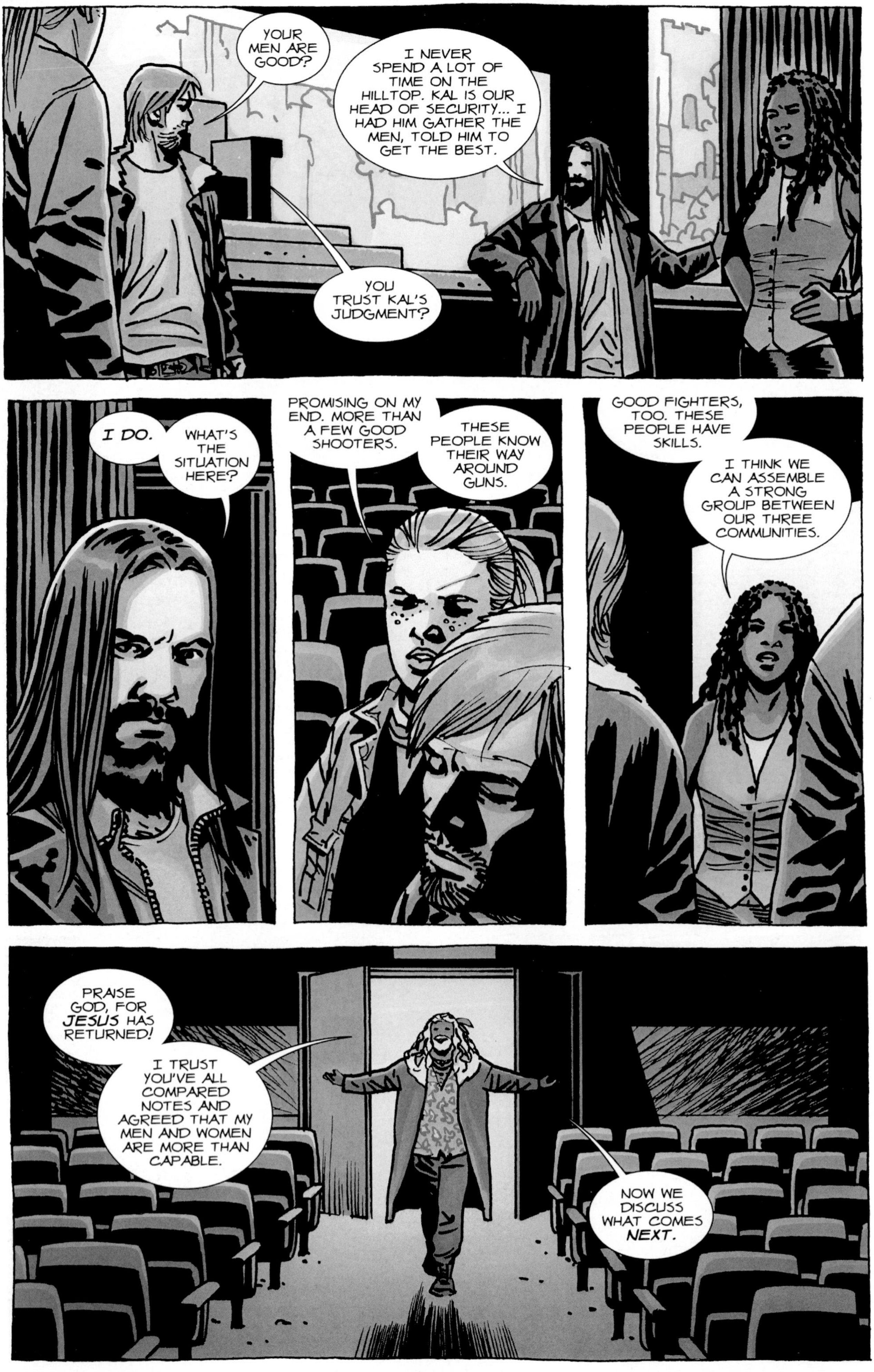
YOUR MEN ARE GOOD?
I NEVER SPEND A LOT OF TIME ON THE HILLTOP. KAL IS OUR HEAD OF SECURITY... I HAD HIM GATHER THE MEN, TOLD HIM TO GET THE BEST.
YOU TRUST KAL'S JUDGMENT?
I DO.
WHAT'S THE SITUATION HERE?
PROMISING ON MY END. MORE THAN A FEW GOOD SHOOTERS.
THESE PEOPLE KNOW THEIR WAY AROUND GUNS.
GOOD FIGHTERS, TOO. THESE PEOPLE HAVE SKILLS.
I THINK WE CAN ASSEMBLE A STRONG GROUP BETWEEN OUR THREE COMMUNITIES.
PRAISE GOD, FOR JESUS HAS RETURNED!
I TRUST YOU'VE ALL COMPARED NOTES AND AGREED THAT MY MEN AND WOMEN ARE MORE THAN CAPABLE.
NOW WE DISCUSS WHAT COMES NEXT.

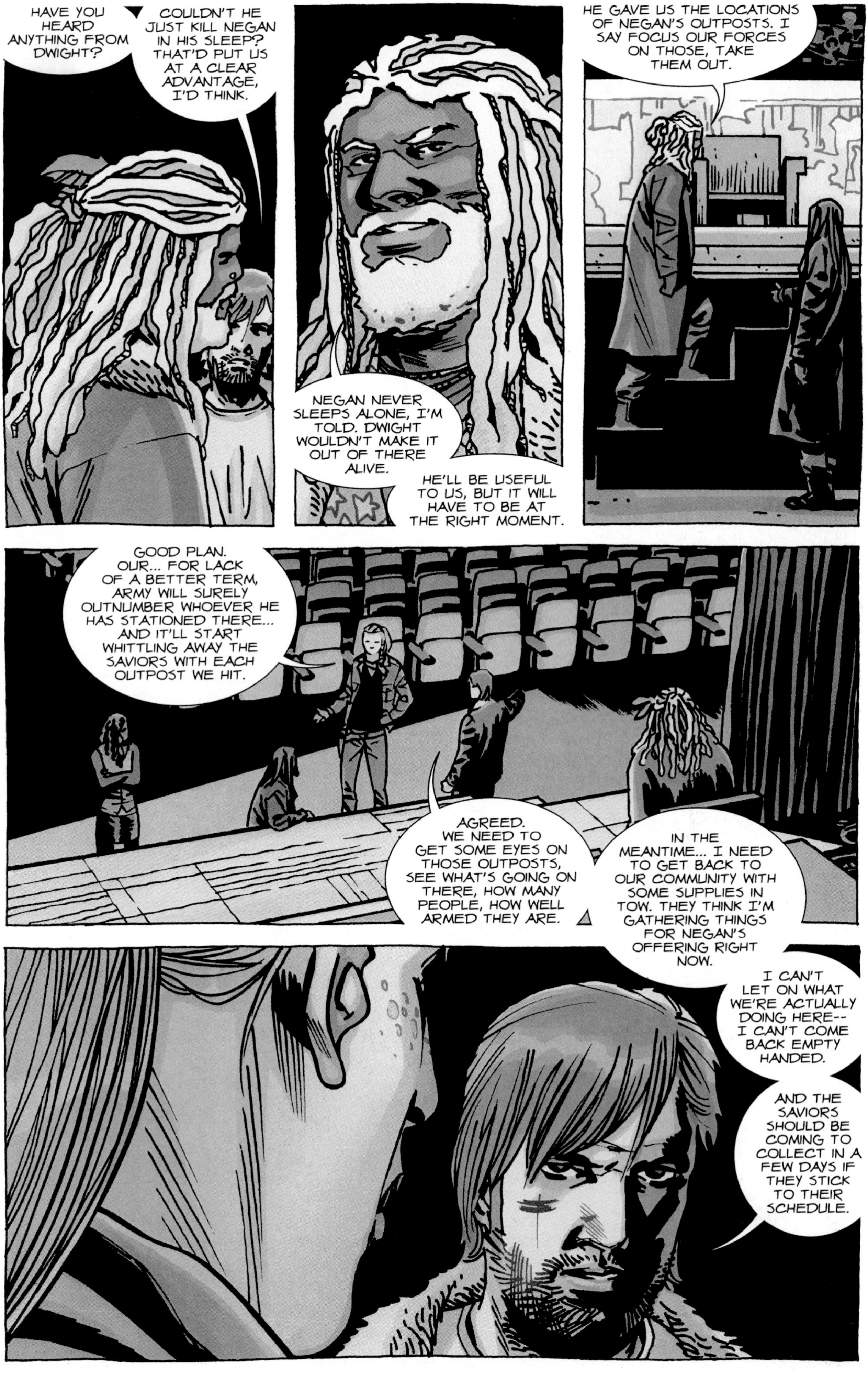
HAVE YOU HEARD ANYTHING FROM DWIGHT?
COULDN'T HE JUST KILL NEGAN IN HIS SLEEP? THAT'D PUT US AT A CLEAR ADVANTAGE, I'D THINK.
NEGAN NEVER SLEEPS ALONE, I'M TOLD. DWIGHT WOULDN'T MAKE IT OUT OF THERE ALIVE.
HE'LL BE USEFUL TO US, BUT IT WILL HAVE TO BE AT THE RIGHT MOMENT.
HE GAVE US THE LOCATIONS OF NEGAN'S OUTPOSTS. I SAY FOCUS OUR FORCES ON THOSE, TAKE THEM OUT.
GOOD PLAN. OUR... FOR LACK OF A BETTER TERM, ARMY WILL SURELY OUTNUMBER WHOEVER HE HAS STATIONED THERE... AND IT'LL START WHITTLING AWAY THE SAVIORS WITH EACH OUTPOST WE HIT.
AGREED. WE NEED TO GET SOME EYES ON THOSE OUTPOSTS, SEE WHAT'S GOING ON THERE, HOW MANY PEOPLE, HOW WELL ARMED THEY ARE.
IN THE MEANTIME... I NEED TO GET BACK TO OUR COMMUNITY WITH SOME SUPPLIES IN TOW. THEY THINK I'M GATHERING THINGS FOR NEGAN'S OFFERING RIGHT NOW.
I CAN'T LET ON WHAT WE'RE ACTUALLY DOING HERE-- I CAN'T COME BACK EMPTY HANDED.
AND THE SAVIORS SHOULD BE COMING TO COLLECT IN A FEW DAYS IF THEY STICK TO THEIR SCHEDULE.

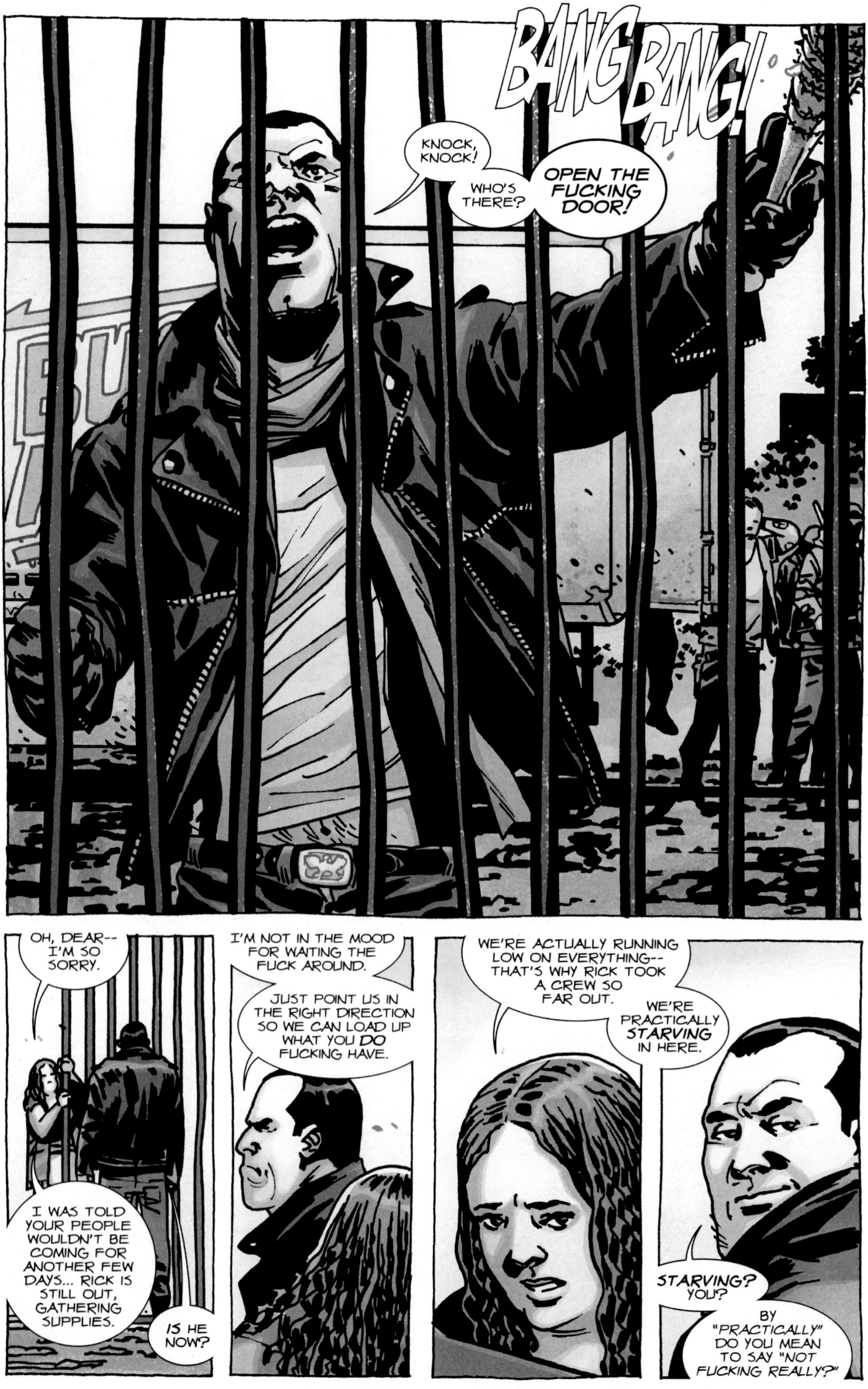
BANG BANG!
KNOCK, KNOCK!
WHO'S THERE?
OPEN THE FUCKING DOOR!
OH, DEAR-- I'M SO SORRY.
I WAS TOLD YOUR PEOPLE WOULDN'T BE COMING FOR ANOTHER FEW DAYS... RICK IS STILL OUT, GATHERING SUPPLIES.
IS HE NOW?
I'M NOT IN THE MOOD FOR WAITING THE FUCK AROUND.
JUST POINT US IN THE RIGHT DIRECTION SO WE CAN LOAD UP WHAT YOU DO FUCKING HAVE.
WE'RE ACTUALLY RUNNING LOW ON EVERYTHING-- THAT'S WHY RICK TOOK A CREW SO FAR OUT.
WE'RE PRACTICALLY STARVING IN HERE.
STARVING? YOU?
BY "PRACTICALLY" DO YOU MEAN TO SAY "NOT FUCKING REALLY?"

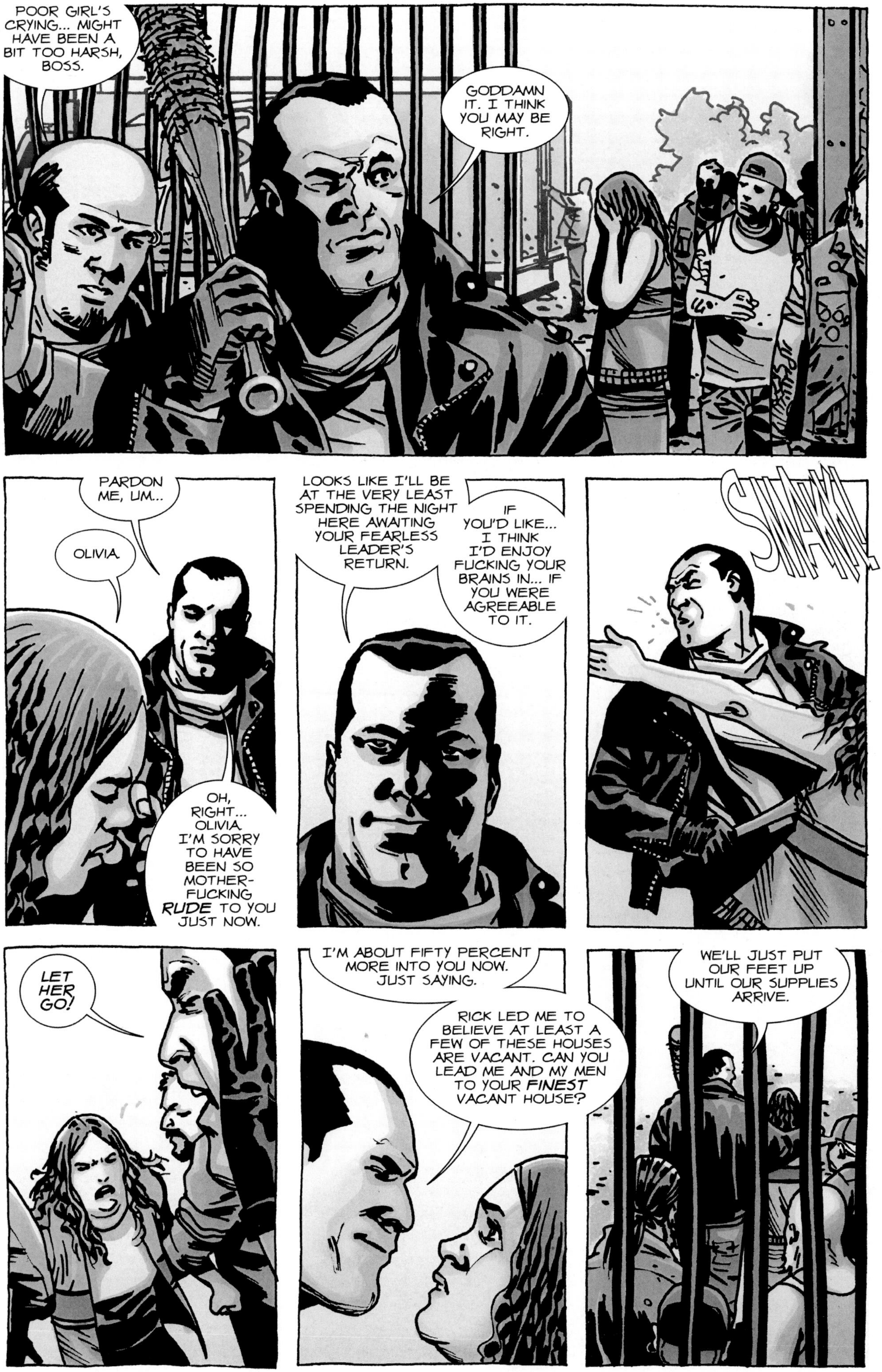
POOR GIRL'S CRYING... MIGHT HAVE BEEN A BIT TOO HARSH, BOSS.
GODDAMN IT. I THINK YOU MAY BE RIGHT.
PARDON ME, UM...
OLIVIA.
OH, RIGHT... OLIVIA. I'M SORRY TO HAVE BEEN SO MOTHER-FUCKING *RUDE* TO YOU JUST NOW.
LOOKS LIKE I'LL BE AT THE VERY LEAST SPENDING THE NIGHT HERE AWAITING YOUR FEARLESS LEADER'S RETURN.
IF YOU'D LIKE... I THINK I'D ENJOY FUCKING YOUR BRAINS IN... IF YOU WERE AGREEABLE TO IT.
SMAKK!
LET HER GO!
I'M ABOUT FIFTY PERCENT MORE INTO YOU NOW. JUST SAYING.
RICK LED ME TO BELIEVE AT LEAST A FEW OF THESE HOUSES ARE VACANT. CAN YOU LEAD ME AND MY MEN TO YOUR *FINEST* VACANT HOUSE?
WE'LL JUST PUT OUR FEET UP UNTIL OUR SUPPLIES ARRIVE.

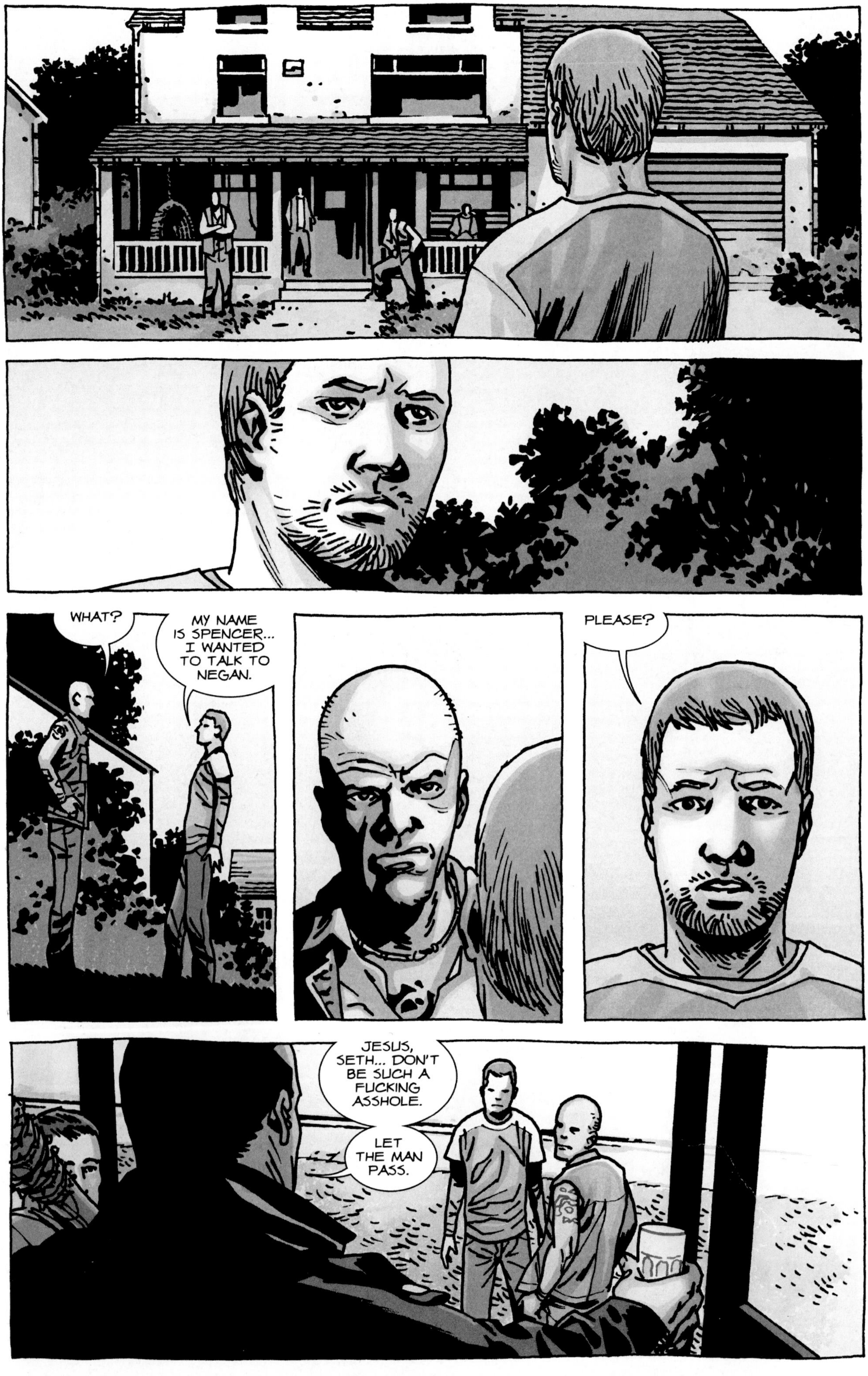
WHAT?
MY NAME IS SPENCER... I WANTED TO TALK TO NEGAN.
PLEASE?
JESUS, SETH... DON'T BE SUCH A FUCKING ASSHOLE.
LET THE MAN PASS.

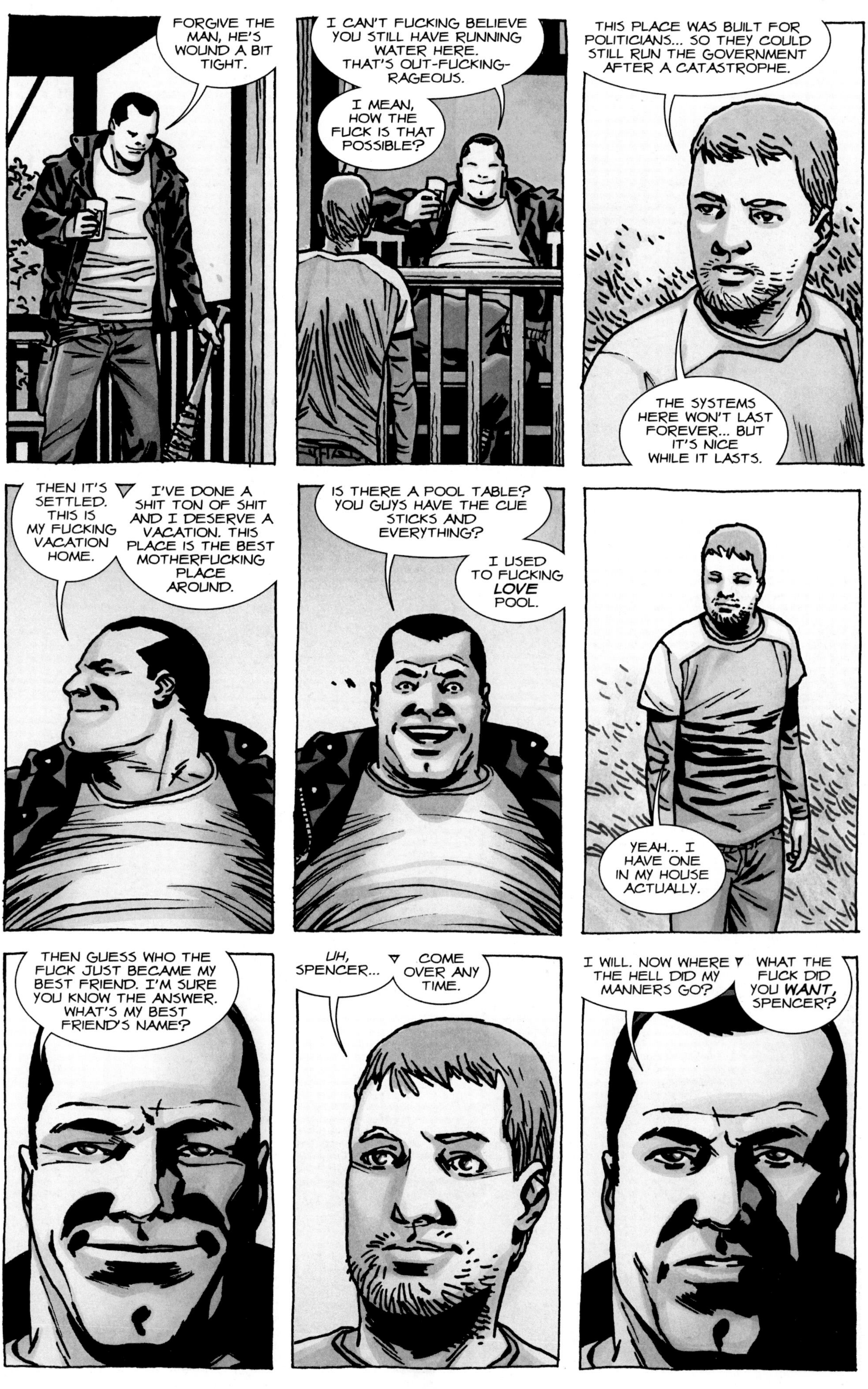
FORGIVE THE MAN, HE'S WOUND A BIT TIGHT.
I CAN'T FUCKING BELIEVE YOU STILL HAVE RUNNING WATER HERE. THAT'S OUT-FUCKING-RAGEOUS.
I MEAN, HOW THE FUCK IS THAT POSSIBLE?
THIS PLACE WAS BUILT FOR POLITICIANS... SO THEY COULD STILL RUN THE GOVERNMENT AFTER A CATASTROPHE.
THE SYSTEMS HERE WON'T LAST FOREVER... BUT IT'S NICE WHILE IT LASTS.
THEN IT'S SETTLED. THIS IS MY FUCKING VACATION HOME.
I'VE DONE A SHIT TON OF SHIT AND I DESERVE A VACATION. THIS PLACE IS THE BEST MOTHERFUCKING PLACE AROUND.
IS THERE A POOL TABLE? YOU GUYS HAVE THE CUE STICKS AND EVERYTHING?
I USED TO FUCKING LOVE POOL.
YEAH... I HAVE ONE IN MY HOUSE ACTUALLY.
THEN GUESS WHO THE FUCK JUST BECAME MY BEST FRIEND. I'M SURE YOU KNOW THE ANSWER. WHAT'S MY BEST FRIEND'S NAME?
UH, SPENCER...
COME OVER ANY TIME.
I WILL. NOW WHERE THE HELL DID MY MANNERS GO?
WHAT THE FUCK DID YOU WANT, SPENCER?

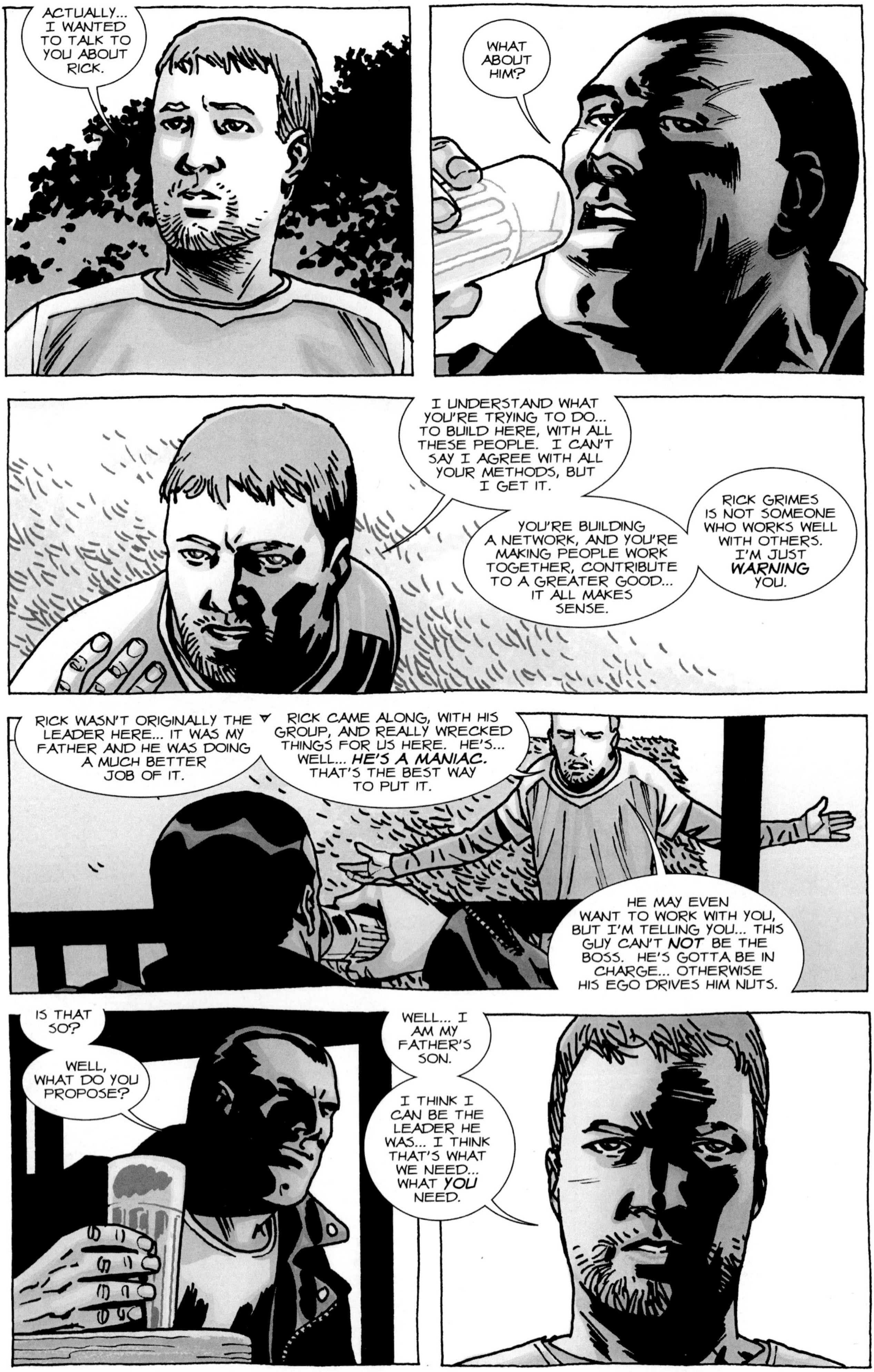

ACTUALLY... I WANTED TO TALK TO YOU ABOUT RICK.
WHAT ABOUT HIM?
I UNDERSTAND WHAT YOU'RE TRYING TO DO... TO BUILD HERE, WITH ALL THESE PEOPLE. I CAN'T SAY I AGREE WITH ALL YOUR METHODS, BUT I GET IT.
YOU'RE BUILDING A NETWORK, AND YOU'RE MAKING PEOPLE WORK TOGETHER, CONTRIBUTE TO A GREATER GOOD... IT ALL MAKES SENSE.
RICK GRIMES IS NOT SOMEONE WHO WORKS WELL WITH OTHERS. I'M JUST ***WARNING*** YOU.
RICK WASN'T ORIGINALLY THE LEADER HERE... IT WAS MY FATHER AND HE WAS DOING A MUCH BETTER JOB OF IT.
RICK CAME ALONG, WITH HIS GROUP, AND REALLY WRECKED THINGS FOR US HERE. HE'S... WELL... ***HE'S A MANIAC.*** THAT'S THE BEST WAY TO PUT IT.
HE MAY EVEN WANT TO WORK WITH YOU, BUT I'M TELLING YOU... THIS GUY CAN'T ***NOT*** BE THE BOSS. HE'S GOTTA BE IN CHARGE... OTHERWISE HIS EGO DRIVES HIM NUTS.
IS THAT SO?
WELL, WHAT DO YOU PROPOSE?
WELL... I AM MY FATHER'S SON.
I THINK I CAN BE THE LEADER HE WAS... I THINK THAT'S WHAT WE NEED... WHAT ***YOU*** NEED.

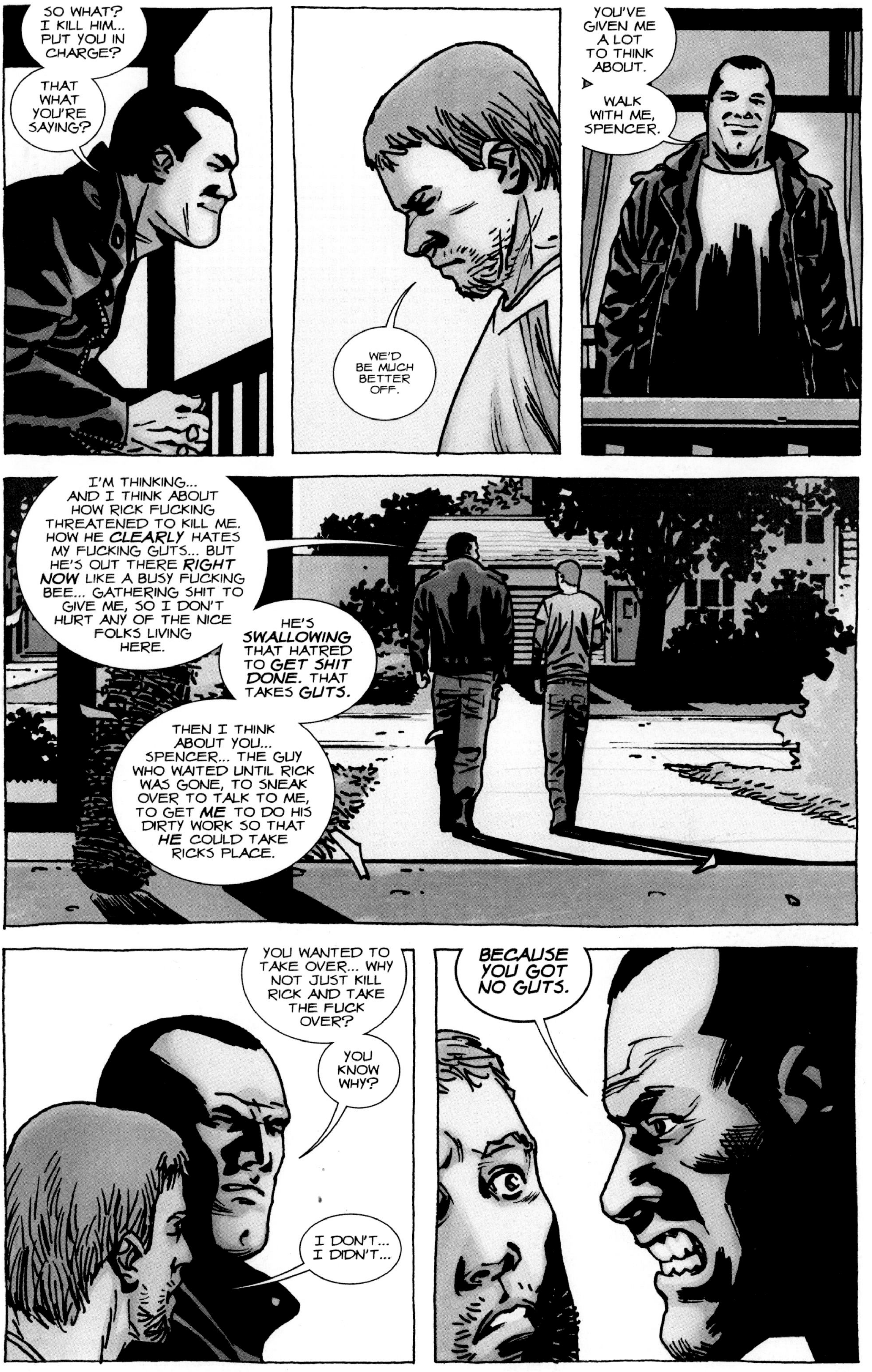
SO WHAT? I KILL HIM... PUT YOU IN CHARGE?
THAT WHAT YOU'RE SAYING?
WE'D BE MUCH BETTER OFF.
YOU'VE GIVEN ME A LOT TO THINK ABOUT.
WALK WITH ME, SPENCER.
I'M THINKING... AND I THINK ABOUT HOW RICK FUCKING THREATENED TO KILL ME. HOW HE CLEARLY HATES MY FUCKING GUTS... BUT HE'S OUT THERE RIGHT NOW LIKE A BUSY FUCKING BEE... GATHERING SHIT TO GIVE ME, SO I DON'T HURT ANY OF THE NICE FOLKS LIVING HERE.
HE'S SWALLOWING THAT HATRED TO GET SHIT DONE. THAT TAKES GUTS.
THEN I THINK ABOUT YOU... SPENCER... THE GUY WHO WAITED UNTIL RICK WAS GONE, TO SNEAK OVER TO TALK TO ME, TO GET ME TO DO HIS DIRTY WORK SO THAT HE COULD TAKE RICKS PLACE.
YOU WANTED TO TAKE OVER... WHY NOT JUST KILL RICK AND TAKE THE FUCK OVER?
YOU KNOW WHY?
I DON'T... I DIDN'T...
BECAUSE YOU GOT NO GUTS.

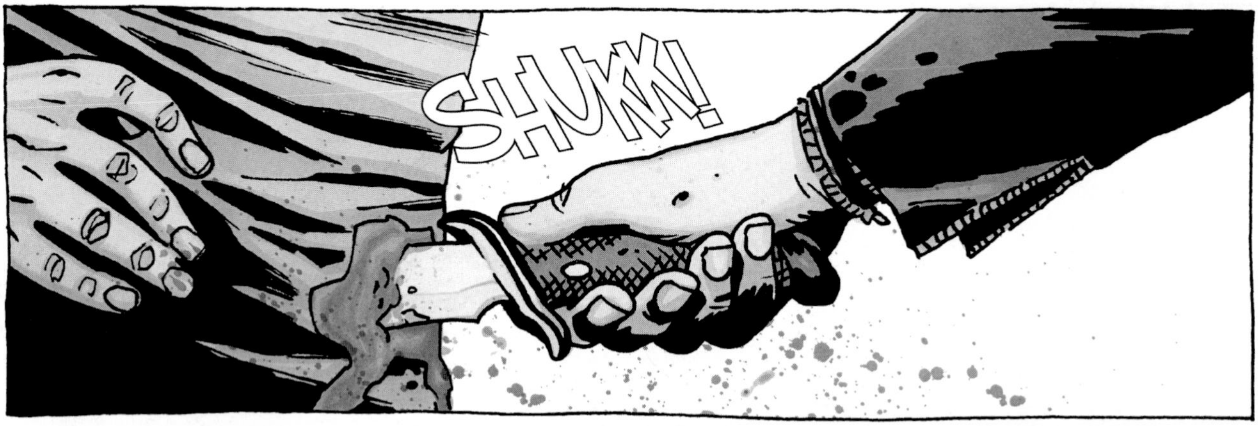
SHUKK!

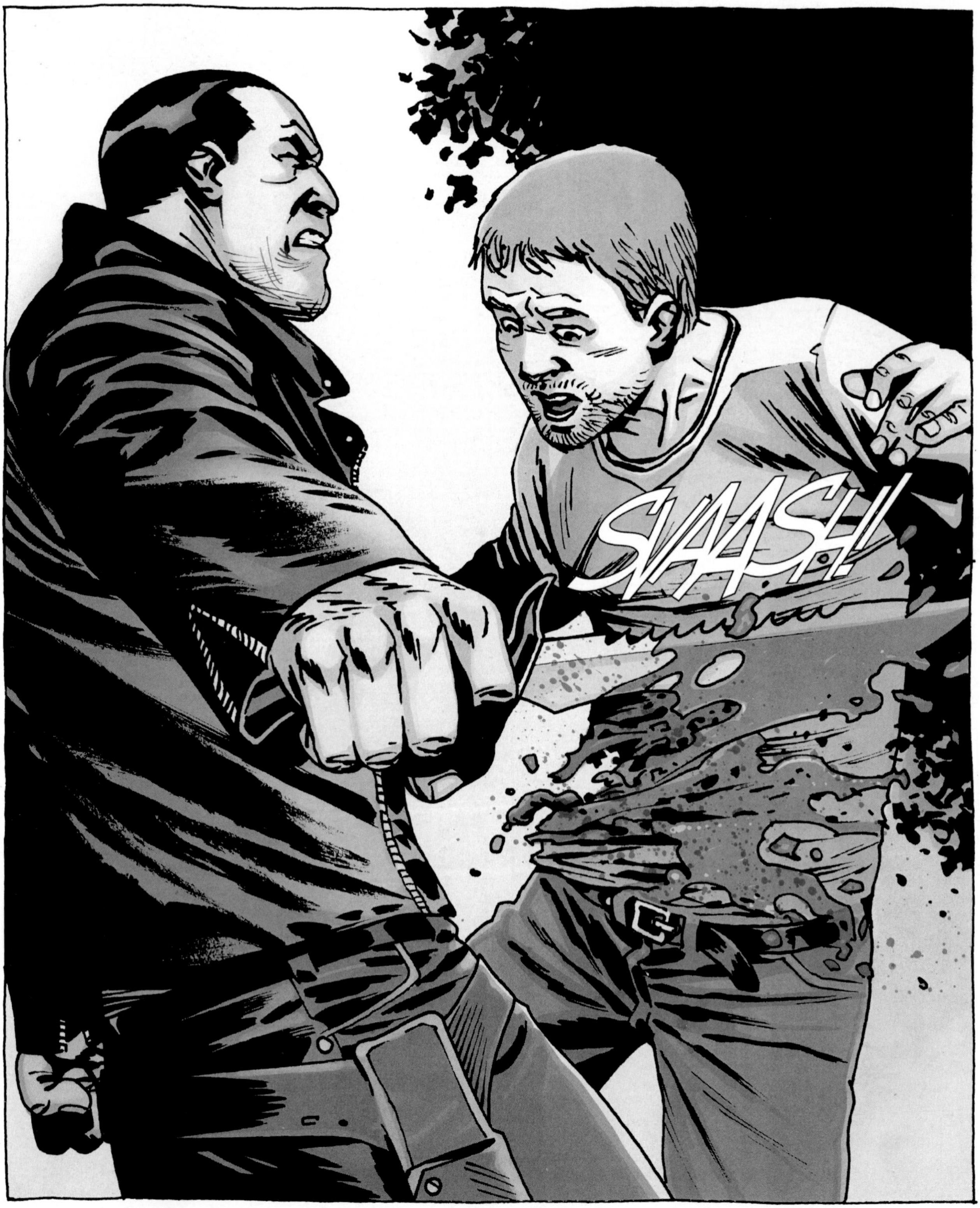
SVAASH!

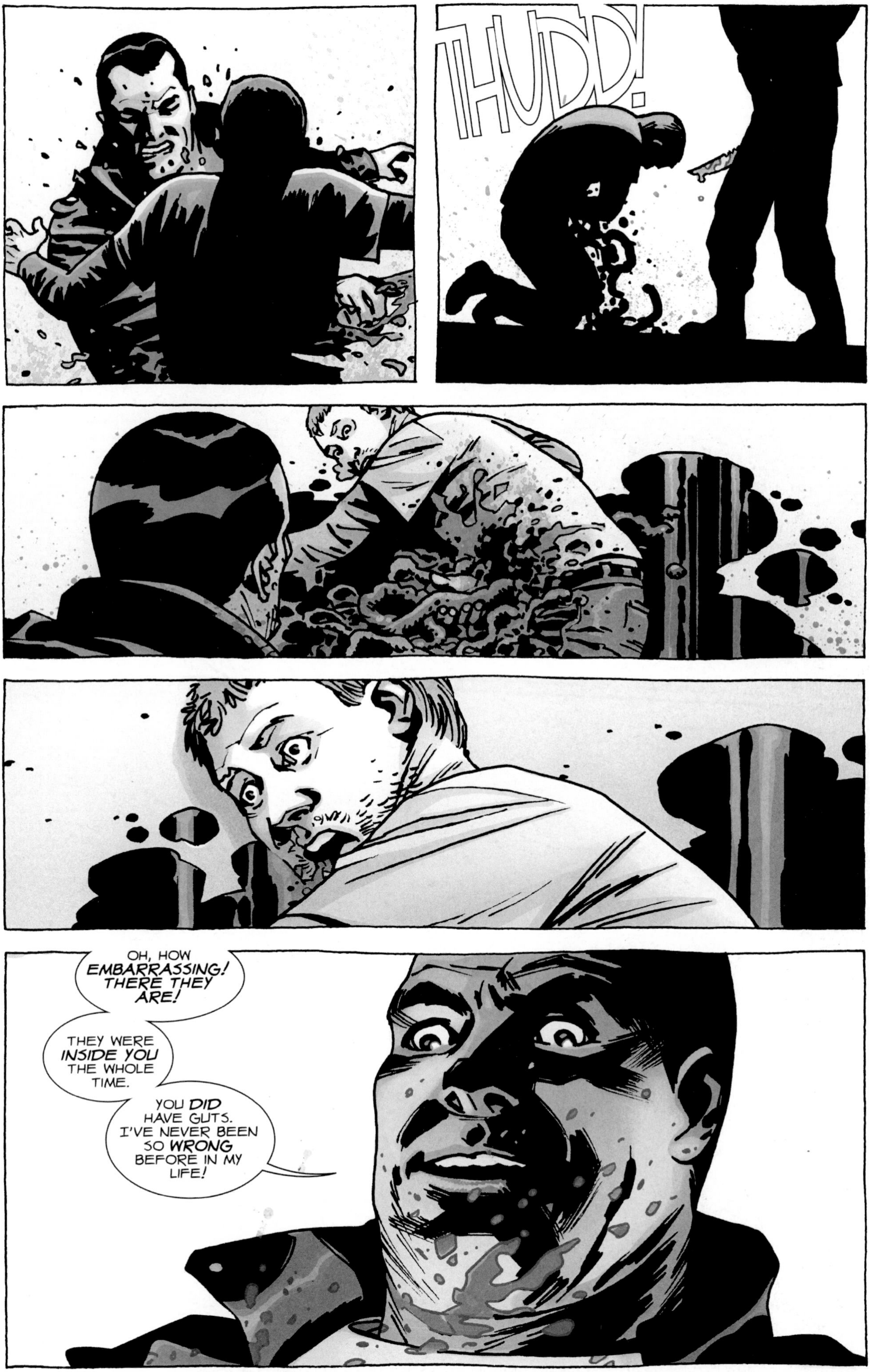
THUDD!
OH, HOW EMBARRASSING! THERE THEY ARE!
THEY WERE INSIDE YOU THE WHOLE TIME.
YOU DID HAVE GUTS. I'VE NEVER BEEN SO WRONG BEFORE IN MY LIFE!

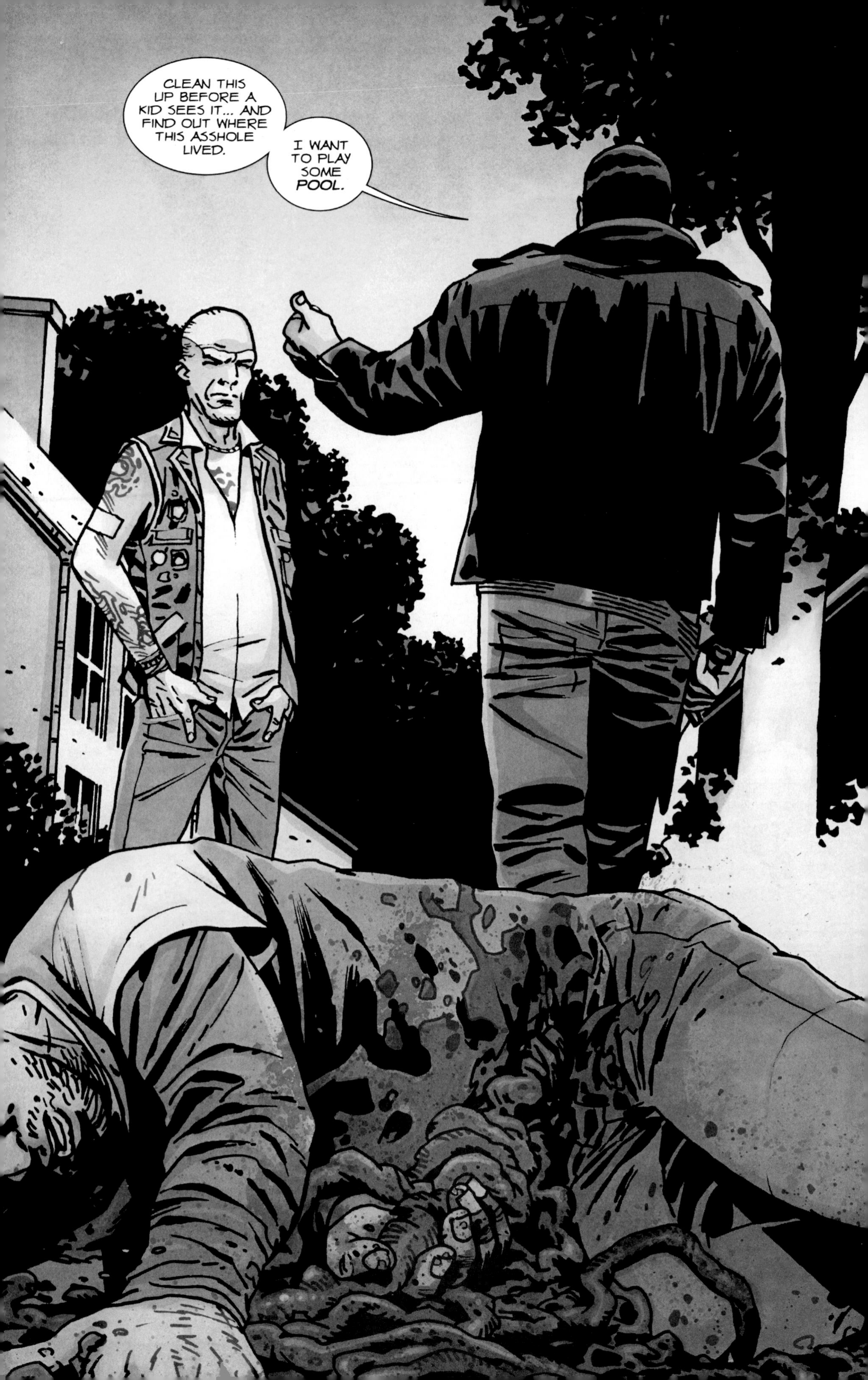
CLEAN THIS UP BEFORE A KID SEES IT... AND FIND OUT WHERE THIS ASSHOLE LIVED.
I WANT TO PLAY SOME *POOL.*

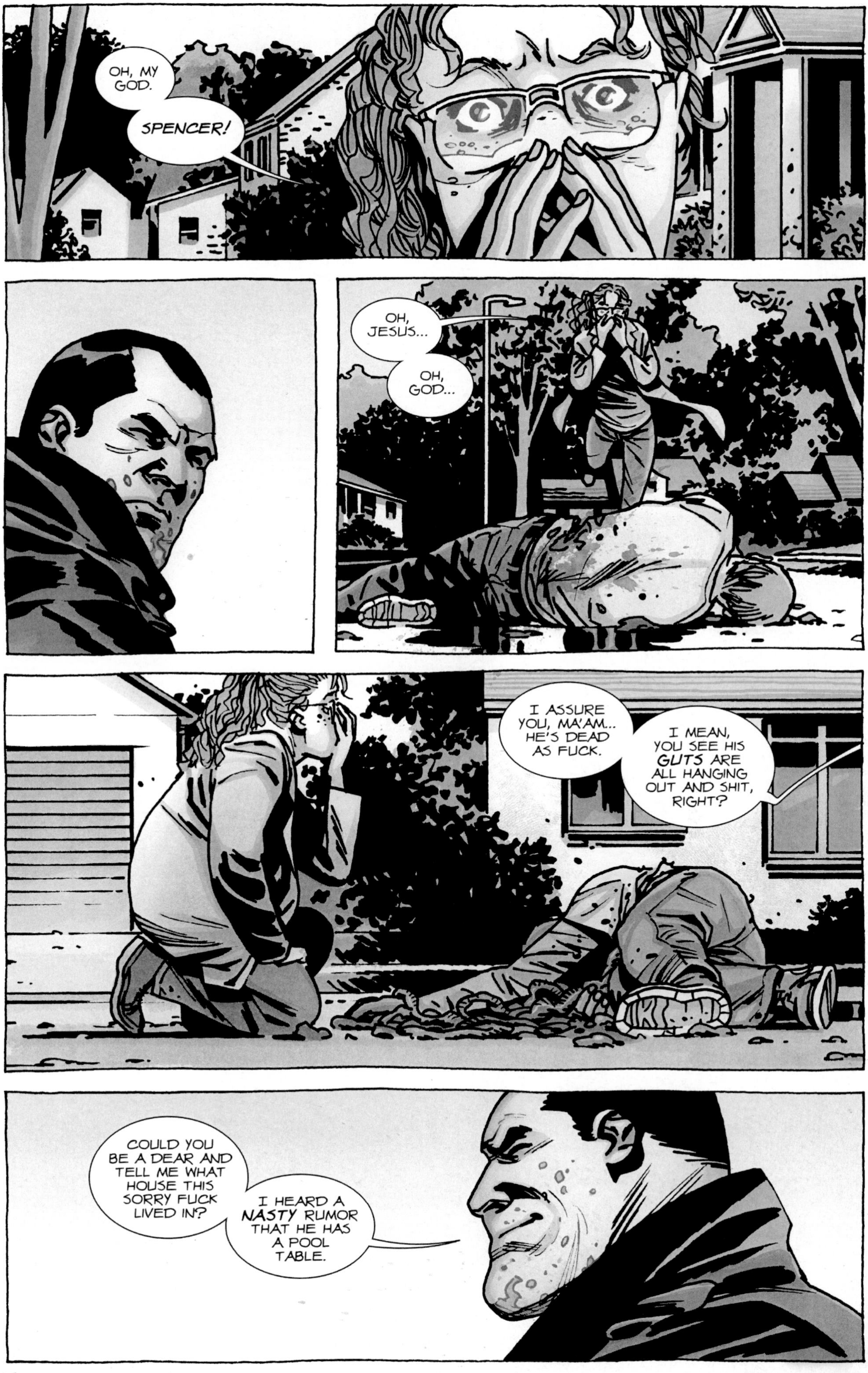
OH, MY GOD.
SPENCER!
OH, JESUS...
OH, GOD...
I ASSURE YOU, MA'AM... HE'S DEAD AS FUCK.
I MEAN, YOU SEE HIS GUTS ARE ALL HANGING OUT AND SHIT, RIGHT?
COULD YOU BE A DEAR AND TELL ME WHAT HOUSE THIS SORRY FUCK LIVED IN?
I HEARD A NASTY RUMOR THAT HE HAS A POOL TABLE.

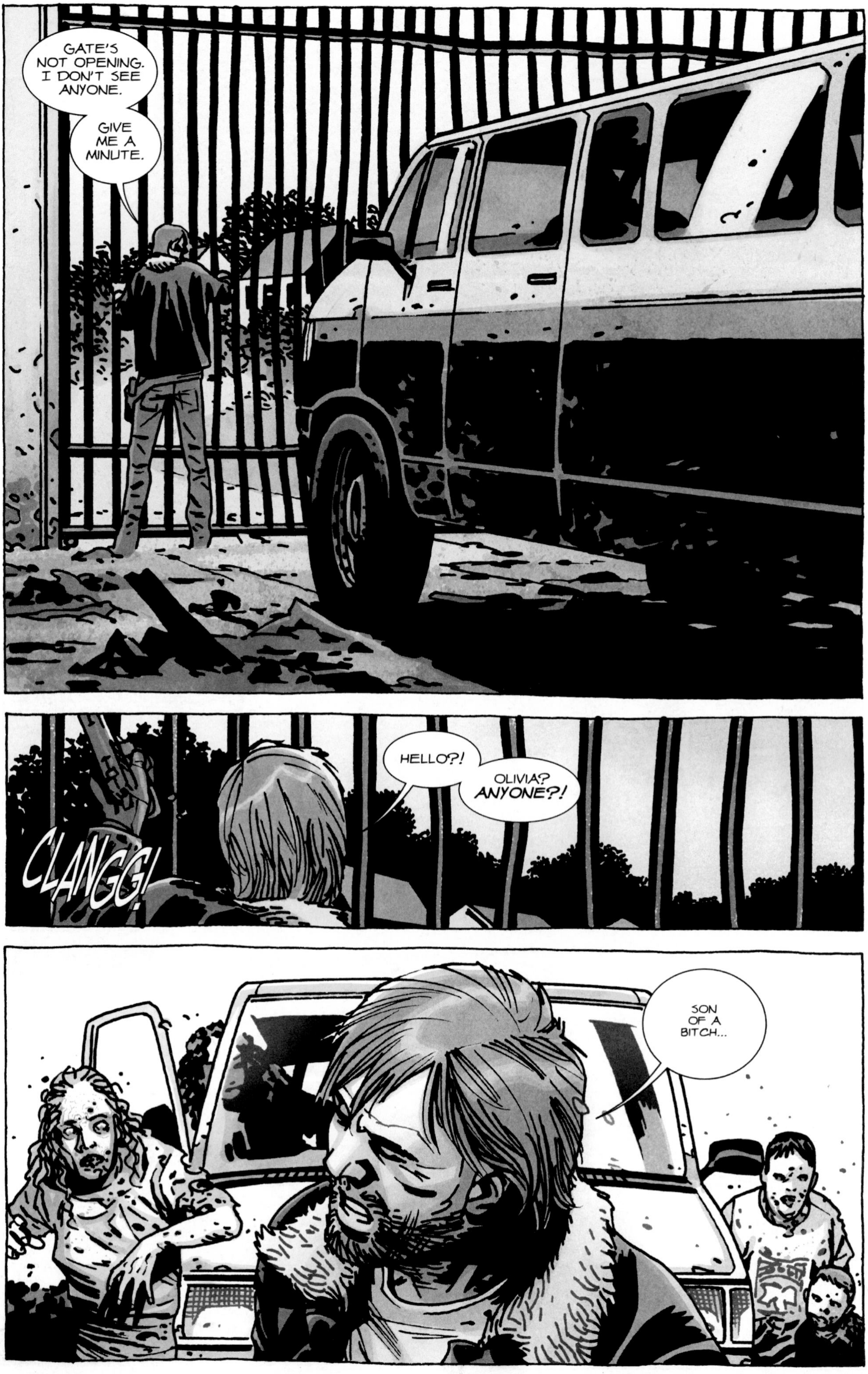
GATE'S NOT OPENING. I DON'T SEE ANYONE.
GIVE ME A MINUTE.
CLANGG!
HELLO?!
OLIVIA? ANYONE?!
SON OF A BITCH...

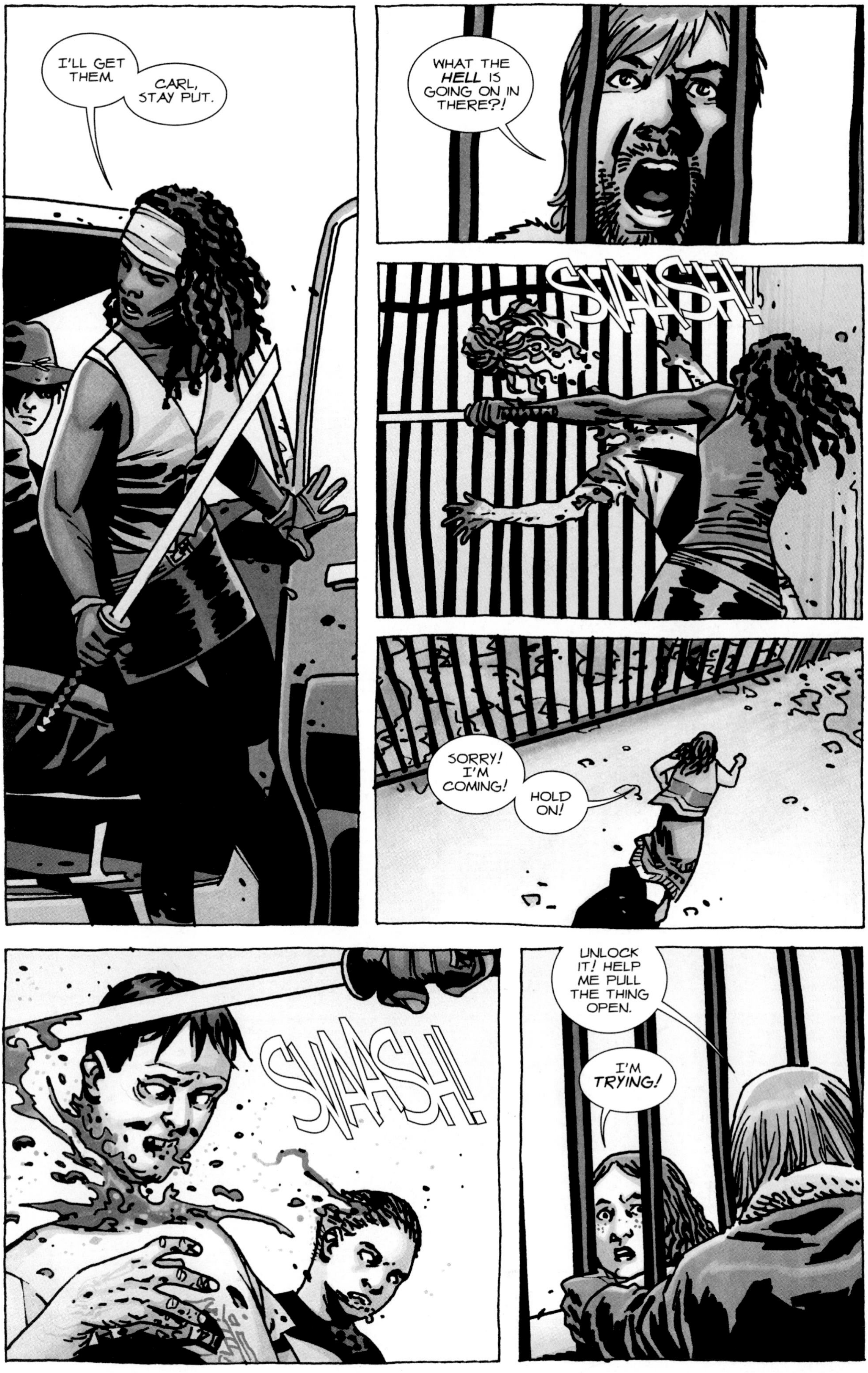
I'LL GET THEM.
CARL, STAY PUT.
WHAT THE *HELL* IS GOING ON IN THERE?!
SWASH!
SORRY! I'M COMING!
HOLD ON!
SWASH!
UNLOCK IT! HELP ME PULL THE THING OPEN.
I'M *TRYING!*

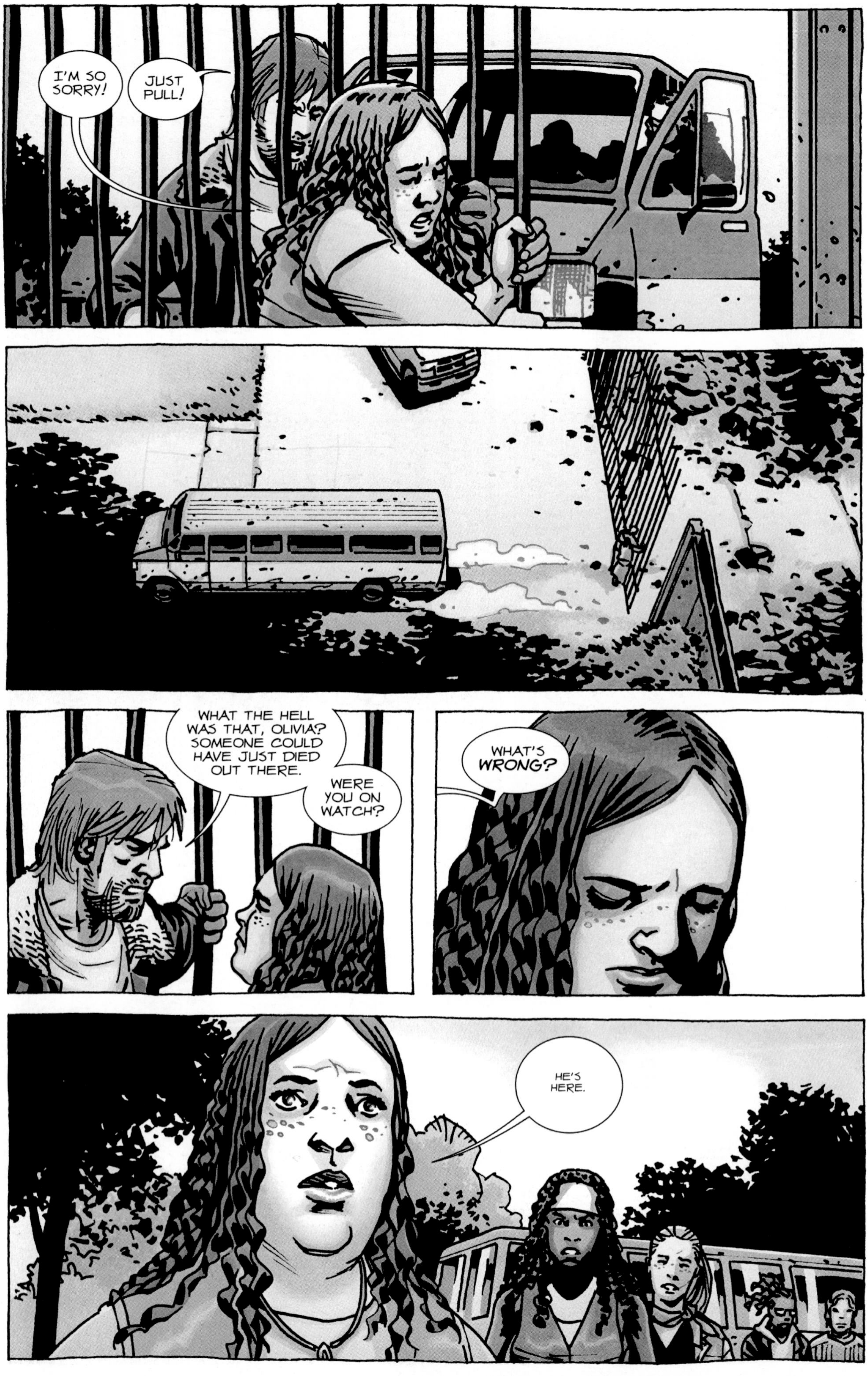
I'M SO SORRY!
JUST PULL!
WHAT THE HELL WAS THAT, OLIVIA? SOMEONE COULD HAVE JUST DIED OUT THERE.
WERE YOU ON WATCH?
WHAT'S WRONG?
HE'S HERE.

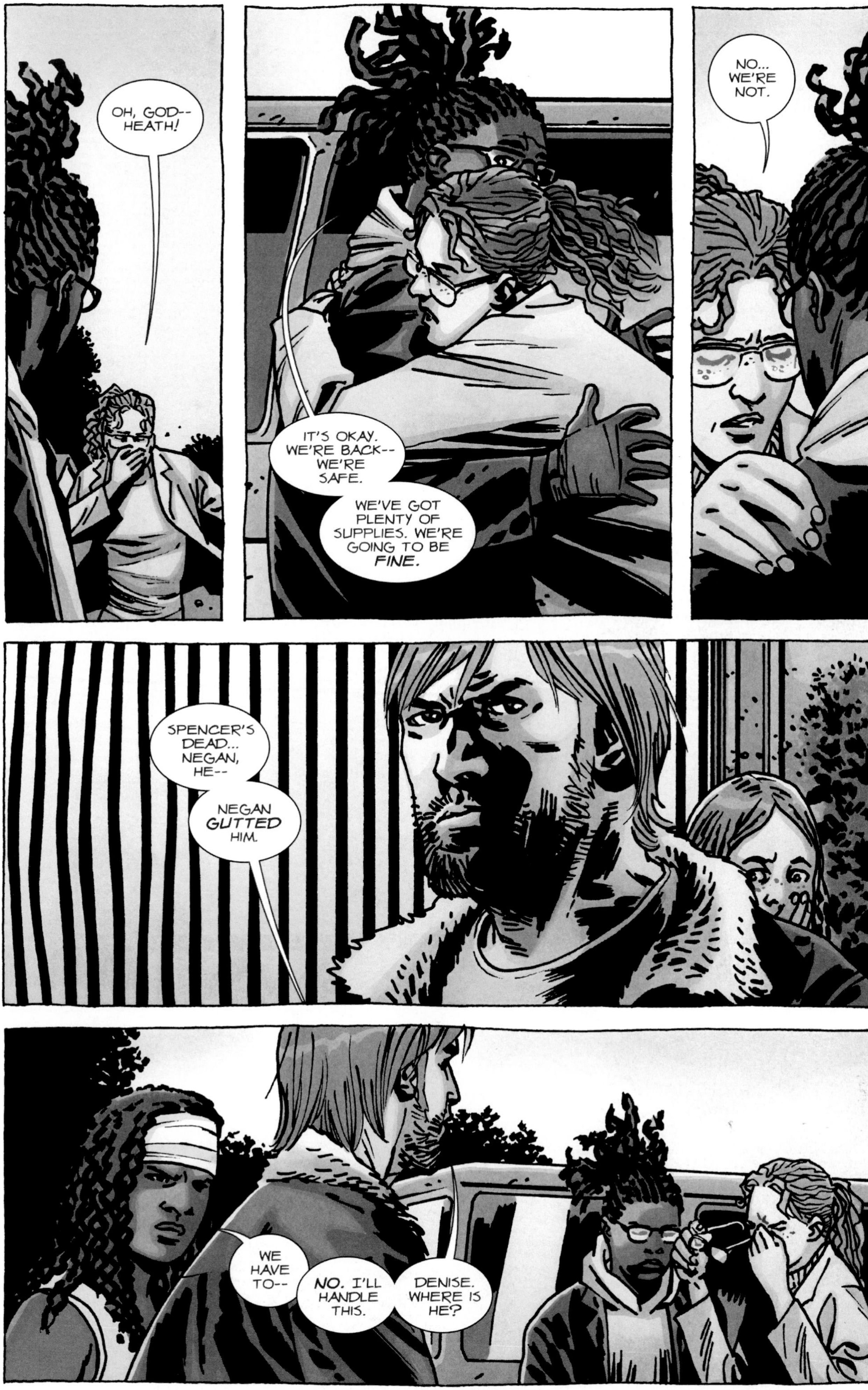
OH, GOD--
HEATH!
IT'S OKAY. WE'RE BACK-- WE'RE SAFE.
WE'VE GOT PLENTY OF SUPPLIES. WE'RE GOING TO BE FINE.
NO... WE'RE NOT.
SPENCER'S DEAD... NEGAN, HE--
NEGAN GUTTED HIM.
DENISE. WHERE IS HE?
NO. I'LL HANDLE THIS.
WE HAVE TO--

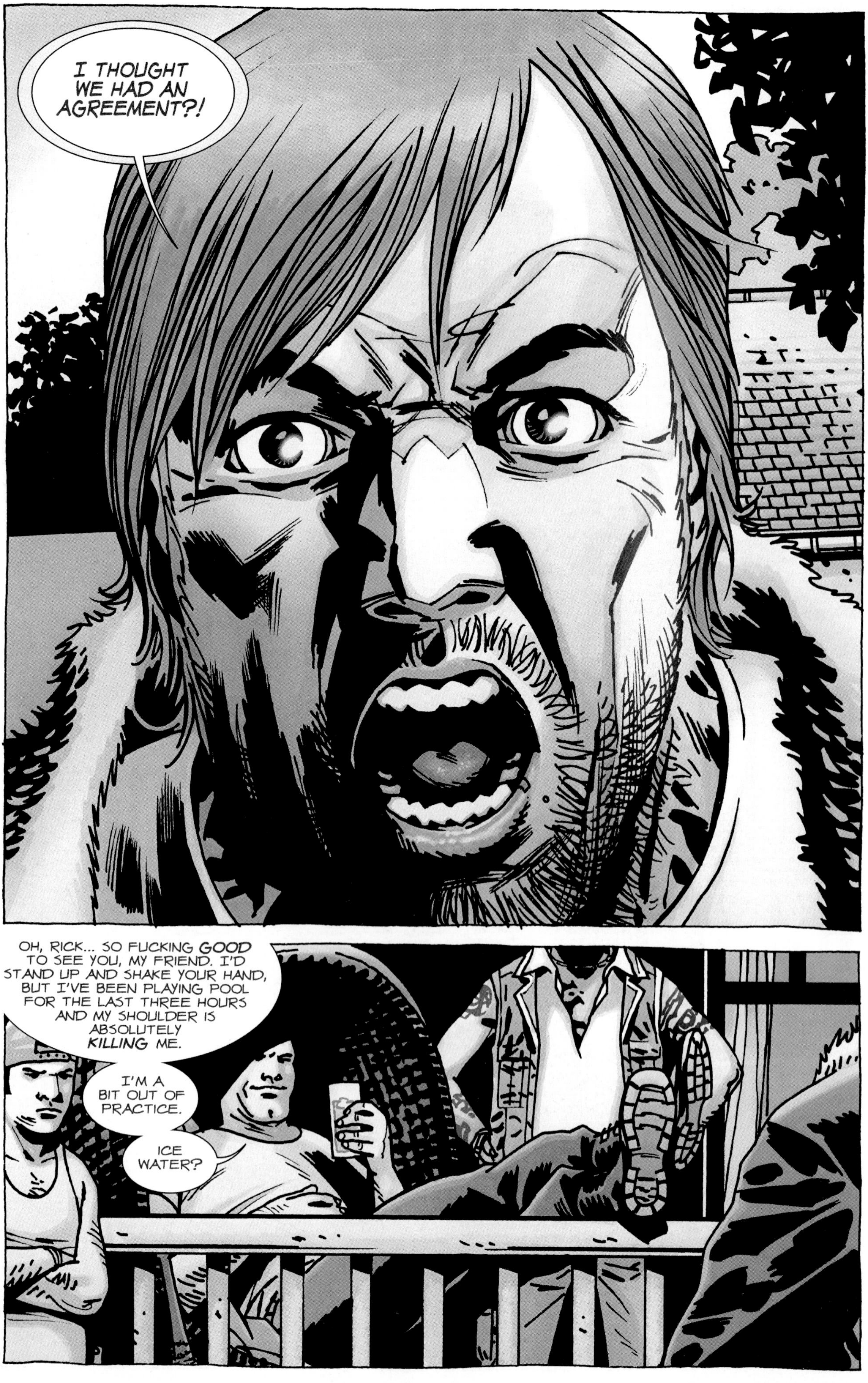
I THOUGHT WE HAD AN AGREEMENT?!
OH, RICK... SO FUCKING GOOD TO SEE YOU, MY FRIEND. I'D STAND UP AND SHAKE YOUR HAND, BUT I'VE BEEN PLAYING POOL FOR THE LAST THREE HOURS AND MY SHOULDER IS ABSOLUTELY KILLING ME.
I'M A BIT OUT OF PRACTICE.
ICE WATER?

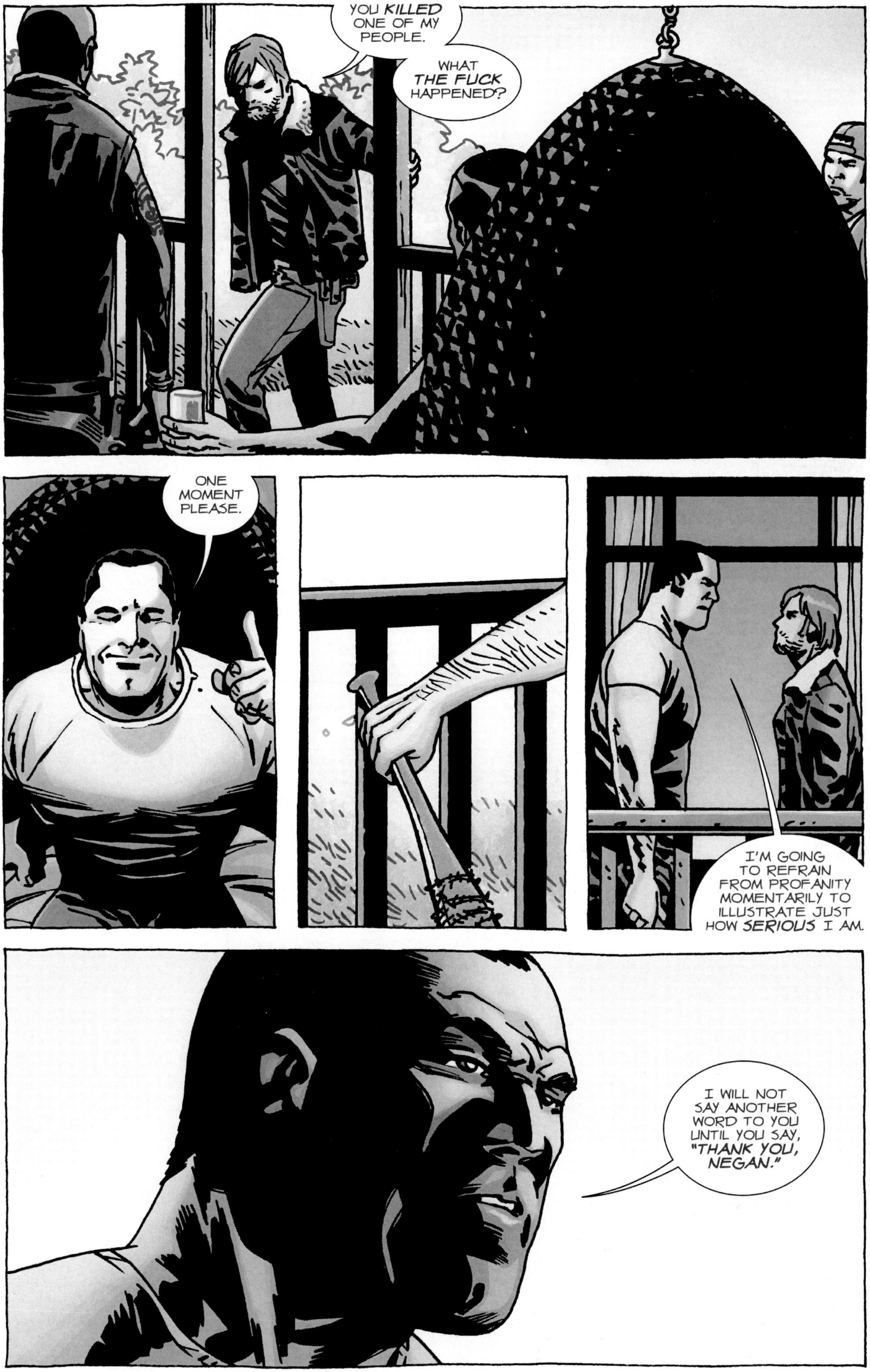
YOU KILLED ONE OF MY PEOPLE.
WHAT THE FUCK HAPPENED?
ONE MOMENT PLEASE.
I'M GOING TO REFRAIN FROM PROFANITY MOMENTARILY TO ILLUSTRATE JUST HOW SERIOUS I AM.
I WILL NOT SAY ANOTHER WORD TO YOU UNTIL YOU SAY, "THANK YOU, NEGAN."

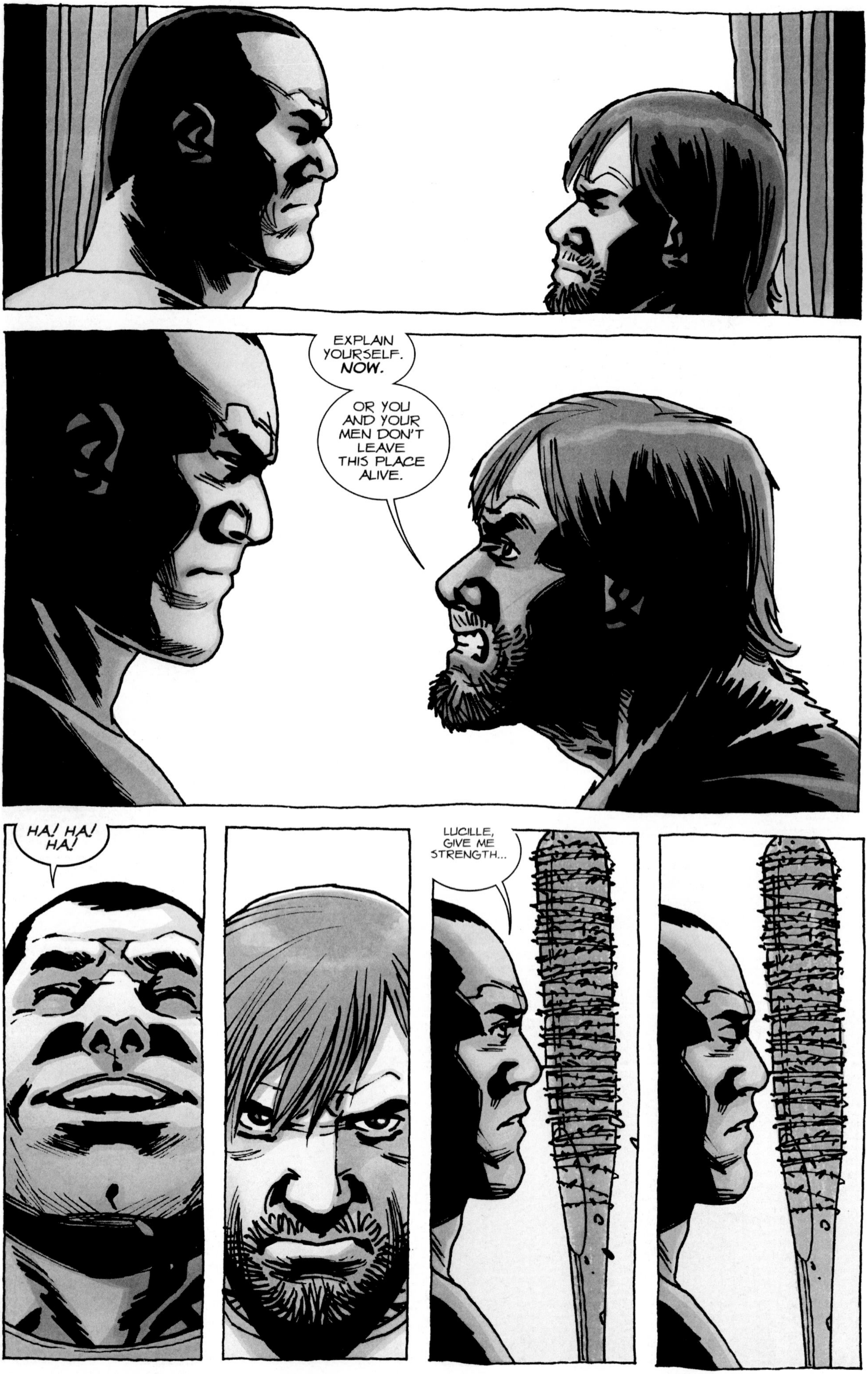
EXPLAIN YOURSELF. NOW.
OR YOU AND YOUR MEN DON'T LEAVE THIS PLACE ALIVE.
HA! HA! HA!
LUCILLE, GIVE ME STRENGTH...

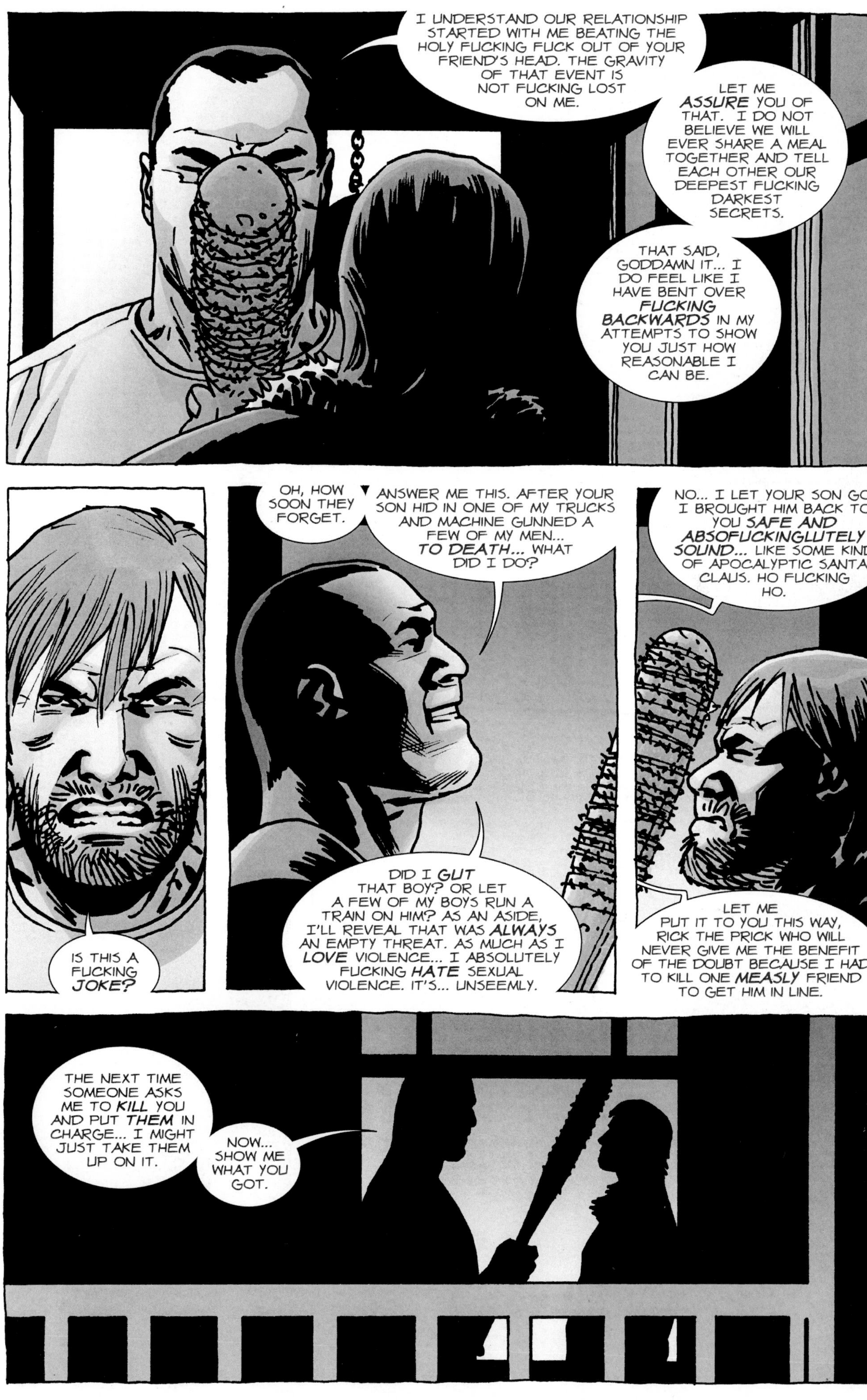
I UNDERSTAND OUR RELATIONSHIP STARTED WITH ME BEATING THE HOLY FUCKING FUCK OUT OF YOUR FRIEND'S HEAD. THE GRAVITY OF THAT EVENT IS NOT FUCKING LOST ON ME.
LET ME ASSURE YOU OF THAT. I DO NOT BELIEVE WE WILL EVER SHARE A MEAL TOGETHER AND TELL EACH OTHER OUR DEEPEST FUCKING DARKEST SECRETS.
THAT SAID, GODDAMN IT... I DO FEEL LIKE I HAVE BENT OVER FUCKING BACKWARDS IN MY ATTEMPTS TO SHOW YOU JUST HOW REASONABLE I CAN BE.
IS THIS A FUCKING JOKE?
OH, HOW SOON THEY FORGET.
ANSWER ME THIS. AFTER YOUR SON HID IN ONE OF MY TRUCKS AND MACHINE GUNNED A FEW OF MY MEN... TO DEATH... WHAT DID I DO?
DID I GUT THAT BOY? OR LET A FEW OF MY BOYS RUN A TRAIN ON HIM? AS AN ASIDE, I'LL REVEAL THAT WAS ALWAYS AN EMPTY THREAT. AS MUCH AS I LOVE VIOLENCE... I ABSOLUTELY FUCKING HATE SEXUAL VIOLENCE. IT'S... UNSEEMLY.
NO... I LET YOUR SON GO, I BROUGHT HIM BACK TO YOU SAFE AND ABSOFUCKINGLUTELY SOUND... LIKE SOME KIND OF APOCALYPTIC SANTA CLAUS. HO FUCKING HO.
LET ME PUT IT TO YOU THIS WAY, RICK THE PRICK WHO WILL NEVER GIVE ME THE BENEFIT OF THE DOUBT BECAUSE I HAD TO KILL ONE MEASLY FRIEND TO GET HIM IN LINE.
THE NEXT TIME SOMEONE ASKS ME TO KILL YOU AND PUT THEM IN CHARGE... I MIGHT JUST TAKE THEM UP ON IT.
NOW... SHOW ME WHAT YOU GOT.

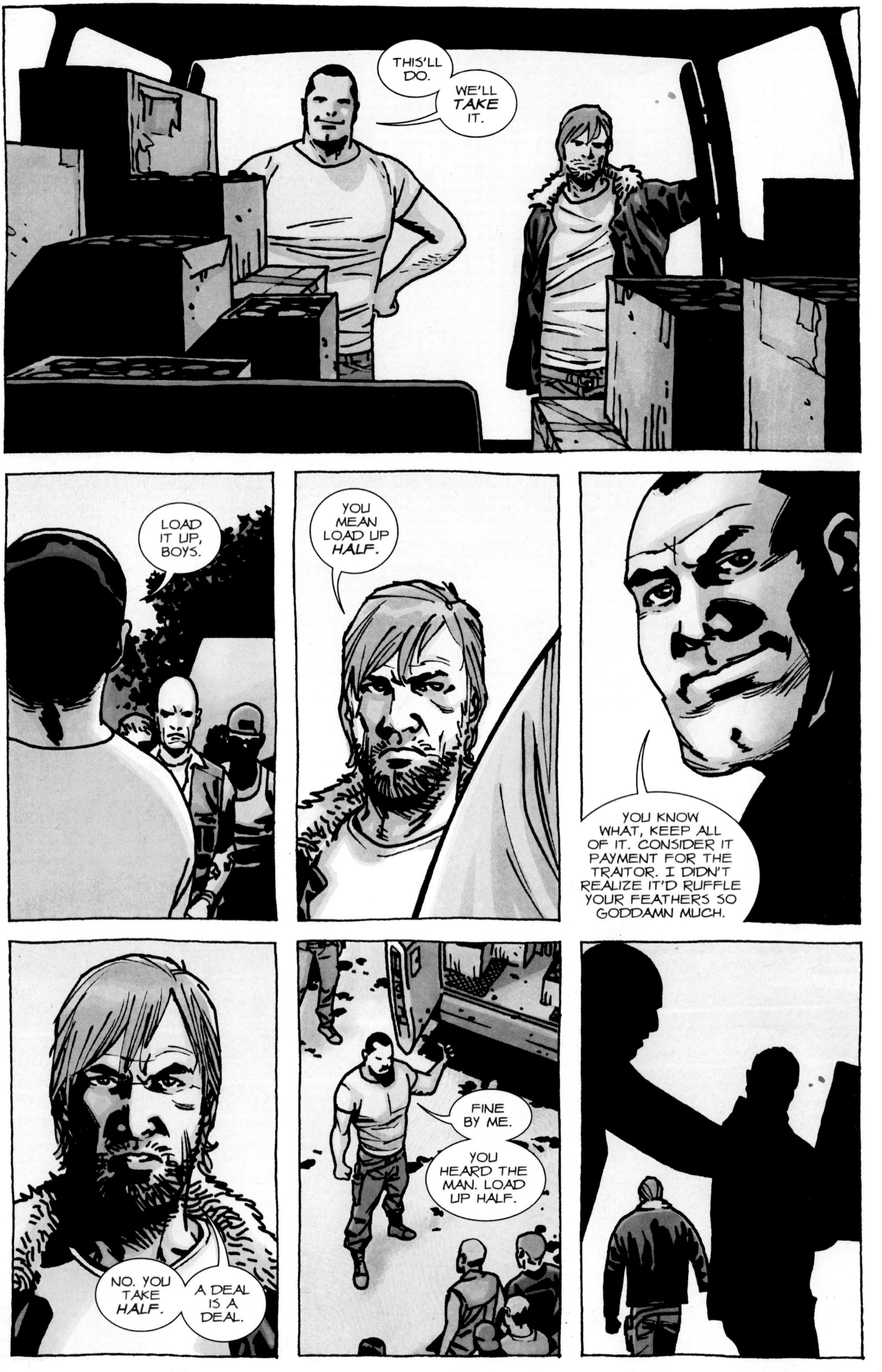
THIS'LL DO.
WE'LL *TAKE* IT.
LOAD IT UP, BOYS.
YOU MEAN LOAD UP *HALF.*
YOU KNOW WHAT, KEEP ALL OF IT. CONSIDER IT PAYMENT FOR THE TRAITOR. I DIDN'T REALIZE IT'D RUFFLE YOUR FEATHERS SO GODDAMN MUCH.
NO. YOU TAKE *HALF.*
A DEAL IS A DEAL.
FINE BY ME.
YOU HEARD THE MAN. LOAD UP HALF.

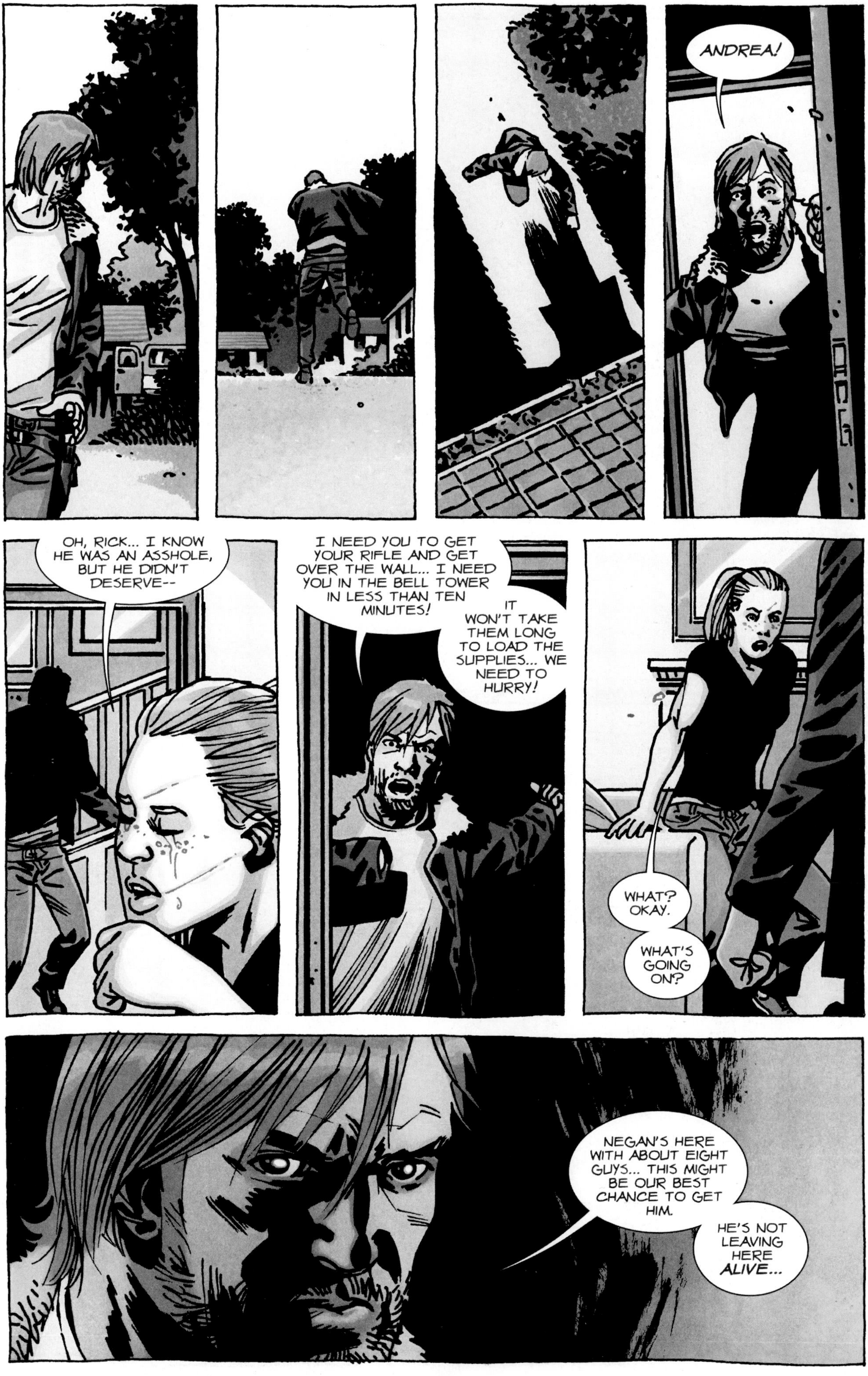
ANDREA!
OH, RICK... I KNOW HE WAS AN ASSHOLE, BUT HE DIDN'T DESERVE--
I NEED YOU TO GET YOUR RIFLE AND GET OVER THE WALL... I NEED YOU IN THE BELL TOWER IN LESS THAN TEN MINUTES!
IT WON'T TAKE THEM LONG TO LOAD THE SUPPLIES... WE NEED TO HURRY!
WHAT? OKAY.
WHAT'S GOING ON?
NEGAN'S HERE WITH ABOUT EIGHT GUYS... THIS MIGHT BE OUR BEST CHANCE TO GET HIM.
HE'S NOT LEAVING HERE ALIVE...

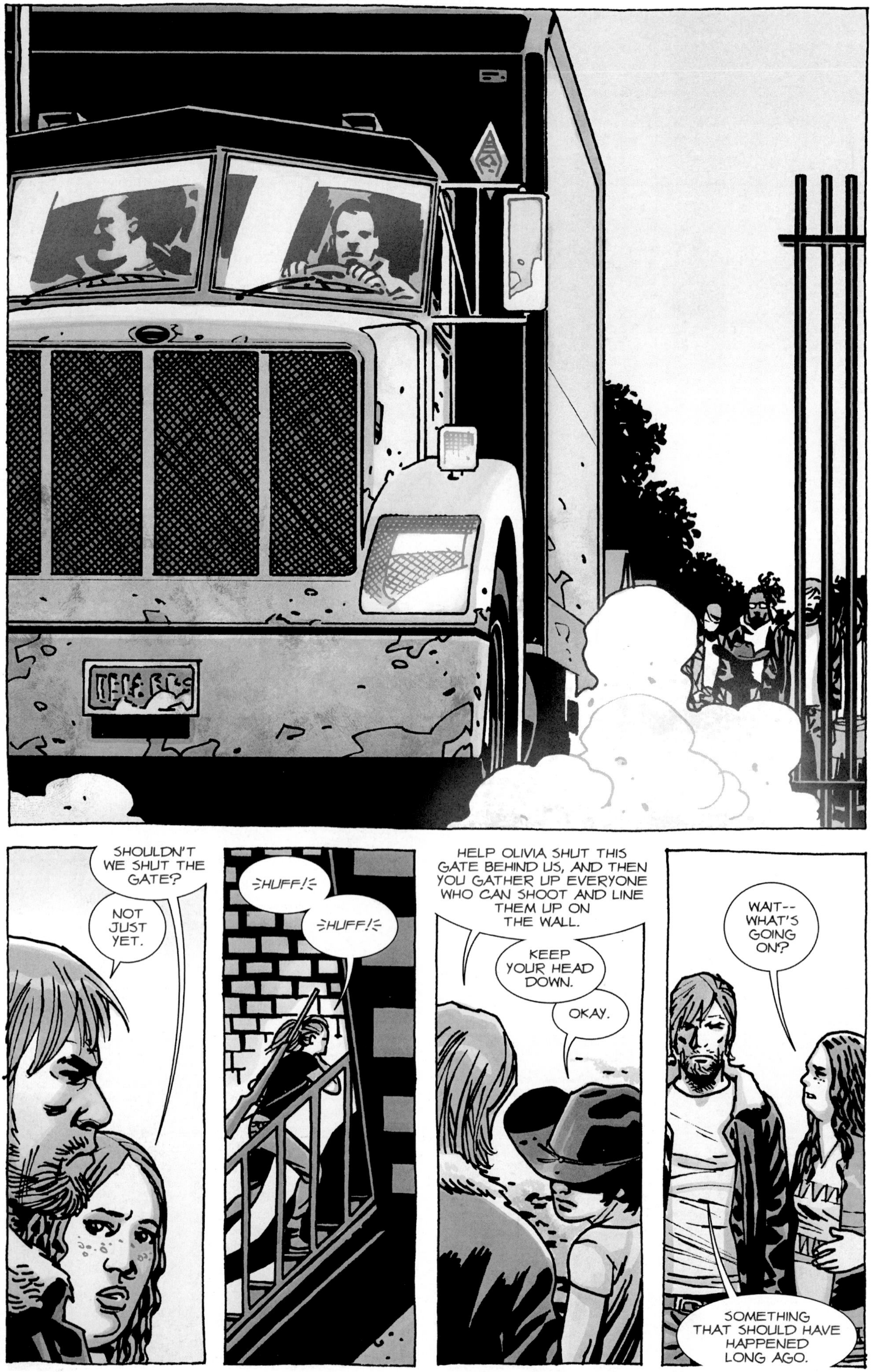

SHOULDN'T WE SHUT THE GATE?
NOT JUST YET.
HUFF!
HUFF!
HELP OLIVIA SHUT THIS GATE BEHIND US, AND THEN YOU GATHER UP EVERYONE WHO CAN SHOOT AND LINE THEM UP ON THE WALL.
KEEP YOUR HEAD DOWN.
OKAY.
WAIT-- WHAT'S GOING ON?
SOMETHING THAT SHOULD HAVE HAPPENED LONG AGO.

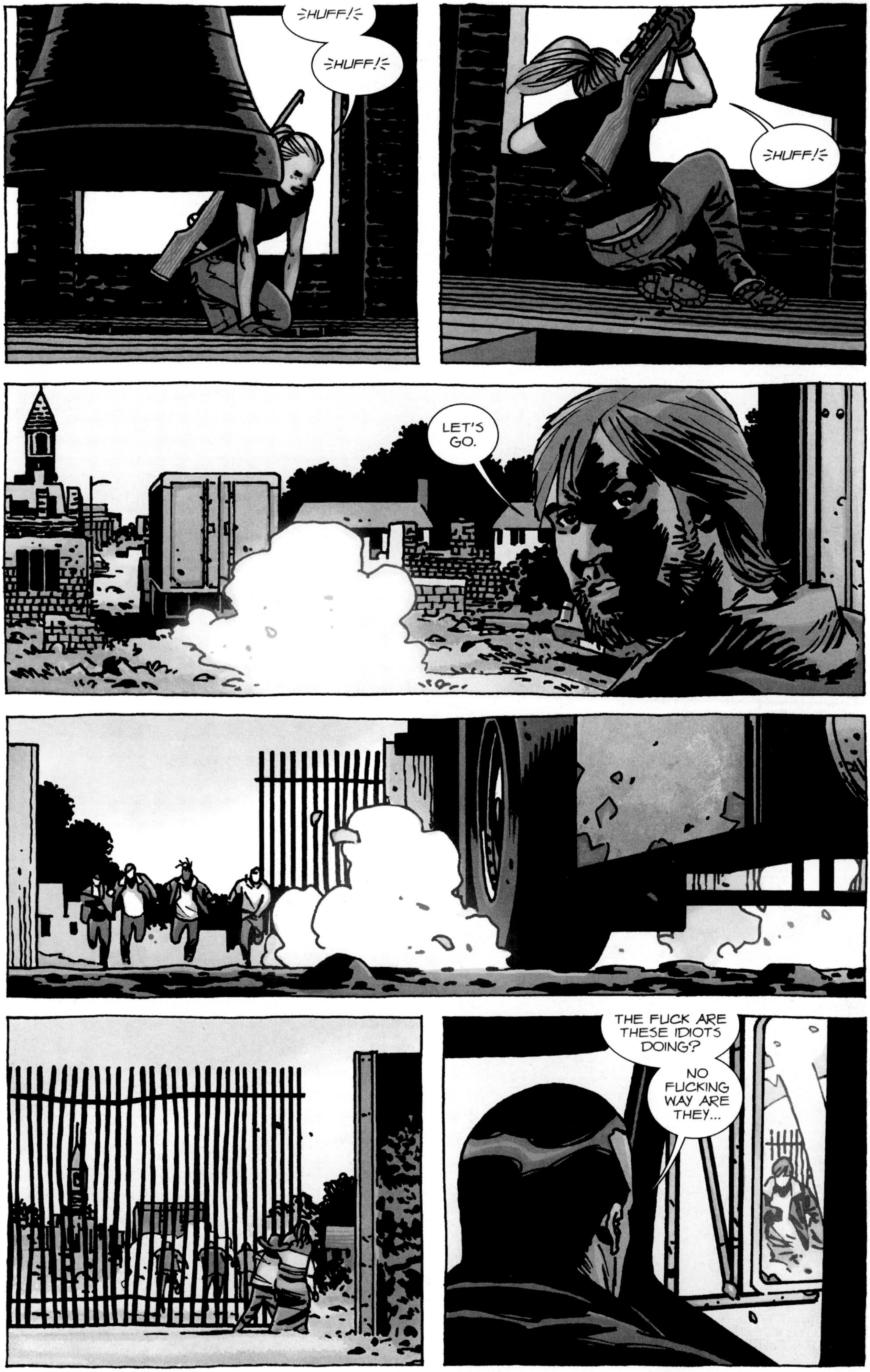

HUFF!
HUFF!
HUFF!
LET'S GO.
THE FUCK ARE THESE IDIOTS DOING?
NO FUCKING WAY ARE THEY...

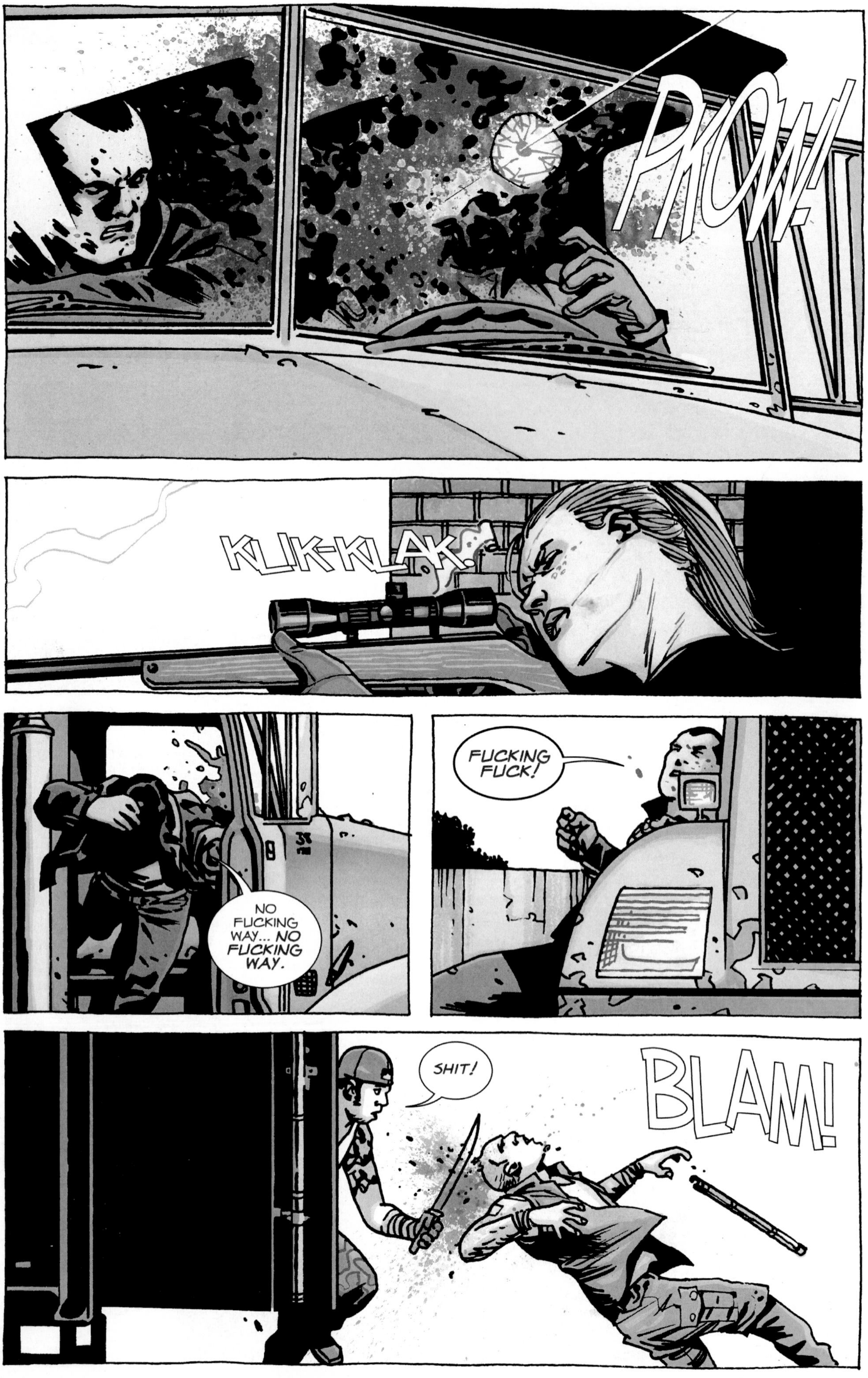
PKOW!
KLIK-KLAK.
NO FUCKING WAY... NO FUCKING WAY.
FUCKING FUCK!
SHIT!
BLAM!

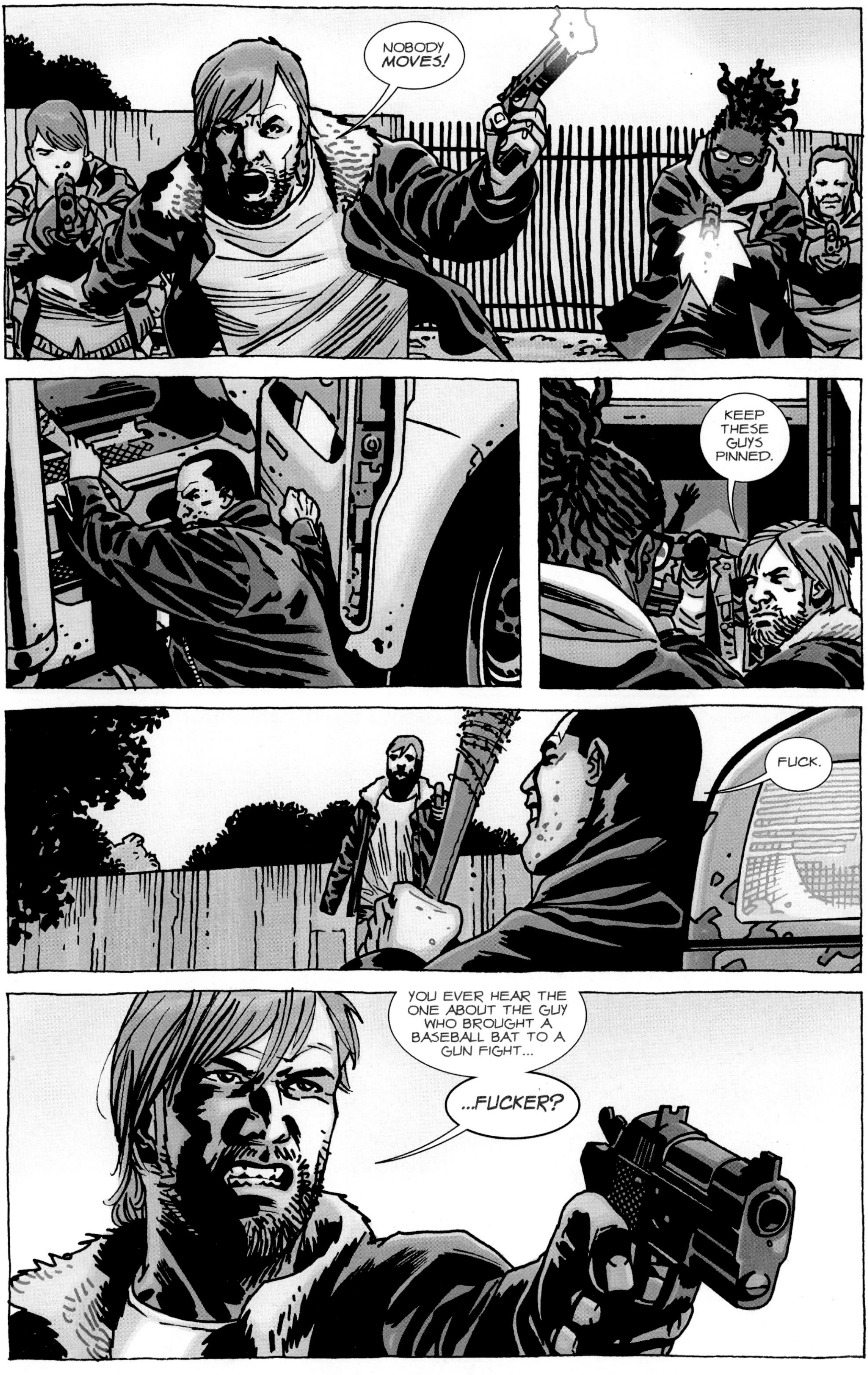
NOBODY MOVES!
KEEP THESE GUYS PINNED.
FUCK.
YOU EVER HEAR THE ONE ABOUT THE GUY WHO BROUGHT A BASEBALL BAT TO A GUN FIGHT...
...FUCKER?

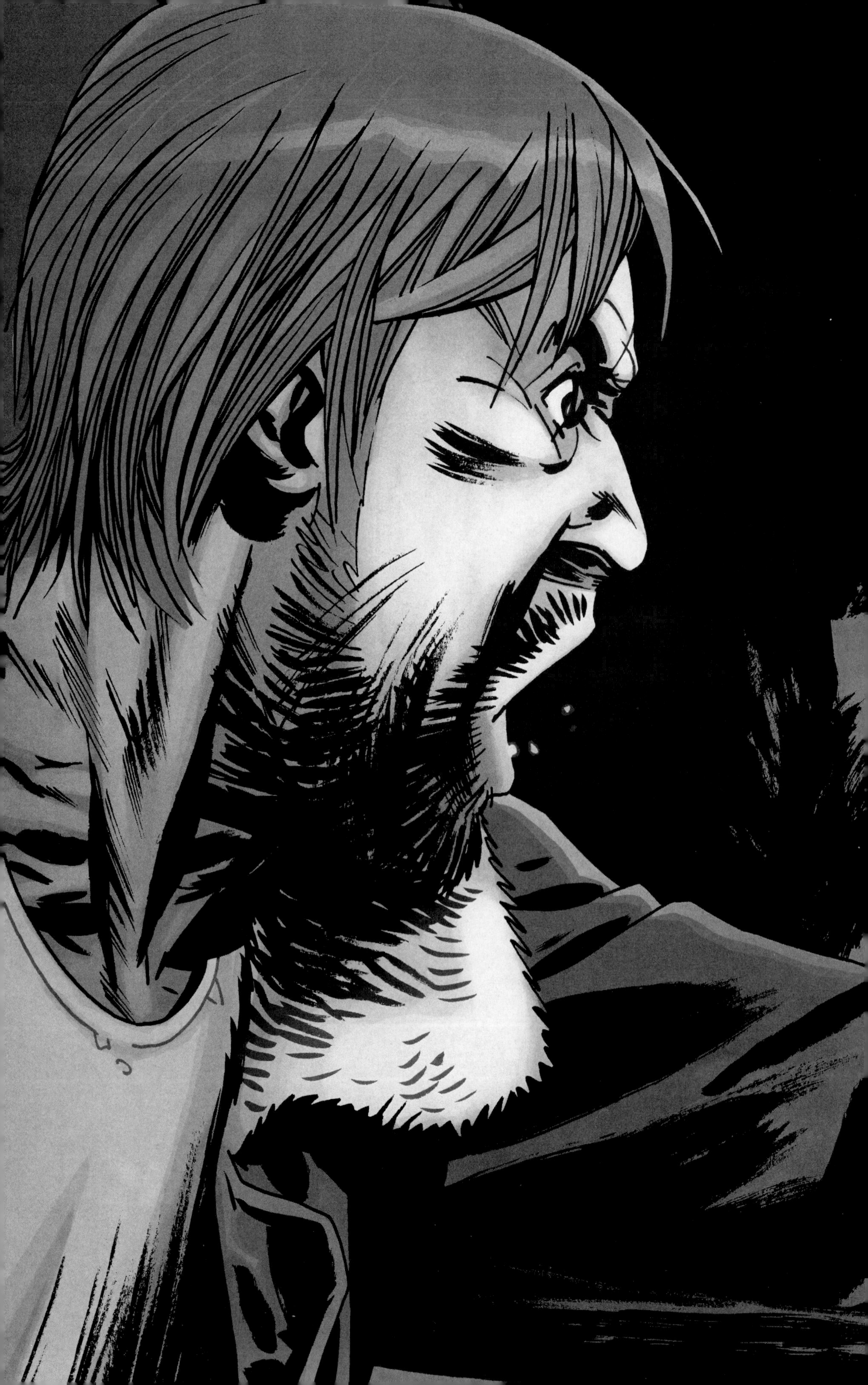

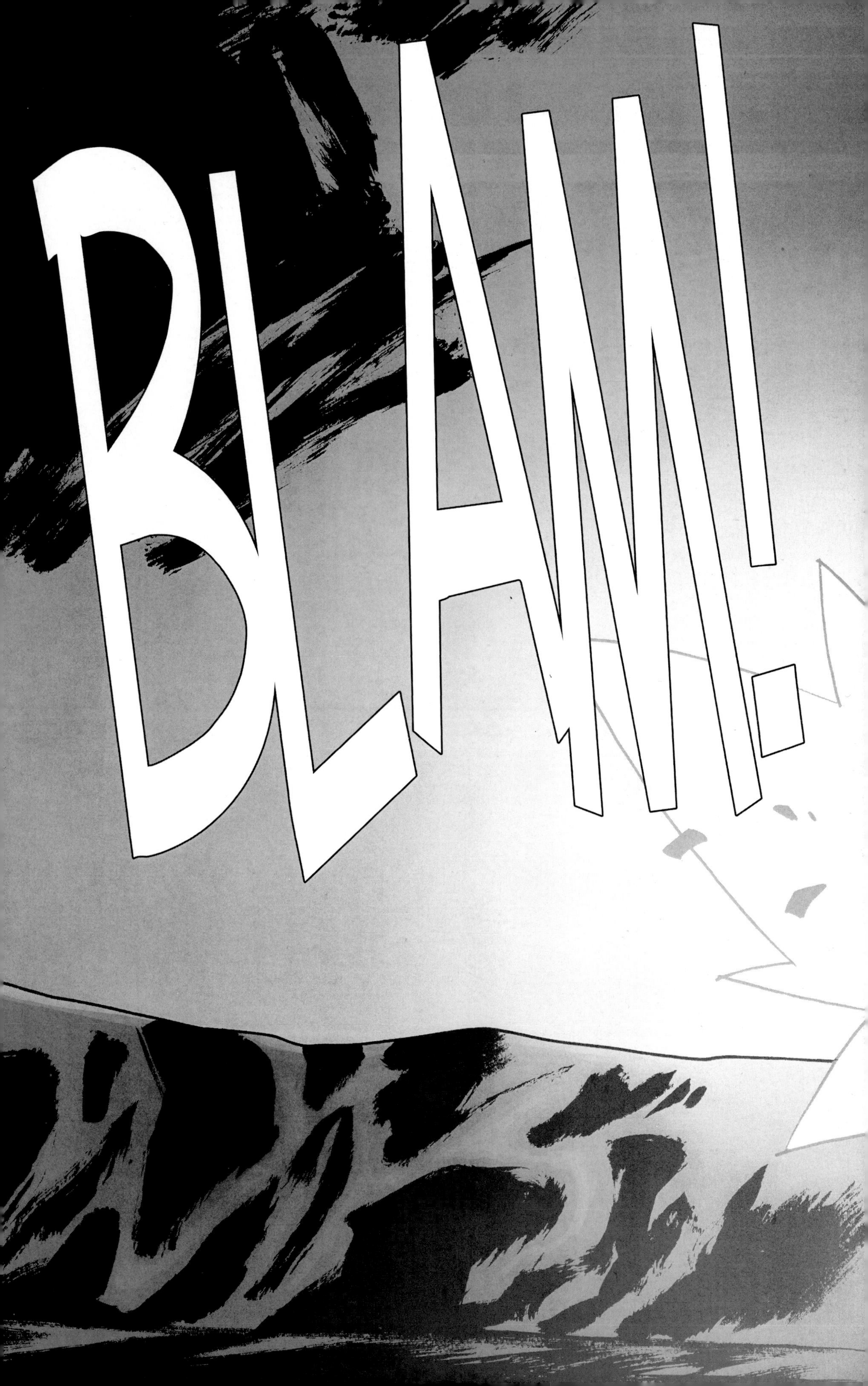
BLAM!

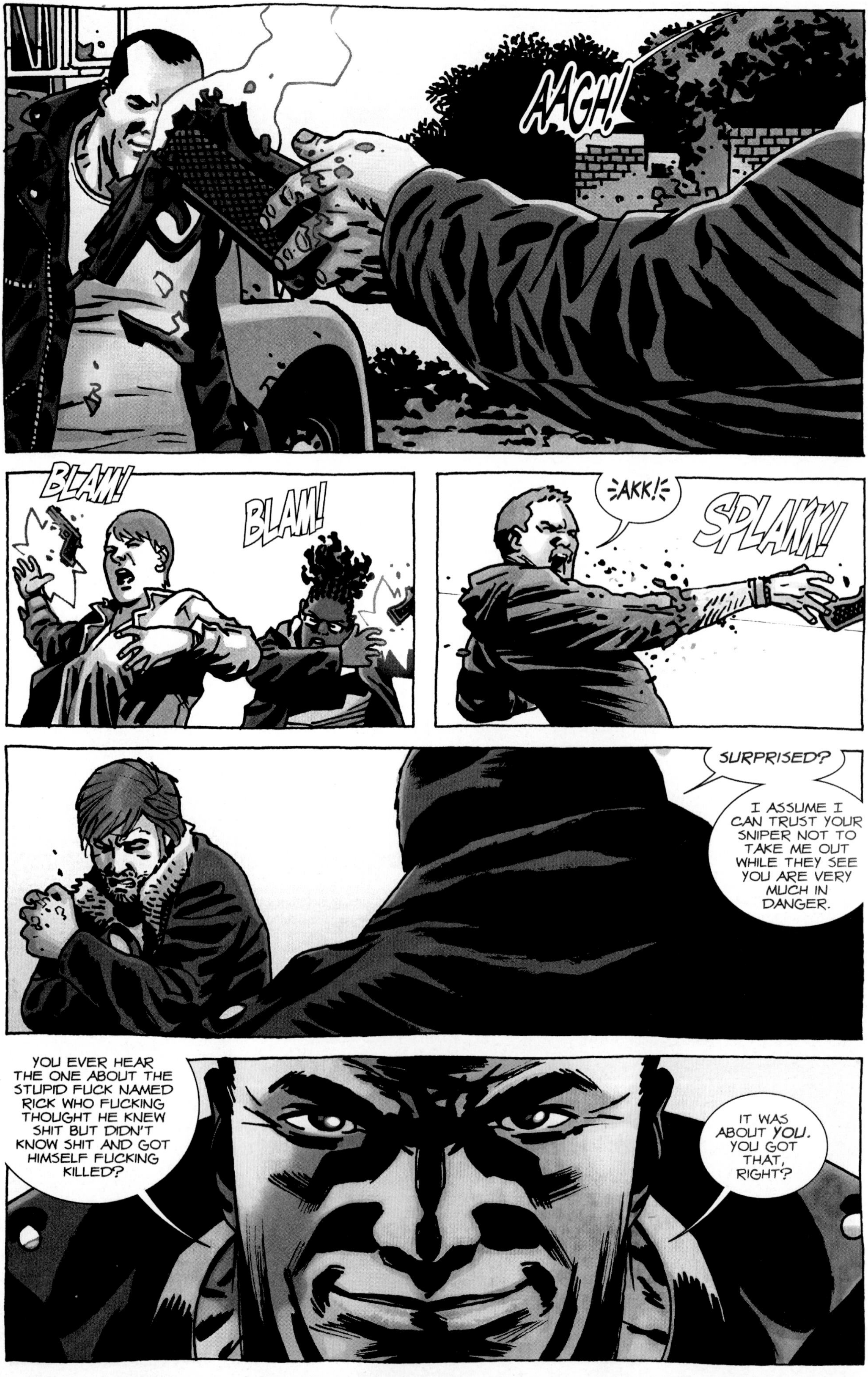
AAGH!
BLAM!
BLAM!
AKK!
SPLAKK!
SURPRISED?
I ASSUME I CAN TRUST YOUR SNIPER NOT TO TAKE ME OUT WHILE THEY SEE YOU ARE VERY MUCH IN DANGER.
YOU EVER HEAR THE ONE ABOUT THE STUPID FUCK NAMED RICK WHO FUCKING THOUGHT HE KNEW SHIT BUT DIDN'T KNOW SHIT AND GOT HIMSELF FUCKING KILLED?
IT WAS ABOUT *YOU*. YOU GOT THAT, RIGHT?

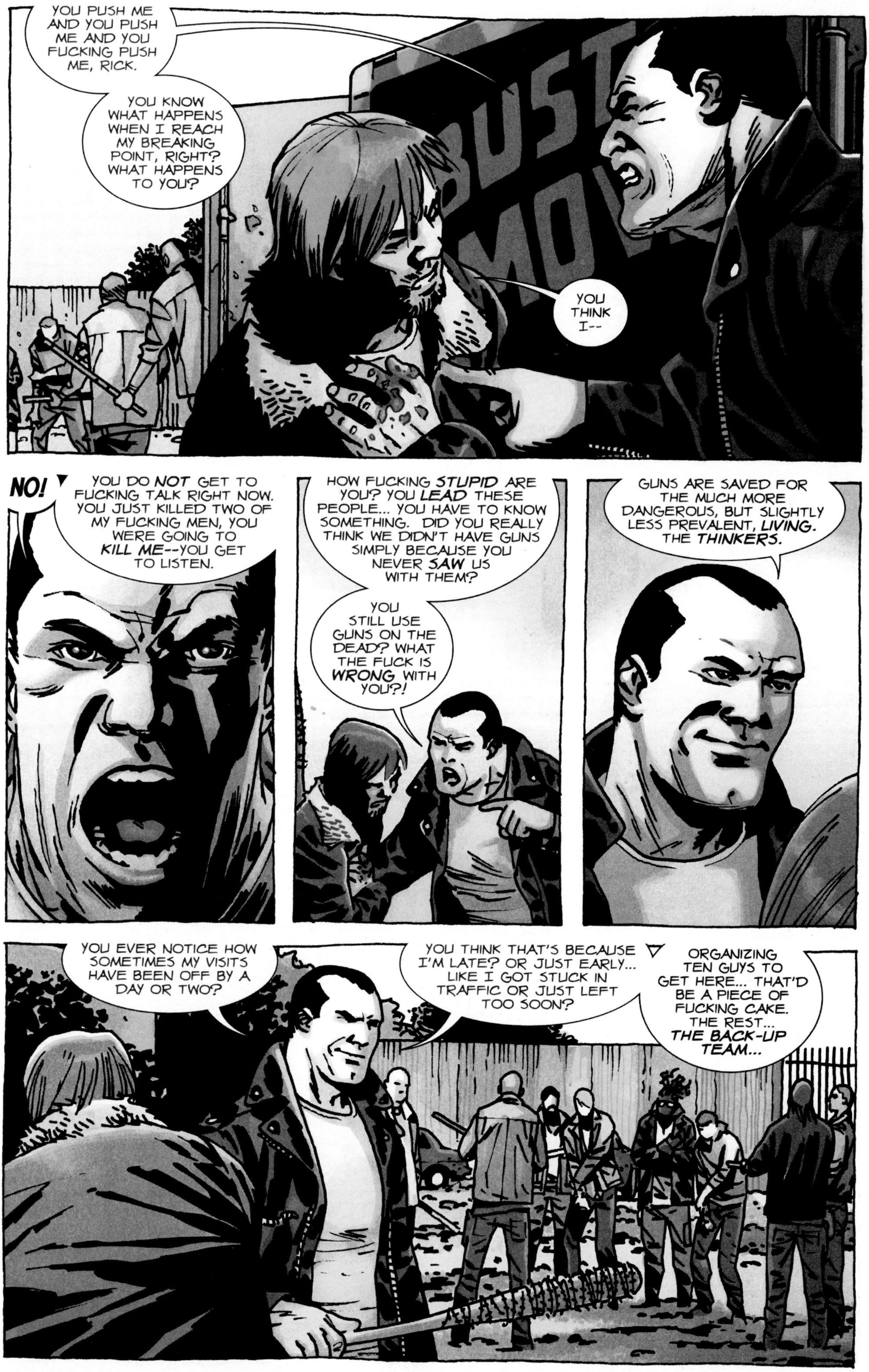
YOU PUSH ME AND YOU PUSH ME AND YOU FUCKING PUSH ME, RICK.
YOU KNOW WHAT HAPPENS WHEN I REACH MY BREAKING POINT, RIGHT? WHAT HAPPENS TO YOU?
YOU THINK I--
NO!
YOU DO NOT GET TO FUCKING TALK RIGHT NOW. YOU JUST KILLED TWO OF MY FUCKING MEN, YOU WERE GOING TO KILL ME--YOU GET TO LISTEN.
HOW FUCKING STUPID ARE YOU? YOU LEAD THESE PEOPLE... YOU HAVE TO KNOW SOMETHING. DID YOU REALLY THINK WE DIDN'T HAVE GUNS SIMPLY BECAUSE YOU NEVER SAW US WITH THEM?
YOU STILL USE GUNS ON THE DEAD? WHAT THE FUCK IS WRONG WITH YOU?!
GUNS ARE SAVED FOR THE MUCH MORE DANGEROUS, BUT SLIGHTLY LESS PREVALENT, LIVING. THE THINKERS.
YOU EVER NOTICE HOW SOMETIMES MY VISITS HAVE BEEN OFF BY A DAY OR TWO?
YOU THINK THAT'S BECAUSE I'M LATE? OR JUST EARLY... LIKE I GOT STUCK IN TRAFFIC OR JUST LEFT TOO SOON?
ORGANIZING TEN GUYS TO GET HERE... THAT'D BE A PIECE OF FUCKING CAKE. THE REST... THE BACK-UP TEAM...

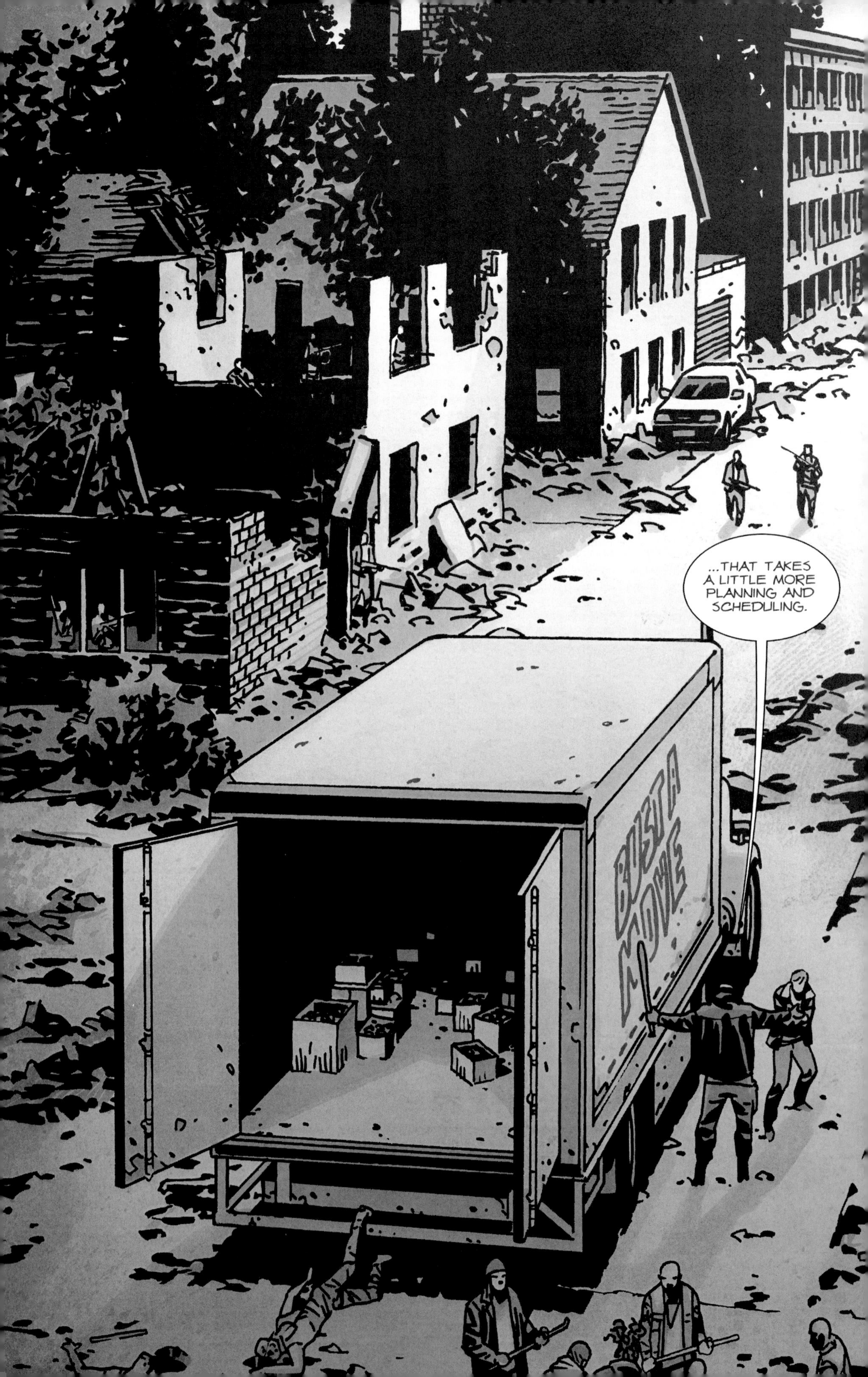
...THAT TAKES A LITTLE MORE PLANNING AND SCHEDULING.
BUST A MOVE

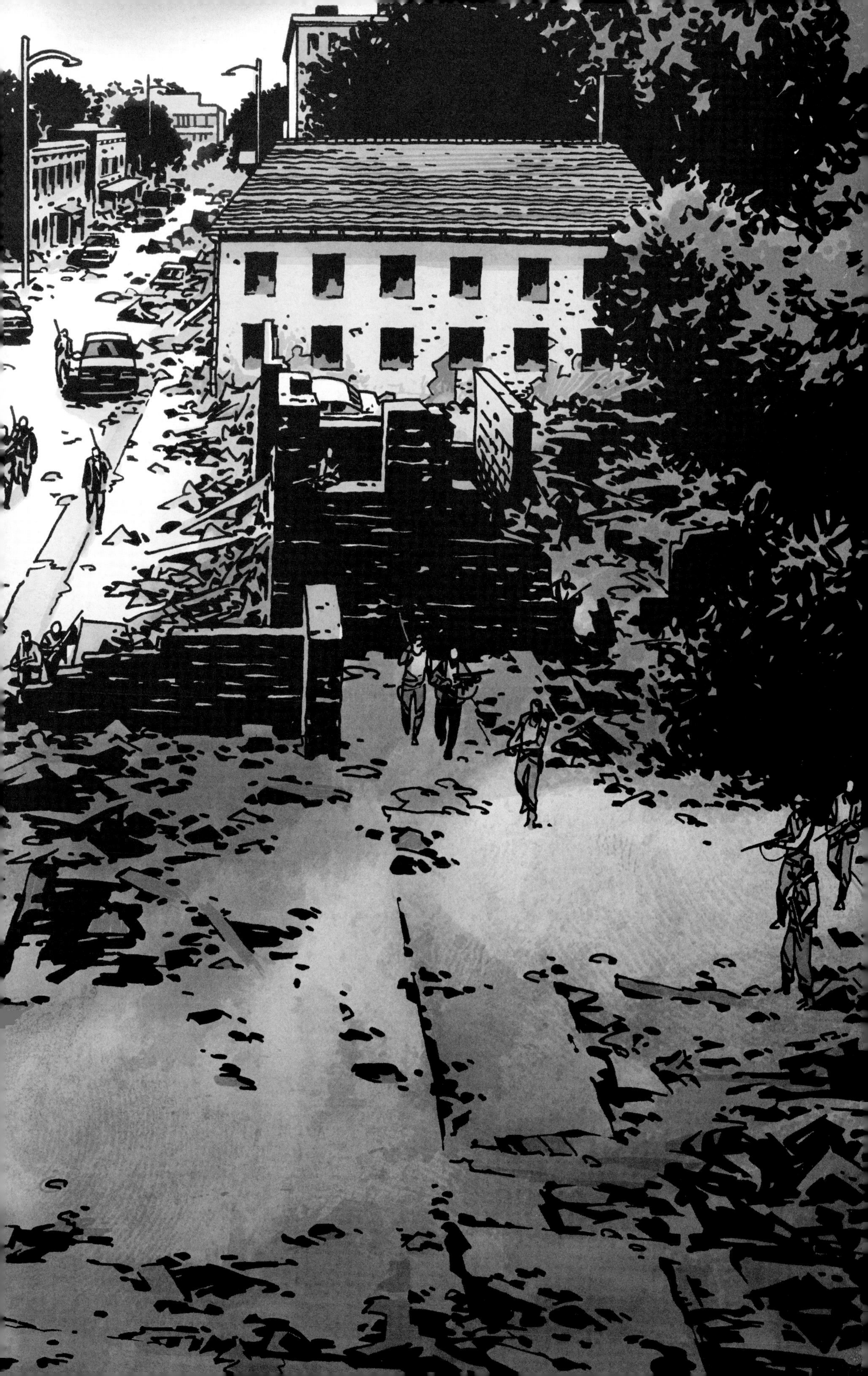

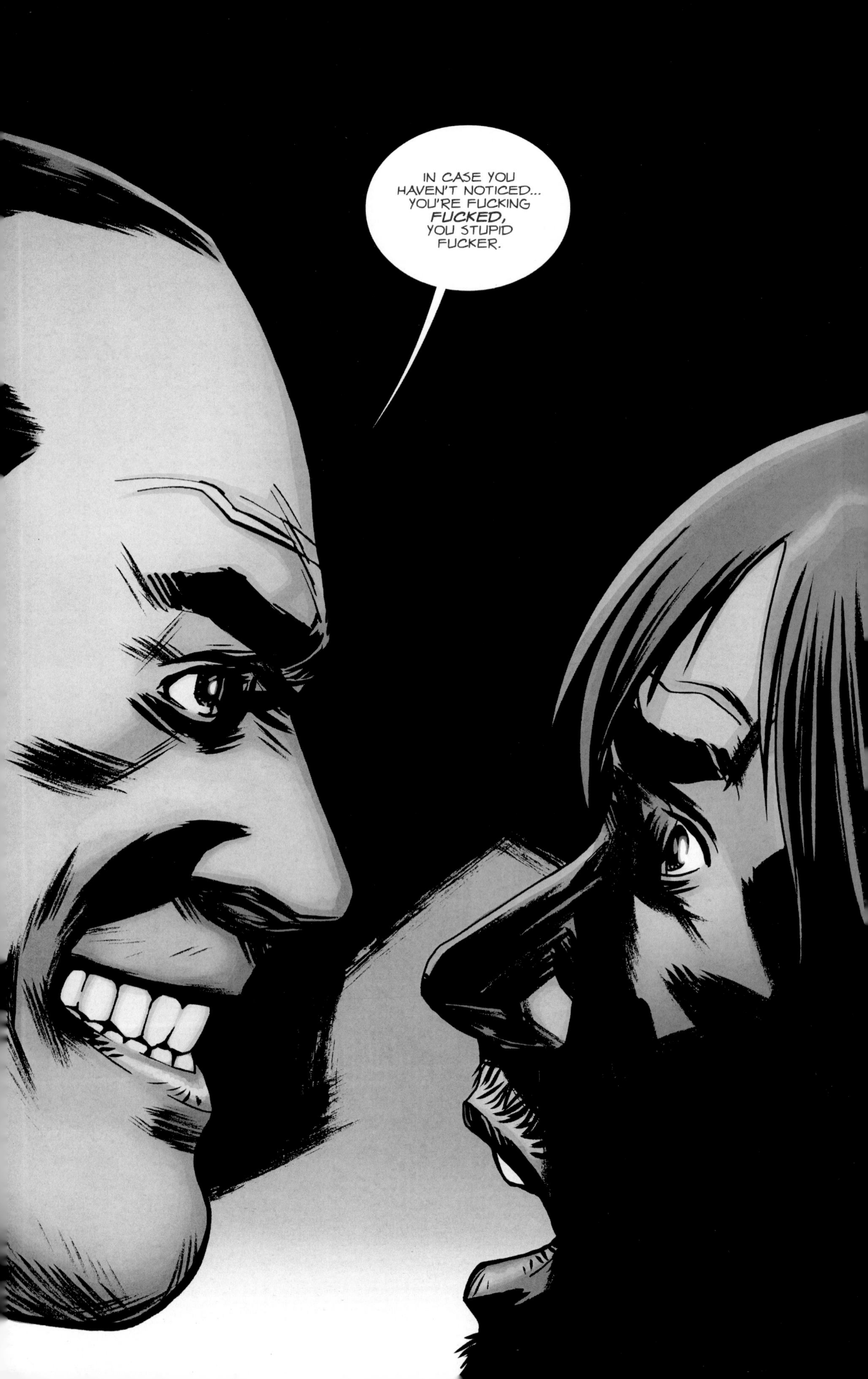
IN CASE YOU HAVEN'T NOTICED... YOU'RE FUCKING *FUCKED,* YOU STUPID FUCKER.

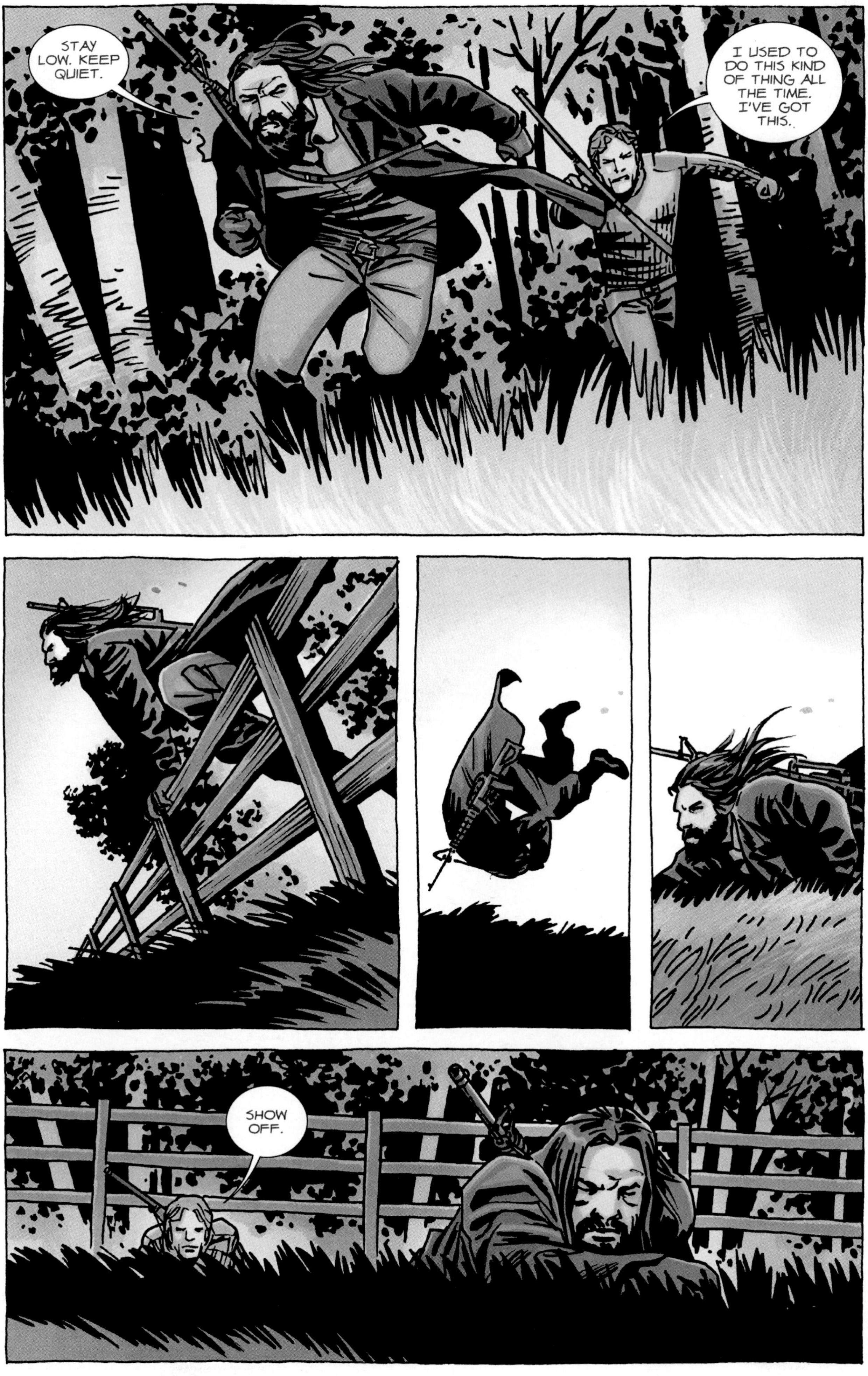
STAY LOW. KEEP QUIET.
I USED TO DO THIS KIND OF THING ALL THE TIME. I'VE GOT THIS.
SHOW OFF.

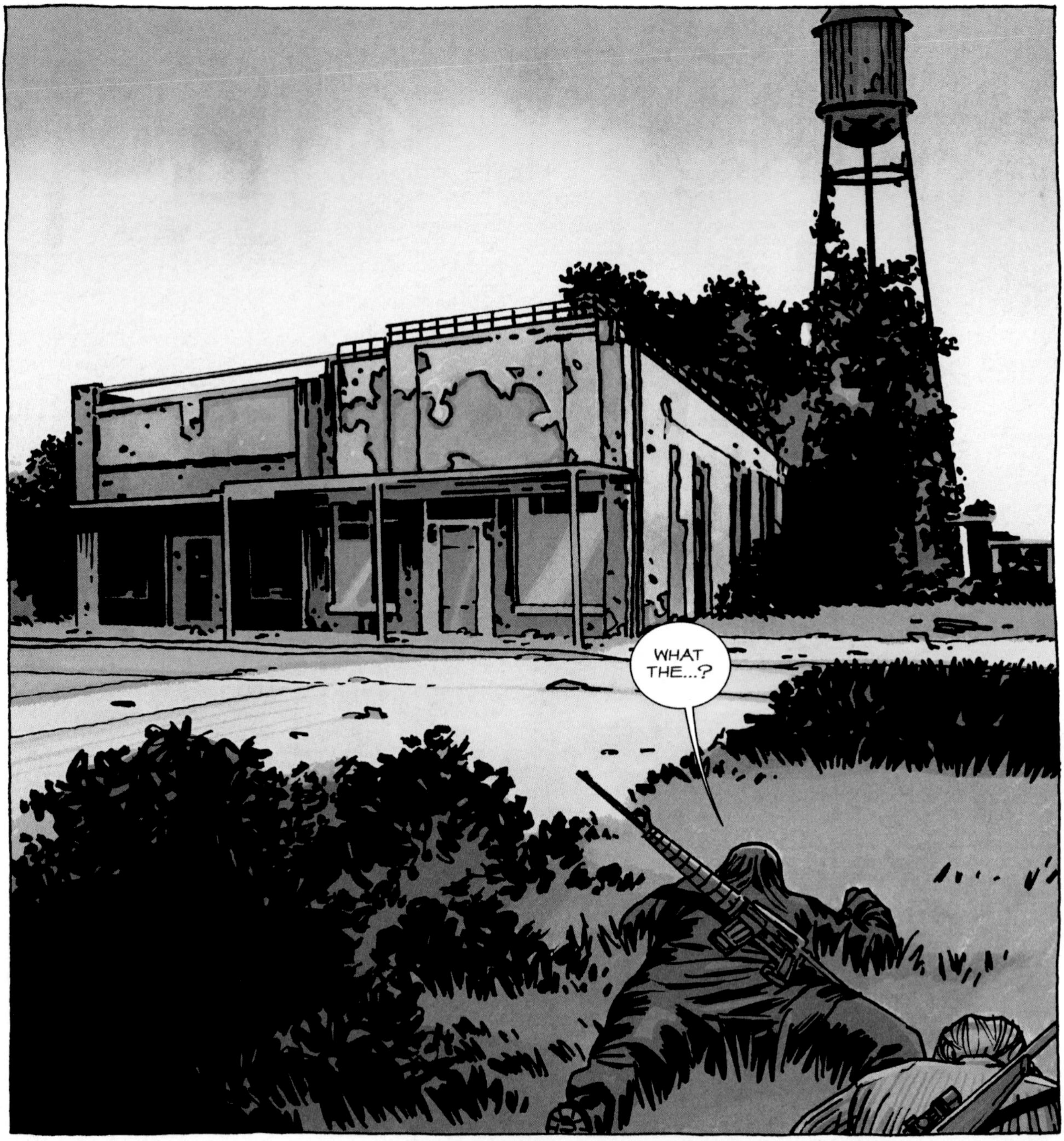
WHAT THE...?

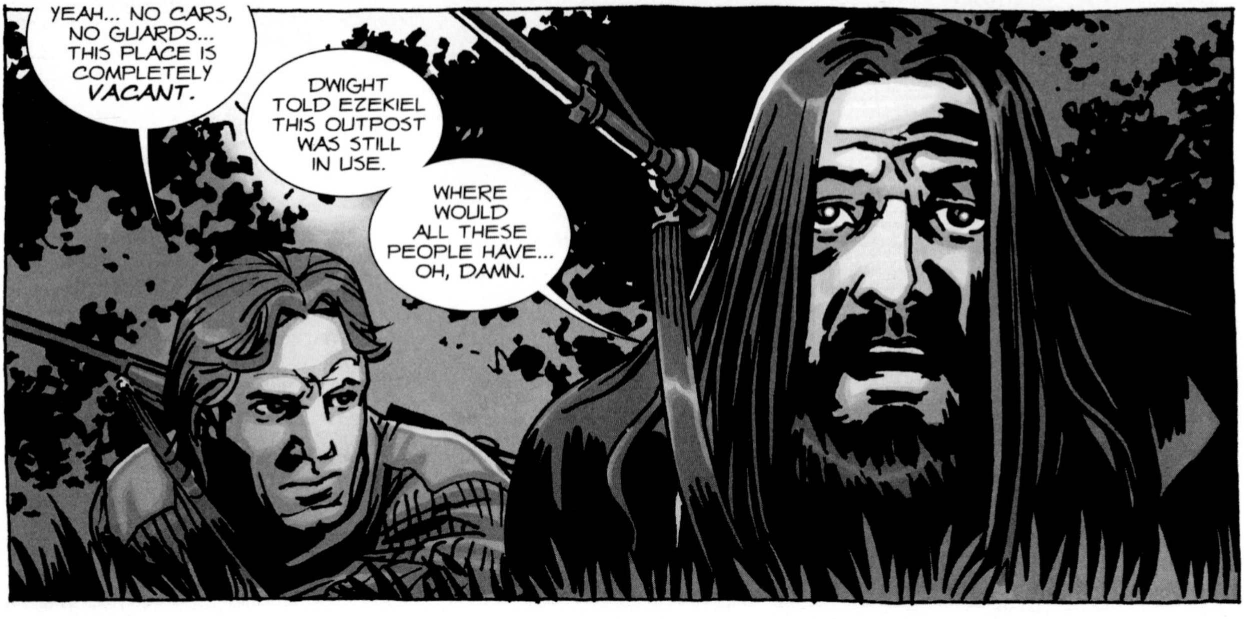
YEAH... NO CARS, NO GUARDS... THIS PLACE IS COMPLETELY ***VACANT.***
DWIGHT TOLD EZEKIEL THIS OUTPOST WAS STILL IN USE.
WHERE WOULD ALL THESE PEOPLE HAVE... OH, DAMN.

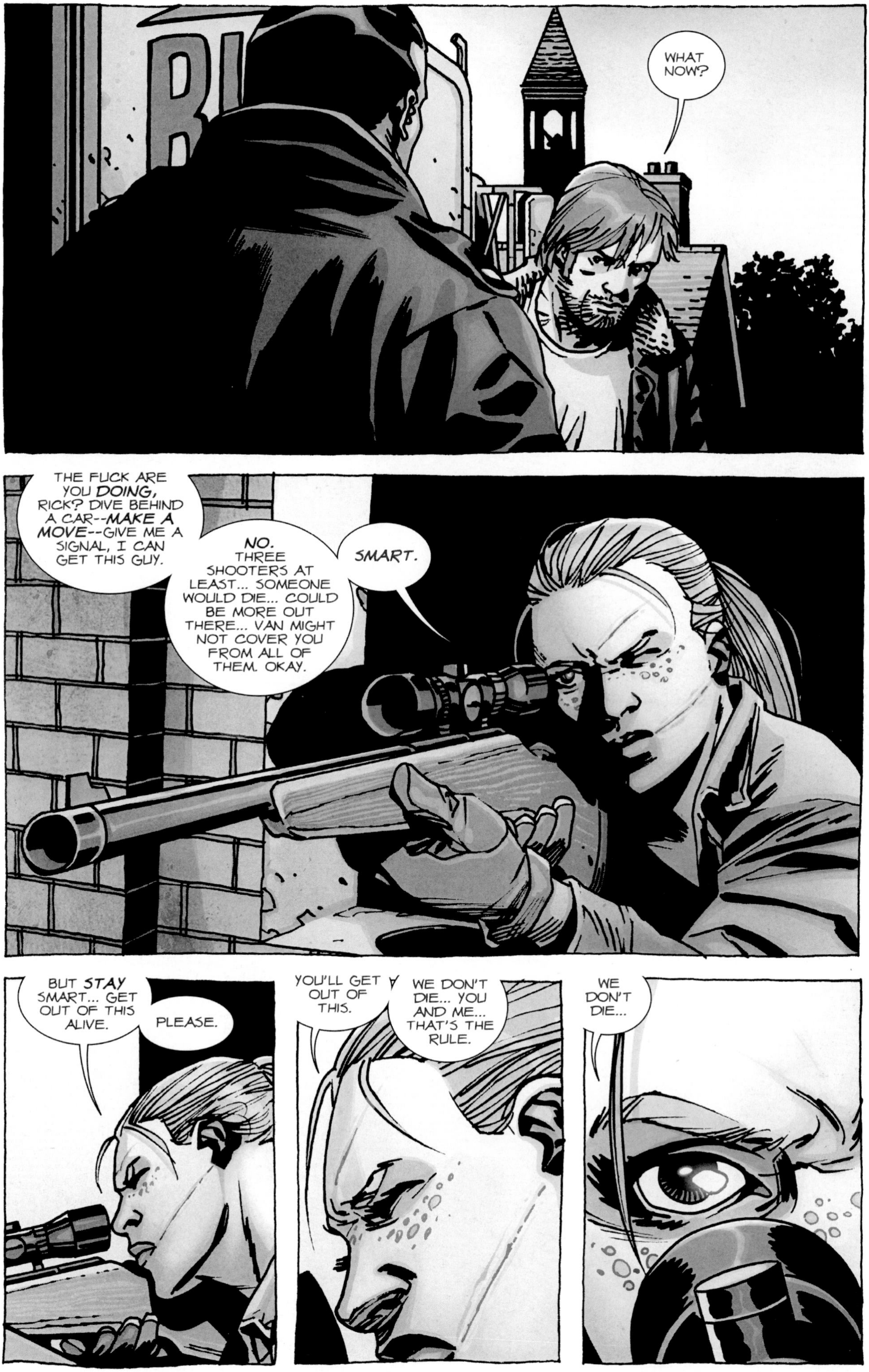

WHAT NOW?
THE FUCK ARE YOU DOING, RICK? DIVE BEHIND A CAR--MAKE A MOVE--GIVE ME A SIGNAL, I CAN GET THIS GUY.
NO. THREE SHOOTERS AT LEAST... SOMEONE WOULD DIE... COULD BE MORE OUT THERE... VAN MIGHT NOT COVER YOU FROM ALL OF THEM. OKAY.
SMART.
BUT STAY SMART... GET OUT OF THIS ALIVE.
PLEASE.
YOU'LL GET OUT OF THIS.
WE DON'T DIE... YOU AND ME... THAT'S THE RULE.
WE DON'T DIE...

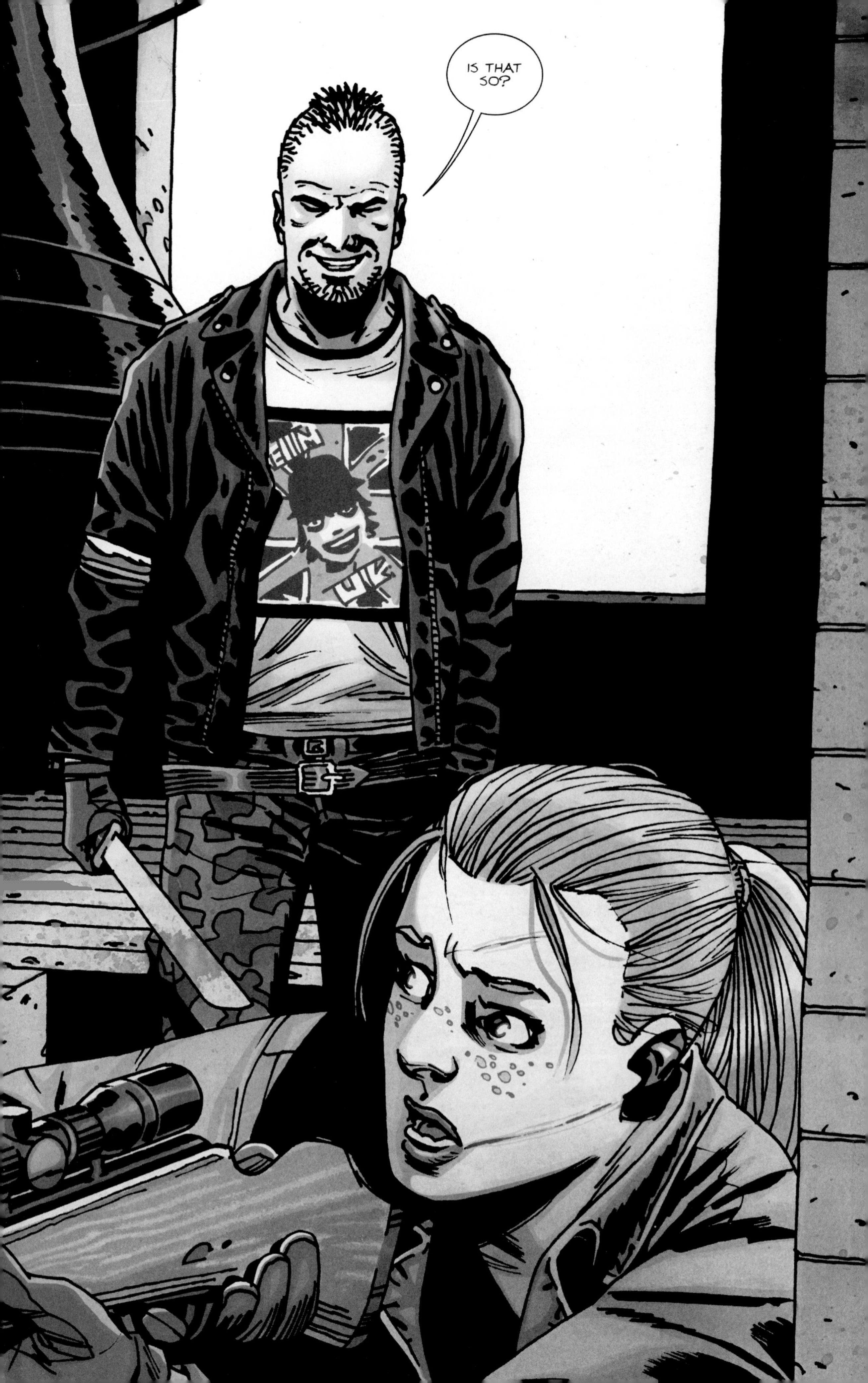
IS THAT SO?

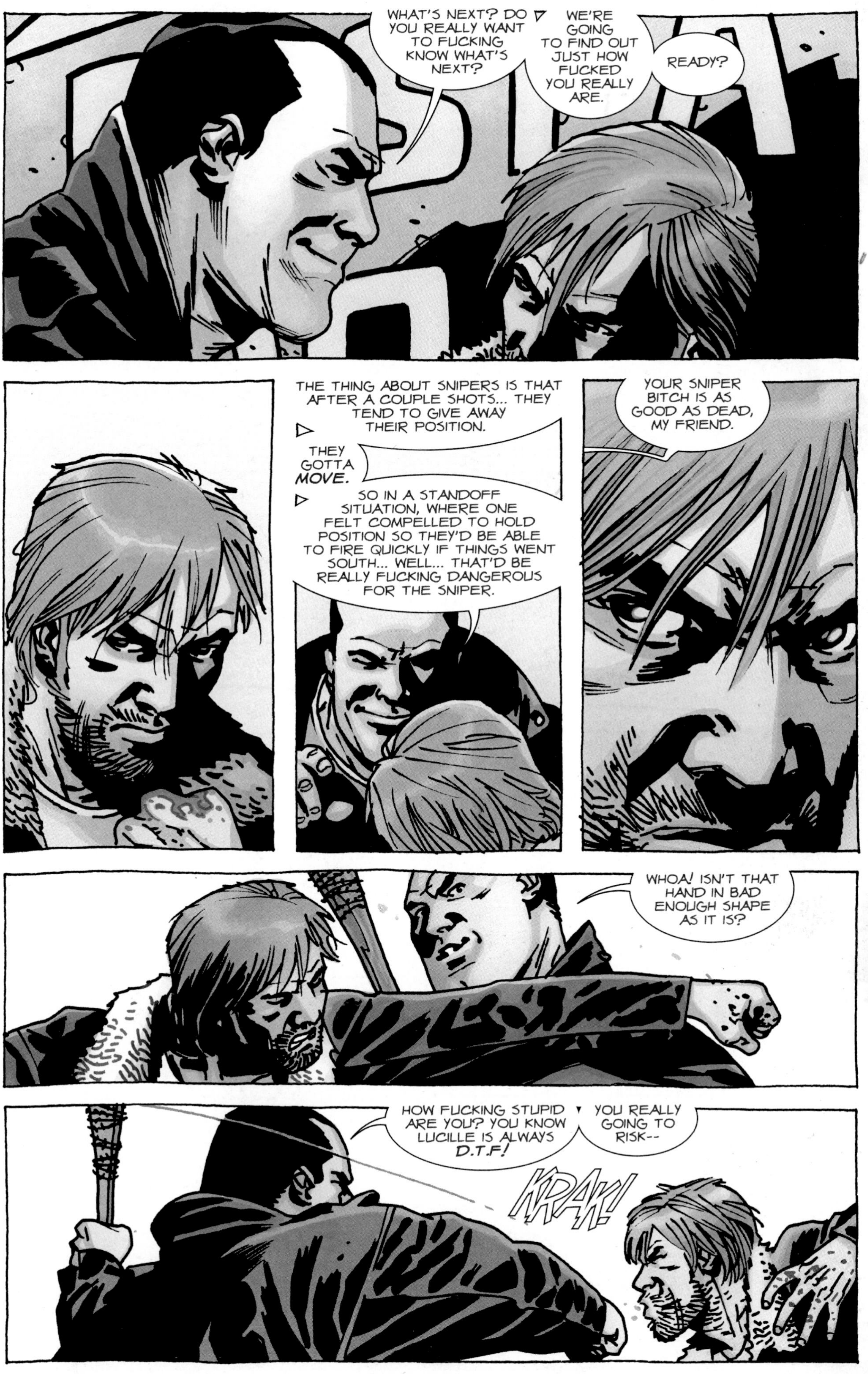
WHAT'S NEXT? DO YOU REALLY WANT TO FUCKING KNOW WHAT'S NEXT?
WE'RE GOING TO FIND OUT JUST HOW FUCKED YOU REALLY ARE.
READY?
THE THING ABOUT SNIPERS IS THAT AFTER A COUPLE SHOTS... THEY TEND TO GIVE AWAY THEIR POSITION.
THEY GOTTA MOVE.
SO IN A STANDOFF SITUATION, WHERE ONE FELT COMPELLED TO HOLD POSITION SO THEY'D BE ABLE TO FIRE QUICKLY IF THINGS WENT SOUTH... WELL... THAT'D BE REALLY FUCKING DANGEROUS FOR THE SNIPER.
YOUR SNIPER BITCH IS AS GOOD AS DEAD, MY FRIEND.
WHOA! ISN'T THAT HAND IN BAD ENOUGH SHAPE AS IT IS?
HOW FUCKING STUPID ARE YOU? YOU KNOW LUCILLE IS ALWAYS D.T.F!
YOU REALLY GOING TO RISK--
KRAK!

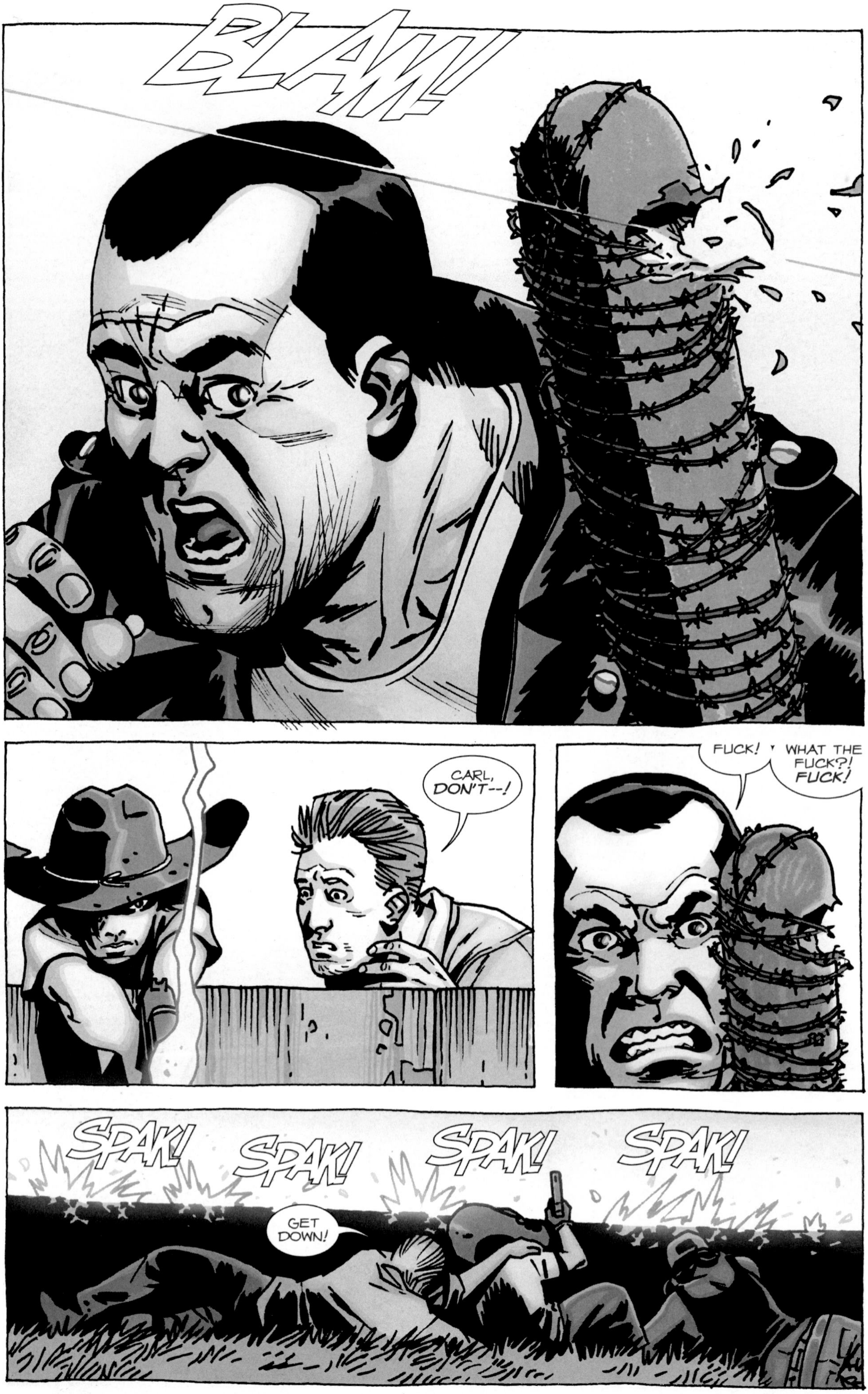
BLAM!
CARL, DON'T--!
FUCK!
WHAT THE FUCK?! FUCK!
SPAK!
SPAK!
SPAK!
SPAK!
GET DOWN!

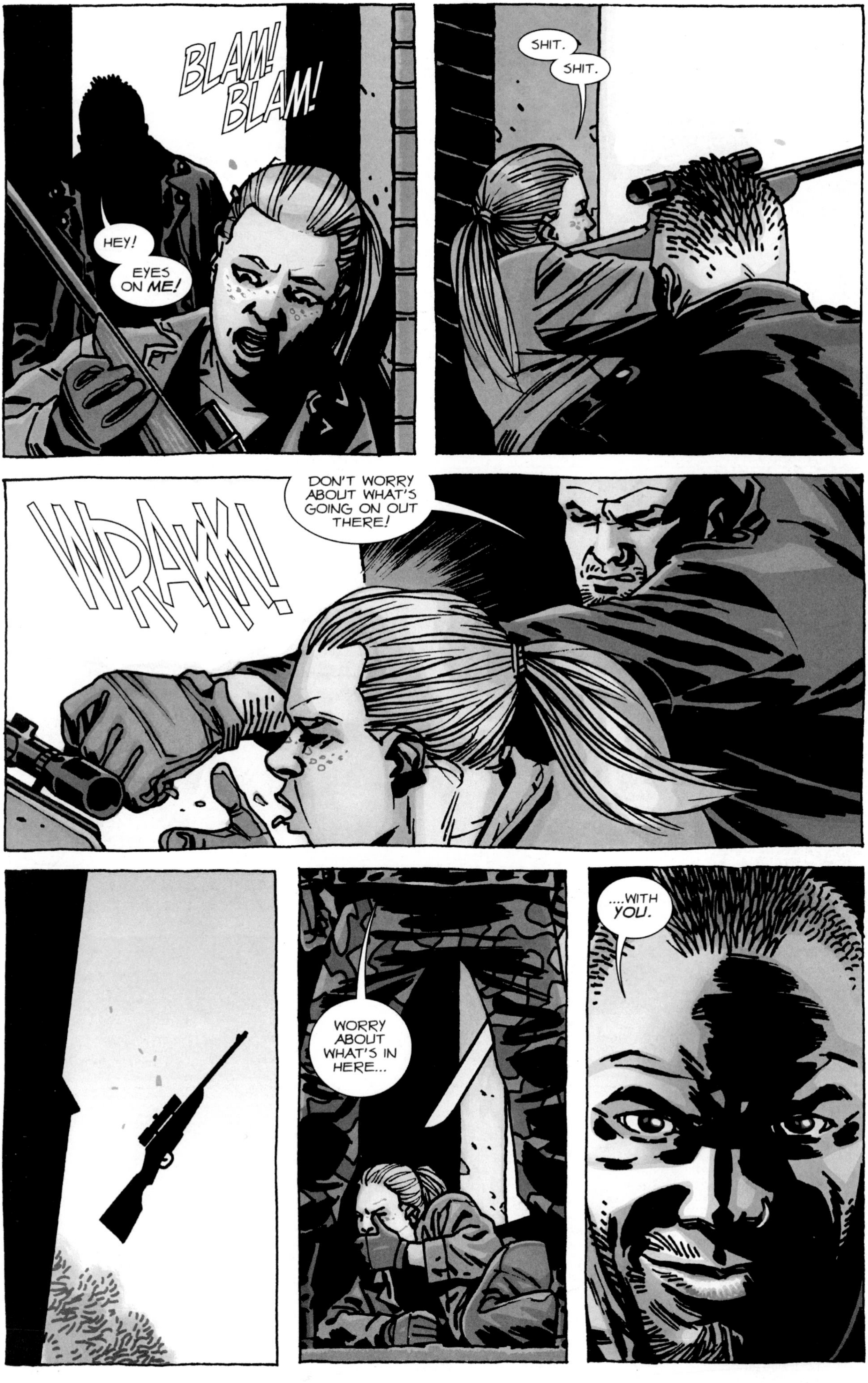
BLAM! BLAM!
HEY!
EYES ON ME!
SHIT.
SHIT.
WRAKK!
DON'T WORRY ABOUT WHAT'S GOING ON OUT THERE!
WORRY ABOUT WHAT'S IN HERE...
....WITH YOU.

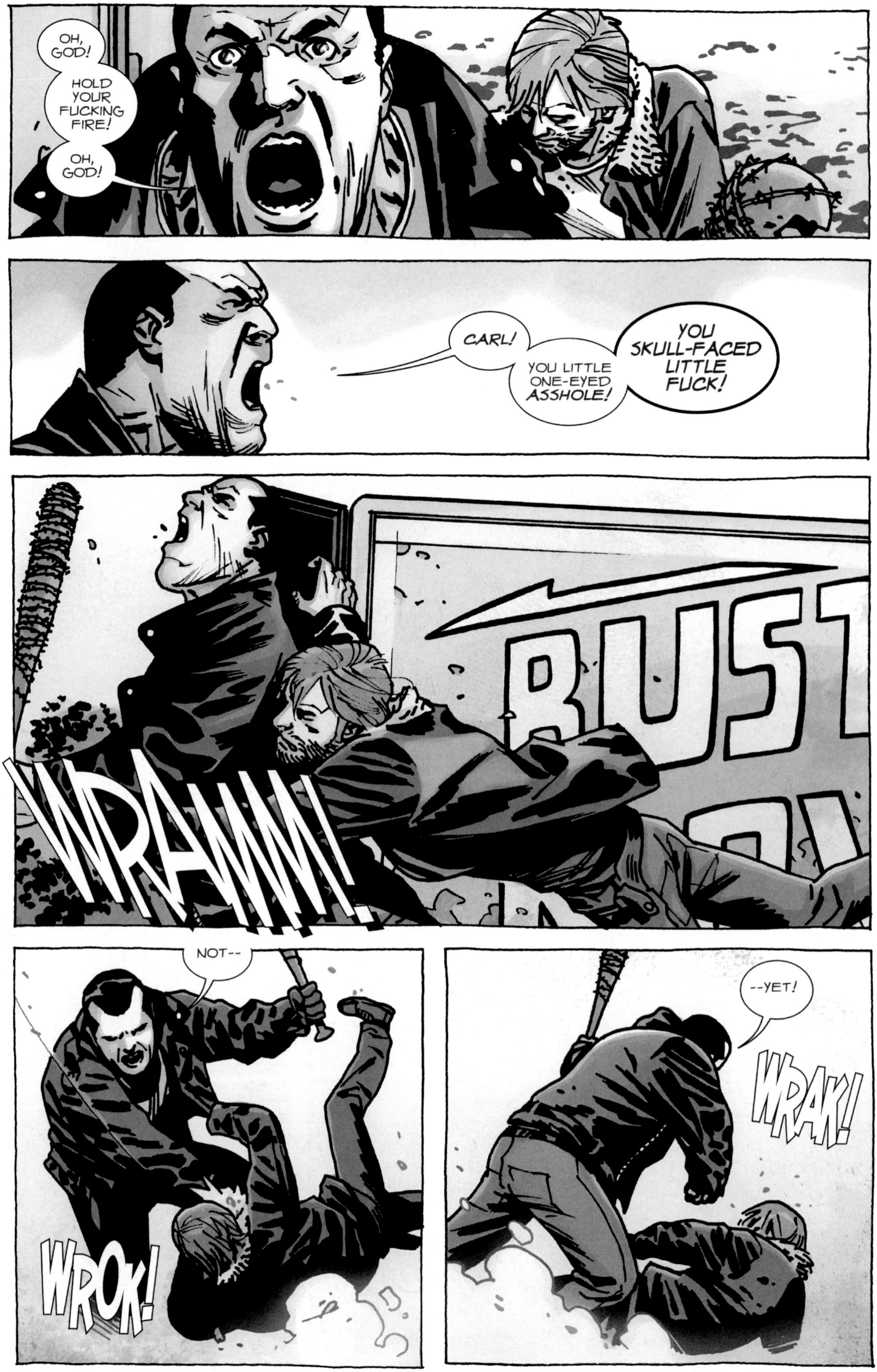
OH, GOD!
HOLD YOUR FUCKING FIRE!
OH, GOD!
CARL!
YOU LITTLE ONE-EYED ASSHOLE!
YOU SKULL-FACED LITTLE FUCK!
BUST
WRAMM!
NOT--
WROK!
--YET!
WRAK!

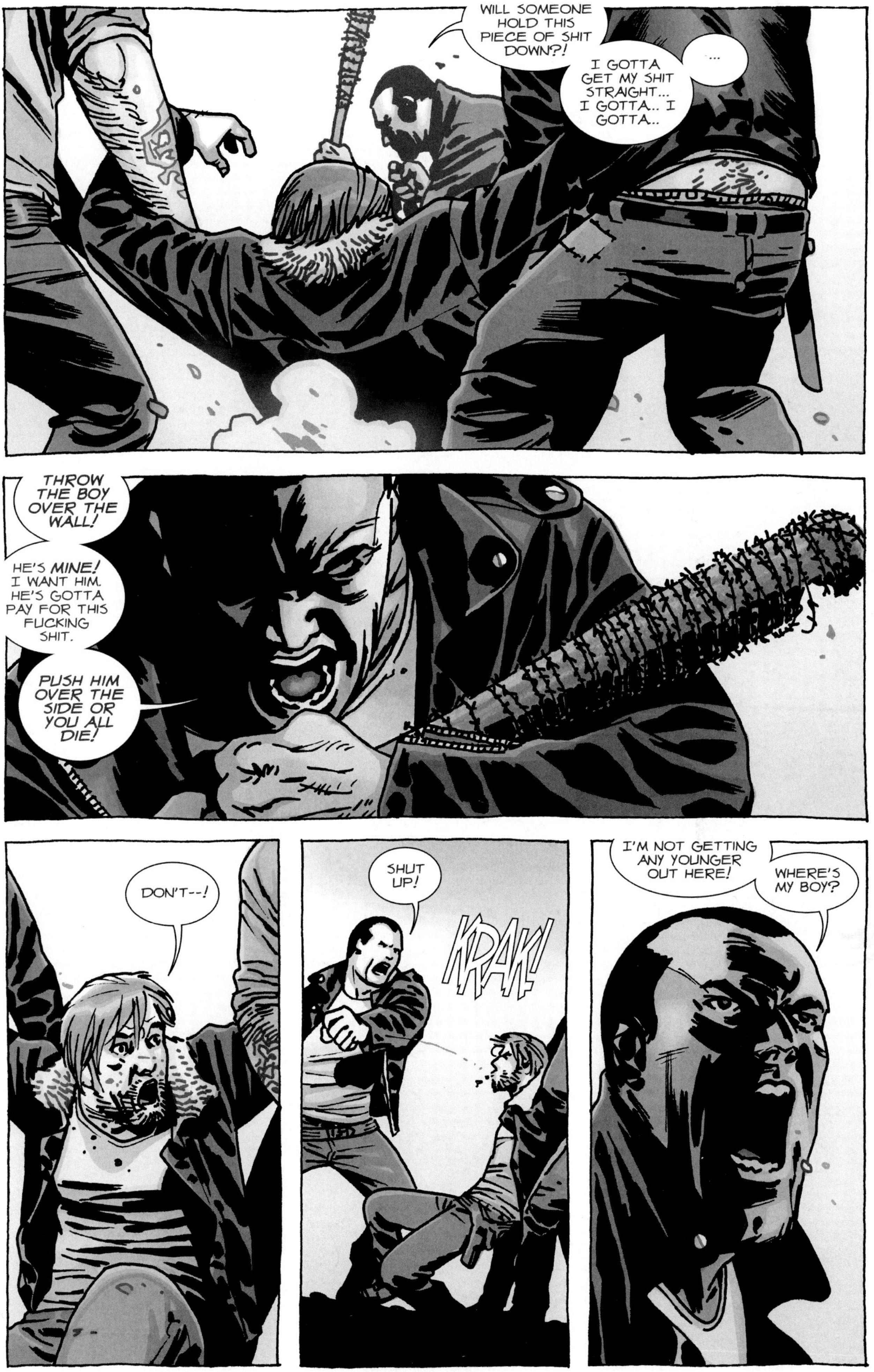
WILL SOMEONE HOLD THIS PIECE OF SHIT DOWN?!
I GOTTA GET MY SHIT STRAIGHT... I GOTTA... I GOTTA...
...
THROW THE BOY OVER THE WALL!
HE'S MINE! I WANT HIM. HE'S GOTTA PAY FOR THIS FUCKING SHIT.
PUSH HIM OVER THE SIDE OR YOU ALL DIE!
DON'T--!
SHUT UP!
KRAK!
I'M NOT GETTING ANY YOUNGER OUT HERE!
WHERE'S MY BOY?

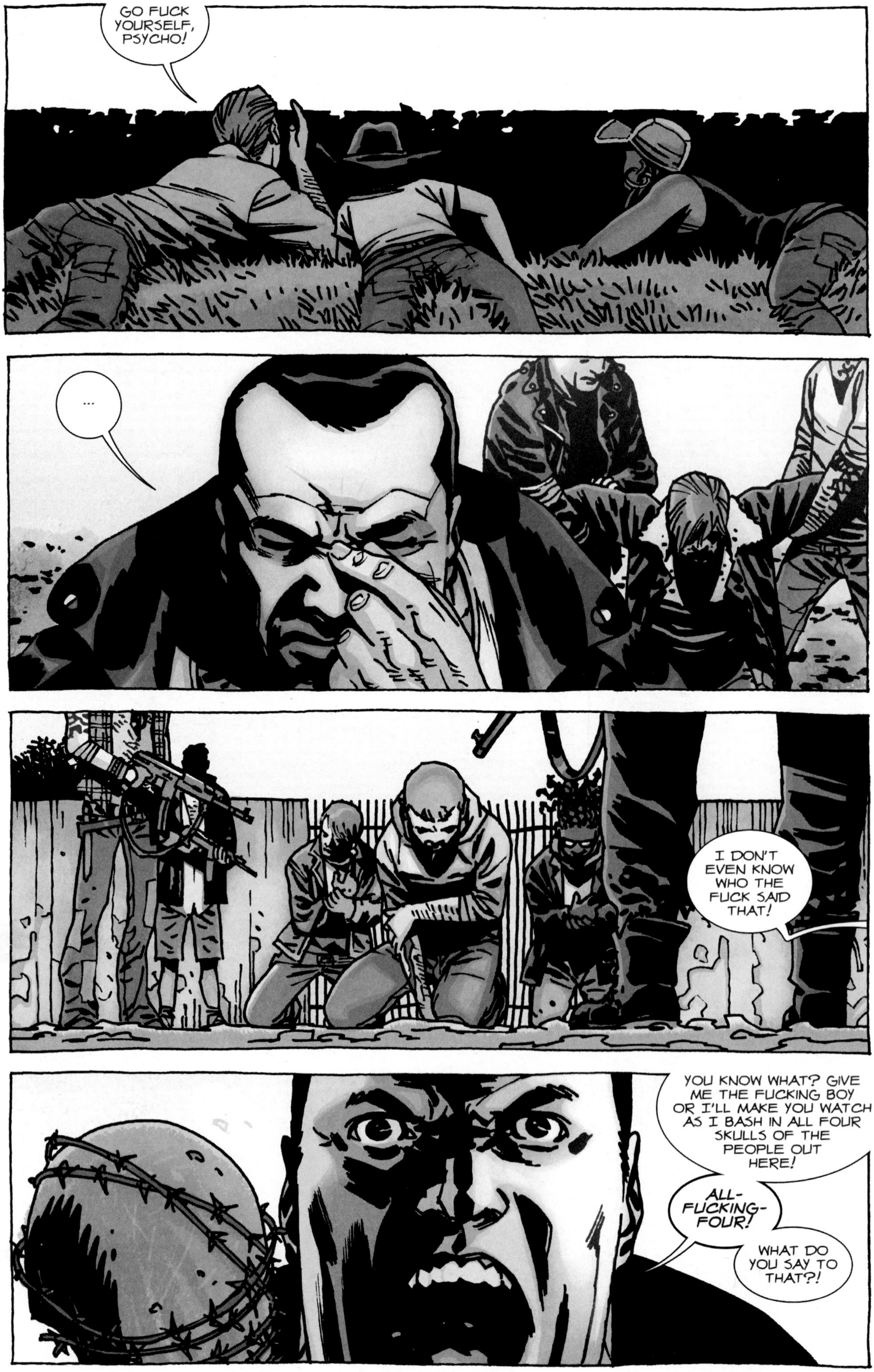
GO FUCK YOURSELF, PSYCHO!
...
I DON'T EVEN KNOW WHO THE FUCK SAID THAT!
YOU KNOW WHAT? GIVE ME THE FUCKING BOY OR I'LL MAKE YOU WATCH AS I BASH IN ALL FOUR SKULLS OF THE PEOPLE OUT HERE!
ALL-FUCKING-FOUR!
WHAT DO YOU SAY TO THAT?!

NAH.

TOO QUICK. I WANT TO SAVOR IT.

YOU READY FOR THIS?

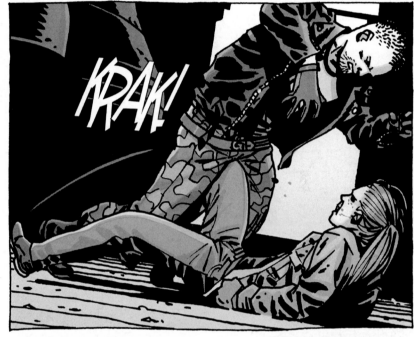

KRAK!

YES.

WRAKK!

LUCKY SHOT.

WHUDD.

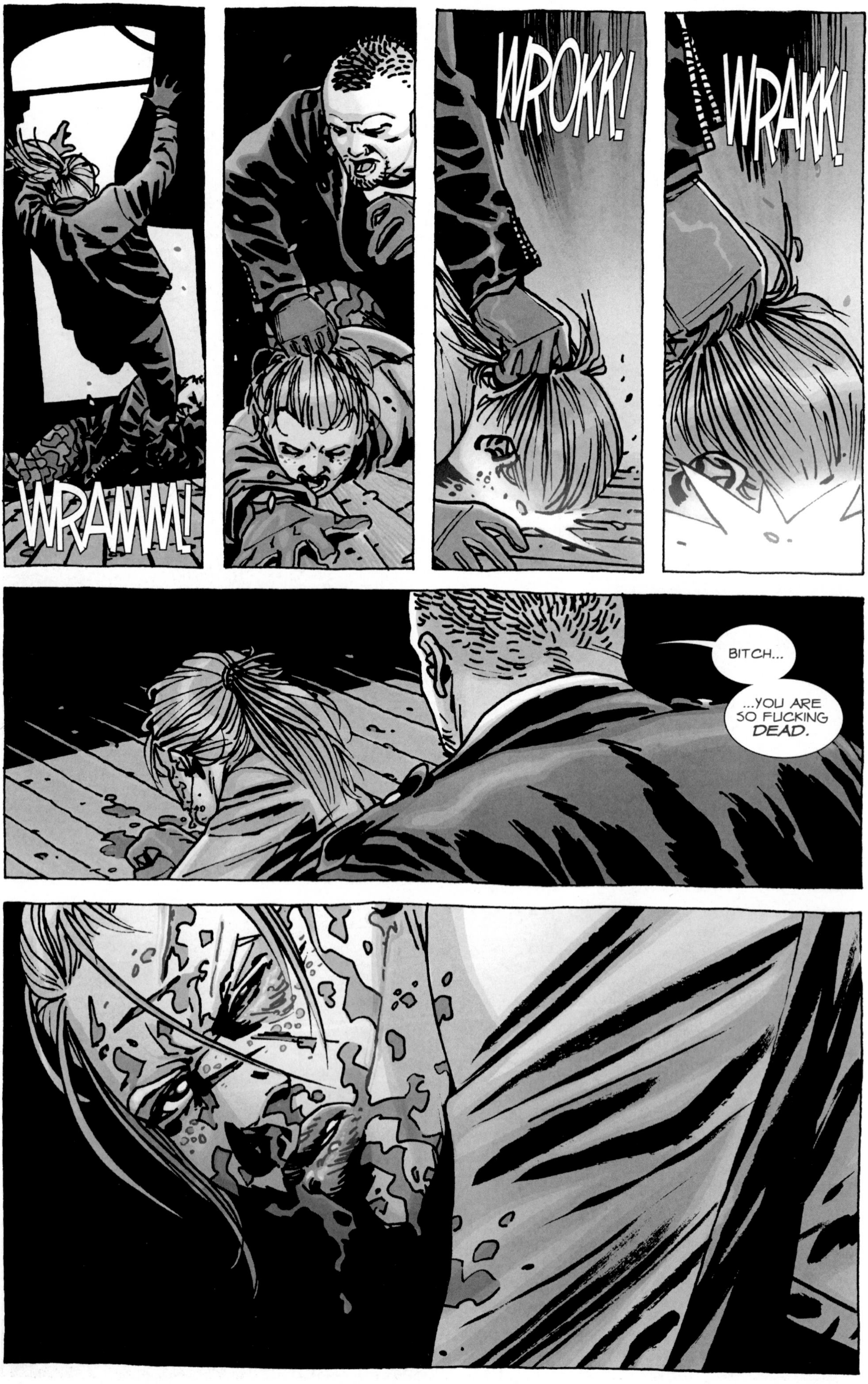
WRAMM!
WROKK!
WRAKK!
BITCH...
...YOU ARE SO FUCKING DEAD.

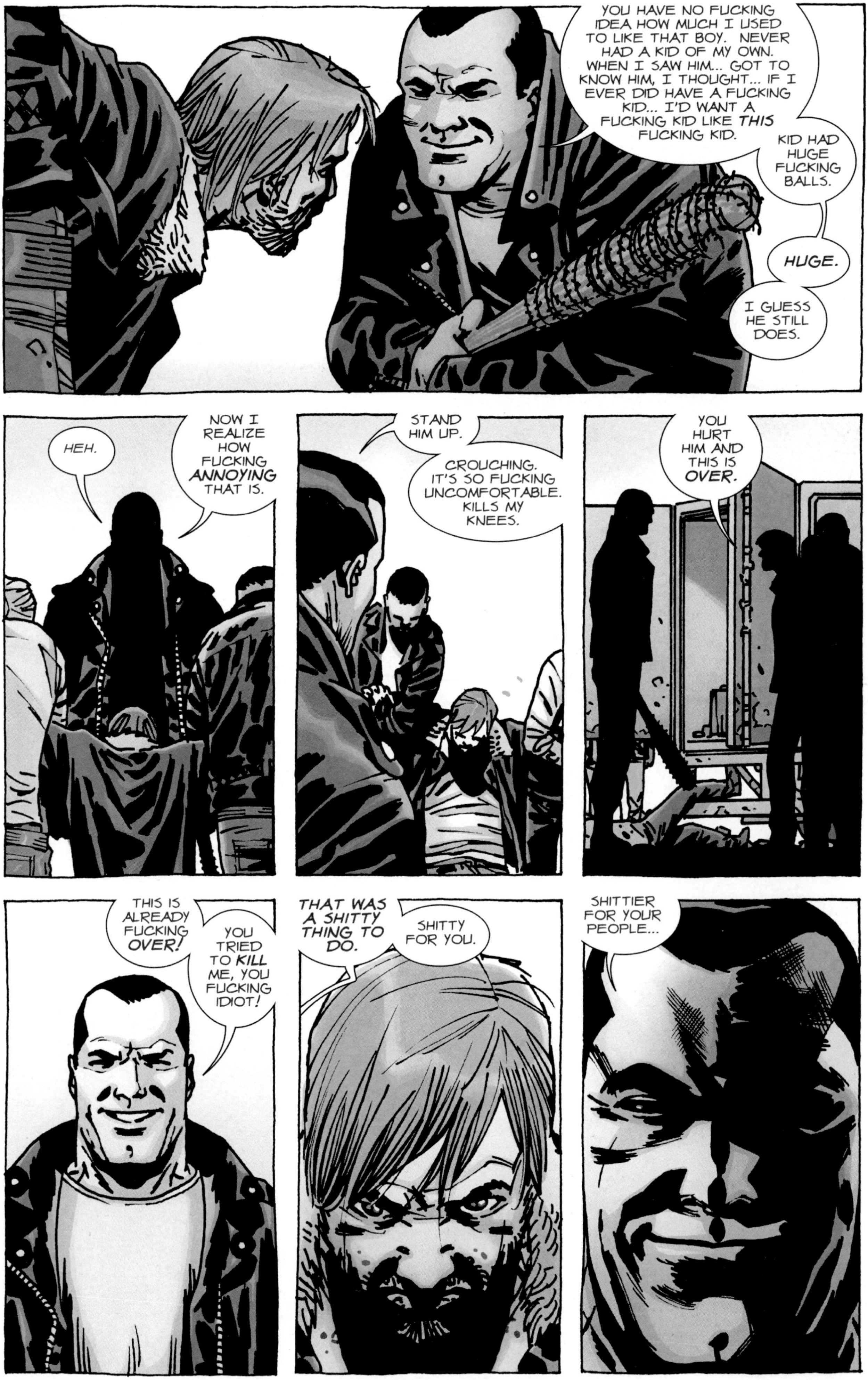

YOU HAVE NO FUCKING IDEA HOW MUCH I USED TO LIKE THAT BOY. NEVER HAD A KID OF MY OWN. WHEN I SAW HIM... GOT TO KNOW HIM, I THOUGHT... IF I EVER DID HAVE A FUCKING KID... I'D WANT A FUCKING KID LIKE THIS FUCKING KID.
KID HAD HUGE FUCKING BALLS.
HUGE.
I GUESS HE STILL DOES.
HEH.
NOW I REALIZE HOW FUCKING ANNOYING THAT IS.
STAND HIM UP.
CROUCHING. IT'S SO FUCKING UNCOMFORTABLE. KILLS MY KNEES.
YOU HURT HIM AND THIS IS OVER.
THIS IS ALREADY FUCKING OVER!
YOU TRIED TO KILL ME, YOU FUCKING IDIOT!
THAT WAS A SHITTY THING TO DO.
SHITTY FOR YOU.
SHITTIER FOR YOUR PEOPLE...

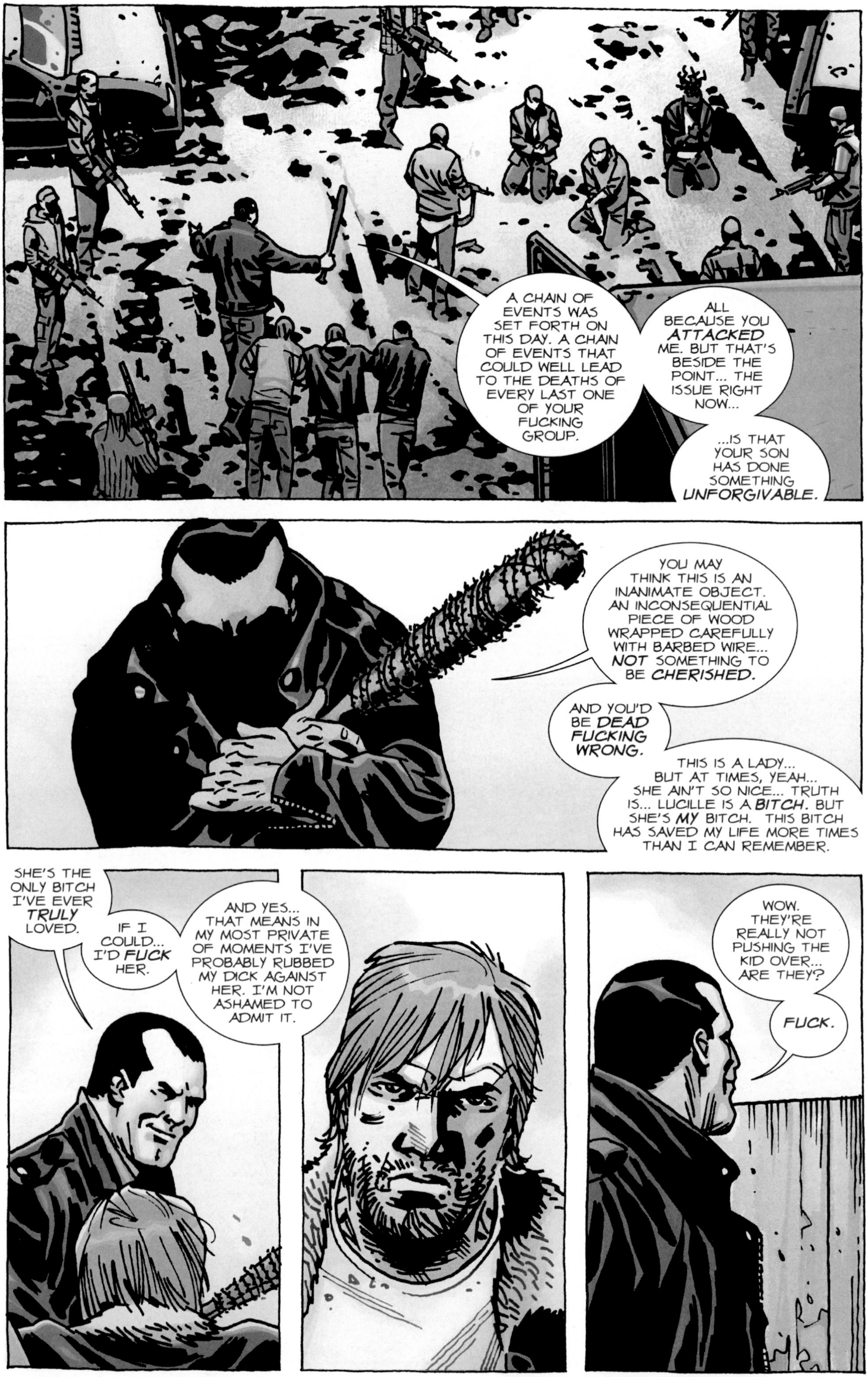
A CHAIN OF EVENTS WAS SET FORTH ON THIS DAY. A CHAIN OF EVENTS THAT COULD WELL LEAD TO THE DEATHS OF EVERY LAST ONE OF YOUR FUCKING GROUP.
ALL BECAUSE YOU ATTACKED ME. BUT THAT'S BESIDE THE POINT... THE ISSUE RIGHT NOW...
...IS THAT YOUR SON HAS DONE SOMETHING UNFORGIVABLE.
YOU MAY THINK THIS IS AN INANIMATE OBJECT. AN INCONSEQUENTIAL PIECE OF WOOD WRAPPED CAREFULLY WITH BARBED WIRE... NOT SOMETHING TO BE CHERISHED.
AND YOU'D BE DEAD FUCKING WRONG.
THIS IS A LADY... BUT AT TIMES, YEAH... SHE AIN'T SO NICE... TRUTH IS... LUCILLE IS A BITCH. BUT SHE'S MY BITCH. THIS BITCH HAS SAVED MY LIFE MORE TIMES THAN I CAN REMEMBER.
SHE'S THE ONLY BITCH I'VE EVER TRULY LOVED.
IF I COULD... I'D FUCK HER.
AND YES... THAT MEANS IN MY MOST PRIVATE OF MOMENTS I'VE PROBABLY RUBBED MY DICK AGAINST HER. I'M NOT ASHAMED TO ADMIT IT.
WOW. THEY'RE REALLY NOT PUSHING THE KID OVER... ARE THEY?
FUCK.

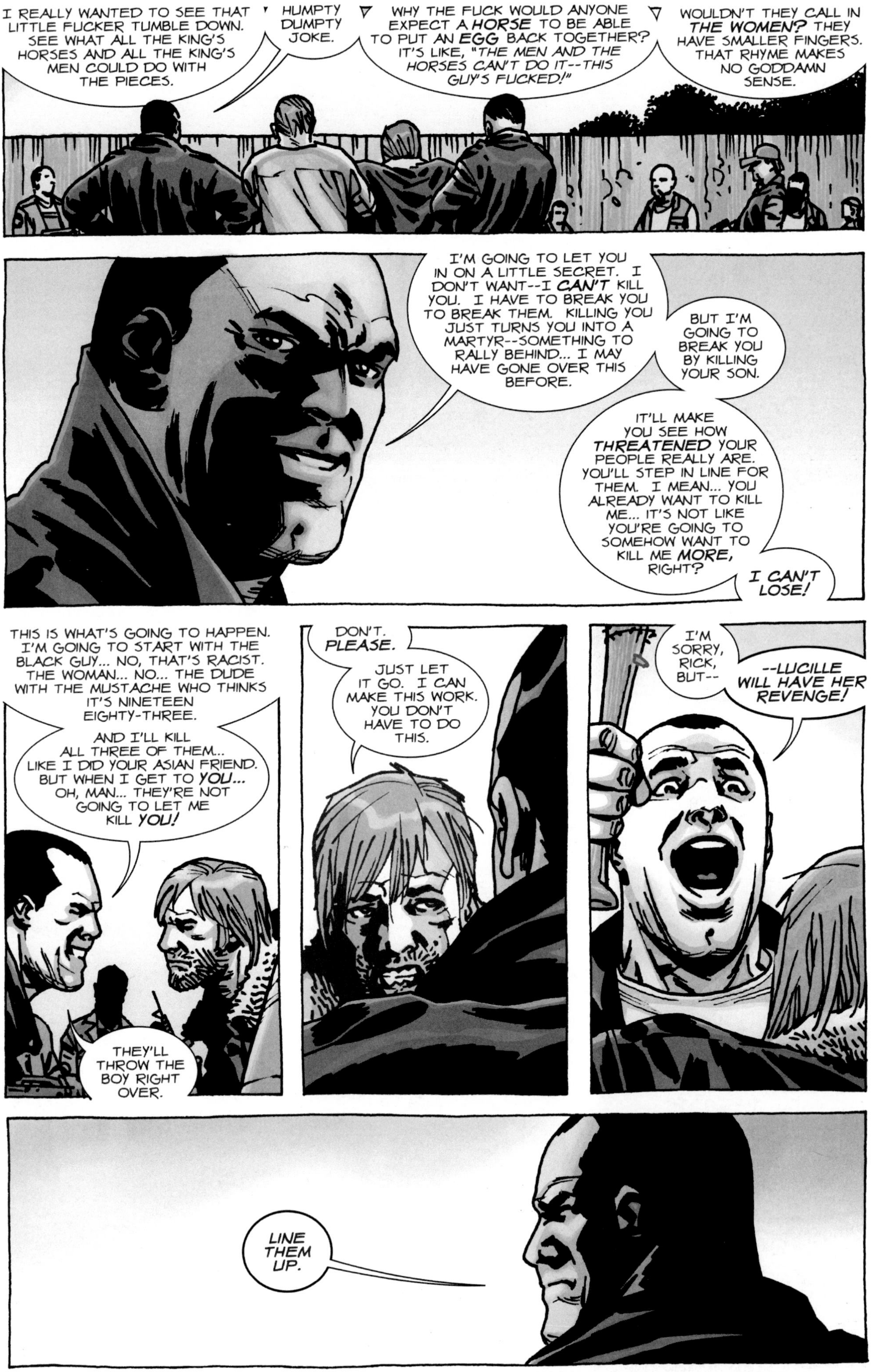
I REALLY WANTED TO SEE THAT LITTLE FUCKER TUMBLE DOWN. SEE WHAT ALL THE KING'S HORSES AND ALL THE KING'S MEN COULD DO WITH THE PIECES.
HUMPTY DUMPTY JOKE.
WHY THE FUCK WOULD ANYONE EXPECT A HORSE TO BE ABLE TO PUT AN EGG BACK TOGETHER? IT'S LIKE, "THE MEN AND THE HORSES CAN'T DO IT--THIS GUY'S FUCKED!"
WOULDN'T THEY CALL IN THE WOMEN? THEY HAVE SMALLER FINGERS. THAT RHYME MAKES NO GODDAMN SENSE.
I'M GOING TO LET YOU IN ON A LITTLE SECRET. I DON'T WANT--I CAN'T KILL YOU. I HAVE TO BREAK YOU TO BREAK THEM. KILLING YOU JUST TURNS YOU INTO A MARTYR--SOMETHING TO RALLY BEHIND... I MAY HAVE GONE OVER THIS BEFORE.
BUT I'M GOING TO BREAK YOU BY KILLING YOUR SON.
IT'LL MAKE YOU SEE HOW THREATENED YOUR PEOPLE REALLY ARE. YOU'LL STEP IN LINE FOR THEM. I MEAN... YOU ALREADY WANT TO KILL ME... IT'S NOT LIKE YOU'RE GOING TO SOMEHOW WANT TO KILL ME MORE, RIGHT?
I CAN'T LOSE!
THIS IS WHAT'S GOING TO HAPPEN. I'M GOING TO START WITH THE BLACK GUY... NO, THAT'S RACIST. THE WOMAN... NO... THE DUDE WITH THE MUSTACHE WHO THINKS IT'S NINETEEN EIGHTY-THREE.
AND I'LL KILL ALL THREE OF THEM... LIKE I DID YOUR ASIAN FRIEND. BUT WHEN I GET TO YOU... OH, MAN... THEY'RE NOT GOING TO LET ME KILL YOU!
THEY'LL THROW THE BOY RIGHT OVER.
DON'T. PLEASE.
JUST LET IT GO. I CAN MAKE THIS WORK. YOU DON'T HAVE TO DO THIS.
I'M SORRY, RICK, BUT--
--LUCILLE WILL HAVE HER REVENGE!
LINE THEM UP.

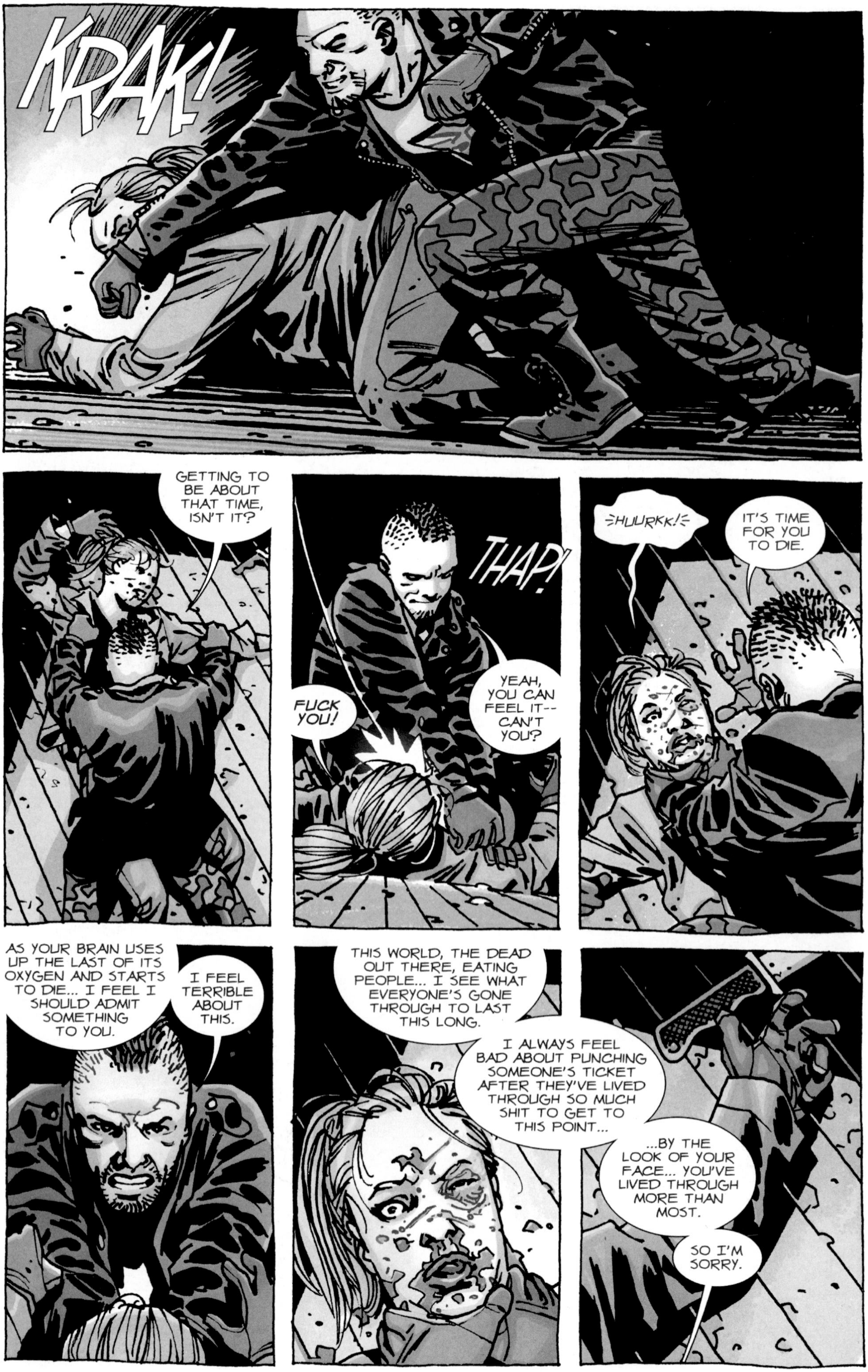
KRAK!
GETTING TO BE ABOUT THAT TIME, ISN'T IT?
THAP!
YEAH, YOU CAN FEEL IT-- CAN'T YOU?
FUCK YOU!
HUURKK!
IT'S TIME FOR YOU TO DIE.
AS YOUR BRAIN USES UP THE LAST OF ITS OXYGEN AND STARTS TO DIE... I FEEL I SHOULD ADMIT SOMETHING TO YOU.
I FEEL TERRIBLE ABOUT THIS.
THIS WORLD, THE DEAD OUT THERE, EATING PEOPLE... I SEE WHAT EVERYONE'S GONE THROUGH TO LAST THIS LONG.
I ALWAYS FEEL BAD ABOUT PUNCHING SOMEONE'S TICKET AFTER THEY'VE LIVED THROUGH SO MUCH SHIT TO GET TO THIS POINT...
...BY THE LOOK OF YOUR FACE... YOU'VE LIVED THROUGH MORE THAN MOST.
SO I'M SORRY.

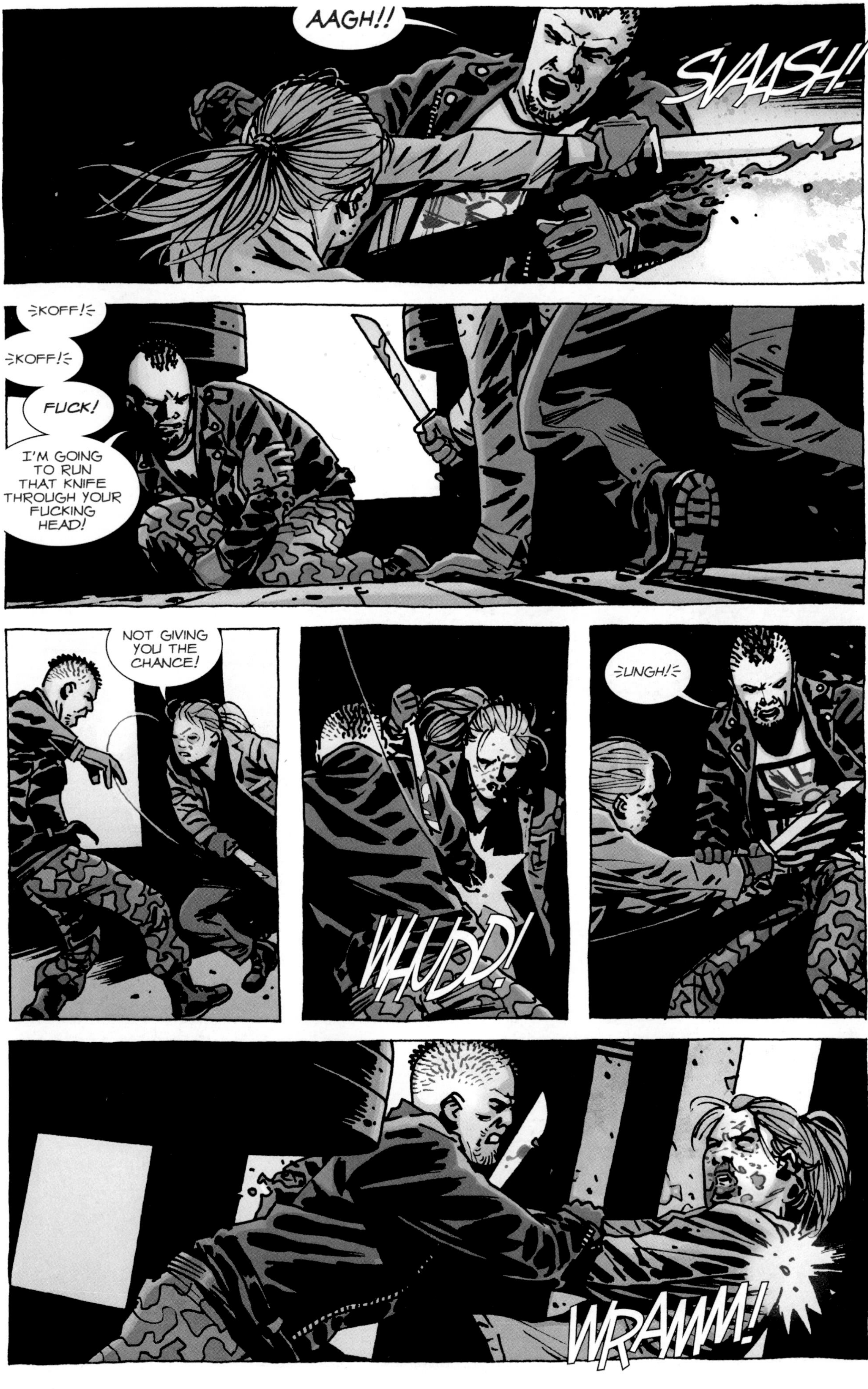
AAGH!!
SVAASH!
KOFF!
KOFF!
FUCK!
I'M GOING TO RUN THAT KNIFE THROUGH YOUR FUCKING HEAD!
NOT GIVING YOU THE CHANCE!
WHUDD!
UNGH!
WRAMM!

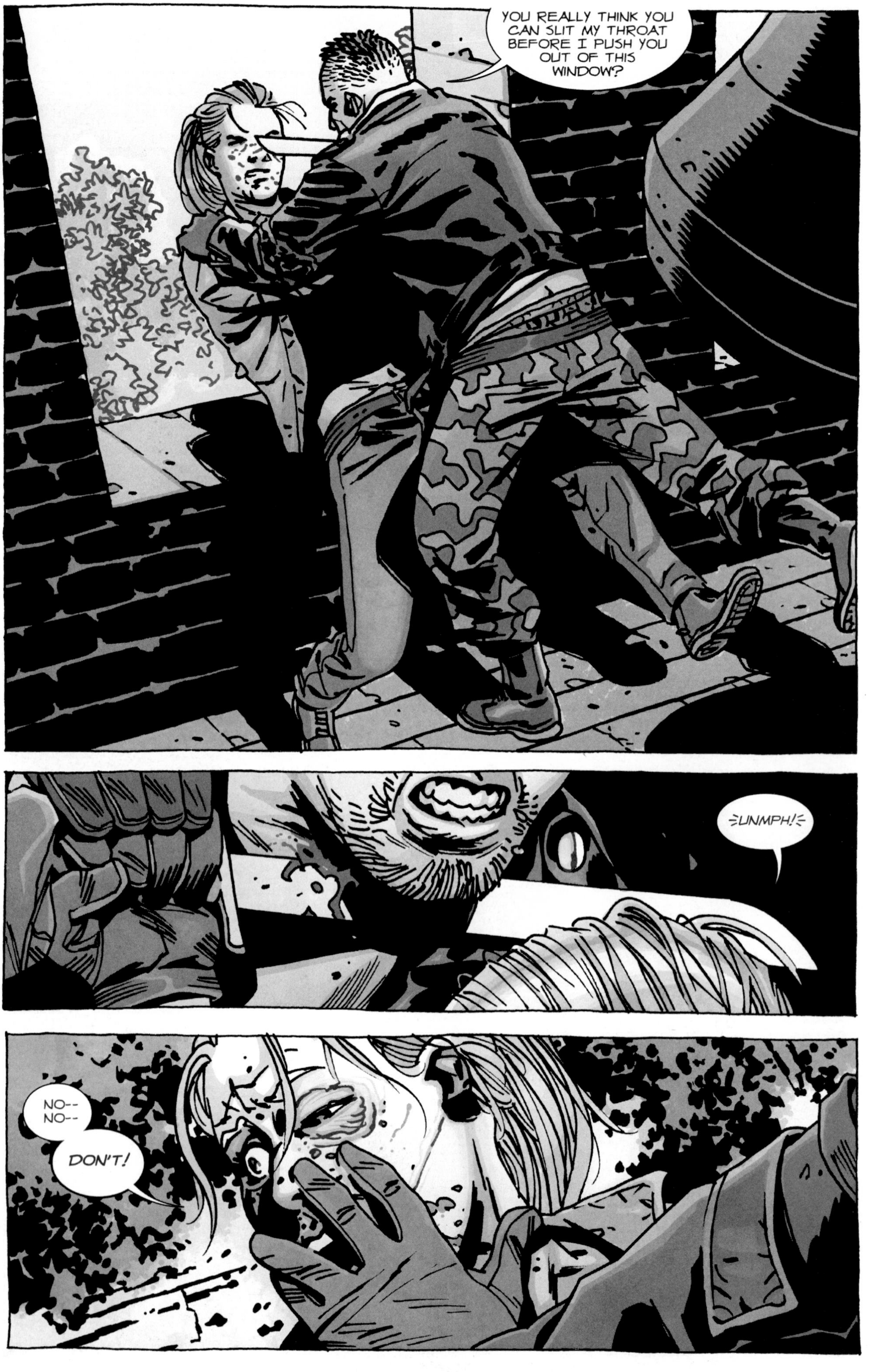
YOU REALLY THINK YOU CAN SLIT MY THROAT BEFORE I PUSH YOU OUT OF THIS WINDOW?
UNMPH!
NO-- NO--
DON'T!

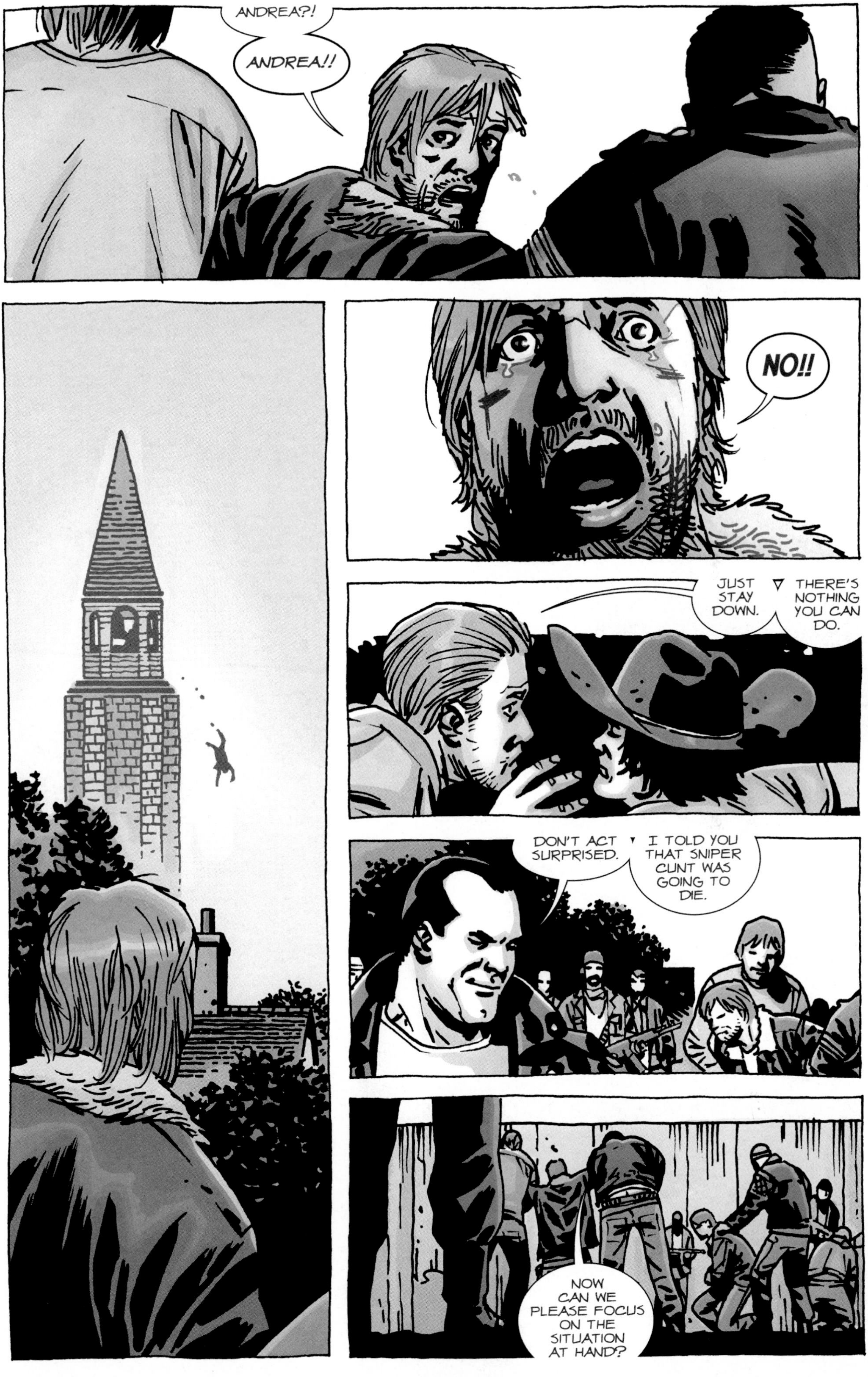
ANDREA?!
ANDREA!!
NO!!
JUST STAY DOWN.
THERE'S NOTHING YOU CAN DO.
DON'T ACT SURPRISED.
I TOLD YOU THAT SNIPER CUNT WAS GOING TO DIE.
NOW CAN WE PLEASE FOCUS ON THE SITUATION AT HAND?

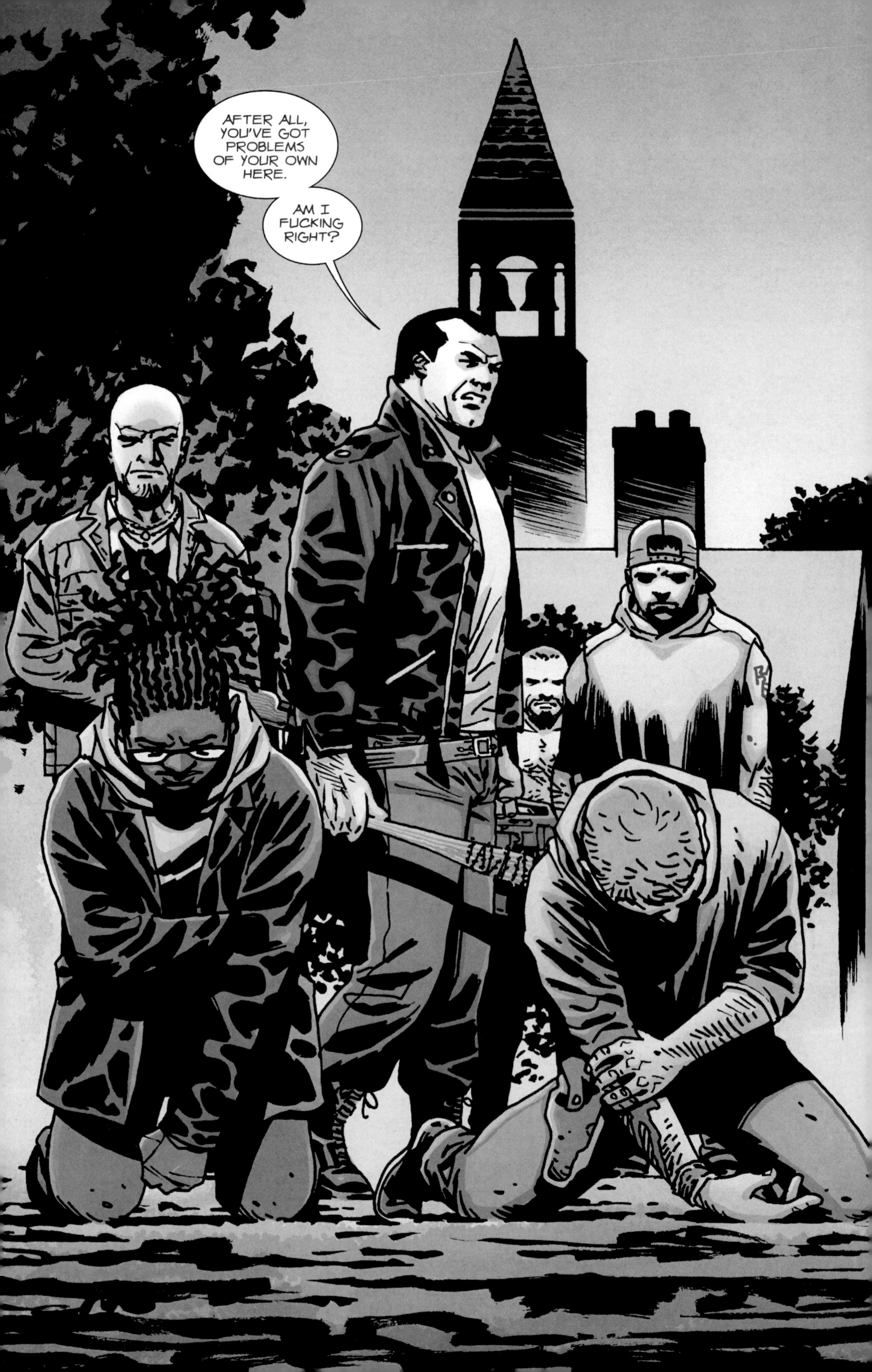
AFTER ALL, YOU'VE GOT PROBLEMS OF YOUR OWN HERE.
AM I FUCKING RIGHT?

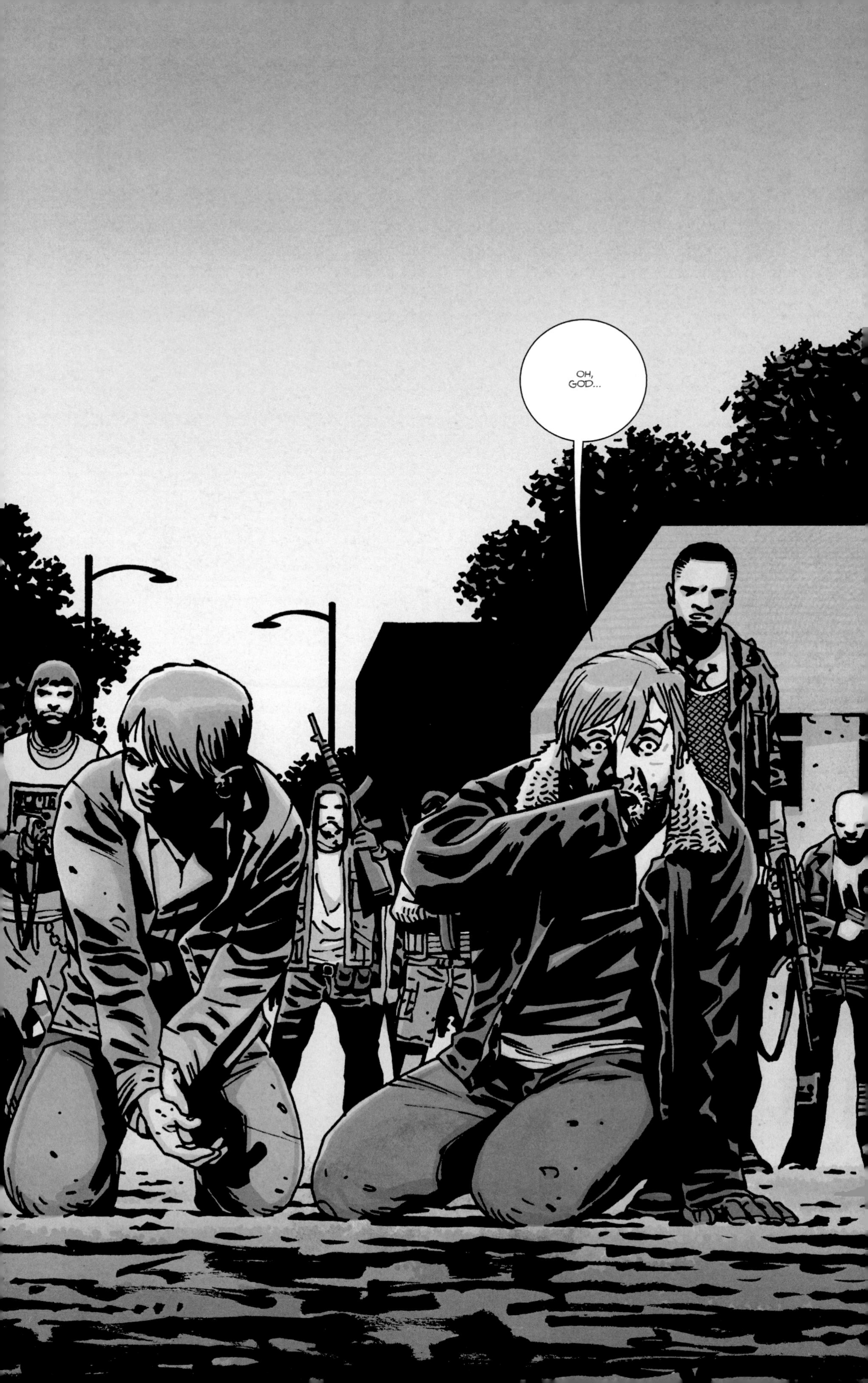
OH, GOD...

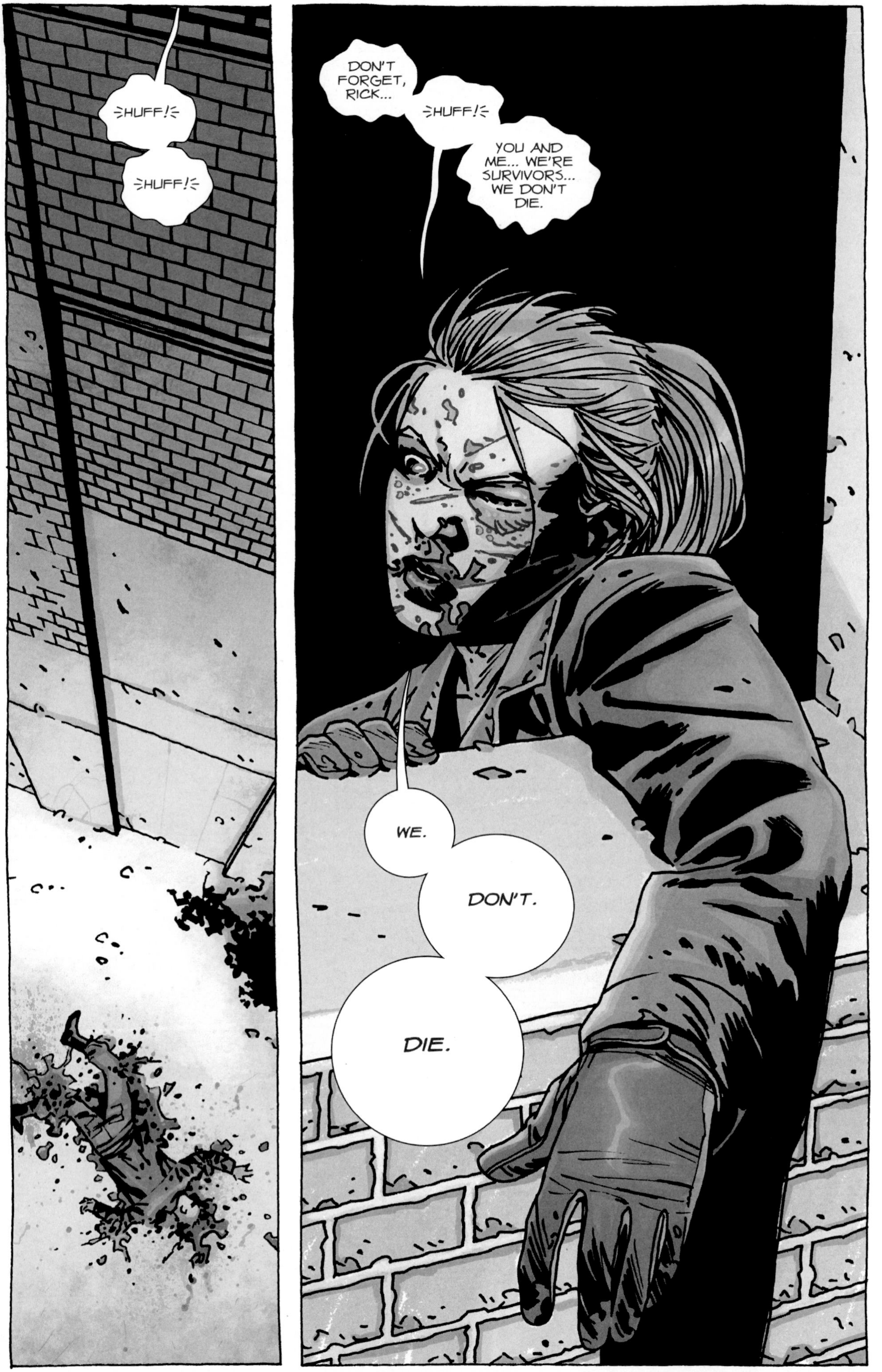

=HUFF!=
=HUFF!=
DON'T FORGET, RICK...
=HUFF!=
YOU AND ME... WE'RE SURVIVORS... WE DON'T DIE.
WE.
DON'T.
DIE.

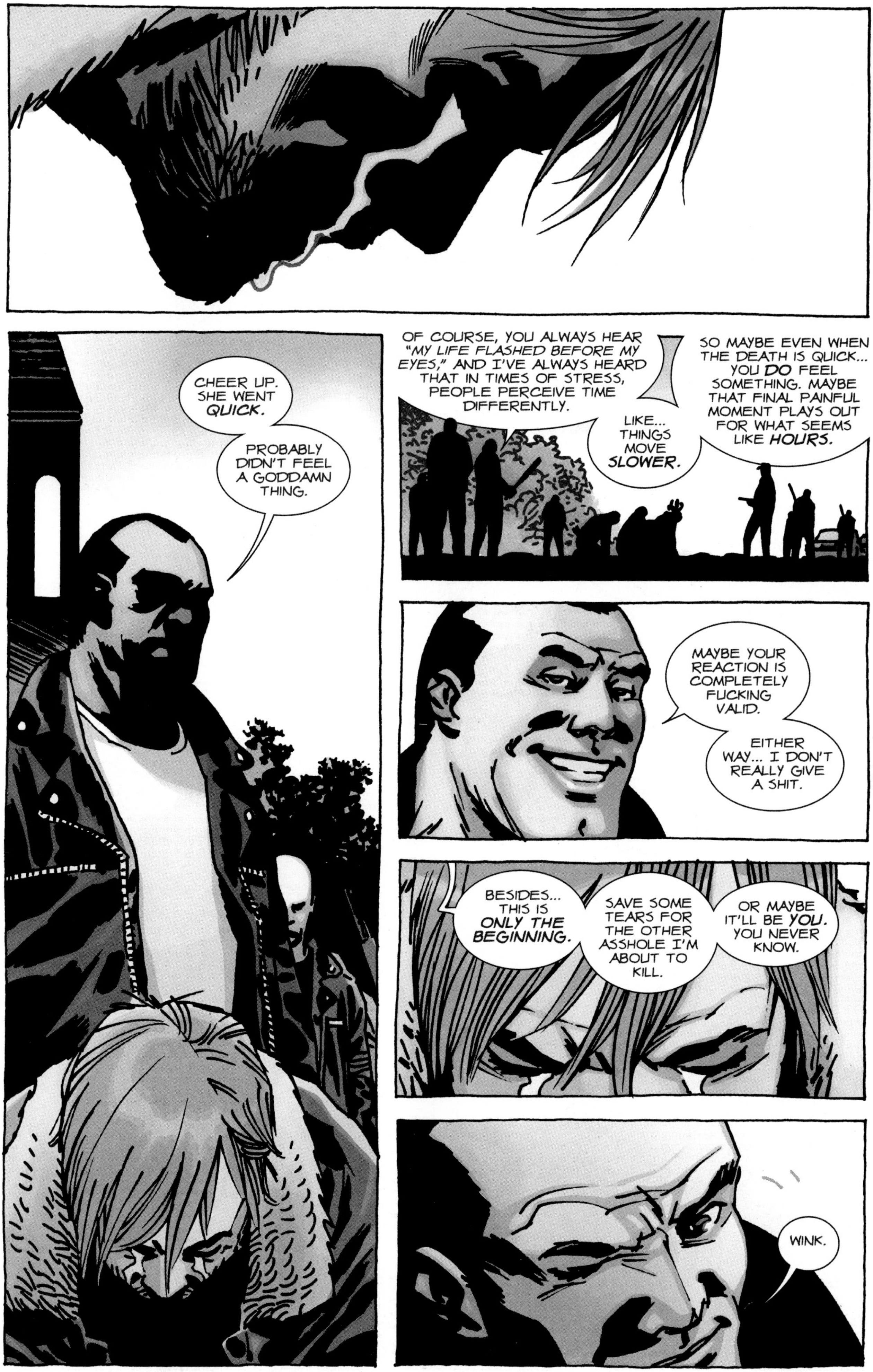
CHEER UP. SHE WENT QUICK.
PROBABLY DIDN'T FEEL A GODDAMN THING.
OF COURSE, YOU ALWAYS HEAR "MY LIFE FLASHED BEFORE MY EYES," AND I'VE ALWAYS HEARD THAT IN TIMES OF STRESS, PEOPLE PERCEIVE TIME DIFFERENTLY.
LIKE... THINGS MOVE SLOWER.
SO MAYBE EVEN WHEN THE DEATH IS QUICK... YOU DO FEEL SOMETHING. MAYBE THAT FINAL PAINFUL MOMENT PLAYS OUT FOR WHAT SEEMS LIKE HOURS.
MAYBE YOUR REACTION IS COMPLETELY FUCKING VALID.
EITHER WAY... I DON'T REALLY GIVE A SHIT.
BESIDES... THIS IS ONLY THE BEGINNING.
SAVE SOME TEARS FOR THE OTHER ASSHOLE I'M ABOUT TO KILL.
OR MAYBE IT'LL BE YOU. YOU NEVER KNOW.
WINK.

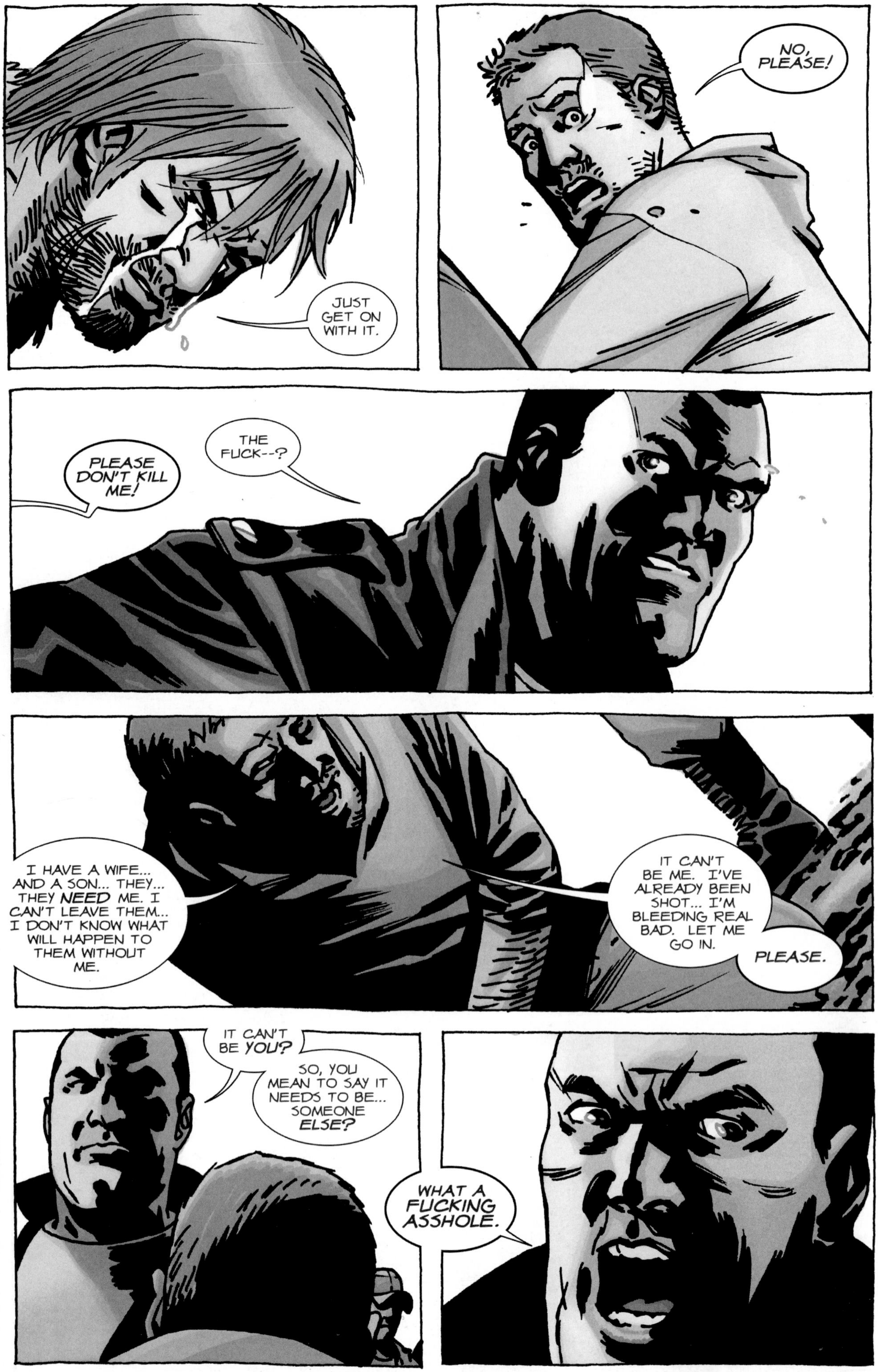
JUST GET ON WITH IT.
NO, PLEASE!
PLEASE DON'T KILL ME!
THE FUCK--?
I HAVE A WIFE... AND A SON... THEY... THEY NEED ME. I CAN'T LEAVE THEM... I DON'T KNOW WHAT WILL HAPPEN TO THEM WITHOUT ME.
IT CAN'T BE ME. I'VE ALREADY BEEN SHOT... I'M BLEEDING REAL BAD. LET ME GO IN.
PLEASE.
IT CAN'T BE YOU?
SO, YOU MEAN TO SAY IT NEEDS TO BE... SOMEONE ELSE?
WHAT A FUCKING ASSHOLE.

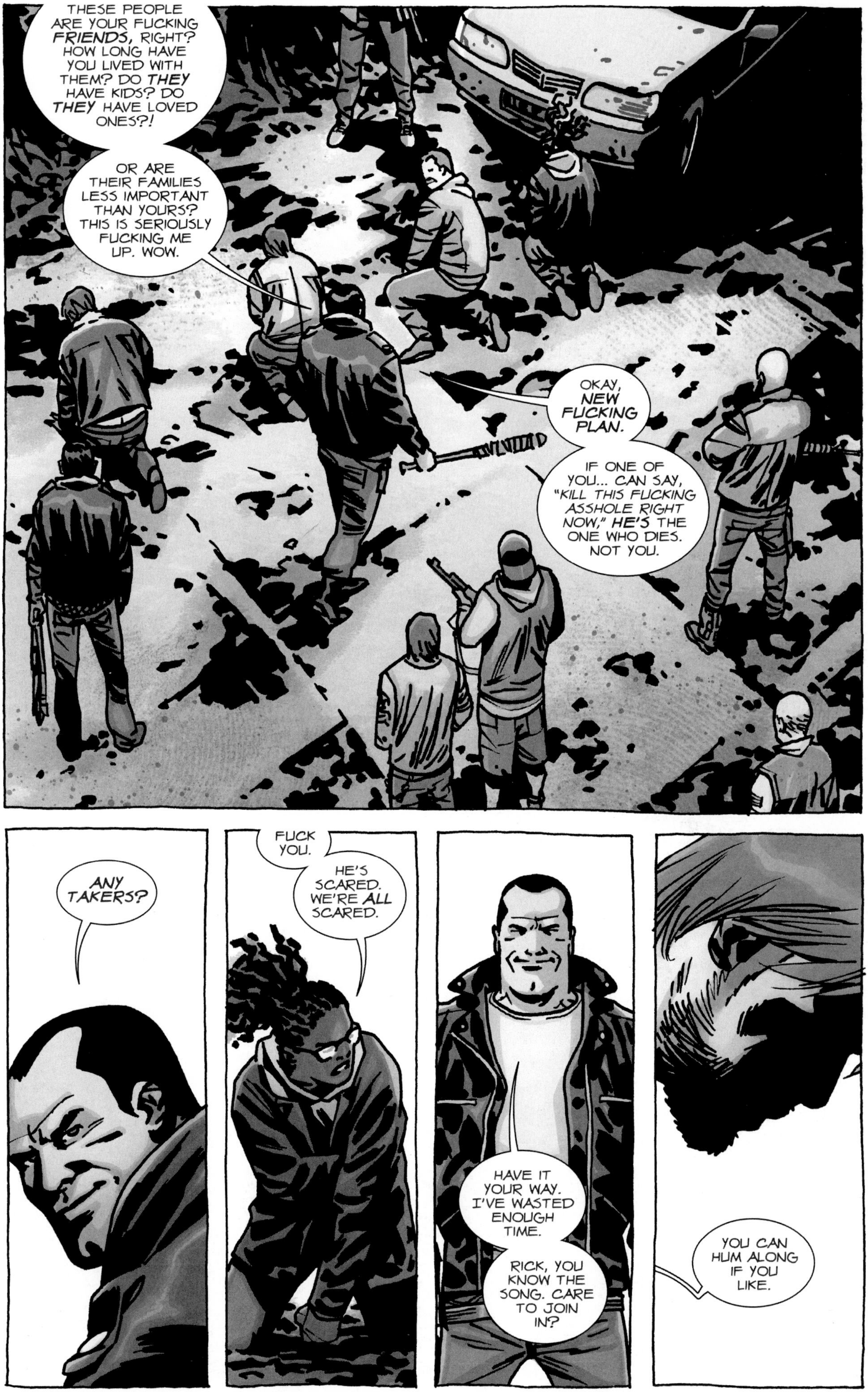
THESE PEOPLE ARE YOUR FUCKING FRIENDS, RIGHT? HOW LONG HAVE YOU LIVED WITH THEM? DO THEY HAVE KIDS? DO THEY HAVE LOVED ONES?!
OR ARE THEIR FAMILIES LESS IMPORTANT THAN YOURS? THIS IS SERIOUSLY FUCKING ME UP. WOW.
OKAY, NEW FUCKING PLAN.
IF ONE OF YOU... CAN SAY, "KILL THIS FUCKING ASSHOLE RIGHT NOW," HE'S THE ONE WHO DIES. NOT YOU.
ANY TAKERS?
FUCK YOU.
HE'S SCARED. WE'RE ALL SCARED.
HAVE IT YOUR WAY. I'VE WASTED ENOUGH TIME.
RICK, YOU KNOW THE SONG. CARE TO JOIN IN?
YOU CAN HUM ALONG IF YOU LIKE.

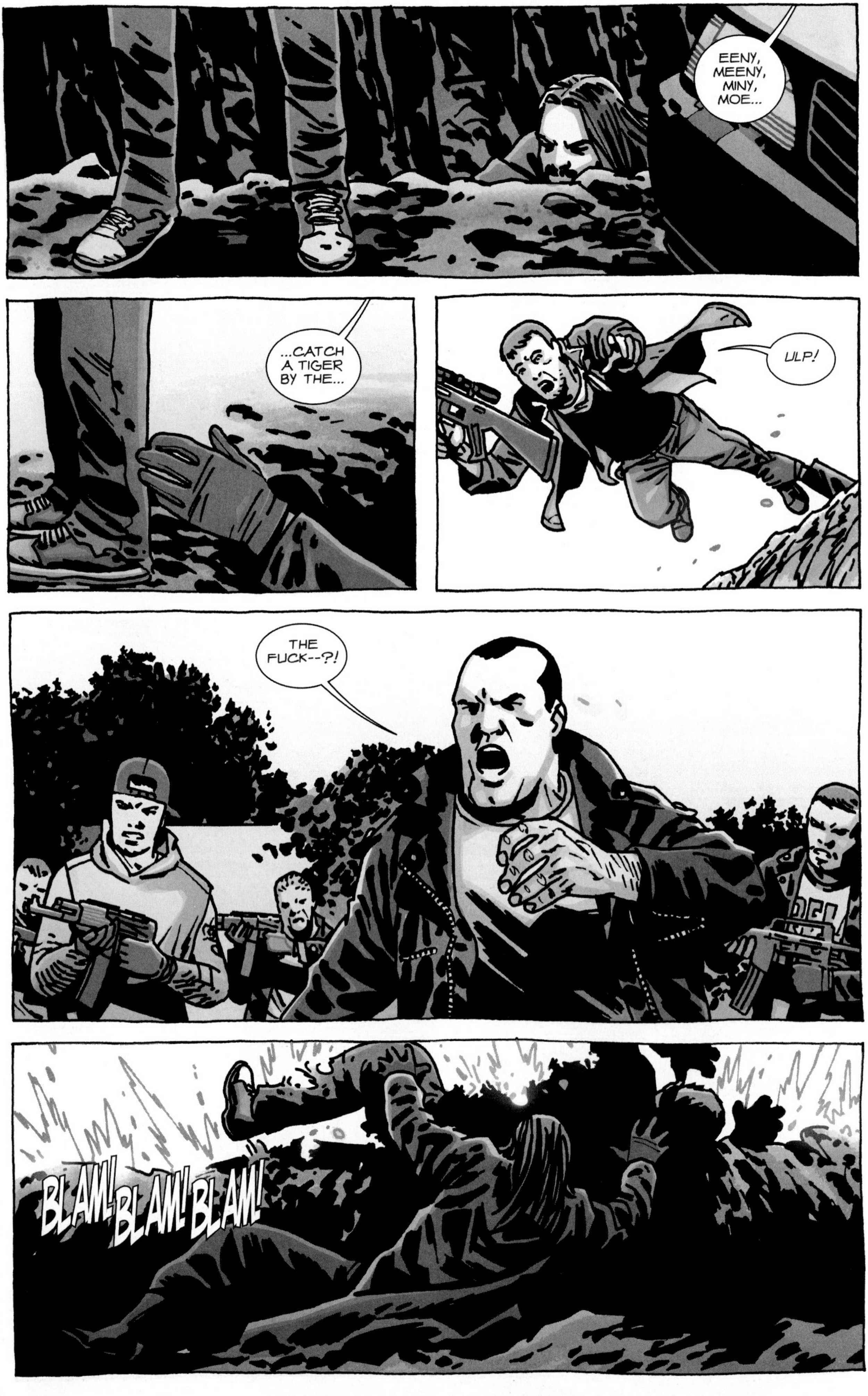
EENY, MEENY, MINY, MOE...
...CATCH A TIGER BY THE...
ULP!
THE FUCK--?!
BLAM! BLAM! BLAM!

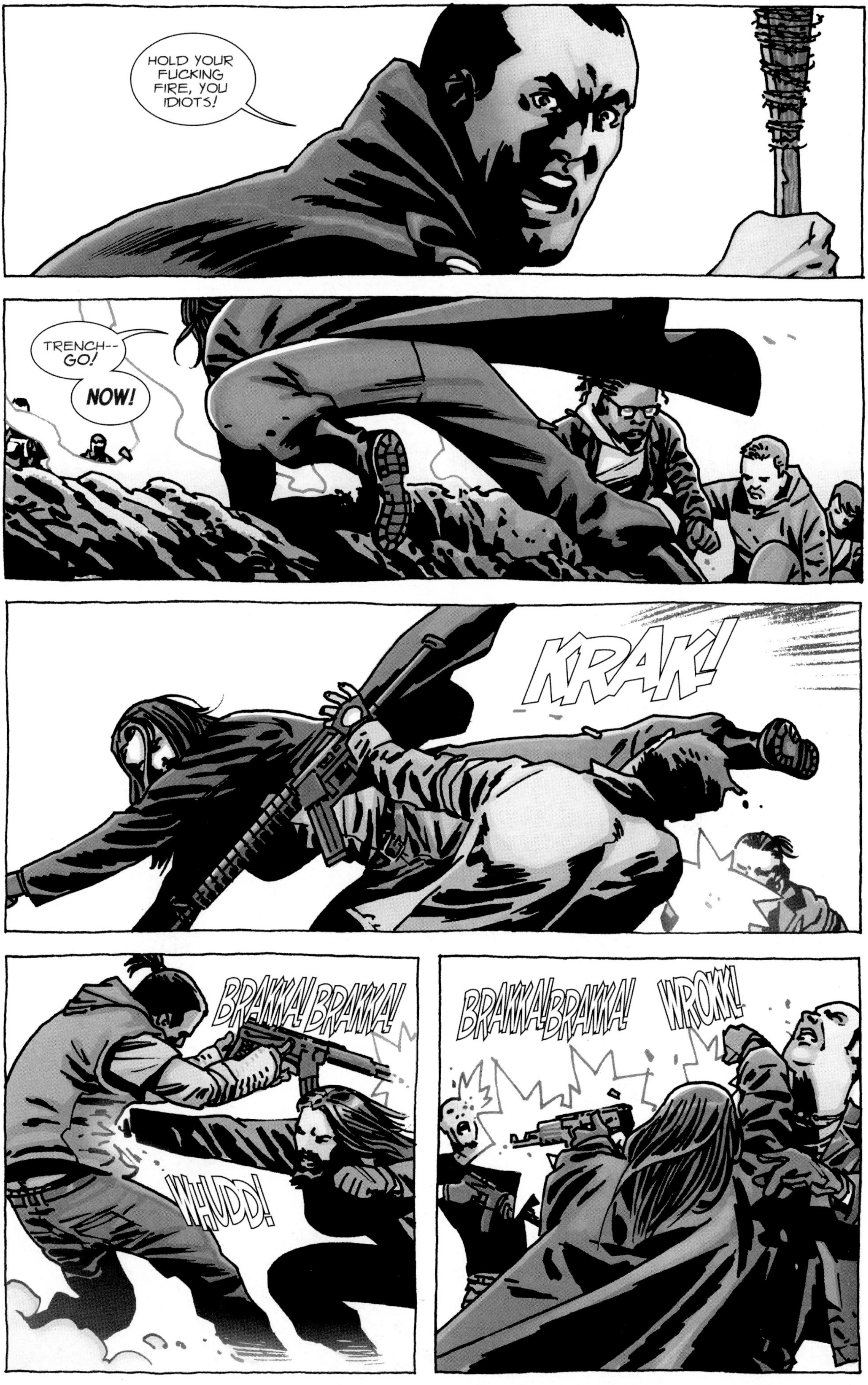
HOLD YOUR FUCKING FIRE, YOU IDIOTS!
TRENCH-- GO!
NOW!
KRAK!
BRAKKA! BRAKKA!
WHUDD!
BRAKKA! BRAKKA!
WROKK!

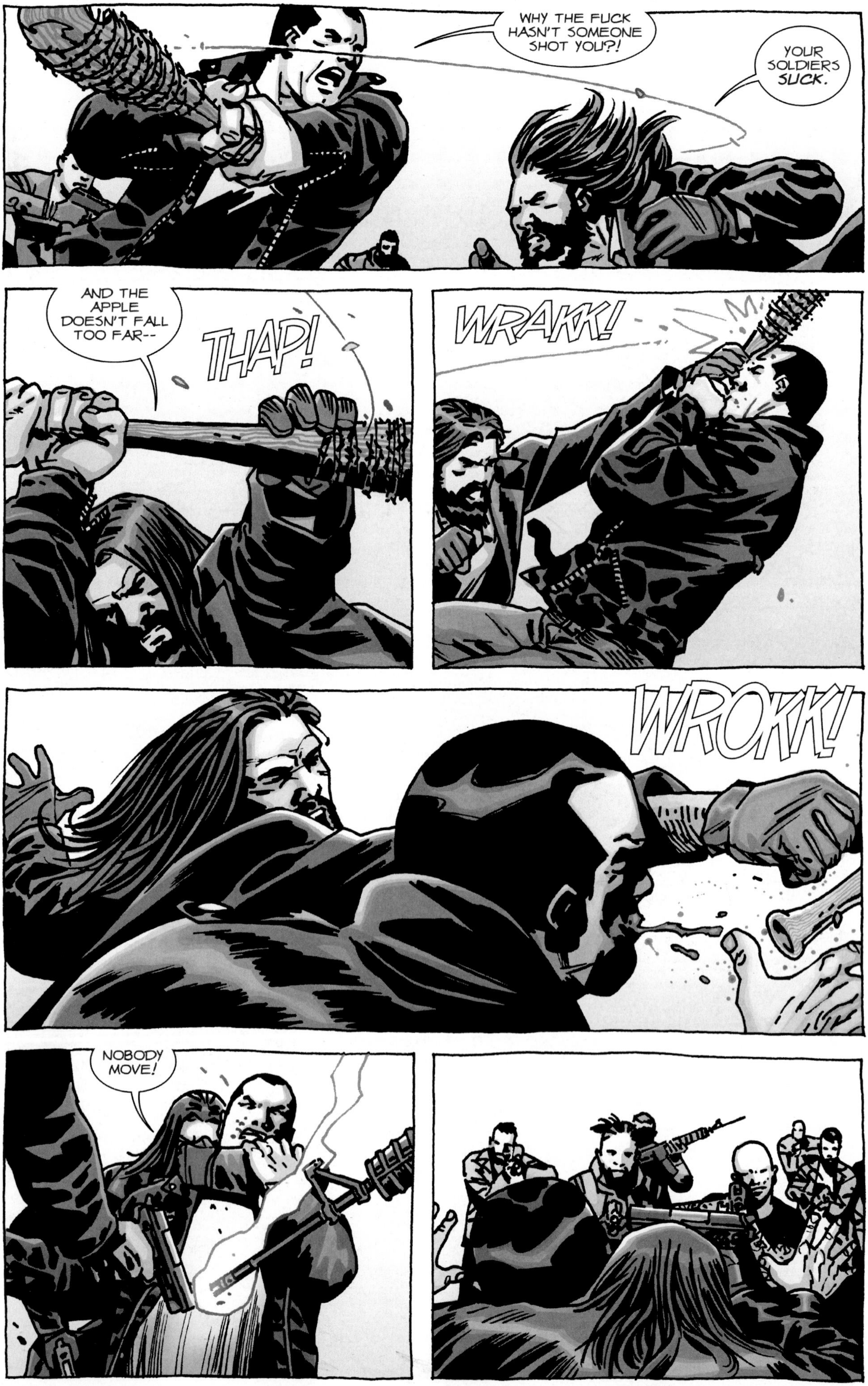
WHY THE FUCK HASN'T SOMEONE SHOT YOU?!
YOUR SOLDIERS SUCK.
AND THE APPLE DOESN'T FALL TOO FAR--
THAP!
WRAKK!
WROKK!
NOBODY MOVE!

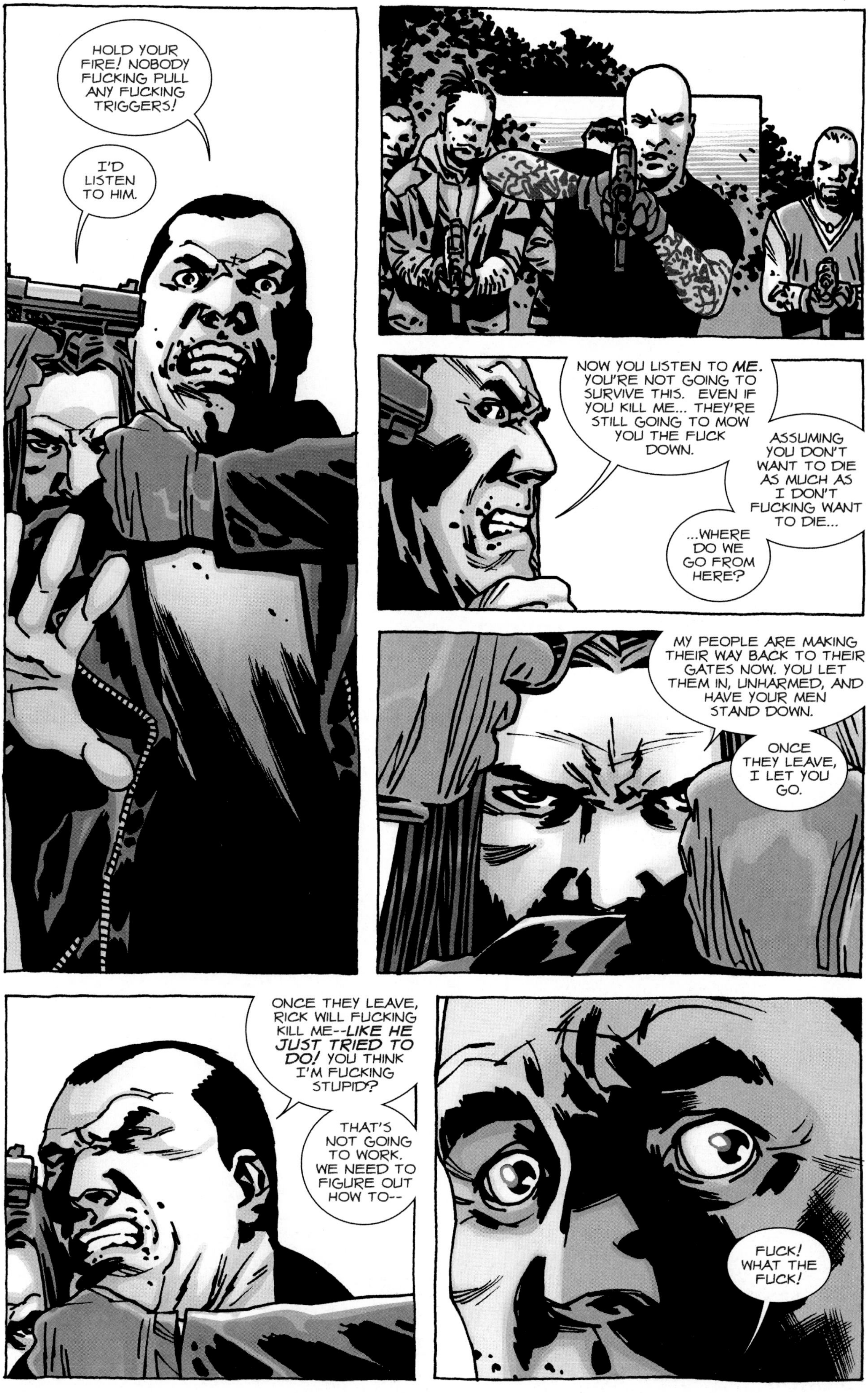
HOLD YOUR FIRE! NOBODY FUCKING PULL ANY FUCKING TRIGGERS!
I'D LISTEN TO HIM.
NOW YOU LISTEN TO ME. YOU'RE NOT GOING TO SURVIVE THIS. EVEN IF YOU KILL ME... THEY'RE STILL GOING TO MOW YOU THE FUCK DOWN.
ASSUMING YOU DON'T WANT TO DIE AS MUCH AS I DON'T FUCKING WANT TO DIE...
...WHERE DO WE GO FROM HERE?
MY PEOPLE ARE MAKING THEIR WAY BACK TO THEIR GATES NOW. YOU LET THEM IN, UNHARMED, AND HAVE YOUR MEN STAND DOWN.
ONCE THEY LEAVE, I LET YOU GO.
ONCE THEY LEAVE, RICK WILL FUCKING KILL ME--LIKE HE JUST TRIED TO DO! YOU THINK I'M FUCKING STUPID?
THAT'S NOT GOING TO WORK. WE NEED TO FIGURE OUT HOW TO--
FUCK! WHAT THE FUCK!

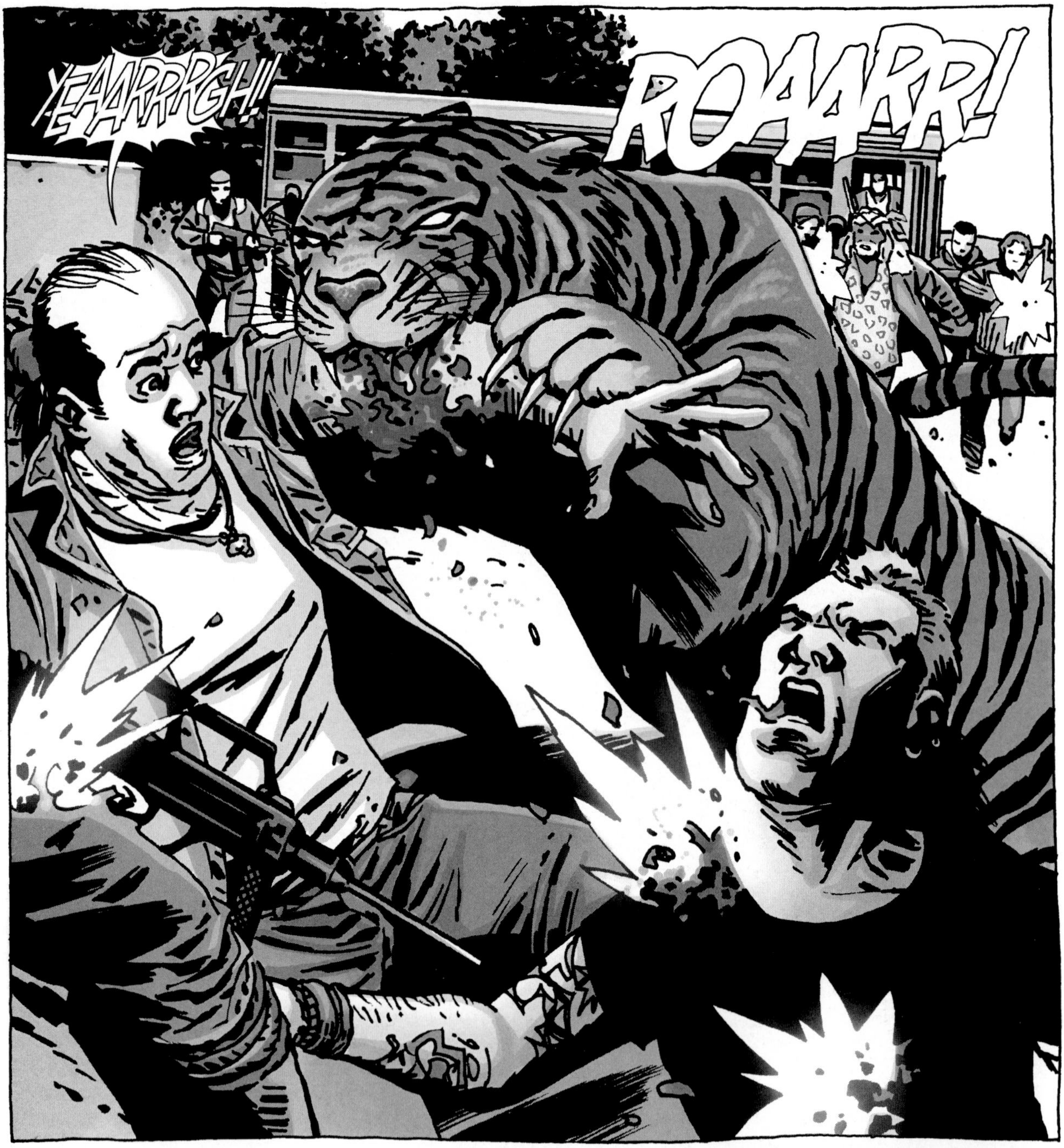
YEAARRRRGH!!
ROAARR!

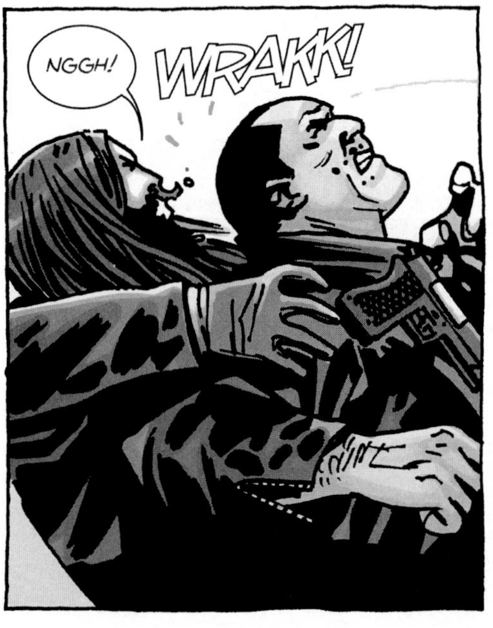
NGGH!
WRAKK!

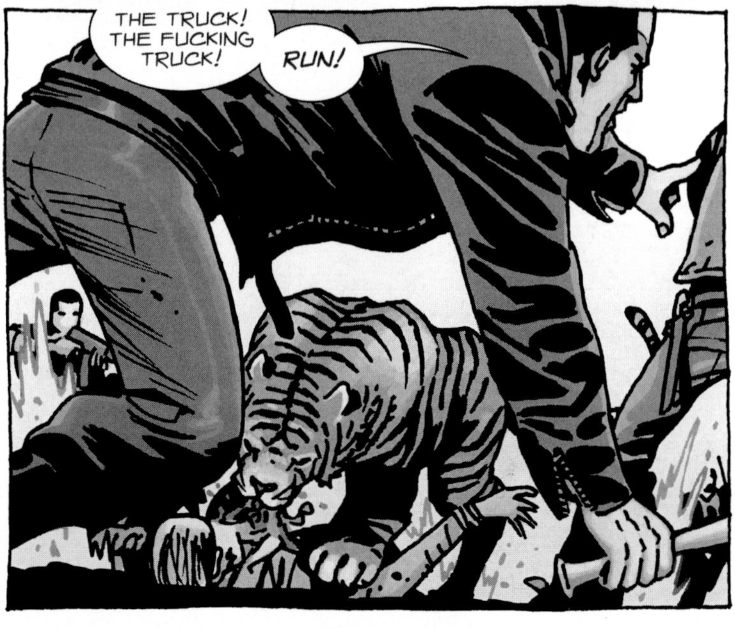
THE TRUCK! THE FUCKING TRUCK!
RUN!

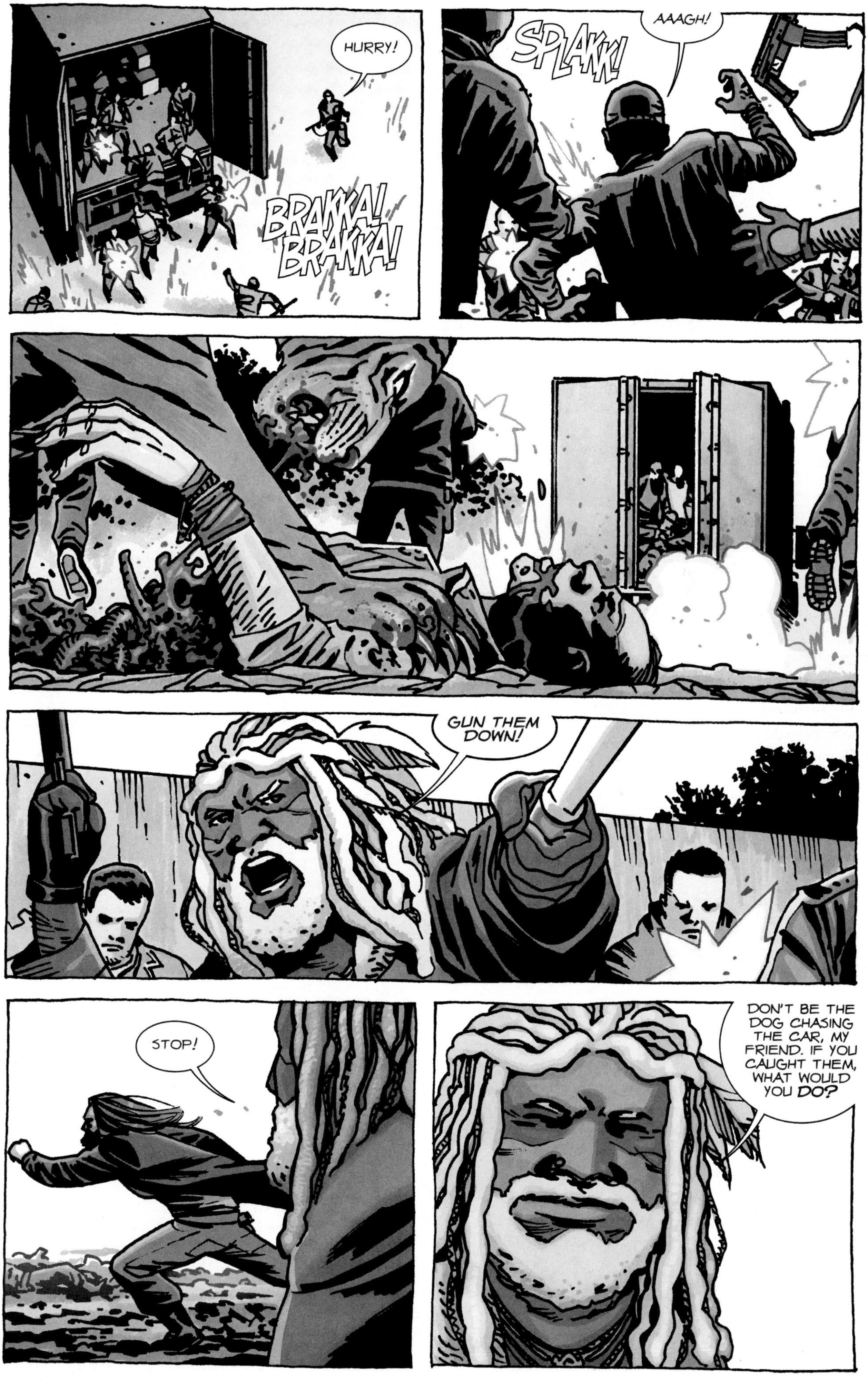
HURRY!
BRAKKA! BRAKKA!
SPLAKK!
AAAGH!
GUN THEM DOWN!
STOP!
DON'T BE THE DOG CHASING THE CAR, MY FRIEND. IF YOU CAUGHT THEM, WHAT WOULD YOU DO?

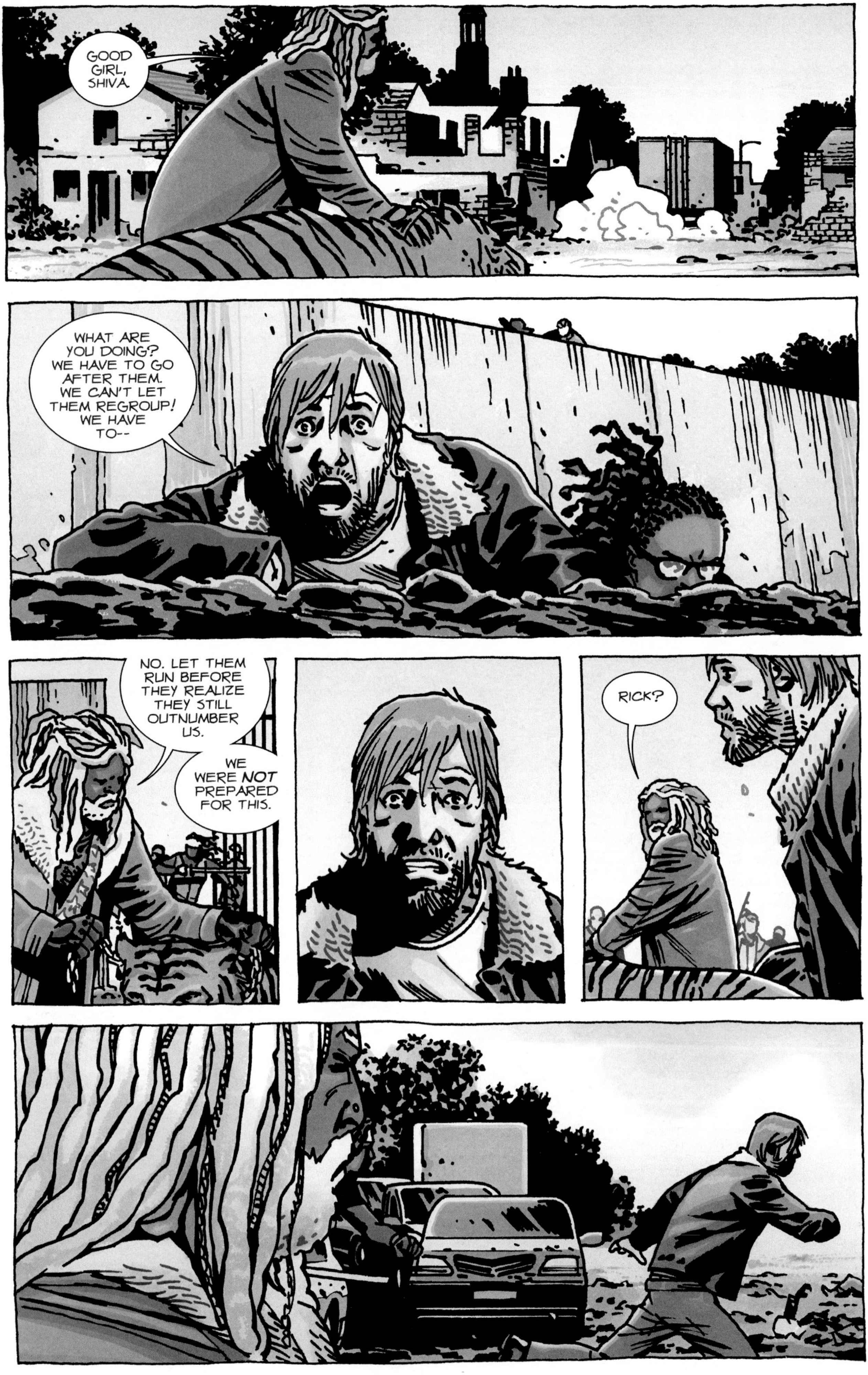
GOOD GIRL, SHIVA.
WHAT ARE YOU DOING? WE HAVE TO GO AFTER THEM. WE CAN'T LET THEM REGROUP! WE HAVE TO--
NO. LET THEM RUN BEFORE THEY REALIZE THEY STILL OUTNUMBER US.
WE WERE NOT PREPARED FOR THIS.
RICK?

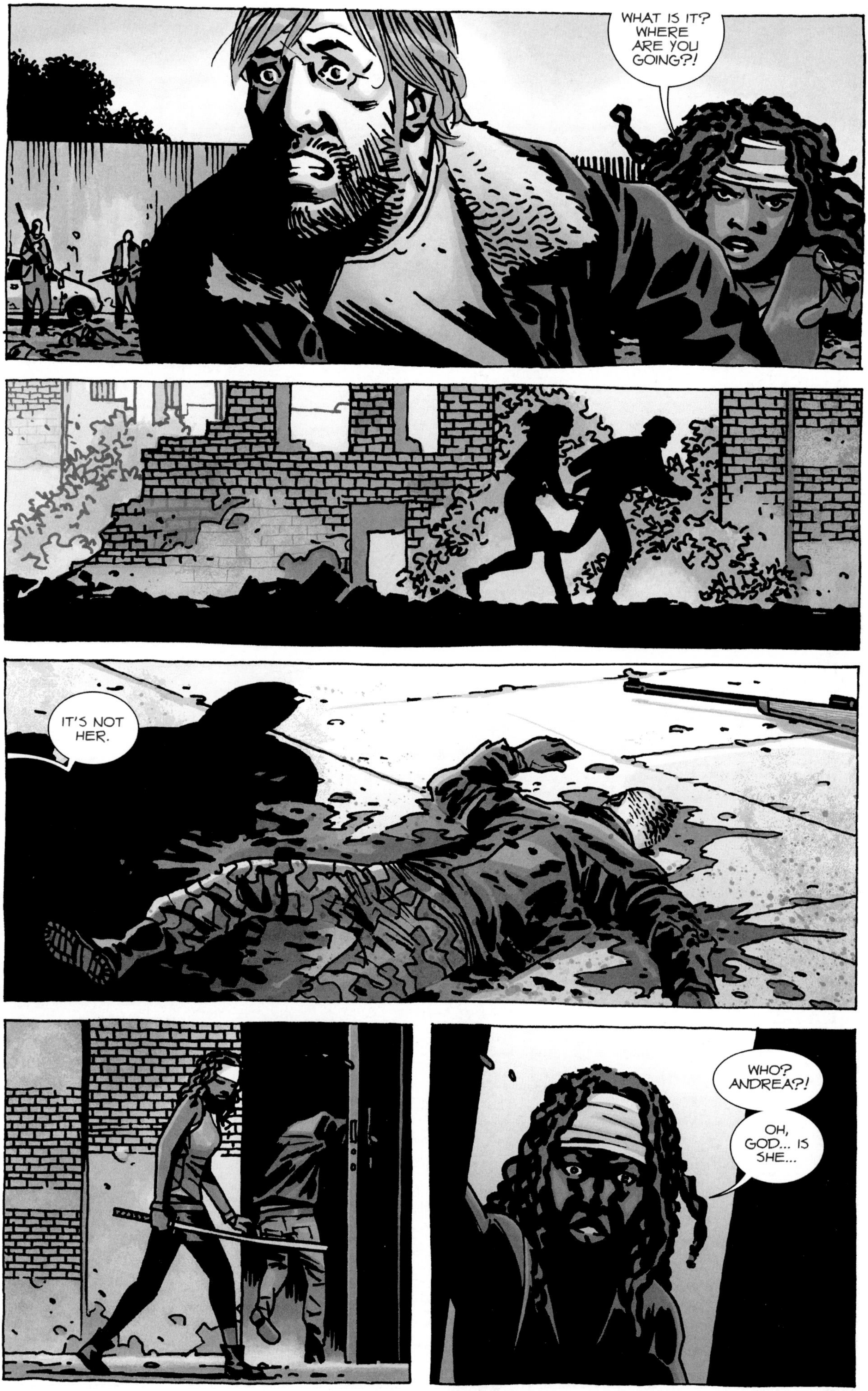
WHAT IS IT? WHERE ARE YOU GOING?!
IT'S NOT HER.
WHO? ANDREA?!
OH, GOD... IS SHE...

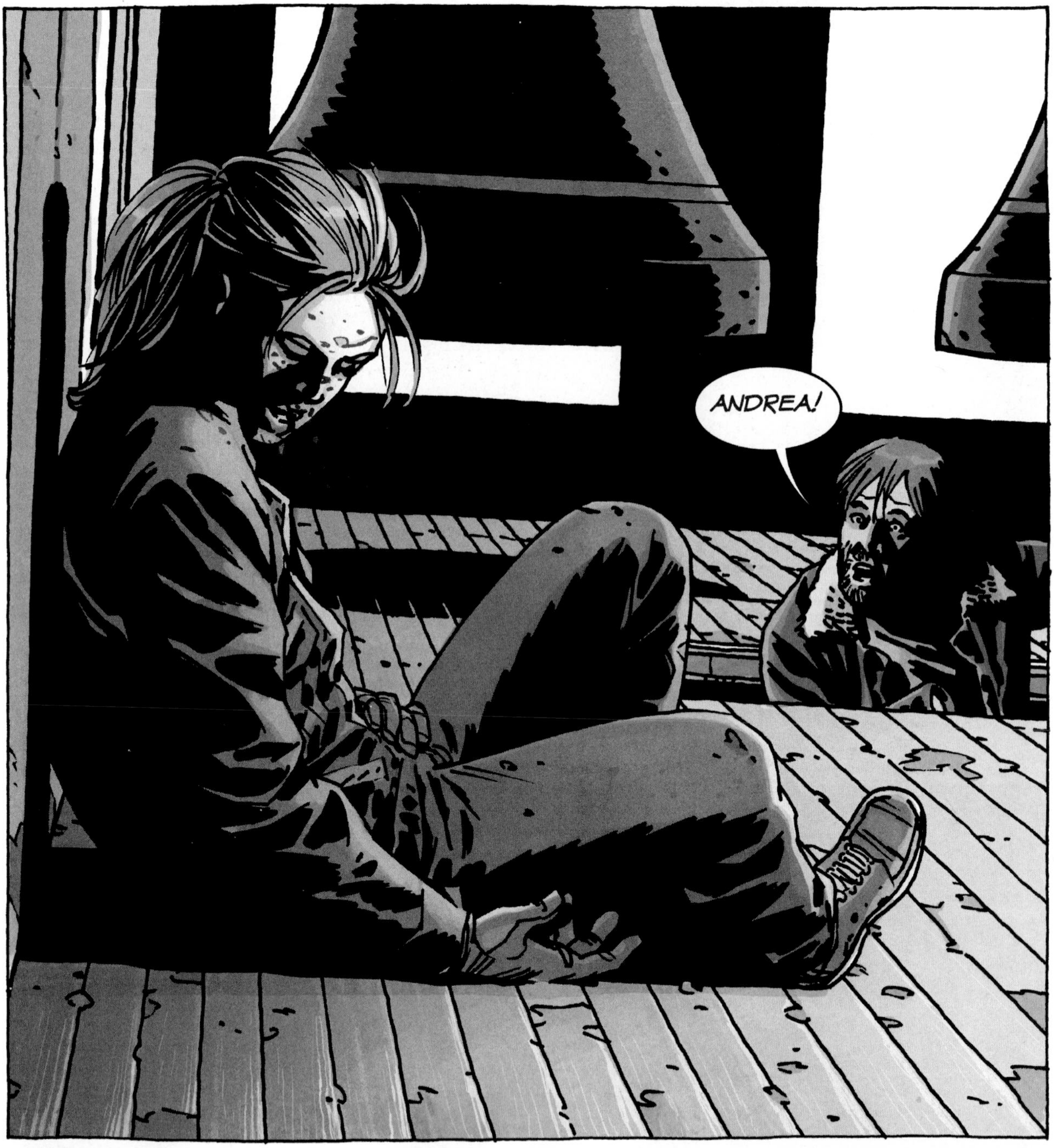
ANDREA!

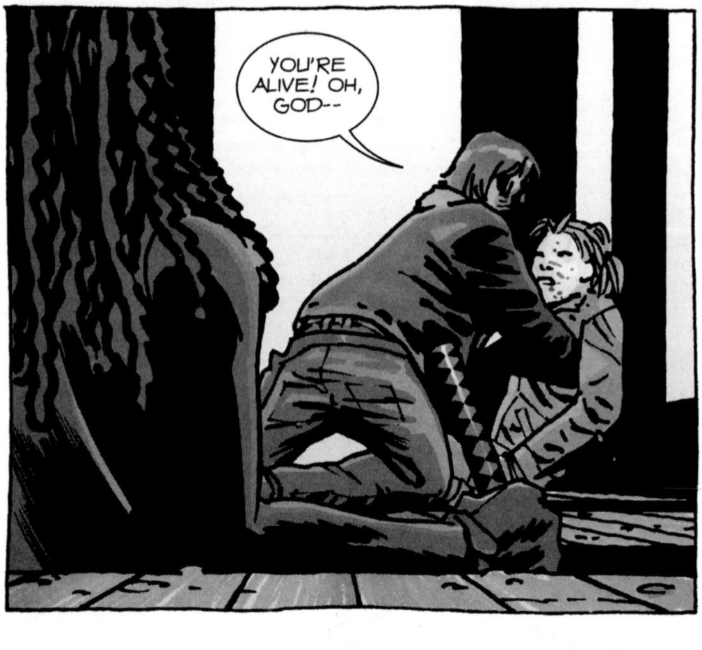
YOU'RE ALIVE! OH, GOD--

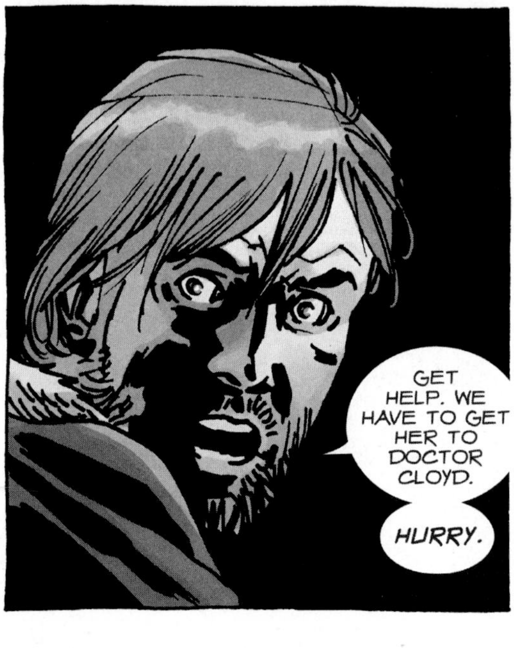
GET HELP. WE HAVE TO GET HER TO DOCTOR CLOYD.
HURRY.

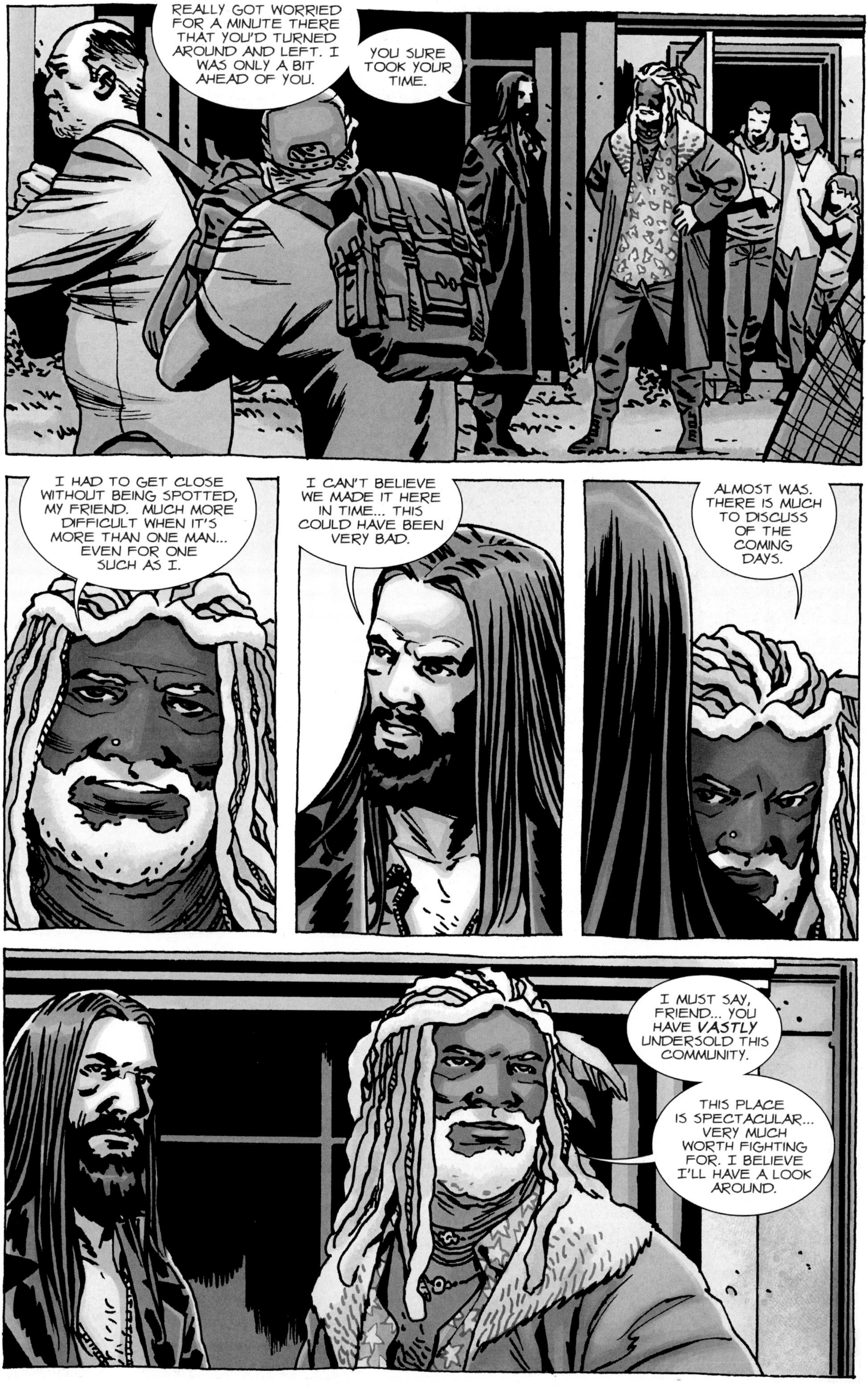
REALLY GOT WORRIED FOR A MINUTE THERE THAT YOU'D TURNED AROUND AND LEFT. I WAS ONLY A BIT AHEAD OF YOU.
YOU SURE TOOK YOUR TIME.
I HAD TO GET CLOSE WITHOUT BEING SPOTTED, MY FRIEND. MUCH MORE DIFFICULT WHEN IT'S MORE THAN ONE MAN... EVEN FOR ONE SUCH AS I.
I CAN'T BELIEVE WE MADE IT HERE IN TIME... THIS COULD HAVE BEEN VERY BAD.
ALMOST WAS. THERE IS MUCH TO DISCUSS OF THE COMING DAYS.
I MUST SAY, FRIEND... YOU HAVE *VASTLY* UNDERSOLD THIS COMMUNITY.
THIS PLACE IS SPECTACULAR... VERY MUCH WORTH FIGHTING FOR. I BELIEVE I'LL HAVE A LOOK AROUND.

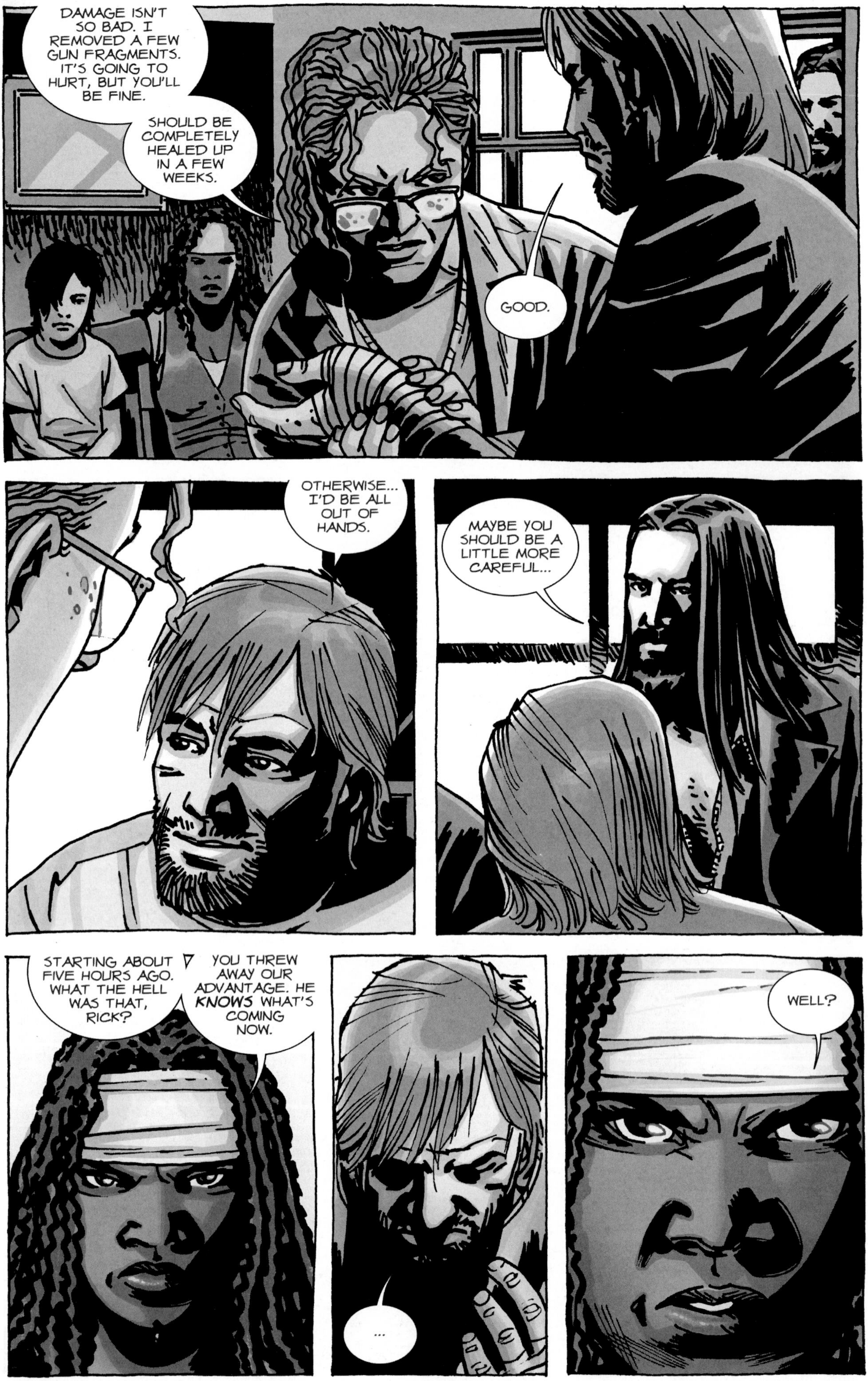
DAMAGE ISN'T SO BAD. I REMOVED A FEW GUN FRAGMENTS. IT'S GOING TO HURT, BUT YOU'LL BE FINE.
SHOULD BE COMPLETELY HEALED UP IN A FEW WEEKS.
GOOD.
OTHERWISE... I'D BE ALL OUT OF HANDS.
MAYBE YOU SHOULD BE A LITTLE MORE CAREFUL...
STARTING ABOUT FIVE HOURS AGO. WHAT THE HELL WAS THAT, RICK?
YOU THREW AWAY OUR ADVANTAGE. HE KNOWS WHAT'S COMING NOW.
...
WELL?

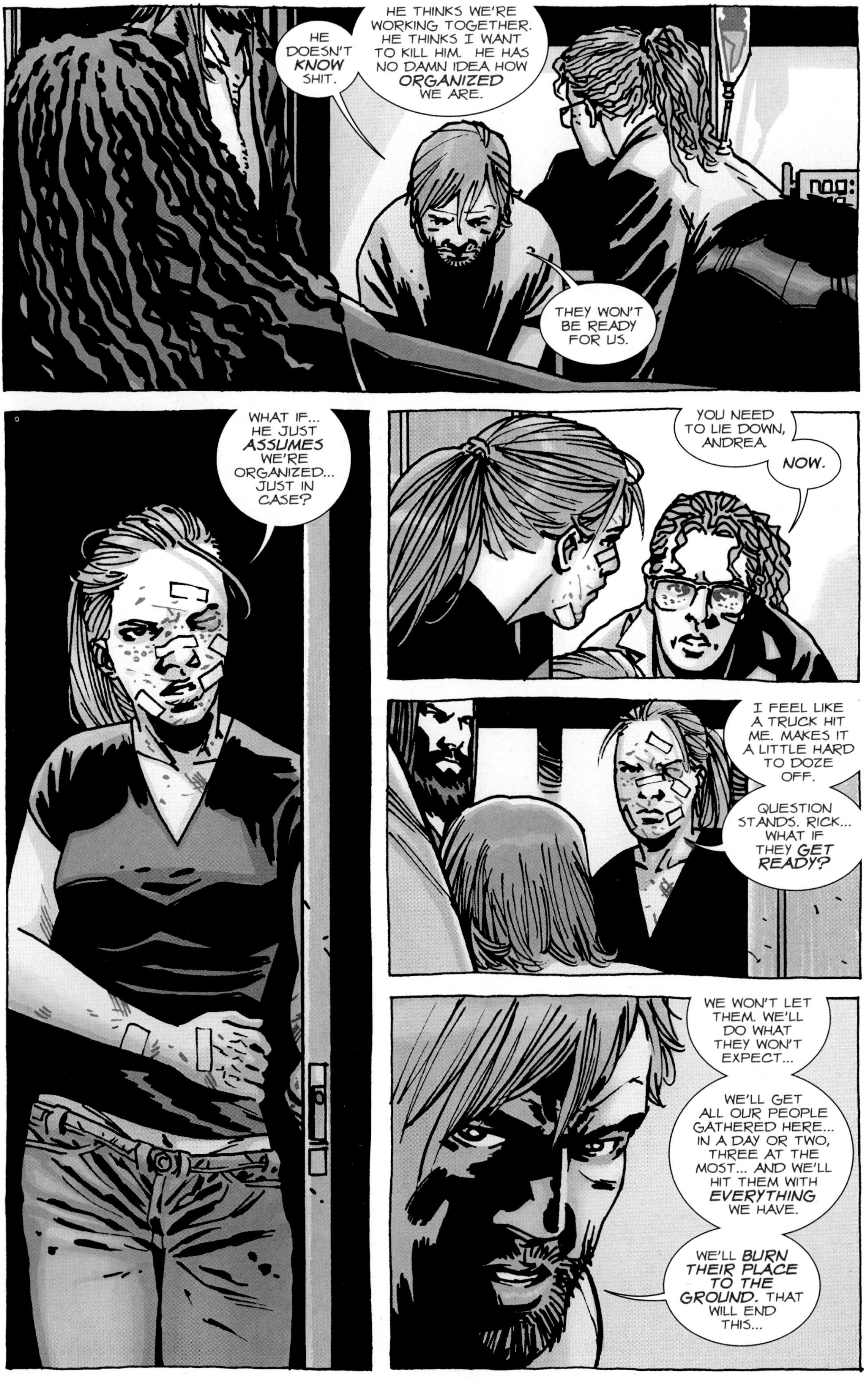

HE DOESN'T KNOW SHIT.
HE THINKS WE'RE WORKING TOGETHER. HE THINKS I WANT TO KILL HIM. HE HAS NO DAMN IDEA HOW ORGANIZED WE ARE.
THEY WON'T BE READY FOR US.
WHAT IF... HE JUST ASSUMES WE'RE ORGANIZED... JUST IN CASE?
YOU NEED TO LIE DOWN, ANDREA.
NOW.
I FEEL LIKE A TRUCK HIT ME. MAKES IT A LITTLE HARD TO DOZE OFF.
QUESTION STANDS. RICK... WHAT IF THEY GET READY?
WE WON'T LET THEM. WE'LL DO WHAT THEY WON'T EXPECT...
WE'LL GET ALL OUR PEOPLE GATHERED HERE... IN A DAY OR TWO, THREE AT THE MOST... AND WE'LL HIT THEM WITH EVERYTHING WE HAVE.
WE'LL BURN THEIR PLACE TO THE GROUND. THAT WILL END THIS...

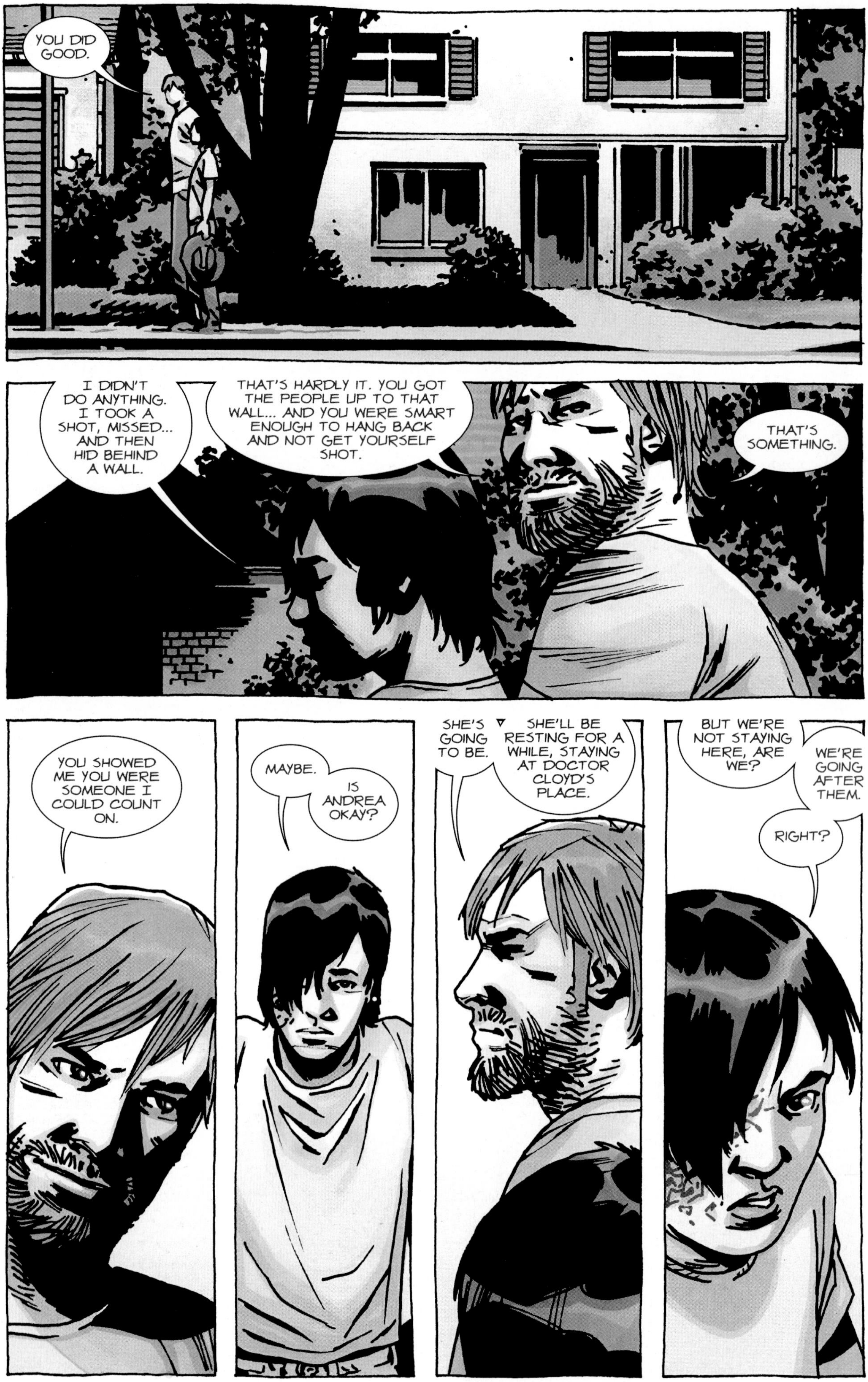
YOU DID GOOD.
I DIDN'T DO ANYTHING. I TOOK A SHOT, MISSED... AND THEN HID BEHIND A WALL.
THAT'S HARDLY IT. YOU GOT THE PEOPLE UP TO THAT WALL... AND YOU WERE SMART ENOUGH TO HANG BACK AND NOT GET YOURSELF SHOT.
THAT'S SOMETHING.
YOU SHOWED ME YOU WERE SOMEONE I COULD COUNT ON.
MAYBE.
IS ANDREA OKAY?
SHE'S GOING TO BE.
SHE'LL BE RESTING FOR A WHILE, STAYING AT DOCTOR CLOYD'S PLACE.
BUT WE'RE NOT STAYING HERE, ARE WE?
WE'RE GOING AFTER THEM.
RIGHT?

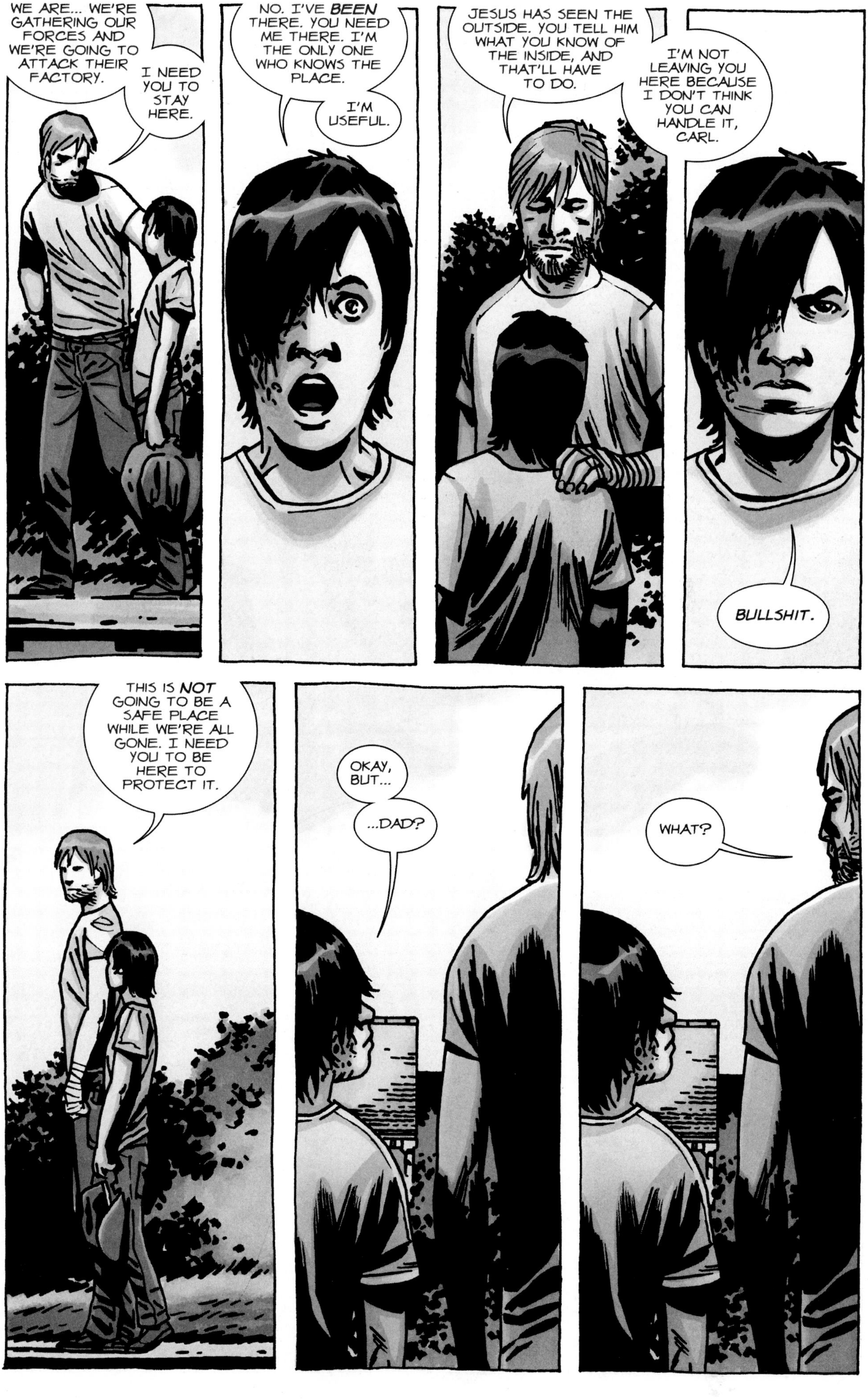
WE ARE... WE'RE GATHERING OUR FORCES AND WE'RE GOING TO ATTACK THEIR FACTORY.
I NEED YOU TO STAY HERE.
NO. I'VE **BEEN** THERE. YOU NEED ME THERE. I'M THE ONLY ONE WHO KNOWS THE PLACE.
I'M USEFUL.
JESUS HAS SEEN THE OUTSIDE. YOU TELL HIM WHAT YOU KNOW OF THE INSIDE, AND THAT'LL HAVE TO DO.
I'M NOT LEAVING YOU HERE BECAUSE I DON'T THINK YOU CAN HANDLE IT, CARL.
BULLSHIT.
THIS IS **NOT** GOING TO BE A SAFE PLACE WHILE WE'RE ALL GONE. I NEED YOU TO BE HERE TO PROTECT IT.
OKAY, BUT...
...DAD?
WHAT?

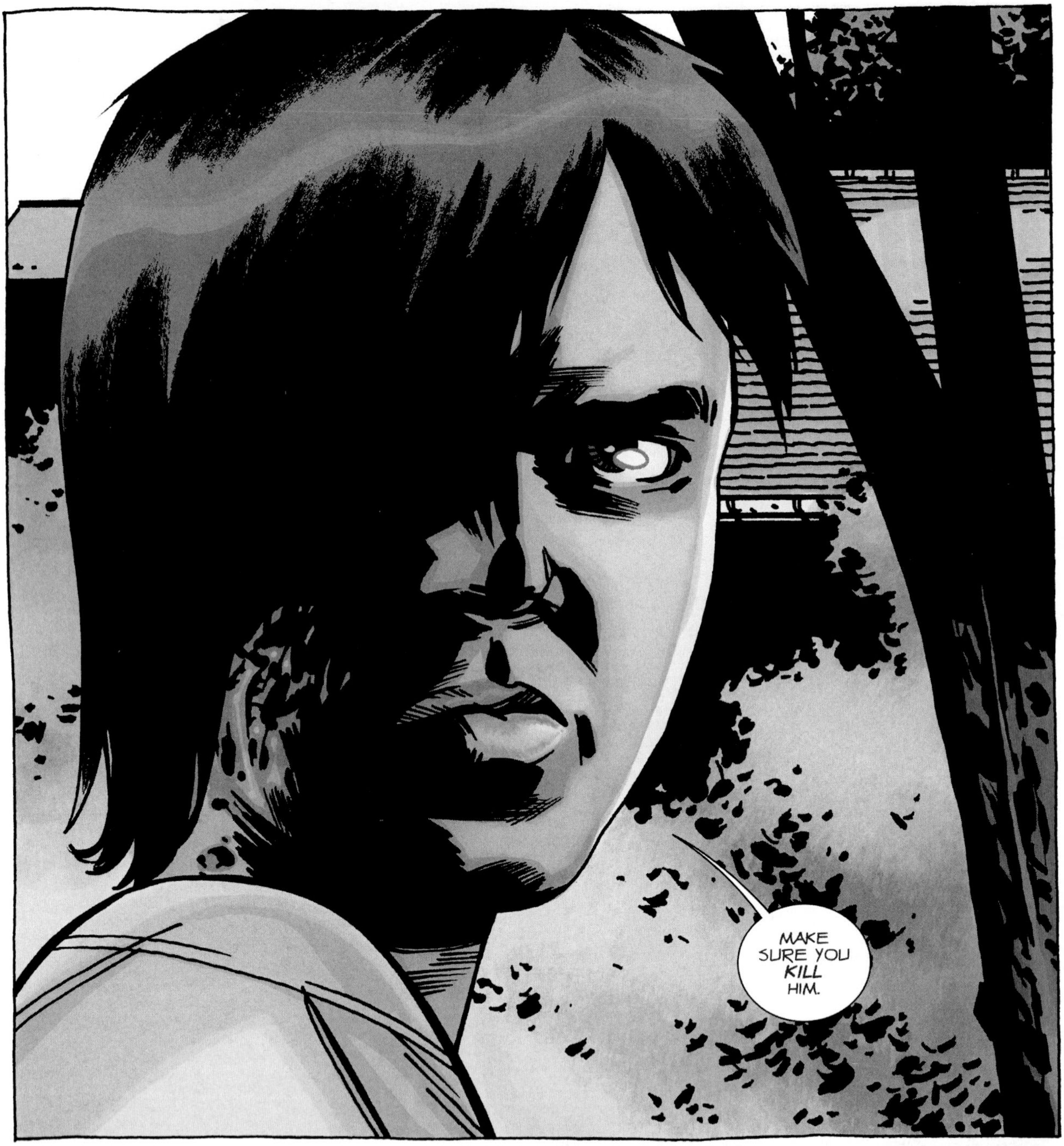
MAKE SURE YOU KILL HIM.

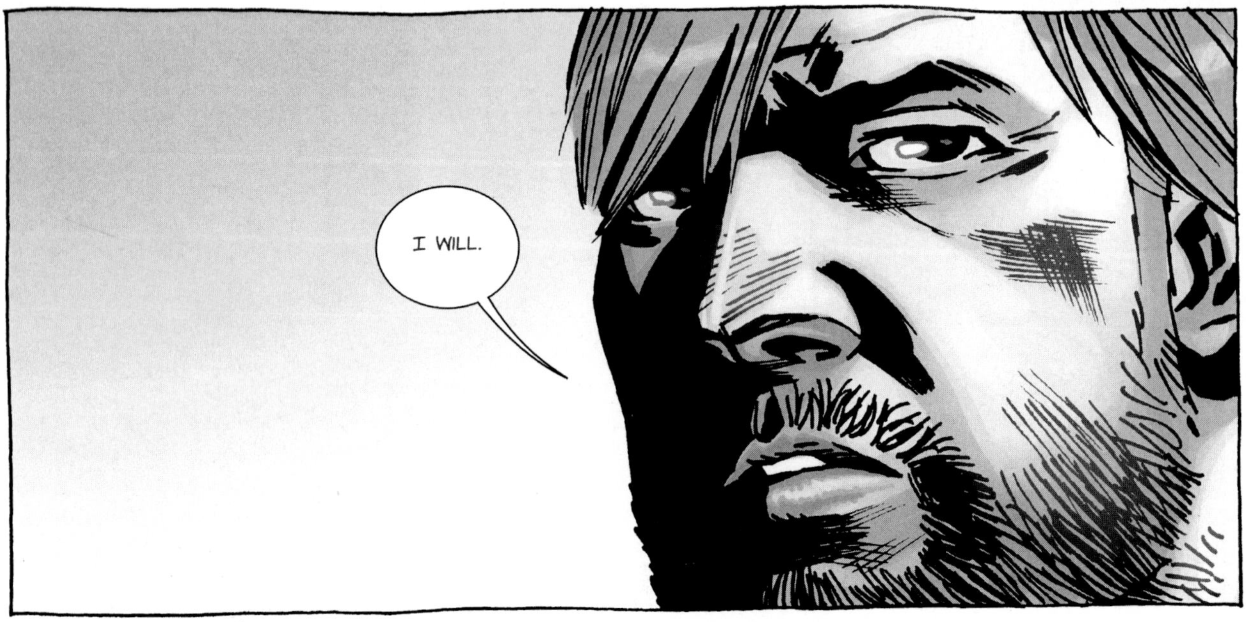
I WILL.

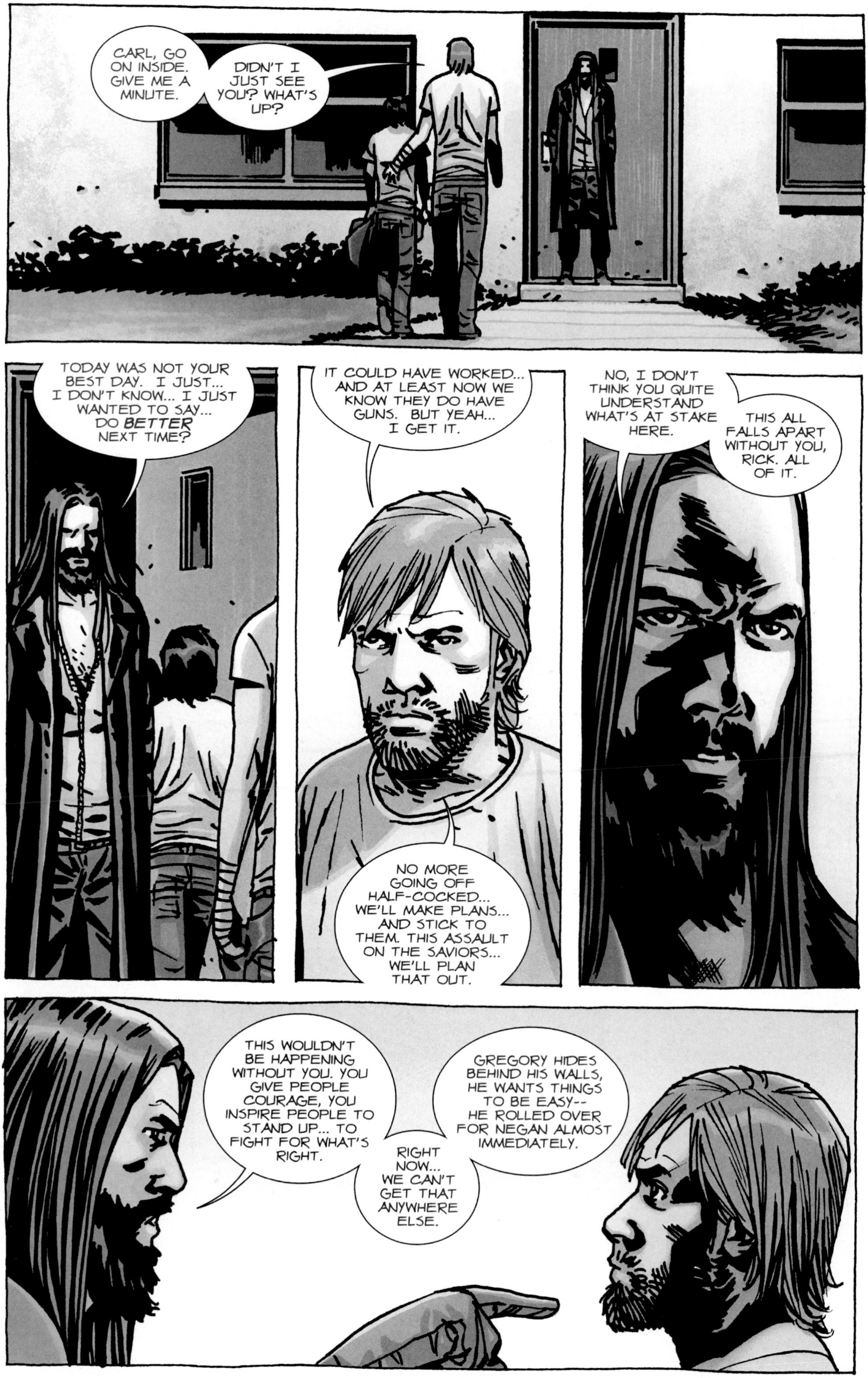
CARL, GO ON INSIDE. GIVE ME A MINUTE.
DIDN'T I JUST SEE YOU? WHAT'S UP?
TODAY WAS NOT YOUR BEST DAY. I JUST... I DON'T KNOW... I JUST WANTED TO SAY... DO BETTER NEXT TIME?
IT COULD HAVE WORKED... AND AT LEAST NOW WE KNOW THEY DO HAVE GUNS. BUT YEAH... I GET IT.
NO MORE GOING OFF HALF-COCKED... WE'LL MAKE PLANS... AND STICK TO THEM. THIS ASSAULT ON THE SAVIORS... WE'LL PLAN THAT OUT.
NO, I DON'T THINK YOU QUITE UNDERSTAND WHAT'S AT STAKE HERE.
THIS ALL FALLS APART WITHOUT YOU, RICK. ALL OF IT.
THIS WOULDN'T BE HAPPENING WITHOUT YOU. YOU GIVE PEOPLE COURAGE, YOU INSPIRE PEOPLE TO STAND UP... TO FIGHT FOR WHAT'S RIGHT.
GREGORY HIDES BEHIND HIS WALLS, HE WANTS THINGS TO BE EASY-- HE ROLLED OVER FOR NEGAN ALMOST IMMEDIATELY.
RIGHT NOW... WE CAN'T GET THAT ANYWHERE ELSE.

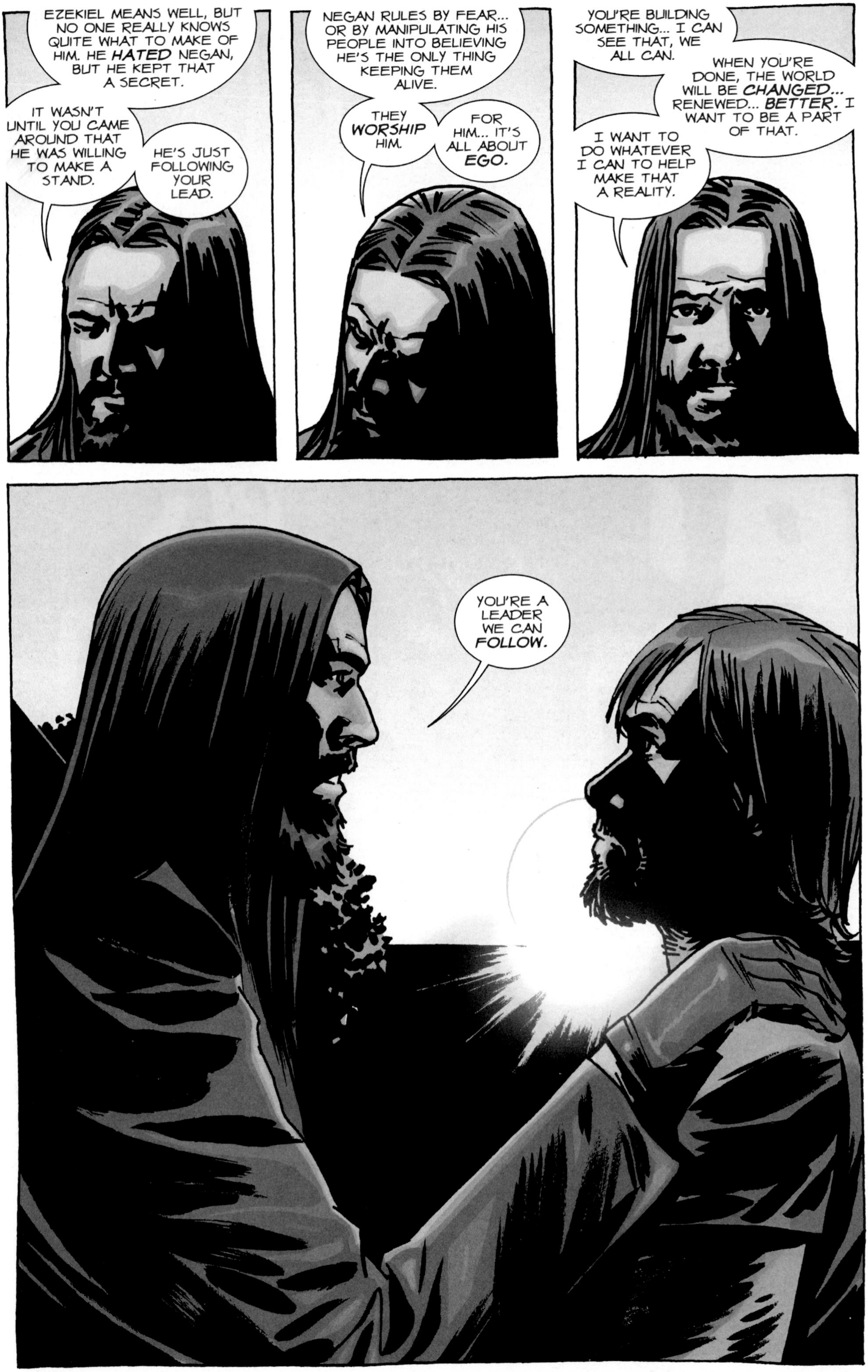
EZEKIEL MEANS WELL, BUT NO ONE REALLY KNOWS QUITE WHAT TO MAKE OF HIM. HE HATED NEGAN, BUT HE KEPT THAT A SECRET.
IT WASN'T UNTIL YOU CAME AROUND THAT HE WAS WILLING TO MAKE A STAND.
HE'S JUST FOLLOWING YOUR LEAD.
NEGAN RULES BY FEAR... OR BY MANIPULATING HIS PEOPLE INTO BELIEVING HE'S THE ONLY THING KEEPING THEM ALIVE.
THEY WORSHIP HIM.
FOR HIM... IT'S ALL ABOUT EGO.
YOU'RE BUILDING SOMETHING... I CAN SEE THAT, WE ALL CAN.
WHEN YOU'RE DONE, THE WORLD WILL BE CHANGED... RENEWED... BETTER. I WANT TO BE A PART OF THAT.
I WANT TO DO WHATEVER I CAN TO HELP MAKE THAT A REALITY.
YOU'RE A LEADER WE CAN FOLLOW.

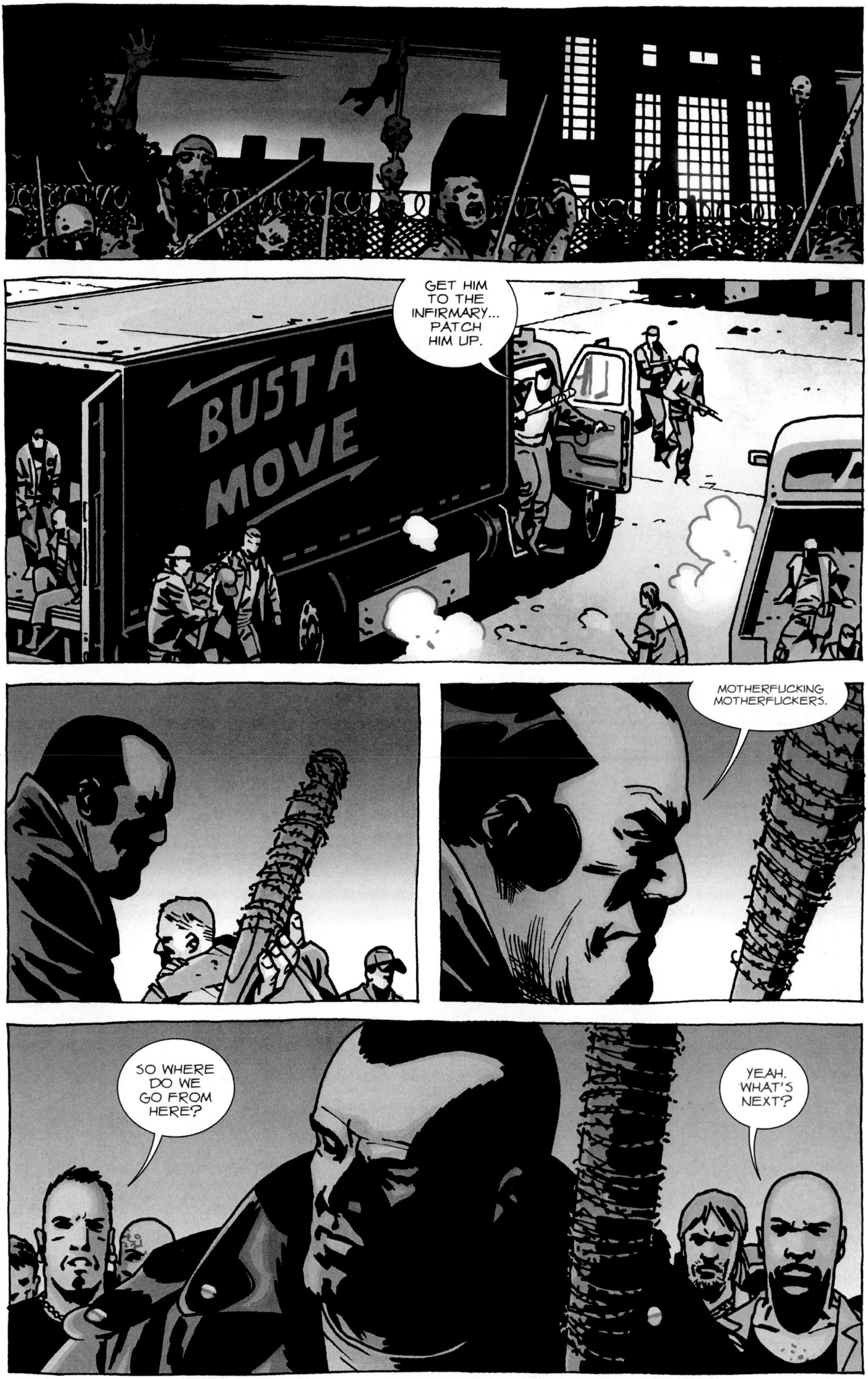
BUST A MOVE
GET HIM TO THE INFIRMARY... PATCH HIM UP.
MOTHERFUCKING MOTHERFUCKERS.
SO WHERE DO WE GO FROM HERE?
YEAH. WHAT'S NEXT?

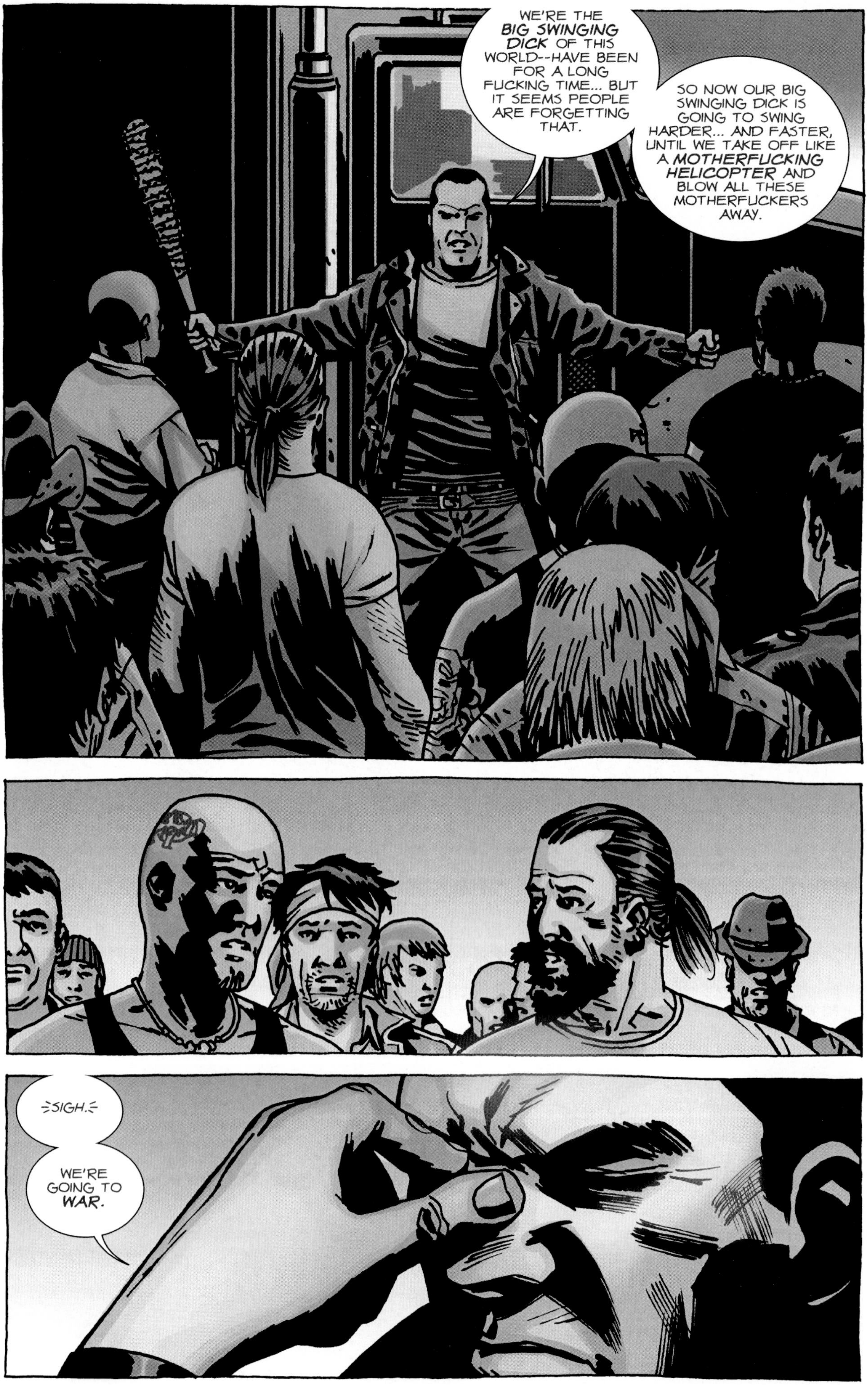
WE'RE THE BIG SWINGING DICK OF THIS WORLD--HAVE BEEN FOR A LONG FUCKING TIME... BUT IT SEEMS PEOPLE ARE FORGETTING THAT.
SO NOW OUR BIG SWINGING DICK IS GOING TO SWING HARDER... AND FASTER, UNTIL WE TAKE OFF LIKE A MOTHERFUCKING HELICOPTER AND BLOW ALL THESE MOTHERFUCKERS AWAY.
SIGH.
WE'RE GOING TO WAR.

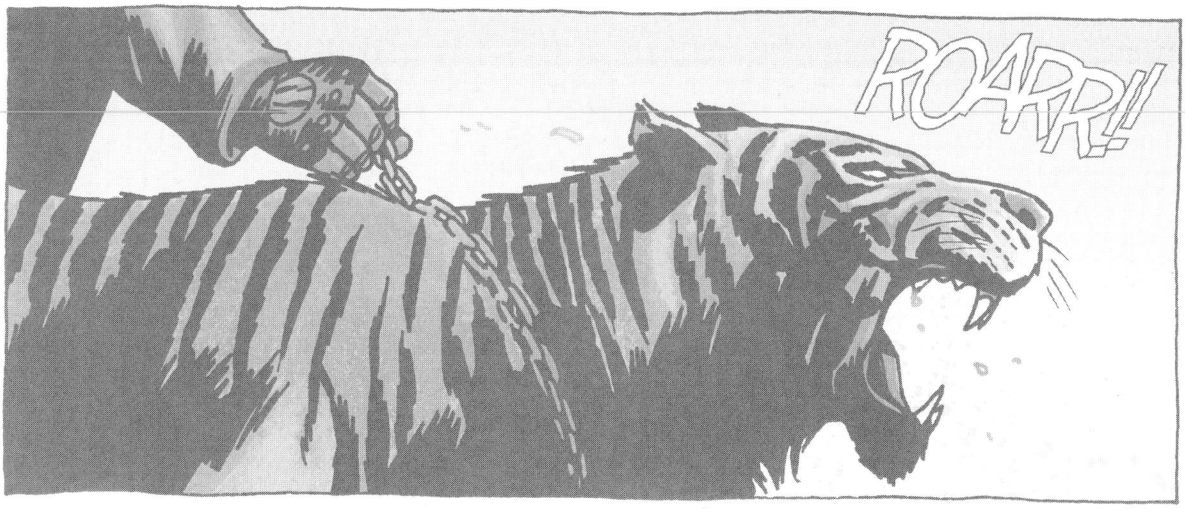
ROARR!!

Chapter Twenty:
All Out War Part One

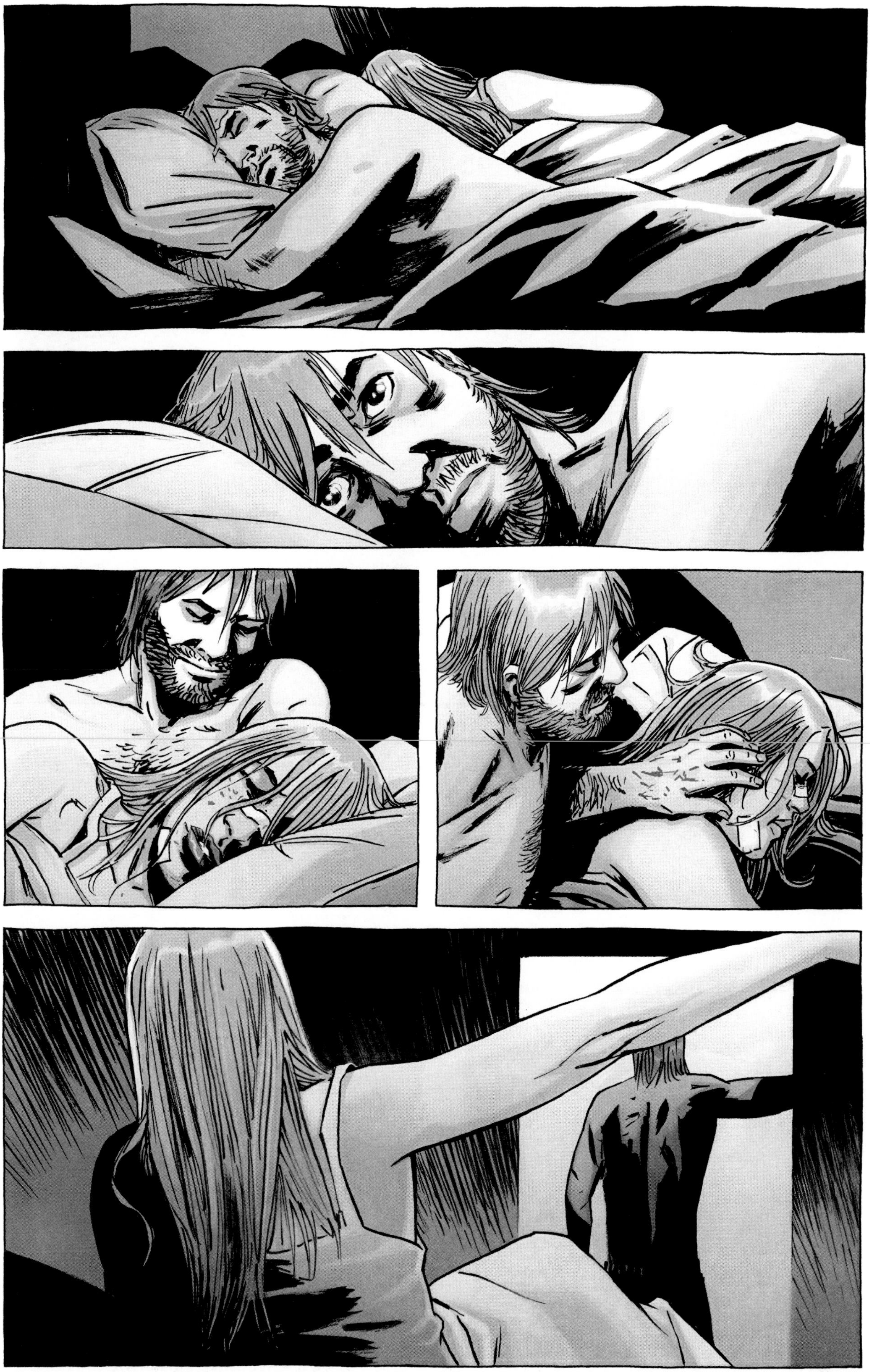

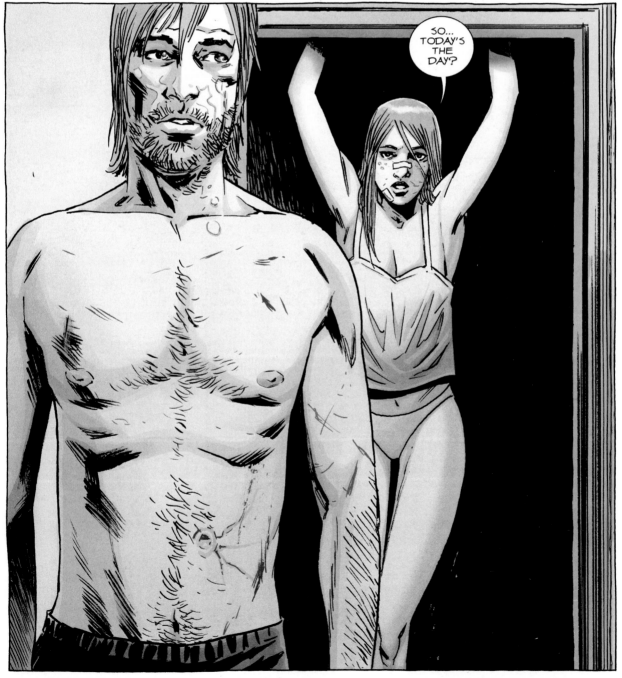

SO...
TODAY'S
THE
DAY?

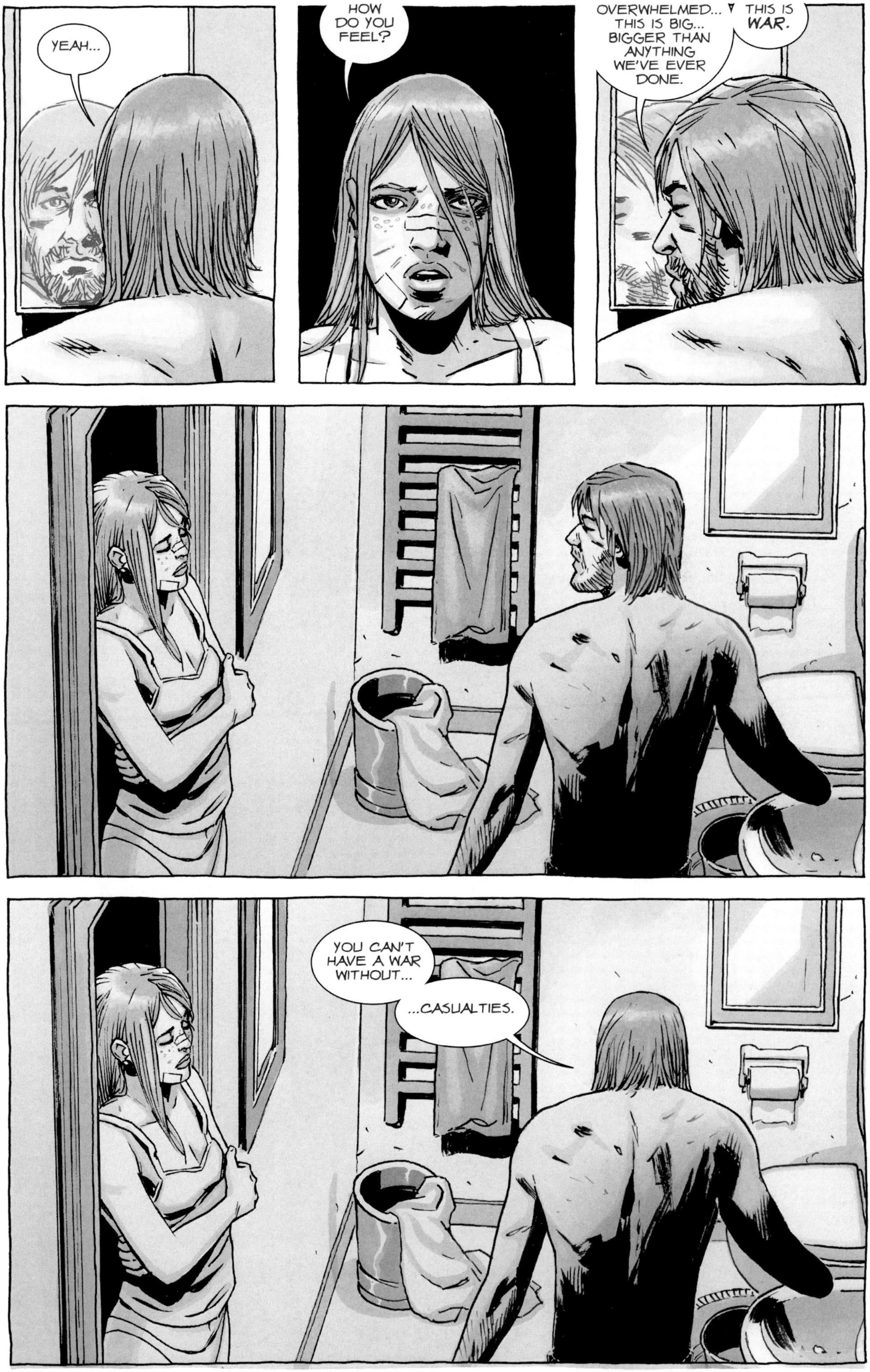
YEAH...
HOW DO YOU FEEL?
OVERWHELMED... THIS IS BIG... BIGGER THAN ANYTHING WE'VE EVER DONE.
THIS IS WAR.
YOU CAN'T HAVE A WAR WITHOUT...
...CASUALTIES.

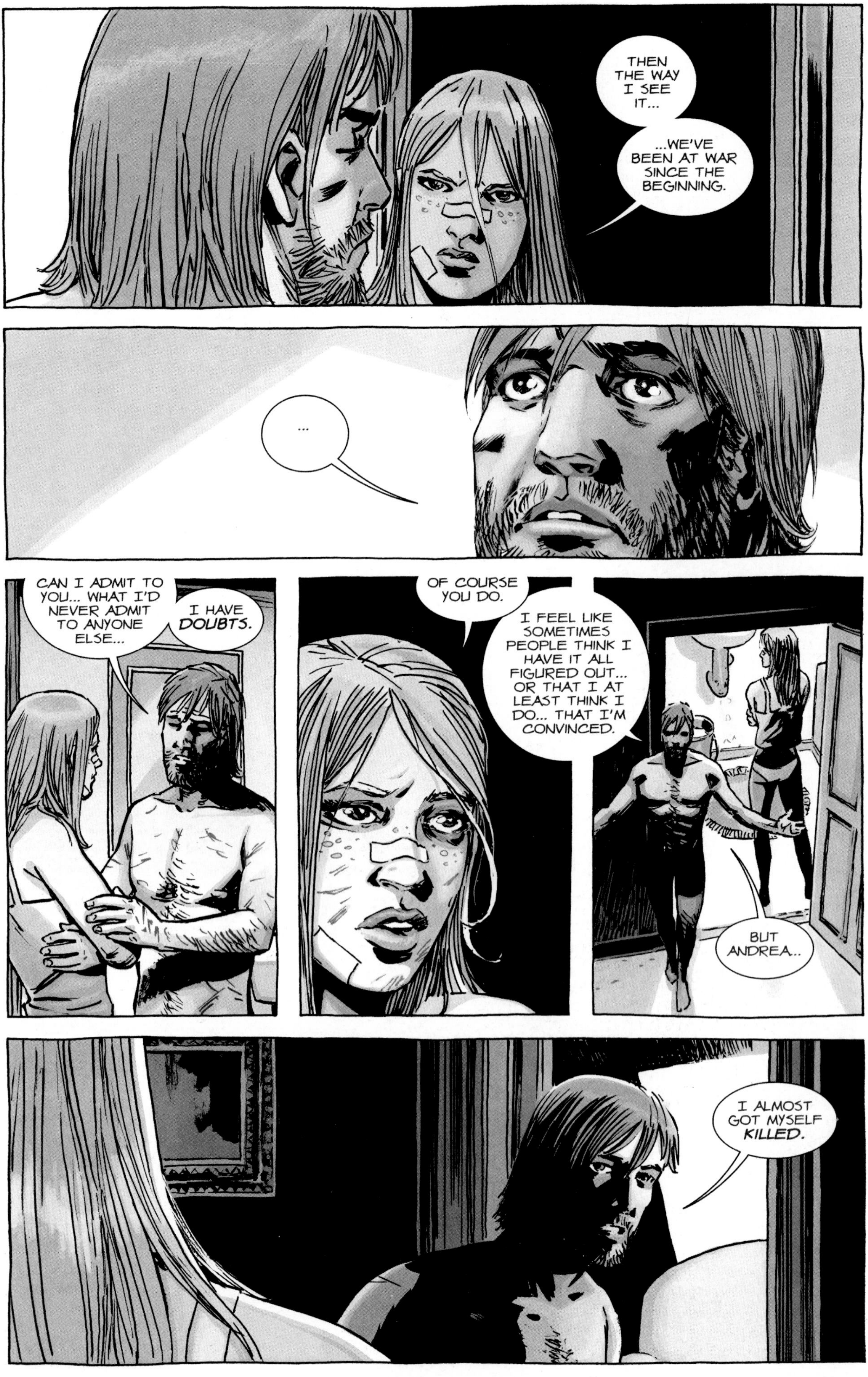
THEN THE WAY I SEE IT...
...WE'VE BEEN AT WAR SINCE THE BEGINNING.
...
CAN I ADMIT TO YOU... WHAT I'D NEVER ADMIT TO ANYONE ELSE...
I HAVE *DOUBTS.*
OF COURSE YOU DO.
I FEEL LIKE SOMETIMES PEOPLE THINK I HAVE IT ALL FIGURED OUT... OR THAT I AT LEAST THINK I DO... THAT I'M CONVINCED.
BUT ANDREA...
I ALMOST GOT MYSELF *KILLED.*

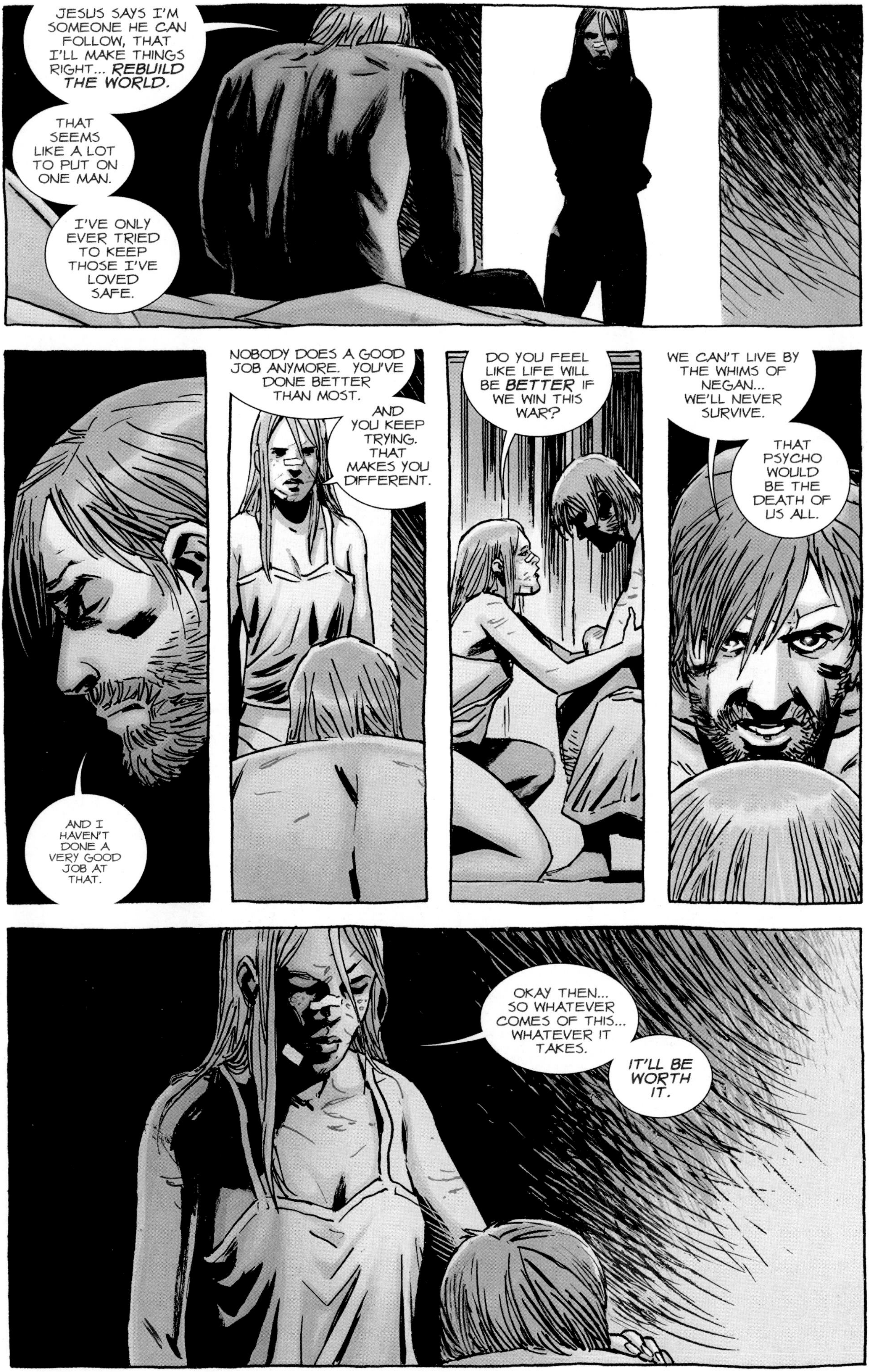
JESUS SAYS I'M SOMEONE HE CAN FOLLOW, THAT I'LL MAKE THINGS RIGHT... REBUILD THE WORLD.
THAT SEEMS LIKE A LOT TO PUT ON ONE MAN.
I'VE ONLY EVER TRIED TO KEEP THOSE I'VE LOVED SAFE.
AND I HAVEN'T DONE A VERY GOOD JOB AT THAT.
NOBODY DOES A GOOD JOB ANYMORE. YOU'VE DONE BETTER THAN MOST.
AND YOU KEEP TRYING. THAT MAKES YOU DIFFERENT.
DO YOU FEEL LIKE LIFE WILL BE BETTER IF WE WIN THIS WAR?
WE CAN'T LIVE BY THE WHIMS OF NEGAN... WE'LL NEVER SURVIVE.
THAT PSYCHO WOULD BE THE DEATH OF US ALL.
OKAY THEN... SO WHATEVER COMES OF THIS... WHATEVER IT TAKES.
IT'LL BE WORTH IT.

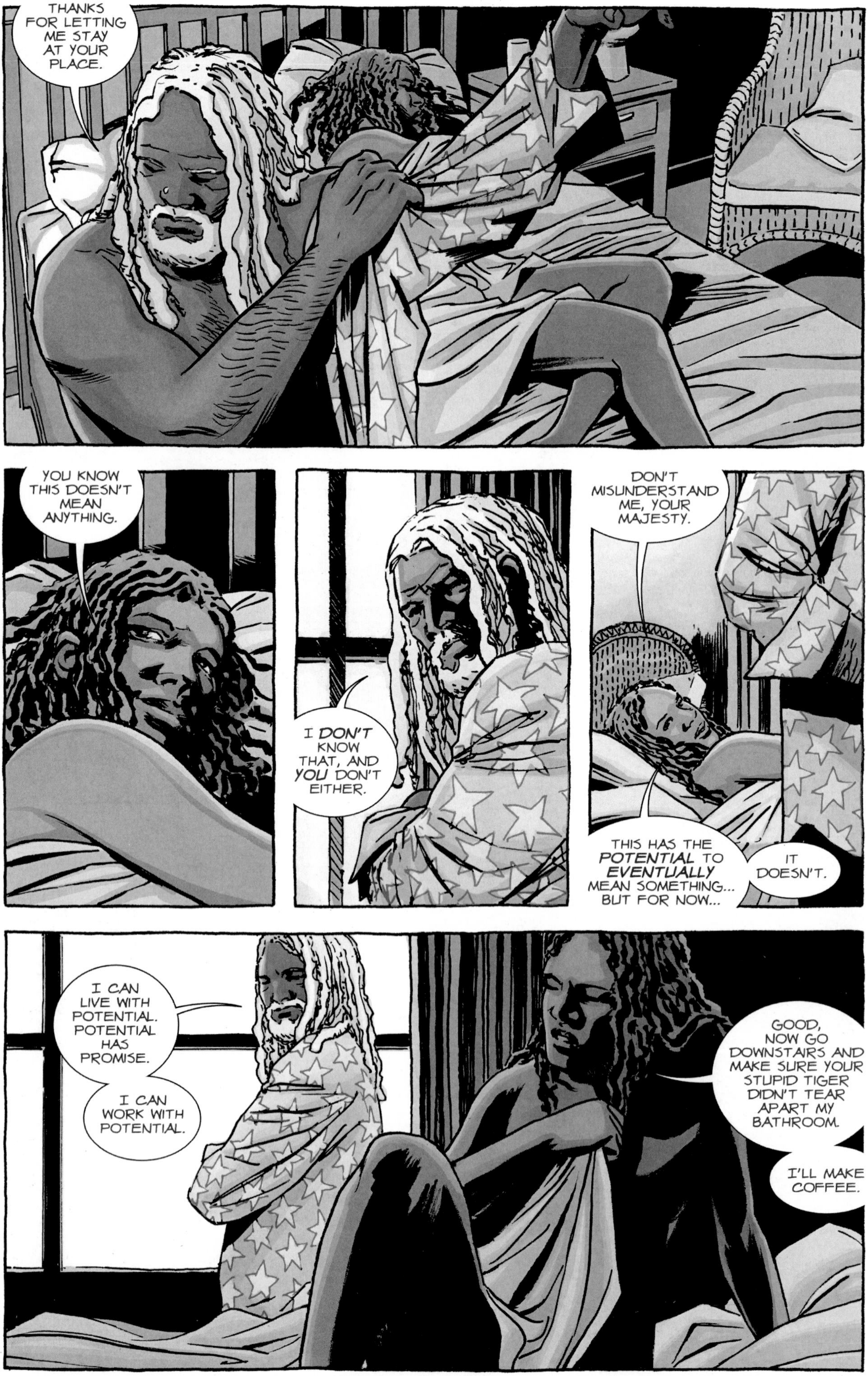
THANKS FOR LETTING ME STAY AT YOUR PLACE.
YOU KNOW THIS DOESN'T MEAN ANYTHING.
I DON'T KNOW THAT, AND YOU DON'T EITHER.
DON'T MISUNDERSTAND ME, YOUR MAJESTY.
THIS HAS THE POTENTIAL TO EVENTUALLY MEAN SOMETHING... BUT FOR NOW...
IT DOESN'T.
I CAN LIVE WITH POTENTIAL. POTENTIAL HAS PROMISE.
I CAN WORK WITH POTENTIAL.
GOOD, NOW GO DOWNSTAIRS AND MAKE SURE YOUR STUPID TIGER DIDN'T TEAR APART MY BATHROOM.
I'LL MAKE COFFEE.

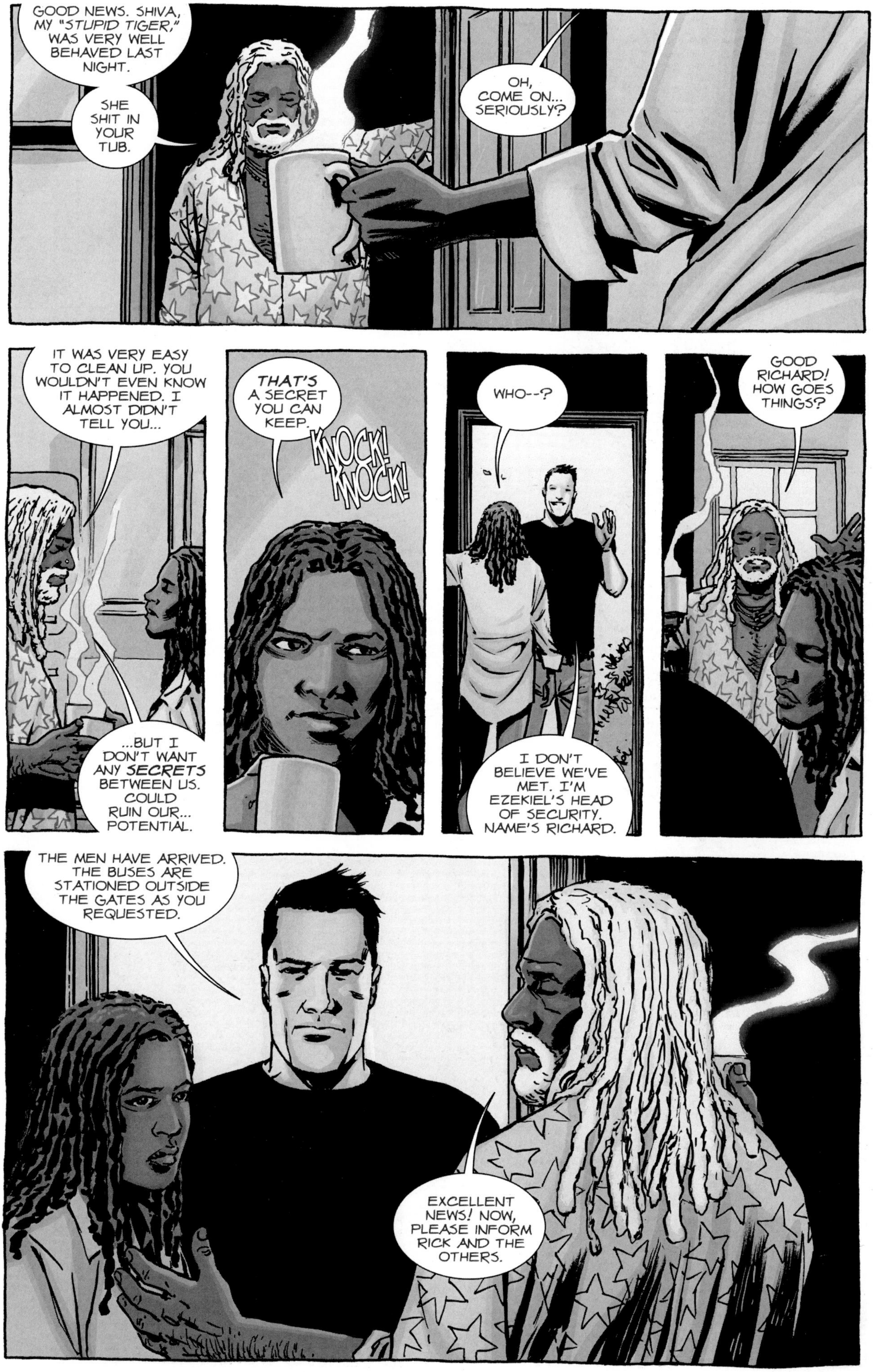
GOOD NEWS. SHIVA, MY "STUPID TIGER," WAS VERY WELL BEHAVED LAST NIGHT.
SHE SHIT IN YOUR TUB.
OH, COME ON... SERIOUSLY?
IT WAS VERY EASY TO CLEAN UP. YOU WOULDN'T EVEN KNOW IT HAPPENED. I ALMOST DIDN'T TELL YOU...
...BUT I DON'T WANT ANY SECRETS BETWEEN US. COULD RUIN OUR... POTENTIAL.
THAT'S A SECRET YOU CAN KEEP.
KNOCK! KNOCK!
WHO--?
I DON'T BELIEVE WE'VE MET. I'M EZEKIEL'S HEAD OF SECURITY. NAME'S RICHARD.
GOOD RICHARD! HOW GOES THINGS?
THE MEN HAVE ARRIVED. THE BUSES ARE STATIONED OUTSIDE THE GATES AS YOU REQUESTED.
EXCELLENT NEWS! NOW, PLEASE INFORM RICK AND THE OTHERS.

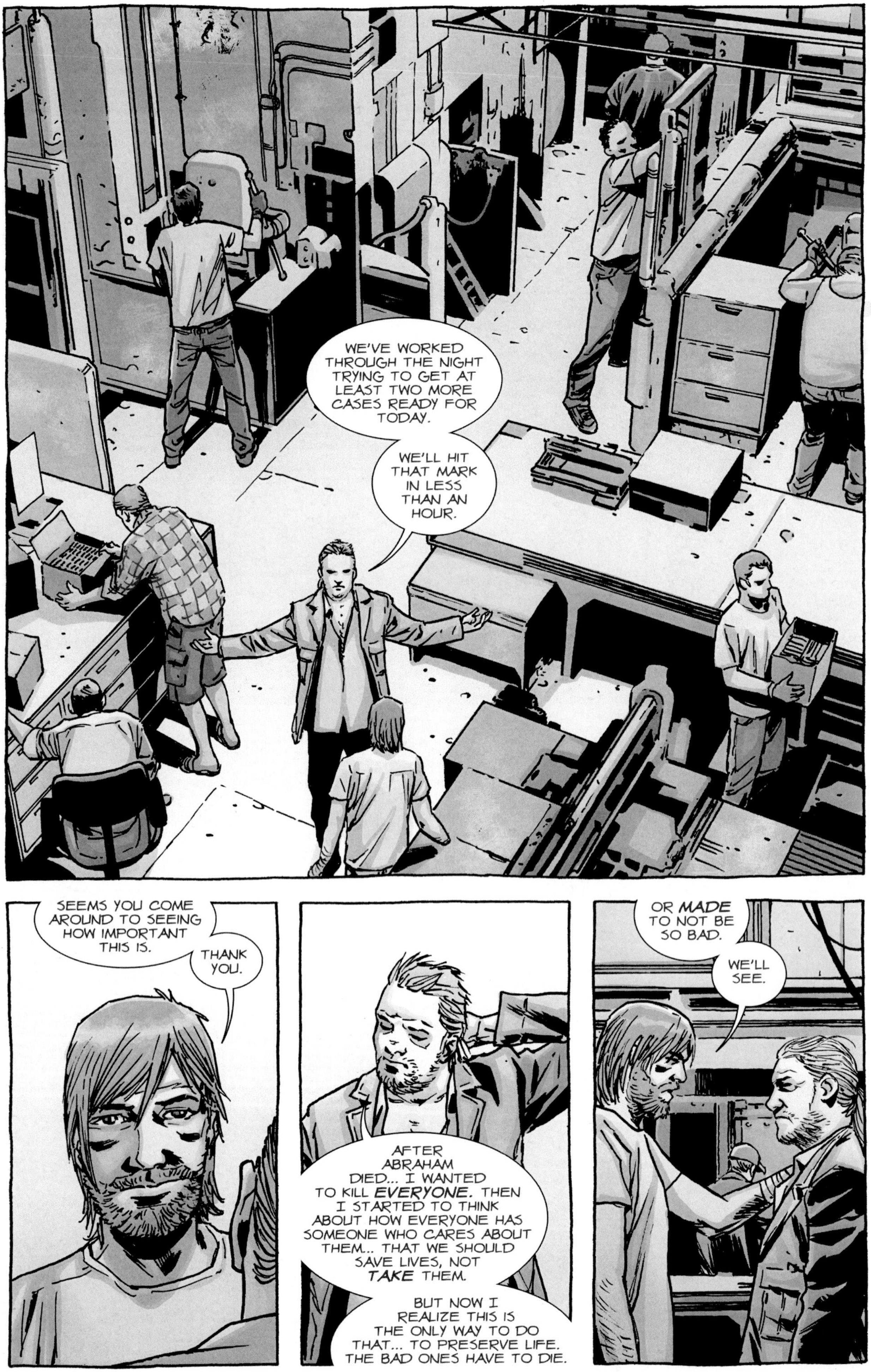
WE'VE WORKED THROUGH THE NIGHT TRYING TO GET AT LEAST TWO MORE CASES READY FOR TODAY.
WE'LL HIT THAT MARK IN LESS THAN AN HOUR.
SEEMS YOU COME AROUND TO SEEING HOW IMPORTANT THIS IS.
THANK YOU.
AFTER ABRAHAM DIED... I WANTED TO KILL EVERYONE. THEN I STARTED TO THINK ABOUT HOW EVERYONE HAS SOMEONE WHO CARES ABOUT THEM... THAT WE SHOULD SAVE LIVES, NOT TAKE THEM.
BUT NOW I REALIZE THIS IS THE ONLY WAY TO DO THAT... TO PRESERVE LIFE. THE BAD ONES HAVE TO DIE.
OR MADE TO NOT BE SO BAD.
WE'LL SEE.

TAKE AS MUCH TIME AS YOU NEED.

THANK YOU, FATHER.

I WANTED TO CALL THIS MEETING TO MAKE SURE THERE WEREN'T ANY LAST MINUTE DETAILS WE WERE OVERLOOKING BEFORE WE DO THIS.

ALL OUR PEOPLE ARE GATHERED, THE SUPPLIES ARE LOADED... WE'RE PREPARED TO MOVE.

MY PEOPLE ARE HERE... WE'RE READY TO GO.

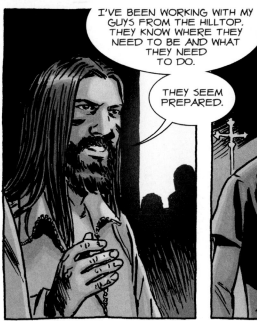

I'VE BEEN WORKING WITH MY GUYS FROM THE HILLTOP. THEY KNOW WHERE THEY NEED TO BE AND WHAT THEY NEED TO DO.

THEY SEEM PREPARED.

GOOD... LET'S GO OVER THE PLAN ONE MORE TIME...

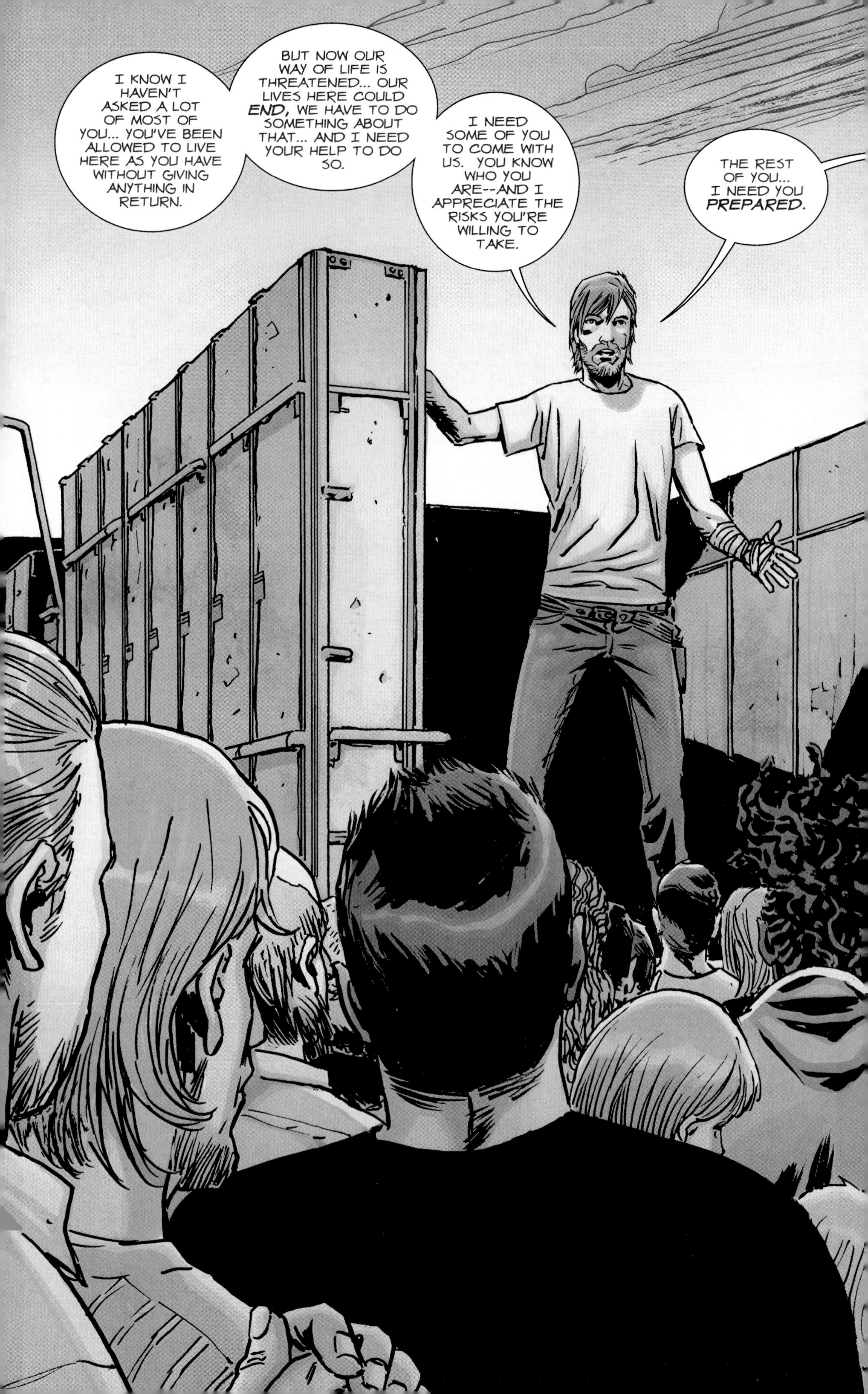
I KNOW I HAVEN'T ASKED A LOT OF MOST OF YOU... YOU'VE BEEN ALLOWED TO LIVE HERE AS YOU HAVE WITHOUT GIVING ANYTHING IN RETURN.
BUT NOW OUR WAY OF LIFE IS THREATENED... OUR LIVES HERE COULD *END,* WE HAVE TO DO SOMETHING ABOUT THAT... AND I NEED YOUR HELP TO DO SO.
I NEED SOME OF YOU TO COME WITH US. YOU KNOW WHO YOU ARE--AND I APPRECIATE THE RISKS YOU'RE WILLING TO TAKE.
THE REST OF YOU... I NEED YOU *PREPARED.*

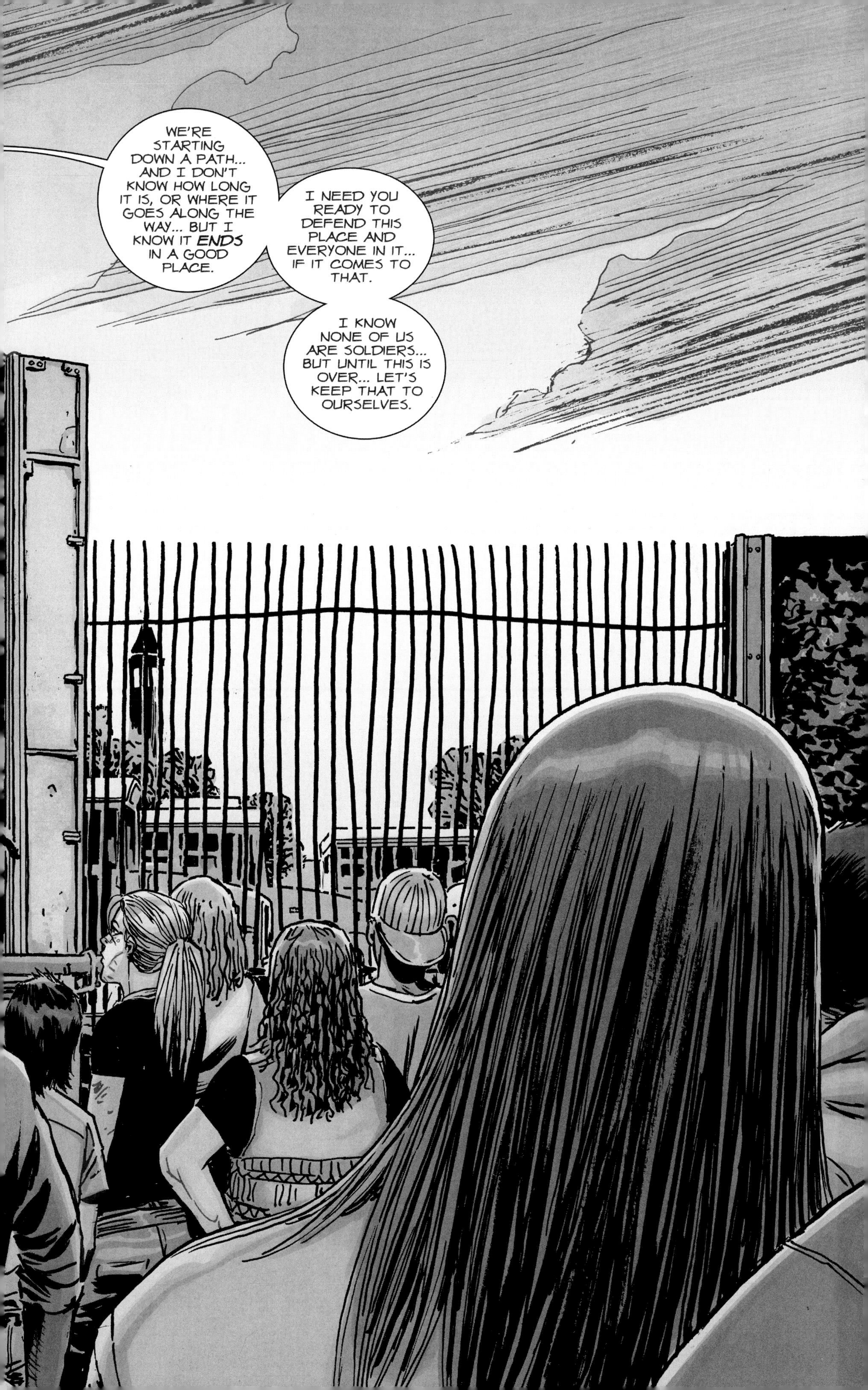
WE'RE STARTING DOWN A PATH... AND I DON'T KNOW HOW LONG IT IS, OR WHERE IT GOES ALONG THE WAY... BUT I KNOW IT ENDS IN A GOOD PLACE.
I NEED YOU READY TO DEFEND THIS PLACE AND EVERYONE IN IT... IF IT COMES TO THAT.
I KNOW NONE OF US ARE SOLDIERS... BUT UNTIL THIS IS OVER... LET'S KEEP THAT TO OURSELVES.

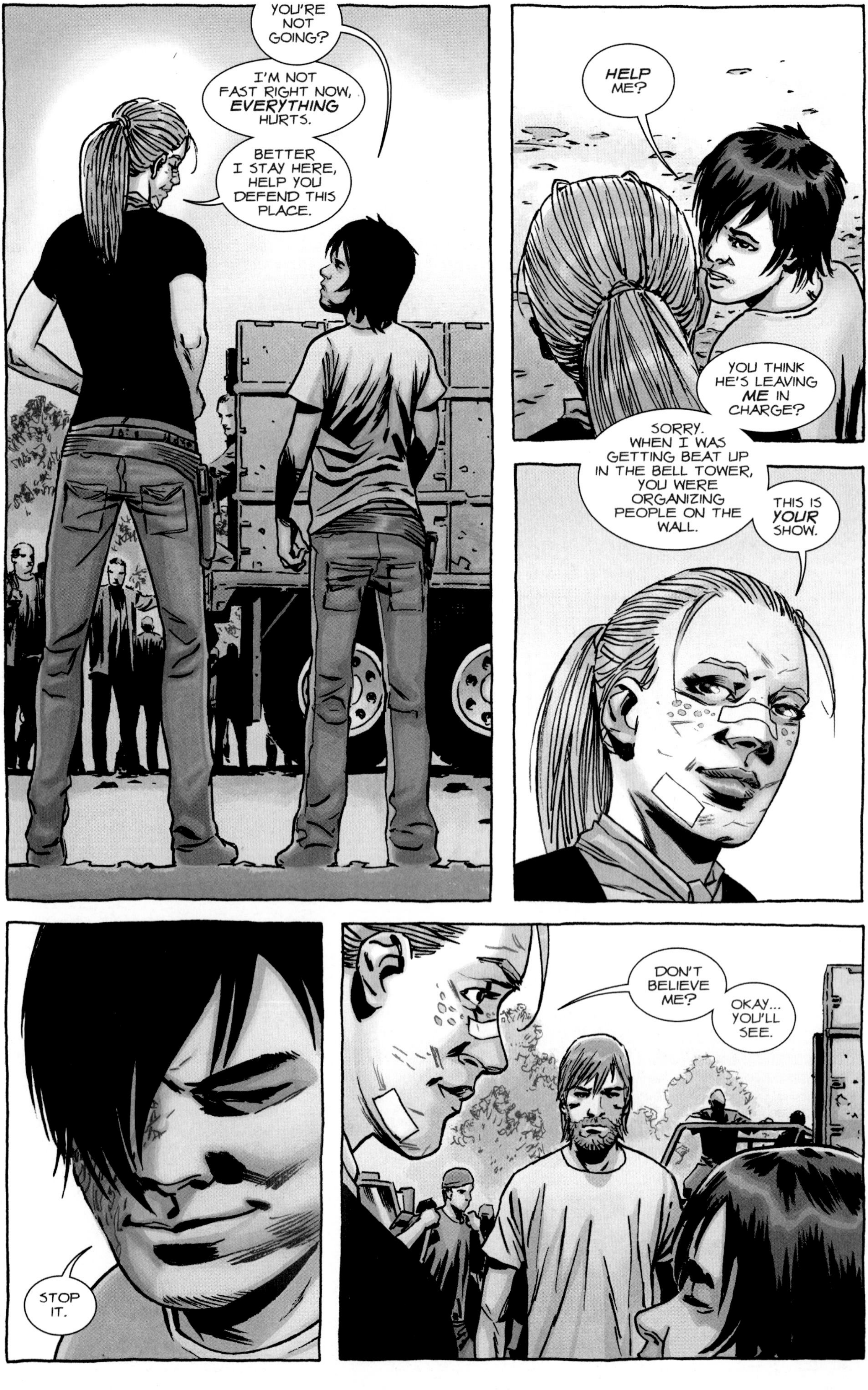
YOU'RE NOT GOING?
I'M NOT FAST RIGHT NOW, EVERYTHING HURTS.
BETTER I STAY HERE, HELP YOU DEFEND THIS PLACE.
HELP ME?
YOU THINK HE'S LEAVING ME IN CHARGE?
SORRY. WHEN I WAS GETTING BEAT UP IN THE BELL TOWER, YOU WERE ORGANIZING PEOPLE ON THE WALL.
THIS IS YOUR SHOW.
STOP IT.
DON'T BELIEVE ME?
OKAY... YOU'LL SEE.

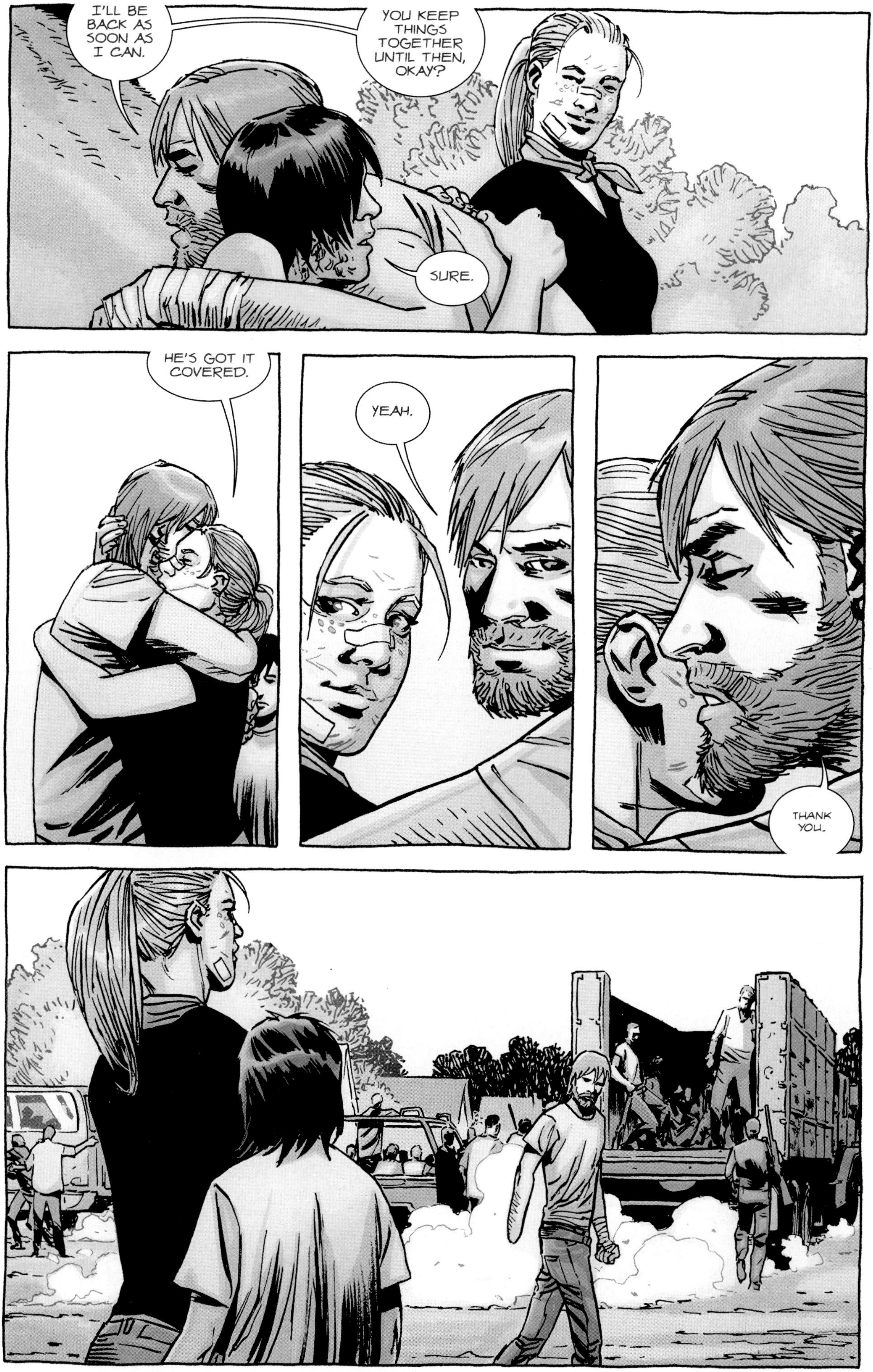
I'LL BE BACK AS SOON AS I CAN.
YOU KEEP THINGS TOGETHER UNTIL THEN, OKAY?
SURE.
HE'S GOT IT COVERED.
YEAH.
THANK YOU.

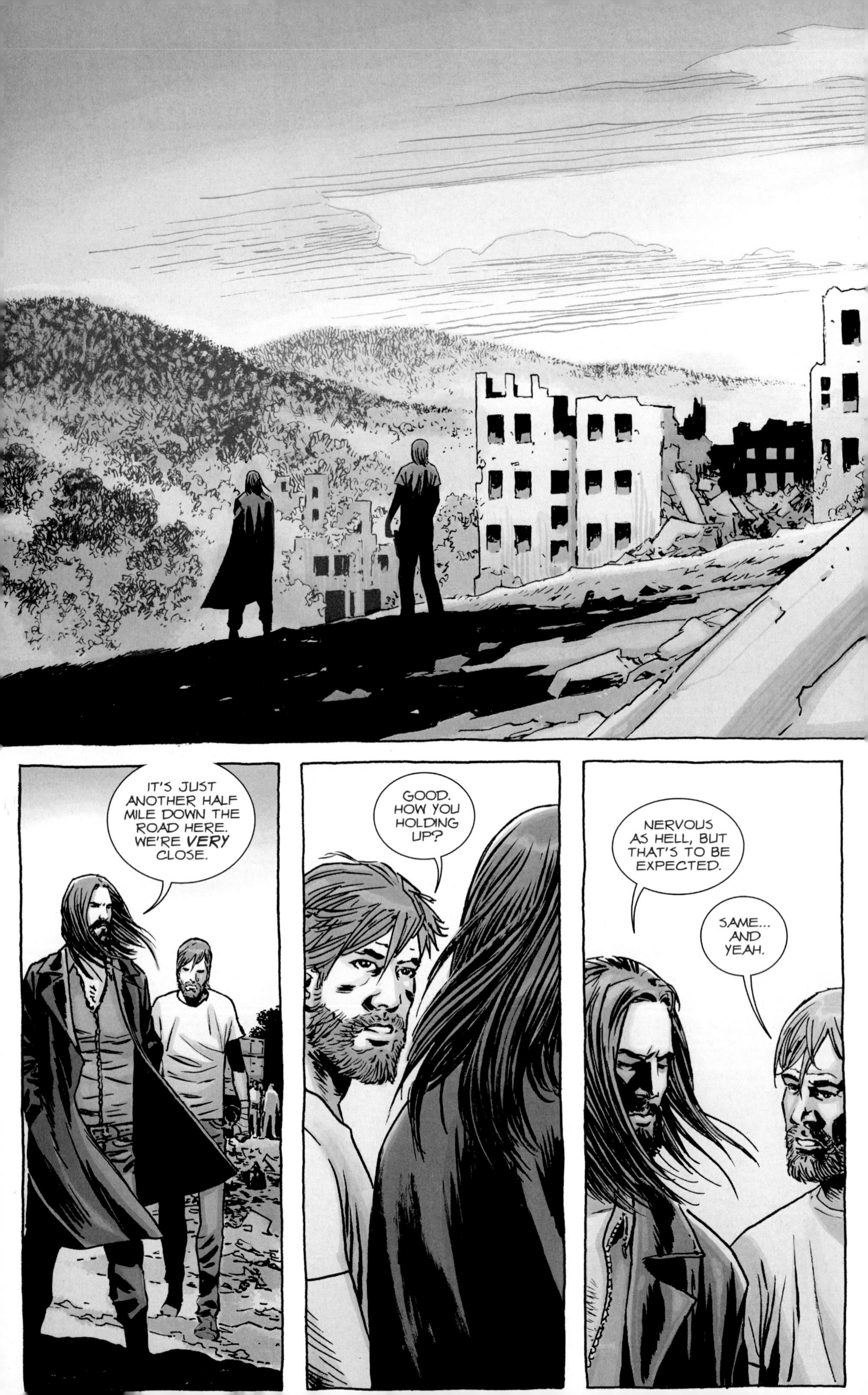
IT'S JUST ANOTHER HALF MILE DOWN THE ROAD HERE. WE'RE *VERY* CLOSE.
GOOD. HOW YOU HOLDING UP?
NERVOUS AS HELL, BUT THAT'S TO BE EXPECTED.
SAME... AND YEAH.

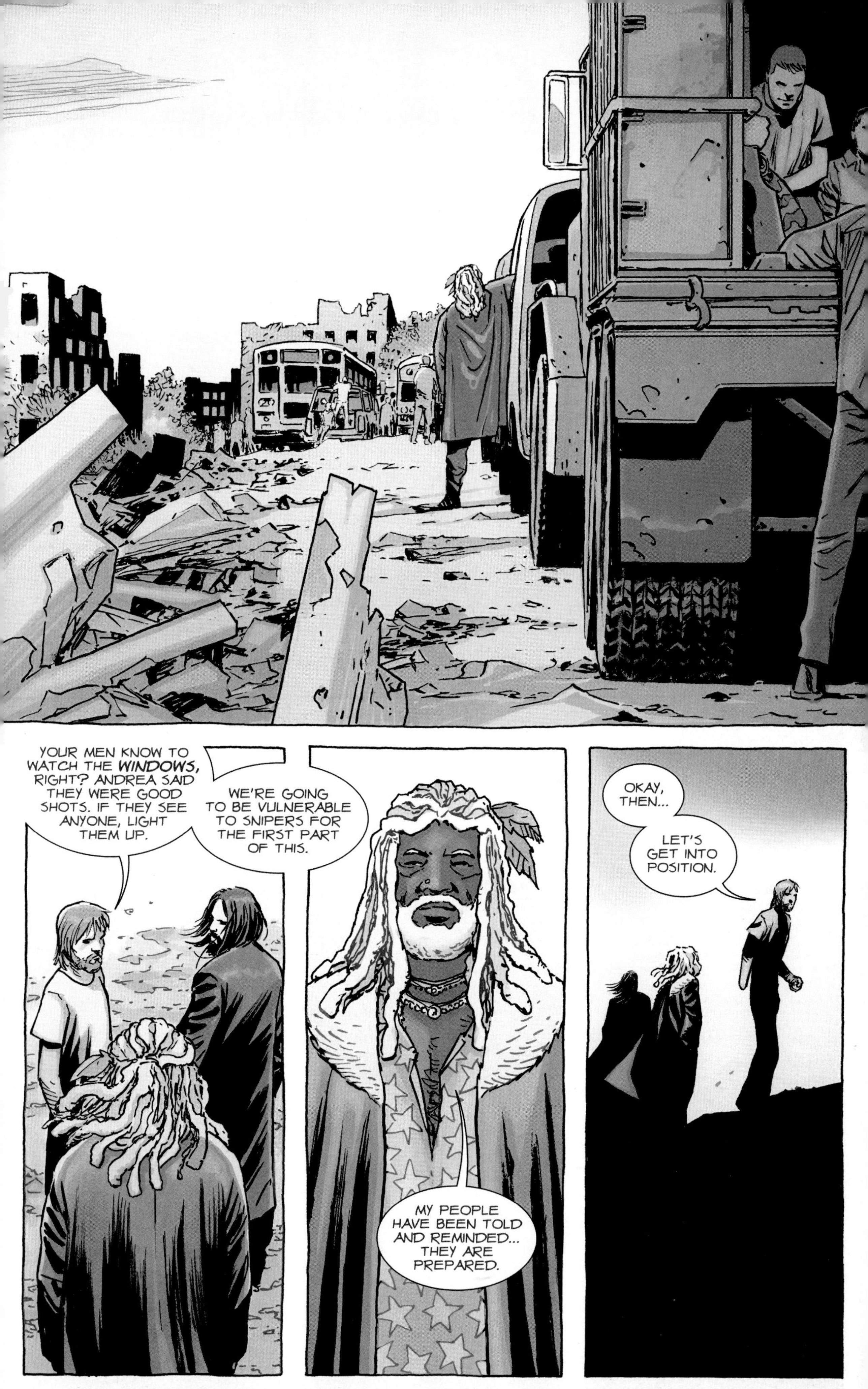
YOUR MEN KNOW TO WATCH THE WINDOWS, RIGHT? ANDREA SAID THEY WERE GOOD SHOTS. IF THEY SEE ANYONE, LIGHT THEM UP.
WE'RE GOING TO BE VULNERABLE TO SNIPERS FOR THE FIRST PART OF THIS.
MY PEOPLE HAVE BEEN TOLD AND REMINDED... THEY ARE PREPARED.
OKAY, THEN...
LET'S GET INTO POSITION.

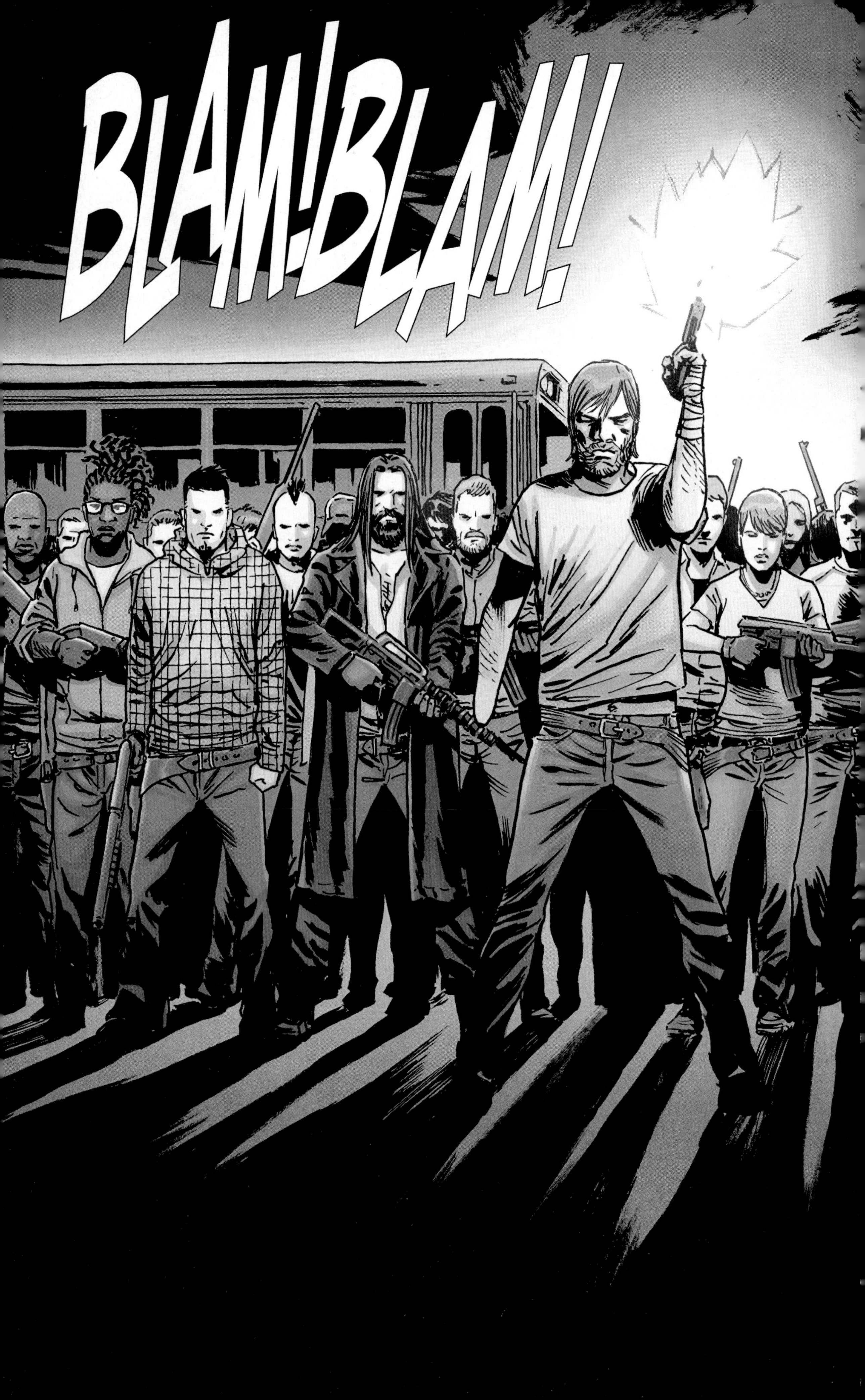
BLAM! BLAM!

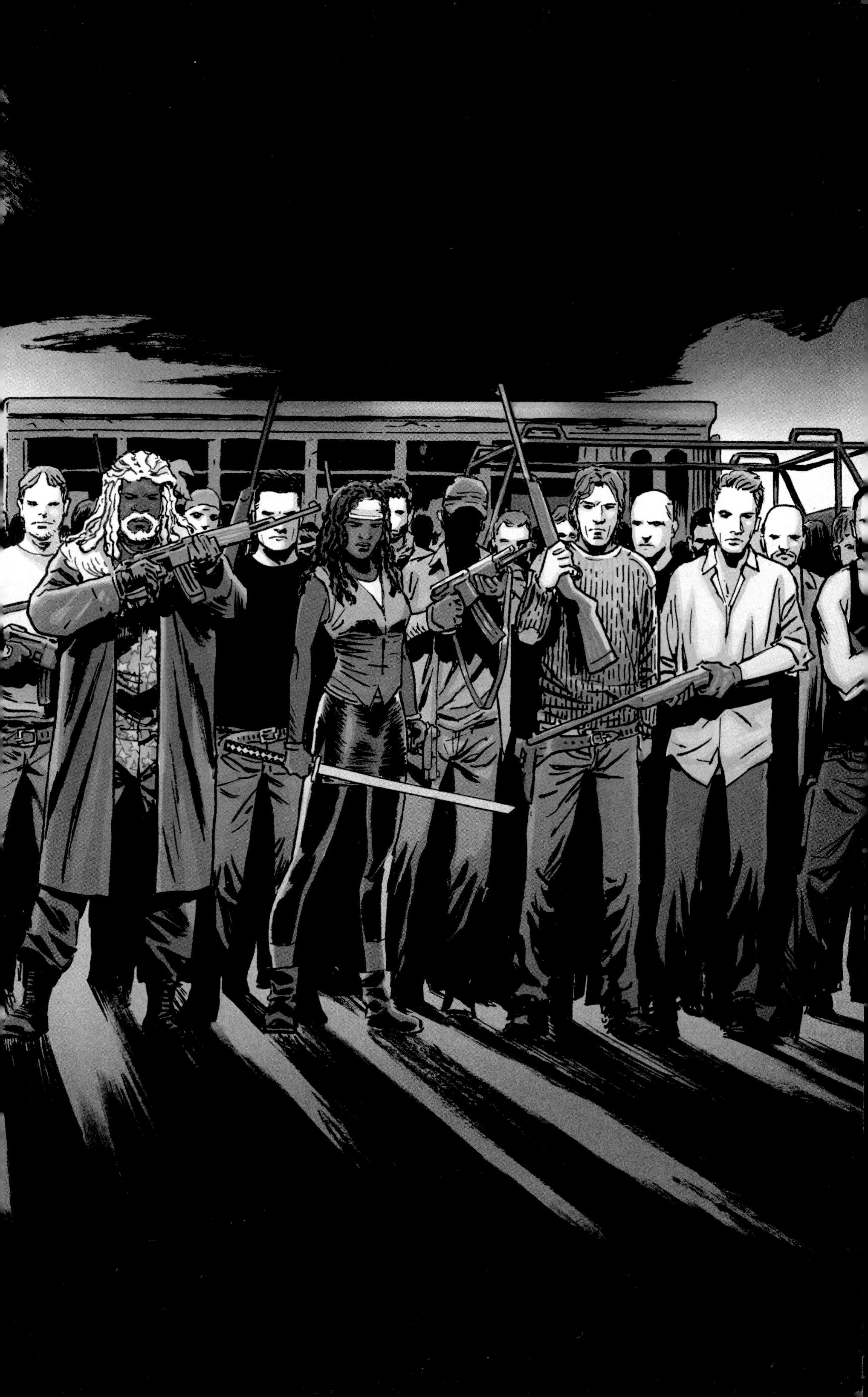

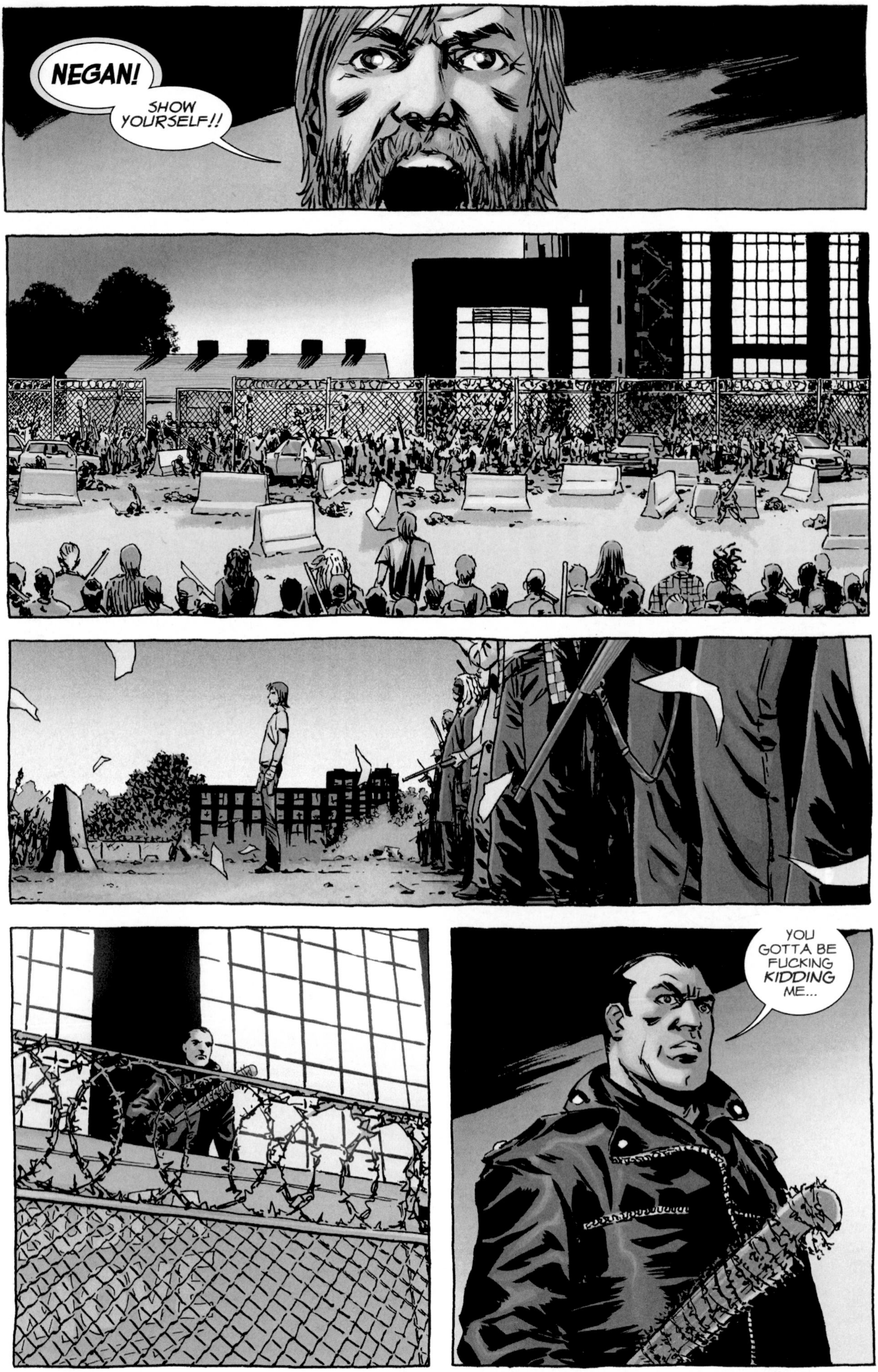

NEGAN!
SHOW YOURSELF!!
YOU GOTTA BE FUCKING KIDDING ME...

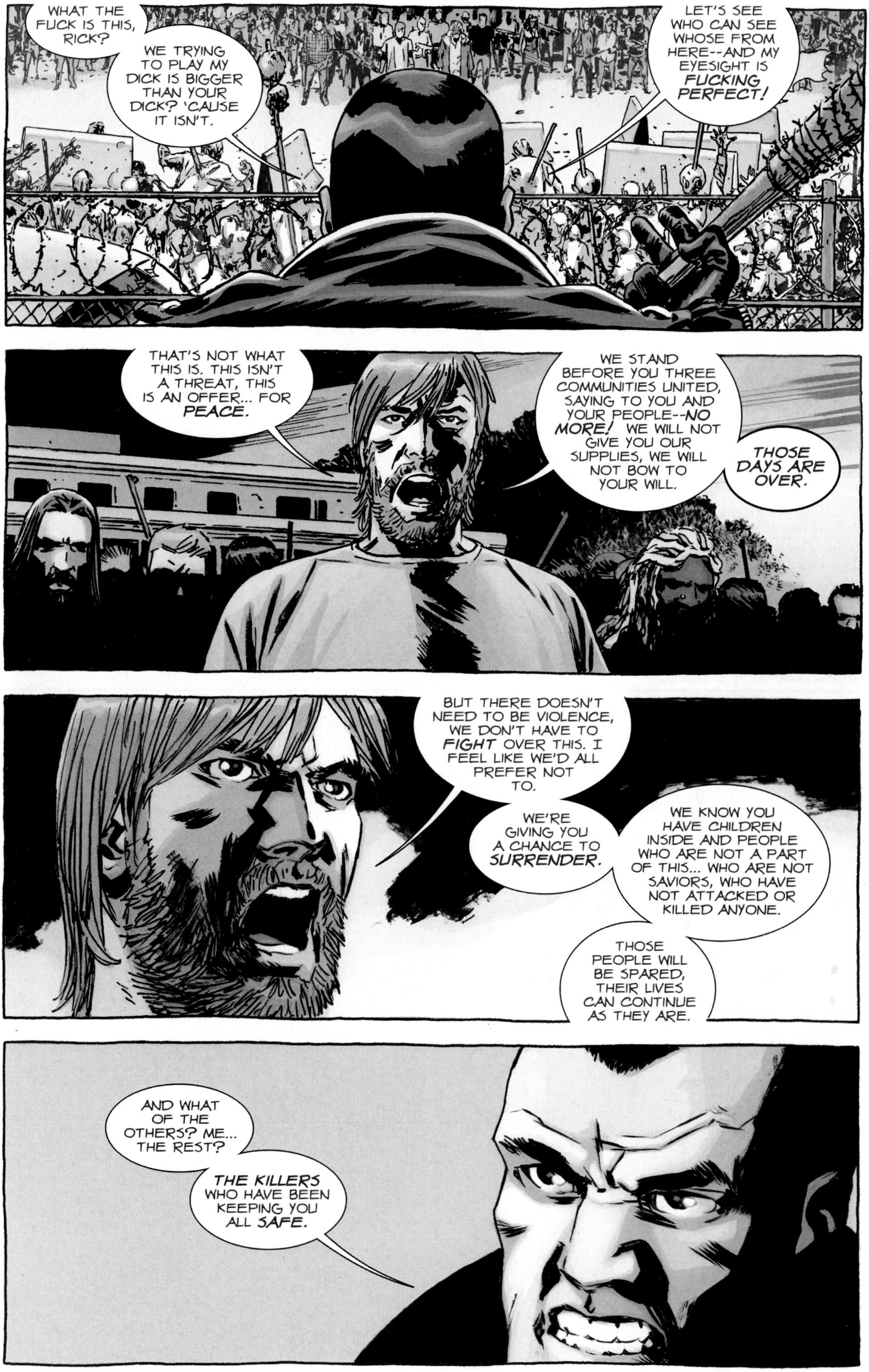
WHAT THE FUCK IS THIS, RICK?
WE TRYING TO PLAY MY DICK IS BIGGER THAN YOUR DICK? 'CAUSE IT ISN'T.
LET'S SEE WHO CAN SEE WHOSE FROM HERE--AND MY EYESIGHT IS FUCKING PERFECT!
THAT'S NOT WHAT THIS IS. THIS ISN'T A THREAT, THIS IS AN OFFER... FOR PEACE.
WE STAND BEFORE YOU THREE COMMUNITIES UNITED, SAYING TO YOU AND YOUR PEOPLE--NO MORE! WE WILL NOT GIVE YOU OUR SUPPLIES, WE WILL NOT BOW TO YOUR WILL.
THOSE DAYS ARE OVER.
BUT THERE DOESN'T NEED TO BE VIOLENCE, WE DON'T HAVE TO FIGHT OVER THIS. I FEEL LIKE WE'D ALL PREFER NOT TO.
WE'RE GIVING YOU A CHANCE TO SURRENDER.
WE KNOW YOU HAVE CHILDREN INSIDE AND PEOPLE WHO ARE NOT A PART OF THIS... WHO ARE NOT SAVIORS, WHO HAVE NOT ATTACKED OR KILLED ANYONE.
THOSE PEOPLE WILL BE SPARED, THEIR LIVES CAN CONTINUE AS THEY ARE.
AND WHAT OF THE OTHERS? ME... THE REST?
THE KILLERS WHO HAVE BEEN KEEPING YOU ALL SAFE.

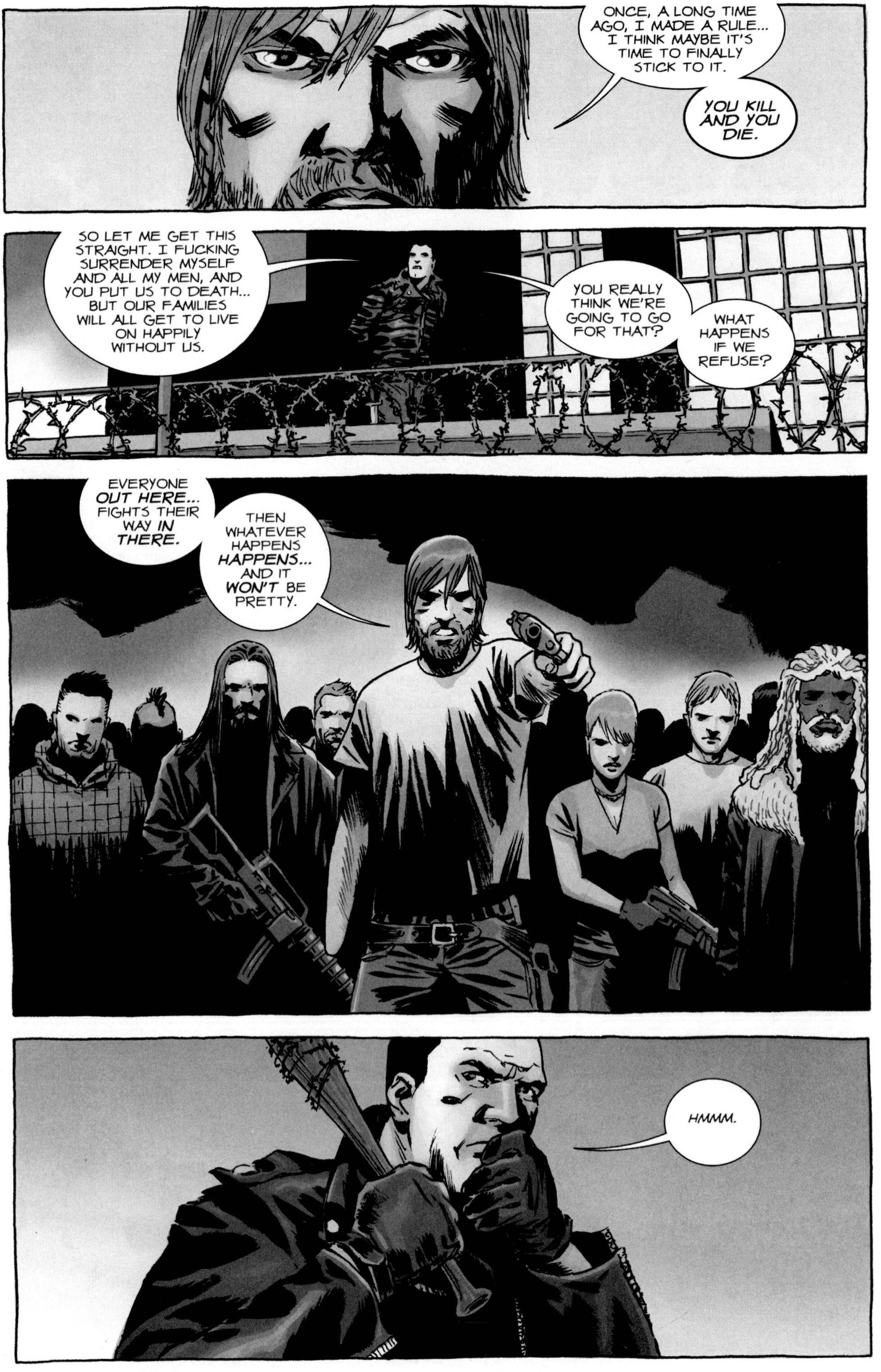
ONCE, A LONG TIME AGO, I MADE A RULE... I THINK MAYBE IT'S TIME TO FINALLY STICK TO IT.
YOU KILL AND YOU DIE.
SO LET ME GET THIS STRAIGHT. I FUCKING SURRENDER MYSELF AND ALL MY MEN, AND YOU PUT US TO DEATH... BUT OUR FAMILIES WILL ALL GET TO LIVE ON HAPPILY WITHOUT US.
YOU REALLY THINK WE'RE GOING TO GO FOR THAT?
WHAT HAPPENS IF WE REFUSE?
EVERYONE OUT HERE... FIGHTS THEIR WAY IN THERE.
THEN WHATEVER HAPPENS HAPPENS... AND IT WON'T BE PRETTY.
HMMM.

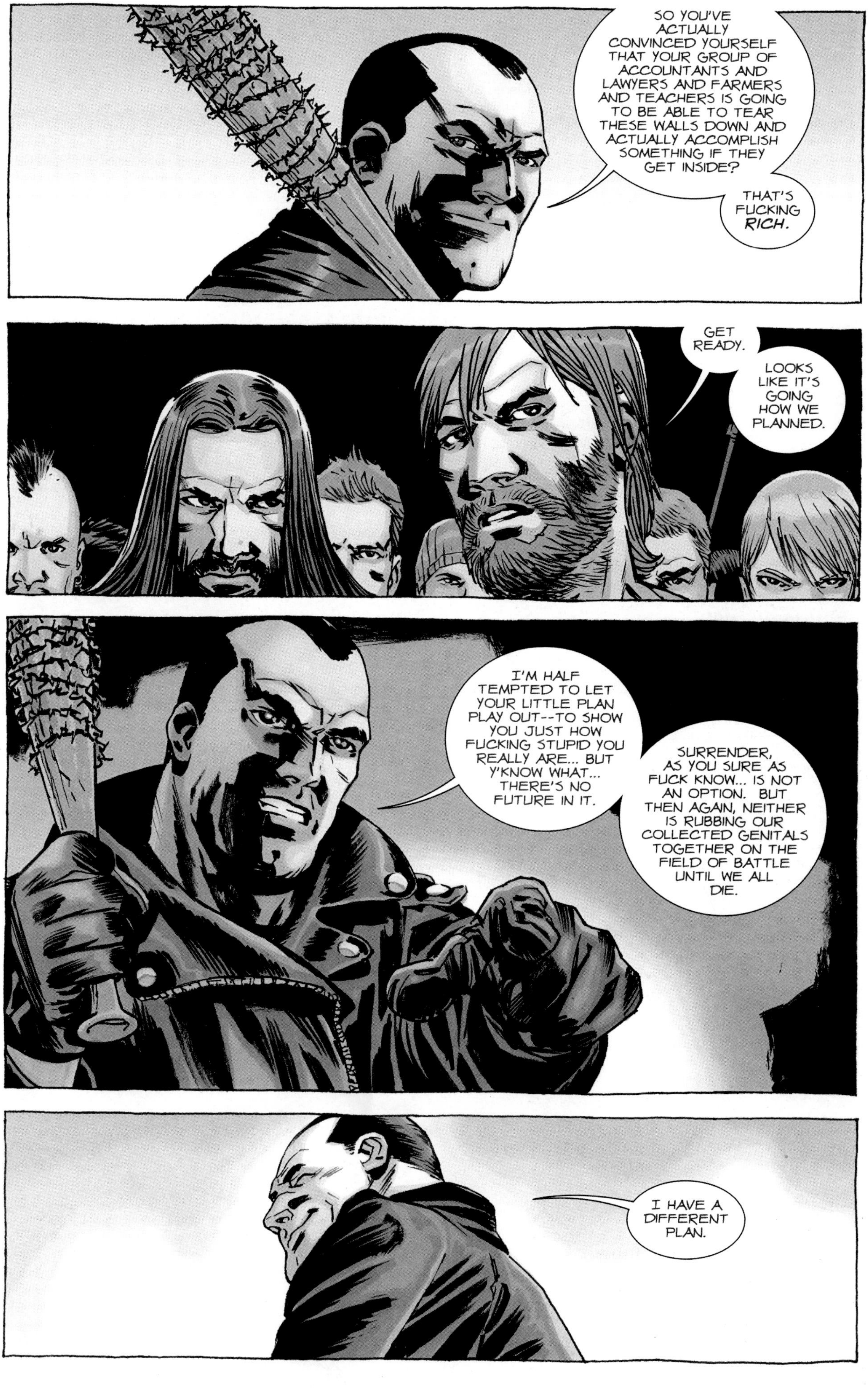
SO YOU'VE ACTUALLY CONVINCED YOURSELF THAT YOUR GROUP OF ACCOUNTANTS AND LAWYERS AND FARMERS AND TEACHERS IS GOING TO BE ABLE TO TEAR THESE WALLS DOWN AND ACTUALLY ACCOMPLISH SOMETHING IF THEY GET INSIDE?
THAT'S FUCKING *RICH.*
GET READY.
LOOKS LIKE IT'S GOING HOW WE PLANNED.
I'M HALF TEMPTED TO LET YOUR LITTLE PLAN PLAY OUT--TO SHOW YOU JUST HOW FUCKING STUPID YOU REALLY ARE... BUT Y'KNOW WHAT... THERE'S NO FUTURE IN IT.
SURRENDER, AS YOU SURE AS FUCK KNOW... IS NOT AN OPTION. BUT THEN AGAIN, NEITHER IS RUBBING OUR COLLECTED GENITALS TOGETHER ON THE FIELD OF BATTLE UNTIL WE ALL DIE.
I HAVE A DIFFERENT PLAN.

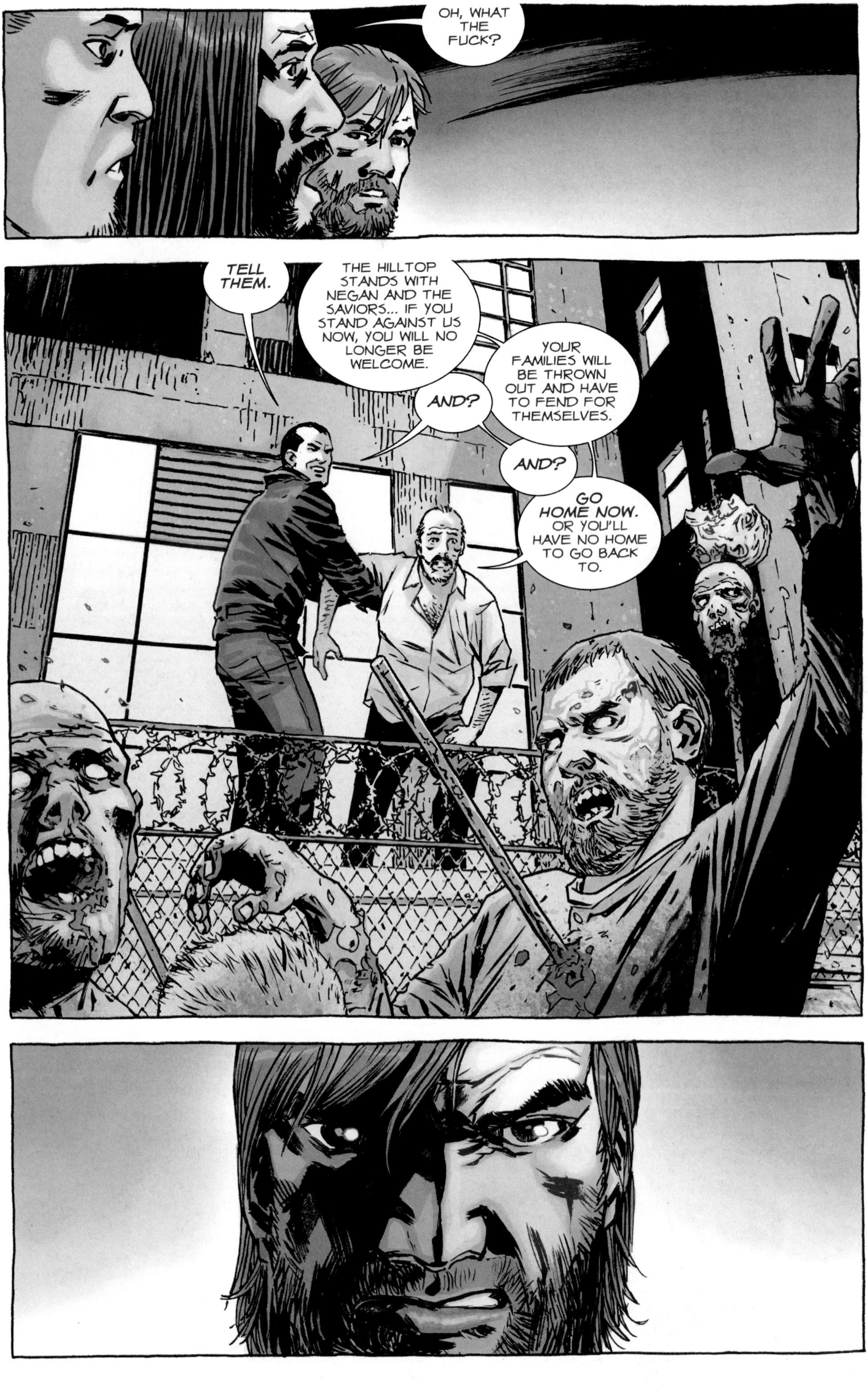
OH, WHAT THE FUCK?
TELL THEM.
THE HILLTOP STANDS WITH NEGAN AND THE SAVIORS... IF YOU STAND AGAINST US NOW, YOU WILL NO LONGER BE WELCOME.
AND?
YOUR FAMILIES WILL BE THROWN OUT AND HAVE TO FEND FOR THEMSELVES.
AND?
GO HOME NOW. OR YOU'LL HAVE NO HOME TO GO BACK TO.

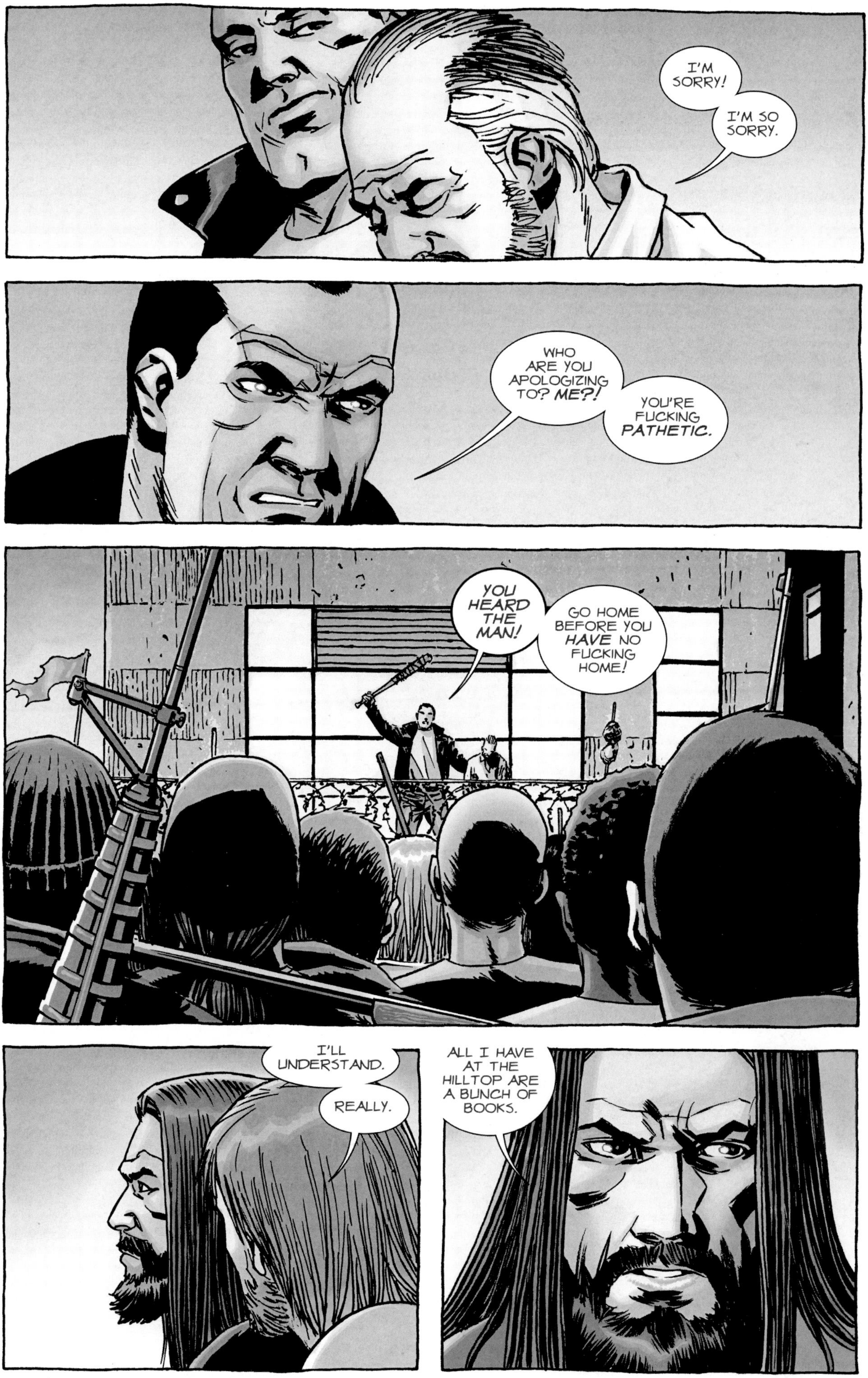
I'M SORRY!
I'M SO SORRY.
WHO ARE YOU APOLOGIZING TO? ME?!
YOU'RE FUCKING PATHETIC.
YOU HEARD THE MAN!
GO HOME BEFORE YOU HAVE NO FUCKING HOME!
I'LL UNDERSTAND.
REALLY.
ALL I HAVE AT THE HILLTOP ARE A BUNCH OF BOOKS.

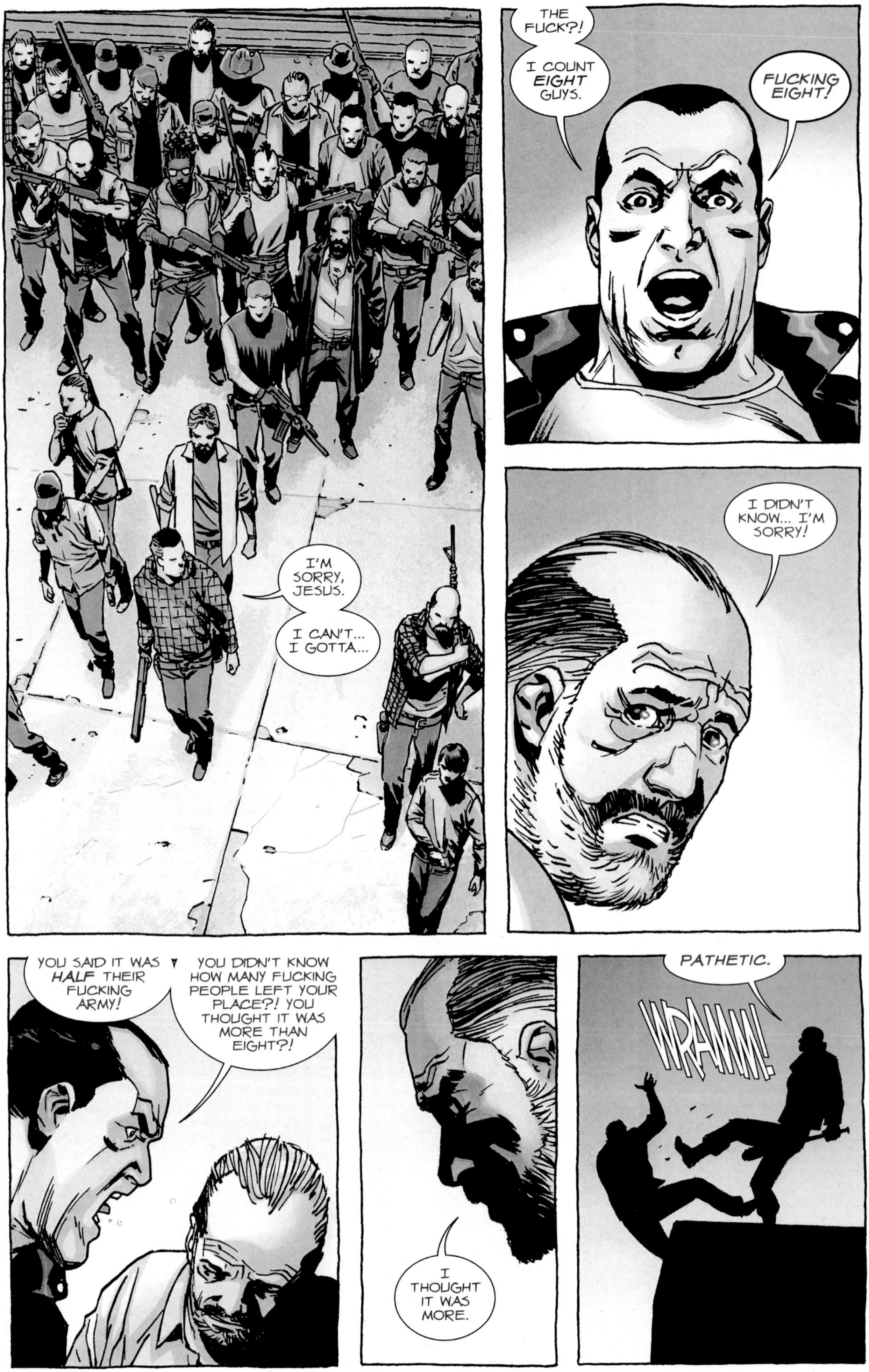
I'M SORRY, JESUS.
I CAN'T... I GOTTA...
THE FUCK?!
I COUNT EIGHT GUYS.
FUCKING EIGHT!
I DIDN'T KNOW... I'M SORRY!
YOU SAID IT WAS HALF THEIR FUCKING ARMY!
YOU DIDN'T KNOW HOW MANY FUCKING PEOPLE LEFT YOUR PLACE?! YOU THOUGHT IT WAS MORE THAN EIGHT?!
I THOUGHT IT WAS MORE.
PATHETIC.
WRAMM!

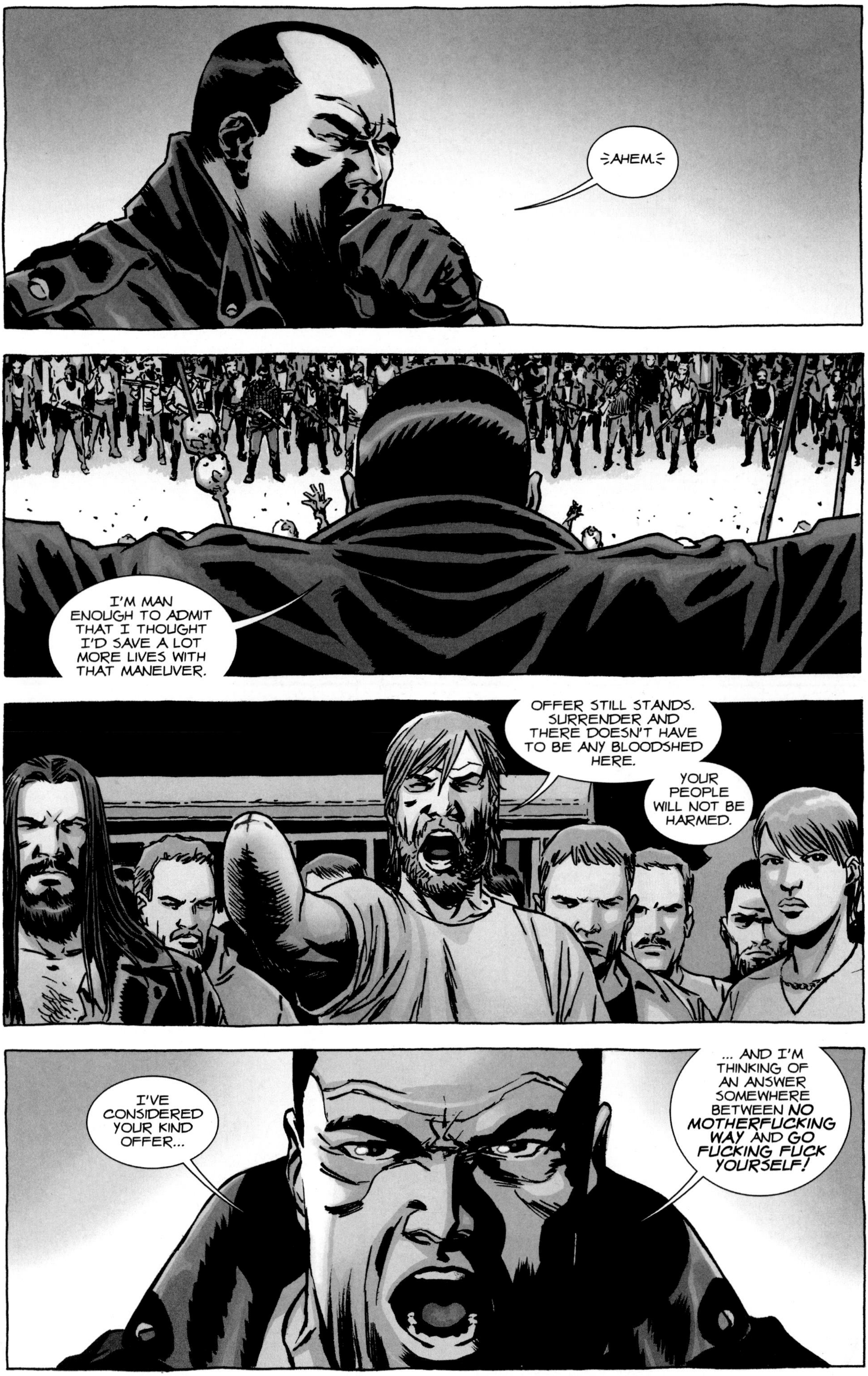
AHEM.
I'M MAN ENOUGH TO ADMIT THAT I THOUGHT I'D SAVE A LOT MORE LIVES WITH THAT MANEUVER.
OFFER STILL STANDS. SURRENDER AND THERE DOESN'T HAVE TO BE ANY BLOODSHED HERE.
YOUR PEOPLE WILL NOT BE HARMED.
I'VE CONSIDERED YOUR KIND OFFER...
... AND I'M THINKING OF AN ANSWER SOMEWHERE BETWEEN NO MOTHERFUCKING WAY AND GO FUCKING FUCK YOURSELF!

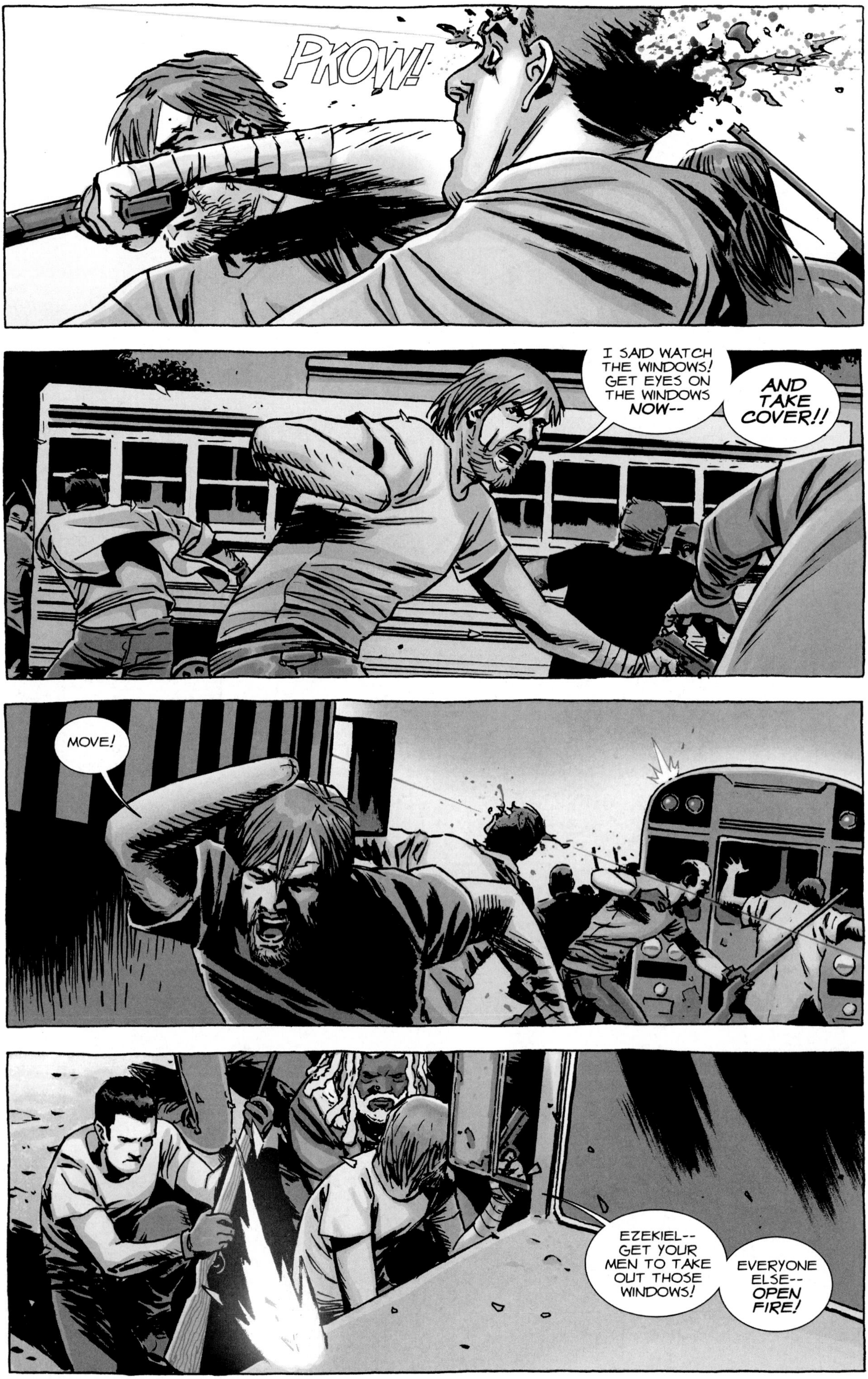
PKOW!
I SAID WATCH THE WINDOWS! GET EYES ON THE WINDOWS NOW--
AND TAKE COVER!!
MOVE!
EZEKIEL-- GET YOUR MEN TO TAKE OUT THOSE WINDOWS!
EVERYONE ELSE-- OPEN FIRE!

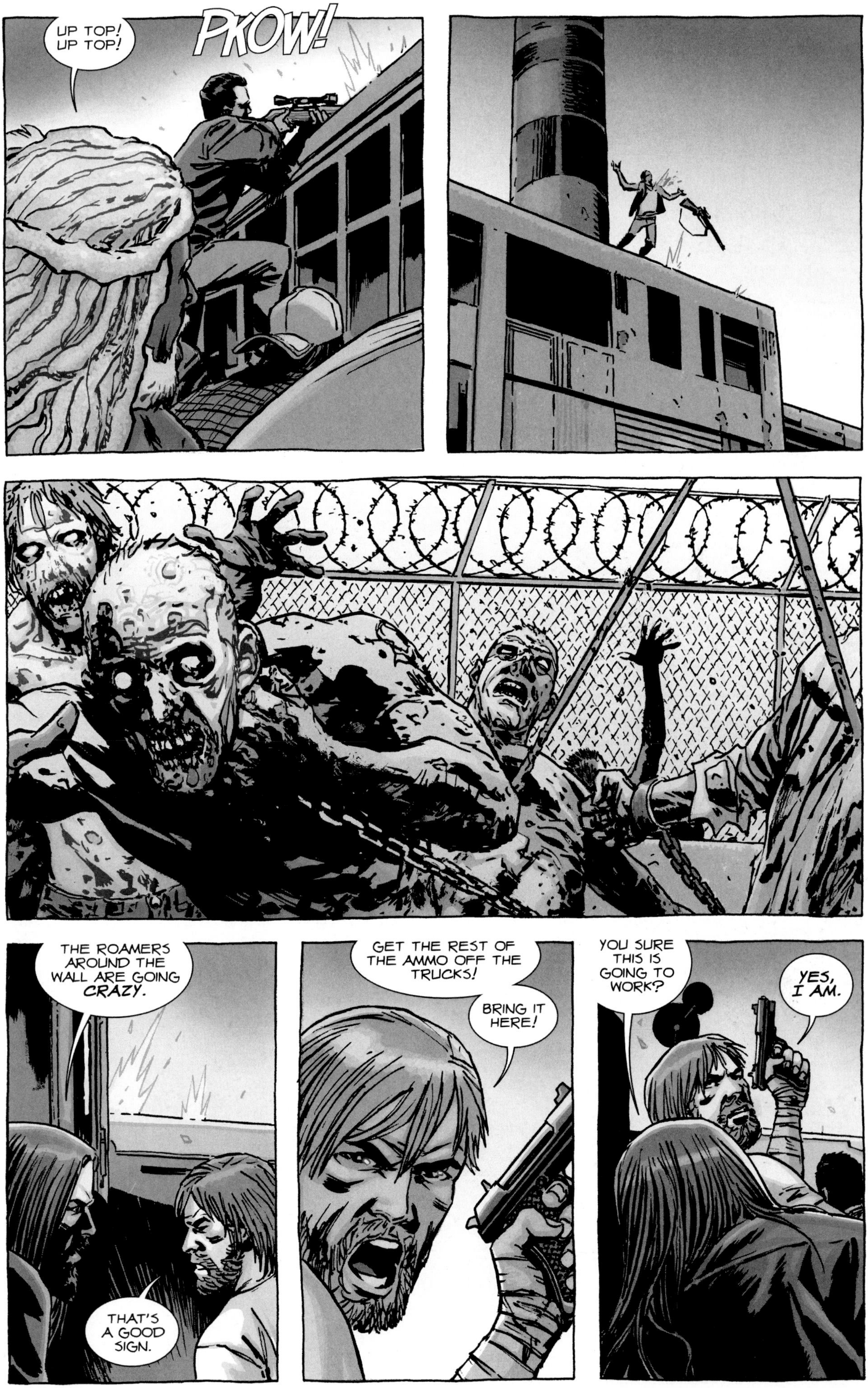
UP TOP! UP TOP!
PKOW!
THE ROAMERS AROUND THE WALL ARE GOING CRAZY.
THAT'S A GOOD SIGN.
GET THE REST OF THE AMMO OFF THE TRUCKS!
BRING IT HERE!
YOU SURE THIS IS GOING TO WORK?
YES, I AM.

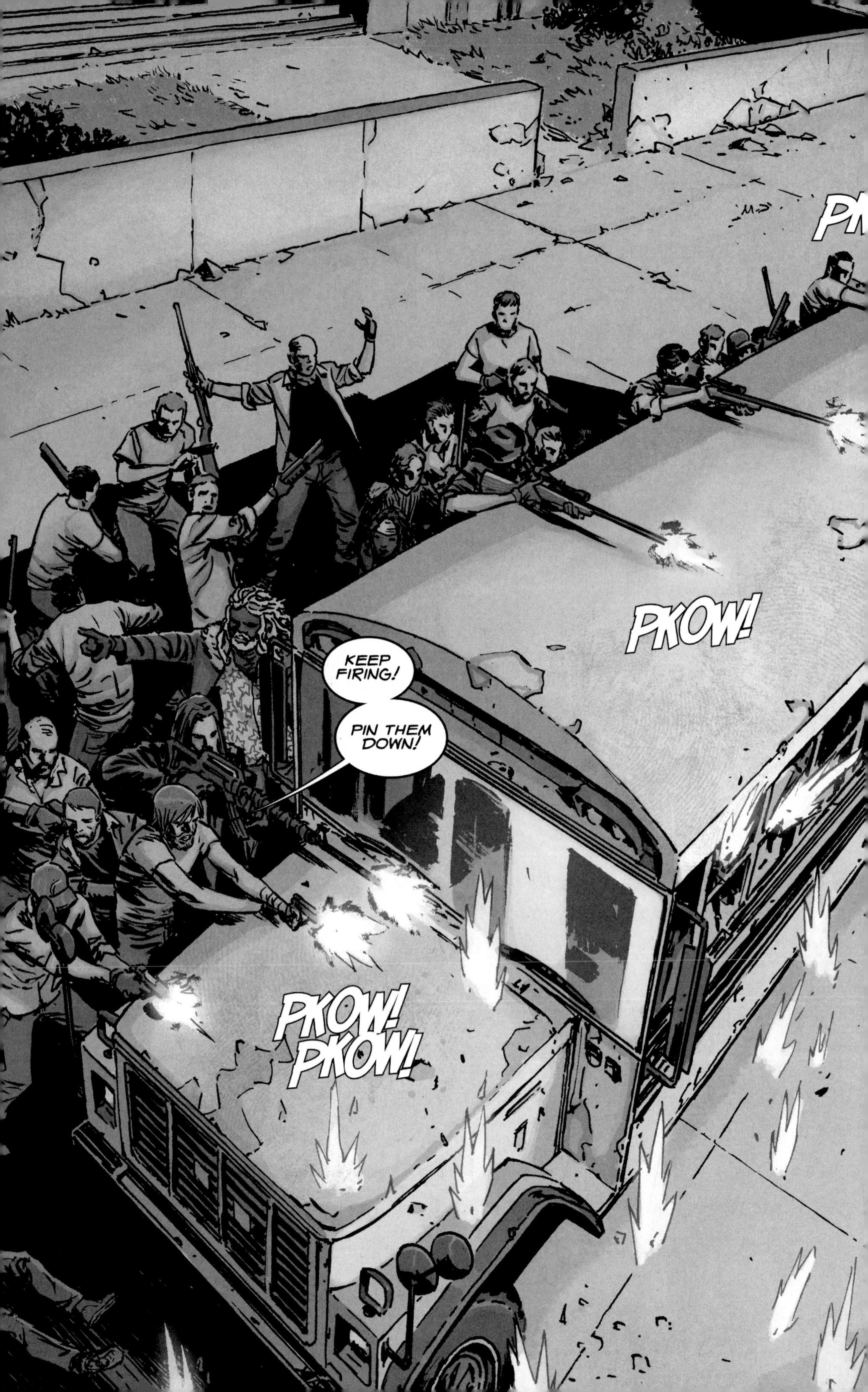
PKOW!
KEEP FIRING!
PIN THEM DOWN!
PKOW! PKOW!

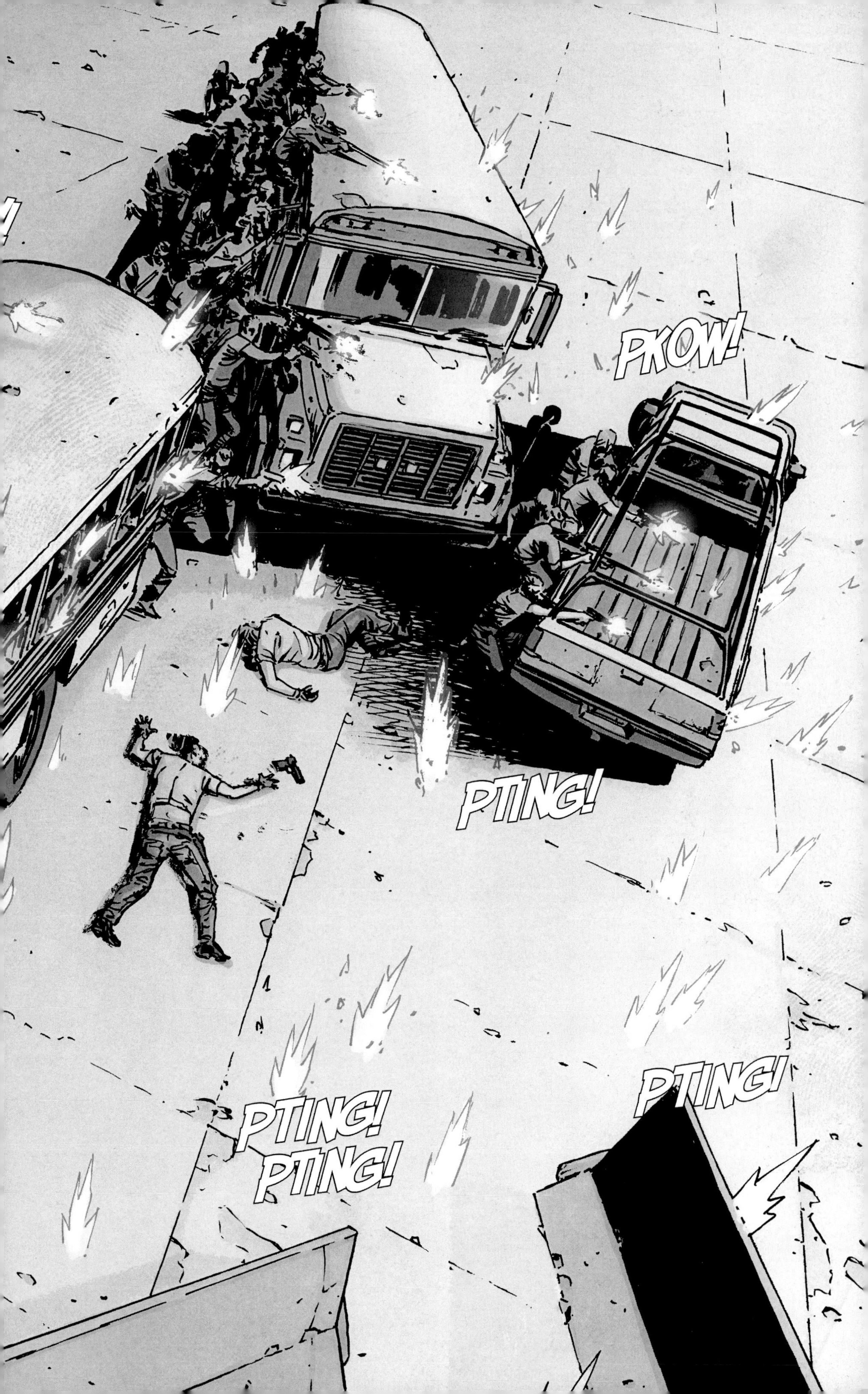
PKOW!
PTING!
PTING!
PTING!
PTING!

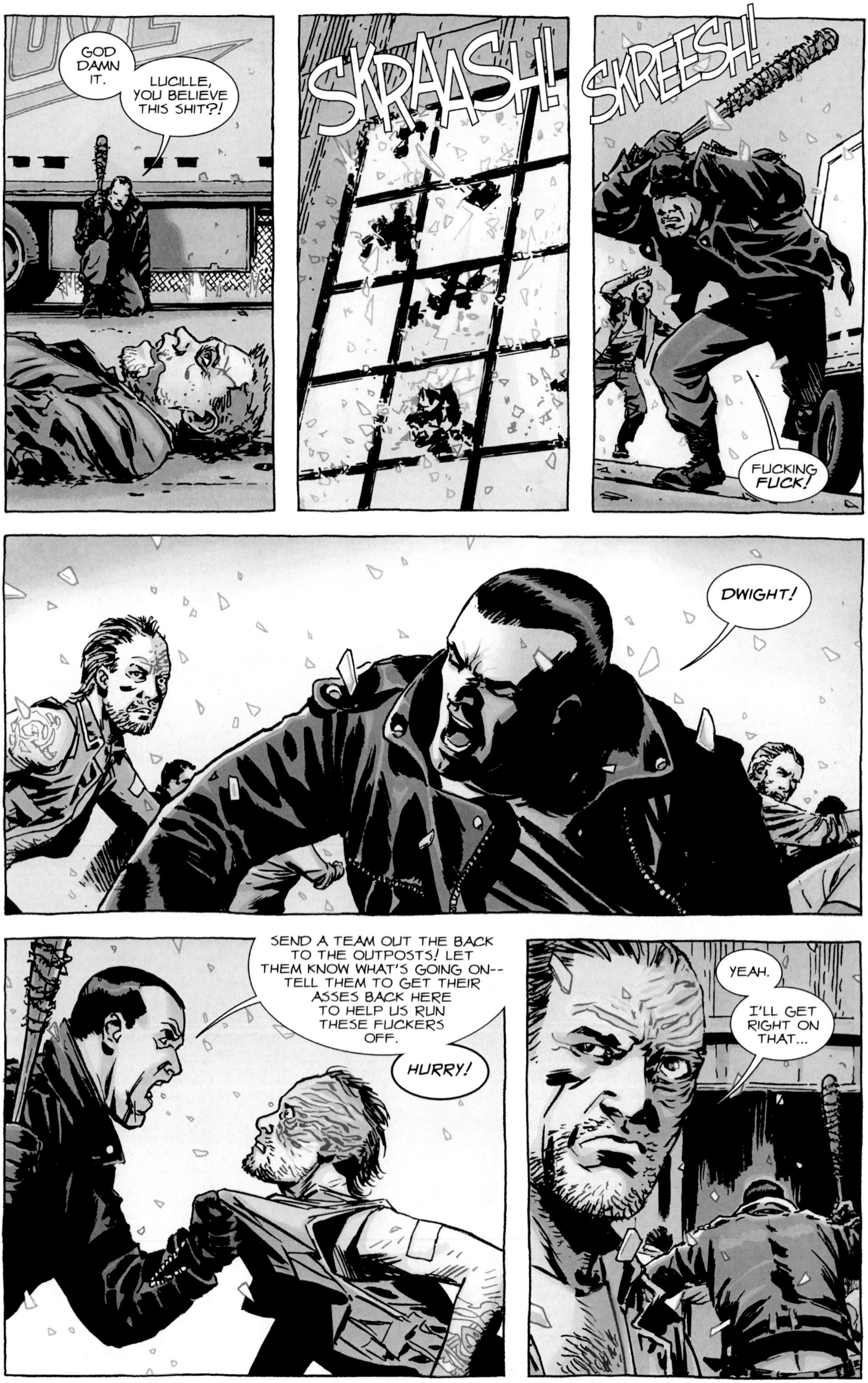
GOD DAMN IT.
LUCILLE, YOU BELIEVE THIS SHIT?!
SKRAASH!
SKREESH!
FUCKING FUCK!
DWIGHT!
SEND A TEAM OUT THE BACK TO THE OUTPOSTS! LET THEM KNOW WHAT'S GOING ON-- TELL THEM TO GET THEIR ASSES BACK HERE TO HELP US RUN THESE FUCKERS OFF.
HURRY!
YEAH.
I'LL GET RIGHT ON THAT...

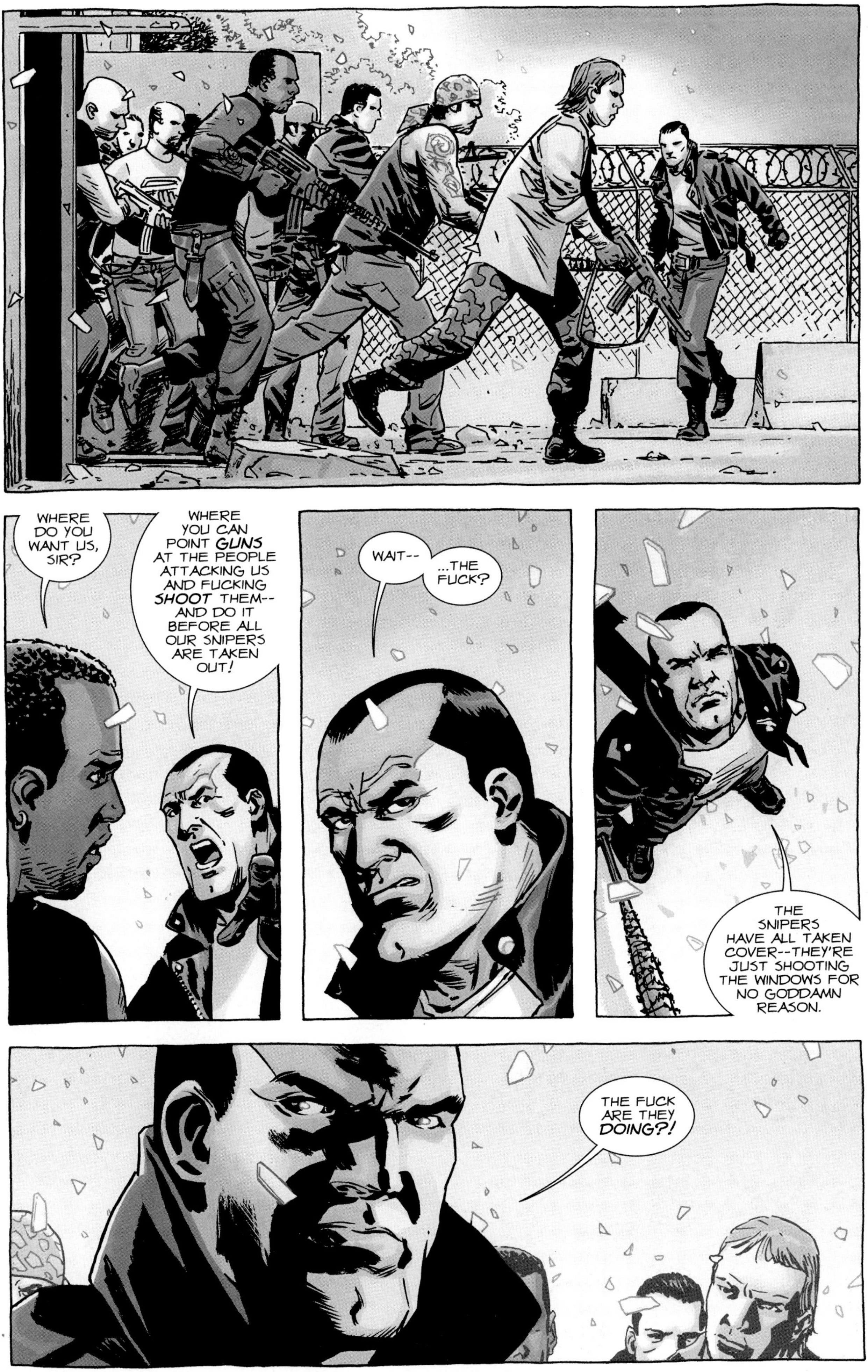
WHERE DO YOU WANT US, SIR?
WHERE YOU CAN POINT GUNS AT THE PEOPLE ATTACKING US AND FUCKING SHOOT THEM-- AND DO IT BEFORE ALL OUR SNIPERS ARE TAKEN OUT!
WAIT--
...THE FUCK?
THE SNIPERS HAVE ALL TAKEN COVER--THEY'RE JUST SHOOTING THE WINDOWS FOR NO GODDAMN REASON.
THE FUCK ARE THEY DOING?!

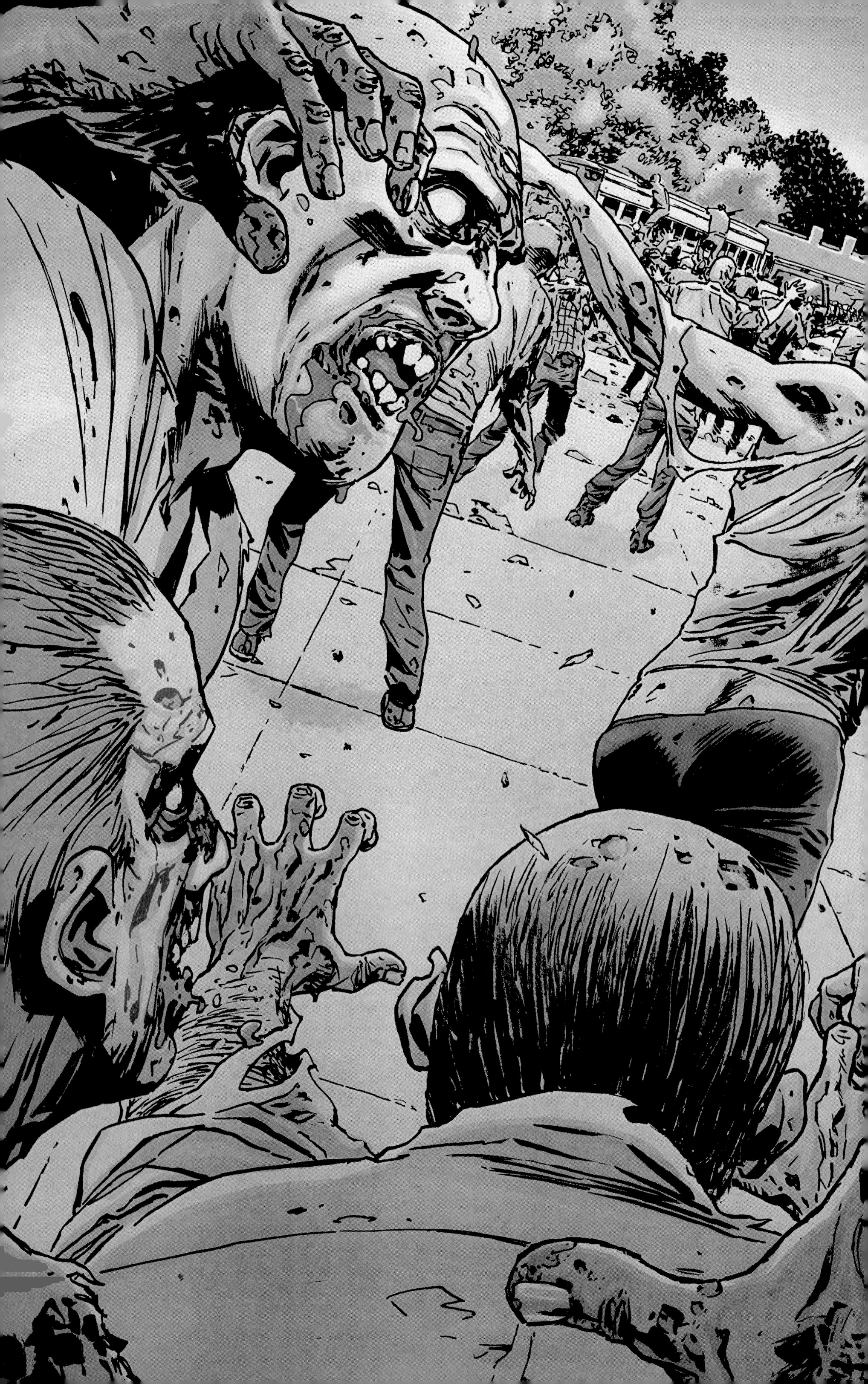

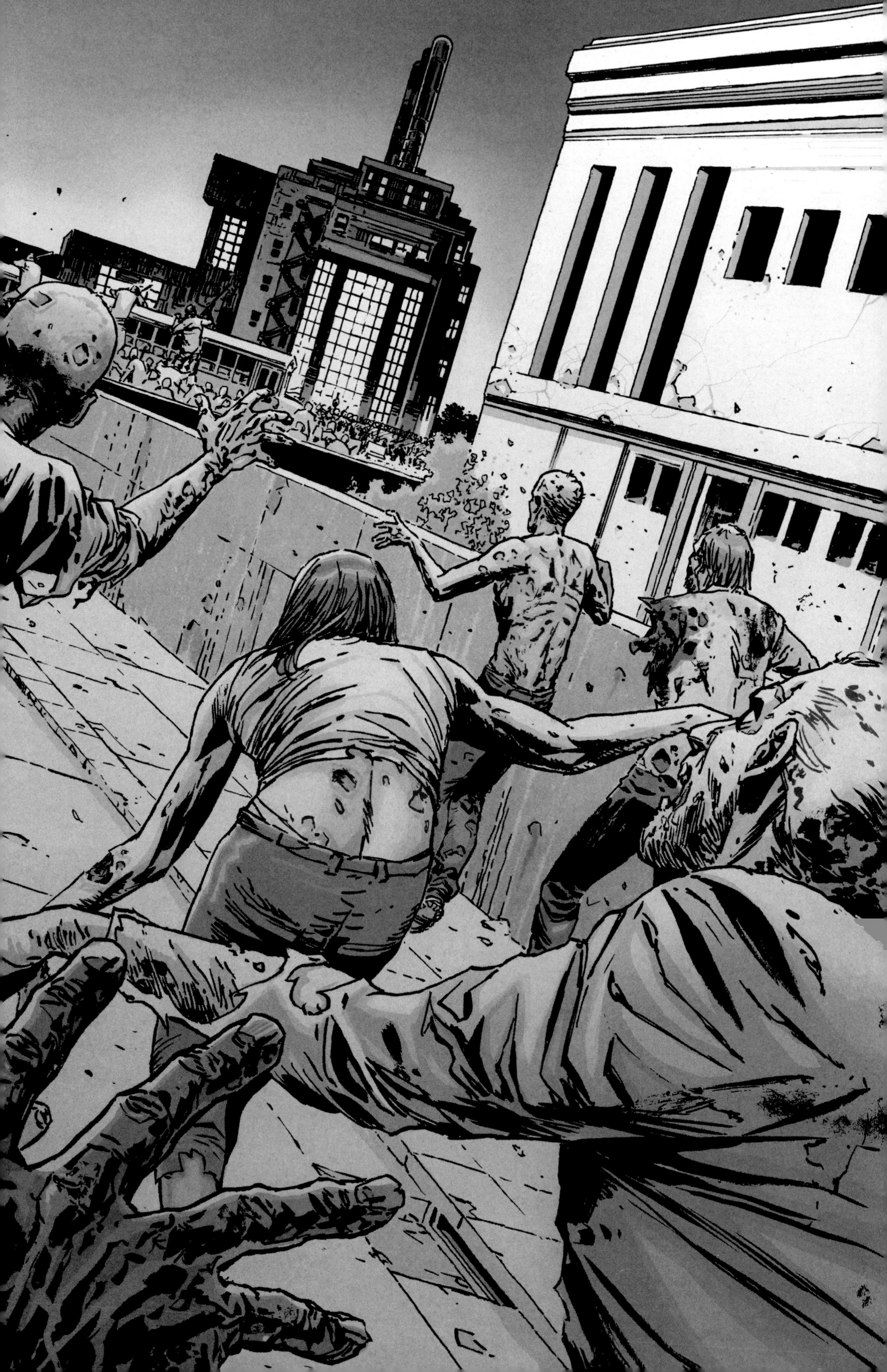

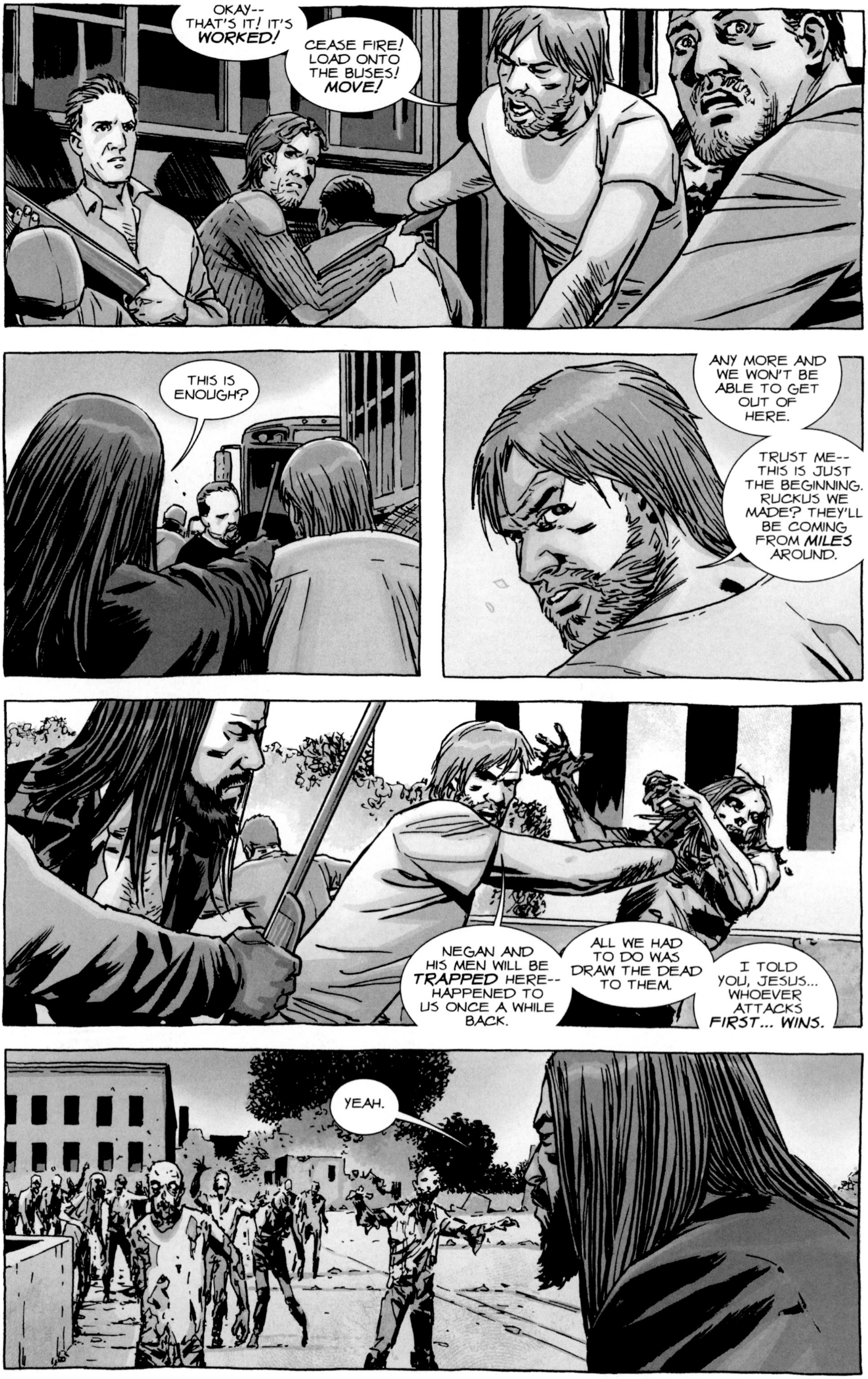
OKAY-- THAT'S IT! IT'S WORKED!
CEASE FIRE! LOAD ONTO THE BUSES! MOVE!
THIS IS ENOUGH?
ANY MORE AND WE WON'T BE ABLE TO GET OUT OF HERE.
TRUST ME-- THIS IS JUST THE BEGINNING. RUCKUS WE MADE? THEY'LL BE COMING FROM MILES AROUND.
NEGAN AND HIS MEN WILL BE TRAPPED HERE-- HAPPENED TO US ONCE A WHILE BACK.
ALL WE HAD TO DO WAS DRAW THE DEAD TO THEM.
I TOLD YOU, JESUS... WHOEVER ATTACKS FIRST... WINS.
YEAH.

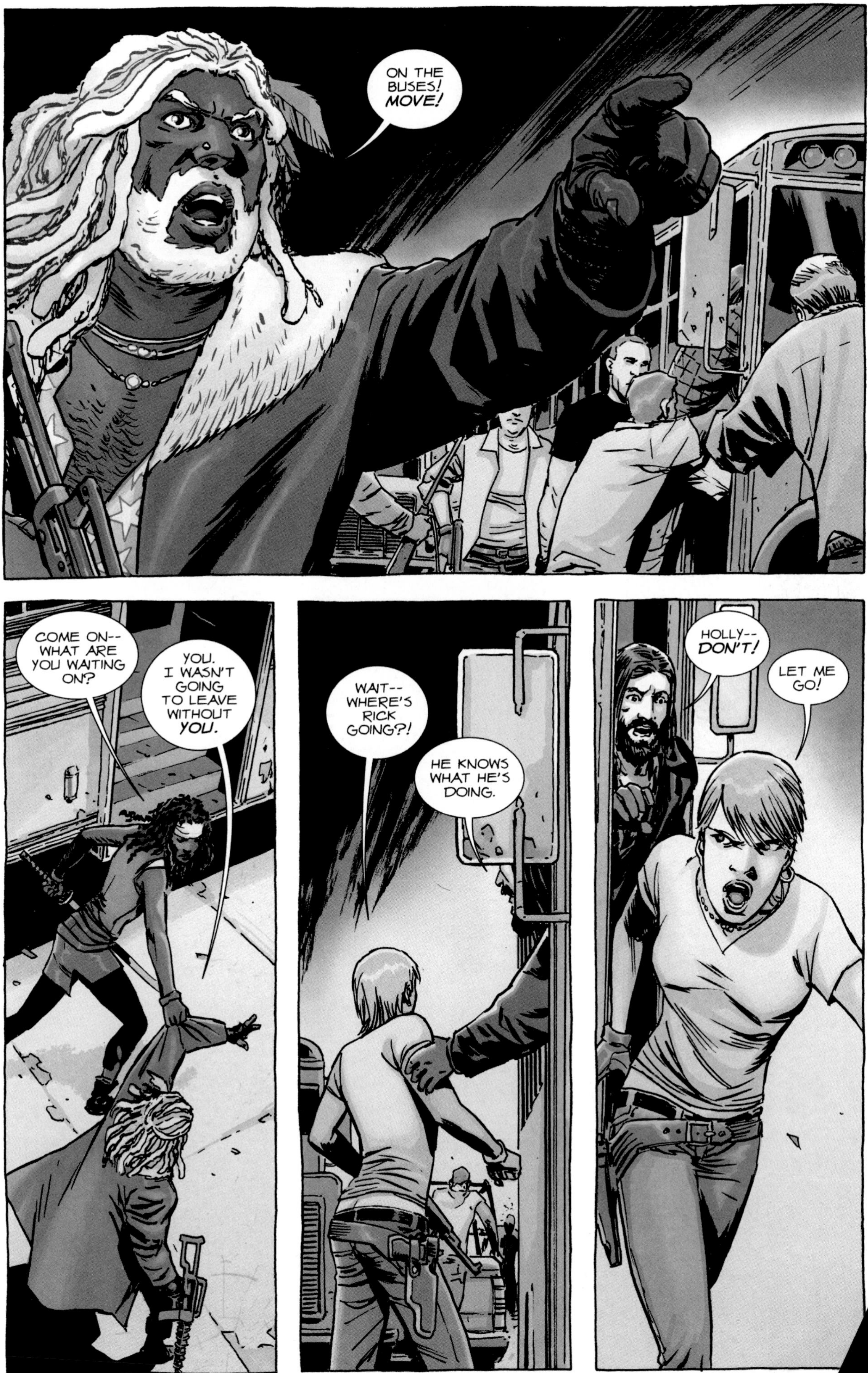
ON THE BUSES! *MOVE!*
COME ON-- WHAT ARE YOU WAITING ON?
YOU. I WASN'T GOING TO LEAVE WITHOUT *YOU.*
WAIT-- WHERE'S RICK GOING?!
HE KNOWS WHAT HE'S DOING.
HOLLY-- *DON'T!*
LET ME GO!

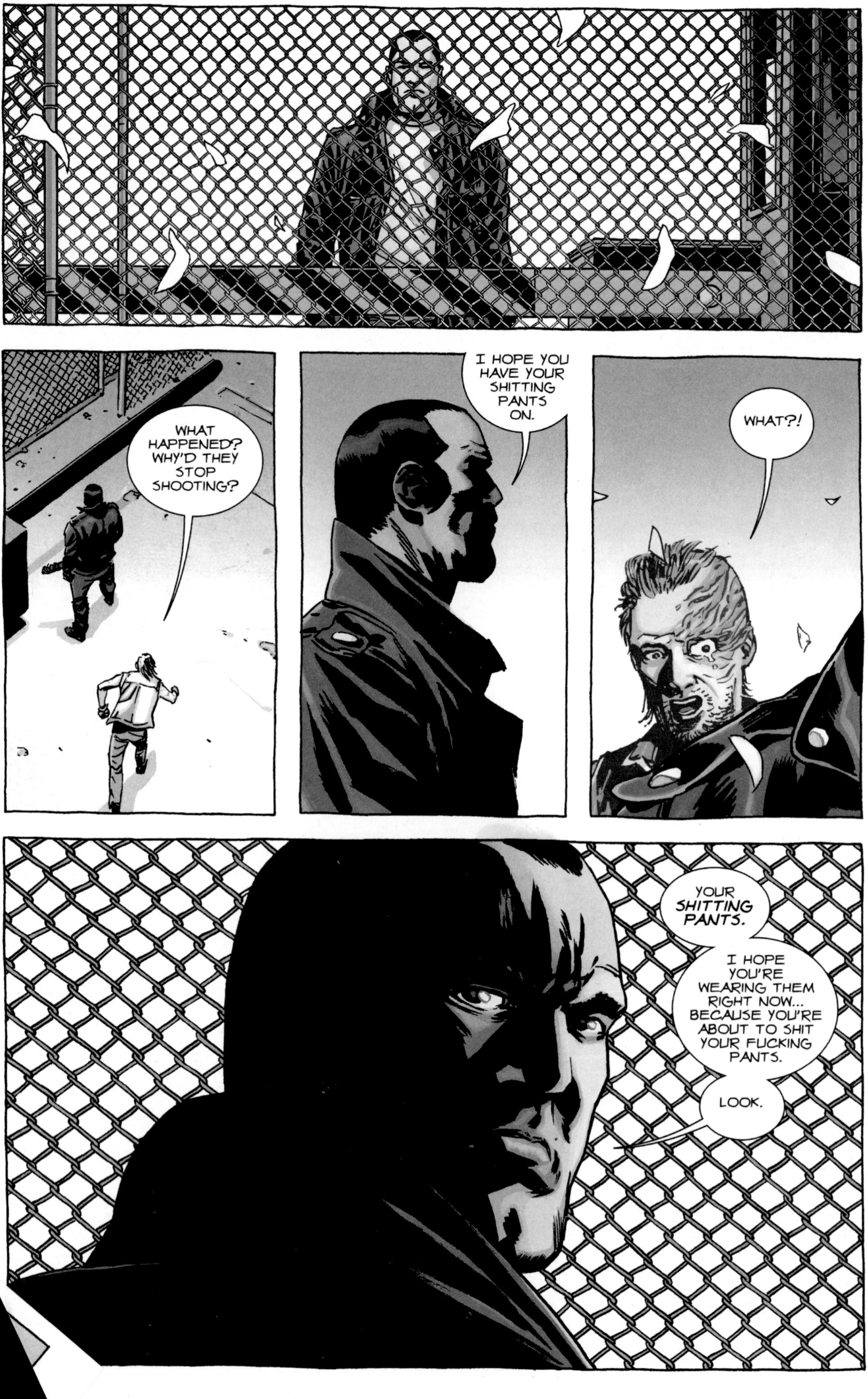
WHAT HAPPENED? WHY'D THEY STOP SHOOTING?
I HOPE YOU HAVE YOUR SHITTING PANTS ON.
WHAT?!
YOUR *SHITTING PANTS.*
I HOPE YOU'RE WEARING THEM RIGHT NOW... BECAUSE YOU'RE ABOUT TO SHIT YOUR FUCKING PANTS.
LOOK.

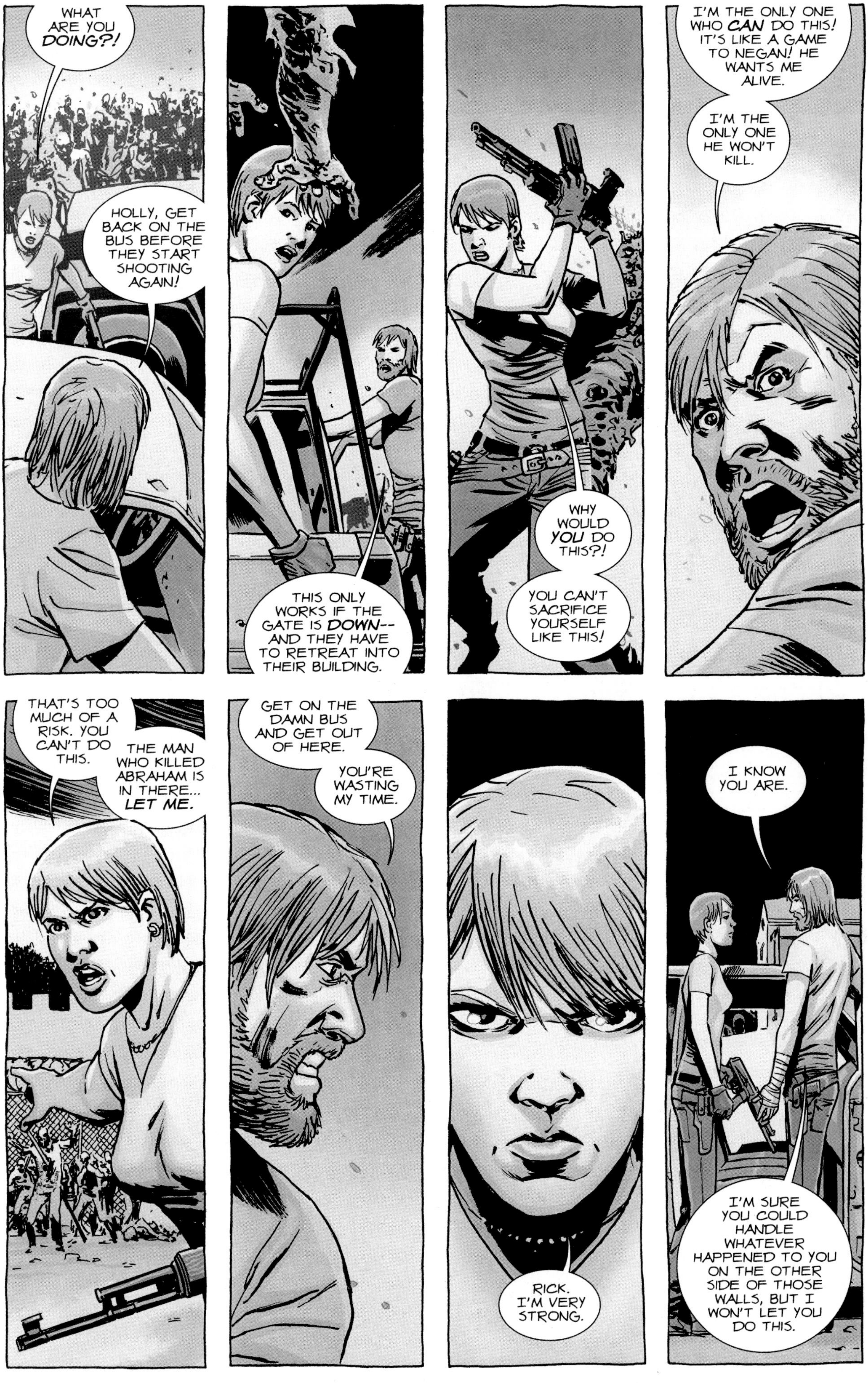
WHAT ARE YOU DOING?!
HOLLY, GET BACK ON THE BUS BEFORE THEY START SHOOTING AGAIN!
THIS ONLY WORKS IF THE GATE IS DOWN-- AND THEY HAVE TO RETREAT INTO THEIR BUILDING.
WHY WOULD YOU DO THIS?!
YOU CAN'T SACRIFICE YOURSELF LIKE THIS!
I'M THE ONLY ONE WHO CAN DO THIS! IT'S LIKE A GAME TO NEGAN! HE WANTS ME ALIVE.
I'M THE ONLY ONE HE WON'T KILL.
THAT'S TOO MUCH OF A RISK. YOU CAN'T DO THIS.
THE MAN WHO KILLED ABRAHAM IS IN THERE... LET ME.
GET ON THE DAMN BUS AND GET OUT OF HERE.
YOU'RE WASTING MY TIME.
RICK. I'M VERY STRONG.
I KNOW YOU ARE.
I'M SURE YOU COULD HANDLE WHATEVER HAPPENED TO YOU ON THE OTHER SIDE OF THOSE WALLS, BUT I WON'T LET YOU DO THIS.

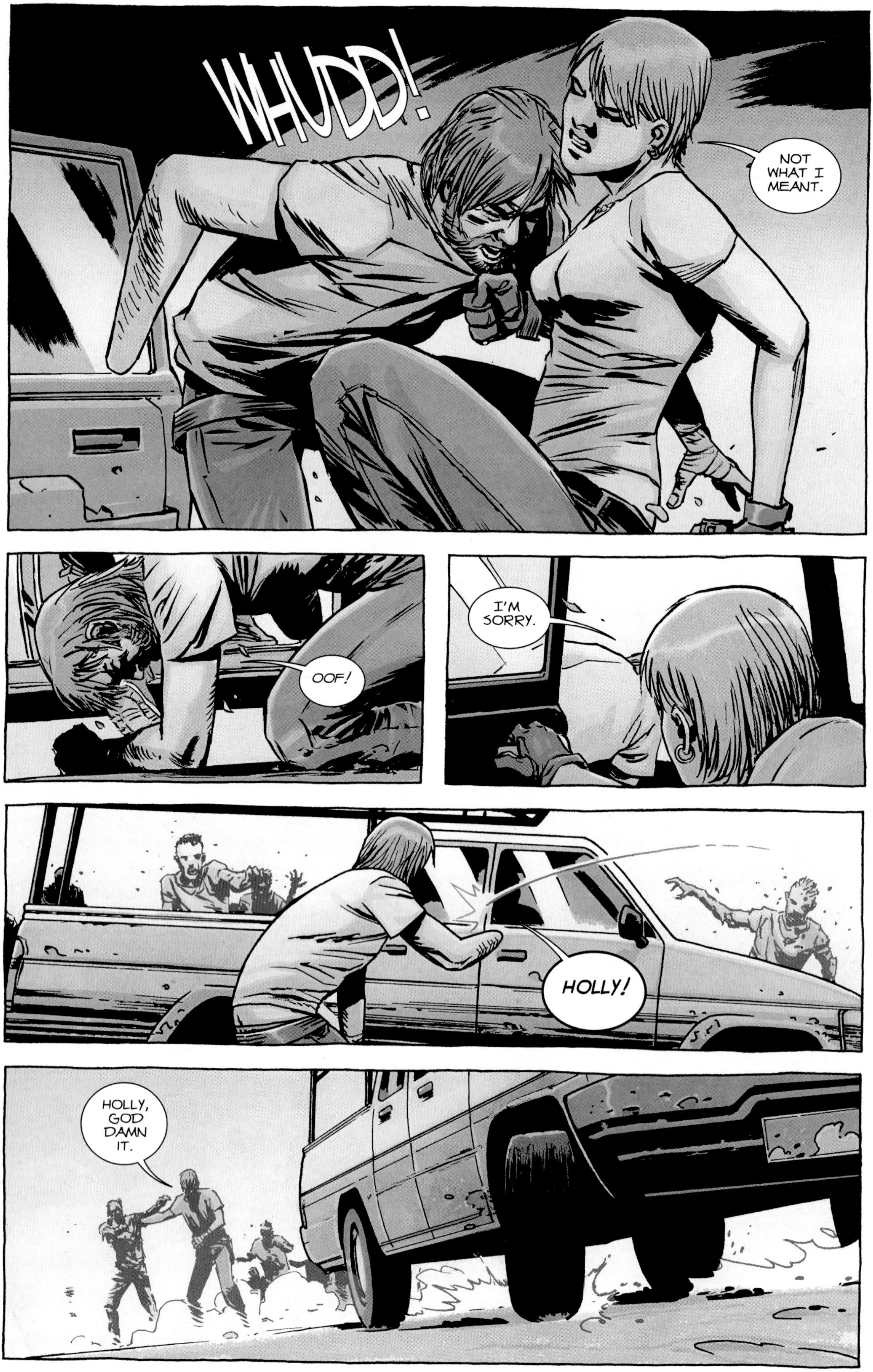
WHUDD!
NOT WHAT I MEANT.
OOF!
I'M SORRY.
HOLLY!
HOLLY, GOD DAMN IT.

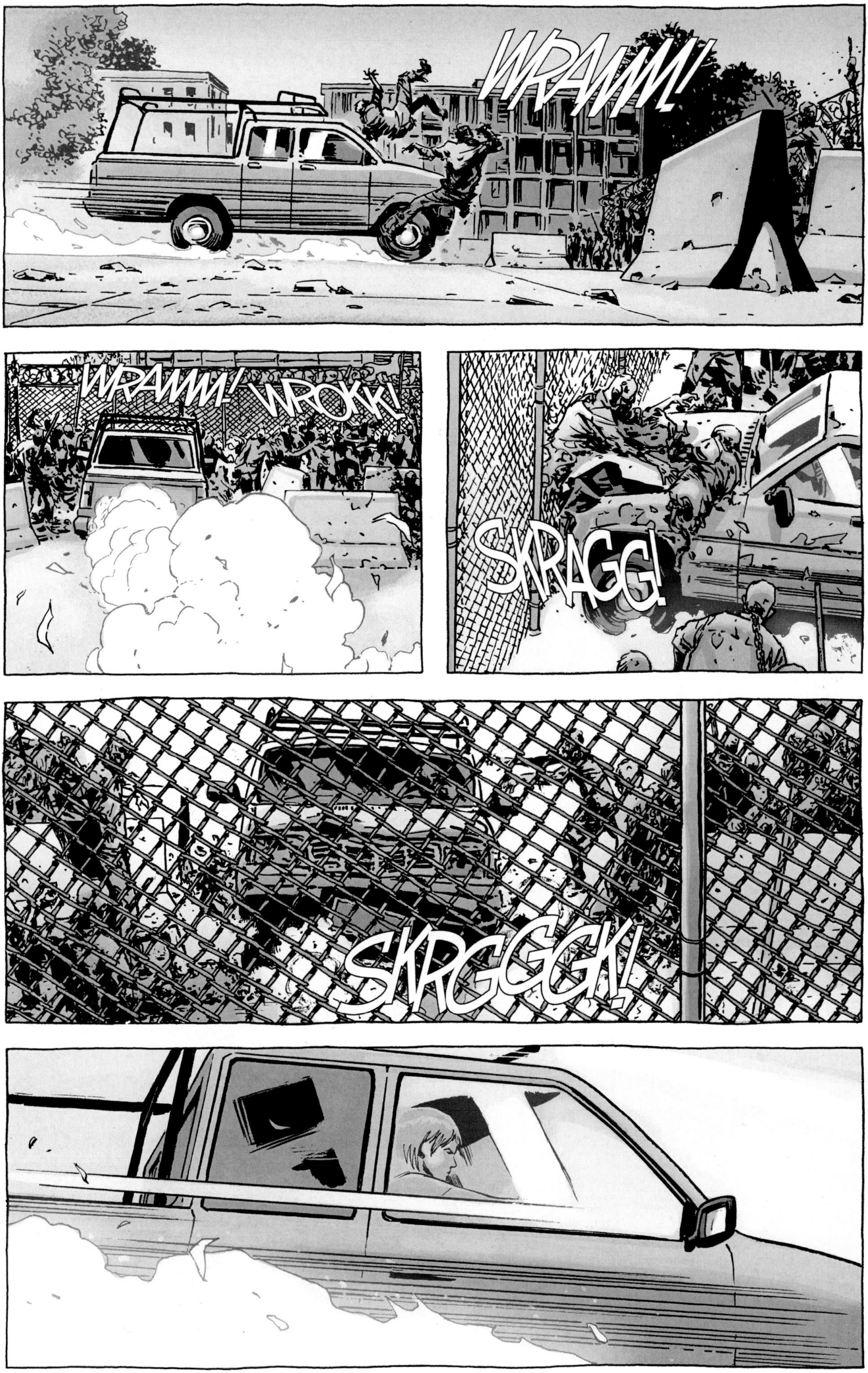
WRAMM!
WRAMM!
WROKK!
SKRAGG!
SKRGGGK!

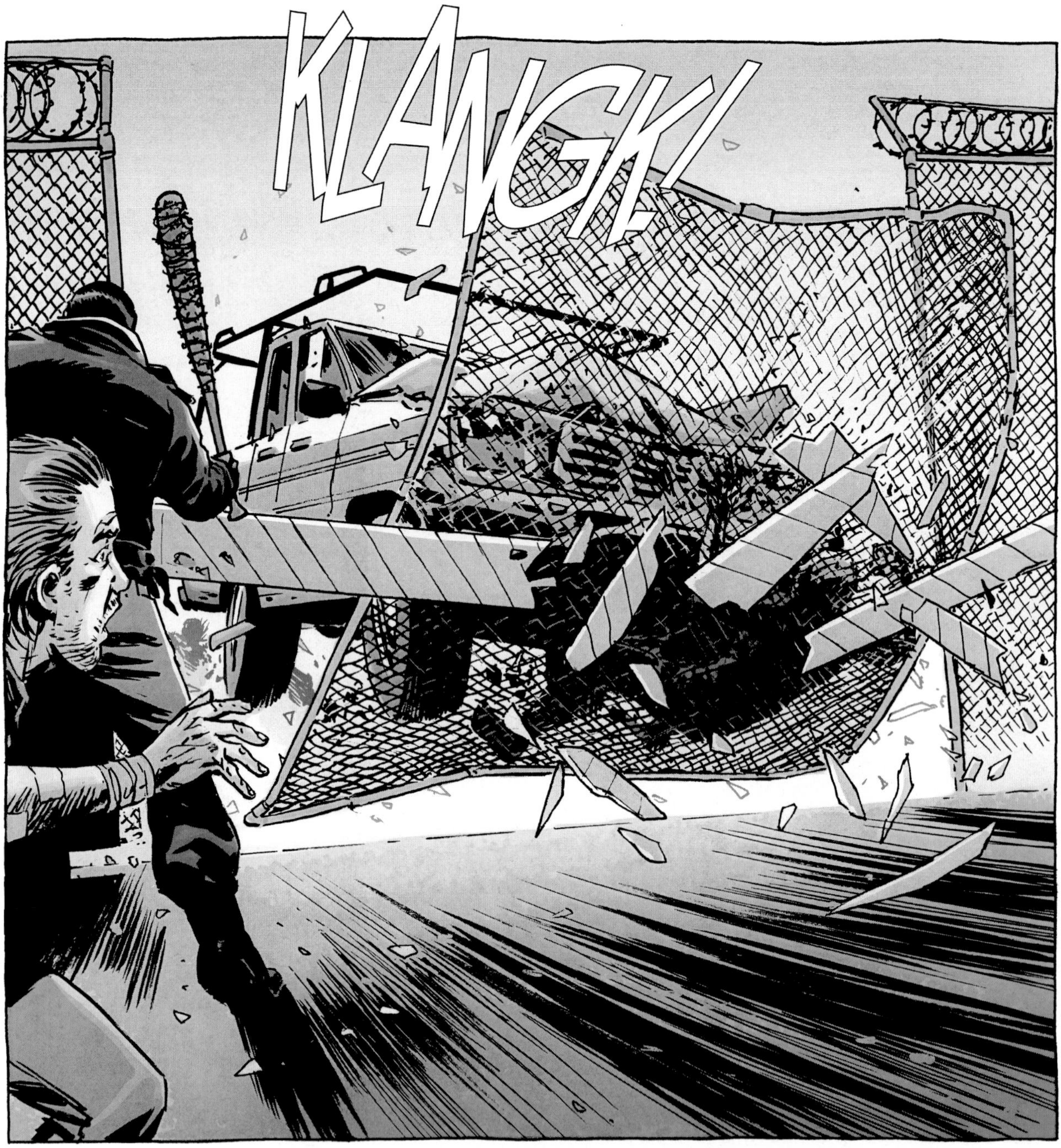
KLANGK!

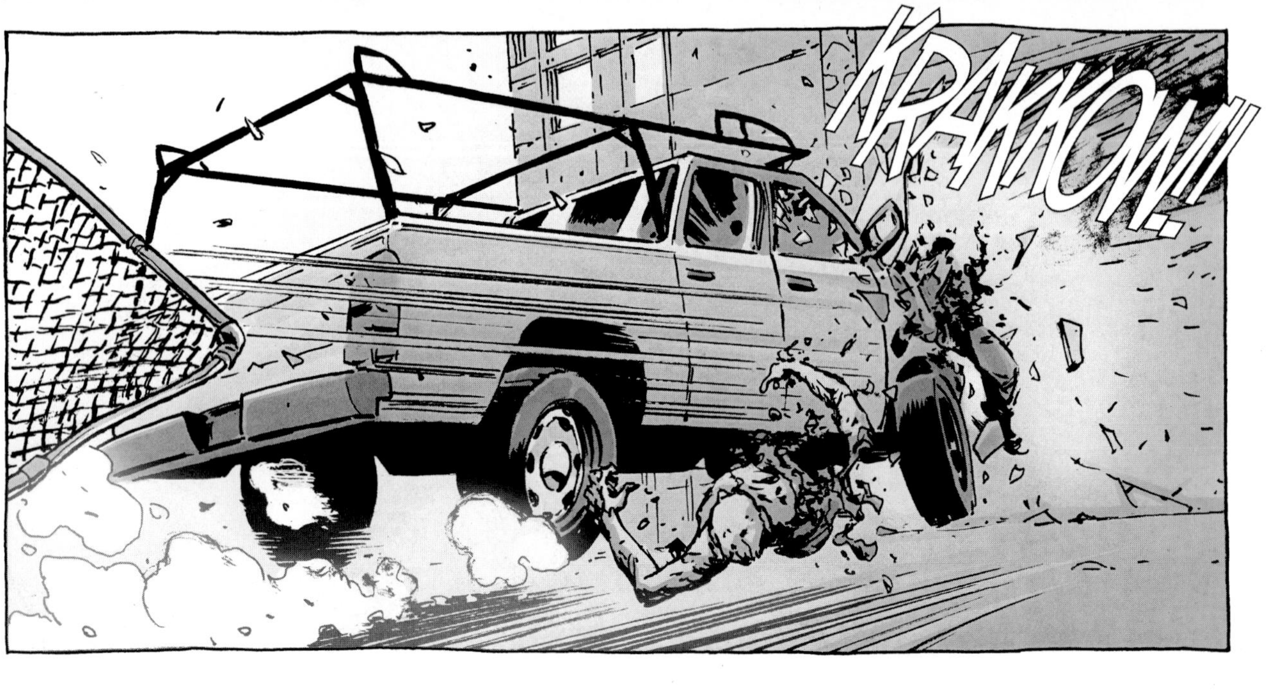
KRAKKOW!!

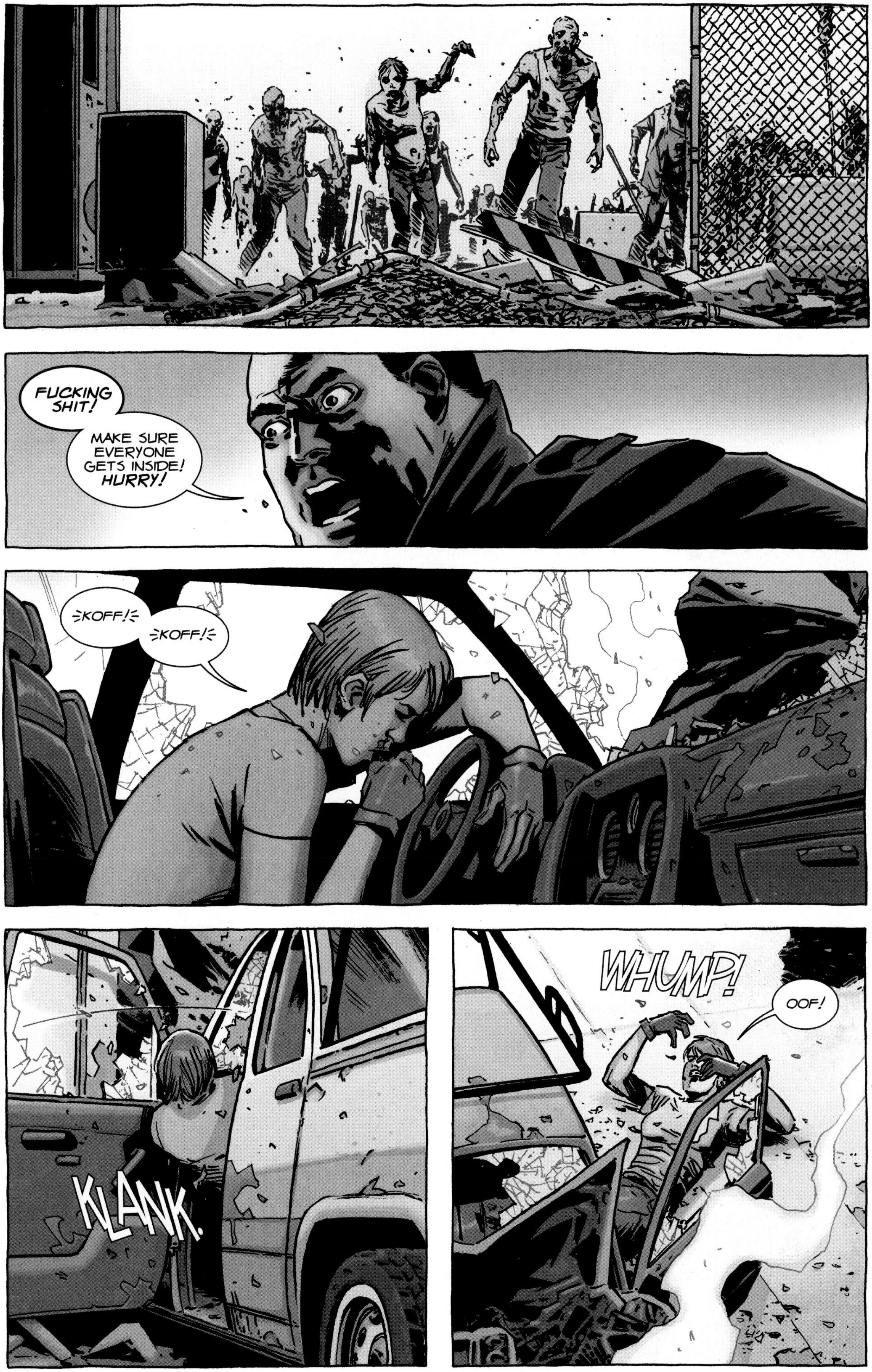
FUCKING SHIT!
MAKE SURE EVERYONE GETS INSIDE! HURRY!
KOFF!
KOFF!
KLANK.
WHUMP!
OOF!

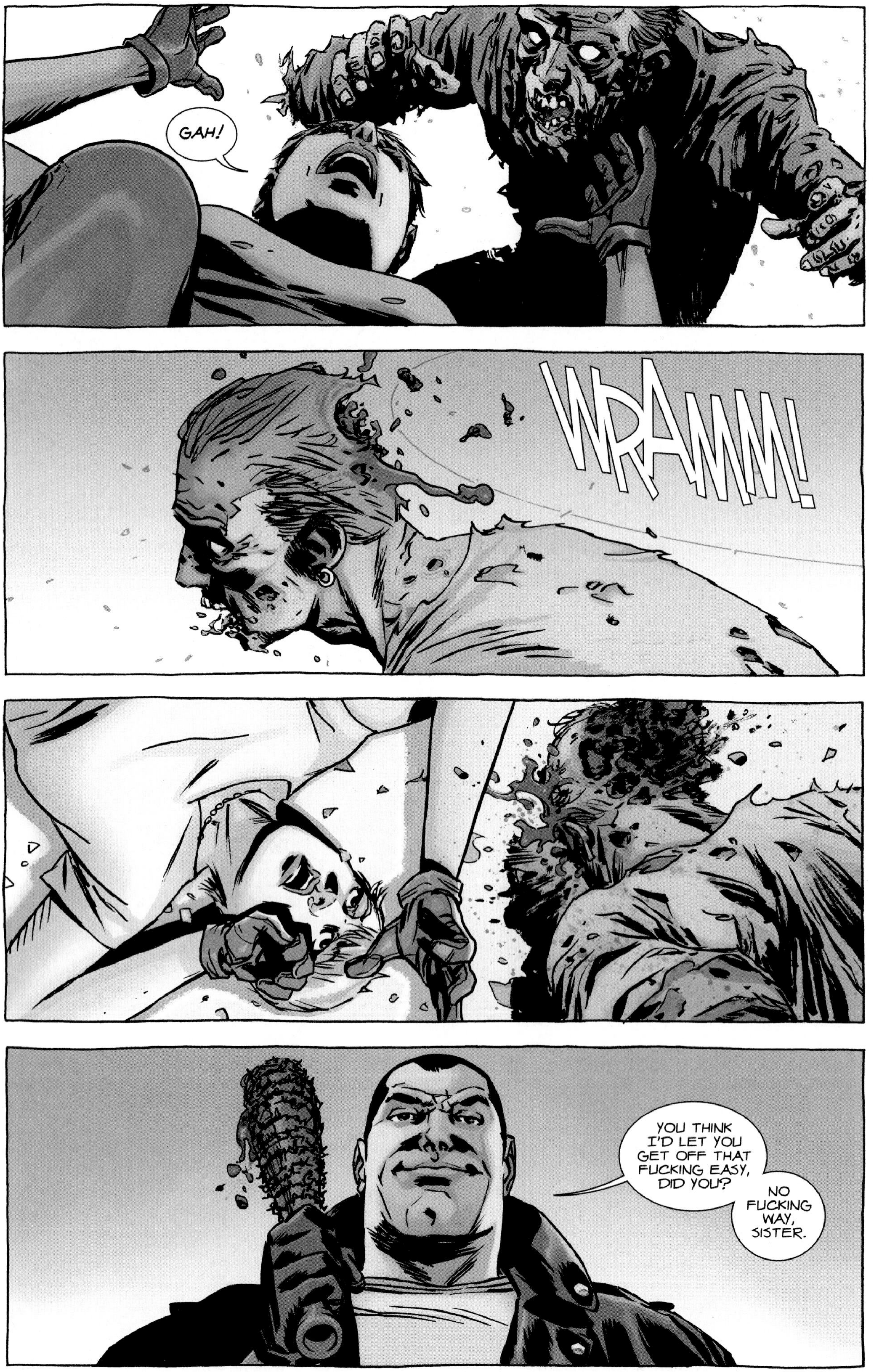
GAH!
WRAMM!
YOU THINK I'D LET YOU GET OFF THAT FUCKING EASY, DID YOU?
NO FUCKING WAY, SISTER.

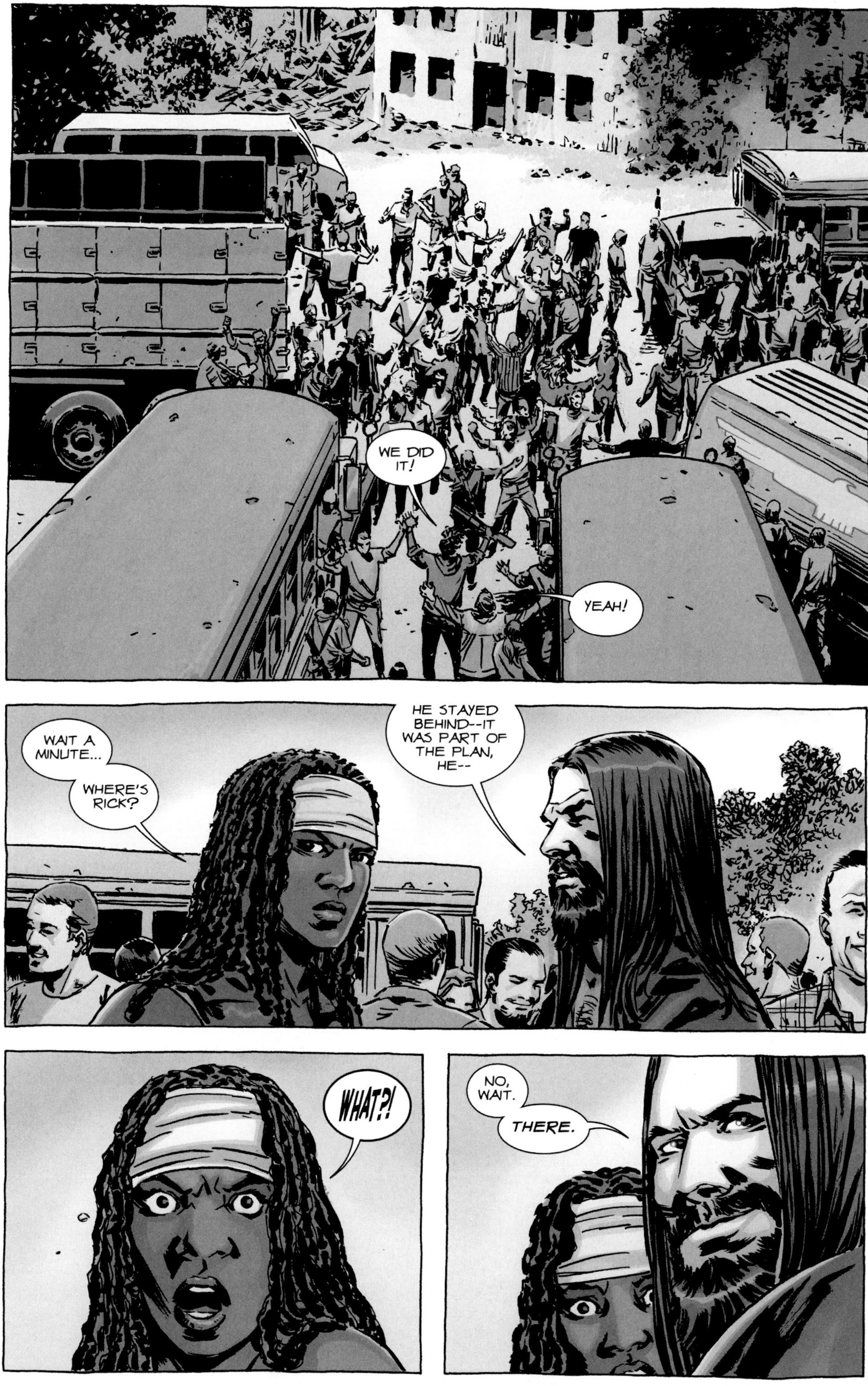
WE DID IT!
YEAH!
WAIT A MINUTE...
WHERE'S RICK?
HE STAYED BEHIND--IT WAS PART OF THE PLAN, HE--
WHAT?!
NO, WAIT.
THERE.

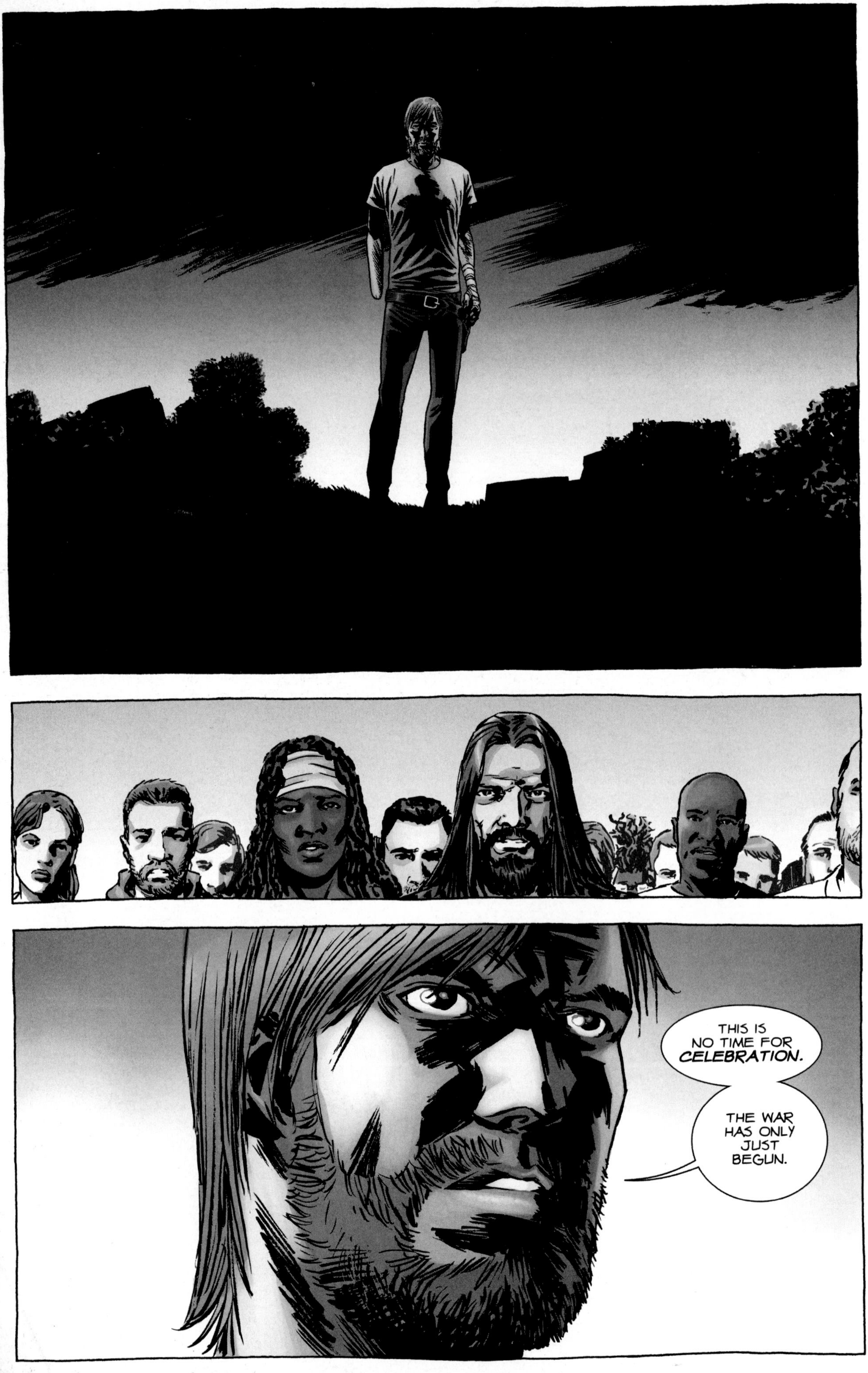
THIS IS NO TIME FOR CELEBRATION.
THE WAR HAS ONLY JUST BEGUN.

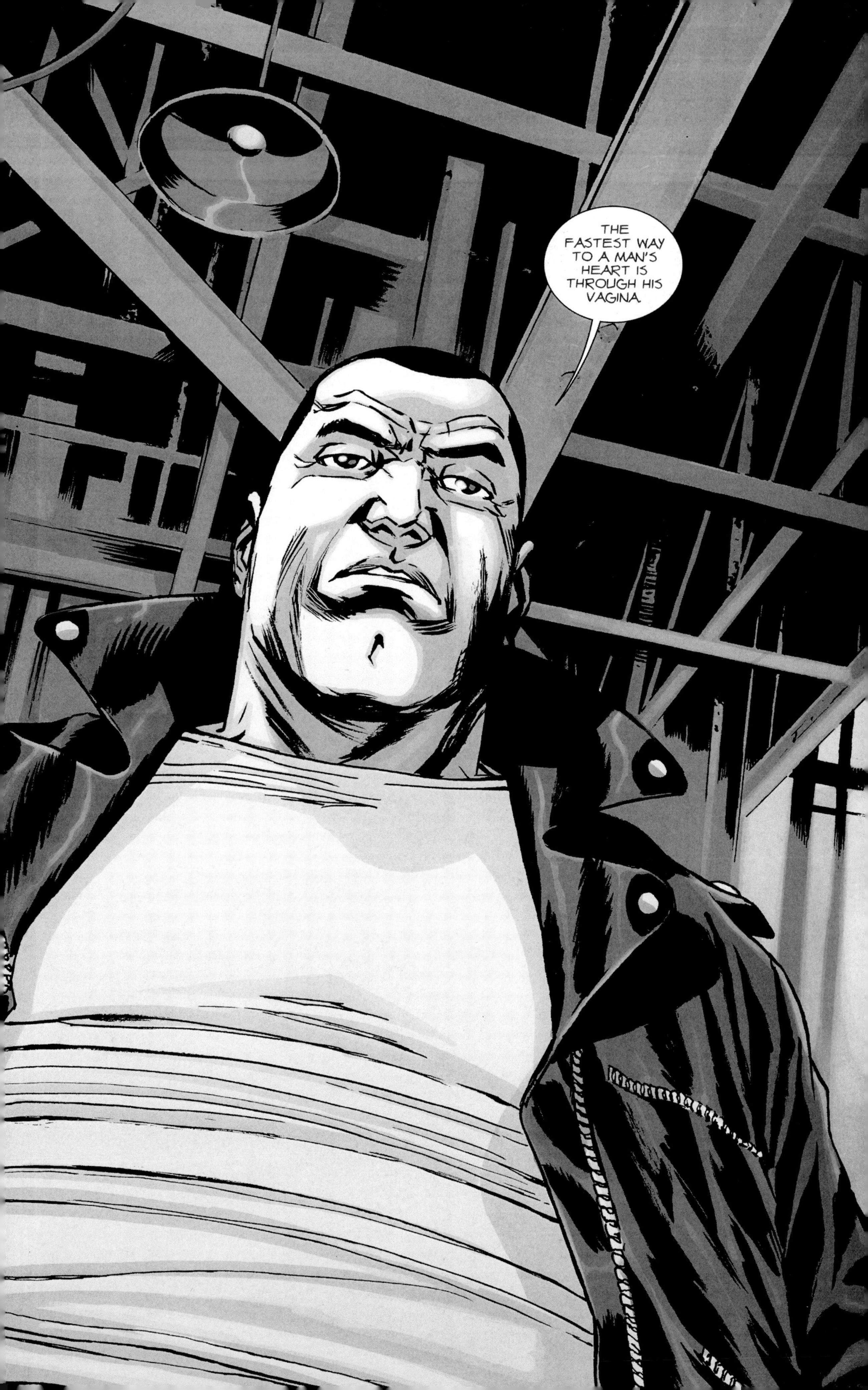
THE FASTEST WAY TO A MAN'S HEART IS THROUGH HIS VAGINA.

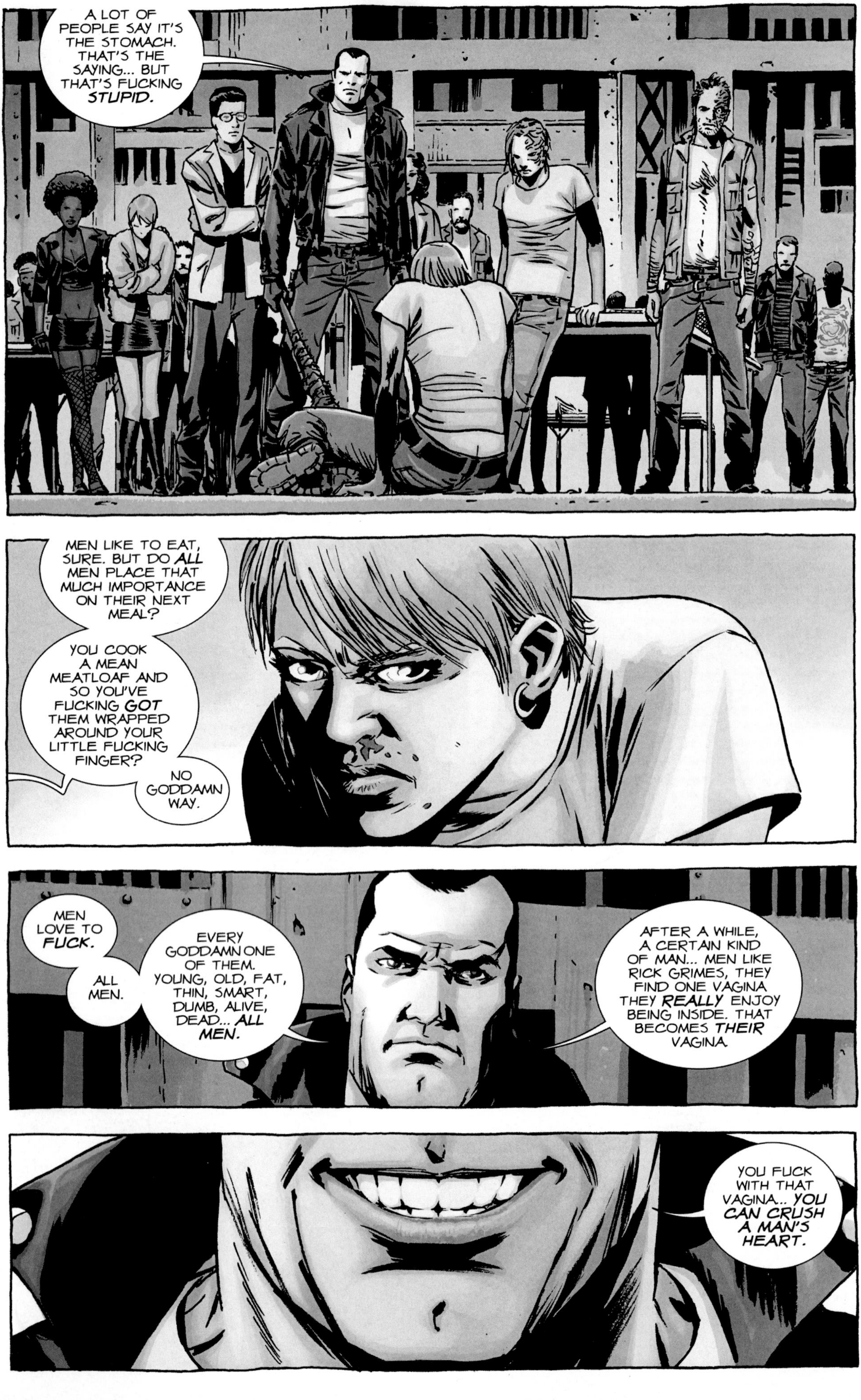
A LOT OF PEOPLE SAY IT'S THE STOMACH. THAT'S THE SAYING... BUT THAT'S FUCKING STUPID.
MEN LIKE TO EAT, SURE. BUT DO ALL MEN PLACE THAT MUCH IMPORTANCE ON THEIR NEXT MEAL?
YOU COOK A MEAN MEATLOAF AND SO YOU'VE FUCKING GOT THEM WRAPPED AROUND YOUR LITTLE FUCKING FINGER?
NO GODDAMN WAY.
MEN LOVE TO FUCK.
ALL MEN.
EVERY GODDAMN ONE OF THEM. YOUNG, OLD, FAT, THIN, SMART, DUMB, ALIVE, DEAD... ALL MEN.
AFTER A WHILE, A CERTAIN KIND OF MAN... MEN LIKE RICK GRIMES, THEY FIND ONE VAGINA THEY REALLY ENJOY BEING INSIDE. THAT BECOMES THEIR VAGINA.
YOU FUCK WITH THAT VAGINA... YOU CAN CRUSH A MAN'S HEART.

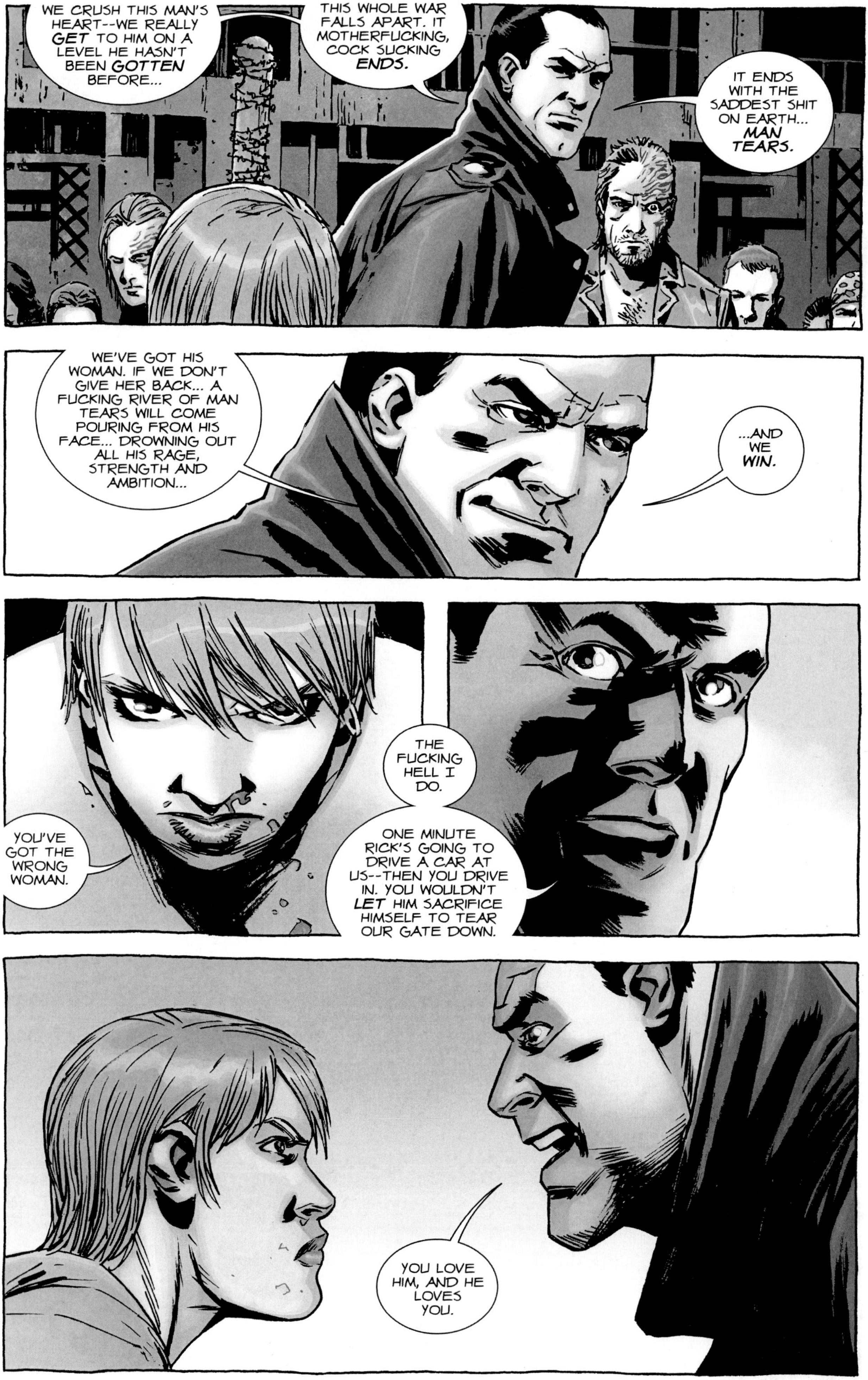
WE CRUSH THIS MAN'S HEART--WE REALLY GET TO HIM ON A LEVEL HE HASN'T BEEN GOTTEN BEFORE...
THIS WHOLE WAR FALLS APART. IT MOTHERFUCKING, COCK SUCKING ENDS.
IT ENDS WITH THE SADDEST SHIT ON EARTH... MAN TEARS.
WE'VE GOT HIS WOMAN. IF WE DON'T GIVE HER BACK... A FUCKING RIVER OF MAN TEARS WILL COME POURING FROM HIS FACE... DROWNING OUT ALL HIS RAGE, STRENGTH AND AMBITION...
...AND WE WIN.
YOU'VE GOT THE WRONG WOMAN.
THE FUCKING HELL I DO.
ONE MINUTE RICK'S GOING TO DRIVE A CAR AT US--THEN YOU DRIVE IN. YOU WOULDN'T LET HIM SACRIFICE HIMSELF TO TEAR OUR GATE DOWN.
YOU LOVE HIM, AND HE LOVES YOU.

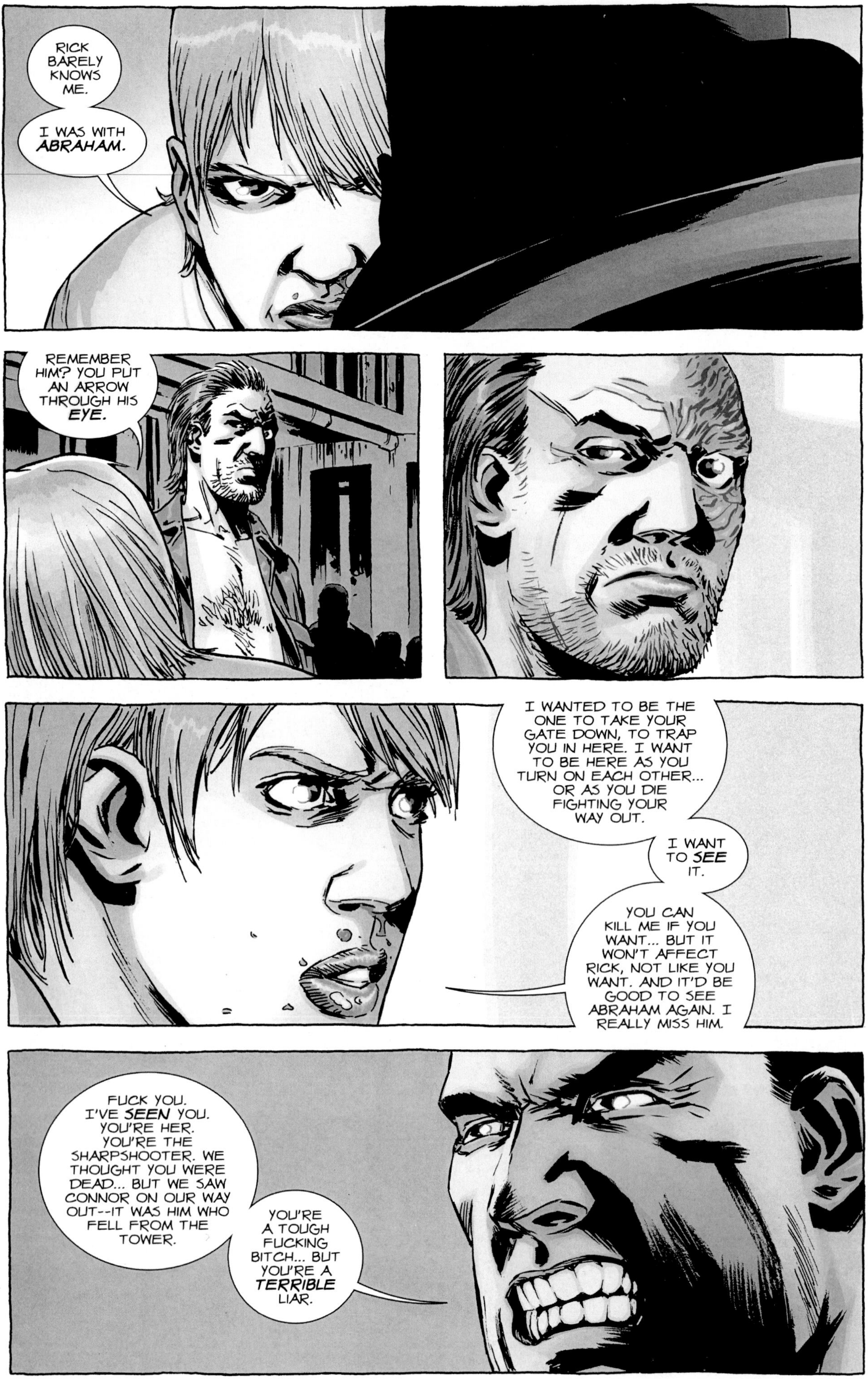
RICK BARELY KNOWS ME.
I WAS WITH ABRAHAM.
REMEMBER HIM? YOU PUT AN ARROW THROUGH HIS EYE.
I WANTED TO BE THE ONE TO TAKE YOUR GATE DOWN, TO TRAP YOU IN HERE. I WANT TO BE HERE AS YOU TURN ON EACH OTHER... OR AS YOU DIE FIGHTING YOUR WAY OUT.
I WANT TO SEE IT.
YOU CAN KILL ME IF YOU WANT... BUT IT WON'T AFFECT RICK, NOT LIKE YOU WANT. AND IT'D BE GOOD TO SEE ABRAHAM AGAIN. I REALLY MISS HIM.
FUCK YOU. I'VE SEEN YOU. YOU'RE HER. YOU'RE THE SHARPSHOOTER. WE THOUGHT YOU WERE DEAD... BUT WE SAW CONNOR ON OUR WAY OUT--IT WAS HIM WHO FELL FROM THE TOWER.
YOU'RE A TOUGH FUCKING BITCH... BUT YOU'RE A TERRIBLE LIAR.

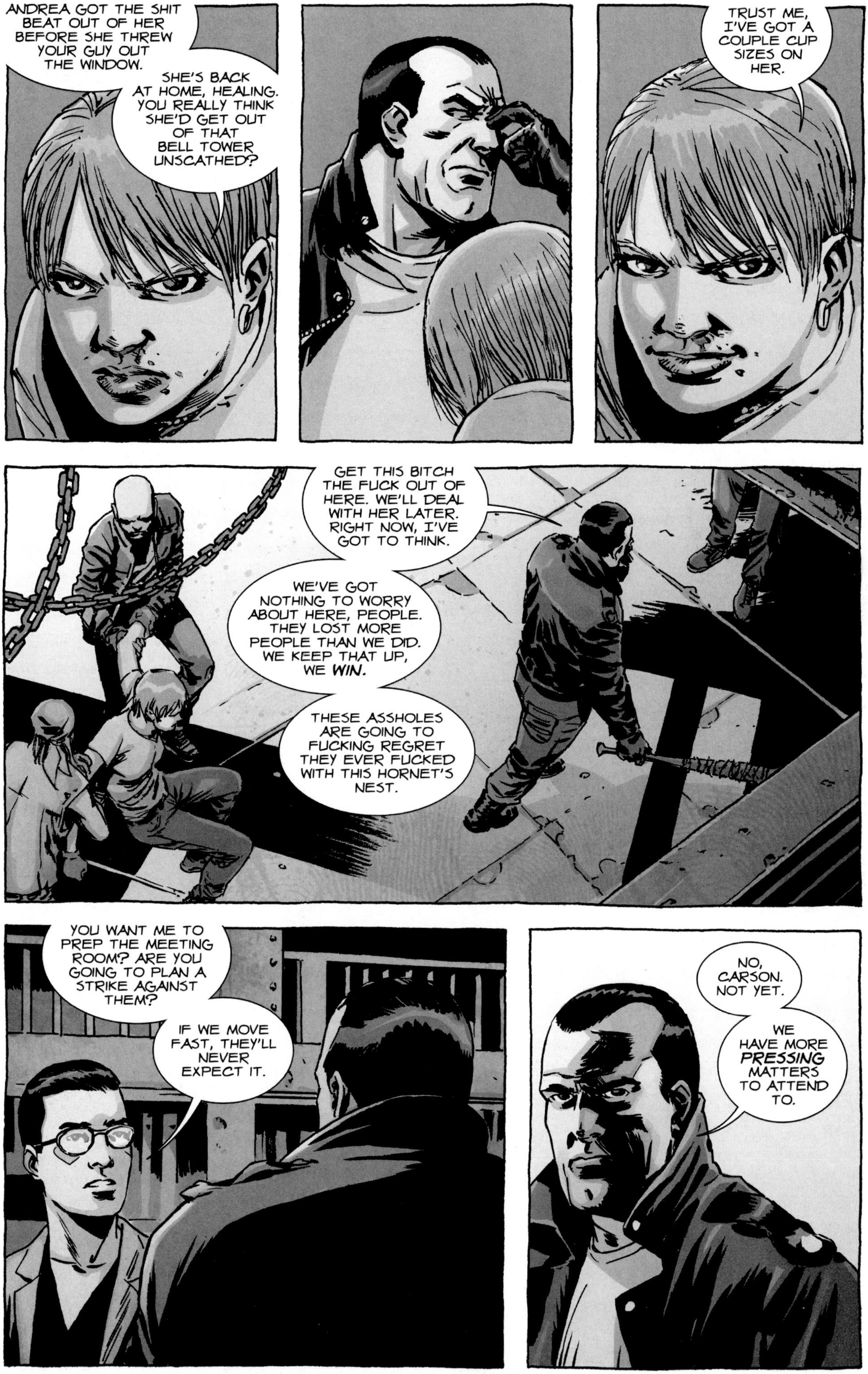
ANDREA GOT THE SHIT BEAT OUT OF HER BEFORE SHE THREW YOUR GUY OUT THE WINDOW.
SHE'S BACK AT HOME, HEALING. YOU REALLY THINK SHE'D GET OUT OF THAT BELL TOWER UNSCATHED?
TRUST ME, I'VE GOT A COUPLE CUP SIZES ON HER.
GET THIS BITCH THE FUCK OUT OF HERE. WE'LL DEAL WITH HER LATER. RIGHT NOW, I'VE GOT TO THINK.
WE'VE GOT NOTHING TO WORRY ABOUT HERE, PEOPLE. THEY LOST MORE PEOPLE THAN WE DID. WE KEEP THAT UP, WE *WIN.*
THESE ASSHOLES ARE GOING TO FUCKING REGRET THEY EVER FUCKED WITH THIS HORNET'S NEST.
YOU WANT ME TO PREP THE MEETING ROOM? ARE YOU GOING TO PLAN A STRIKE AGAINST THEM?
IF WE MOVE FAST, THEY'LL NEVER EXPECT IT.
NO, CARSON. NOT YET.
WE HAVE MORE ***PRESSING*** MATTERS TO ATTEND TO.

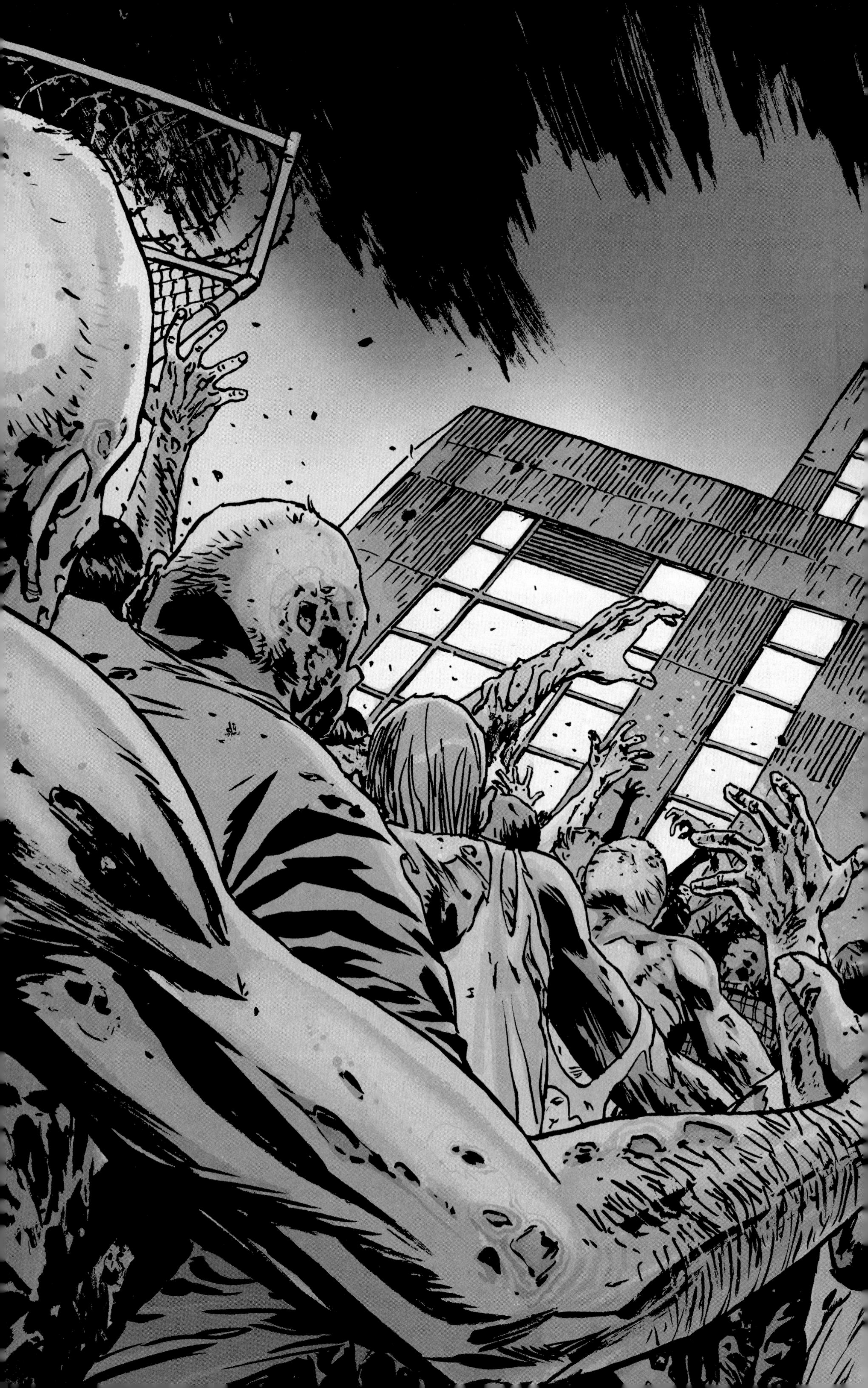

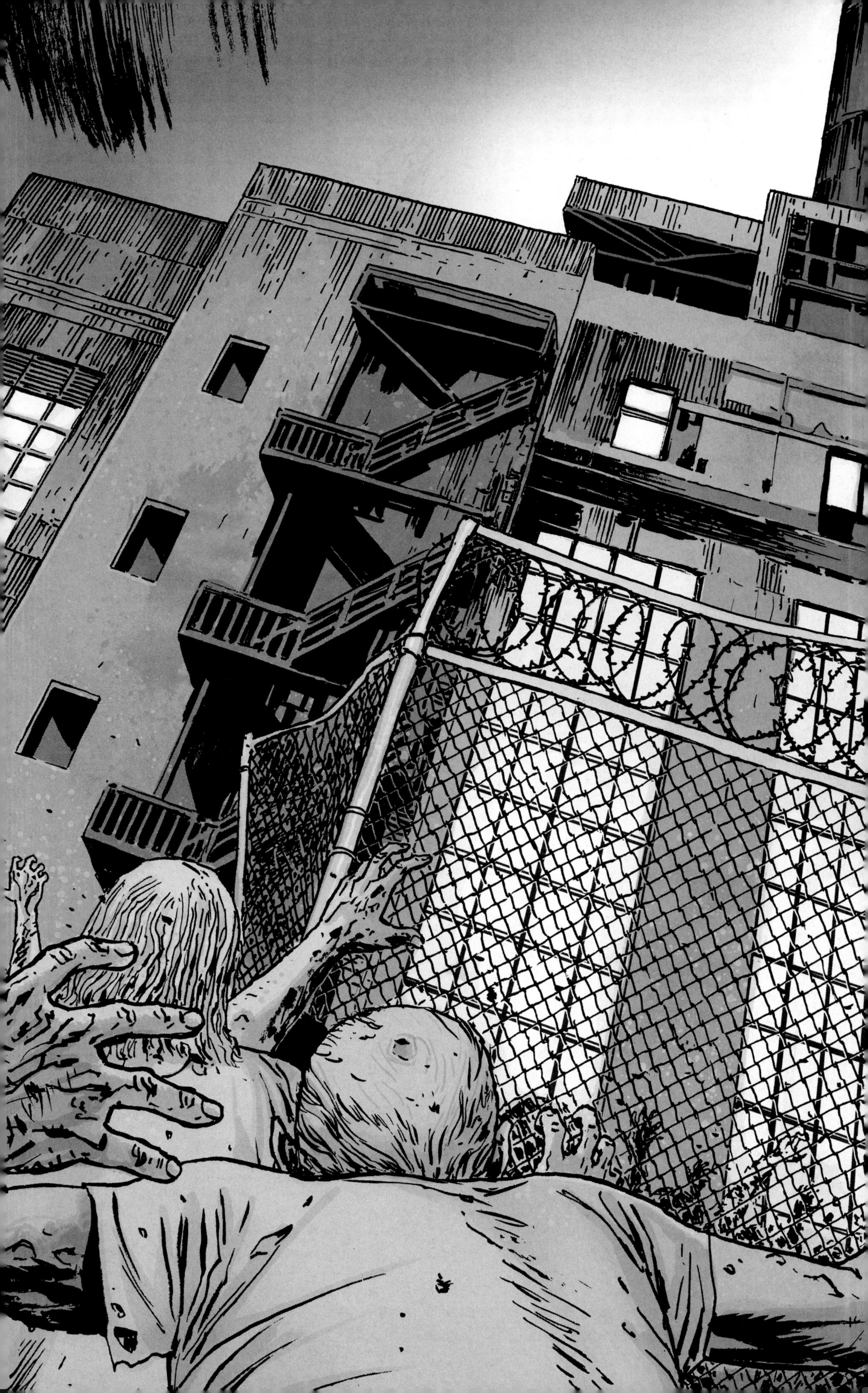

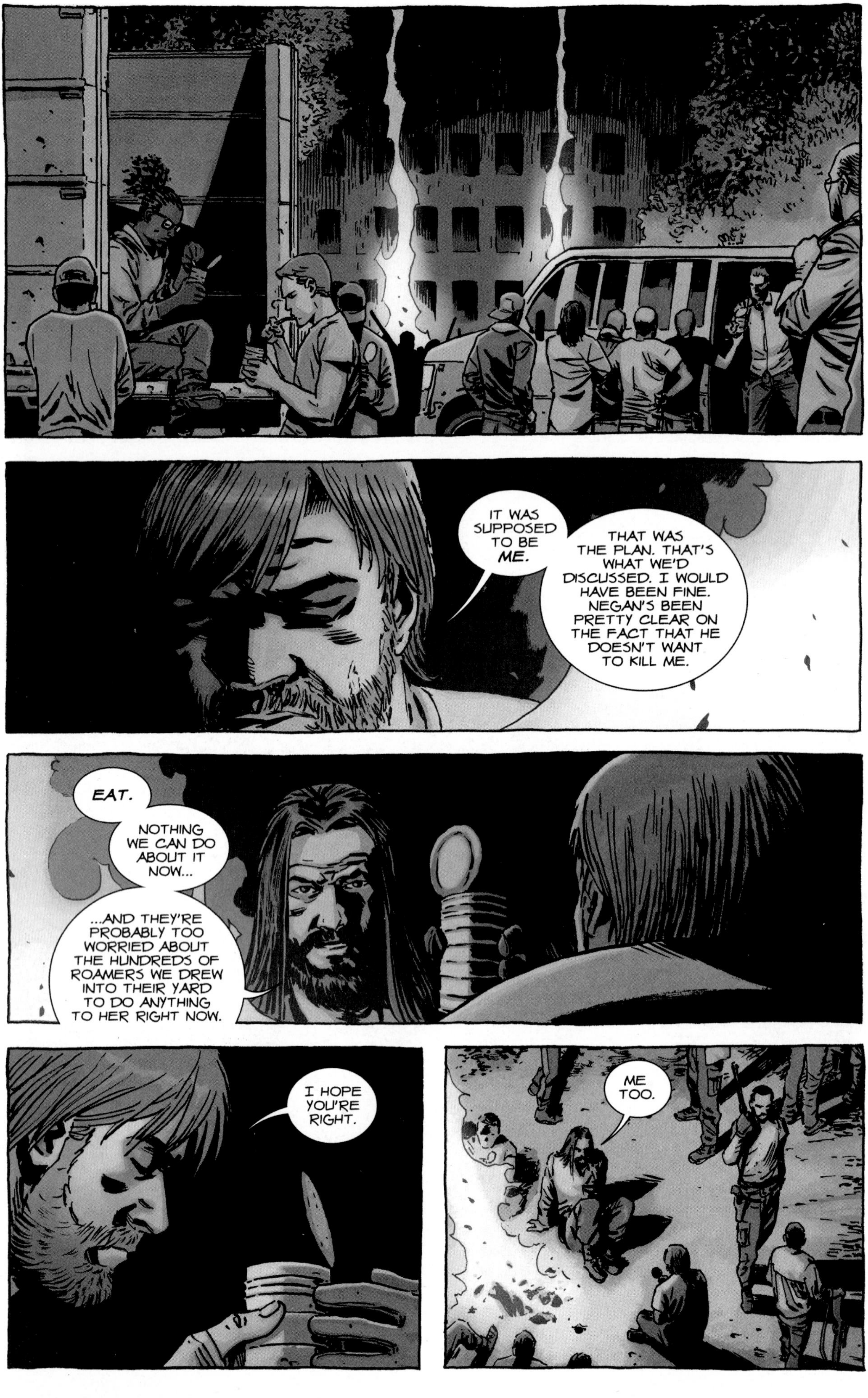
IT WAS SUPPOSED TO BE ME.
THAT WAS THE PLAN. THAT'S WHAT WE'D DISCUSSED. I WOULD HAVE BEEN FINE. NEGAN'S BEEN PRETTY CLEAR ON THE FACT THAT HE DOESN'T WANT TO KILL ME.
EAT.
NOTHING WE CAN DO ABOUT IT NOW...
...AND THEY'RE PROBABLY TOO WORRIED ABOUT THE HUNDREDS OF ROAMERS WE DREW INTO THEIR YARD TO DO ANYTHING TO HER RIGHT NOW.
I HOPE YOU'RE RIGHT.
ME TOO.

SNARRL!

GRUH.

THAT GONNA MAKE HIM SICK?

HER. SHIVA IS A GIRL.

BUT NO. TIGERS HAVE BEEN KNOWN TO EAT FAR WORSE.

WHATEVER IS IN THEM THAT MAKES US GET UP AND WALK SEEMS TO HAVE NO EFFECT ON ANIMALS.

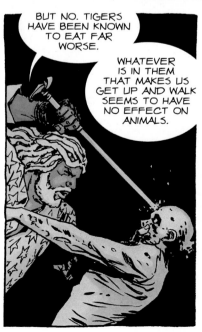

HM.

THAT SAID, I WOULDN'T SMELL HER BREATH ANYTIME SOON.

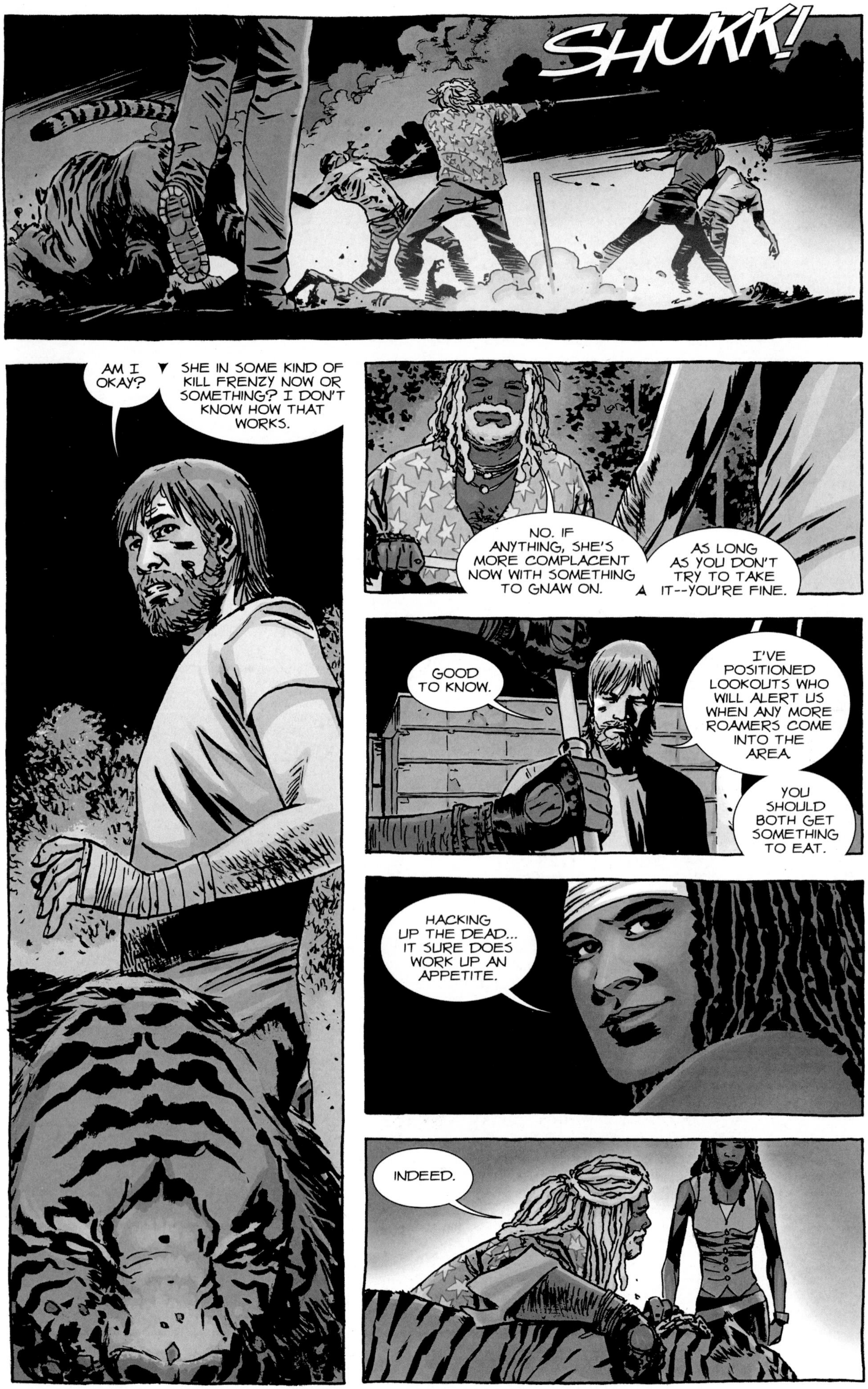
SHUKK!
AM I OKAY?
SHE IN SOME KIND OF KILL FRENZY NOW OR SOMETHING? I DON'T KNOW HOW THAT WORKS.
NO. IF ANYTHING, SHE'S MORE COMPLACENT NOW WITH SOMETHING TO GNAW ON.
AS LONG AS YOU DON'T TRY TO TAKE IT--YOU'RE FINE.
GOOD TO KNOW.
I'VE POSITIONED LOOKOUTS WHO WILL ALERT US WHEN ANY MORE ROAMERS COME INTO THE AREA.
YOU SHOULD BOTH GET SOMETHING TO EAT.
HACKING UP THE DEAD... IT SURE DOES WORK UP AN APPETITE.
INDEED.

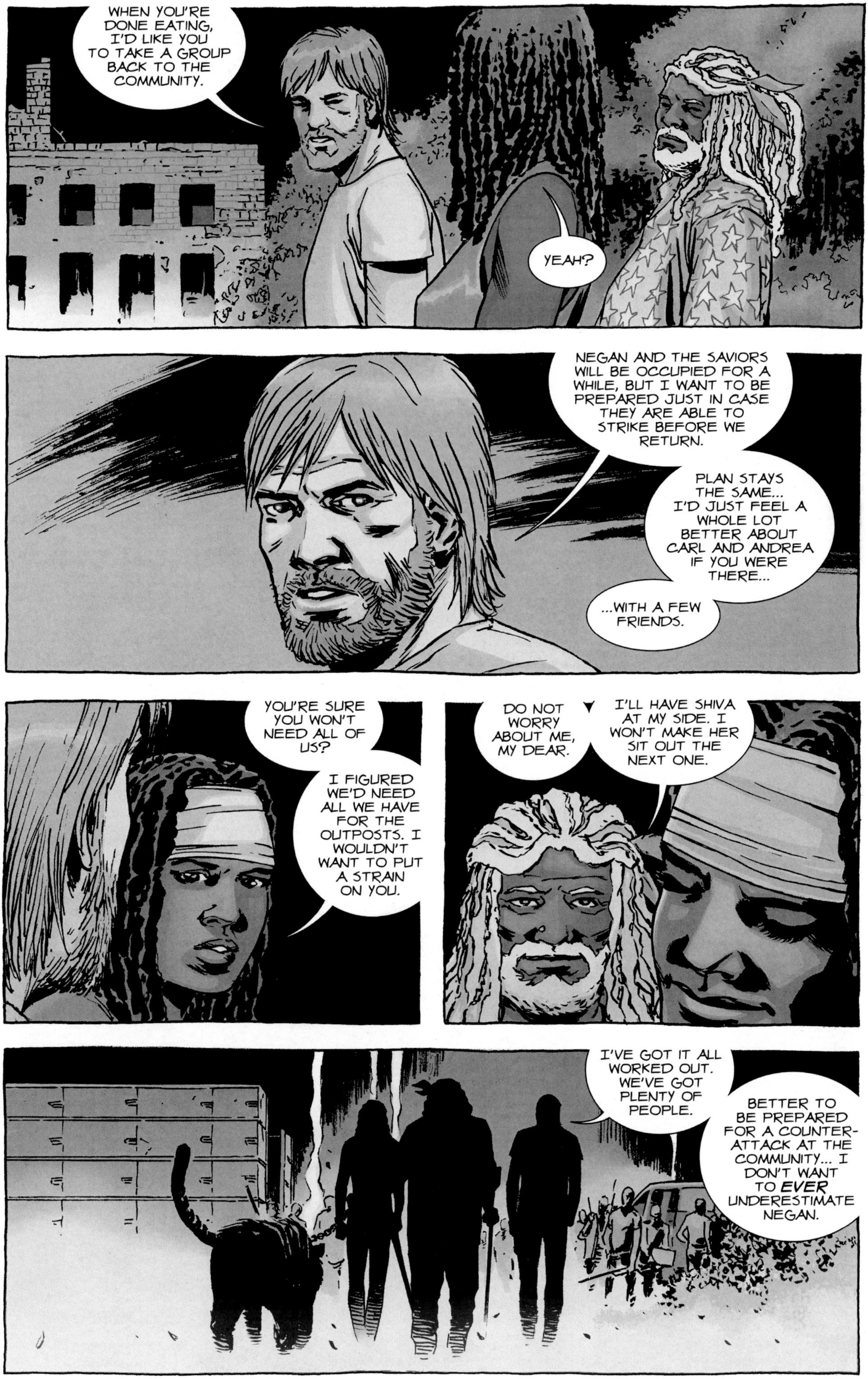
WHEN YOU'RE DONE EATING, I'D LIKE YOU TO TAKE A GROUP BACK TO THE COMMUNITY.
YEAH?
NEGAN AND THE SAVIORS WILL BE OCCUPIED FOR A WHILE, BUT I WANT TO BE PREPARED JUST IN CASE THEY ARE ABLE TO STRIKE BEFORE WE RETURN.
PLAN STAYS THE SAME... I'D JUST FEEL A WHOLE LOT BETTER ABOUT CARL AND ANDREA IF YOU WERE THERE...
...WITH A FEW FRIENDS.
YOU'RE SURE YOU WON'T NEED ALL OF US?
I FIGURED WE'D NEED ALL WE HAVE FOR THE OUTPOSTS. I WOULDN'T WANT TO PUT A STRAIN ON YOU.
DO NOT WORRY ABOUT ME, MY DEAR.
I'LL HAVE SHIVA AT MY SIDE. I WON'T MAKE HER SIT OUT THE NEXT ONE.
I'VE GOT IT ALL WORKED OUT. WE'VE GOT PLENTY OF PEOPLE.
BETTER TO BE PREPARED FOR A COUNTER-ATTACK AT THE COMMUNITY... I DON'T WANT TO EVER UNDERESTIMATE NEGAN.

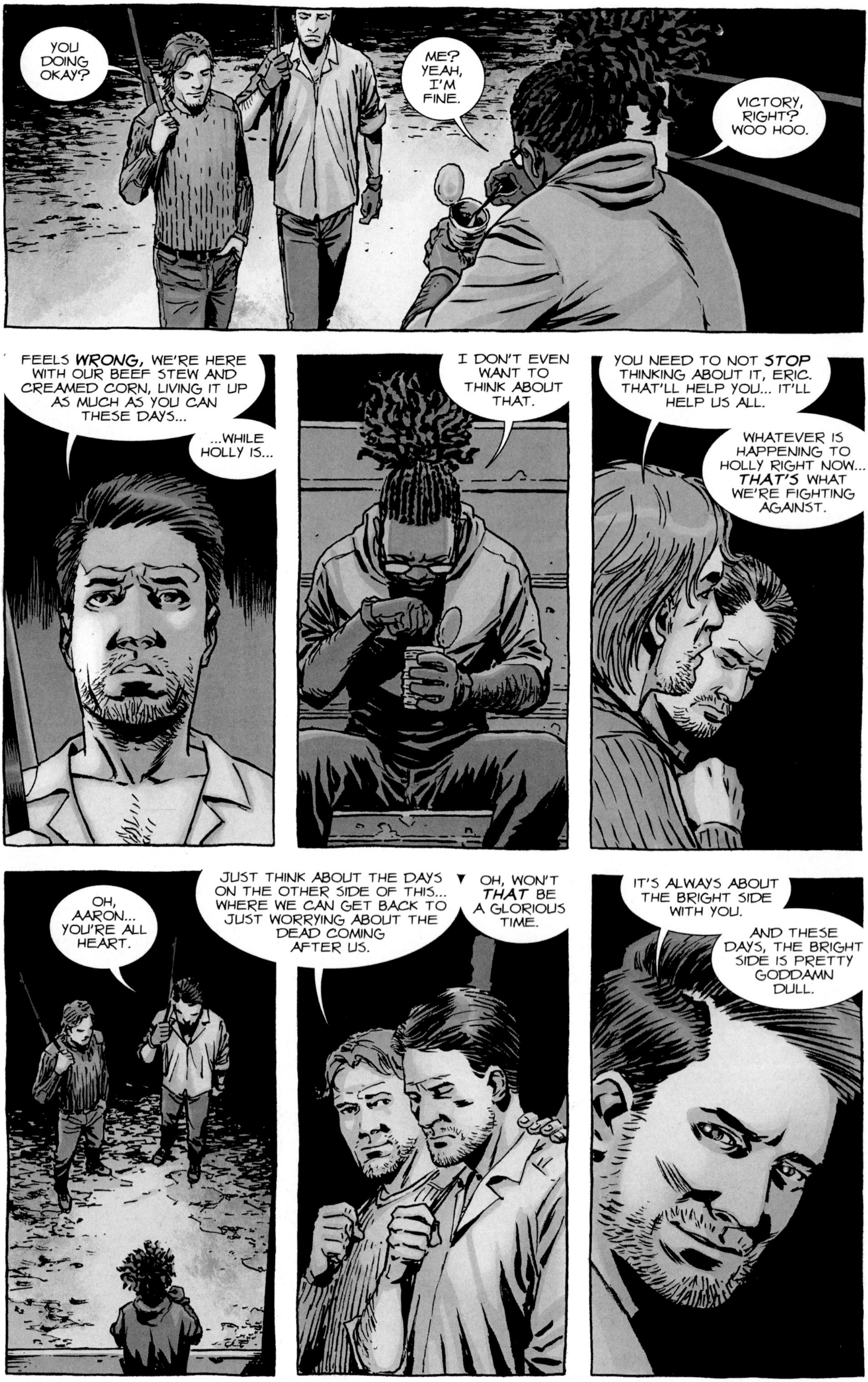
YOU DOING OKAY?
ME? YEAH, I'M FINE.
VICTORY, RIGHT? WOO HOO.
FEELS WRONG, WE'RE HERE WITH OUR BEEF STEW AND CREAMED CORN, LIVING IT UP AS MUCH AS YOU CAN THESE DAYS...
...WHILE HOLLY IS...
I DON'T EVEN WANT TO THINK ABOUT THAT.
YOU NEED TO NOT STOP THINKING ABOUT IT, ERIC. THAT'LL HELP YOU... IT'LL HELP US ALL.
WHATEVER IS HAPPENING TO HOLLY RIGHT NOW... THAT'S WHAT WE'RE FIGHTING AGAINST.
OH, AARON... YOU'RE ALL HEART.
JUST THINK ABOUT THE DAYS ON THE OTHER SIDE OF THIS... WHERE WE CAN GET BACK TO JUST WORRYING ABOUT THE DEAD COMING AFTER US.
OH, WON'T THAT BE A GLORIOUS TIME.
IT'S ALWAYS ABOUT THE BRIGHT SIDE WITH YOU.
AND THESE DAYS, THE BRIGHT SIDE IS PRETTY GODDAMN DULL.

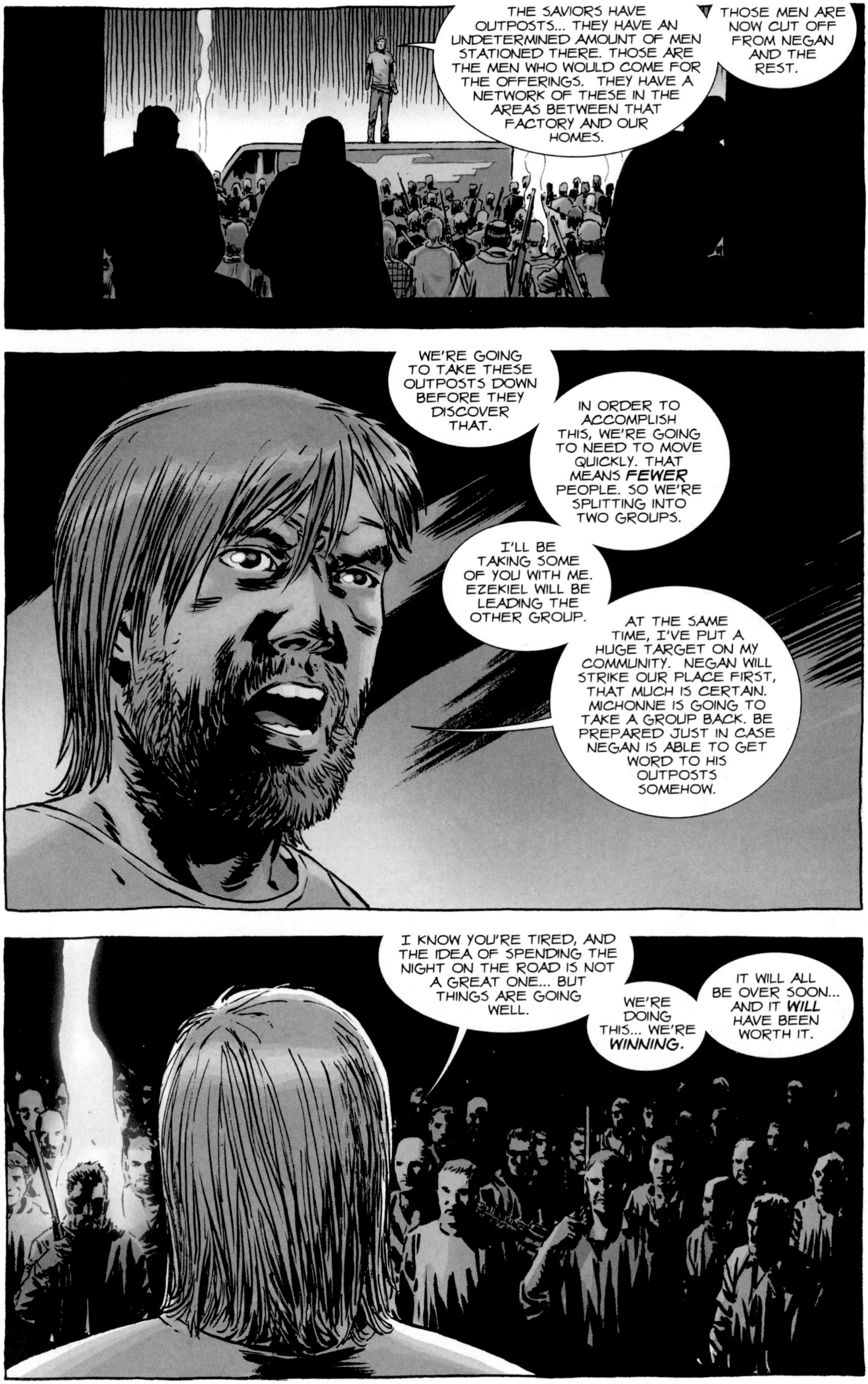
THE SAVIORS HAVE OUTPOSTS... THEY HAVE AN UNDETERMINED AMOUNT OF MEN STATIONED THERE. THOSE ARE THE MEN WHO WOULD COME FOR THE OFFERINGS. THEY HAVE A NETWORK OF THESE IN THE AREAS BETWEEN THAT FACTORY AND OUR HOMES.
THOSE MEN ARE NOW CUT OFF FROM NEGAN AND THE REST.
WE'RE GOING TO TAKE THESE OUTPOSTS DOWN BEFORE THEY DISCOVER THAT.
IN ORDER TO ACCOMPLISH THIS, WE'RE GOING TO NEED TO MOVE QUICKLY. THAT MEANS FEWER PEOPLE. SO WE'RE SPLITTING INTO TWO GROUPS.
I'LL BE TAKING SOME OF YOU WITH ME. EZEKIEL WILL BE LEADING THE OTHER GROUP.
AT THE SAME TIME, I'VE PUT A HUGE TARGET ON MY COMMUNITY. NEGAN WILL STRIKE OUR PLACE FIRST, THAT MUCH IS CERTAIN. MICHONNE IS GOING TO TAKE A GROUP BACK. BE PREPARED JUST IN CASE NEGAN IS ABLE TO GET WORD TO HIS OUTPOSTS SOMEHOW.
I KNOW YOU'RE TIRED, AND THE IDEA OF SPENDING THE NIGHT ON THE ROAD IS NOT A GREAT ONE... BUT THINGS ARE GOING WELL.
WE'RE DOING THIS... WE'RE WINNING.
IT WILL ALL BE OVER SOON... AND IT WILL HAVE BEEN WORTH IT.

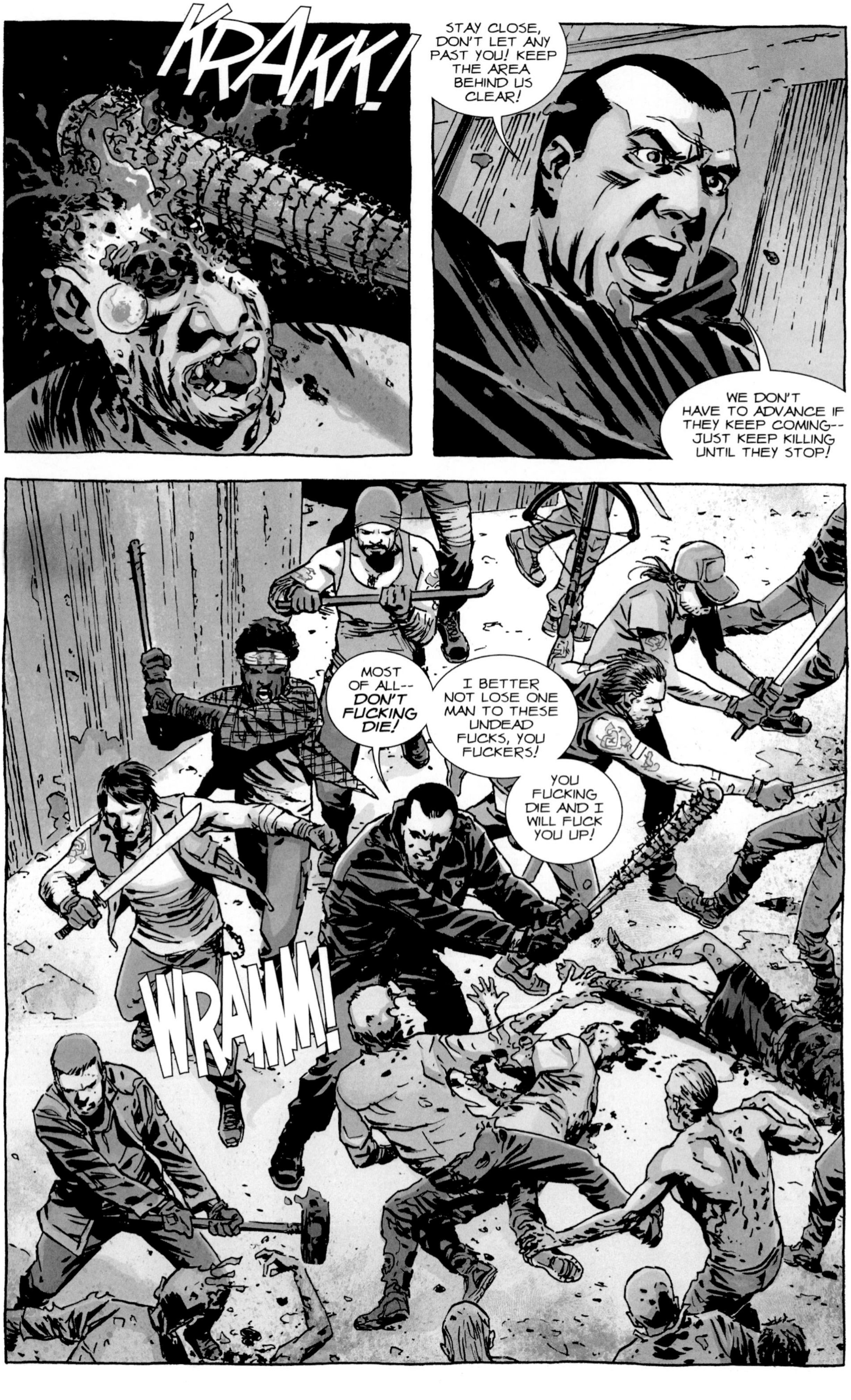
KRAKK!
STAY CLOSE, DON'T LET ANY PAST YOU! KEEP THE AREA BEHIND US CLEAR!
WE DON'T HAVE TO ADVANCE IF THEY KEEP COMING-- JUST KEEP KILLING UNTIL THEY STOP!
I BETTER NOT LOSE ONE MAN TO THESE UNDEAD FUCKS, YOU FUCKERS!
YOU FUCKING DIE AND I WILL FUCK YOU UP!
MOST OF ALL-- DON'T FUCKING DIE!
WRAMM!

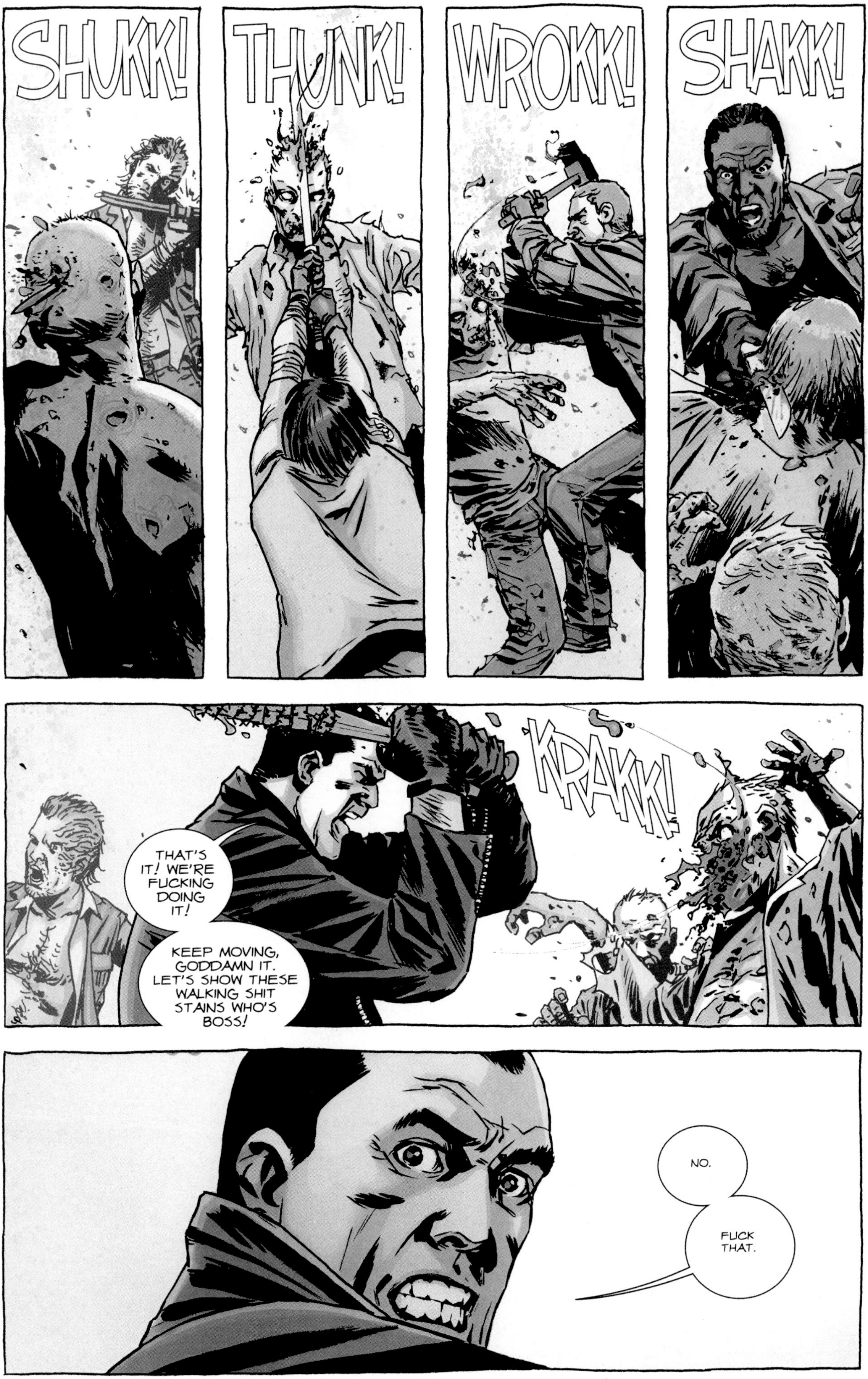
SHUKK!
THUNK!
WROKK!
SHAKK!
KRAKK!
THAT'S IT! WE'RE FUCKING DOING IT!
KEEP MOVING, GODDAMN IT. LET'S SHOW THESE WALKING SHIT STAINS WHO'S BOSS!
NO.
FUCK THAT.

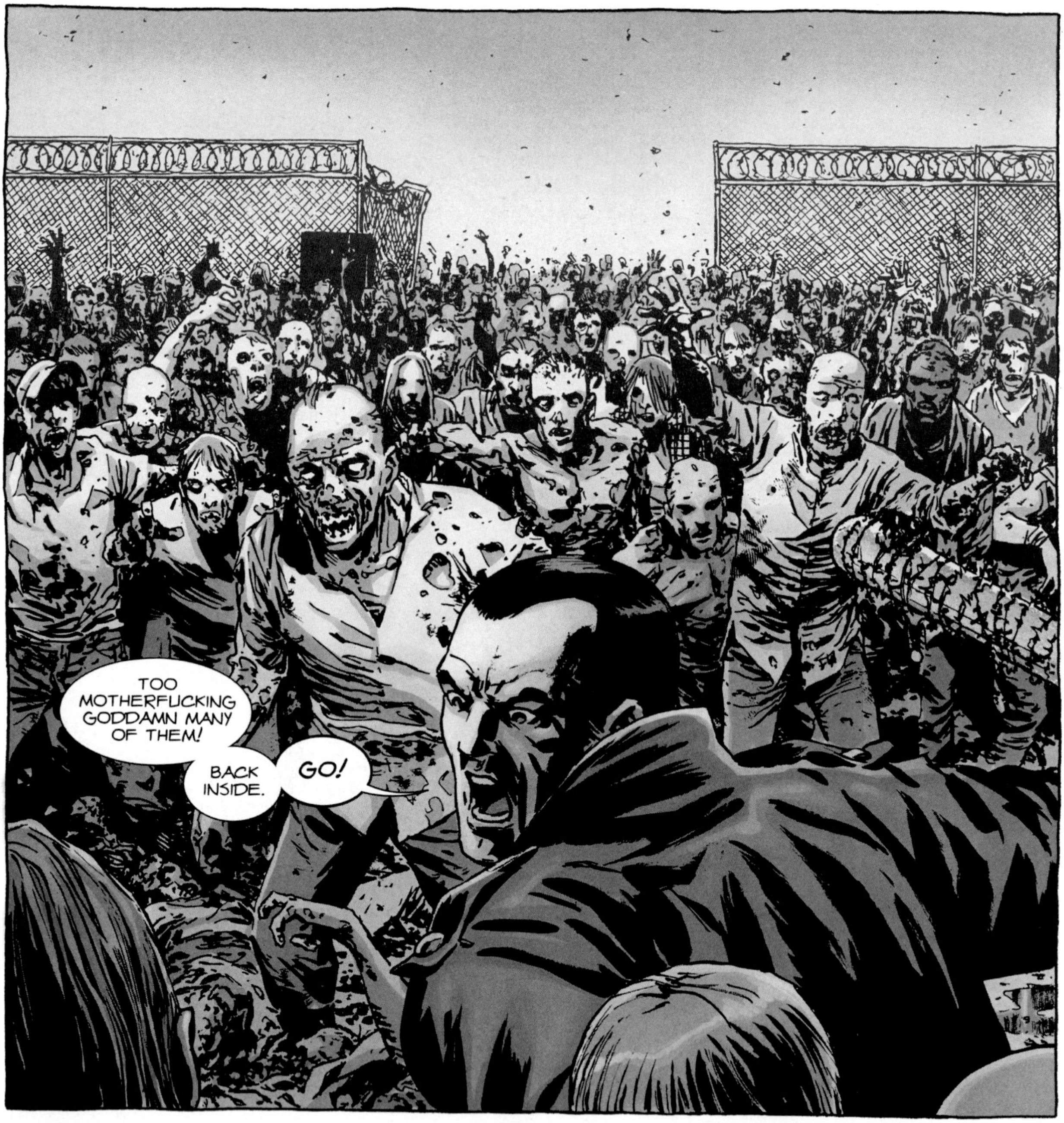
TOO MOTHERFUCKING GODDAMN MANY OF THEM!
BACK INSIDE.
GO!

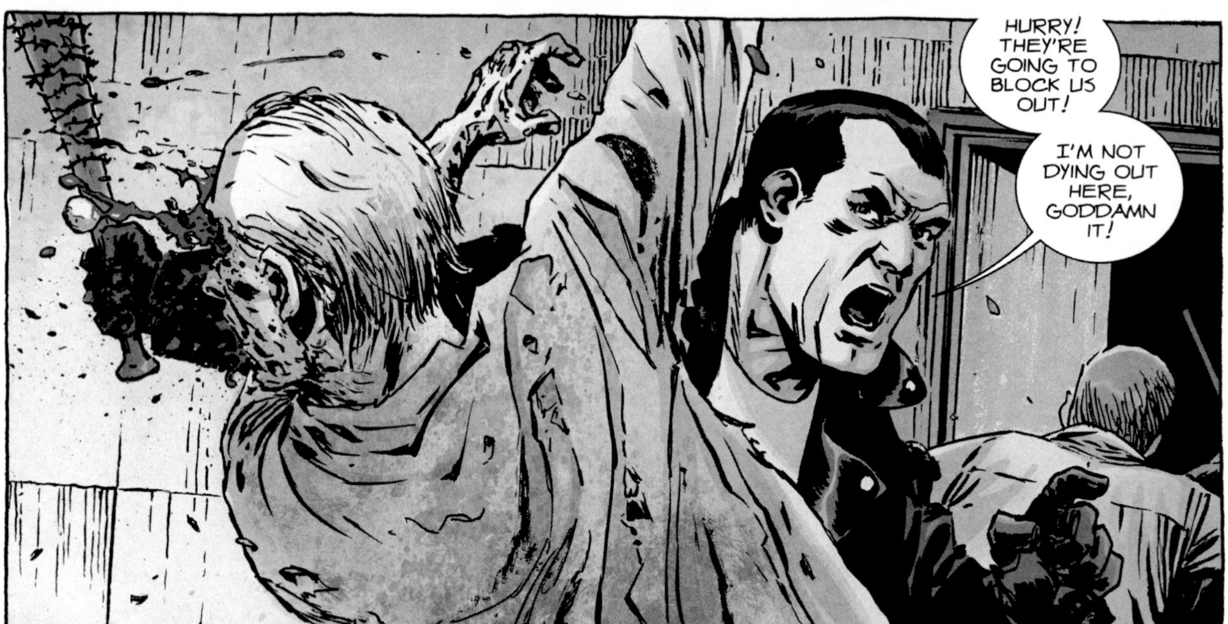
HURRY! THEY'RE GOING TO BLOCK US OUT!
I'M NOT DYING OUT HERE, GODDAMN IT!

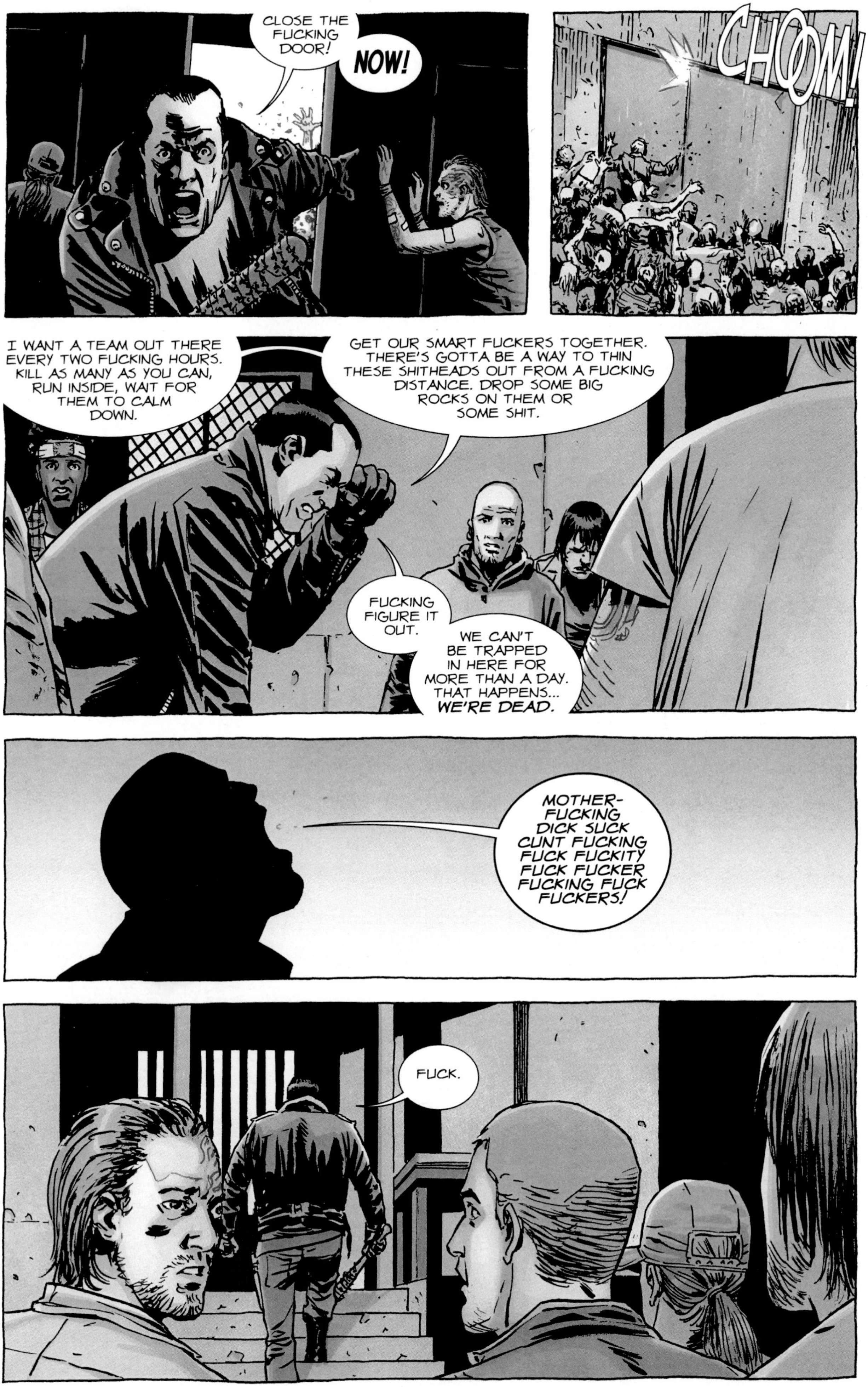
CLOSE THE FUCKING DOOR!
NOW!
CHOOM!
I WANT A TEAM OUT THERE EVERY TWO FUCKING HOURS. KILL AS MANY AS YOU CAN, RUN INSIDE, WAIT FOR THEM TO CALM DOWN.
GET OUR SMART FUCKERS TOGETHER. THERE'S GOTTA BE A WAY TO THIN THESE SHITHEADS OUT FROM A FUCKING DISTANCE. DROP SOME BIG ROCKS ON THEM OR SOME SHIT.
FUCKING FIGURE IT OUT.
WE CAN'T BE TRAPPED IN HERE FOR MORE THAN A DAY. THAT HAPPENS... WE'RE DEAD.
MOTHER-FUCKING DICK SUCK CUNT FUCKING FUCK FUCKITY FUCK FUCKER FUCKING FUCK FUCKERS!
FUCK.

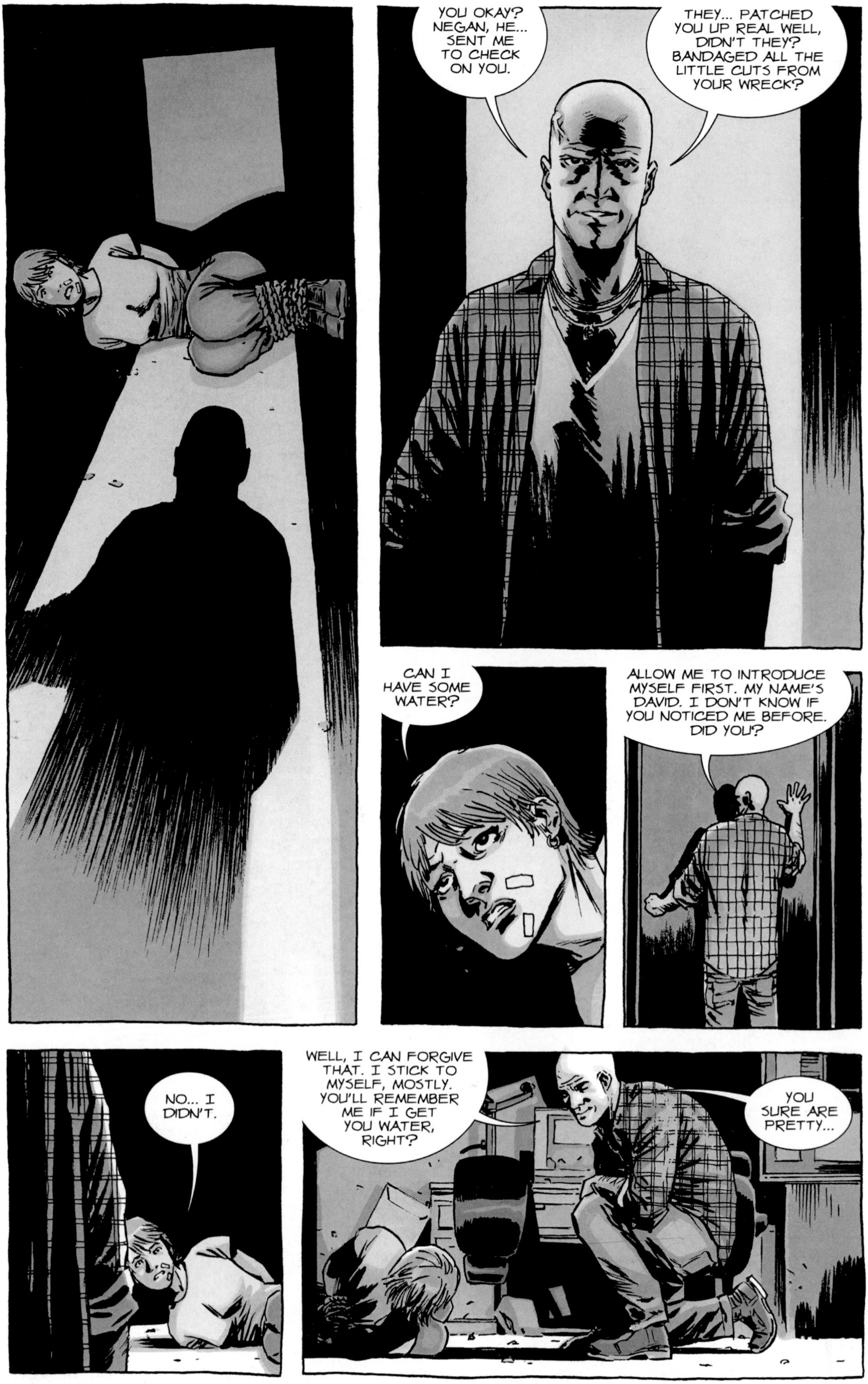
YOU OKAY? NEGAN, HE... SENT ME TO CHECK ON YOU.
THEY... PATCHED YOU UP REAL WELL, DIDN'T THEY? BANDAGED ALL THE LITTLE CUTS FROM YOUR WRECK?
CAN I HAVE SOME WATER?
ALLOW ME TO INTRODUCE MYSELF FIRST. MY NAME'S DAVID. I DON'T KNOW IF YOU NOTICED ME BEFORE. DID YOU?
NO... I DIDN'T.
WELL, I CAN FORGIVE THAT. I STICK TO MYSELF, MOSTLY. YOU'LL REMEMBER ME IF I GET YOU WATER, RIGHT?
YOU SURE ARE PRETTY...

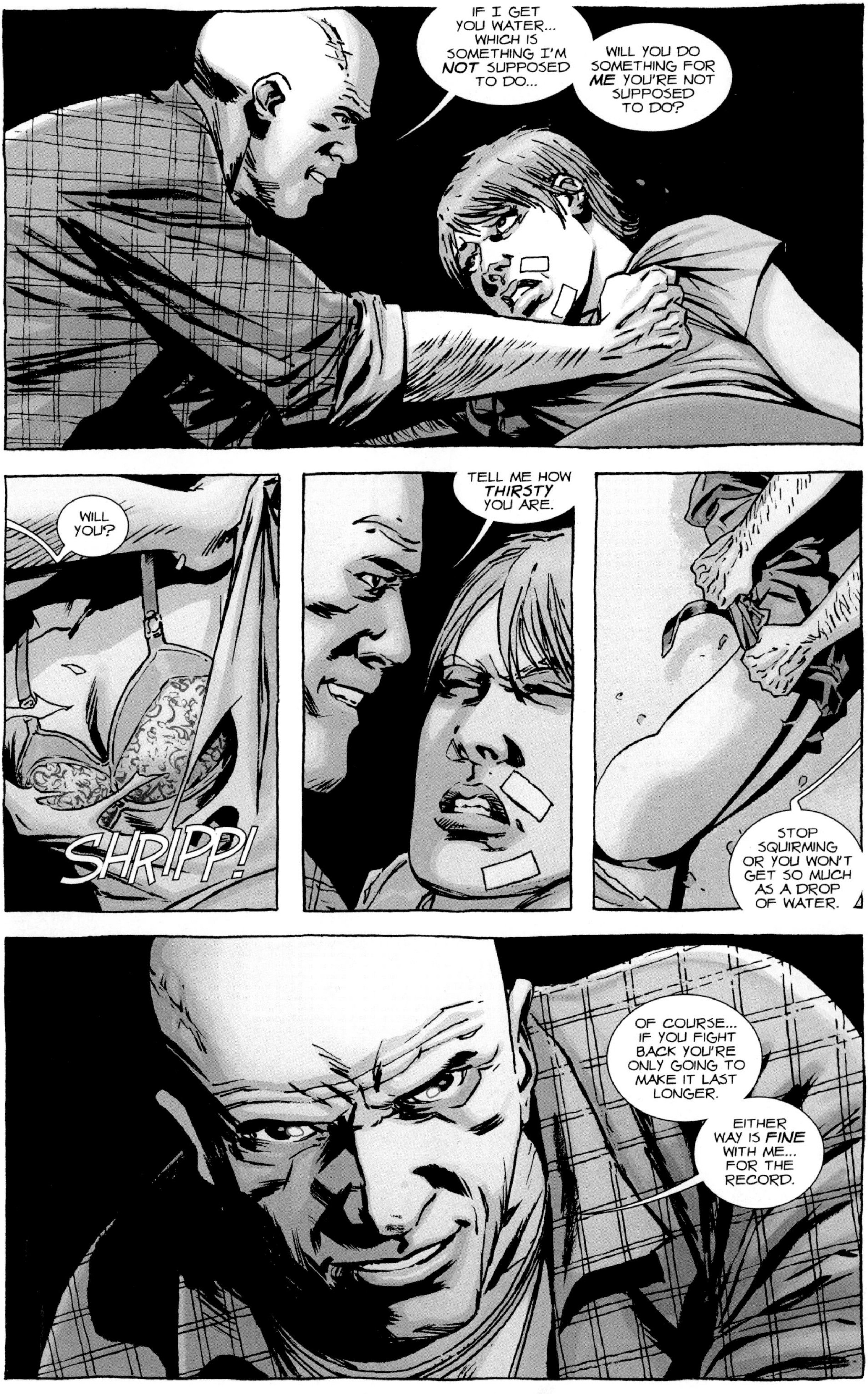
IF I GET YOU WATER... WHICH IS SOMETHING I'M NOT SUPPOSED TO DO...
WILL YOU DO SOMETHING FOR ME YOU'RE NOT SUPPOSED TO DO?
WILL YOU?
SHRIPP!
TELL ME HOW THIRSTY YOU ARE.
STOP SQUIRMING OR YOU WON'T GET SO MUCH AS A DROP OF WATER.
OF COURSE... IF YOU FIGHT BACK YOU'RE ONLY GOING TO MAKE IT LAST LONGER.
EITHER WAY IS FINE WITH ME... FOR THE RECORD.

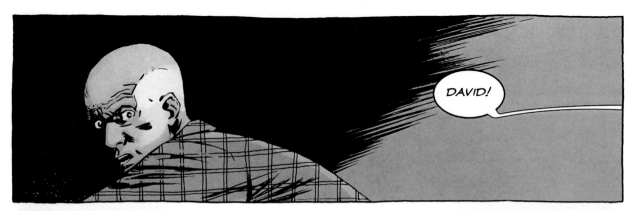

DAVID!

WHAT THE FUCKING FUCK ARE YOU DOING IN HERE?!

NEGAN, SIR--

I--

DO YOU REALLY THINK I NEED YOU TO ANSWER THAT? I CAN FUCKING SEE YOU'RE TRYING TO *RAPE* THIS WOMAN.

YOU WERE GOING TO FUCKING RAPE THIS WOMAN, WEREN'T YOU?!

...

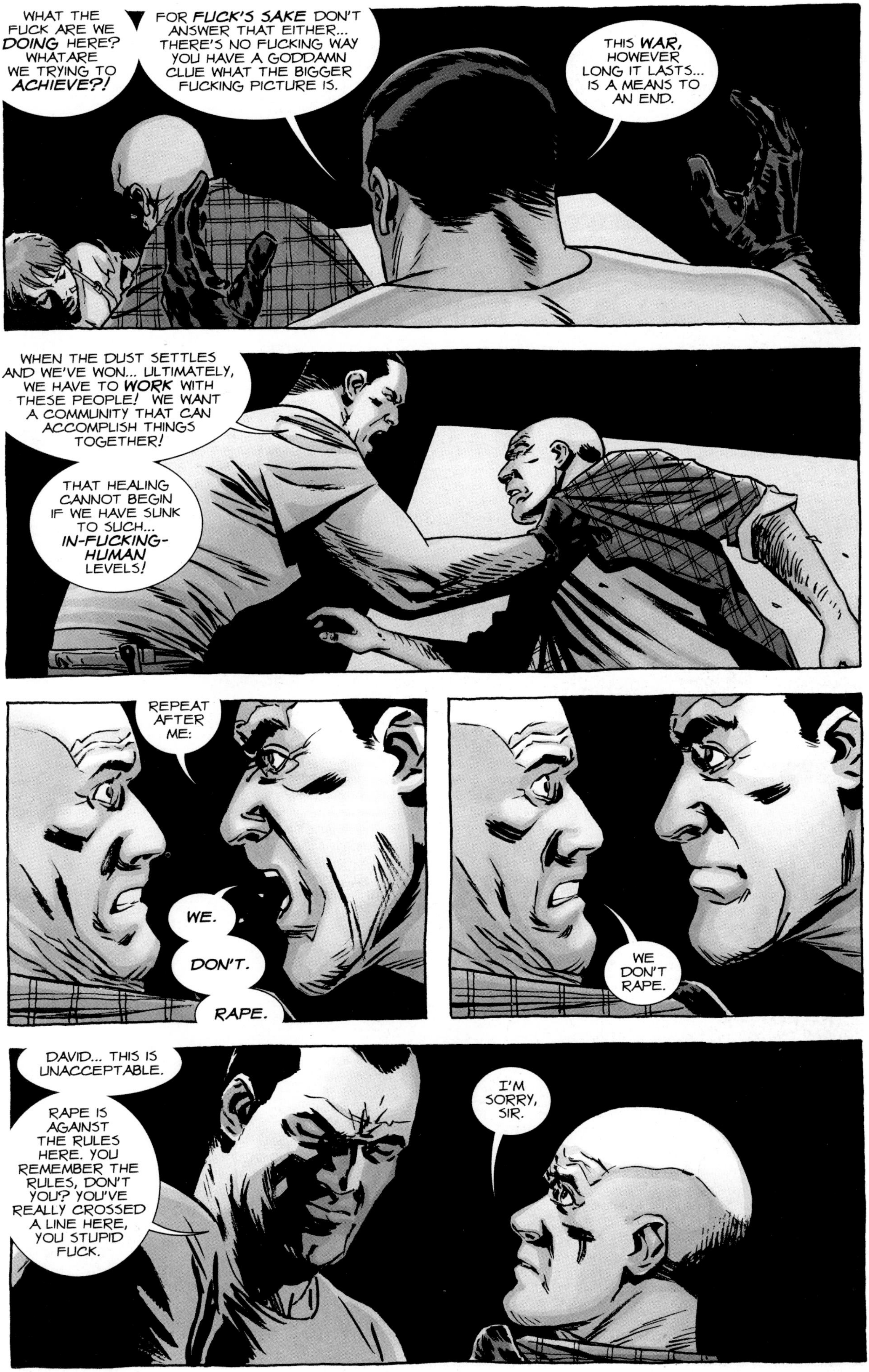

WHAT THE FUCK ARE WE DOING HERE? WHATARE WE TRYING TO ACHIEVE?!
FOR FUCK'S SAKE DON'T ANSWER THAT EITHER... THERE'S NO FUCKING WAY YOU HAVE A GODDAMN CLUE WHAT THE BIGGER FUCKING PICTURE IS.
THIS WAR, HOWEVER LONG IT LASTS... IS A MEANS TO AN END.
WHEN THE DUST SETTLES AND WE'VE WON... ULTIMATELY, WE HAVE TO WORK WITH THESE PEOPLE! WE WANT A COMMUNITY THAT CAN ACCOMPLISH THINGS TOGETHER!
THAT HEALING CANNOT BEGIN IF WE HAVE SUNK TO SUCH... IN-FUCKING-HUMAN LEVELS!
REPEAT AFTER ME:
WE.
DON'T.
RAPE.
WE DON'T RAPE.
DAVID... THIS IS UNACCEPTABLE.
RAPE IS AGAINST THE RULES HERE. YOU REMEMBER THE RULES, DON'T YOU? YOU'VE REALLY CROSSED A LINE HERE, YOU STUPID FUCK.
I'M SORRY, SIR.

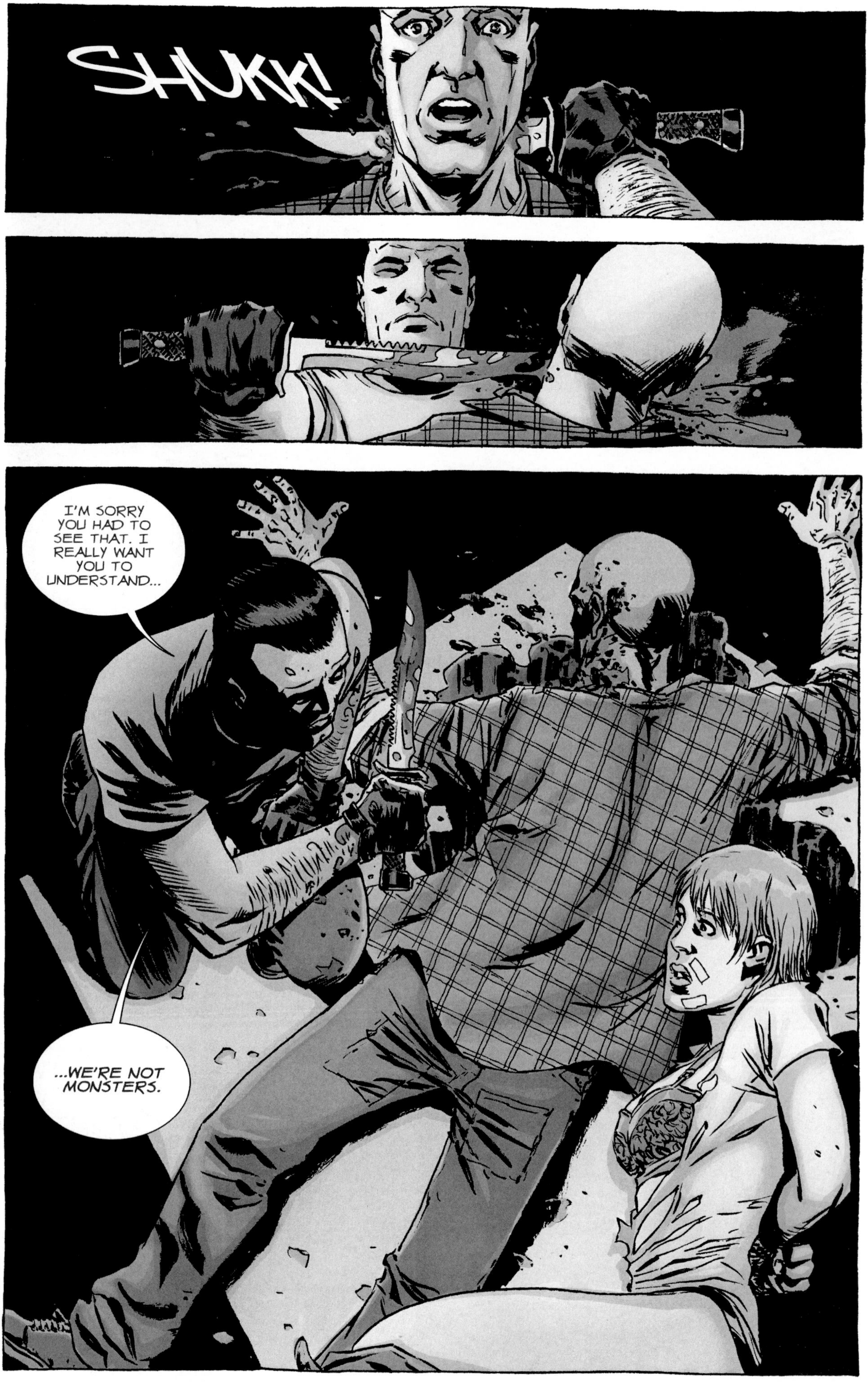
SHUKK!
I'M SORRY YOU HAD TO SEE THAT. I REALLY WANT YOU TO UNDERSTAND...
...WE'RE NOT MONSTERS.

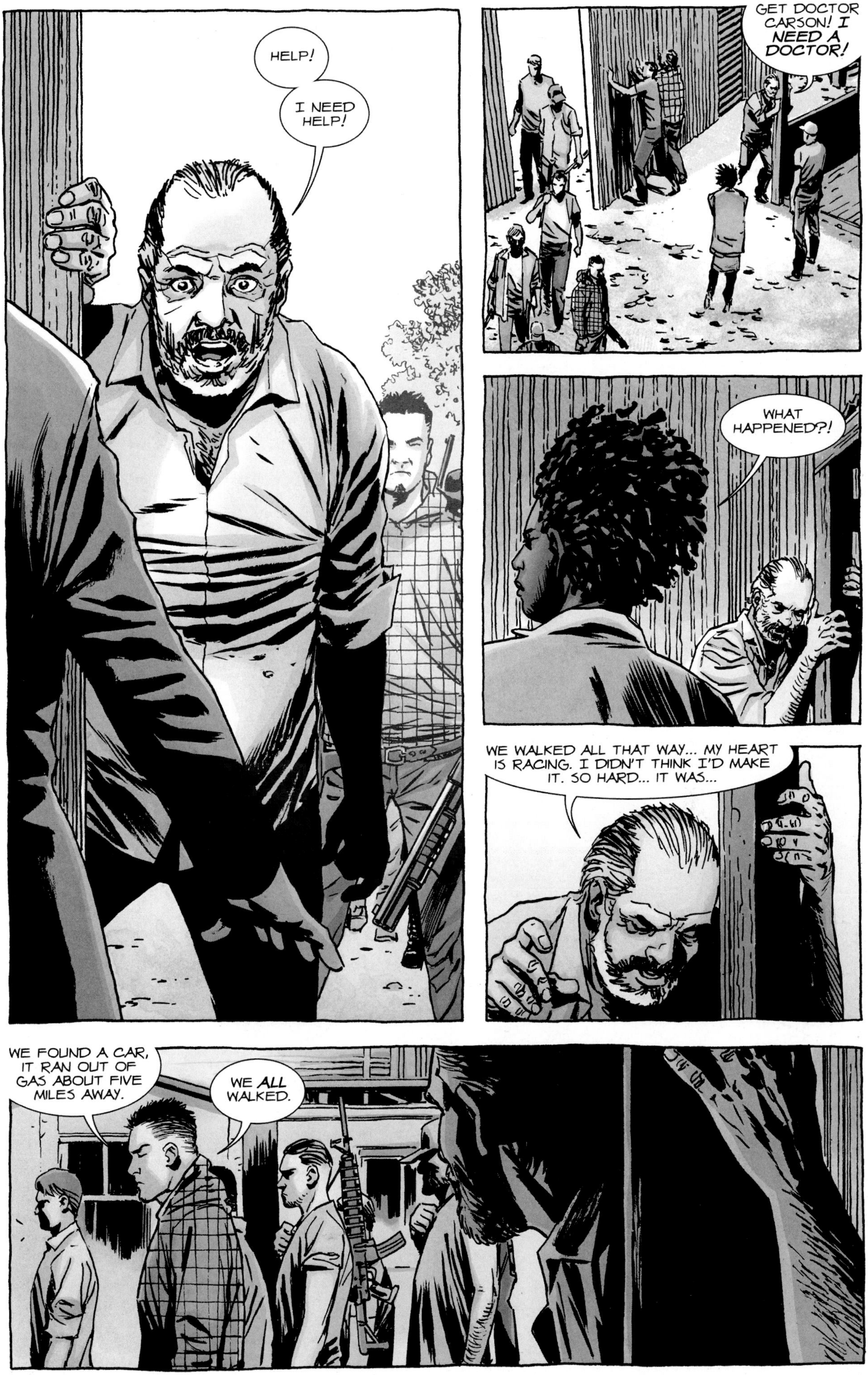
HELP!
I NEED HELP!
GET DOCTOR CARSON! I NEED A DOCTOR!
WHAT HAPPENED?!
WE WALKED ALL THAT WAY... MY HEART IS RACING. I DIDN'T THINK I'D MAKE IT. SO HARD... IT WAS...
WE FOUND A CAR, IT RAN OUT OF GAS ABOUT FIVE MILES AWAY.
WE ALL WALKED.

WHAT HAPPENED? WHY ARE YOU HERE?

IS IT OVER? IS *NEGAN* DEAD?

YOU *KNEW?*

WHAT?

MY MEN DISAPPEARED. SAVIORS CAME TO PICK ME UP, TELL ME THEY'D BEEN DUPED INTO SOME KIND OF CONFLICT... I WAS COMPLETELY IN THE DARK ON...

BUT YOU *KNEW?*

YOU'RE SAYING YOU DIDN'T *KNOW?*

ARE YOU *PRETENDING* JESUS DIDN'T TELL YOU WHAT WAS HAPPENING?

PRETENDING?! WHAT ARE YOU TRYING TO SAY?!

WHO ARE YOU TO TALK TO ME LIKE THIS?! I DON'T EVEN KNOW WHO YOU ARE!

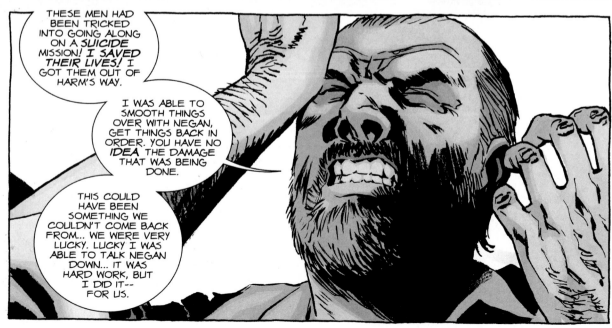

THESE MEN HAD BEEN TRICKED INTO GOING ALONG ON A *SUICIDE* MISSION! *I SAVED THEIR LIVES!* I GOT THEM OUT OF HARM'S WAY.

I WAS ABLE TO SMOOTH THINGS OVER WITH NEGAN, GET THINGS BACK IN ORDER. YOU HAVE NO *IDEA* THE DAMAGE THAT WAS BEING DONE.

THIS COULD HAVE BEEN SOMETHING WE COULDN'T COME BACK FROM... WE WERE VERY LUCKY. LUCKY I WAS ABLE TO TALK NEGAN DOWN... IT WAS HARD WORK, BUT I DID IT-- FOR US.

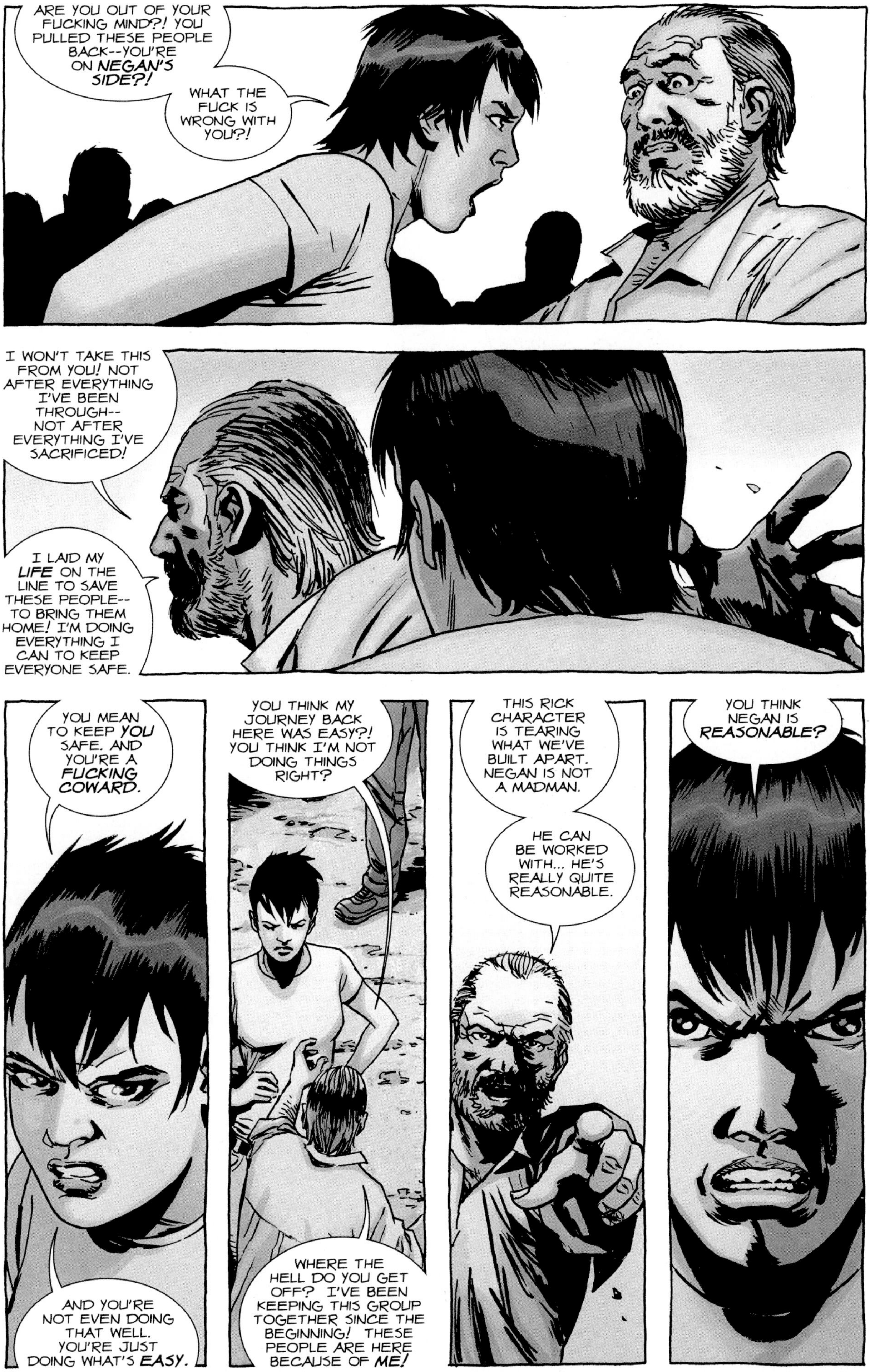
ARE YOU OUT OF YOUR FUCKING MIND?! YOU PULLED THESE PEOPLE BACK--YOU'RE ON NEGAN'S SIDE?!
WHAT THE FUCK IS WRONG WITH YOU?!
I WON'T TAKE THIS FROM YOU! NOT AFTER EVERYTHING I'VE BEEN THROUGH-- NOT AFTER EVERYTHING I'VE SACRIFICED!
I LAID MY LIFE ON THE LINE TO SAVE THESE PEOPLE-- TO BRING THEM HOME! I'M DOING EVERYTHING I CAN TO KEEP EVERYONE SAFE.
YOU MEAN TO KEEP YOU SAFE. AND YOU'RE A FUCKING COWARD.
AND YOU'RE NOT EVEN DOING THAT WELL. YOU'RE JUST DOING WHAT'S EASY.
YOU THINK MY JOURNEY BACK HERE WAS EASY?! YOU THINK I'M NOT DOING THINGS RIGHT?
WHERE THE HELL DO YOU GET OFF? I'VE BEEN KEEPING THIS GROUP TOGETHER SINCE THE BEGINNING! THESE PEOPLE ARE HERE BECAUSE OF ME!
THIS RICK CHARACTER IS TEARING WHAT WE'VE BUILT APART. NEGAN IS NOT A MADMAN.
HE CAN BE WORKED WITH... HE'S REALLY QUITE REASONABLE.
YOU THINK NEGAN IS REASONABLE?

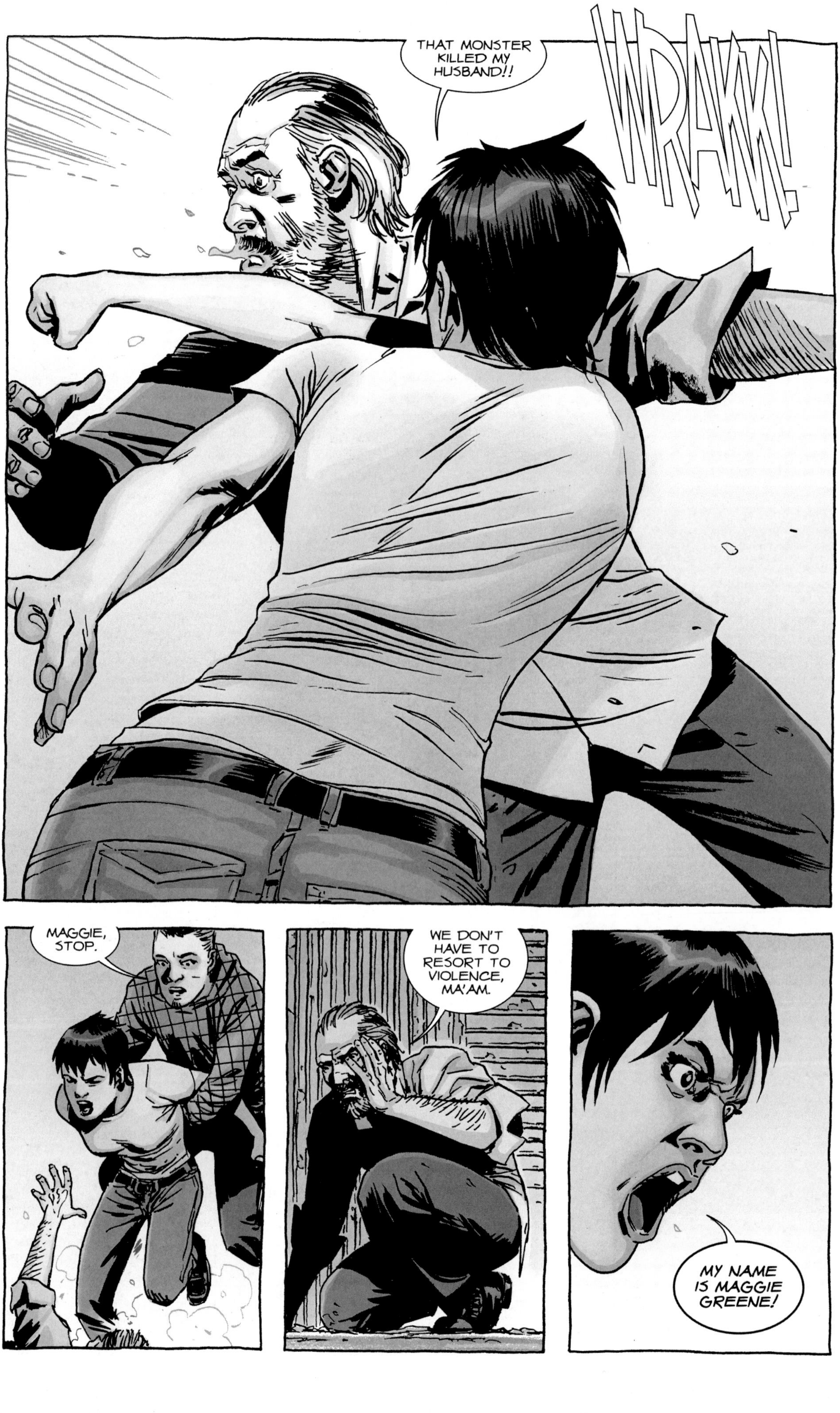
THAT MONSTER KILLED MY HUSBAND!!
WRAKK!
MAGGIE, STOP.
WE DON'T HAVE TO RESORT TO VIOLENCE, MA'AM.
MY NAME IS MAGGIE GREENE!

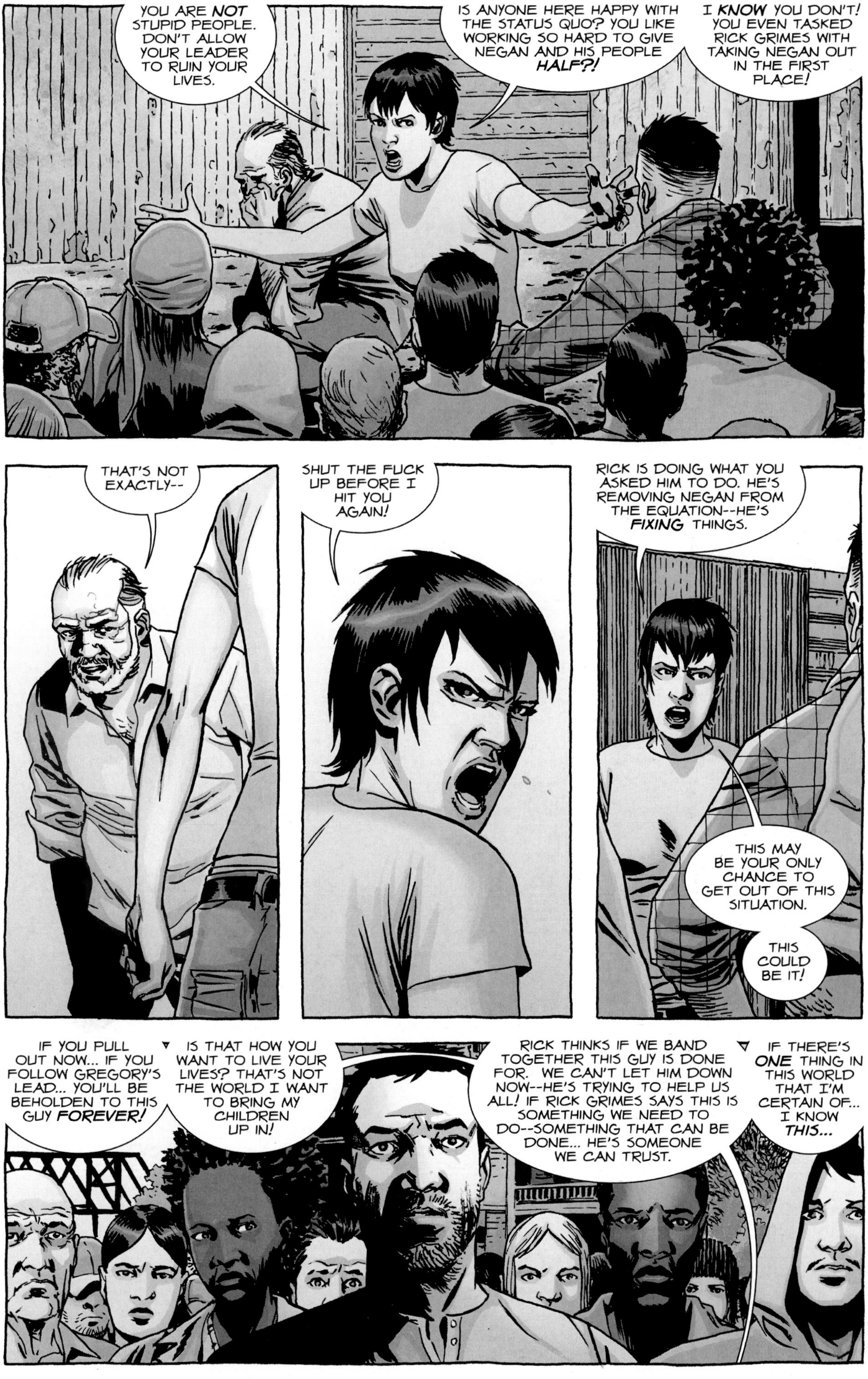
YOU ARE NOT STUPID PEOPLE. DON'T ALLOW YOUR LEADER TO RUIN YOUR LIVES.
IS ANYONE HERE HAPPY WITH THE STATUS QUO? YOU LIKE WORKING SO HARD TO GIVE NEGAN AND HIS PEOPLE HALF?!
I KNOW YOU DON'T! YOU EVEN TASKED RICK GRIMES WITH TAKING NEGAN OUT IN THE FIRST PLACE!
THAT'S NOT EXACTLY--
SHUT THE FUCK UP BEFORE I HIT YOU AGAIN!
RICK IS DOING WHAT YOU ASKED HIM TO DO. HE'S REMOVING NEGAN FROM THE EQUATION--HE'S FIXING THINGS.
THIS MAY BE YOUR ONLY CHANCE TO GET OUT OF THIS SITUATION.
THIS COULD BE IT!
IF YOU PULL OUT NOW... IF YOU FOLLOW GREGORY'S LEAD... YOU'LL BE BEHOLDEN TO THIS GUY FOREVER!
IS THAT HOW YOU WANT TO LIVE YOUR LIVES? THAT'S NOT THE WORLD I WANT TO BRING MY CHILDREN UP IN!
RICK THINKS IF WE BAND TOGETHER THIS GUY IS DONE FOR. WE CAN'T LET HIM DOWN NOW--HE'S TRYING TO HELP US ALL! IF RICK GRIMES SAYS THIS IS SOMETHING WE NEED TO DO--SOMETHING THAT CAN BE DONE... HE'S SOMEONE WE CAN TRUST.
IF THERE'S ONE THING IN THIS WORLD THAT I'M CERTAIN OF... I KNOW THIS...

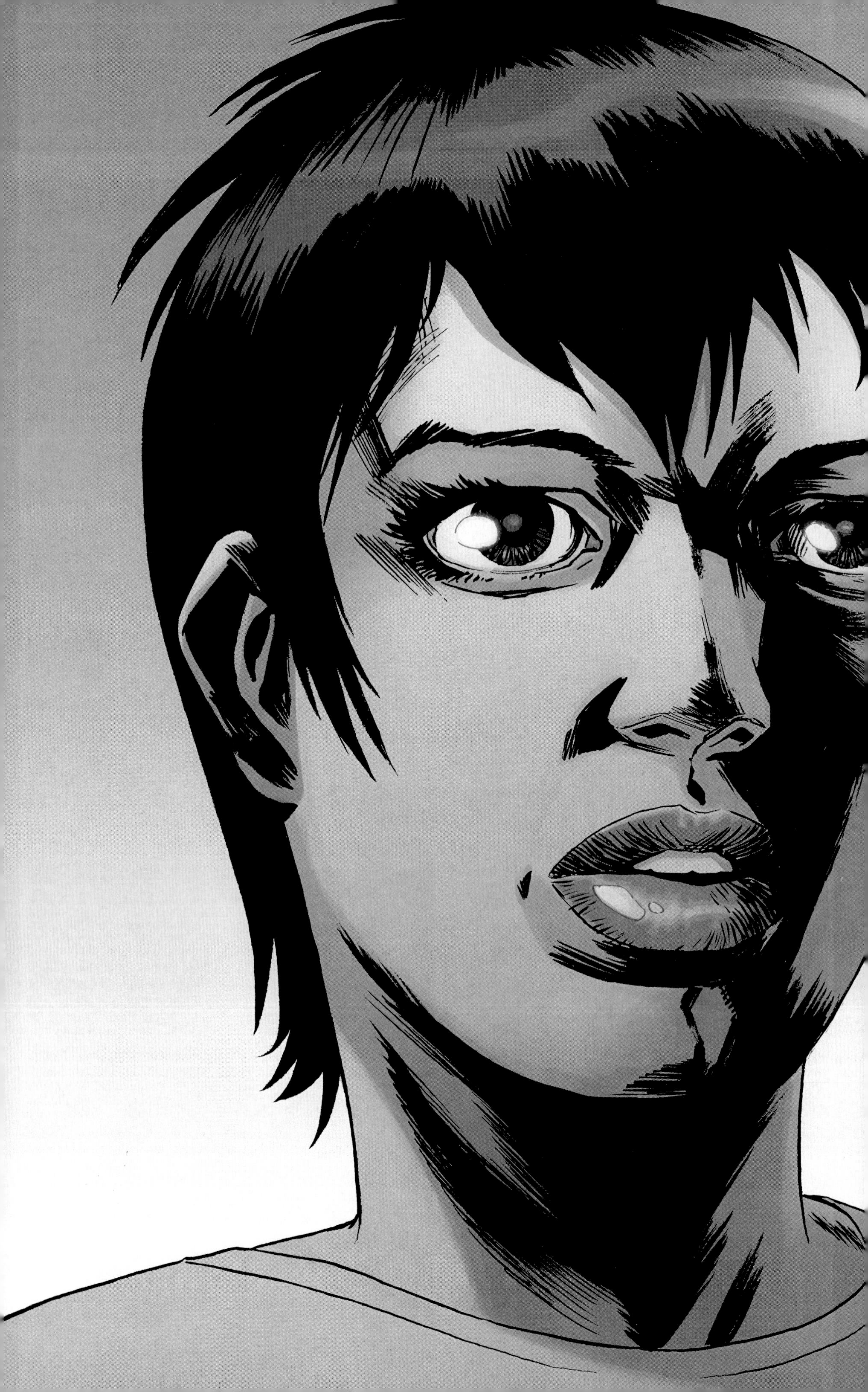

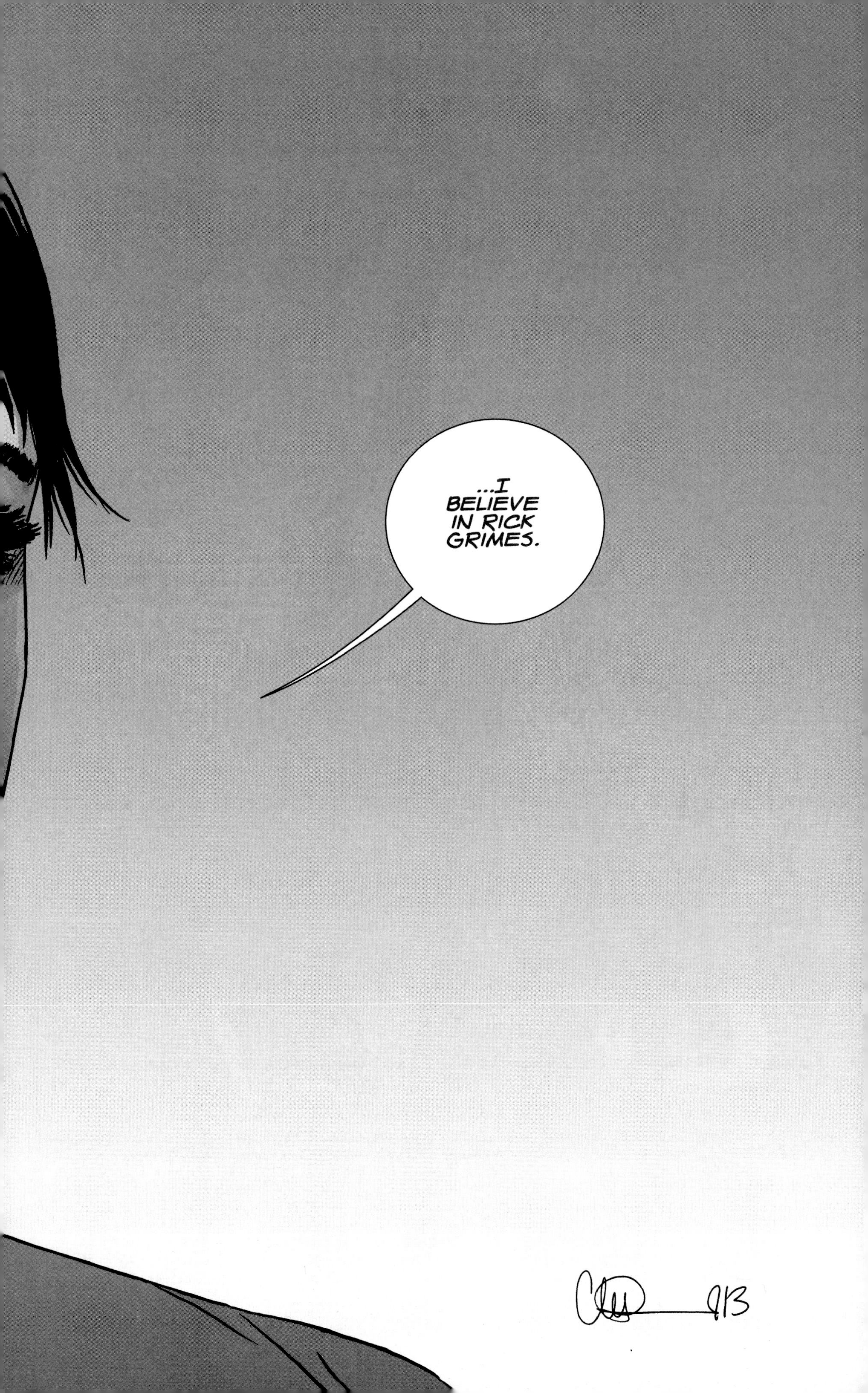
...I BELIEVE IN RICK GRIMES.

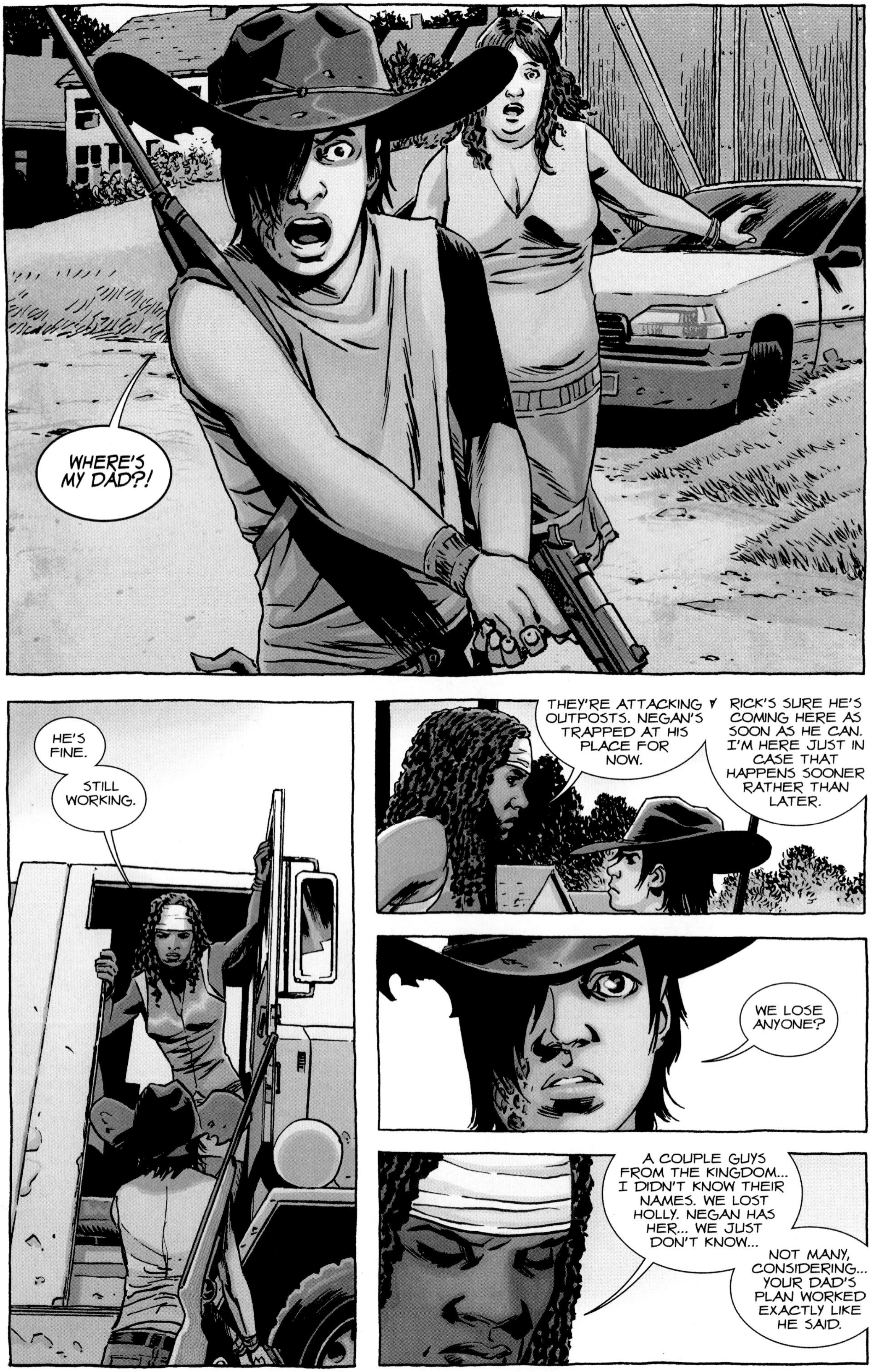
WHERE'S MY DAD?!
HE'S FINE.
STILL WORKING.
THEY'RE ATTACKING OUTPOSTS. NEGAN'S TRAPPED AT HIS PLACE FOR NOW.
RICK'S SURE HE'S COMING HERE AS SOON AS HE CAN. I'M HERE JUST IN CASE THAT HAPPENS SOONER RATHER THAN LATER.
WE LOSE ANYONE?
A COUPLE GUYS FROM THE KINGDOM... I DIDN'T KNOW THEIR NAMES. WE LOST HOLLY. NEGAN HAS HER... WE JUST DON'T KNOW...
NOT MANY, CONSIDERING... YOUR DAD'S PLAN WORKED EXACTLY LIKE HE SAID.

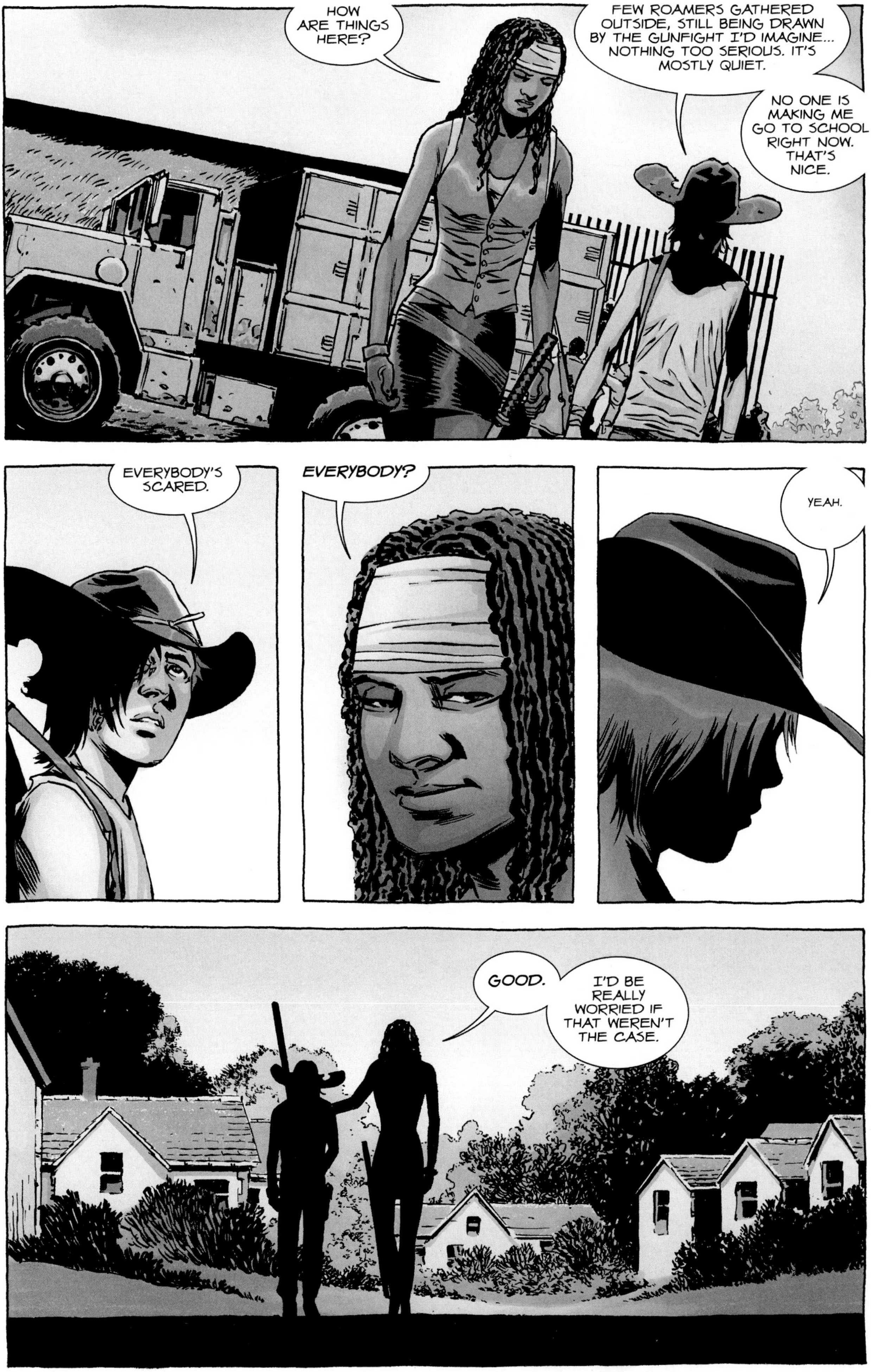
HOW ARE THINGS HERE?
FEW ROAMERS GATHERED OUTSIDE, STILL BEING DRAWN BY THE GUNFIGHT I'D IMAGINE... NOTHING TOO SERIOUS. IT'S MOSTLY QUIET.
NO ONE IS MAKING ME GO TO SCHOOL RIGHT NOW. THAT'S NICE.
EVERYBODY'S SCARED.
EVERYBODY?
YEAH.
GOOD.
I'D BE REALLY WORRIED IF THAT WEREN'T THE CASE.

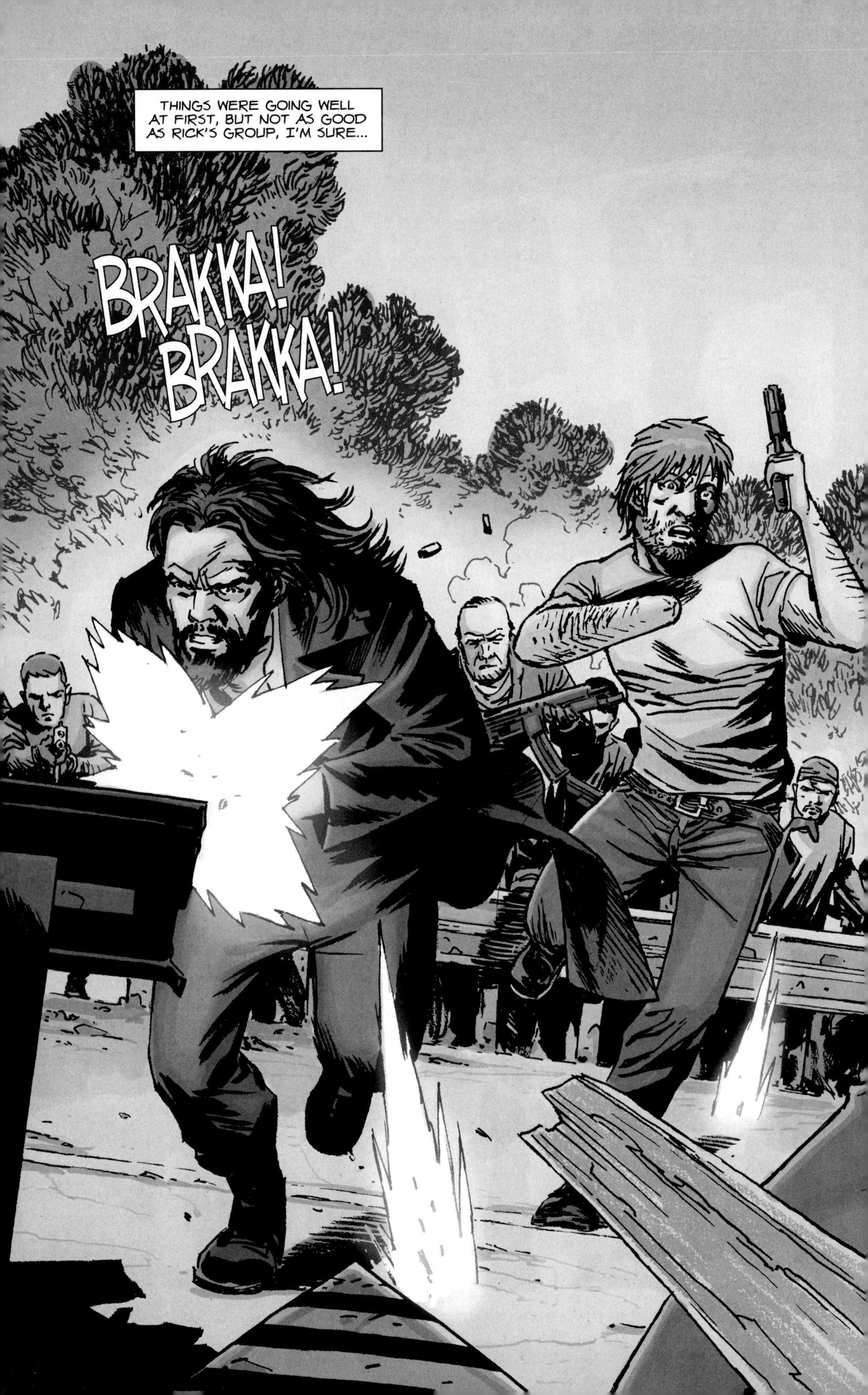
THINGS WERE GOING WELL AT FIRST, BUT NOT AS GOOD AS RICK'S GROUP, I'M SURE...
BRAKKA! BRAKKA!

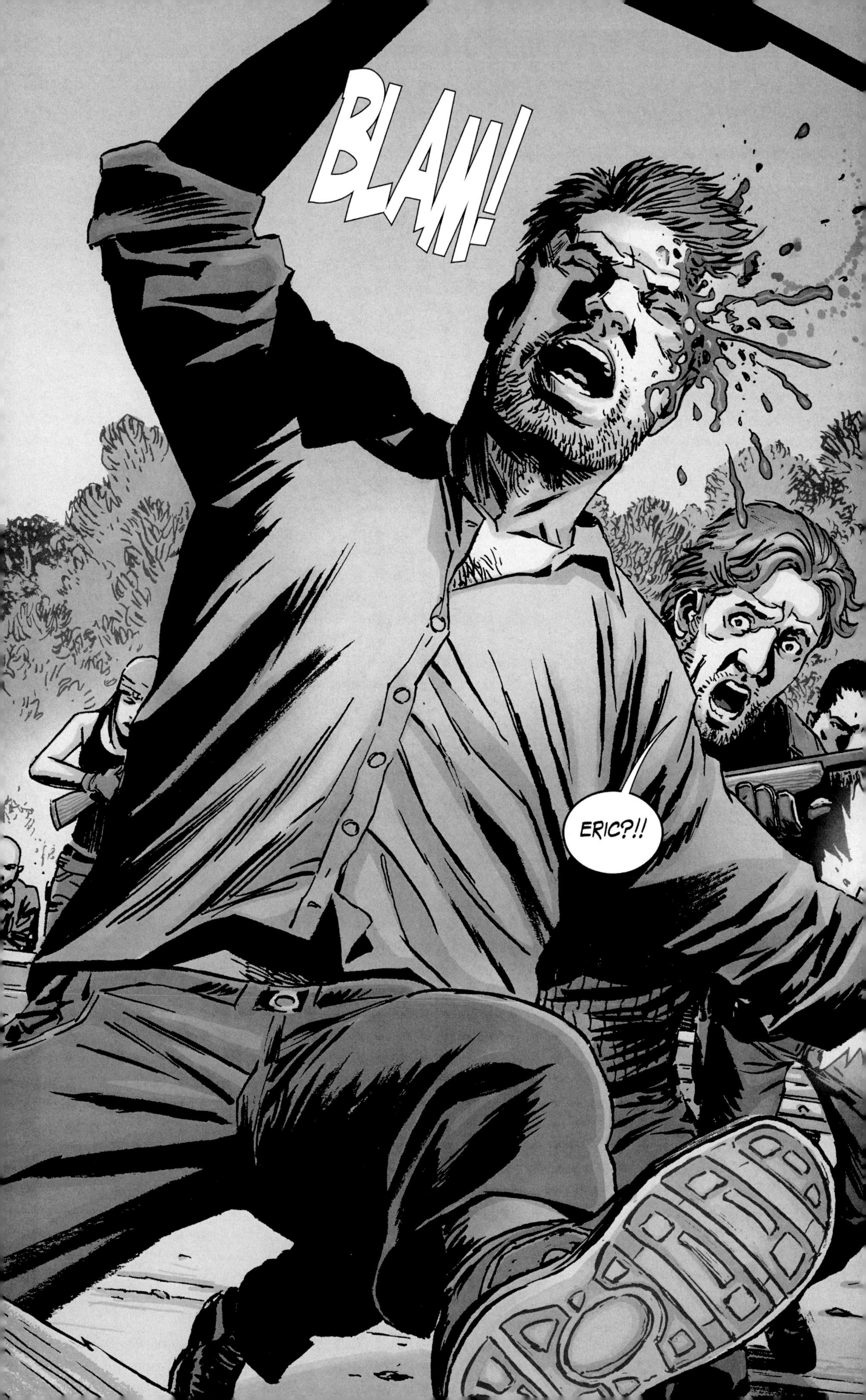
BLAM!
ERIC?!!

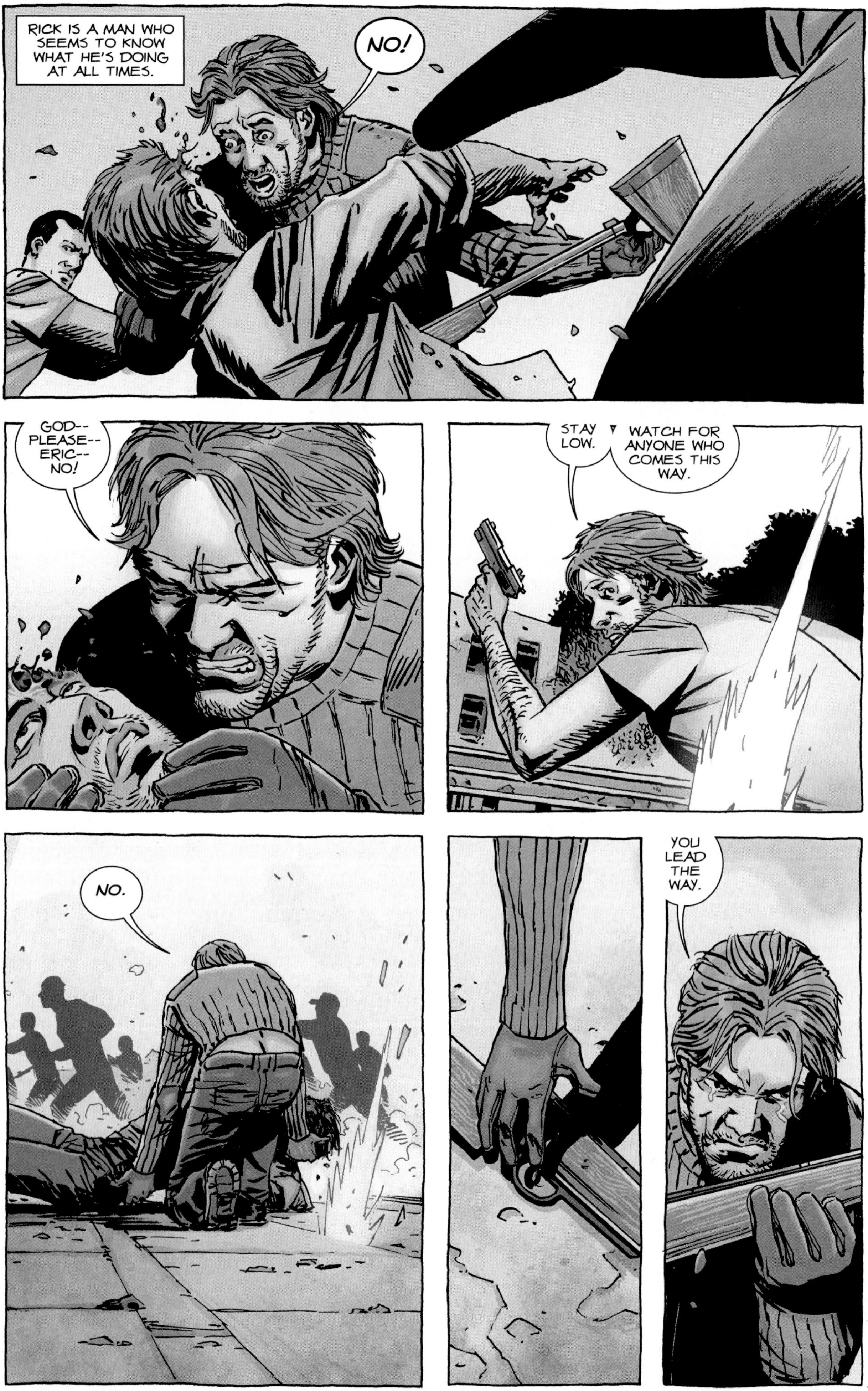
RICK IS A MAN WHO SEEMS TO KNOW WHAT HE'S DOING AT ALL TIMES.
NO!
GOD-- PLEASE-- ERIC-- NO!
STAY LOW.
WATCH FOR ANYONE WHO COMES THIS WAY.
NO.
YOU LEAD THE WAY.

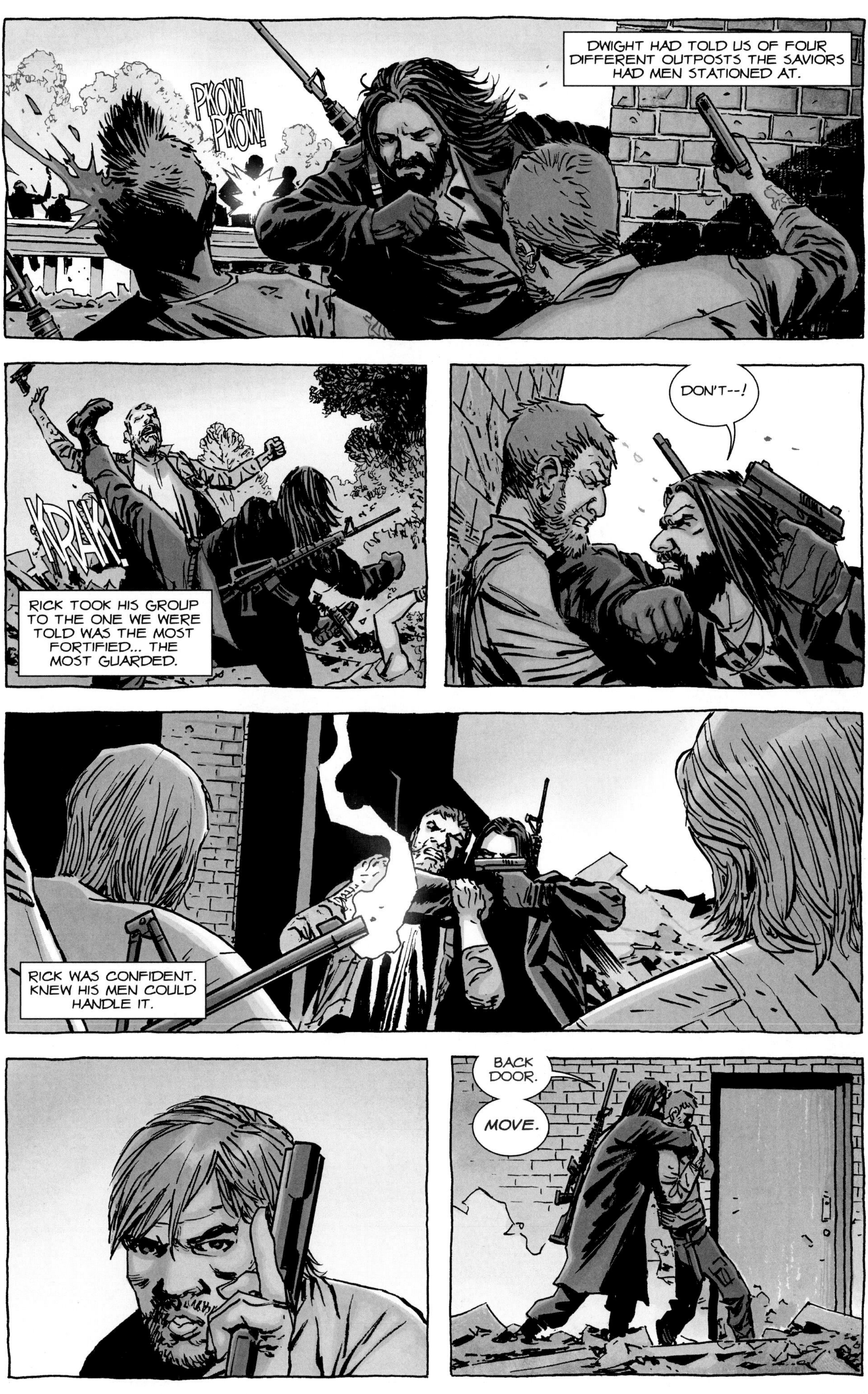
DWIGHT HAD TOLD US OF FOUR DIFFERENT OUTPOSTS THE SAVIORS HAD MEN STATIONED AT.
PKOW! PKOW!
KRAK!
RICK TOOK HIS GROUP TO THE ONE WE WERE TOLD WAS THE MOST FORTIFIED... THE MOST GUARDED.
DON'T--!
RICK WAS CONFIDENT. KNEW HIS MEN COULD HANDLE IT.
BACK DOOR.
MOVE.

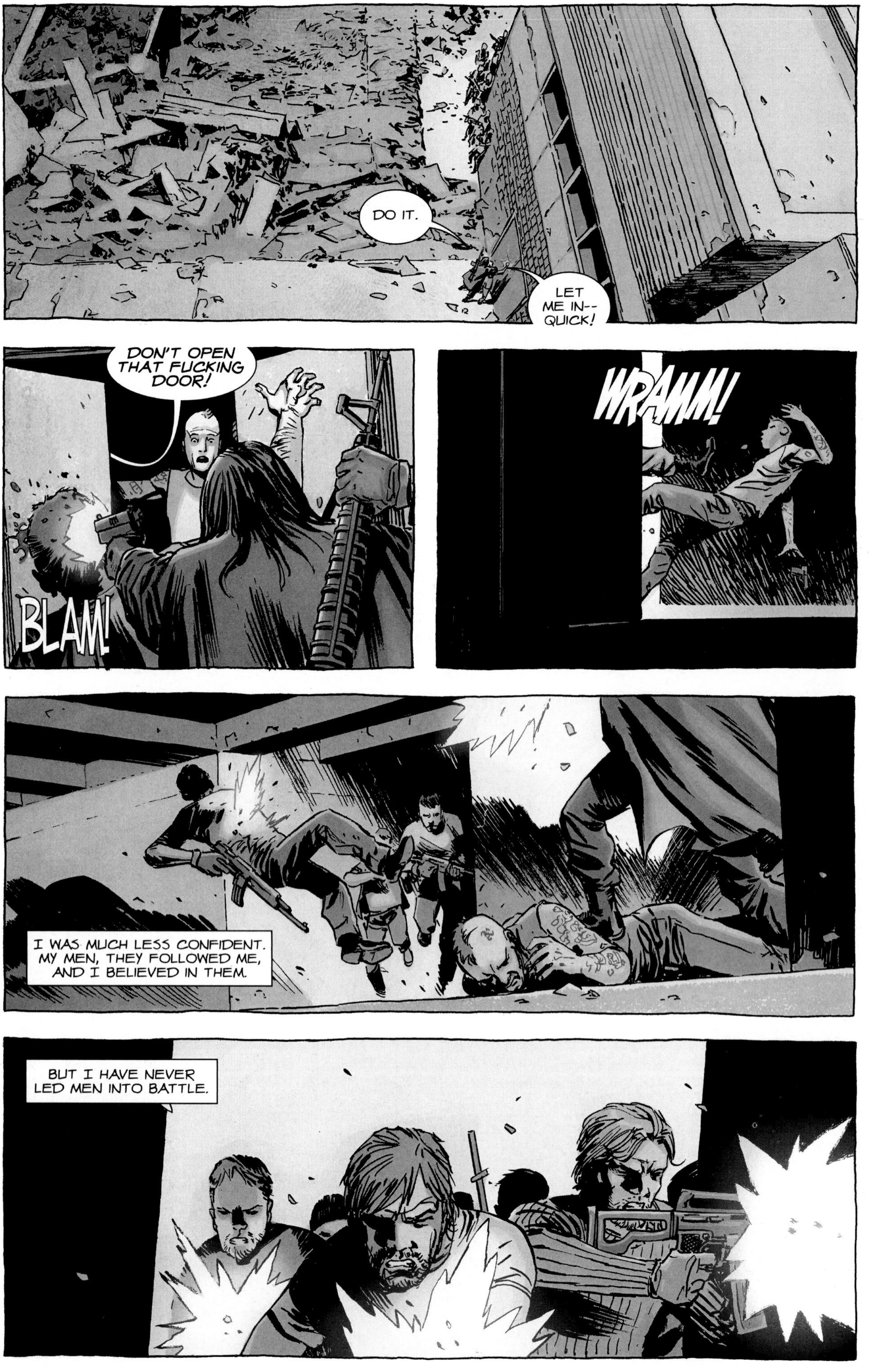
DO IT.
LET ME IN-- QUICK!
DON'T OPEN THAT FUCKING DOOR!
BLAM!
WRAMM!
I WAS MUCH LESS CONFIDENT. MY MEN, THEY FOLLOWED ME, AND I BELIEVED IN THEM.
BUT I HAVE NEVER LED MEN INTO BATTLE.

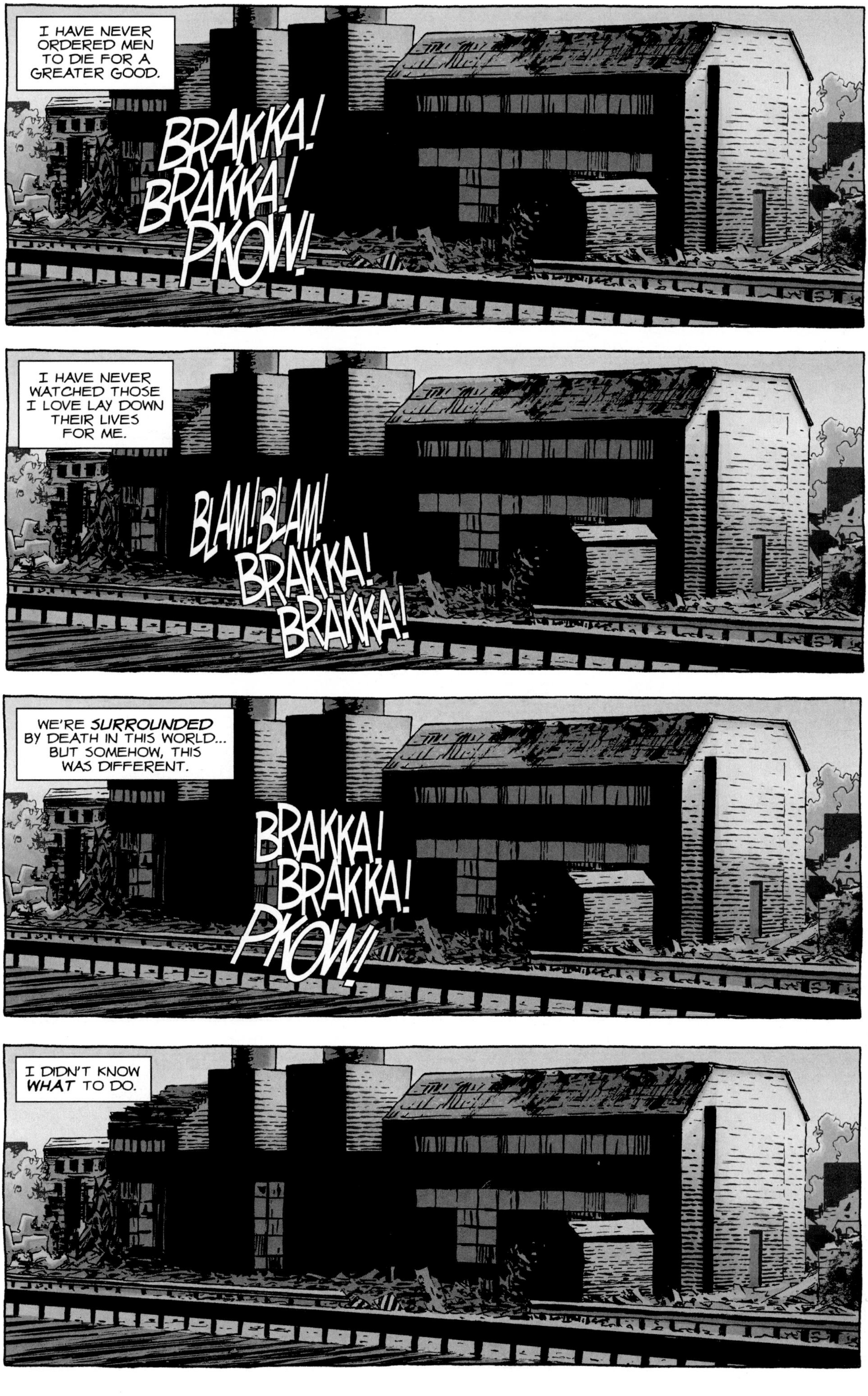
I HAVE NEVER ORDERED MEN TO DIE FOR A GREATER GOOD.
BRAKKA! BRAKKA! PKOW!
I HAVE NEVER WATCHED THOSE I LOVE LAY DOWN THEIR LIVES FOR ME.
BLAM! BLAM! BRAKKA! BRAKKA!
WE'RE *SURROUNDED* BY DEATH IN THIS WORLD... BUT SOMEHOW, THIS WAS DIFFERENT.
BRAKKA! BRAKKA! PKOW!
I DIDN'T KNOW **WHAT** TO DO.

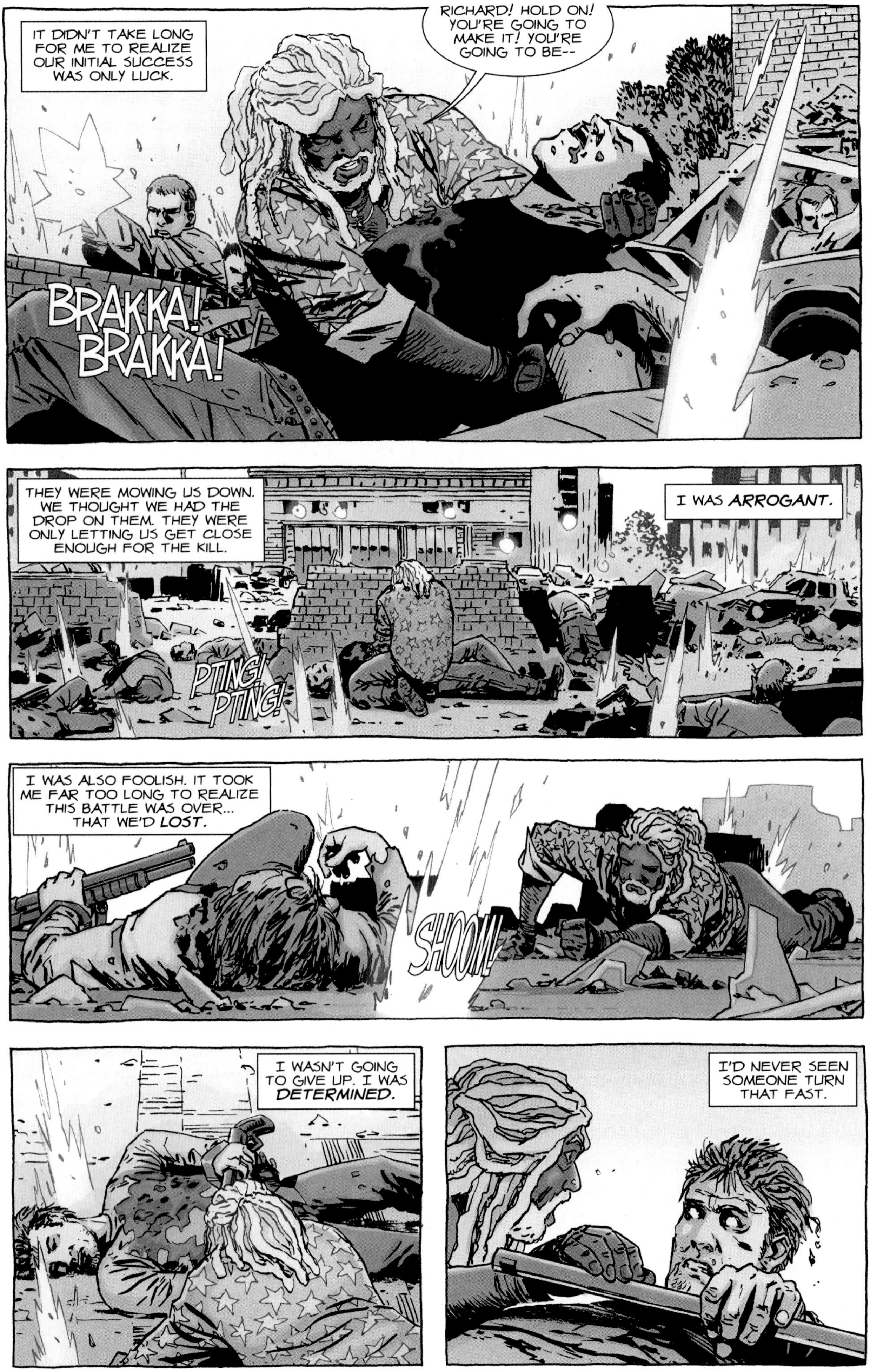
IT DIDN'T TAKE LONG FOR ME TO REALIZE OUR INITIAL SUCCESS WAS ONLY LUCK.
RICHARD! HOLD ON! YOU'RE GOING TO MAKE IT! YOU'RE GOING TO BE--
BRAKKA! BRAKKA!
THEY WERE MOWING US DOWN. WE THOUGHT WE HAD THE DROP ON THEM. THEY WERE ONLY LETTING US GET CLOSE ENOUGH FOR THE KILL.
I WAS ARROGANT.
PTING! PTING!
I WAS ALSO FOOLISH. IT TOOK ME FAR TOO LONG TO REALIZE THIS BATTLE WAS OVER... THAT WE'D LOST.
SHOOM!
I WASN'T GOING TO GIVE UP. I WAS DETERMINED.
I'D NEVER SEEN SOMEONE TURN THAT FAST.

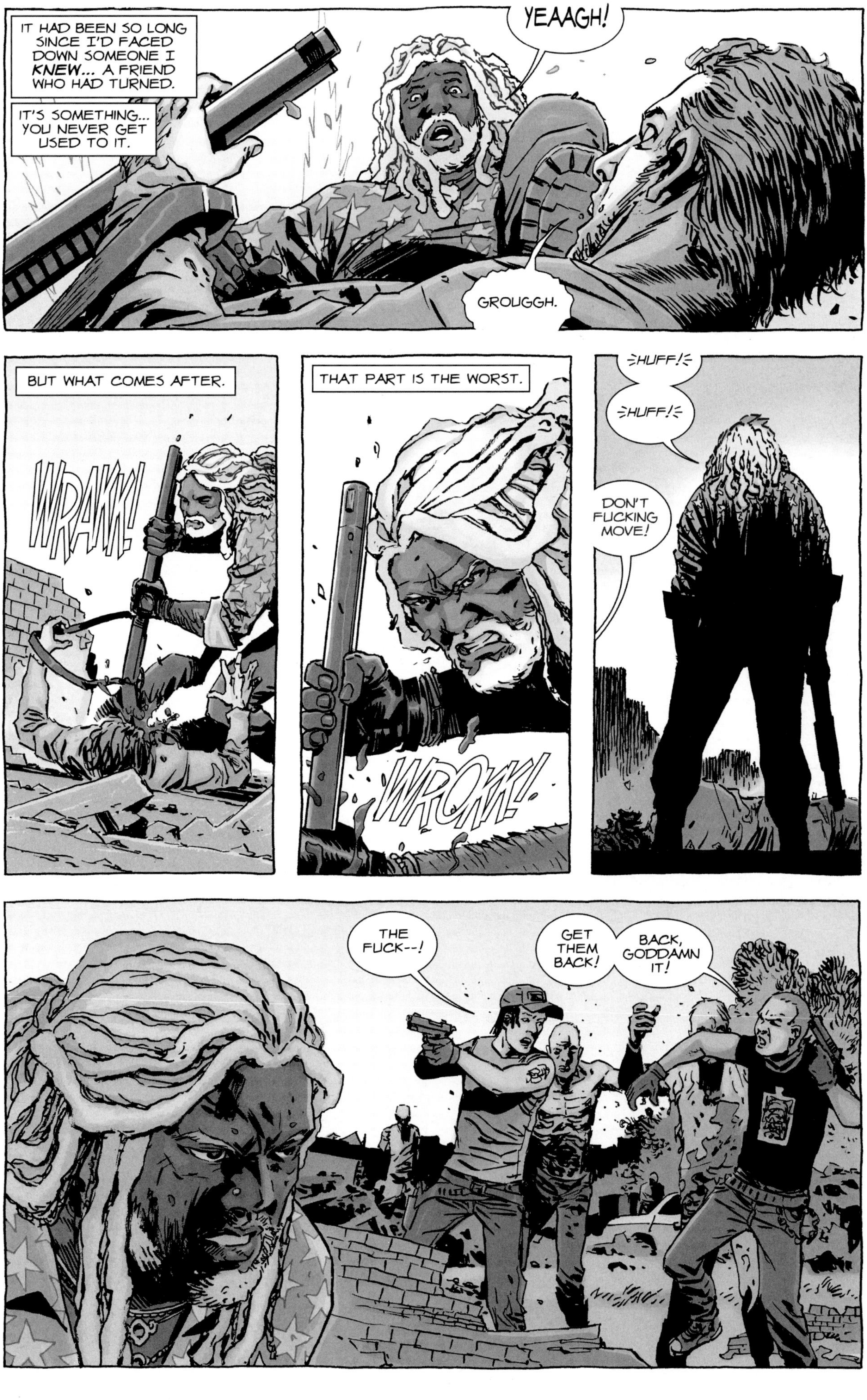
IT HAD BEEN SO LONG SINCE I'D FACED DOWN SOMEONE I **KNEW...** A FRIEND WHO HAD TURNED.
IT'S SOMETHING... YOU NEVER GET USED TO IT.
YEAAGH!
GROUGGH.
BUT WHAT COMES AFTER.
WRAKK!
THAT PART IS THE WORST.
WROKK!
HUFF!
HUFF!
DON'T FUCKING MOVE!
THE FUCK--!
GET THEM BACK!
BACK, GODDAMN IT!

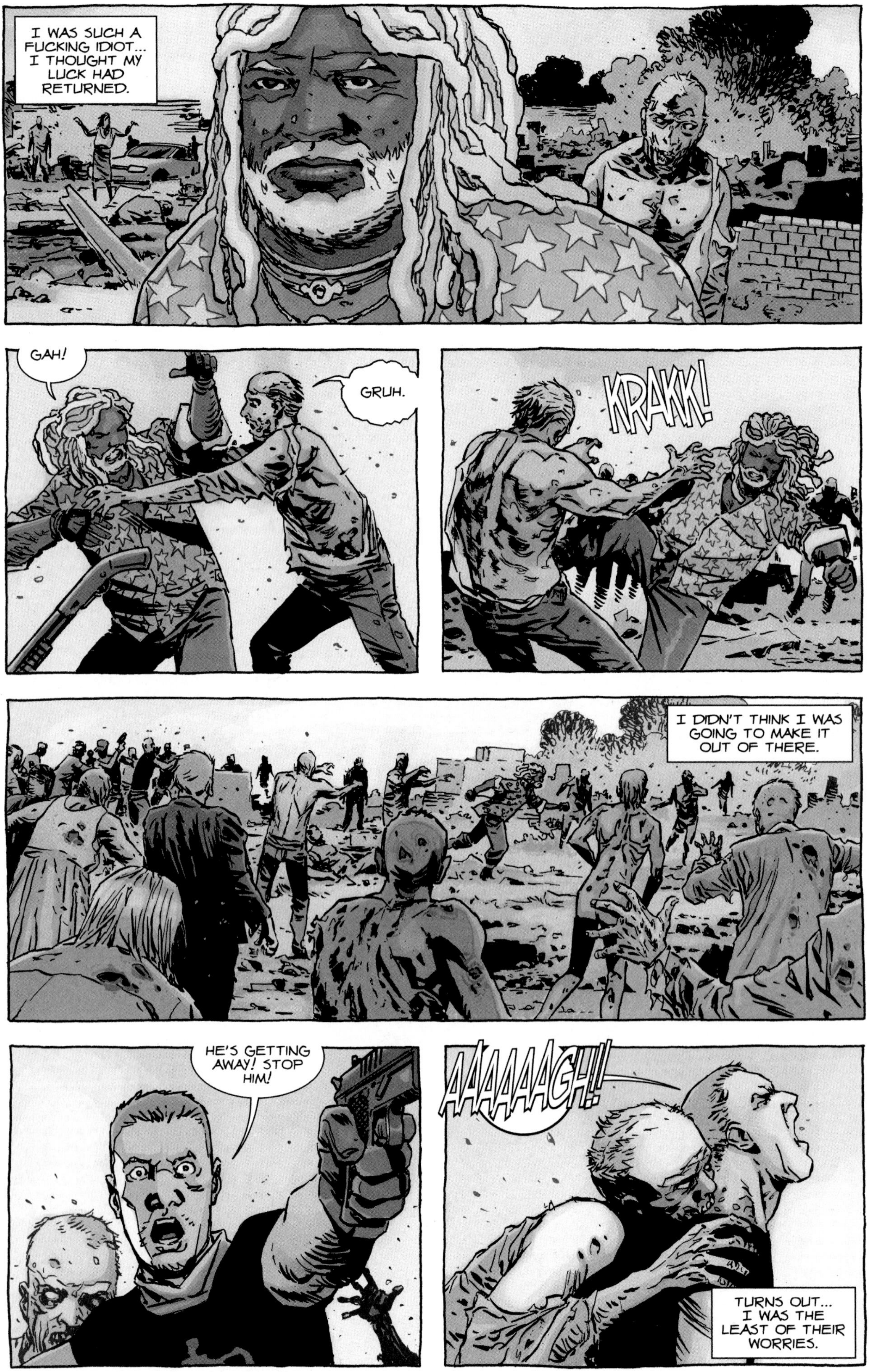
I WAS SUCH A FUCKING IDIOT... I THOUGHT MY LUCK HAD RETURNED.
GAH!
GRUH.
KRAKK!
I DIDN'T THINK I WAS GOING TO MAKE IT OUT OF THERE.
HE'S GETTING AWAY! STOP HIM!
AAAAAAGH!!
TURNS OUT... I WAS THE LEAST OF THEIR WORRIES.

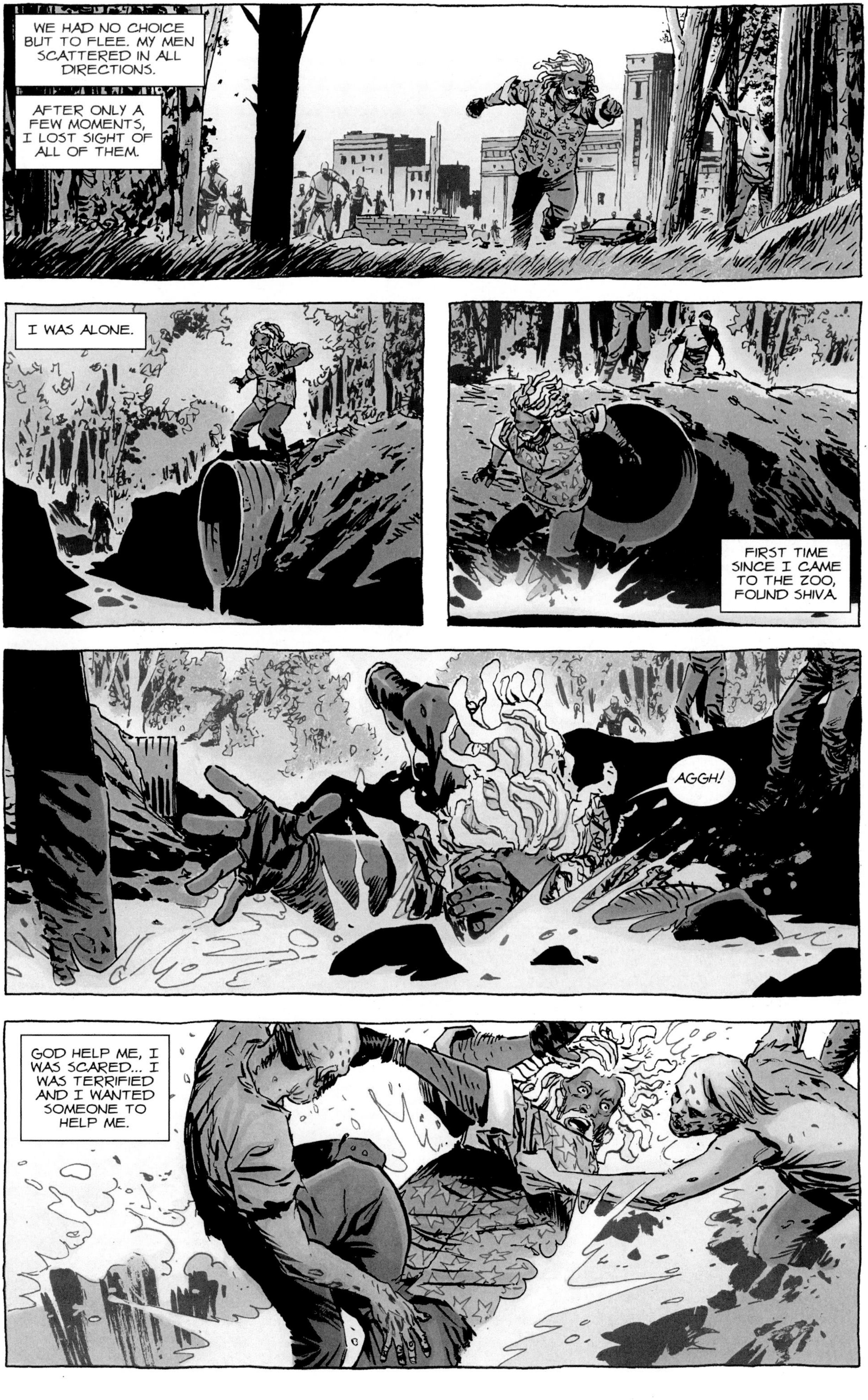
WE HAD NO CHOICE BUT TO FLEE. MY MEN SCATTERED IN ALL DIRECTIONS.
AFTER ONLY A FEW MOMENTS, I LOST SIGHT OF ALL OF THEM.
I WAS ALONE.
FIRST TIME SINCE I CAME TO THE ZOO, FOUND SHIVA
AGGH!
GOD HELP ME, I WAS SCARED... I WAS TERRIFIED AND I WANTED SOMEONE TO HELP ME.

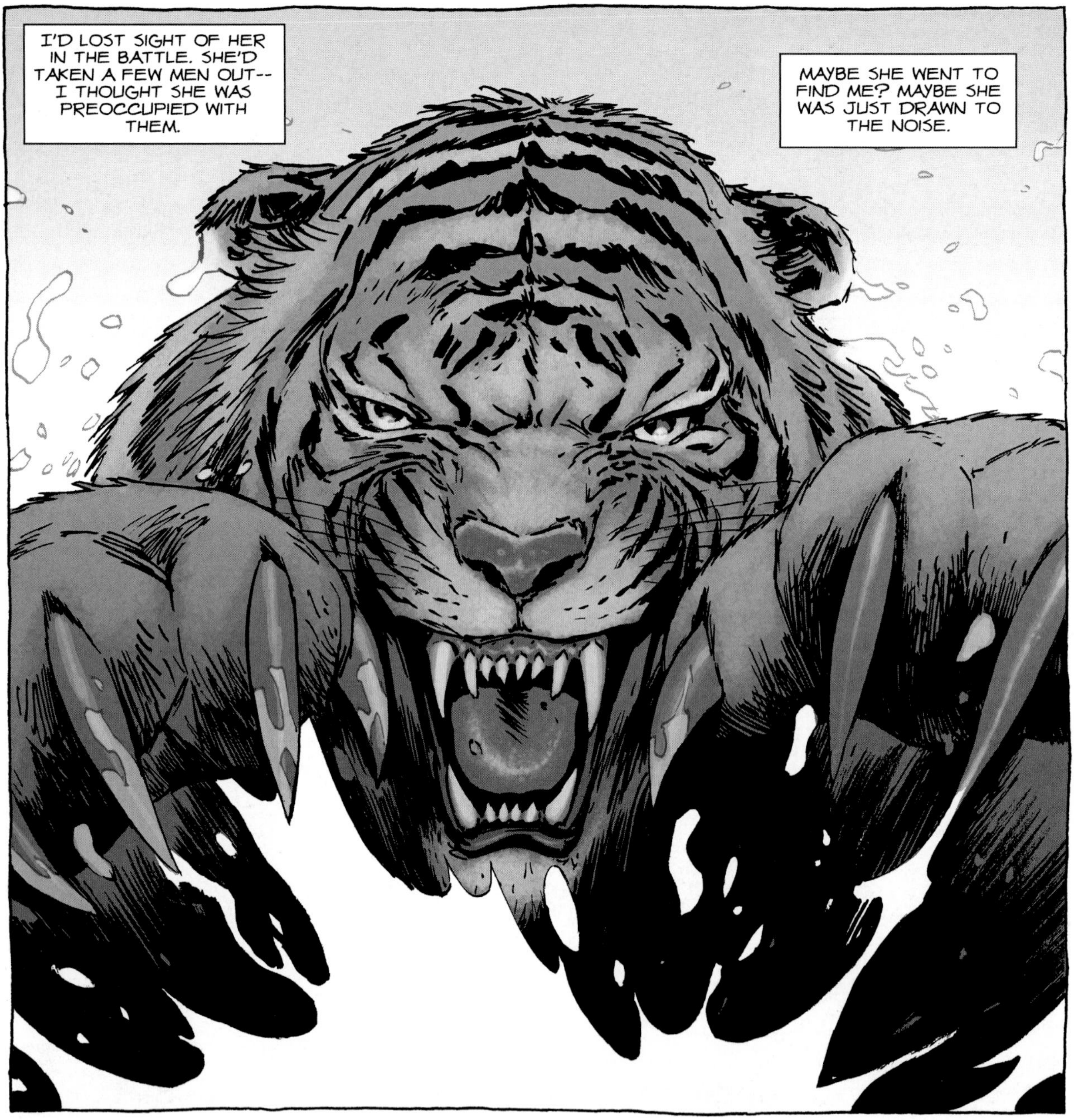
I'D LOST SIGHT OF HER IN THE BATTLE. SHE'D TAKEN A FEW MEN OUT-- I THOUGHT SHE WAS PREOCCUPIED WITH THEM.
MAYBE SHE WENT TO FIND ME? MAYBE SHE WAS JUST DRAWN TO THE NOISE.

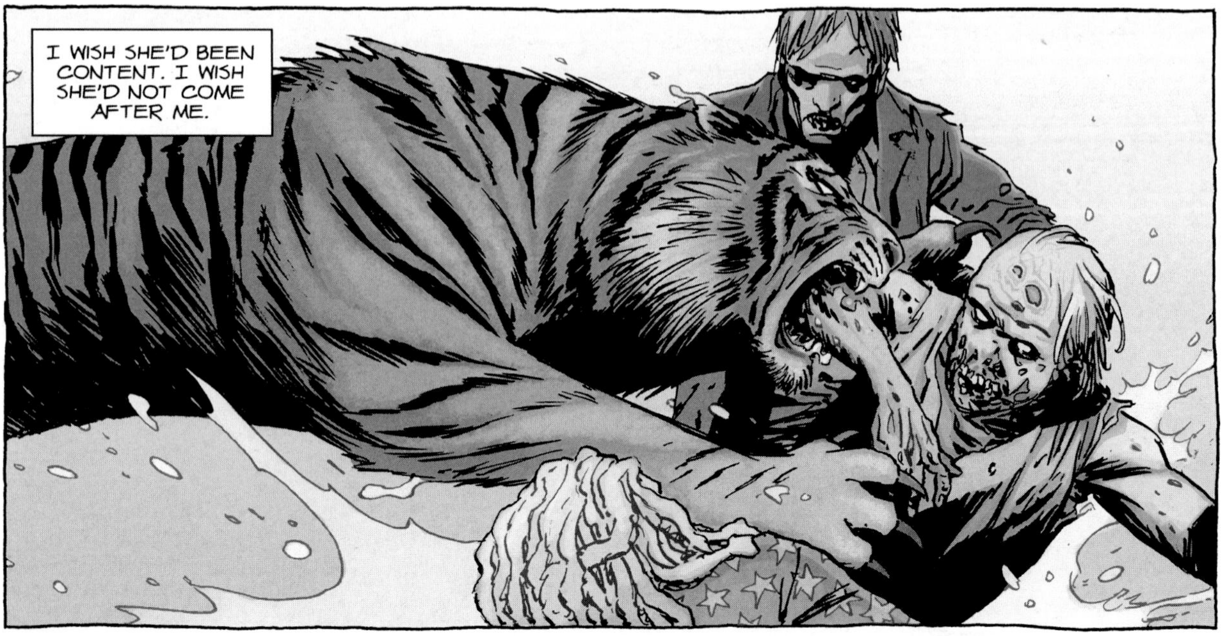
I WISH SHE'D BEEN CONTENT. I WISH SHE'D NOT COME AFTER ME.

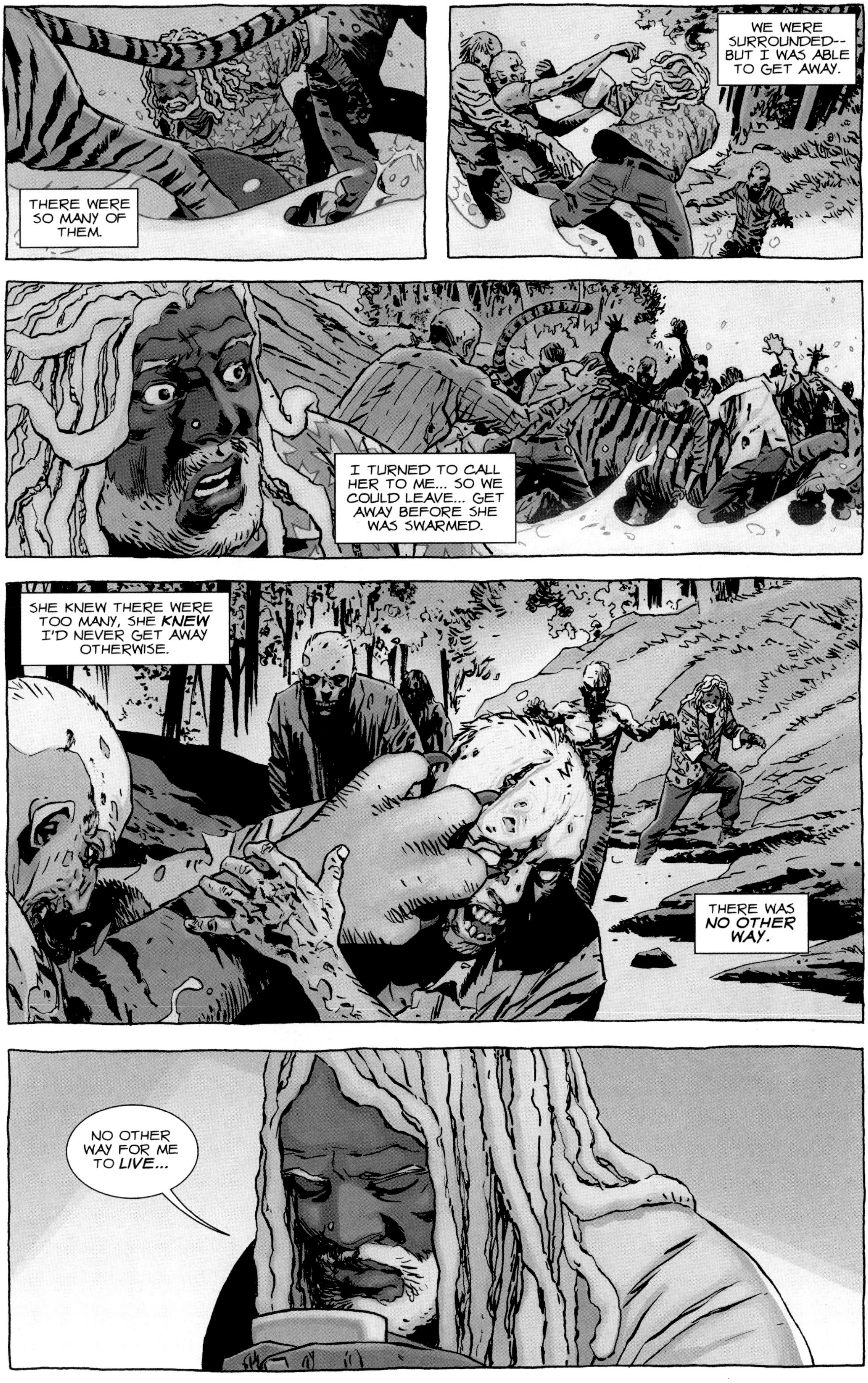

THERE WERE SO MANY OF THEM.
WE WERE SURROUNDED-- BUT I WAS ABLE TO GET AWAY.
I TURNED TO CALL HER TO ME... SO WE COULD LEAVE... GET AWAY BEFORE SHE WAS SWARMED.
SHE KNEW THERE WERE TOO MANY, SHE KNEW I'D NEVER GET AWAY OTHERWISE.
THERE WAS NO OTHER WAY.
NO OTHER WAY FOR ME TO LIVE...

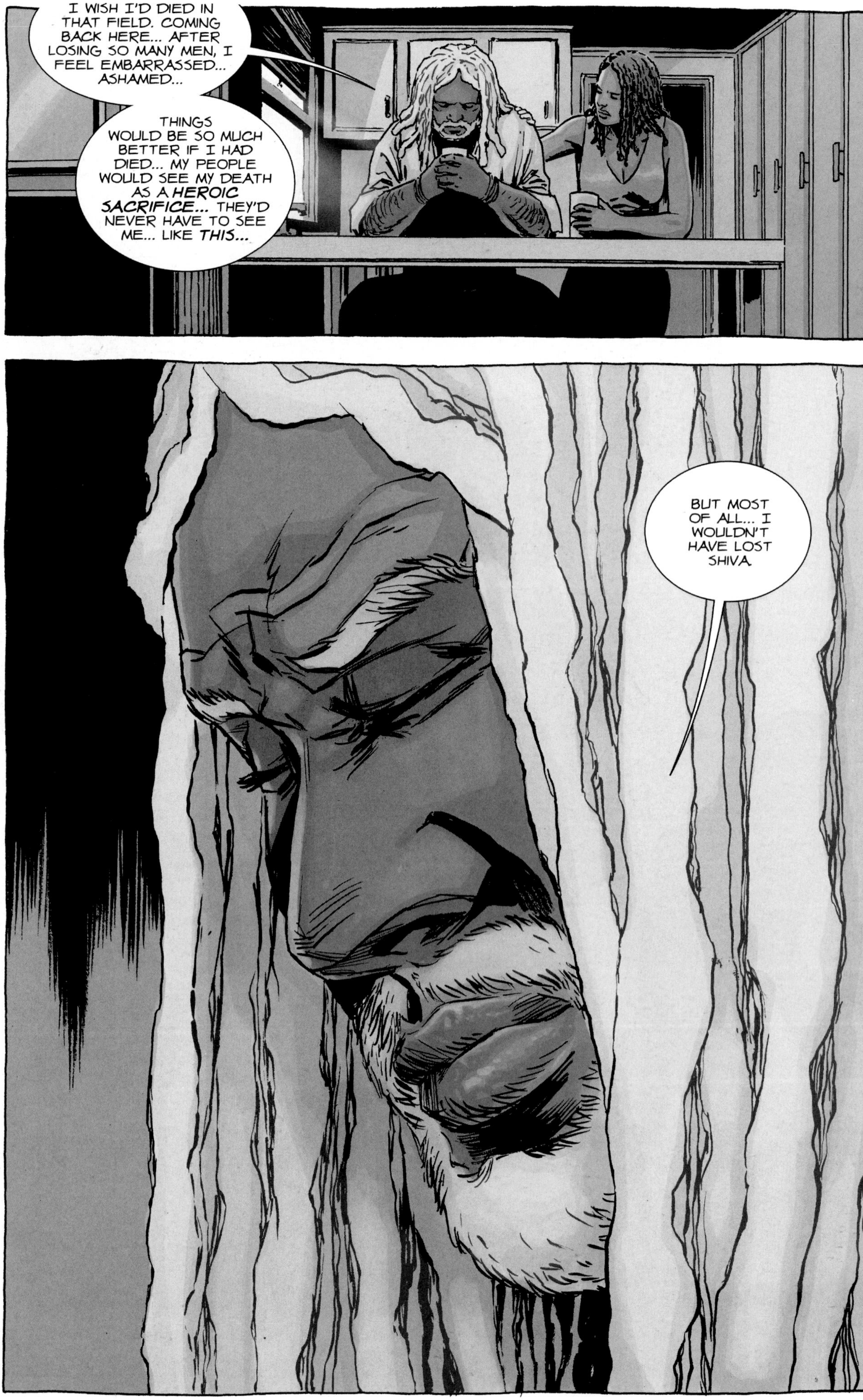
I WISH I'D DIED IN THAT FIELD. COMING BACK HERE... AFTER LOSING SO MANY MEN, I FEEL EMBARRASSED... ASHAMED...
THINGS WOULD BE SO MUCH BETTER IF I HAD DIED... MY PEOPLE WOULD SEE MY DEATH AS A *HEROIC SACRIFICE...* THEY'D NEVER HAVE TO SEE ME... LIKE *THIS...*
BUT MOST OF ALL... I WOULDN'T HAVE LOST SHIVA.

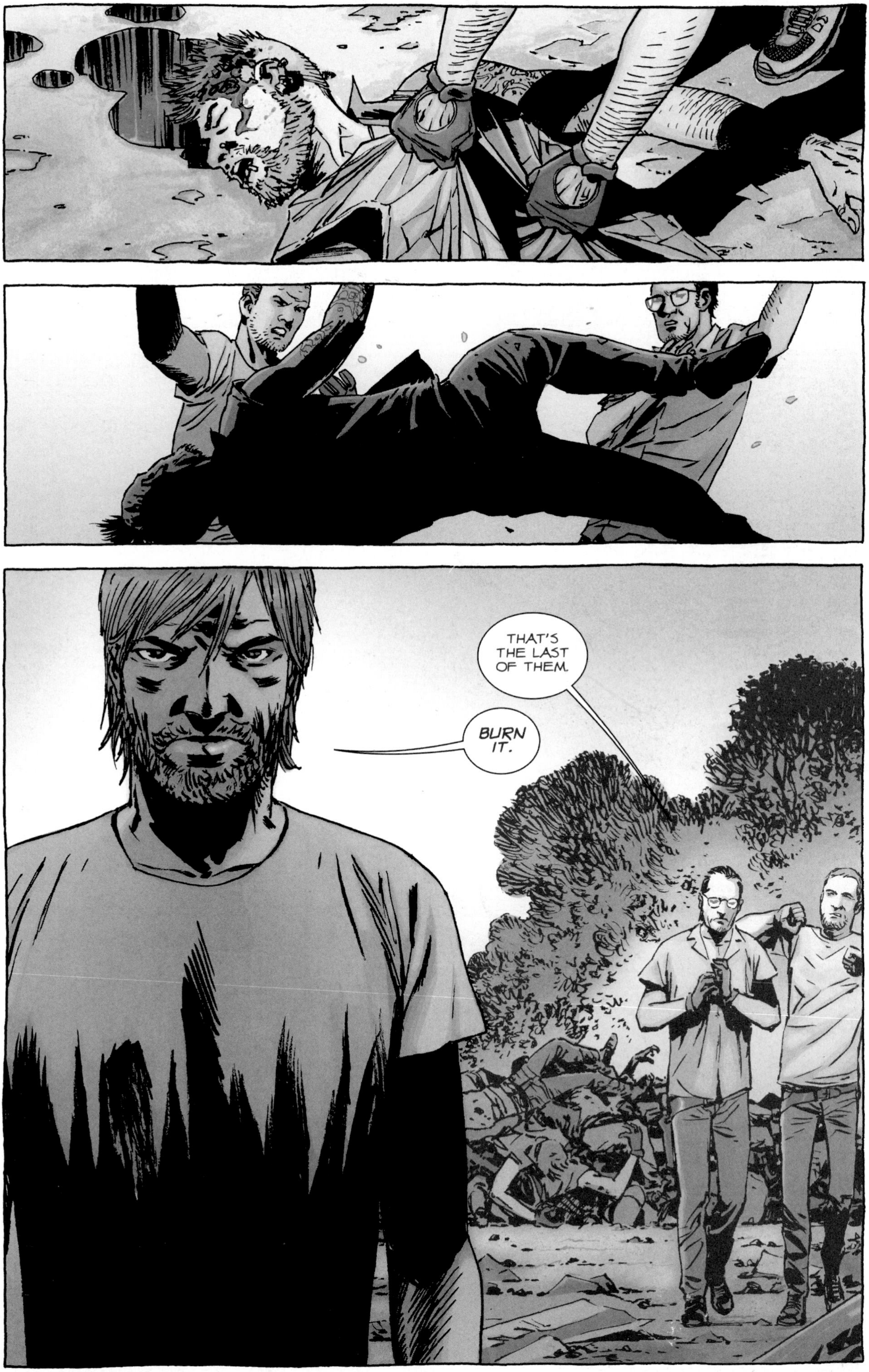
THAT'S THE LAST OF THEM.
BURN IT.

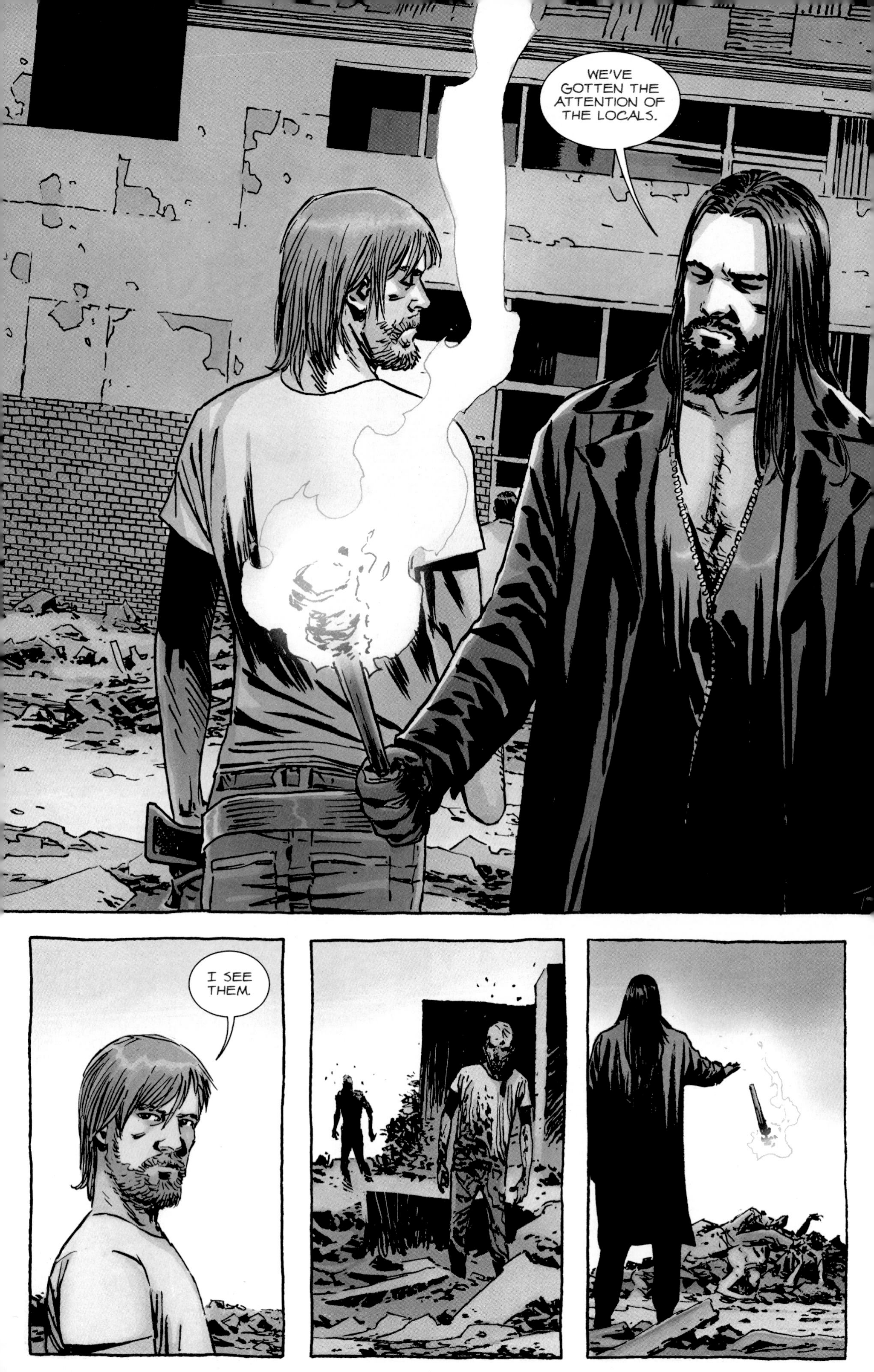
WE'VE GOTTEN THE ATTENTION OF THE LOCALS.
I SEE THEM.

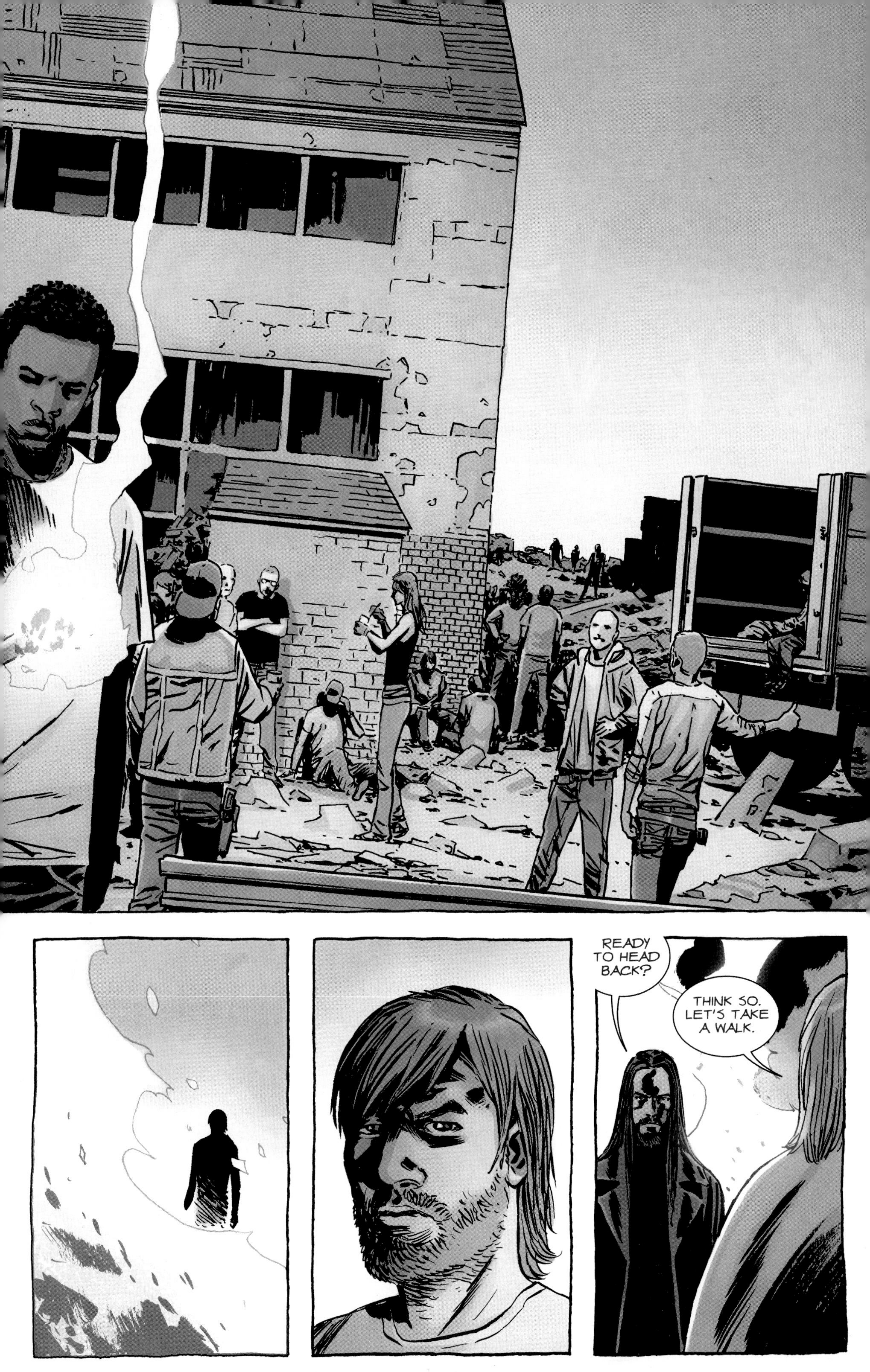
READY TO HEAD BACK?
THINK SO. LET'S TAKE A WALK.

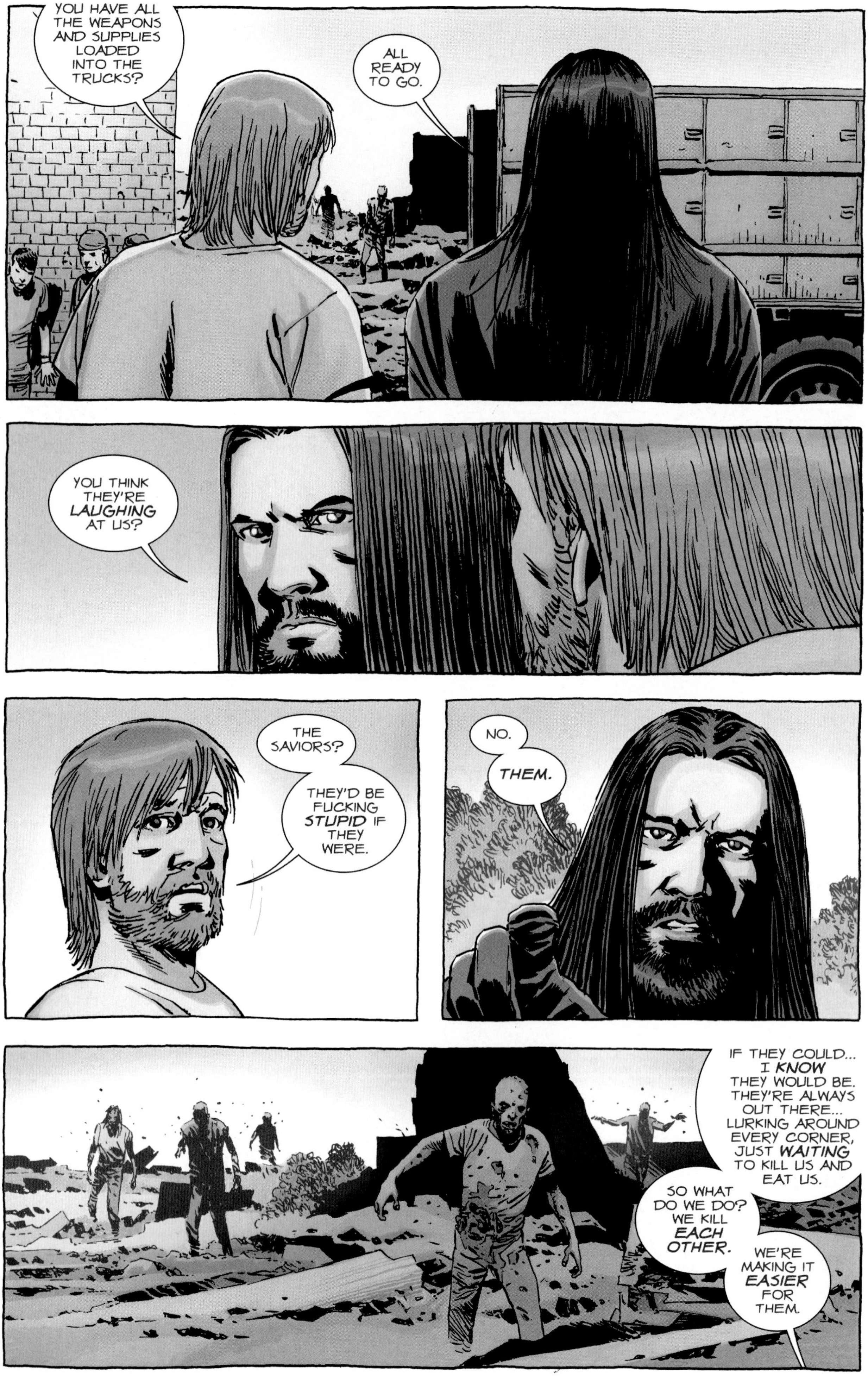
YOU HAVE ALL THE WEAPONS AND SUPPLIES LOADED INTO THE TRUCKS?
ALL READY TO GO.
YOU THINK THEY'RE LAUGHING AT US?
THE SAVIORS?
THEY'D BE FUCKING STUPID IF THEY WERE.
NO.
THEM.
IF THEY COULD... I KNOW THEY WOULD BE. THEY'RE ALWAYS OUT THERE... LURKING AROUND EVERY CORNER, JUST WAITING TO KILL US AND EAT US.
SO WHAT DO WE DO? WE KILL EACH OTHER.
WE'RE MAKING IT EASIER FOR THEM.

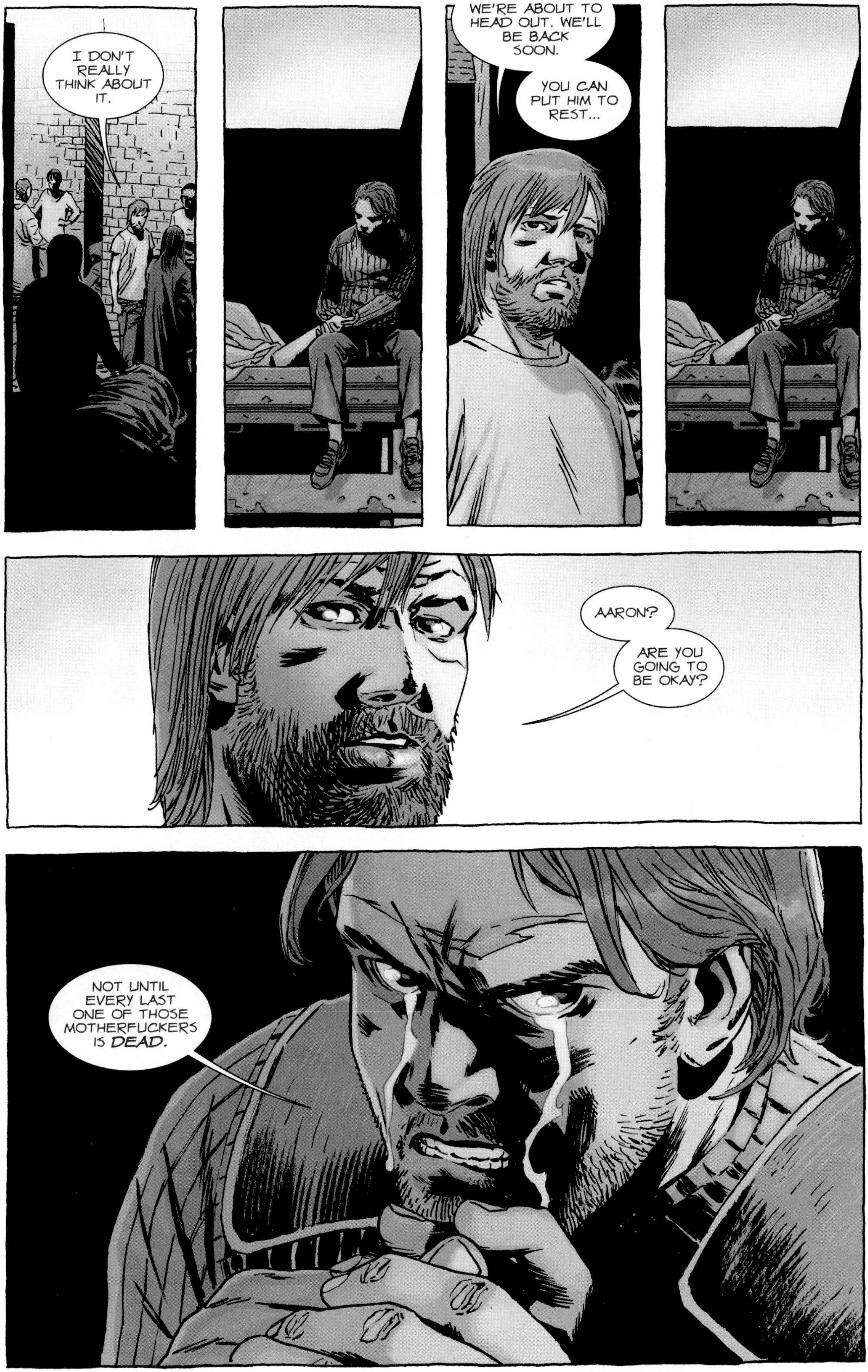
I DON'T REALLY THINK ABOUT IT.
WE'RE ABOUT TO HEAD OUT. WE'LL BE BACK SOON.
YOU CAN PUT HIM TO REST...
AARON?
ARE YOU GOING TO BE OKAY?
NOT UNTIL EVERY LAST ONE OF THOSE MOTHERFUCKERS IS *DEAD.*

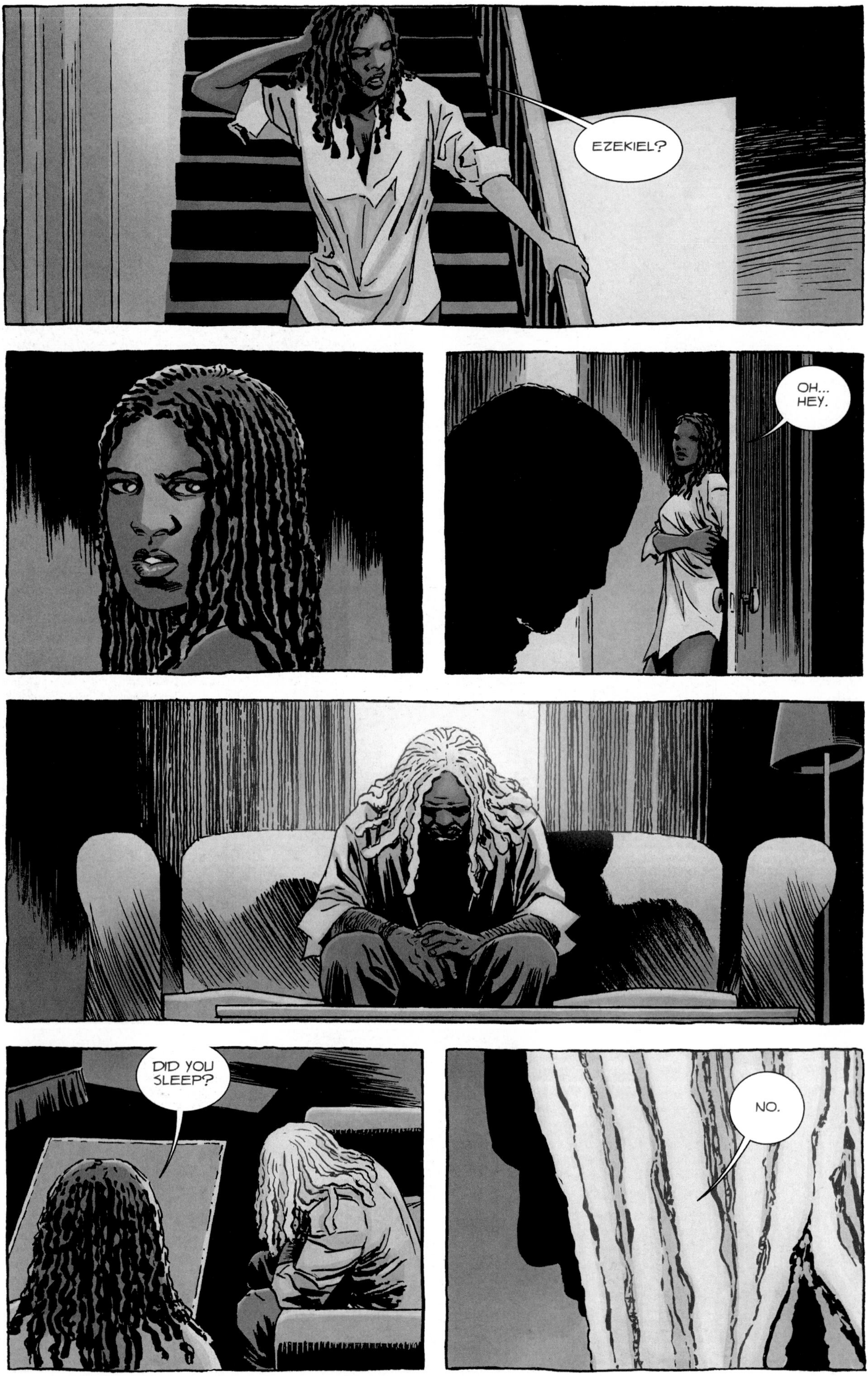
EZEKIEL?
OH... HEY.
DID YOU SLEEP?
NO.

AS I TOLD YOU BEFORE... I LOST LOVED ONES IN THE BEGINNING.

FRIENDS.

NOT FAMILY. I NEVER REALLY HAD A FAMILY. MY FATHER... HE WAS DEAD TO ME AT A VERY EARLY AGE. MY MOTHER NEVER REALLY EARNED THE TITLE.

WOMEN IN MY LIFE... IT JUST NEVER SEEMED TO WORK OUT.

SHIVA, THOSE PEOPLE I LOST... RICHARD... THAT WAS AS CLOSE AS I'VE EVER GOTTEN TO FAMILY.

YOU DIDN'T KNOW HIM... BUT RICHARD, HE WAS THE BACKBONE OF MY KINGDOM... I KEPT A DISTANCE... TO MAINTAIN MY... STUPID FUCKING PERSONA.

HE WAS MY EYES AND EARS.

THOSE PEOPLE LOOKED TO ME FOR GUIDANCE...

THEY WERE LOOKING RIGHT AT ME, LOOKING ME RIGHT IN THE EYES... SAYING "HELP ME," SAYING "WHAT DO I DO," AS THEY WERE GUNNED DOWN RIGHT IN FRONT OF ME.

AND SHIVA... SHE DIDN'T DESERVE THAT... IT WAS MY JOB TO PROTECT HER...

SHE PROBABLY DIDN'T EVEN KNOW... DIDN'T KNOW THAT I LET HER SACRIFICE HERSELF FOR ME.

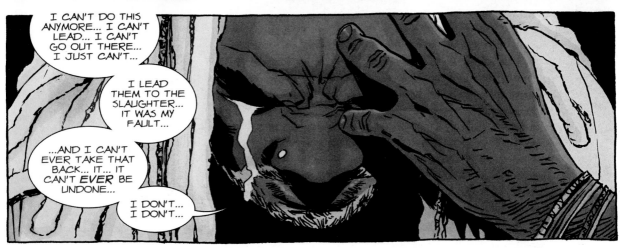

I CAN'T DO THIS ANYMORE... I CAN'T LEAD... I CAN'T GO OUT THERE... I JUST CAN'T...

I LEAD THEM TO THE SLAUGHTER... IT WAS MY FAULT...

...AND I CAN'T EVER TAKE THAT BACK... IT... IT CAN'T EVER BE UNDONE...

I DON'T... I DON'T...

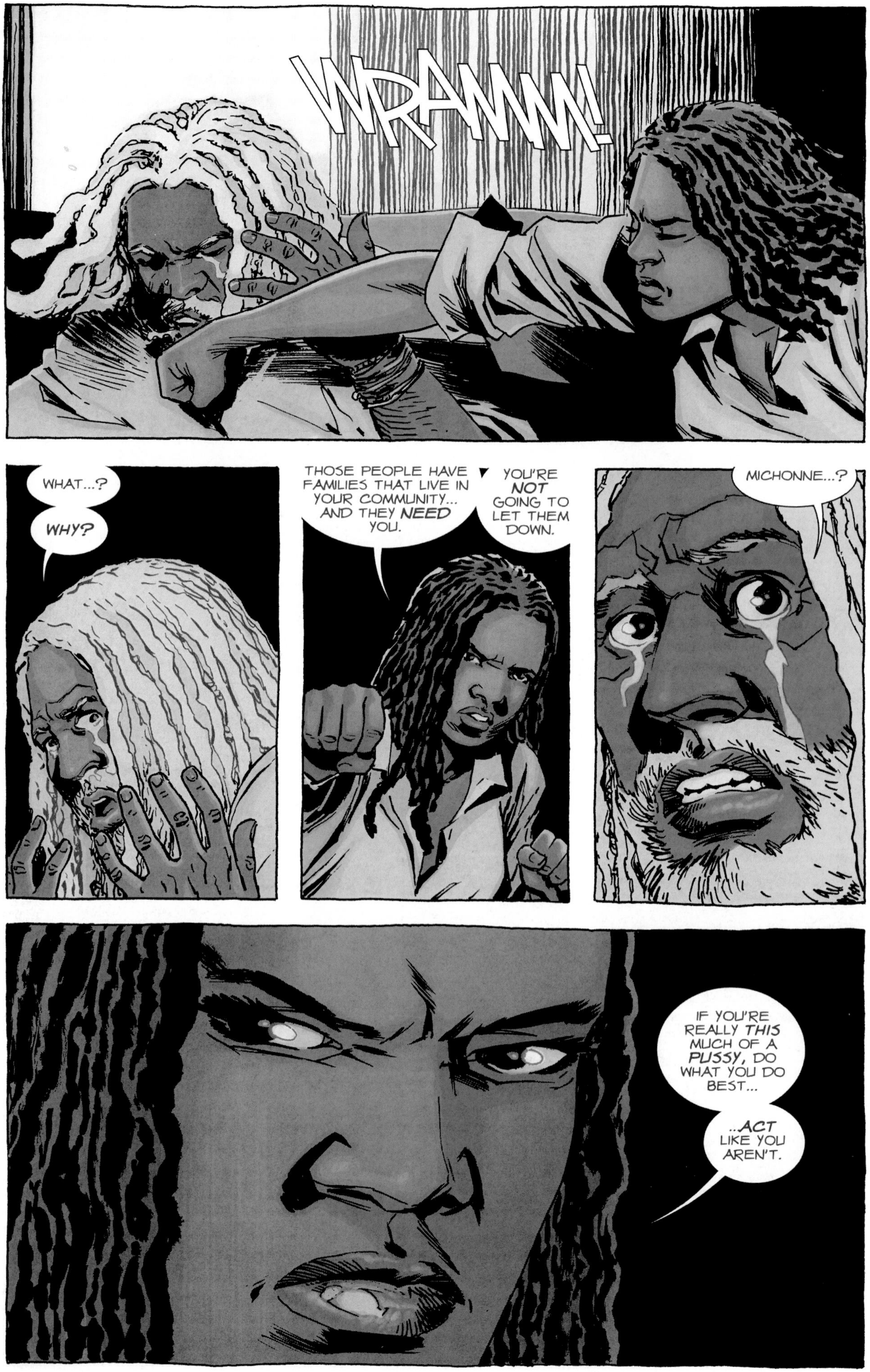
WRAMM!
WHAT...?
WHY?
THOSE PEOPLE HAVE FAMILIES THAT LIVE IN YOUR COMMUNITY... AND THEY NEED YOU.
YOU'RE NOT GOING TO LET THEM DOWN.
MICHONNE...?
IF YOU'RE REALLY THIS MUCH OF A PUSSY, DO WHAT YOU DO BEST...
...ACT LIKE YOU AREN'T.

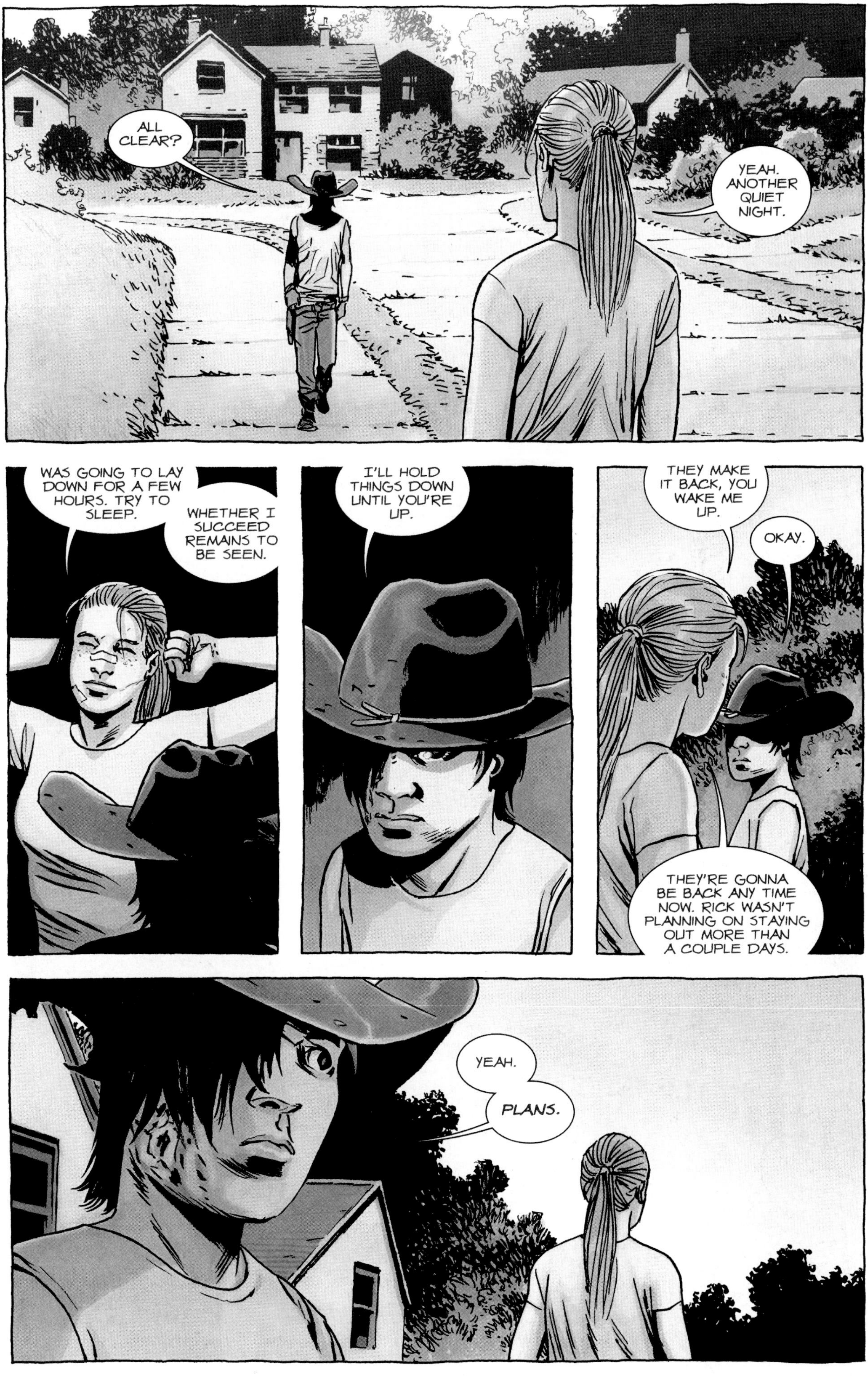
ALL CLEAR?
YEAH. ANOTHER QUIET NIGHT.
WAS GOING TO LAY DOWN FOR A FEW HOURS. TRY TO SLEEP.
WHETHER I SUCCEED REMAINS TO BE SEEN.
I'LL HOLD THINGS DOWN UNTIL YOU'RE UP.
THEY MAKE IT BACK, YOU WAKE ME UP.
OKAY.
THEY'RE GONNA BE BACK ANY TIME NOW. RICK WASN'T PLANNING ON STAYING OUT MORE THAN A COUPLE DAYS.
YEAH.
PLANS.

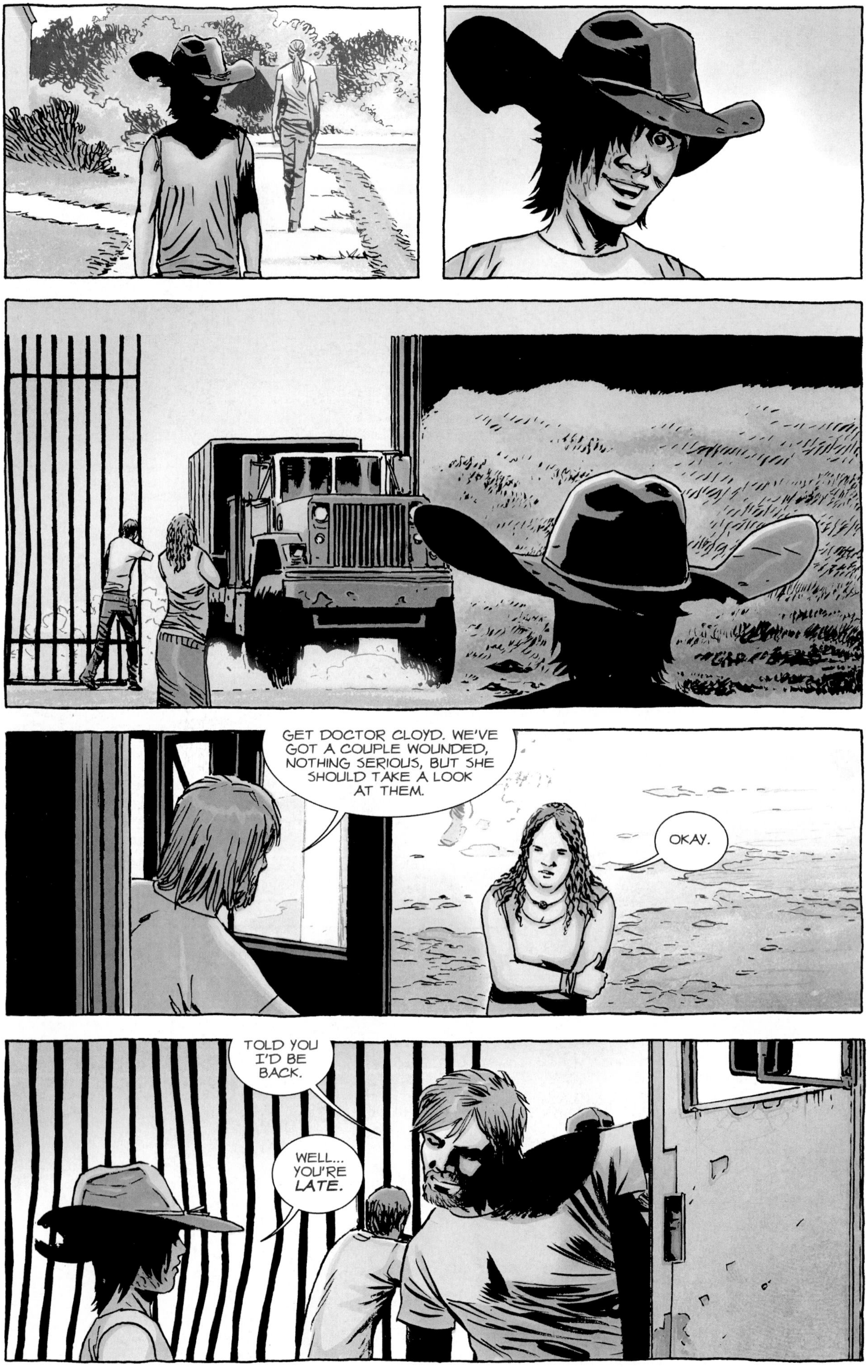
GET DOCTOR CLOYD. WE'VE GOT A COUPLE WOUNDED, NOTHING SERIOUS, BUT SHE SHOULD TAKE A LOOK AT THEM.
OKAY.
TOLD YOU I'D BE BACK.
WELL... YOU'RE *LATE*.

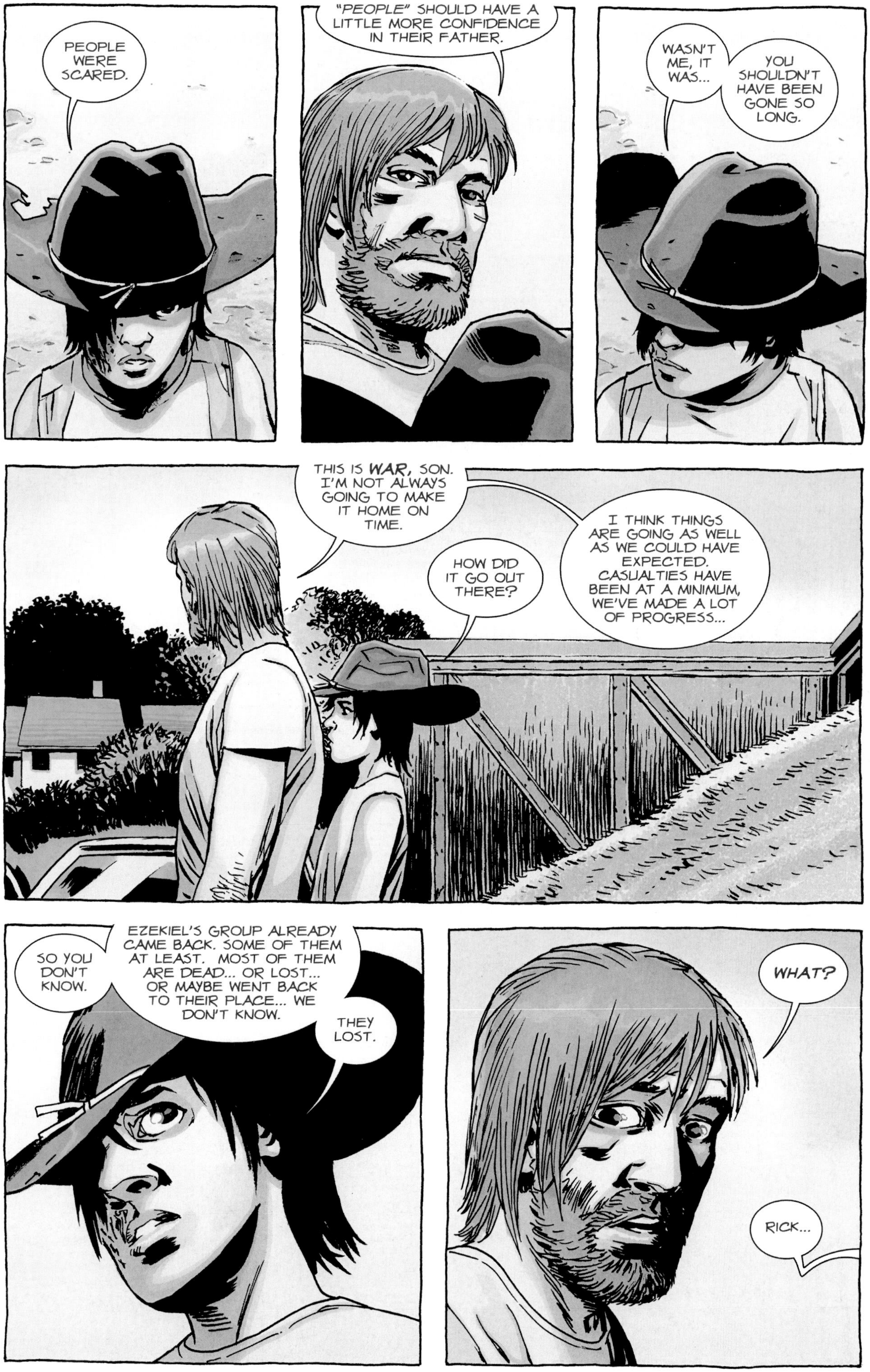
PEOPLE WERE SCARED.
"PEOPLE" SHOULD HAVE A LITTLE MORE CONFIDENCE IN THEIR FATHER.
WASN'T ME, IT WAS...
YOU SHOULDN'T HAVE BEEN GONE SO LONG.
THIS IS WAR, SON. I'M NOT ALWAYS GOING TO MAKE IT HOME ON TIME.
HOW DID IT GO OUT THERE?
I THINK THINGS ARE GOING AS WELL AS WE COULD HAVE EXPECTED. CASUALTIES HAVE BEEN AT A MINIMUM, WE'VE MADE A LOT OF PROGRESS...
SO YOU DON'T KNOW.
EZEKIEL'S GROUP ALREADY CAME BACK. SOME OF THEM AT LEAST. MOST OF THEM ARE DEAD... OR LOST... OR MAYBE WENT BACK TO THEIR PLACE... WE DON'T KNOW.
THEY LOST.
WHAT?
RICK...

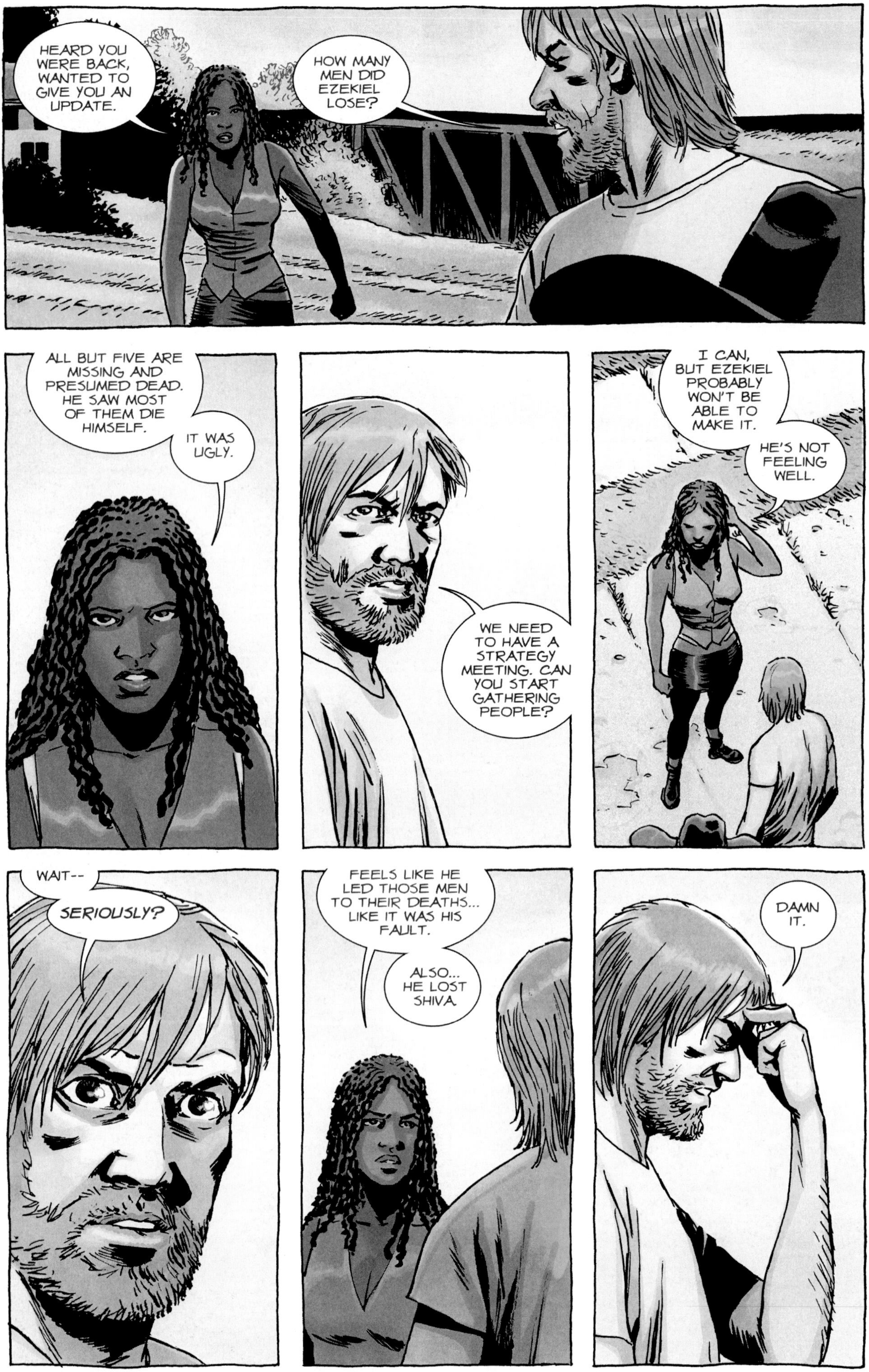
HEARD YOU WERE BACK, WANTED TO GIVE YOU AN UPDATE.
HOW MANY MEN DID EZEKIEL LOSE?
ALL BUT FIVE ARE MISSING AND PRESUMED DEAD. HE SAW MOST OF THEM DIE HIMSELF.
IT WAS UGLY.
WE NEED TO HAVE A STRATEGY MEETING. CAN YOU START GATHERING PEOPLE?
I CAN, BUT EZEKIEL PROBABLY WON'T BE ABLE TO MAKE IT.
HE'S NOT FEELING WELL.
WAIT--
SERIOUSLY?
FEELS LIKE HE LED THOSE MEN TO THEIR DEATHS... LIKE IT WAS HIS FAULT.
ALSO... HE LOST SHIVA.
DAMN IT.

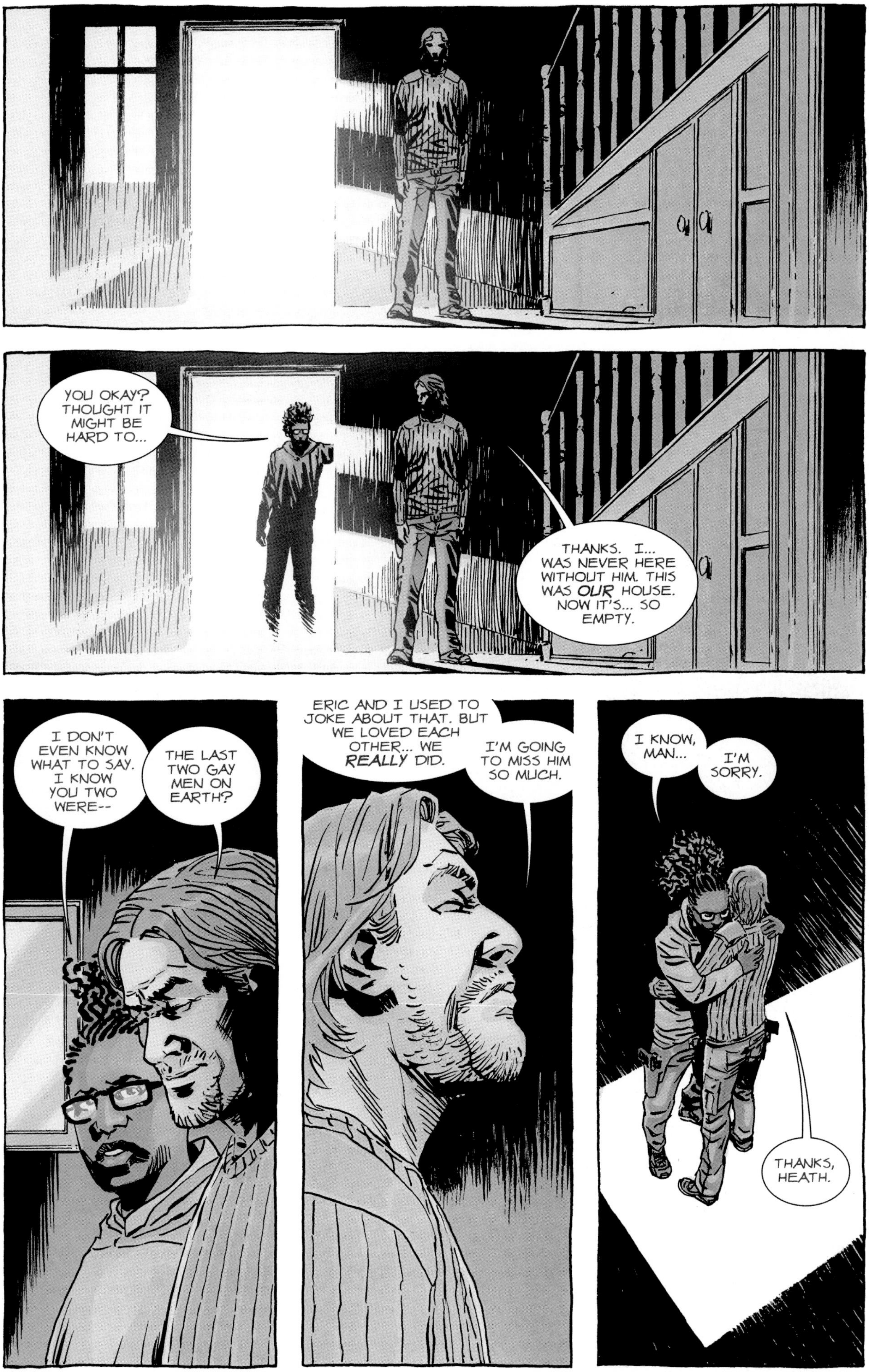
YOU OKAY? THOUGHT IT MIGHT BE HARD TO...
THANKS. I... WAS NEVER HERE WITHOUT HIM. THIS WAS OUR HOUSE. NOW IT'S... SO EMPTY.
I DON'T EVEN KNOW WHAT TO SAY. I KNOW YOU TWO WERE--
THE LAST TWO GAY MEN ON EARTH?
ERIC AND I USED TO JOKE ABOUT THAT. BUT WE LOVED EACH OTHER... WE REALLY DID.
I'M GOING TO MISS HIM SO MUCH.
I KNOW, MAN...
I'M SORRY.
THANKS, HEATH.

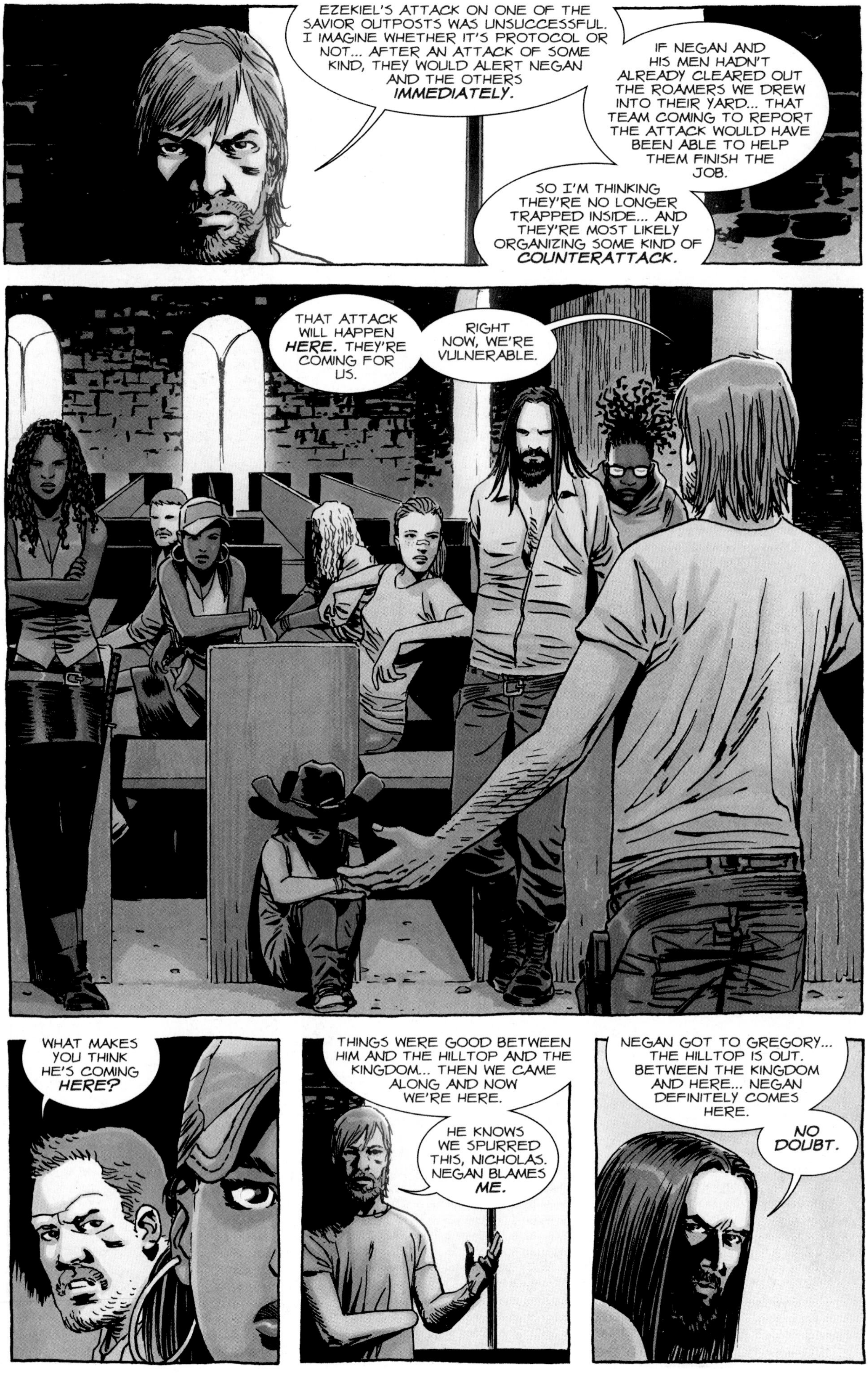
EZEKIEL'S ATTACK ON ONE OF THE SAVIOR OUTPOSTS WAS UNSUCCESSFUL. I IMAGINE WHETHER IT'S PROTOCOL OR NOT... AFTER AN ATTACK OF SOME KIND, THEY WOULD ALERT NEGAN AND THE OTHERS IMMEDIATELY.
IF NEGAN AND HIS MEN HADN'T ALREADY CLEARED OUT THE ROAMERS WE DREW INTO THEIR YARD... THAT TEAM COMING TO REPORT THE ATTACK WOULD HAVE BEEN ABLE TO HELP THEM FINISH THE JOB.
SO I'M THINKING THEY'RE NO LONGER TRAPPED INSIDE... AND THEY'RE MOST LIKELY ORGANIZING SOME KIND OF COUNTERATTACK.
THAT ATTACK WILL HAPPEN HERE. THEY'RE COMING FOR US.
RIGHT NOW, WE'RE VULNERABLE.
WHAT MAKES YOU THINK HE'S COMING HERE?
THINGS WERE GOOD BETWEEN HIM AND THE HILLTOP AND THE KINGDOM... THEN WE CAME ALONG AND NOW WE'RE HERE.
HE KNOWS WE SPURRED THIS, NICHOLAS. NEGAN BLAMES ME.
NEGAN GOT TO GREGORY... THE HILLTOP IS OUT. BETWEEN THE KINGDOM AND HERE... NEGAN DEFINITELY COMES HERE.
NO DOUBT.

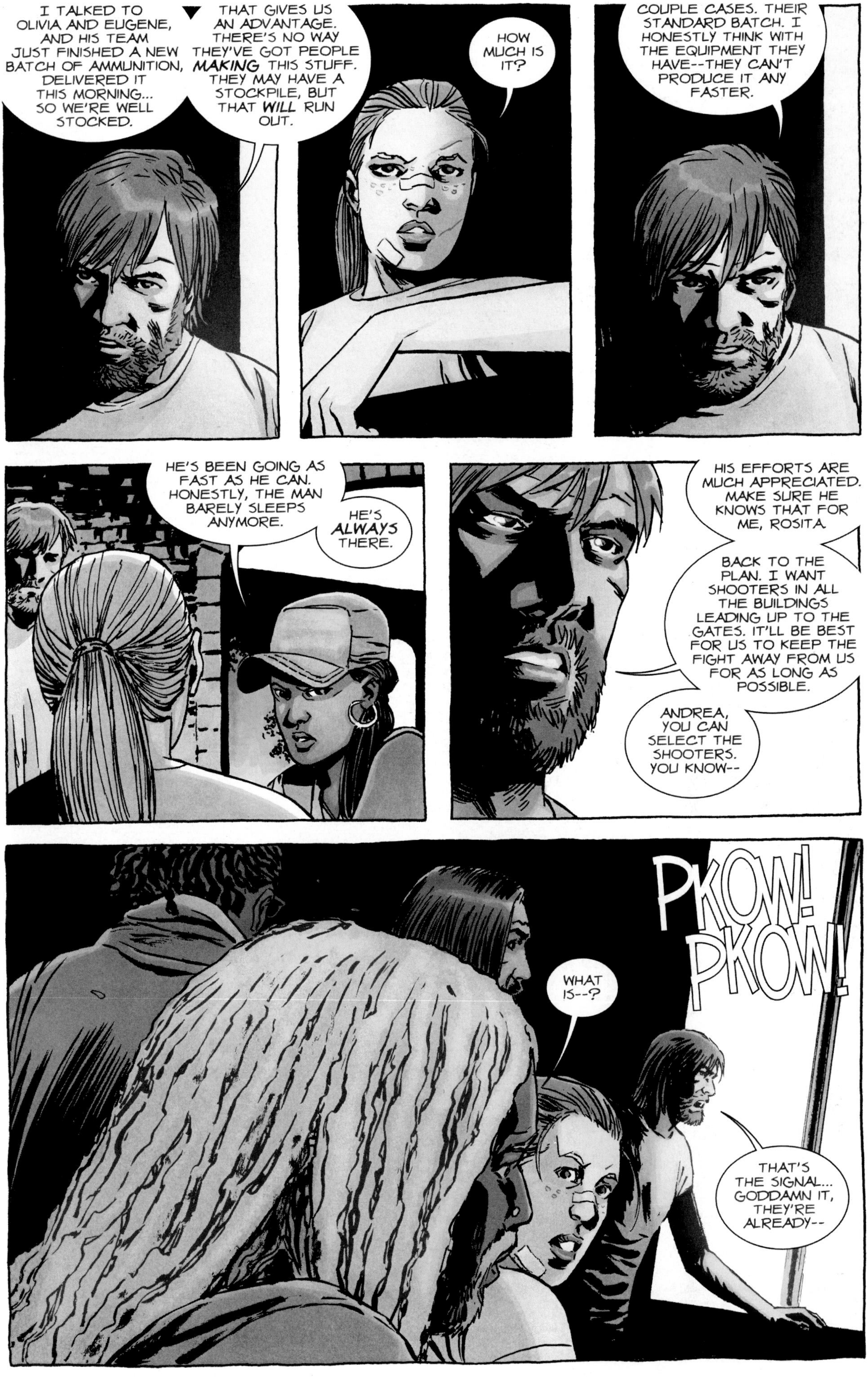
I TALKED TO OLIVIA AND EUGENE, AND HIS TEAM JUST FINISHED A NEW BATCH OF AMMUNITION, DELIVERED IT THIS MORNING... SO WE'RE WELL STOCKED.
THAT GIVES US AN ADVANTAGE. THERE'S NO WAY THEY'VE GOT PEOPLE MAKING THIS STUFF. THEY MAY HAVE A STOCKPILE, BUT THAT WILL RUN OUT.
HOW MUCH IS IT?
COUPLE CASES. THEIR STANDARD BATCH. I HONESTLY THINK WITH THE EQUIPMENT THEY HAVE--THEY CAN'T PRODUCE IT ANY FASTER.
HE'S BEEN GOING AS FAST AS HE CAN. HONESTLY, THE MAN BARELY SLEEPS ANYMORE.
HE'S ALWAYS THERE.
HIS EFFORTS ARE MUCH APPRECIATED. MAKE SURE HE KNOWS THAT FOR ME, ROSITA.
BACK TO THE PLAN. I WANT SHOOTERS IN ALL THE BUILDINGS LEADING UP TO THE GATES. IT'LL BE BEST FOR US TO KEEP THE FIGHT AWAY FROM US FOR AS LONG AS POSSIBLE.
ANDREA, YOU CAN SELECT THE SHOOTERS. YOU KNOW--
PKOW! PKOW!
WHAT IS--?
THAT'S THE SIGNAL... GODDAMN IT, THEY'RE ALREADY--

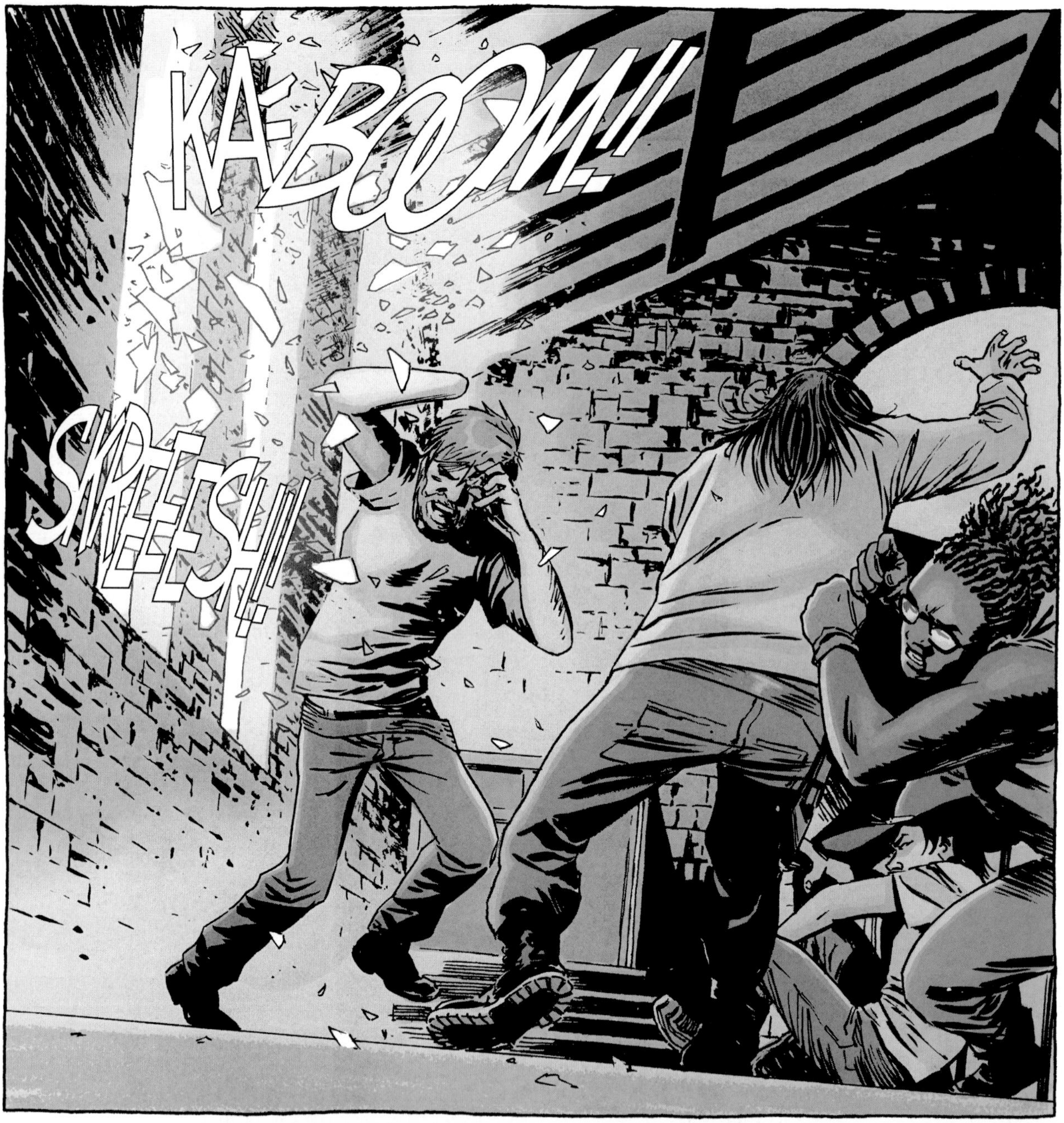
KA-BOOM!!
SKREEESH!!

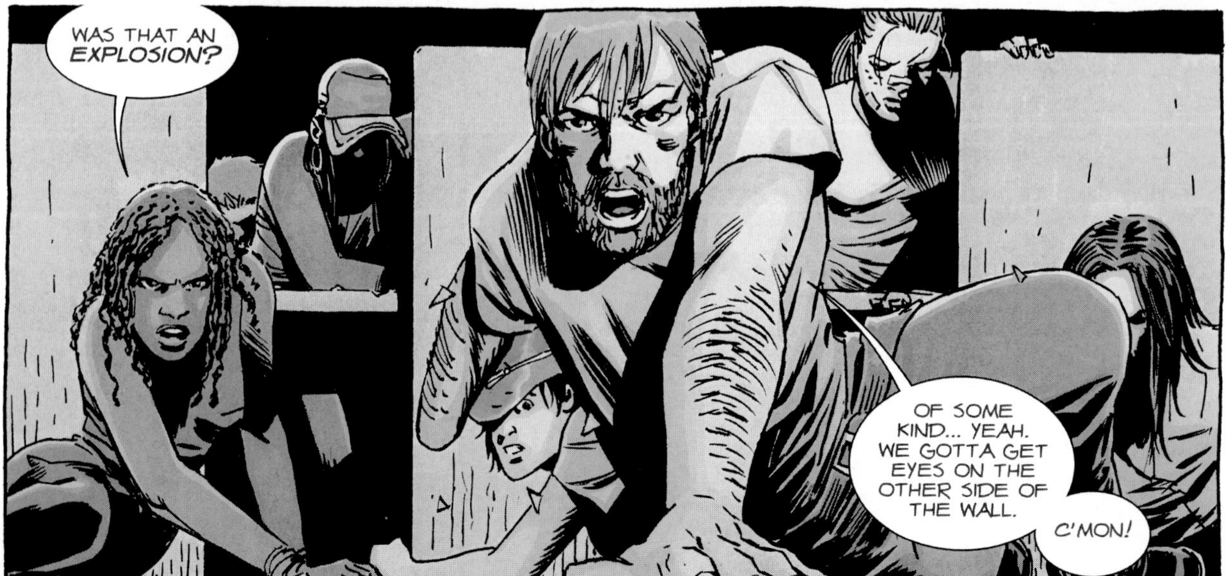
WAS THAT AN *EXPLOSION?*
OF SOME KIND... YEAH. WE GOTTA GET EYES ON THE OTHER SIDE OF THE WALL.
C'MON!

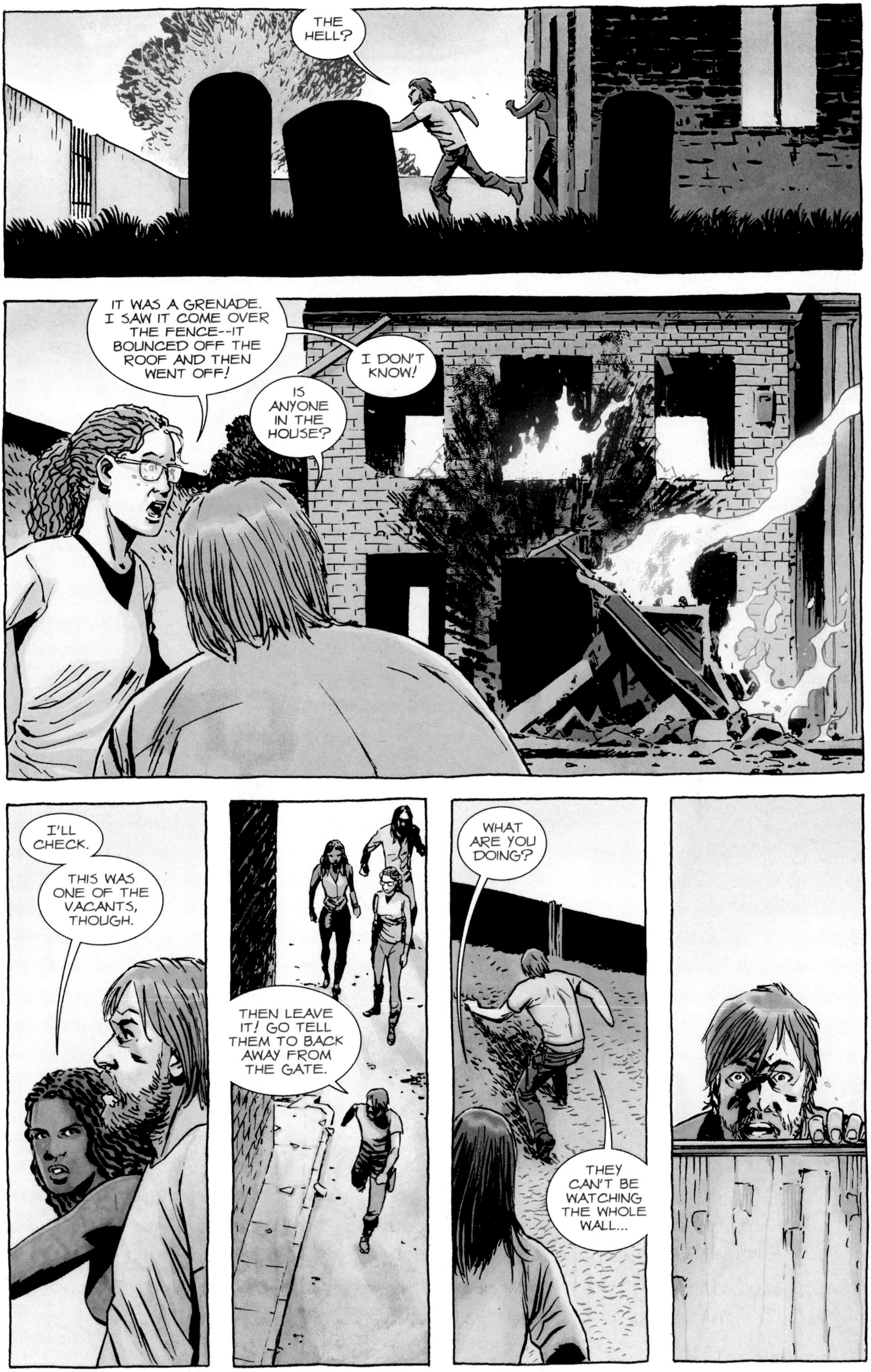
THE HELL?
IT WAS A GRENADE. I SAW IT COME OVER THE FENCE--IT BOUNCED OFF THE ROOF AND THEN WENT OFF!
IS ANYONE IN THE HOUSE?
I DON'T KNOW!
I'LL CHECK.
THIS WAS ONE OF THE VACANTS, THOUGH.
THEN LEAVE IT! GO TELL THEM TO BACK AWAY FROM THE GATE.
WHAT ARE YOU DOING?
THEY CAN'T BE WATCHING THE WHOLE WALL...

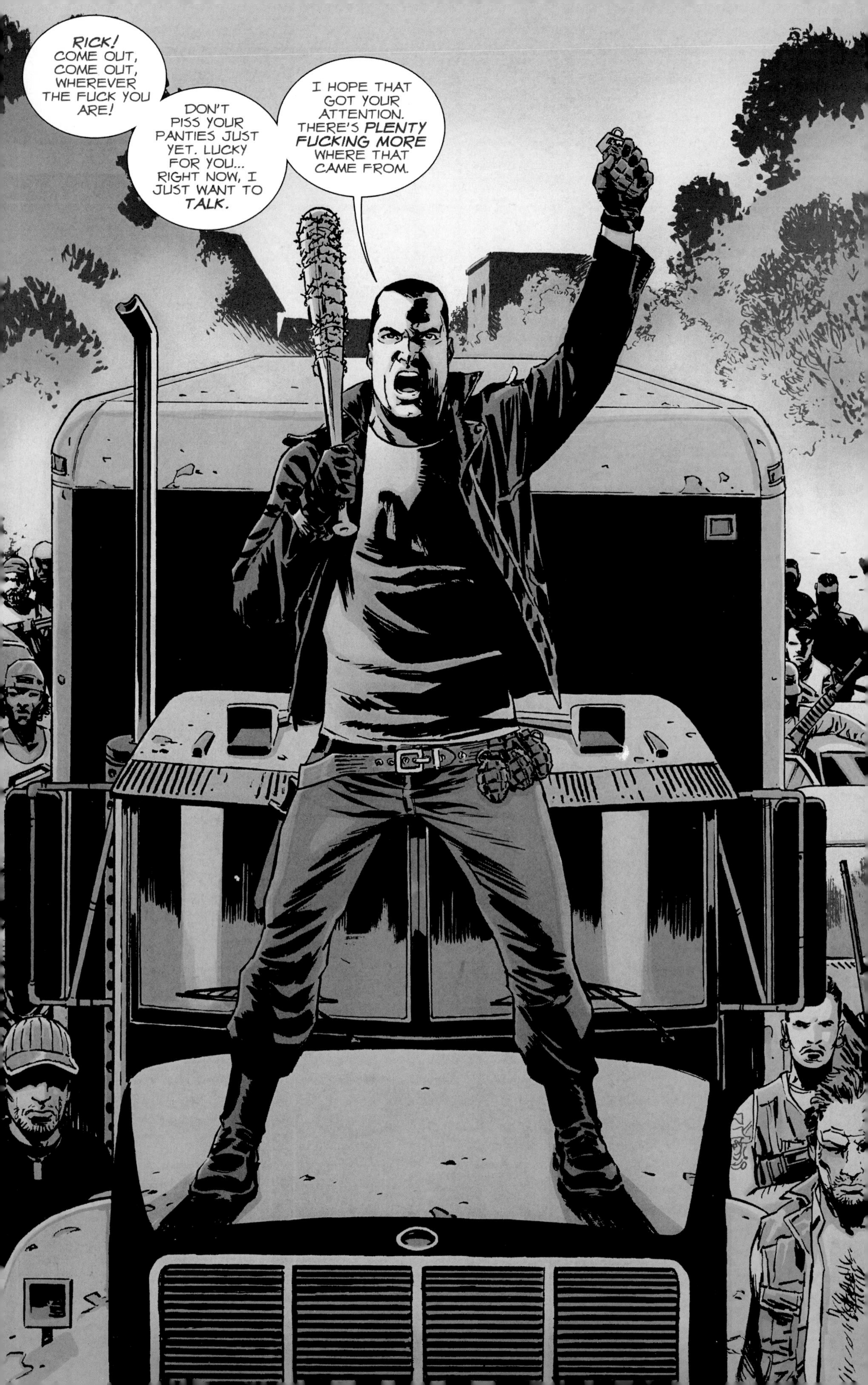
RICK! COME OUT, COME OUT, WHEREVER THE FUCK YOU ARE!
DON'T PISS YOUR PANTIES JUST YET. LUCKY FOR YOU... RIGHT NOW, I JUST WANT TO TALK.
I HOPE THAT GOT YOUR ATTENTION. THERE'S PLENTY FUCKING MORE WHERE THAT CAME FROM.

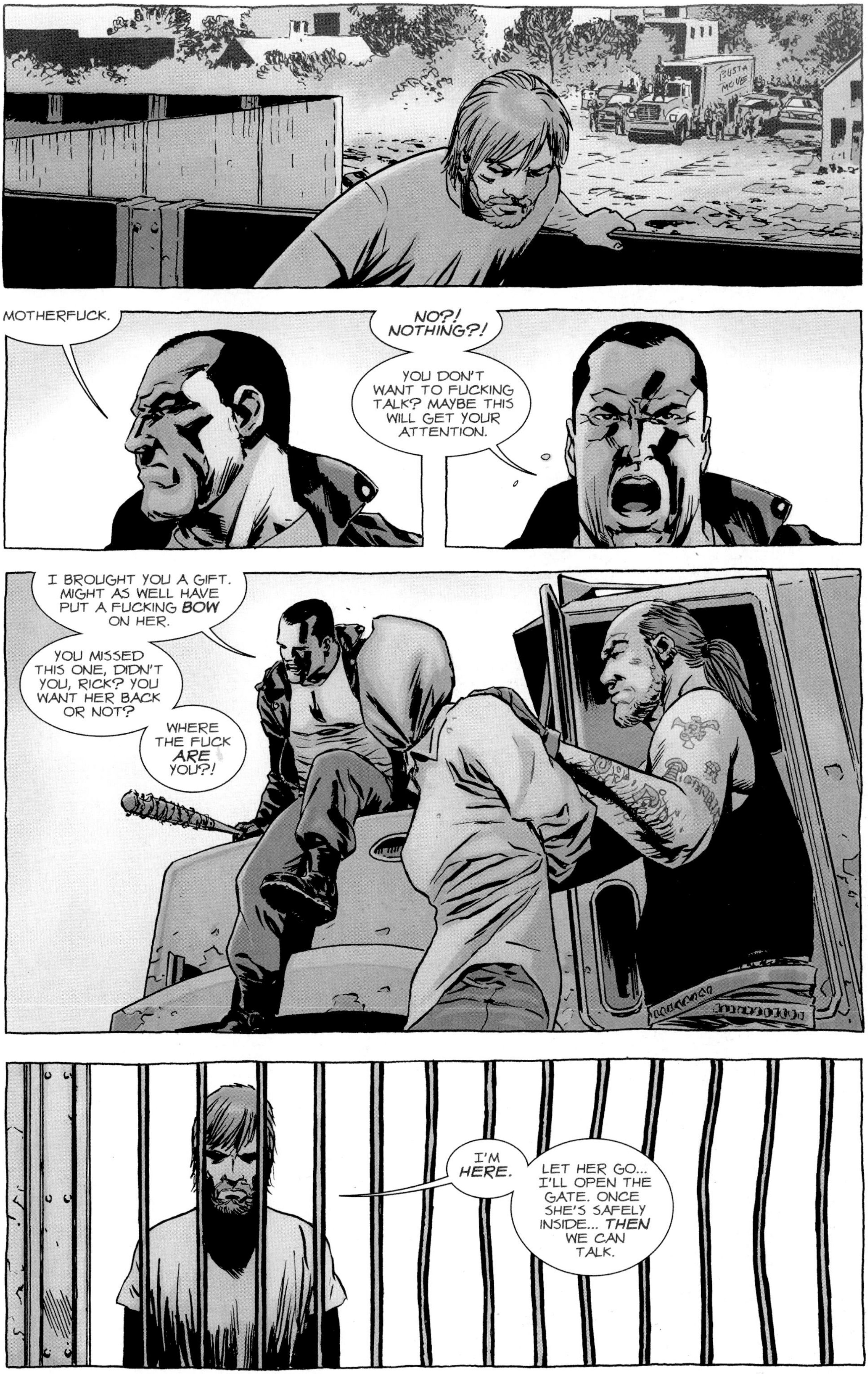

BUSTA MOVE
MOTHERFUCK.
NO?! NOTHING?!
YOU DON'T WANT TO FUCKING TALK? MAYBE THIS WILL GET YOUR ATTENTION.
I BROUGHT YOU A GIFT. MIGHT AS WELL HAVE PUT A FUCKING BOW ON HER.
YOU MISSED THIS ONE, DIDN'T YOU, RICK? YOU WANT HER BACK OR NOT?
WHERE THE FUCK ARE YOU?!
I'M HERE.
LET HER GO... I'LL OPEN THE GATE. ONCE SHE'S SAFELY INSIDE... THEN WE CAN TALK.

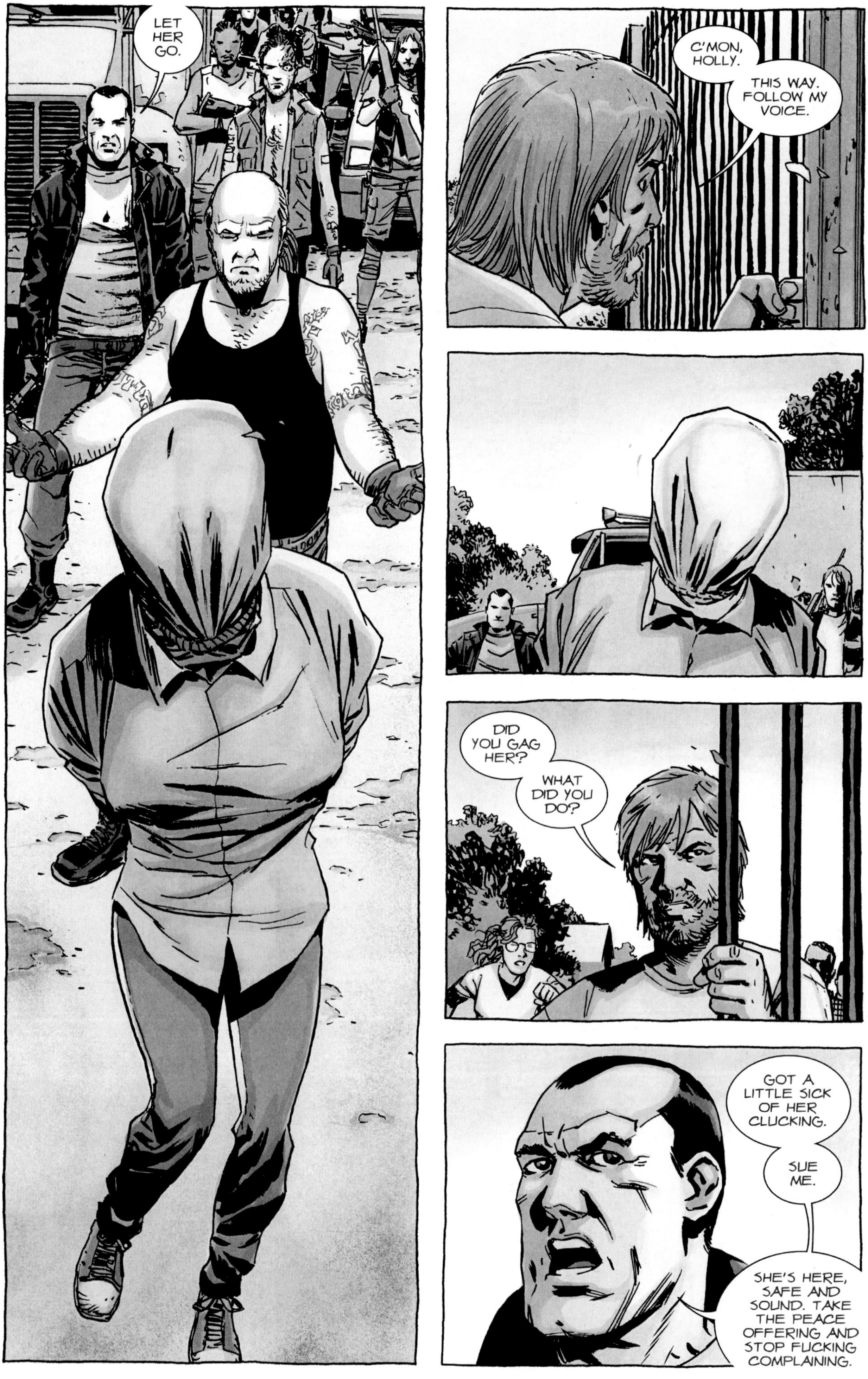
LET HER GO.
C'MON, HOLLY.
THIS WAY. FOLLOW MY VOICE.
DID YOU GAG HER?
WHAT DID YOU DO?
GOT A LITTLE SICK OF HER CLUCKING.
SUE ME.
SHE'S HERE, SAFE AND SOUND. TAKE THE PEACE OFFERING AND STOP FUCKING COMPLAINING.

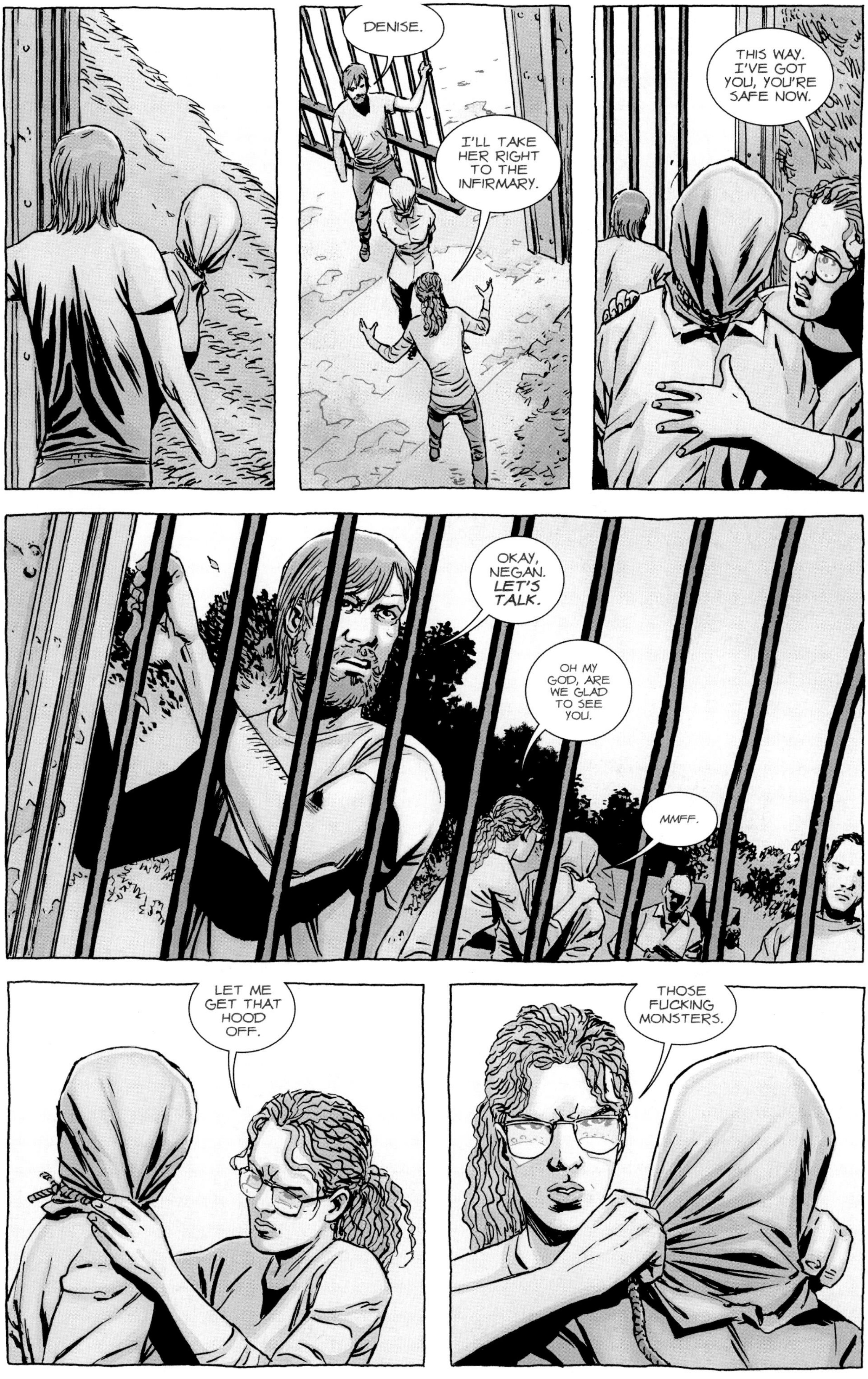
DENISE.
I'LL TAKE HER RIGHT TO THE INFIRMARY.
THIS WAY. I'VE GOT YOU, YOU'RE SAFE NOW.
OKAY, NEGAN. *LET'S TALK.*
OH MY GOD, ARE WE GLAD TO SEE YOU.
MMFF.
LET ME GET THAT HOOD OFF.
THOSE FUCKING MONSTERS.

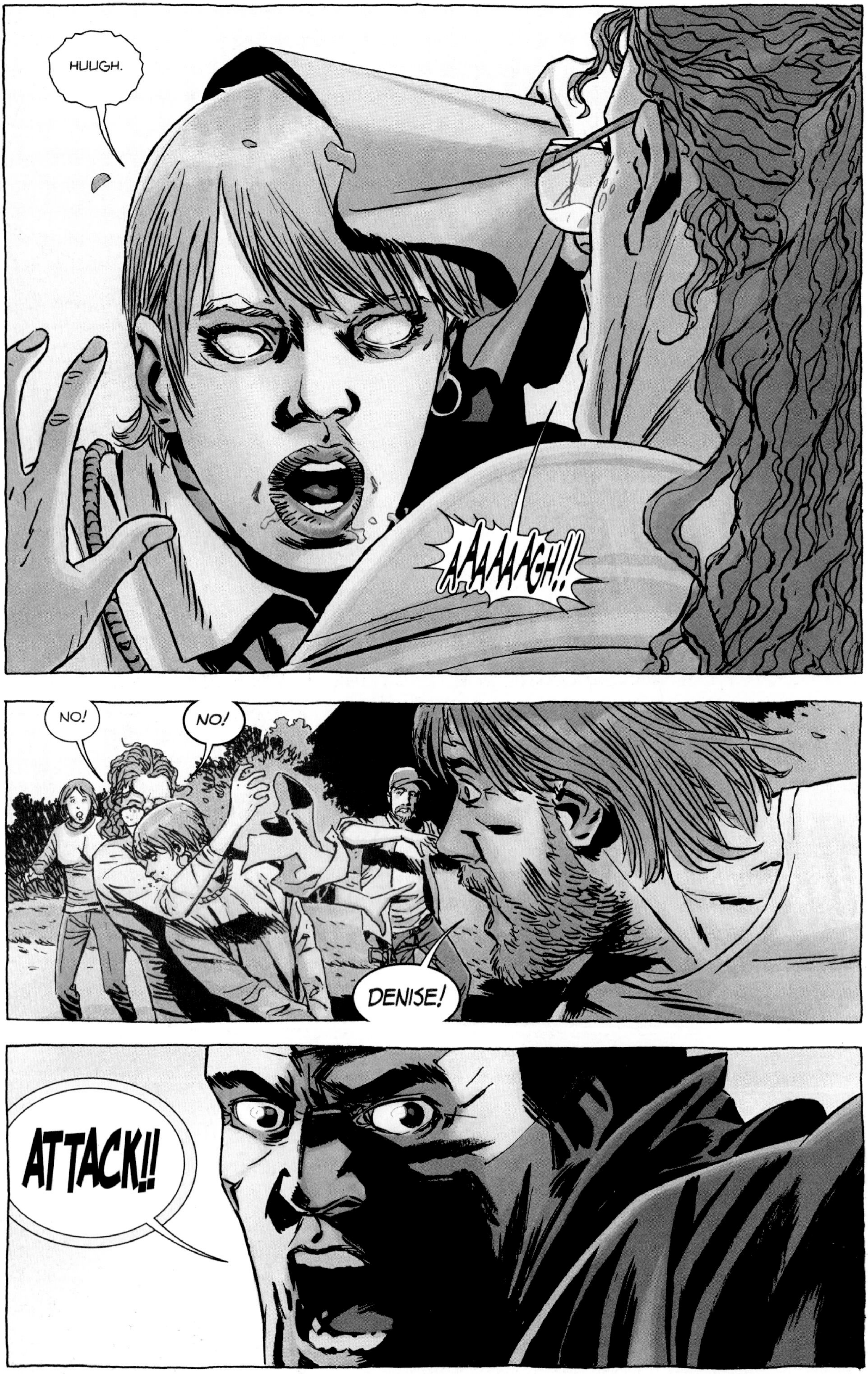
HUUGH.
AAAAAAGH!!
NO!
NO!
DENISE!
ATTACK!!

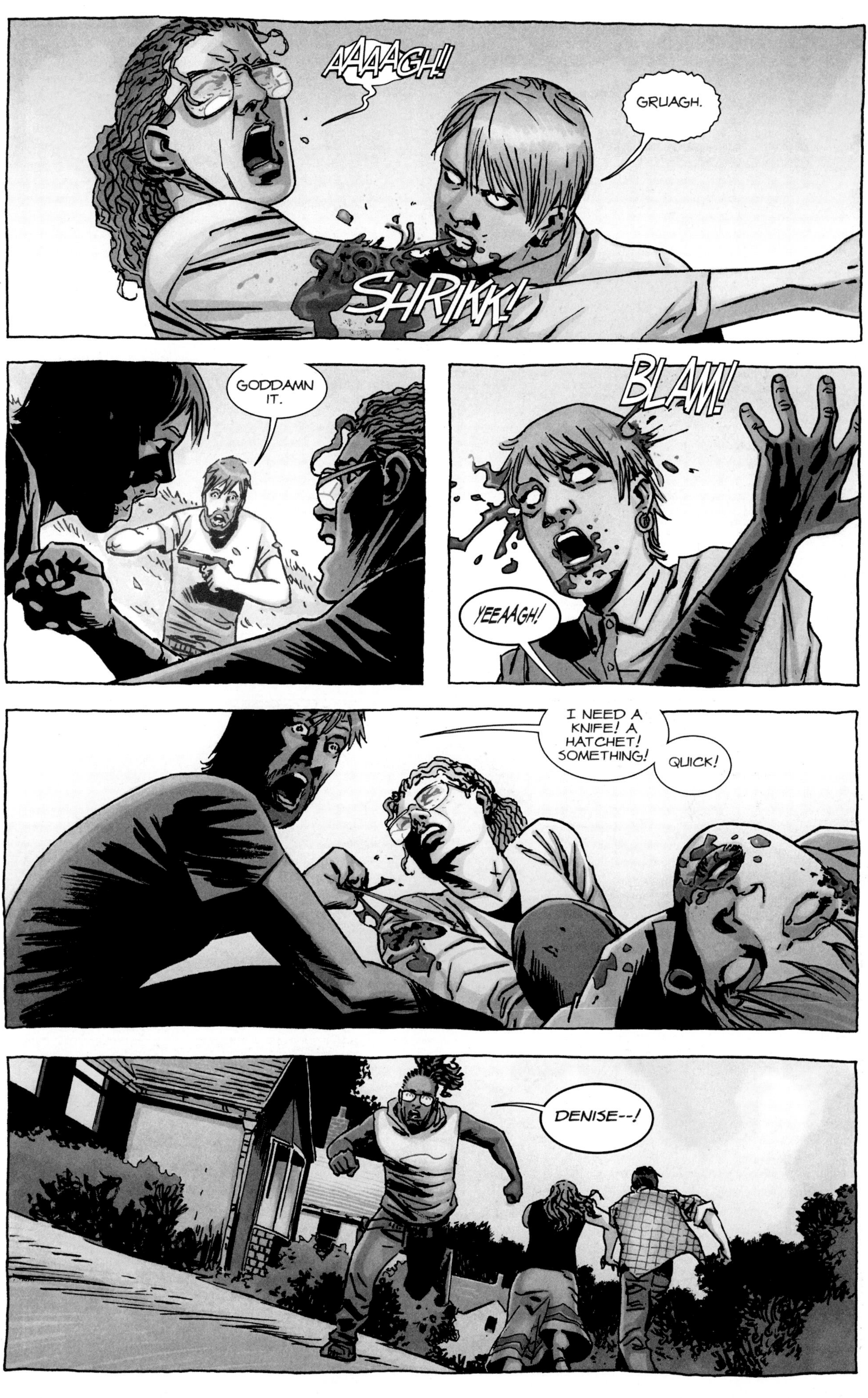
AAAAGH!!
GRUAGH.
SHRIKK!
GODDAMN IT.
BLAM!
YEEAAGH!
I NEED A KNIFE! A HATCHET! SOMETHING!
QUICK!
DENISE--!

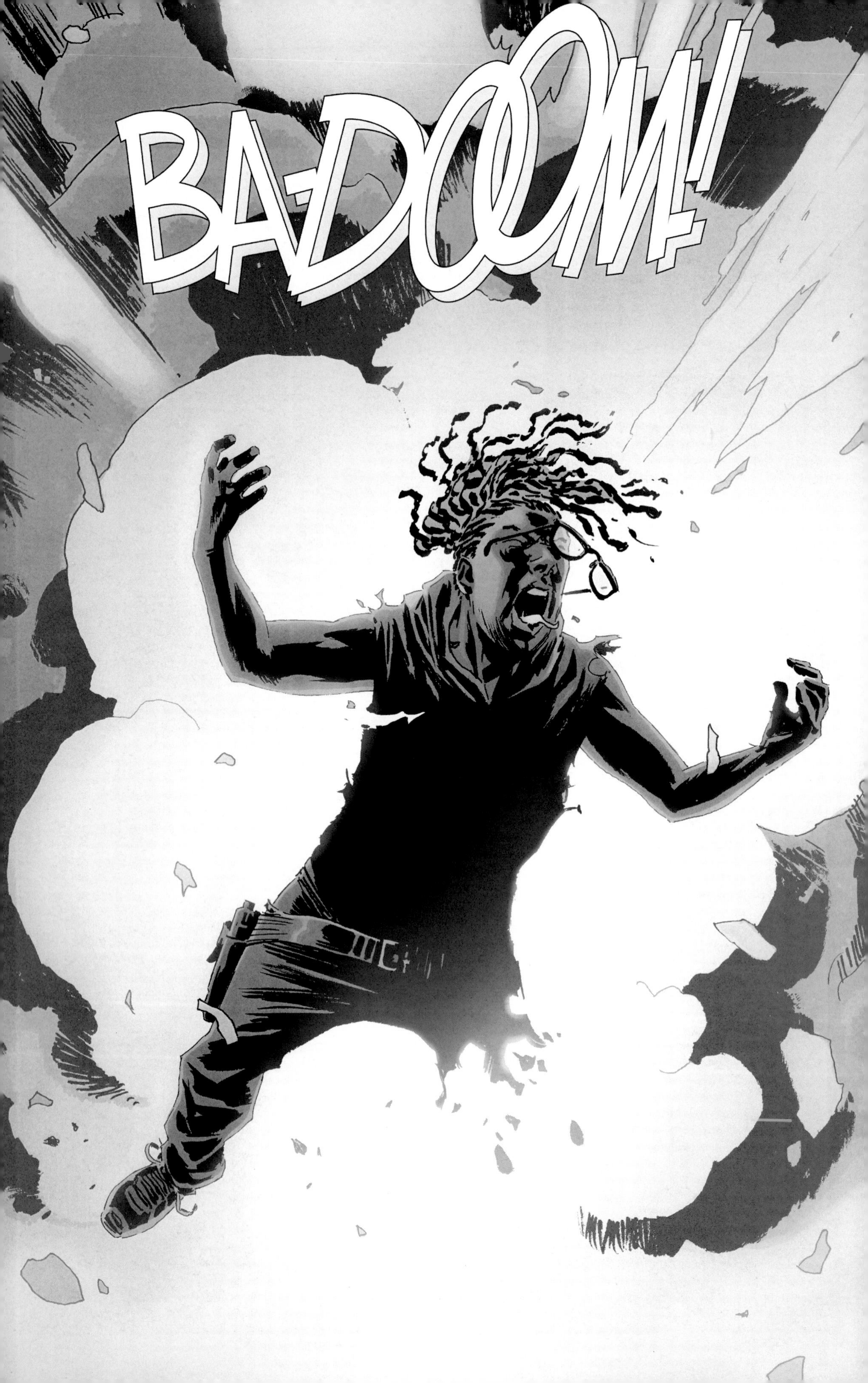
BA-DOOM!

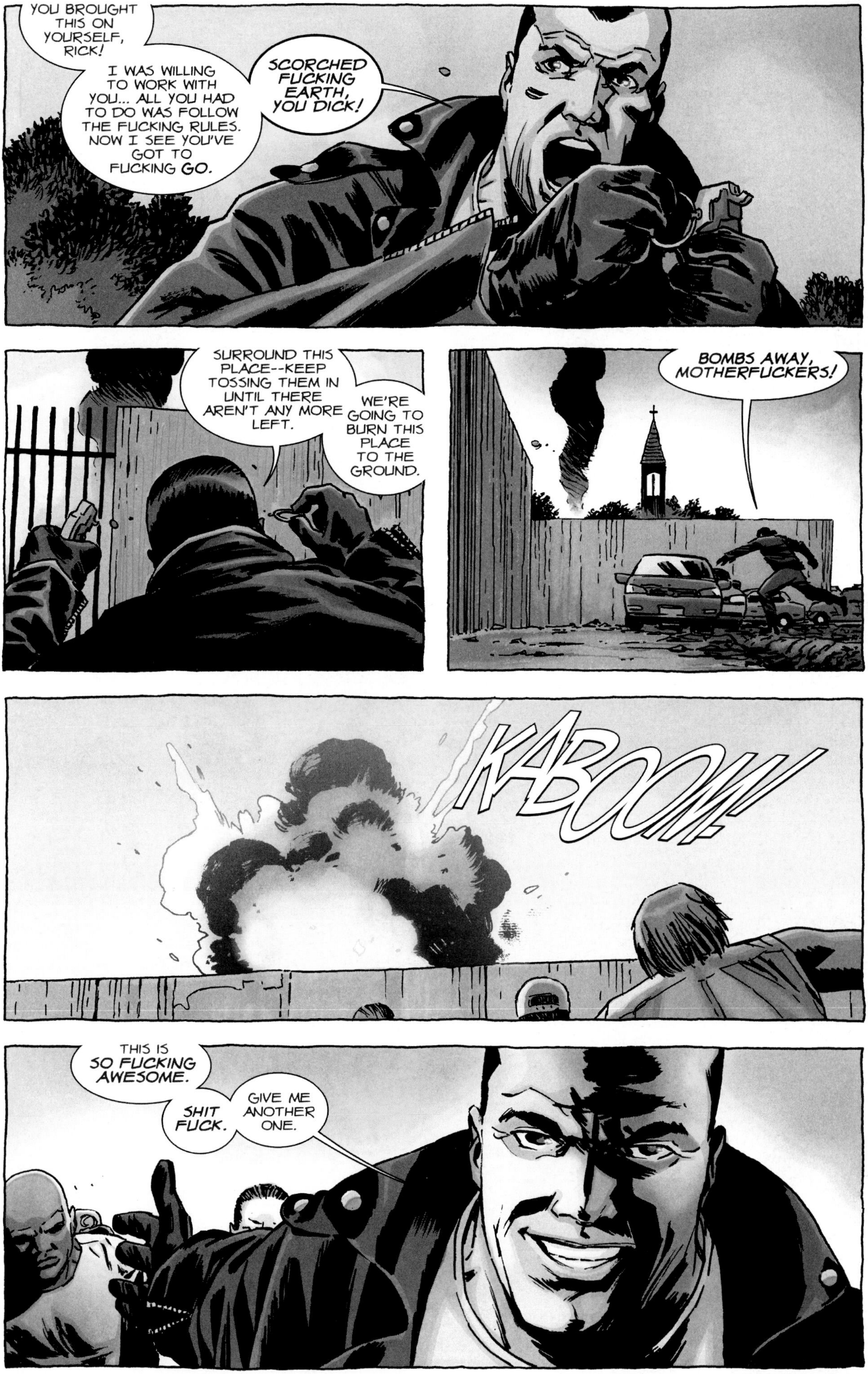
YOU BROUGHT THIS ON YOURSELF, RICK!
I WAS WILLING TO WORK WITH YOU... ALL YOU HAD TO DO WAS FOLLOW THE FUCKING RULES. NOW I SEE YOU'VE GOT TO FUCKING GO.
SCORCHED FUCKING EARTH, YOU DICK!
SURROUND THIS PLACE--KEEP TOSSING THEM IN UNTIL THERE AREN'T ANY MORE LEFT.
WE'RE GOING TO BURN THIS PLACE TO THE GROUND.
BOMBS AWAY, MOTHERFUCKERS!
KABOOM!
THIS IS SO FUCKING AWESOME.
SHIT FUCK.
GIVE ME ANOTHER ONE.

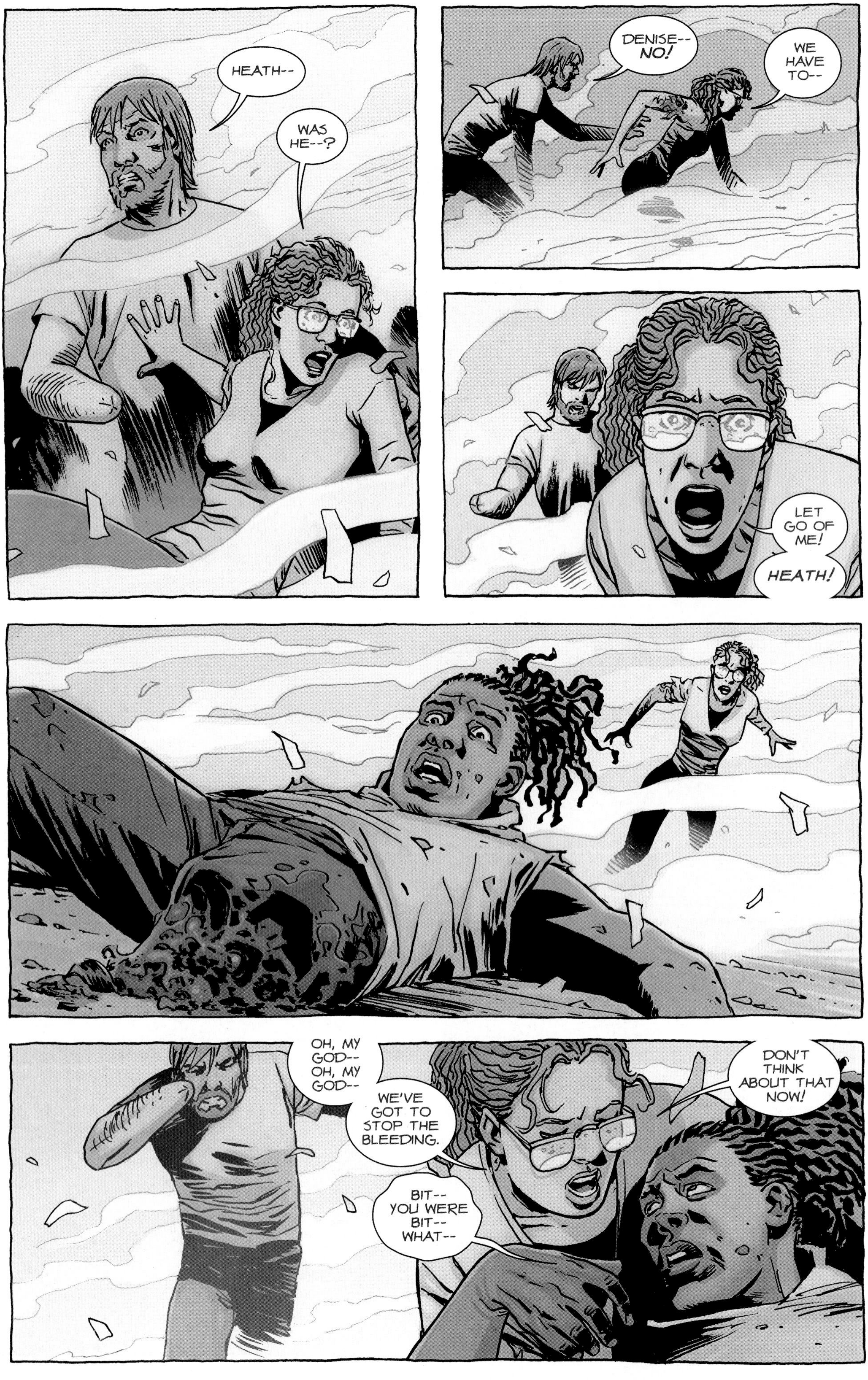
HEATH--
WAS HE--?
DENISE-- NO!
WE HAVE TO--
LET GO OF ME!
HEATH!
OH, MY GOD-- OH, MY GOD--
WE'VE GOT TO STOP THE BLEEDING.
BIT-- YOU WERE BIT-- WHAT--
DON'T THINK ABOUT THAT NOW!

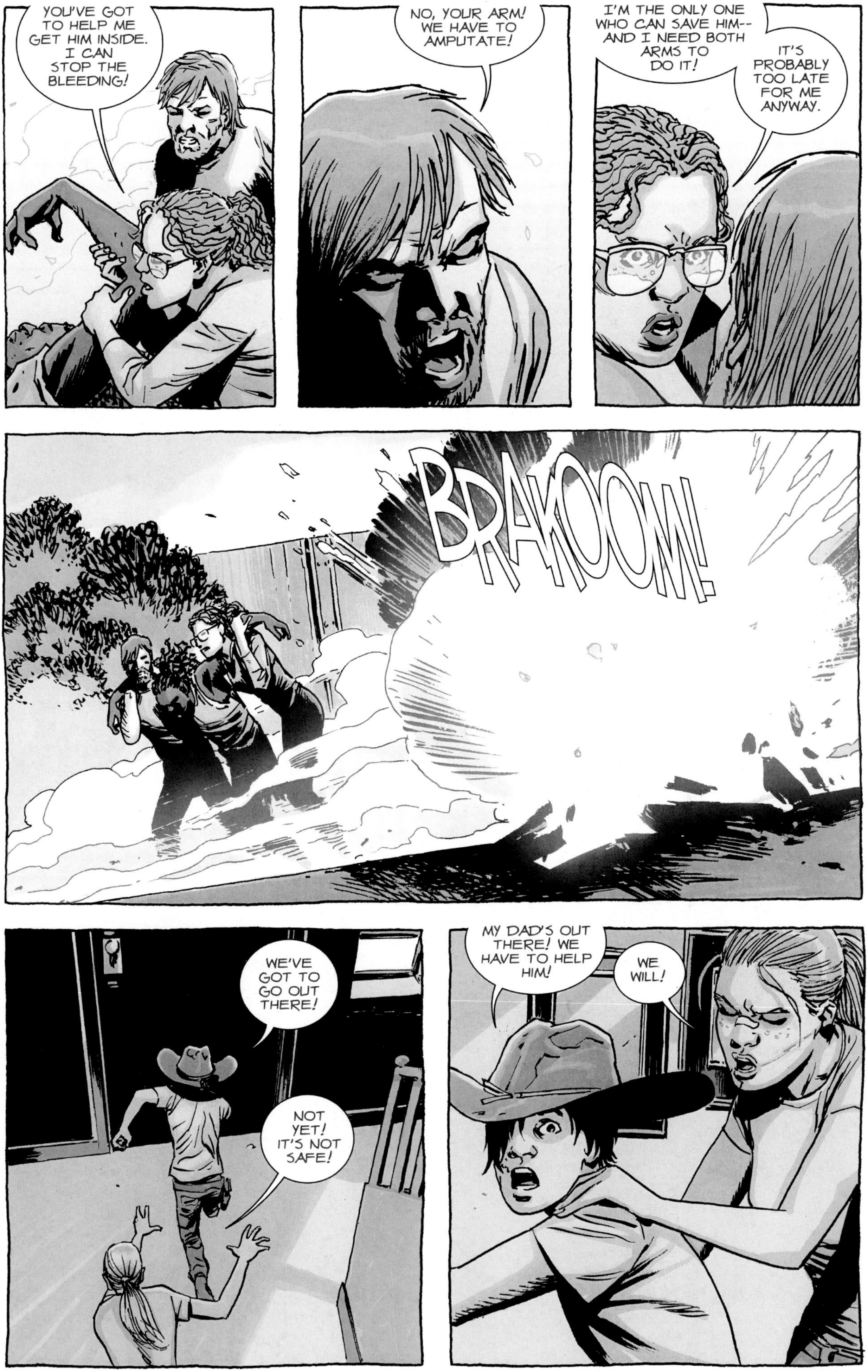
YOU'VE GOT TO HELP ME GET HIM INSIDE. I CAN STOP THE BLEEDING!
NO, YOUR ARM! WE HAVE TO AMPUTATE!
I'M THE ONLY ONE WHO CAN SAVE HIM-- AND I NEED BOTH ARMS TO DO IT!
IT'S PROBABLY TOO LATE FOR ME ANYWAY.
BRAKOOM!
WE'VE GOT TO GO OUT THERE!
NOT YET! IT'S NOT SAFE!
MY DAD'S OUT THERE! WE HAVE TO HELP HIM!
WE WILL!

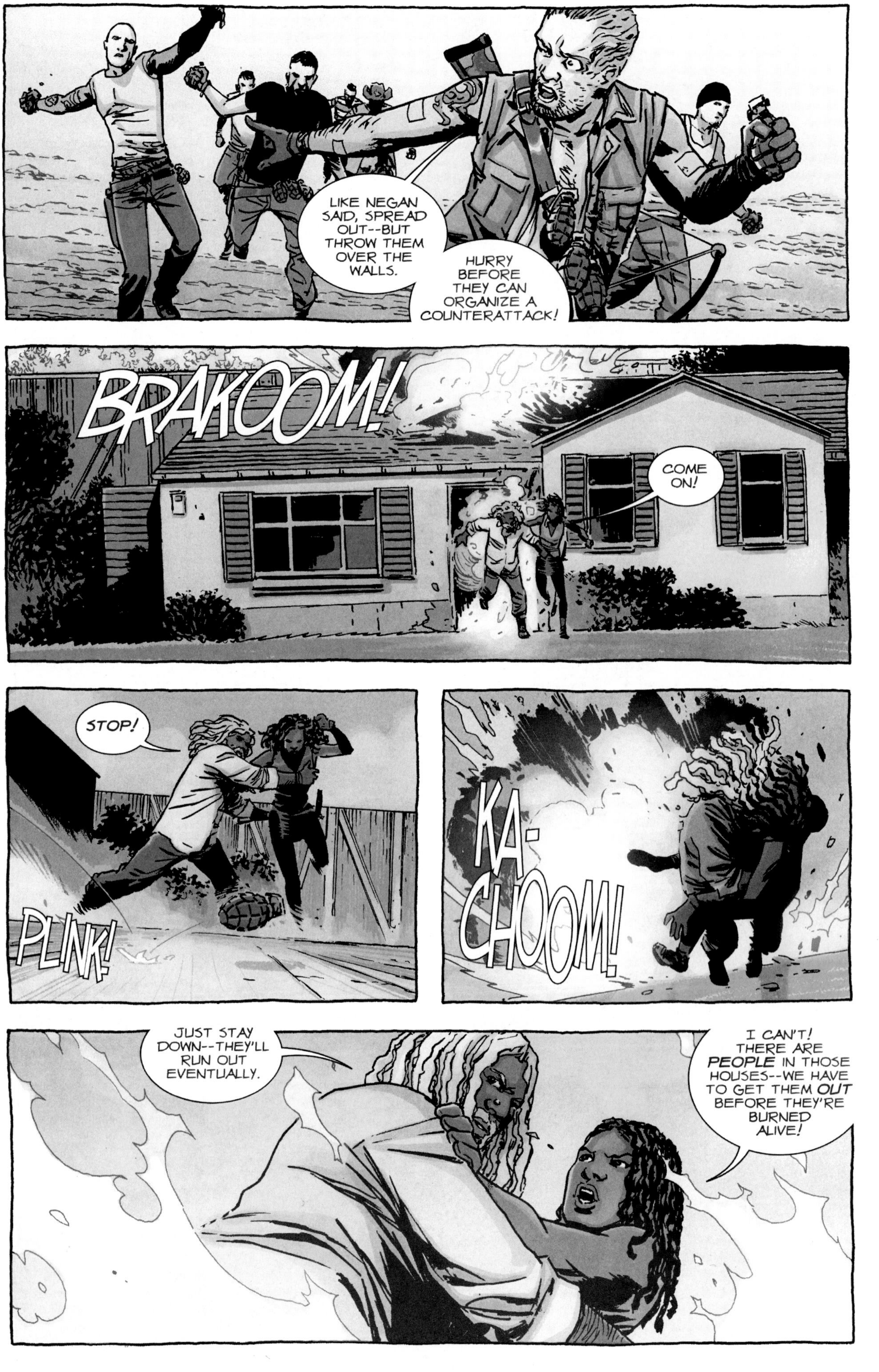
LIKE NEGAN SAID, SPREAD OUT--BUT THROW THEM OVER THE WALLS.
HURRY BEFORE THEY CAN ORGANIZE A COUNTERATTACK!
BRAKOOM!
COME ON!
STOP!
PLINK!
KA-CHOOM!
JUST STAY DOWN--THEY'LL RUN OUT EVENTUALLY.
I CAN'T! THERE ARE *PEOPLE* IN THOSE HOUSES--WE HAVE TO GET THEM *OUT* BEFORE THEY'RE BURNED ALIVE!

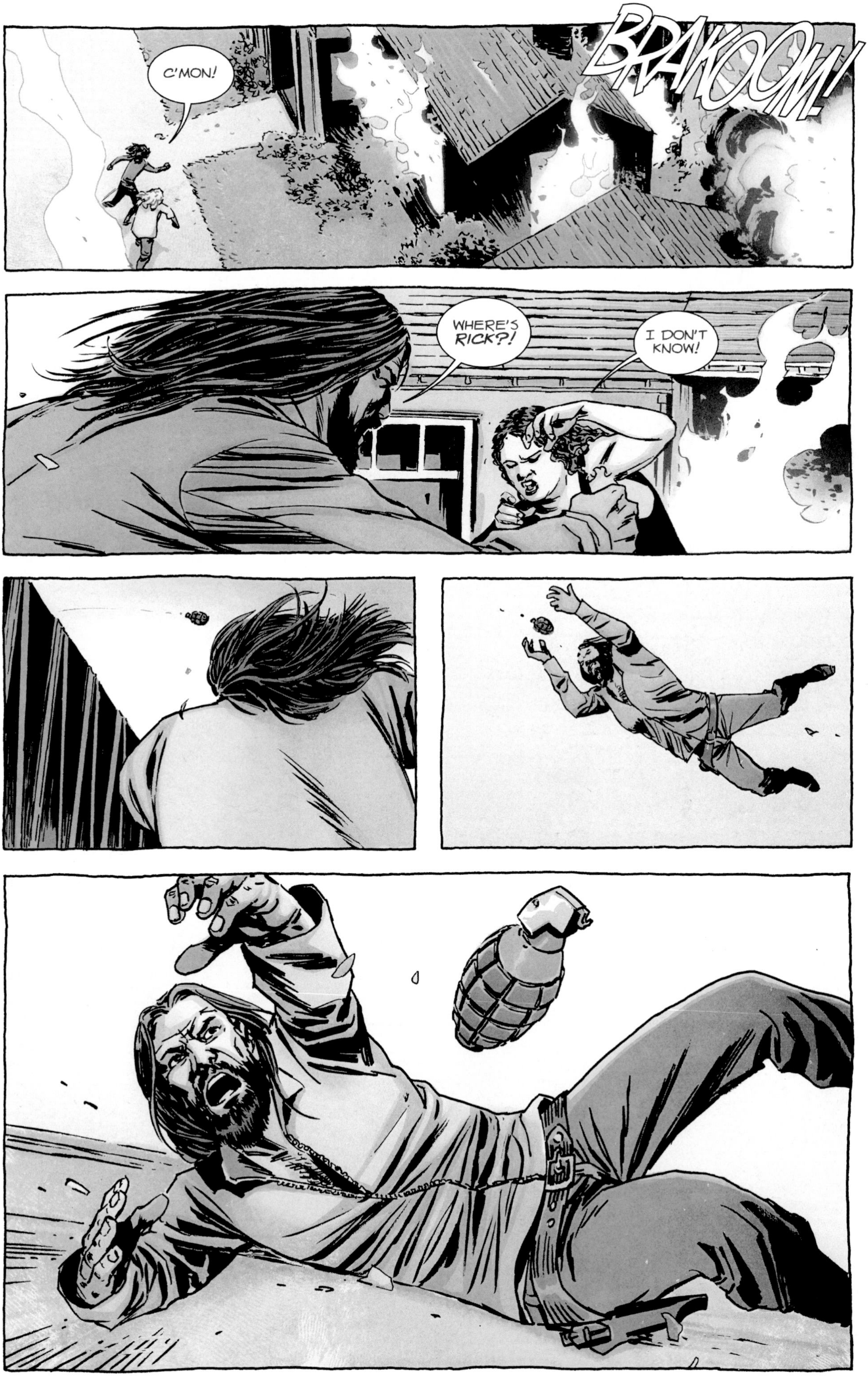

C'MON!
BRAKOOM!
WHERE'S RICK?!
I DON'T KNOW!

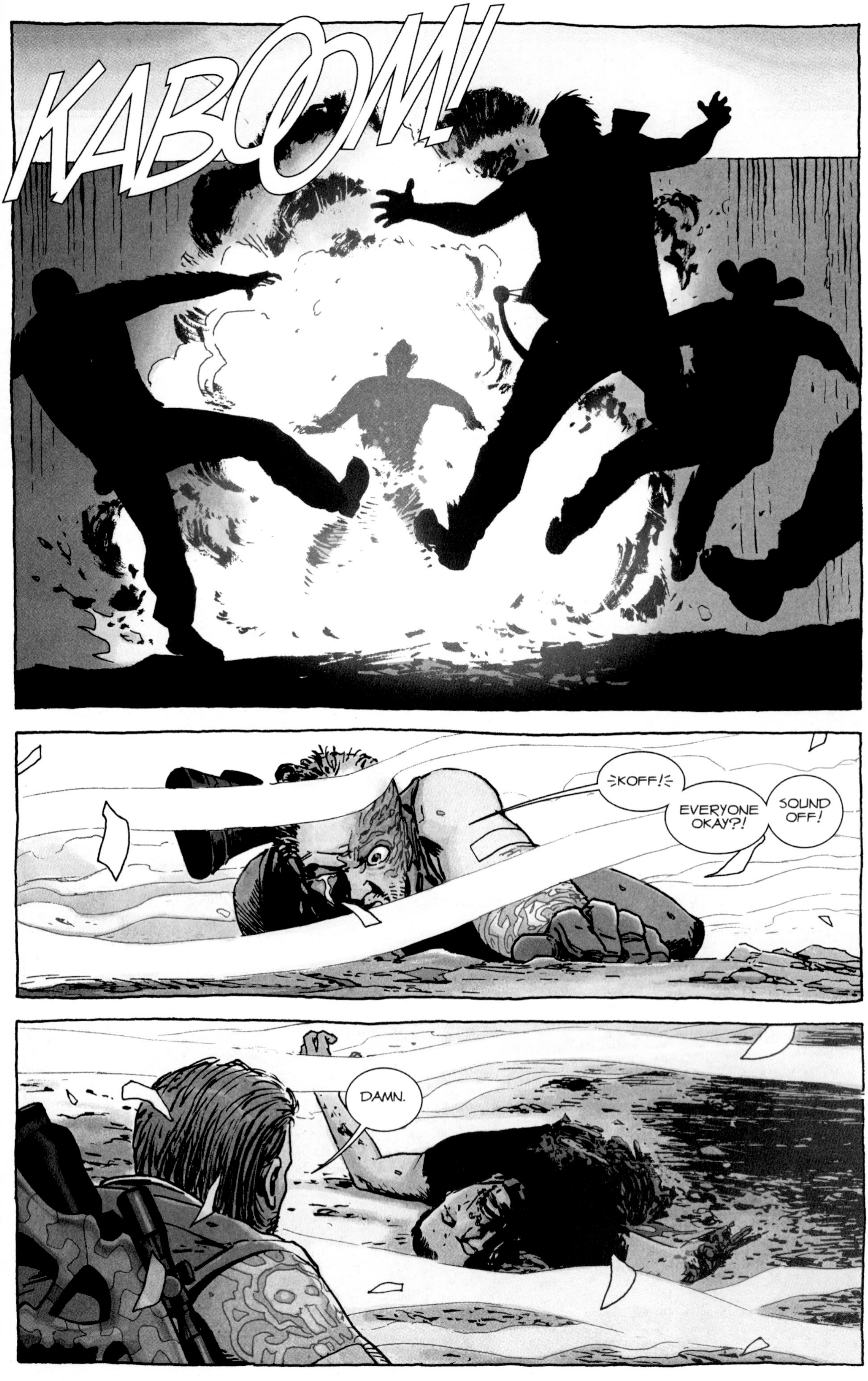
KABOOM!
-KOFF!-
EVERYONE OKAY?!
SOUND OFF!
DAMN.

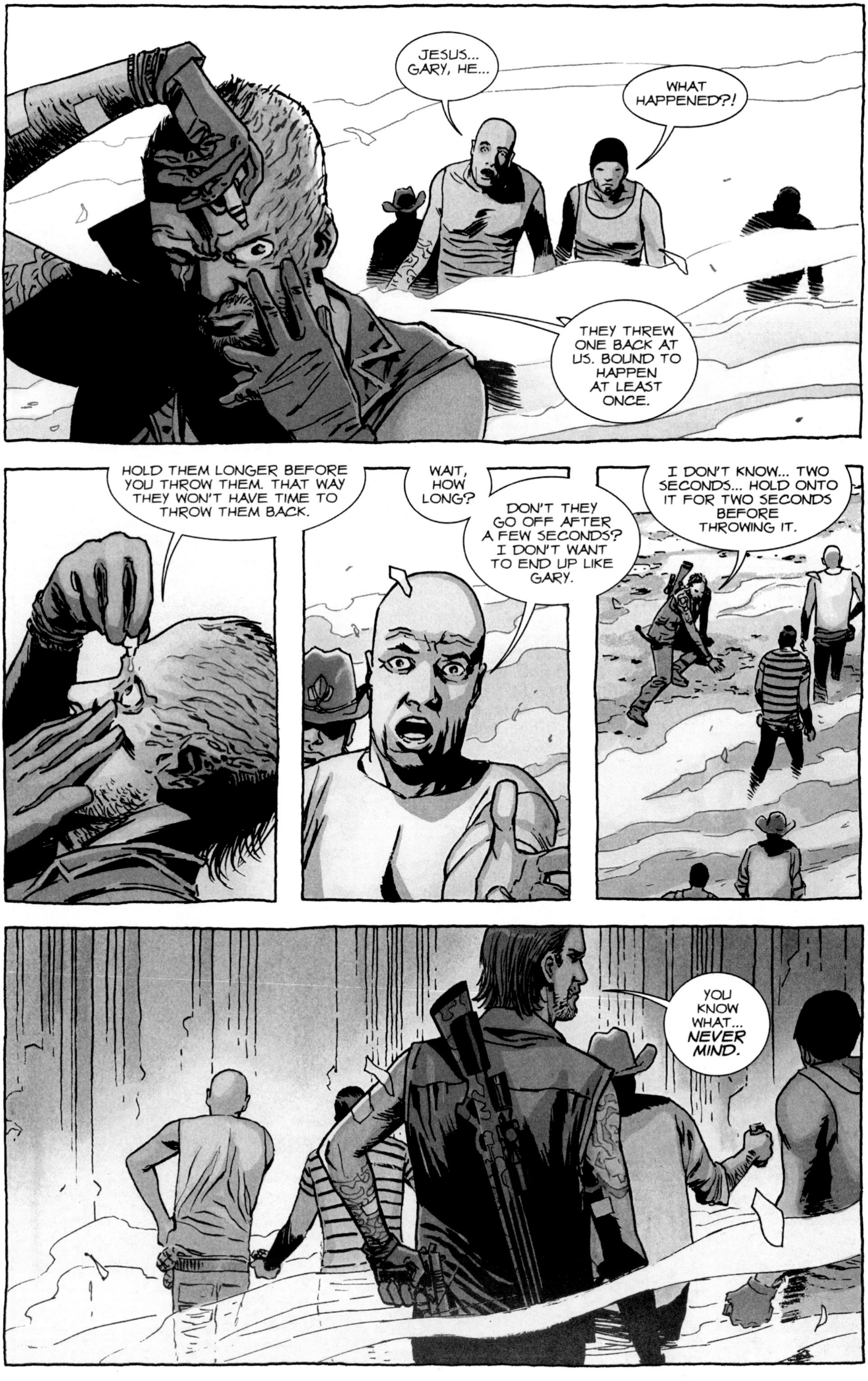
JESUS... GARY, HE...
WHAT HAPPENED?!
THEY THREW ONE BACK AT US. BOUND TO HAPPEN AT LEAST ONCE.
HOLD THEM LONGER BEFORE YOU THROW THEM. THAT WAY THEY WON'T HAVE TIME TO THROW THEM BACK.
WAIT, HOW LONG?
DON'T THEY GO OFF AFTER A FEW SECONDS? I DON'T WANT TO END UP LIKE GARY.
I DON'T KNOW... TWO SECONDS... HOLD ONTO IT FOR TWO SECONDS BEFORE THROWING IT.
YOU KNOW WHAT... NEVER MIND.

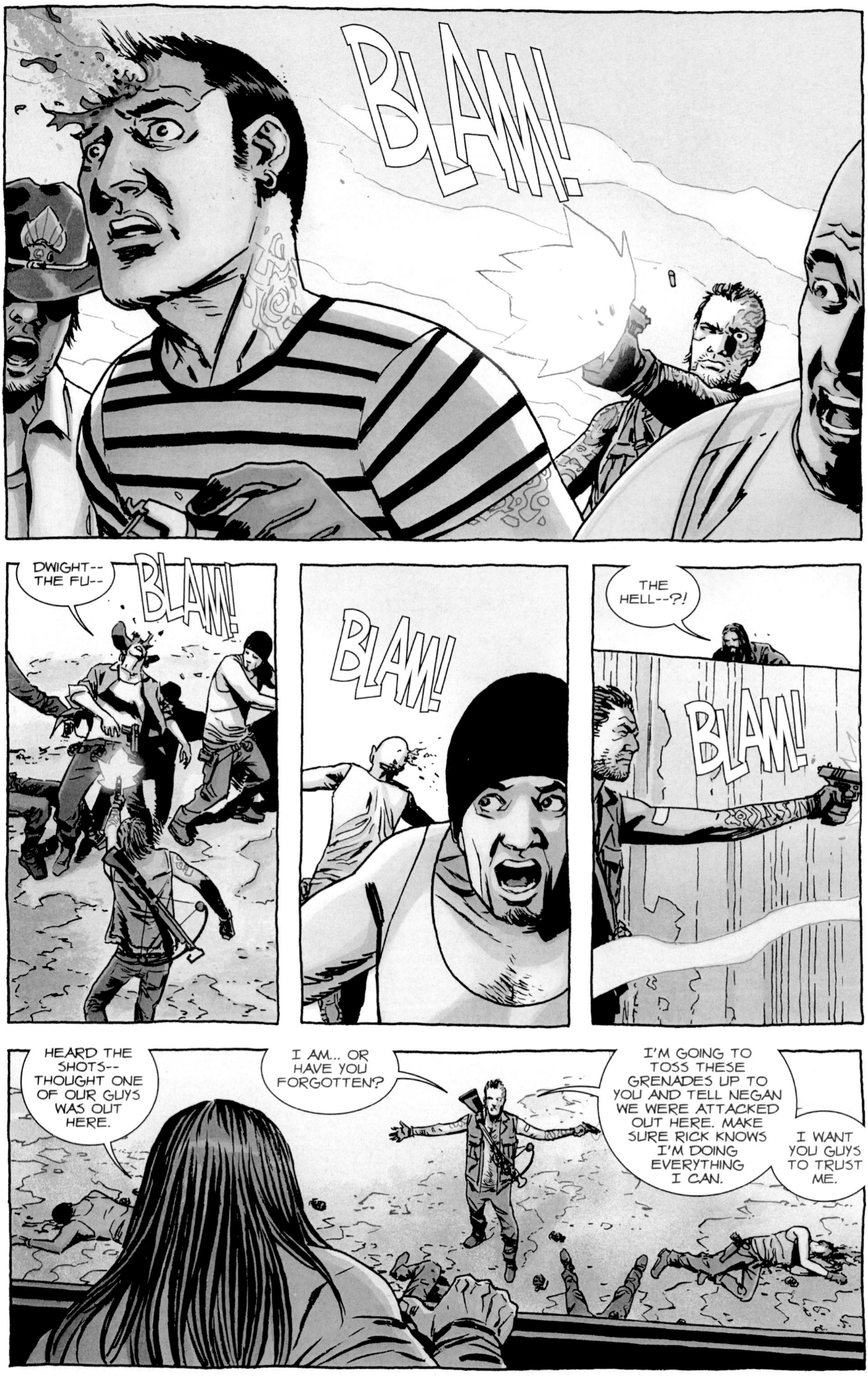
BLAM!
DWIGHT-- THE FU--
BLAM!
BLAM!
THE HELL--?!
BLAM!
HEARD THE SHOTS-- THOUGHT ONE OF OUR GUYS WAS OUT HERE.
I AM... OR HAVE YOU FORGOTTEN?
I'M GOING TO TOSS THESE GRENADES UP TO YOU AND TELL NEGAN WE WERE ATTACKED OUT HERE. MAKE SURE RICK KNOWS I'M DOING EVERYTHING I CAN.
I WANT YOU GUYS TO TRUST ME.

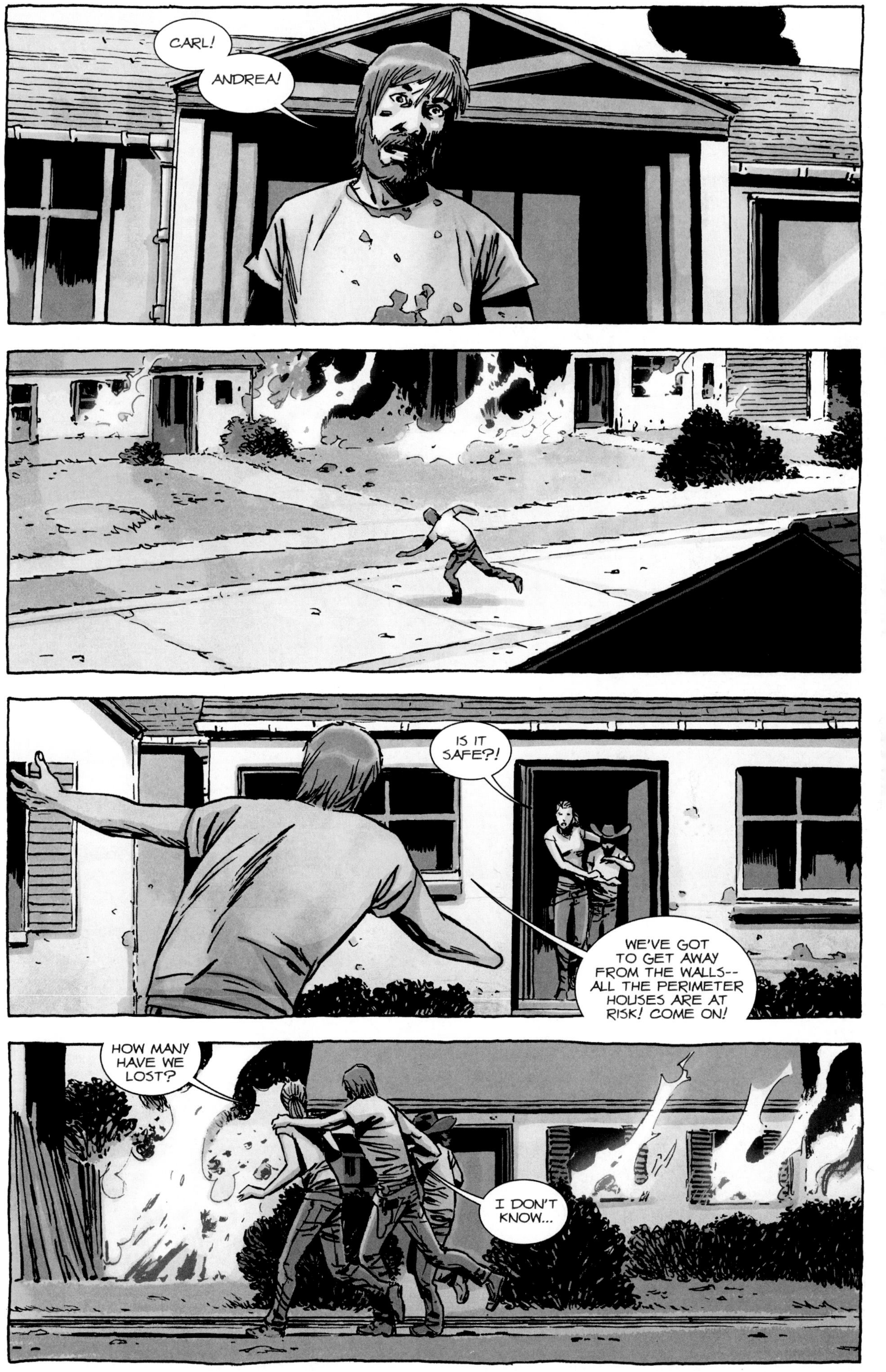
CARL!
ANDREA!
IS IT SAFE?!
WE'VE GOT TO GET AWAY FROM THE WALLS-- ALL THE PERIMETER HOUSES ARE AT RISK! COME ON!
HOW MANY HAVE WE LOST?
I DON'T KNOW...

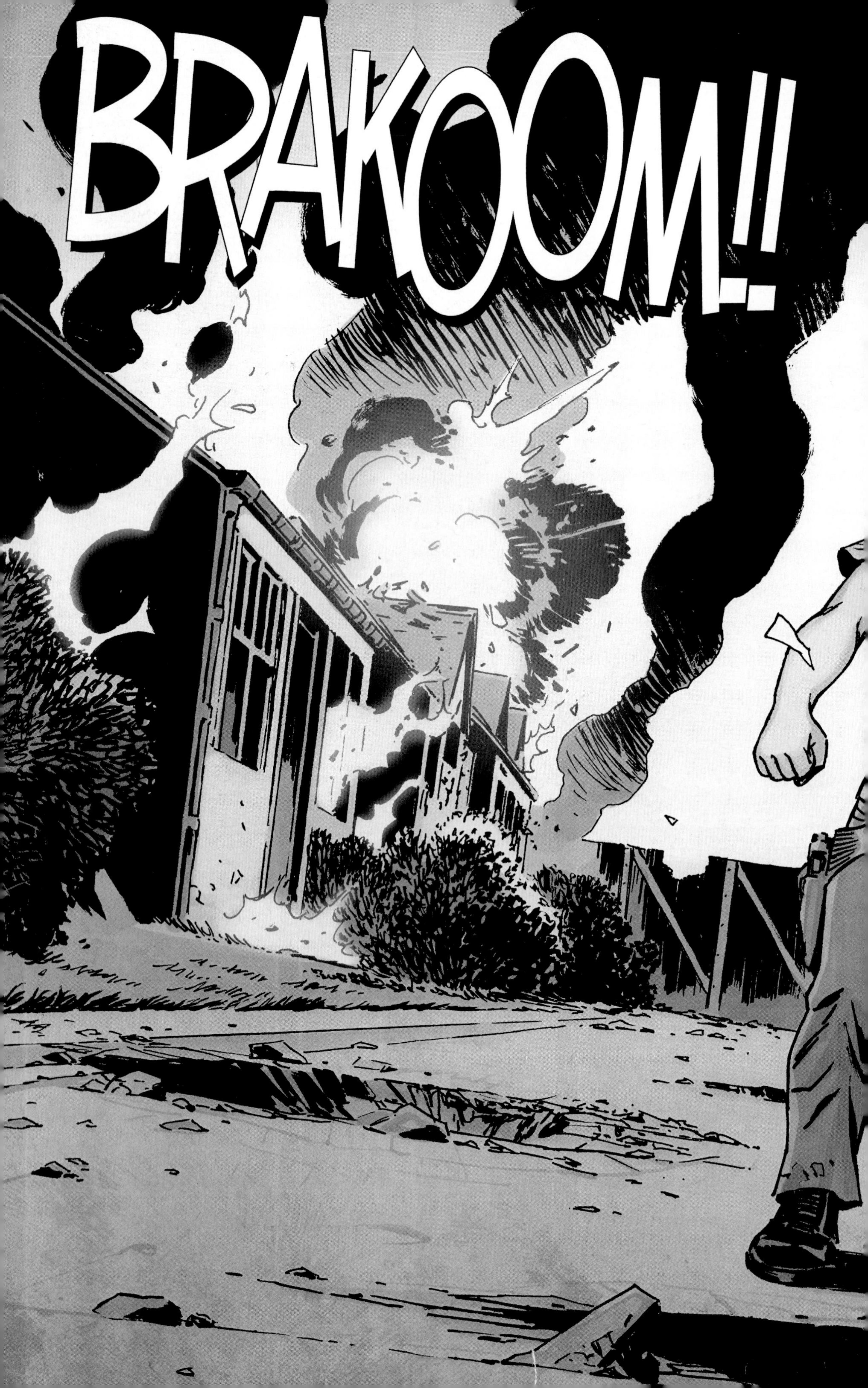
BRAKOOM!!

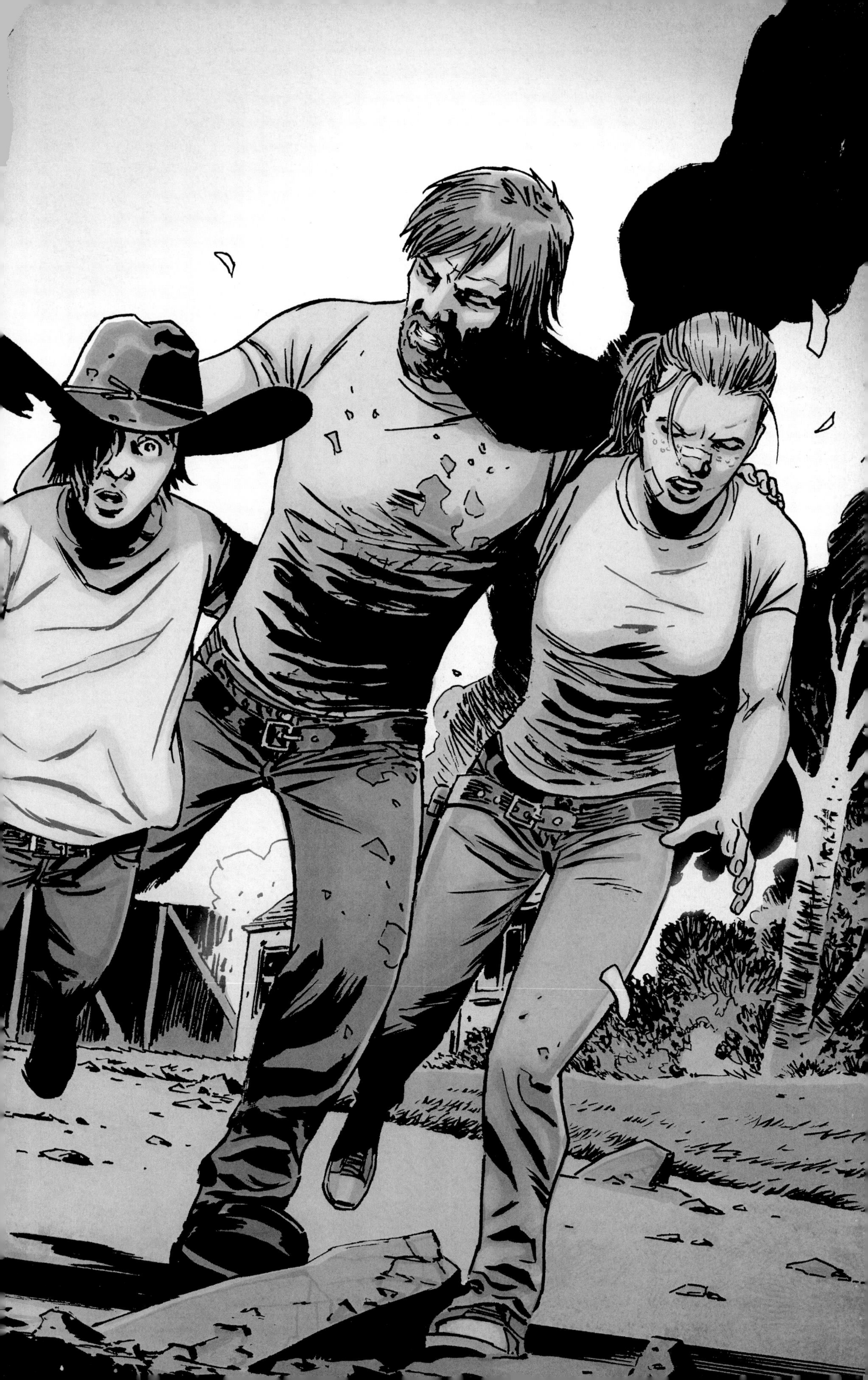

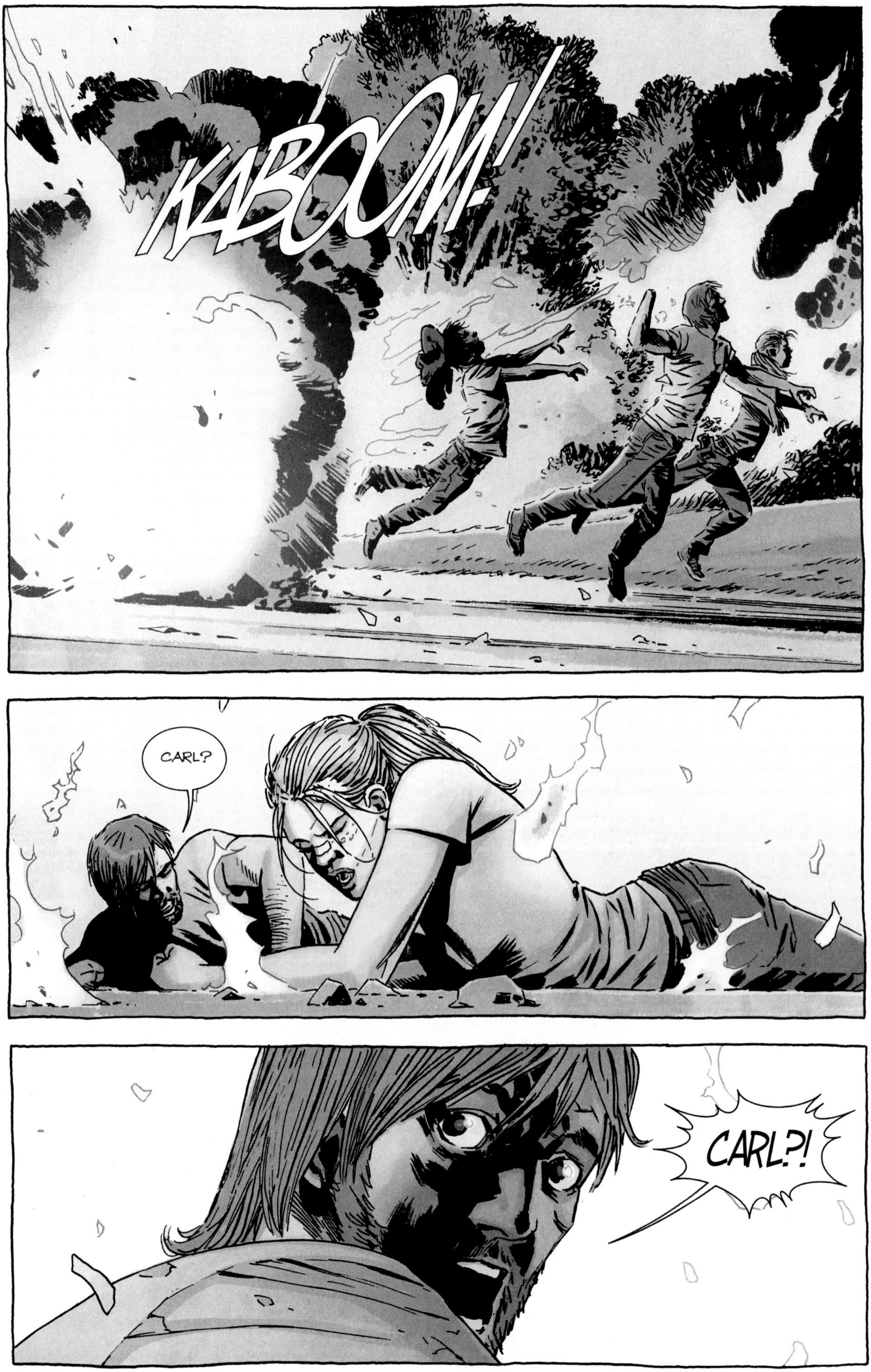
KABOOM!
CARL?
CARL?!

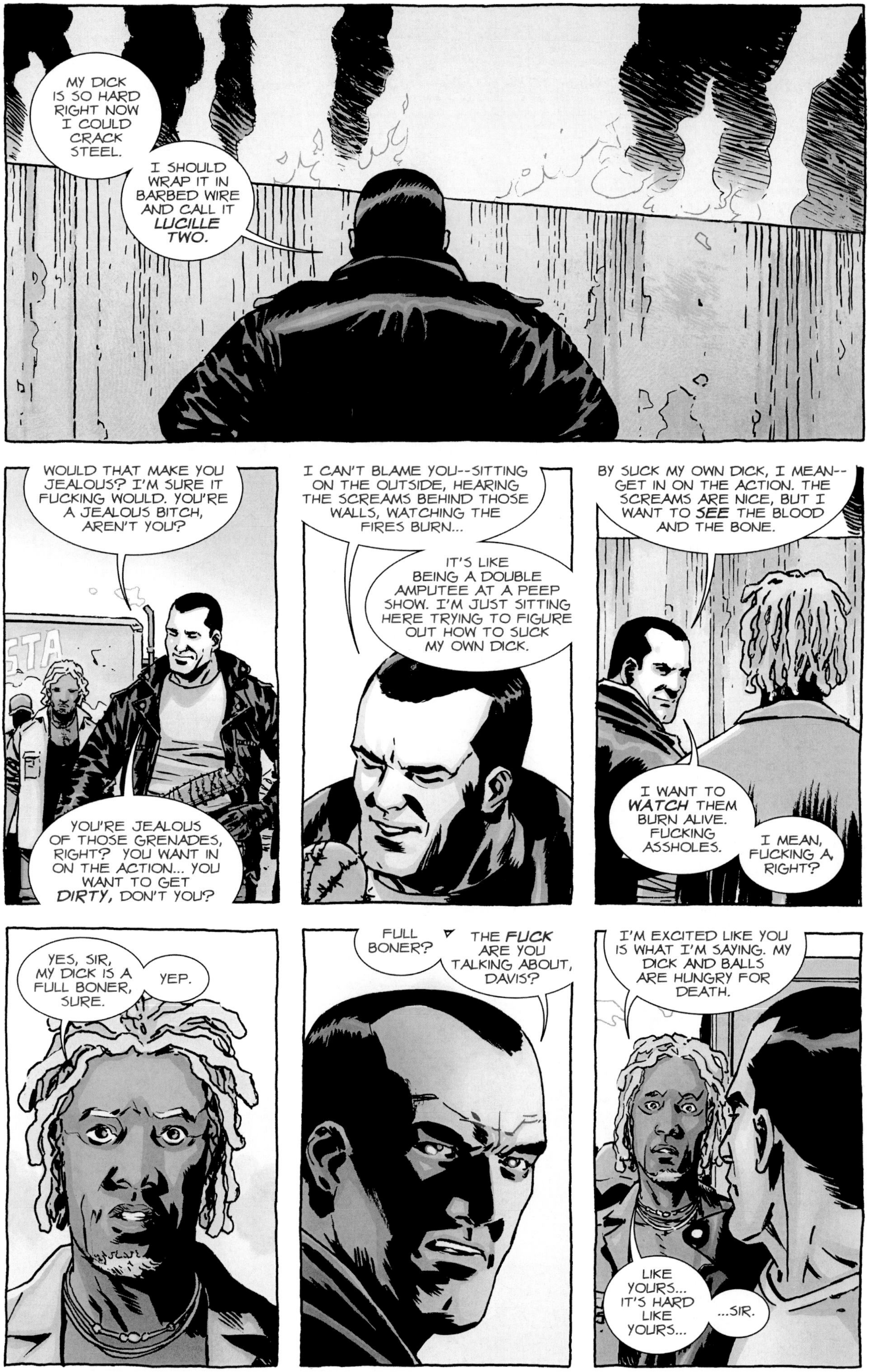

MY DICK IS SO HARD RIGHT NOW I COULD CRACK STEEL.
I SHOULD WRAP IT IN BARBED WIRE AND CALL IT LUCILLE TWO.
WOULD THAT MAKE YOU JEALOUS? I'M SURE IT FUCKING WOULD. YOU'RE A JEALOUS BITCH, AREN'T YOU?
YOU'RE JEALOUS OF THOSE GRENADES, RIGHT? YOU WANT IN ON THE ACTION... YOU WANT TO GET DIRTY, DON'T YOU?
I CAN'T BLAME YOU--SITTING ON THE OUTSIDE, HEARING THE SCREAMS BEHIND THOSE WALLS, WATCHING THE FIRES BURN...
IT'S LIKE BEING A DOUBLE AMPUTEE AT A PEEP SHOW. I'M JUST SITTING HERE TRYING TO FIGURE OUT HOW TO SUCK MY OWN DICK.
BY SUCK MY OWN DICK, I MEAN--GET IN ON THE ACTION. THE SCREAMS ARE NICE, BUT I WANT TO SEE THE BLOOD AND THE BONE.
I WANT TO WATCH THEM BURN ALIVE. FUCKING ASSHOLES.
I MEAN, FUCKING A, RIGHT?
YES, SIR, MY DICK IS A FULL BONER, SURE.
YEP.
FULL BONER?
THE FUCK ARE YOU TALKING ABOUT, DAVIS?
I'M EXCITED LIKE YOU IS WHAT I'M SAYING. MY DICK AND BALLS ARE HUNGRY FOR DEATH.
LIKE YOURS... IT'S HARD LIKE YOURS...
...SIR.

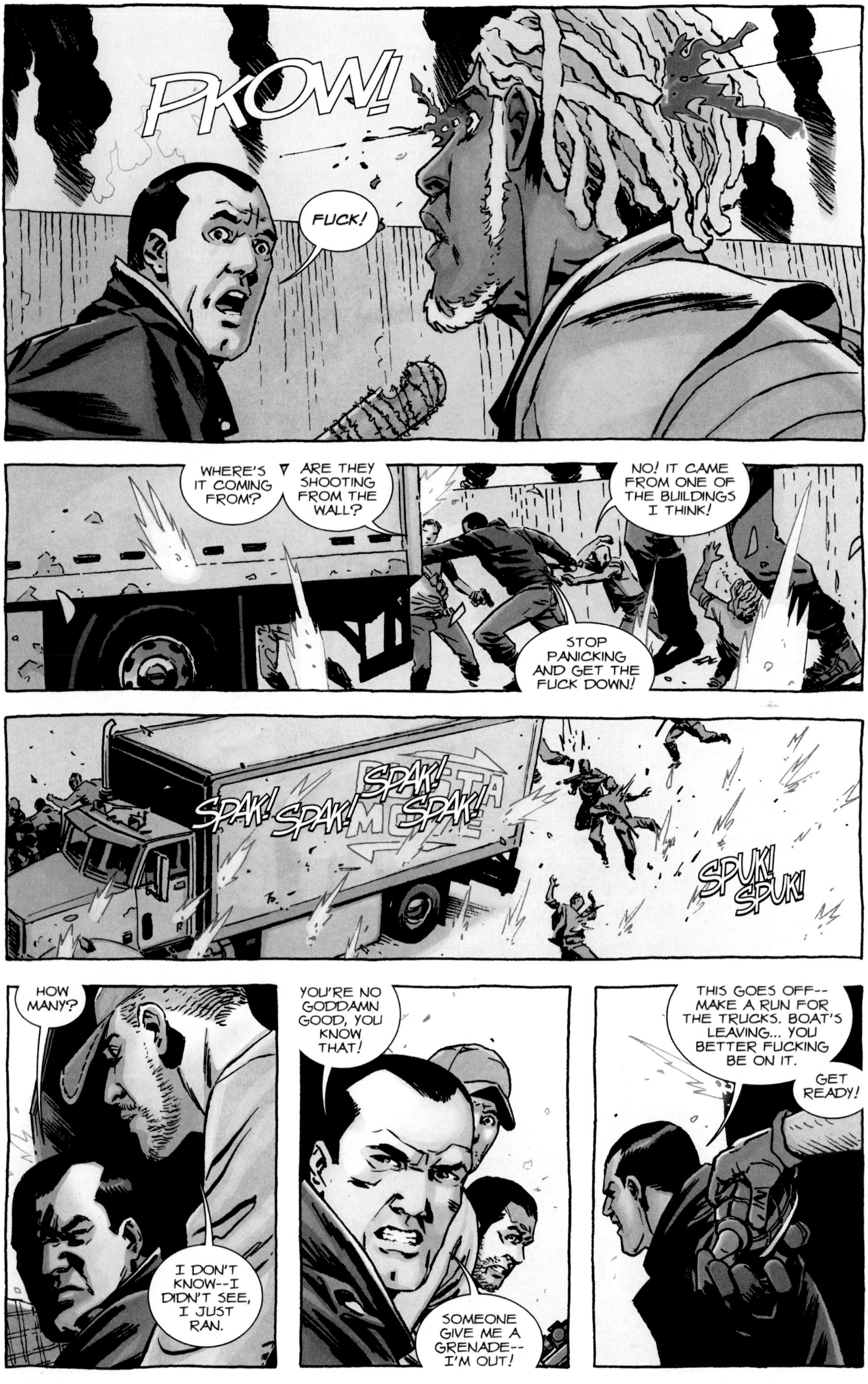
PKOW!
FUCK!
WHERE'S IT COMING FROM?
ARE THEY SHOOTING FROM THE WALL?
NO! IT CAME FROM ONE OF THE BUILDINGS I THINK!
STOP PANICKING AND GET THE FUCK DOWN!
SPAK! SPAK! SPAK! SPAK!
SPUK! SPUK!
HOW MANY?
I DON'T KNOW--I DIDN'T SEE, I JUST RAN.
YOU'RE NO GODDAMN GOOD, YOU KNOW THAT!
SOMEONE GIVE ME A GRENADE-- I'M OUT!
THIS GOES OFF-- MAKE A RUN FOR THE TRUCKS. BOAT'S LEAVING... YOU BETTER FUCKING BE ON IT.
GET READY!

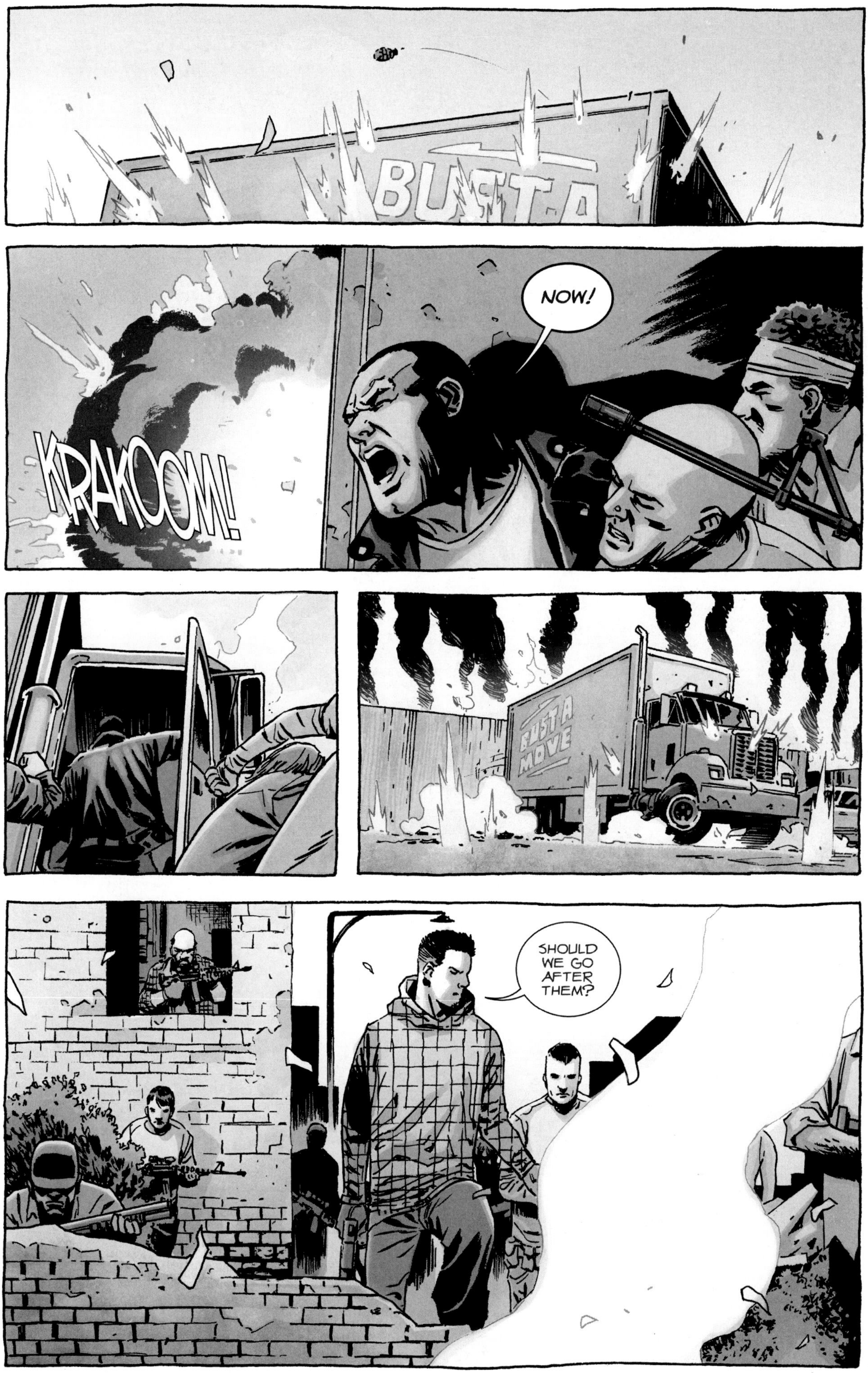
BUST-A
KRAKOOM!
NOW!
BUST A MOVE
SHOULD WE GO AFTER THEM?

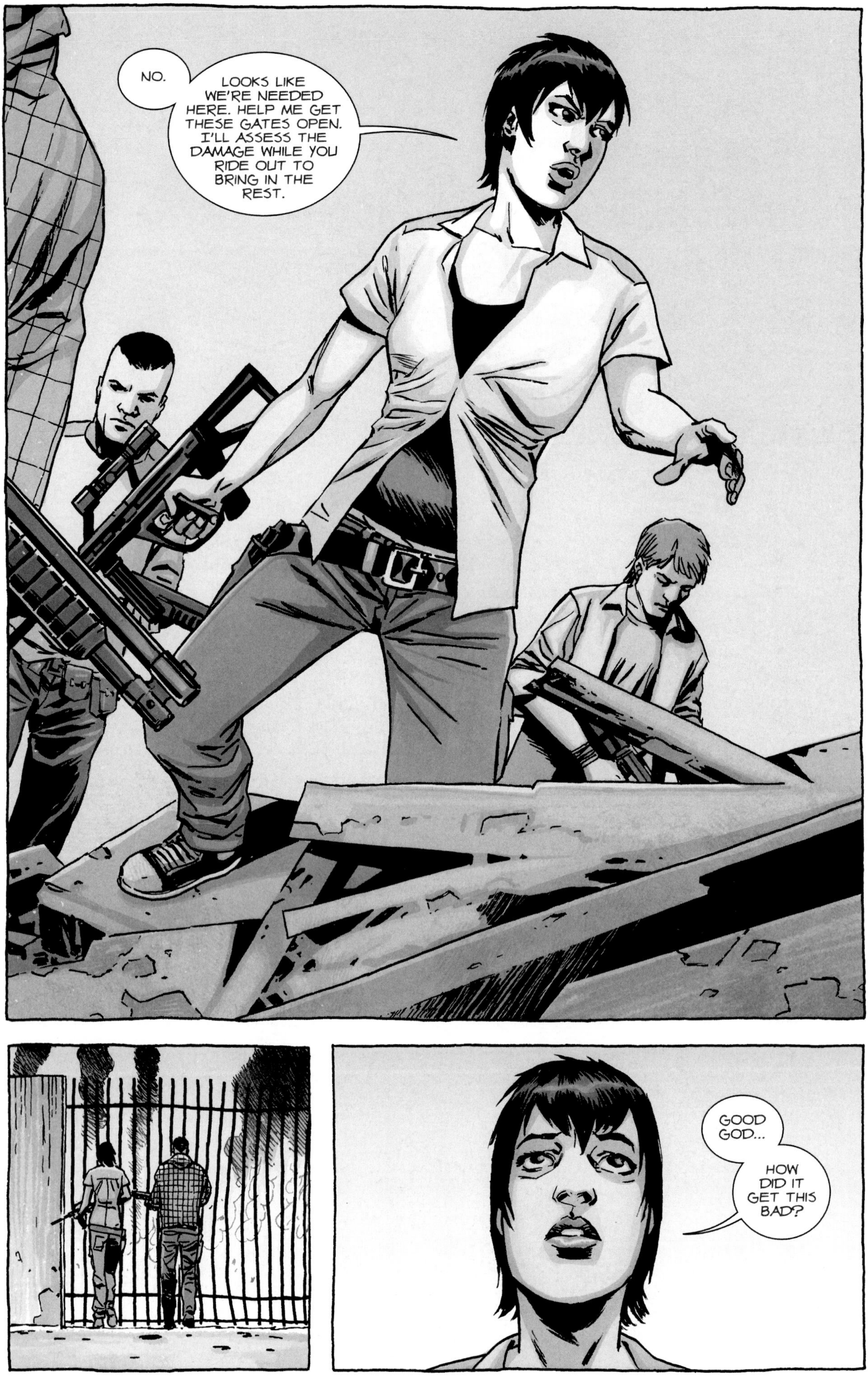
NO.
LOOKS LIKE WE'RE NEEDED HERE. HELP ME GET THESE GATES OPEN. I'LL ASSESS THE DAMAGE WHILE YOU RIDE OUT TO BRING IN THE REST.
GOOD GOD...
HOW DID IT GET THIS BAD?

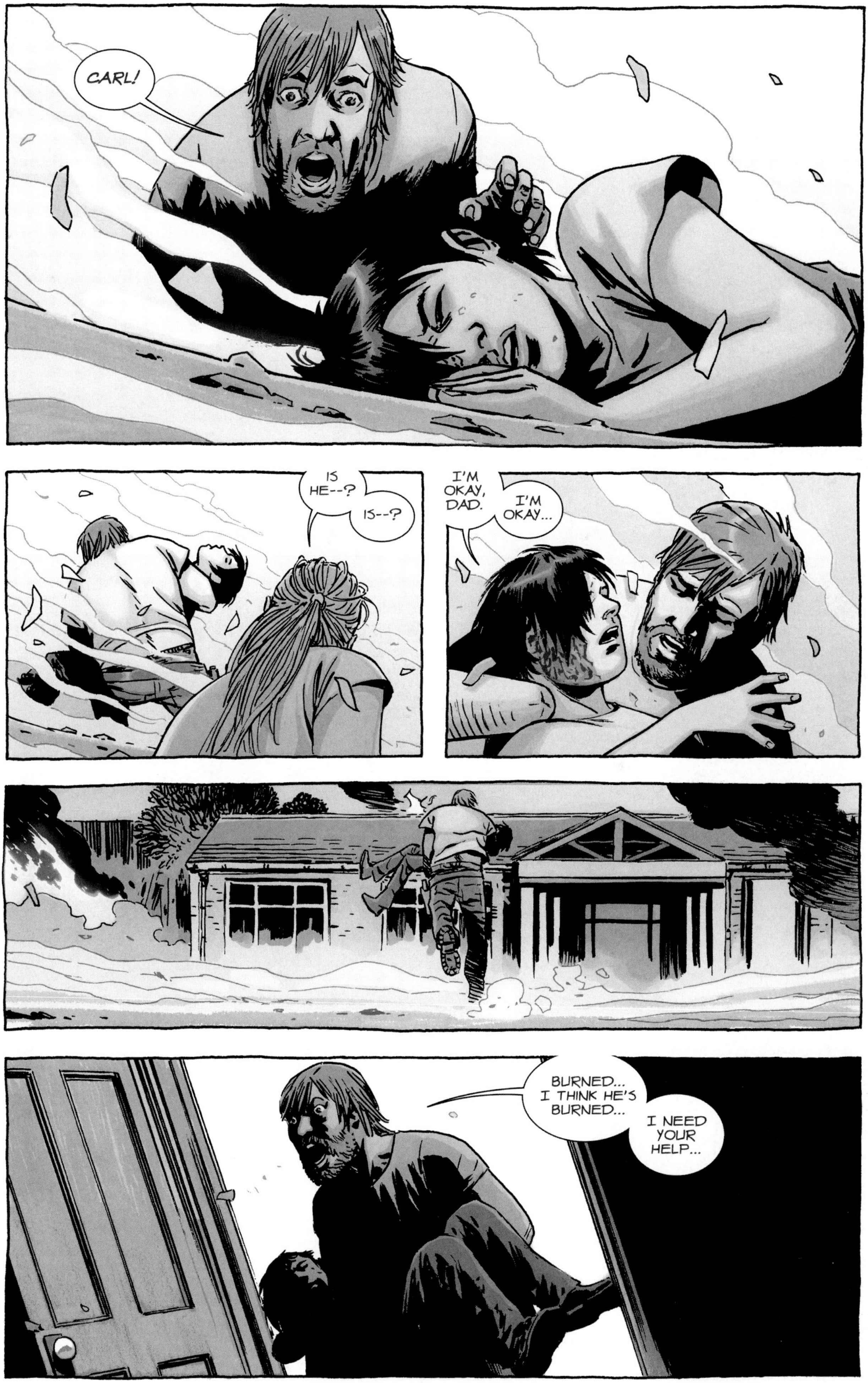
CARL!
IS HE--?
IS--?
I'M OKAY, DAD.
I'M OKAY...
BURNED... I THINK HE'S BURNED...
I NEED YOUR HELP...

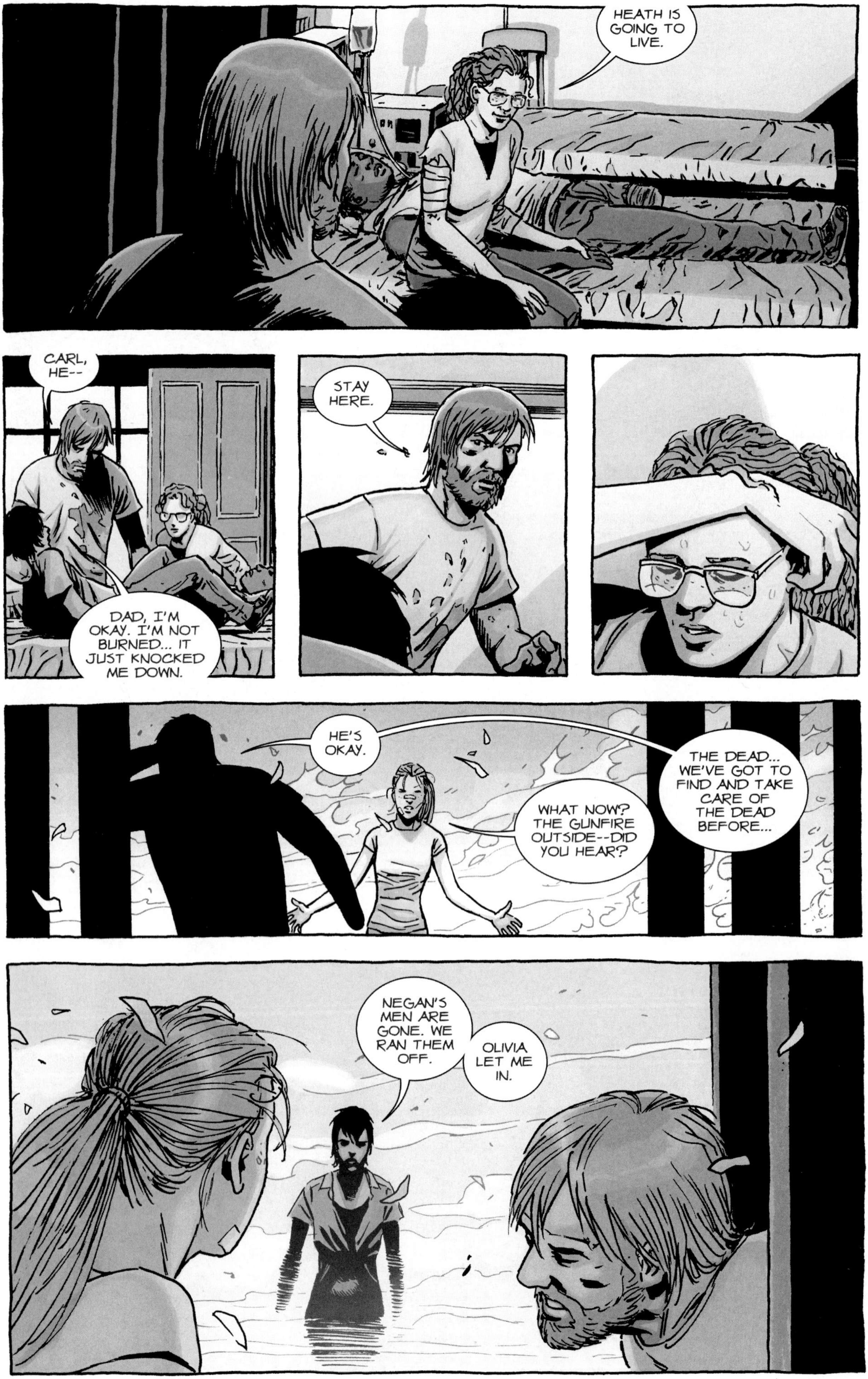
HEATH IS GOING TO LIVE.
CARL, HE--
DAD, I'M OKAY. I'M NOT BURNED... IT JUST KNOCKED ME DOWN.
STAY HERE.
HE'S OKAY.
THE DEAD... WE'VE GOT TO FIND AND TAKE CARE OF THE DEAD BEFORE...
WHAT NOW? THE GUNFIRE OUTSIDE--DID YOU HEAR?
NEGAN'S MEN ARE GONE. WE RAN THEM OFF.
OLIVIA LET ME IN.

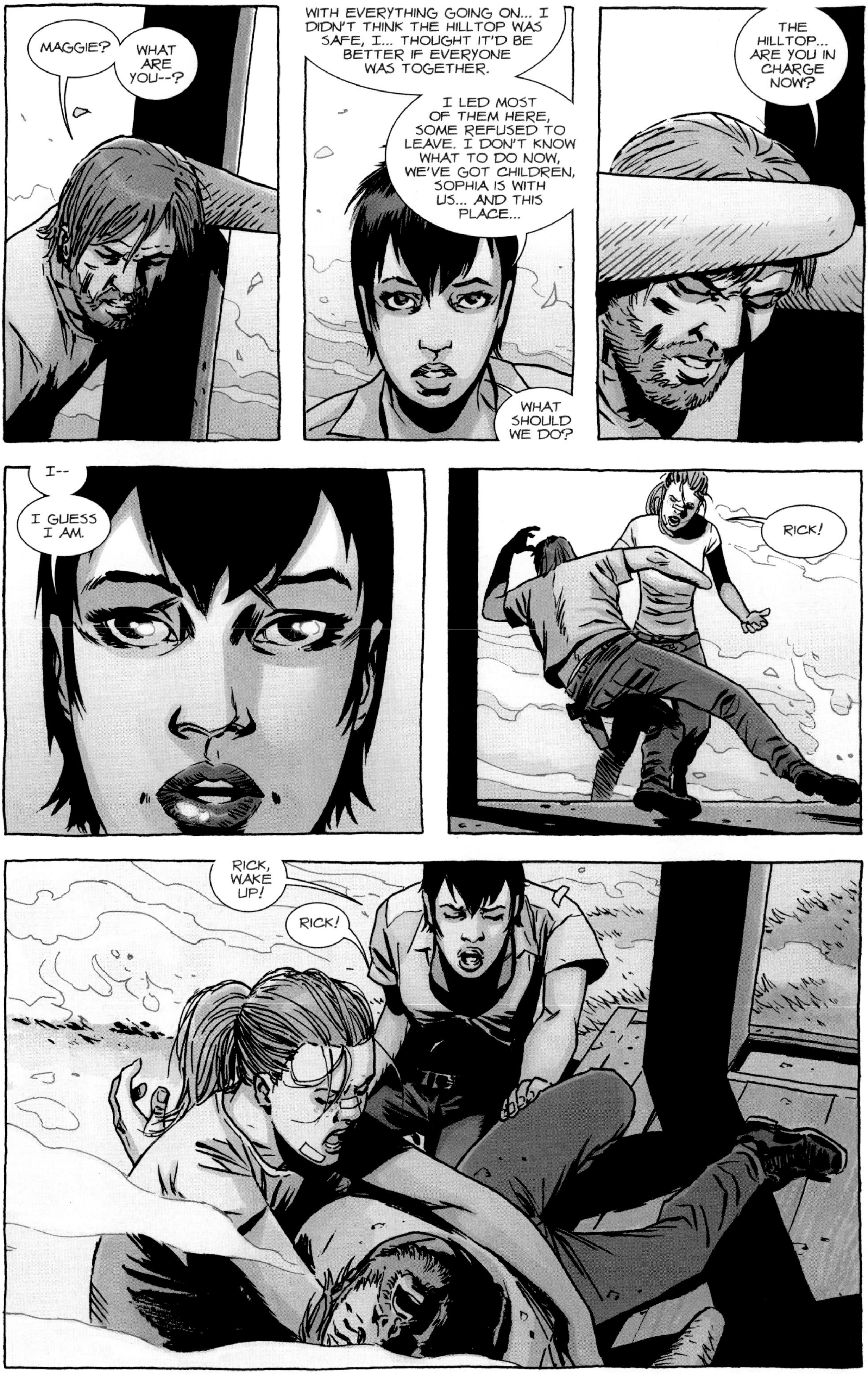
MAGGIE?
WHAT ARE YOU--?
WITH EVERYTHING GOING ON... I DIDN'T THINK THE HILLTOP WAS SAFE, I... THOUGHT IT'D BE BETTER IF EVERYONE WAS TOGETHER.
I LED MOST OF THEM HERE, SOME REFUSED TO LEAVE. I DON'T KNOW WHAT TO DO NOW, WE'VE GOT CHILDREN, SOPHIA IS WITH US... AND THIS PLACE...
WHAT SHOULD WE DO?
THE HILLTOP... ARE YOU IN CHARGE NOW?
I--
I GUESS I AM.
RICK!
RICK, WAKE UP!
RICK!

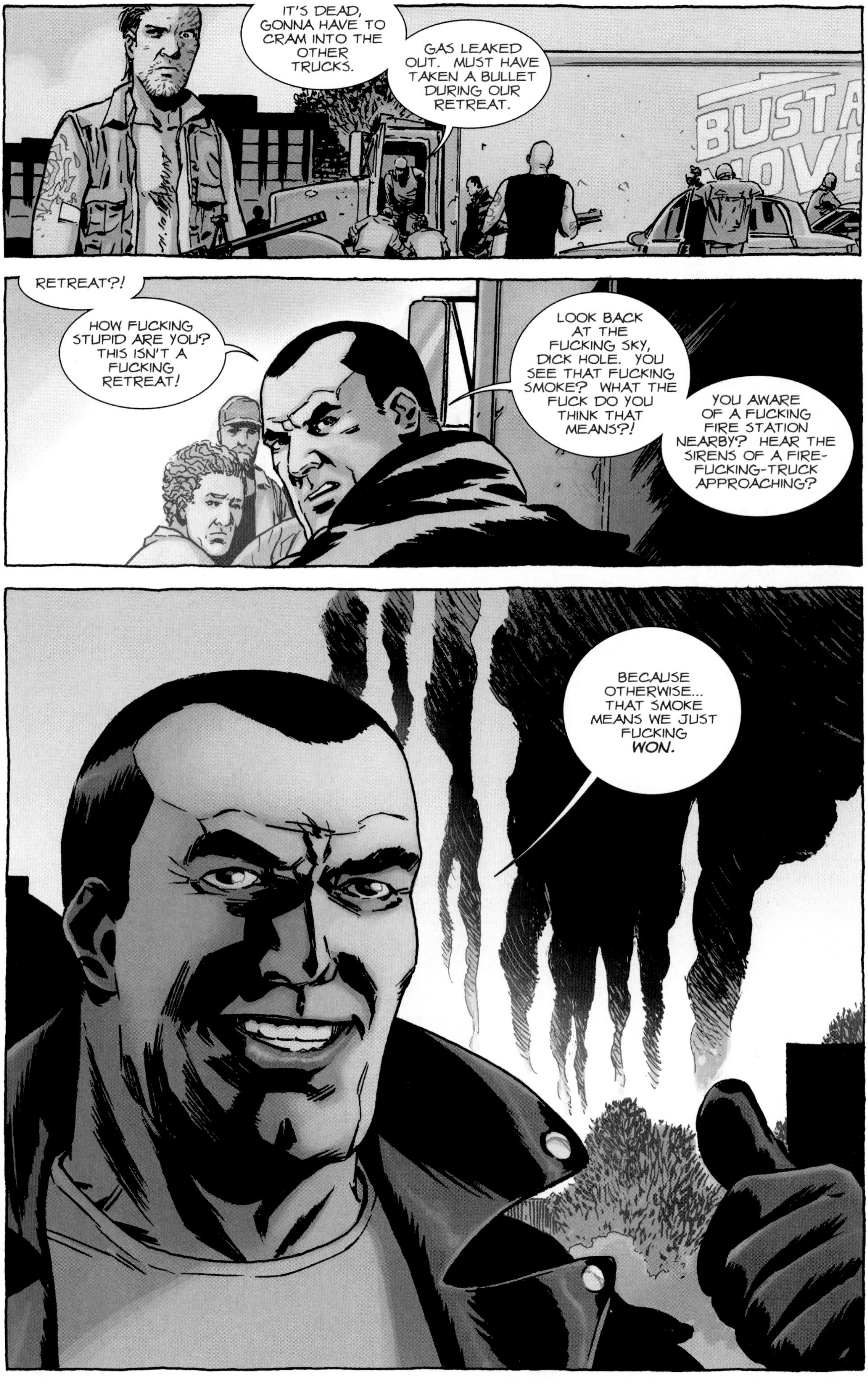

IT'S DEAD, GONNA HAVE TO CRAM INTO THE OTHER TRUCKS.
GAS LEAKED OUT. MUST HAVE TAKEN A BULLET DURING OUR RETREAT.
BUSTA
RETREAT?!
HOW FUCKING STUPID ARE YOU? THIS ISN'T A FUCKING RETREAT!
LOOK BACK AT THE FUCKING SKY, DICK HOLE. YOU SEE THAT FUCKING SMOKE? WHAT THE FUCK DO YOU THINK THAT MEANS?!
YOU AWARE OF A FUCKING FIRE STATION NEARBY? HEAR THE SIRENS OF A FIRE-FUCKING-TRUCK APPROACHING?
BECAUSE OTHERWISE... THAT SMOKE MEANS WE JUST FUCKING **WON.**

TO BE CONTINUED...

Sketchbook

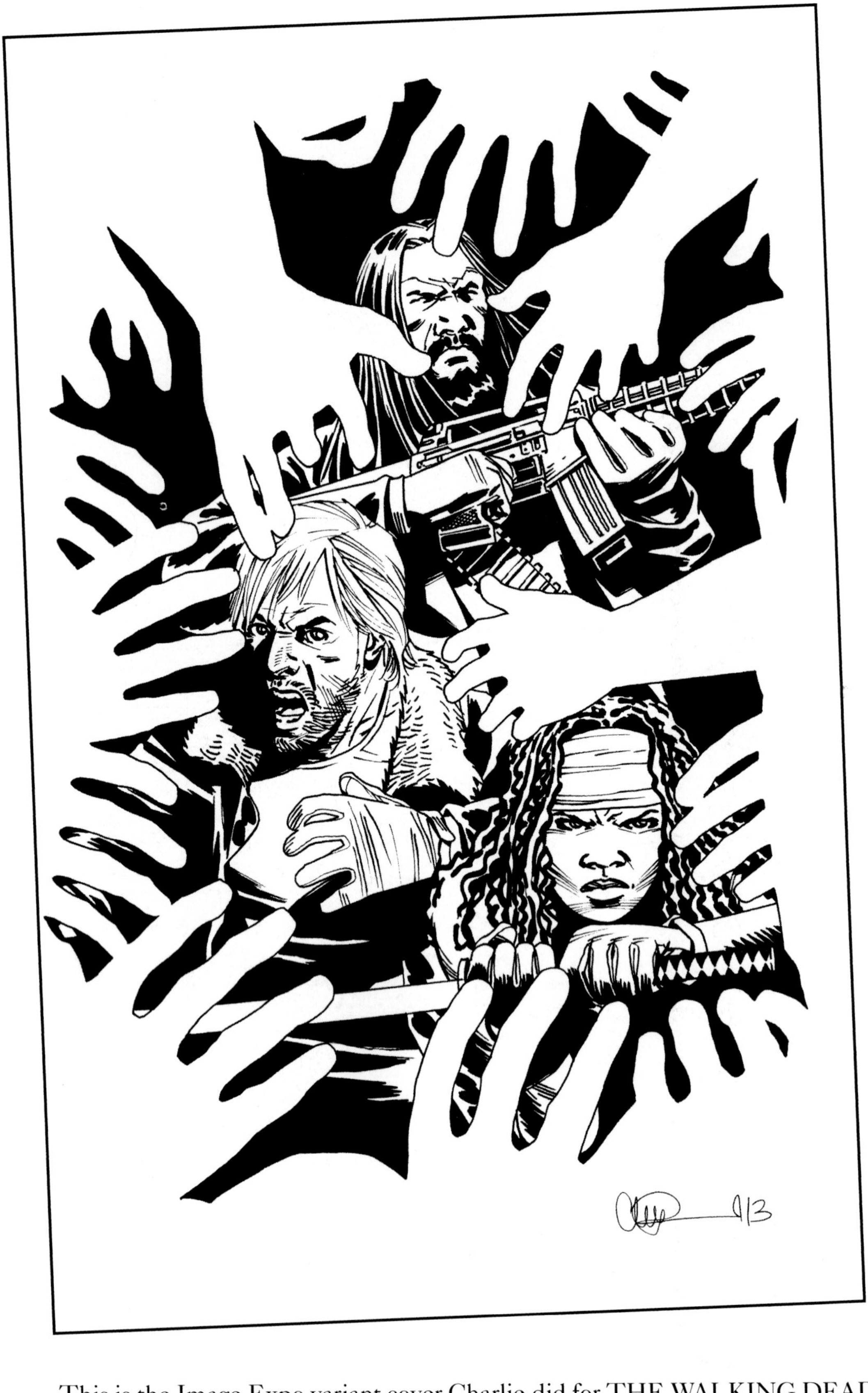

This is the Image Expo variant cover Charlie did for THE WALKING DEAD #112 . It was the first of our new semi-regular Image Expo shows, and where we announced ALL OUT WAR. If you look closely, you can probably see some hands.

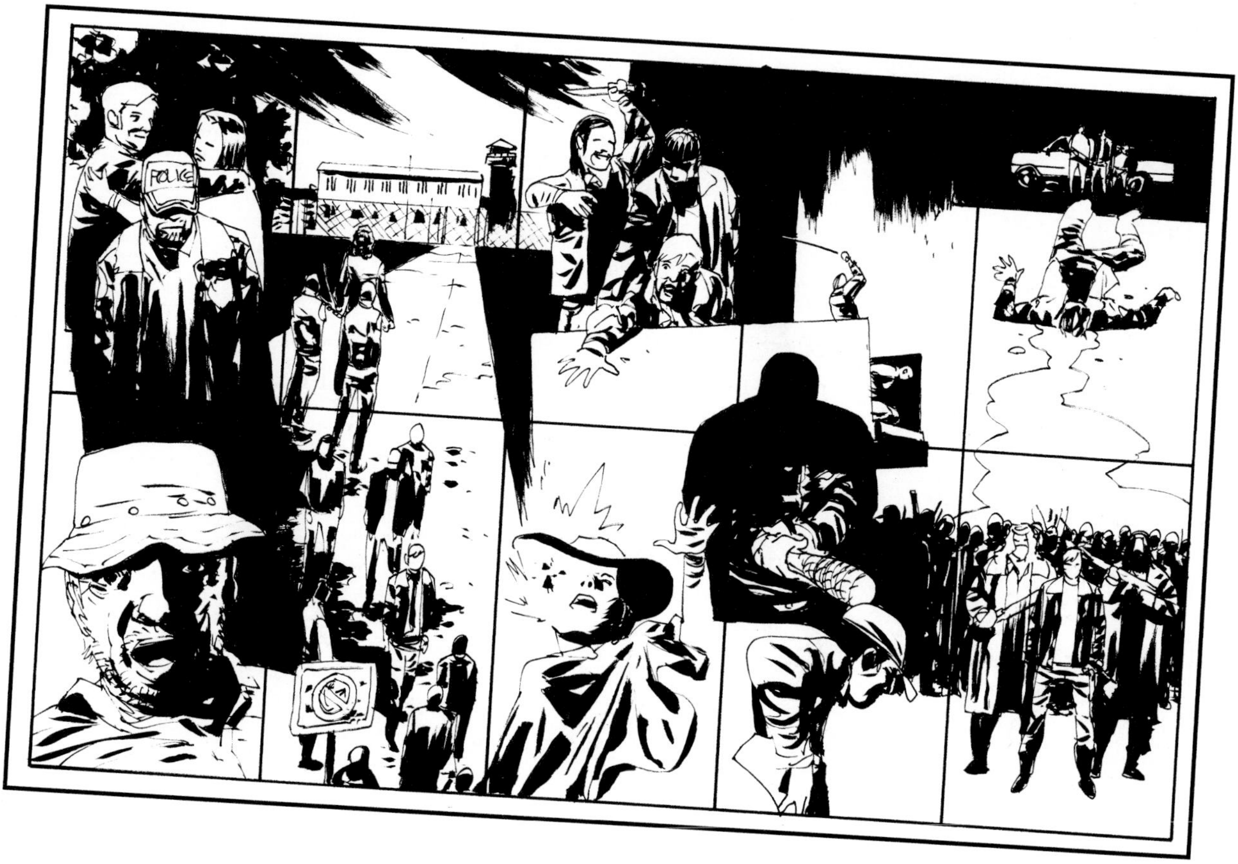
POLICE

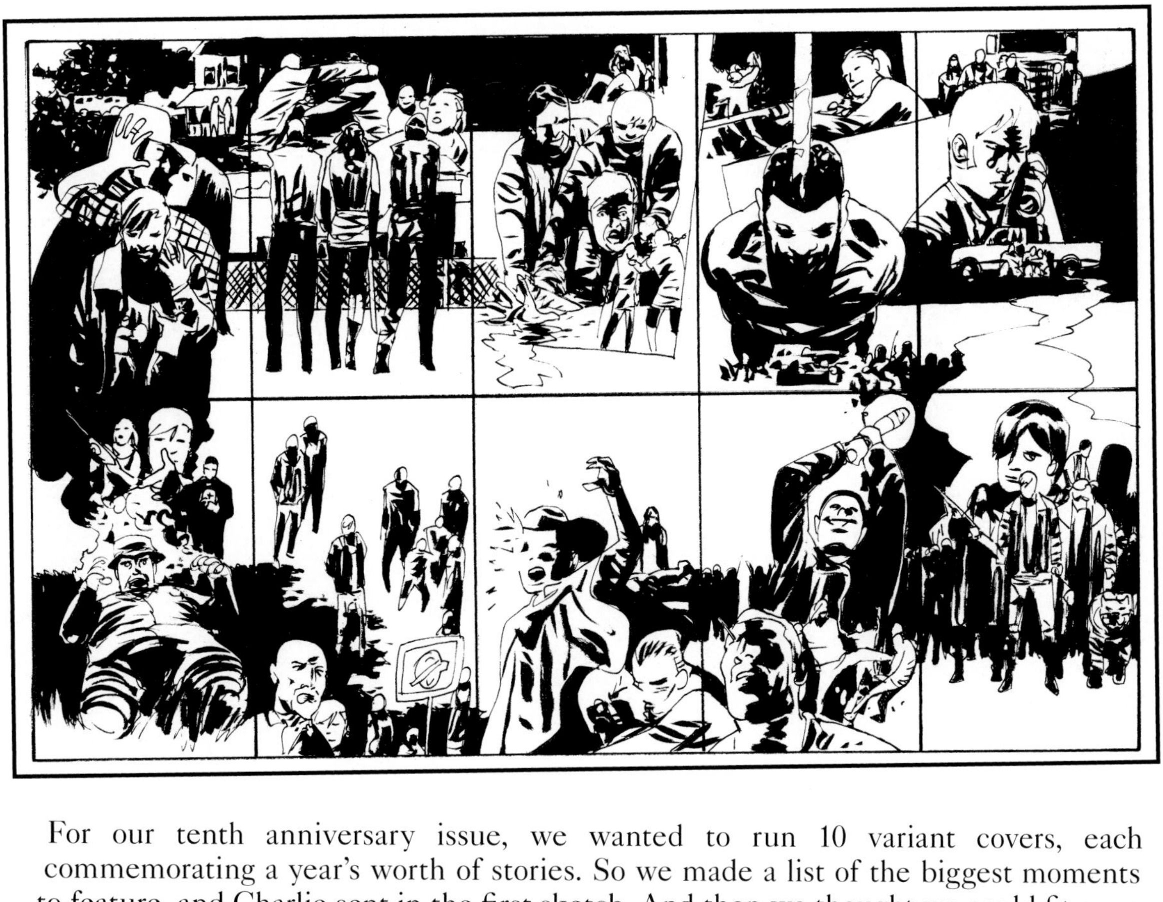

For our tenth anniversary issue, we wanted to run 10 variant covers, each commemorating a year's worth of stories. So we made a list of the biggest moments to feature, and Charlie sent in the first sketch. And then we thought we could fit even more moments in, and Charlie drew another sketch and that's the one we went with.

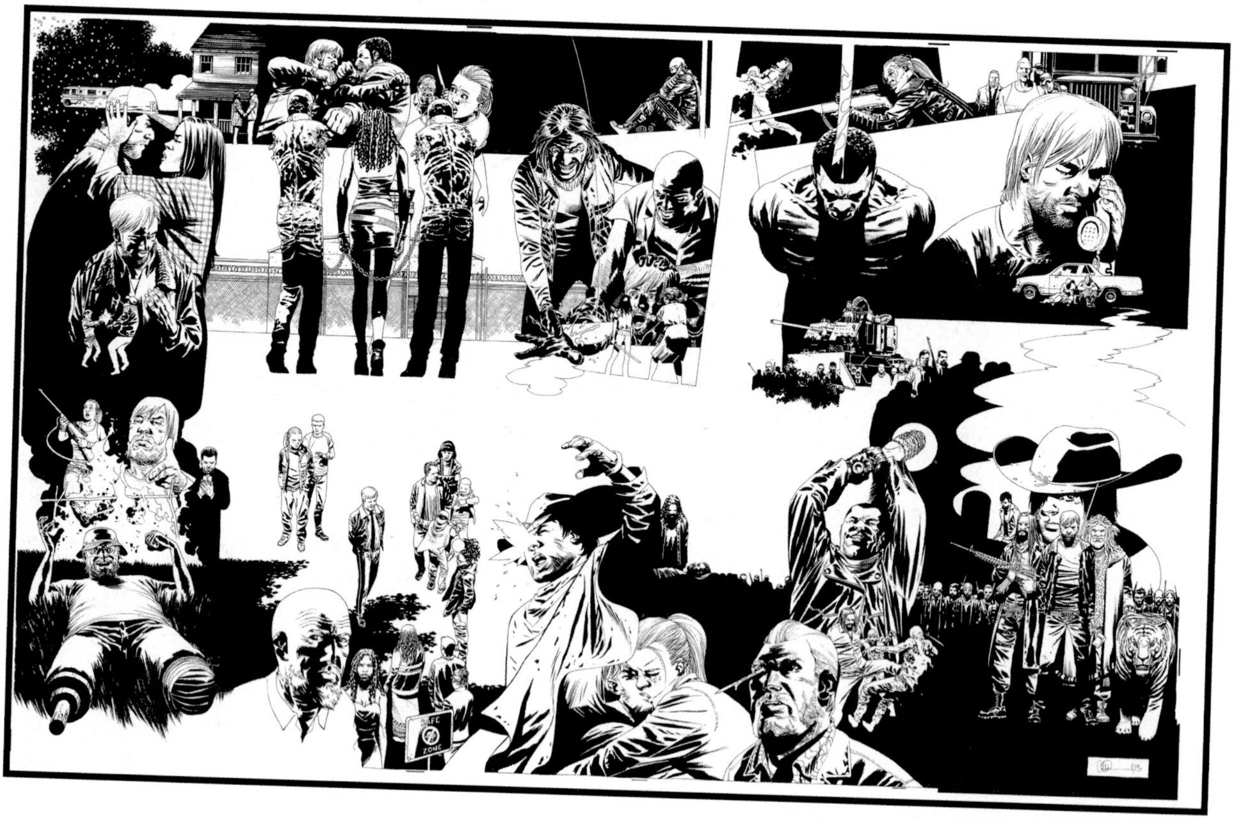

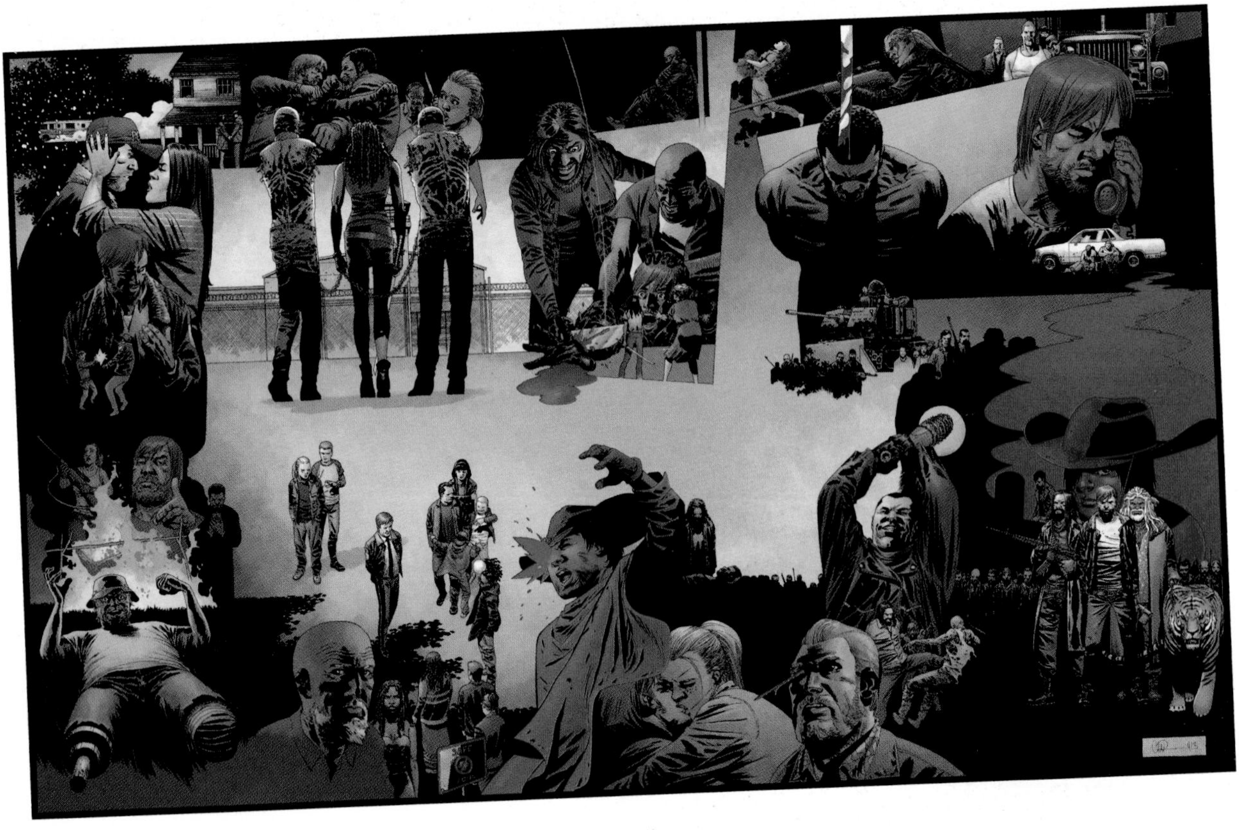

After that, Charlie inked it and Dave Stewart colored it, and that's how comics are made. The original covers are now hanging in the Skybound office.

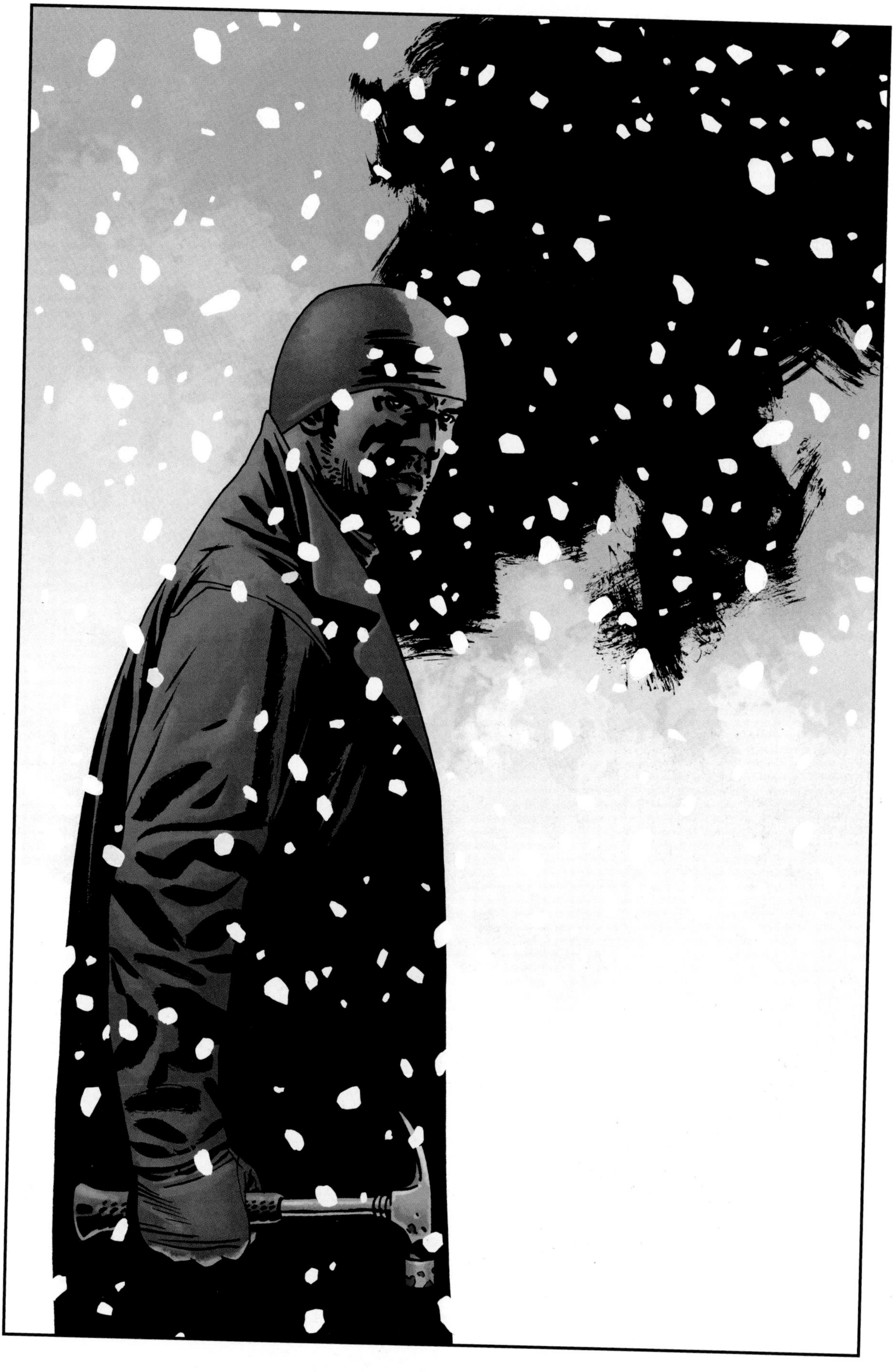

This is the cover for the TYREESE SPECIAL... which collected Tyreese's first appearance in issue 7 as well as a brand new Tyreese short story. This was colored by Dave Stewart, too.

These four Faction logos were designed by the super talented Clark Orr. We wanted to do something different to promote ALL OUT WAR, and let fans support their favorite group.

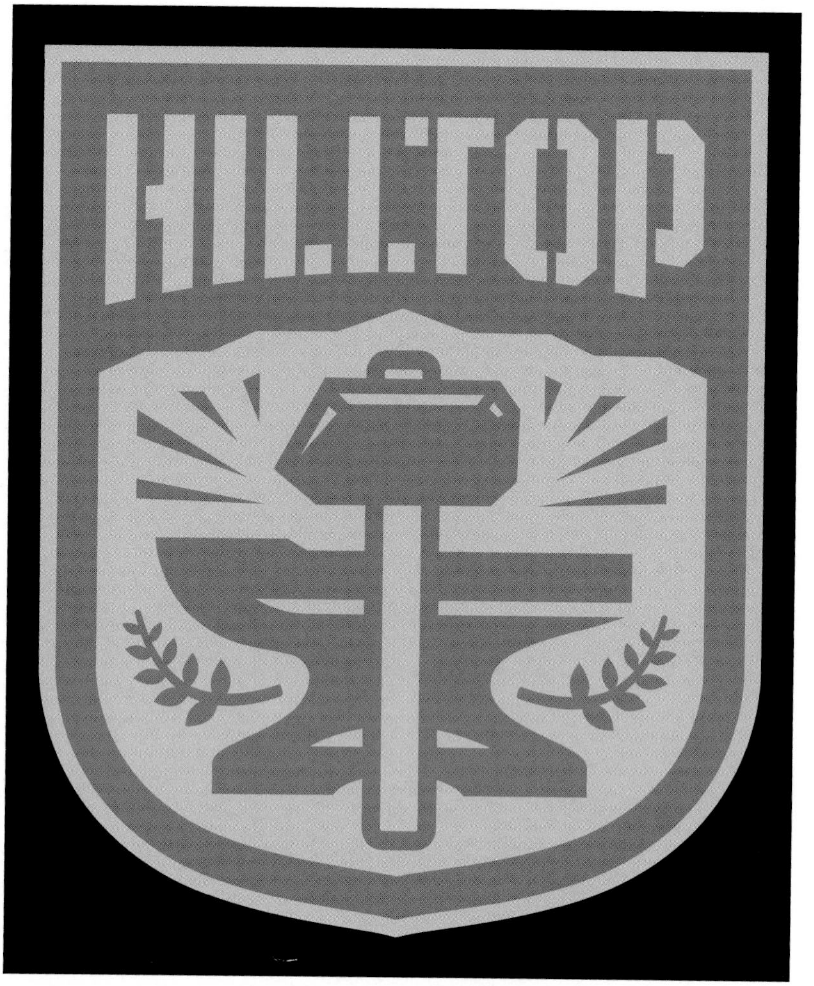
HILLTOP

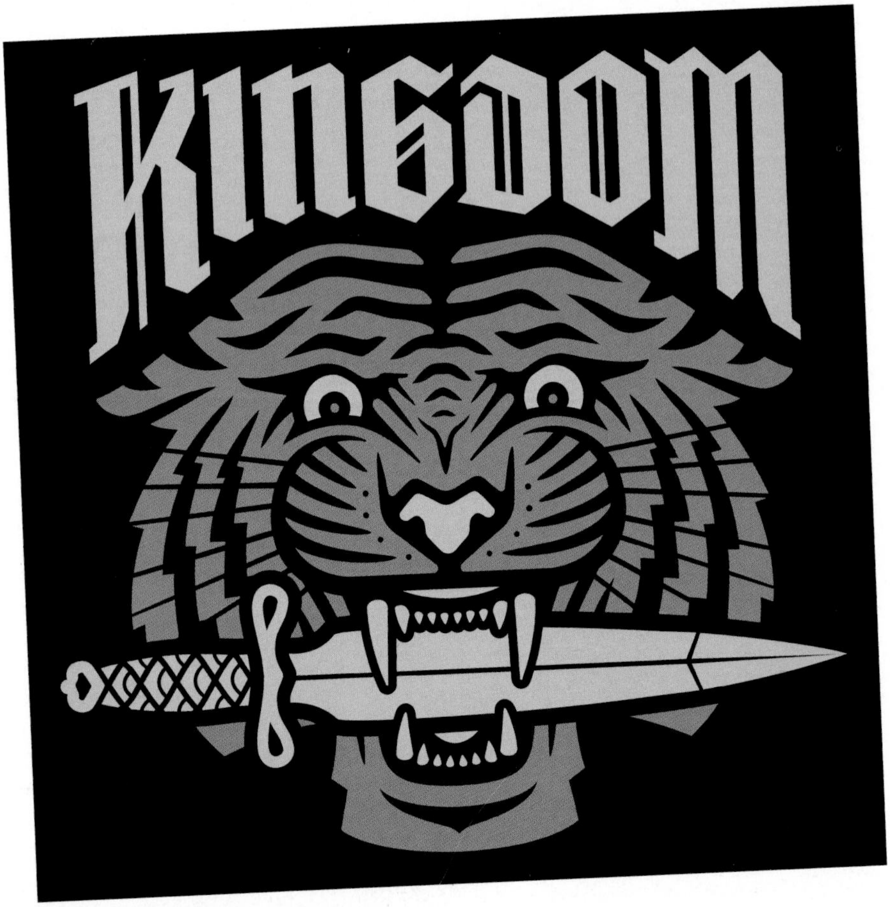
KINGDOM

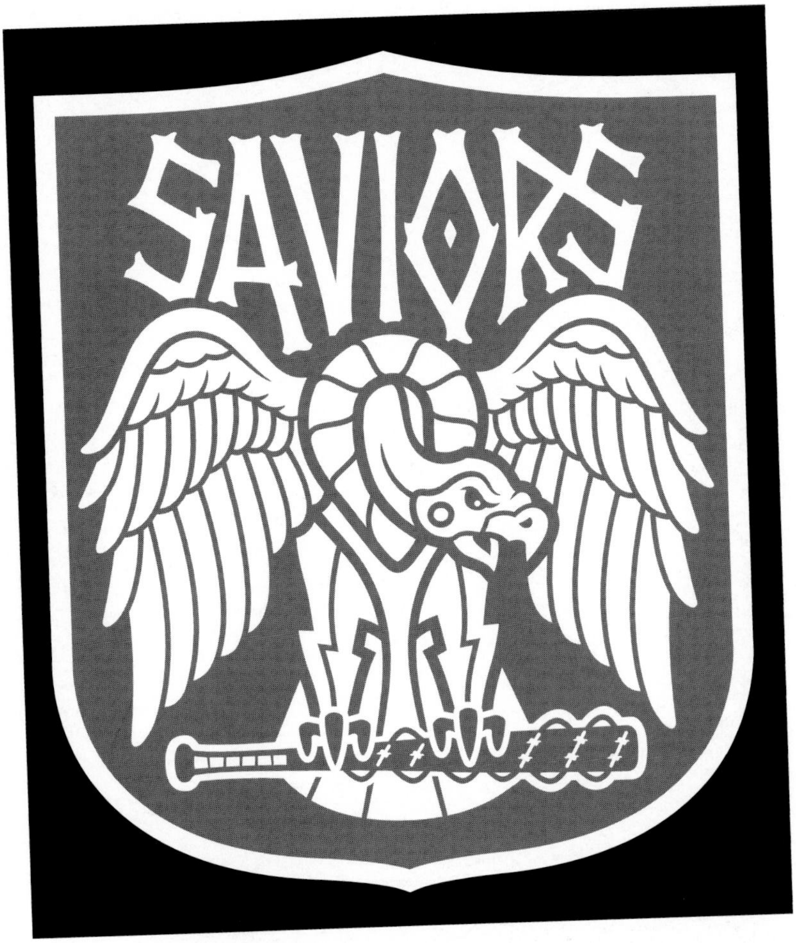
SAVIORS

So we started selling t-shirts, hats and messenger bags that all feature these cool logos.

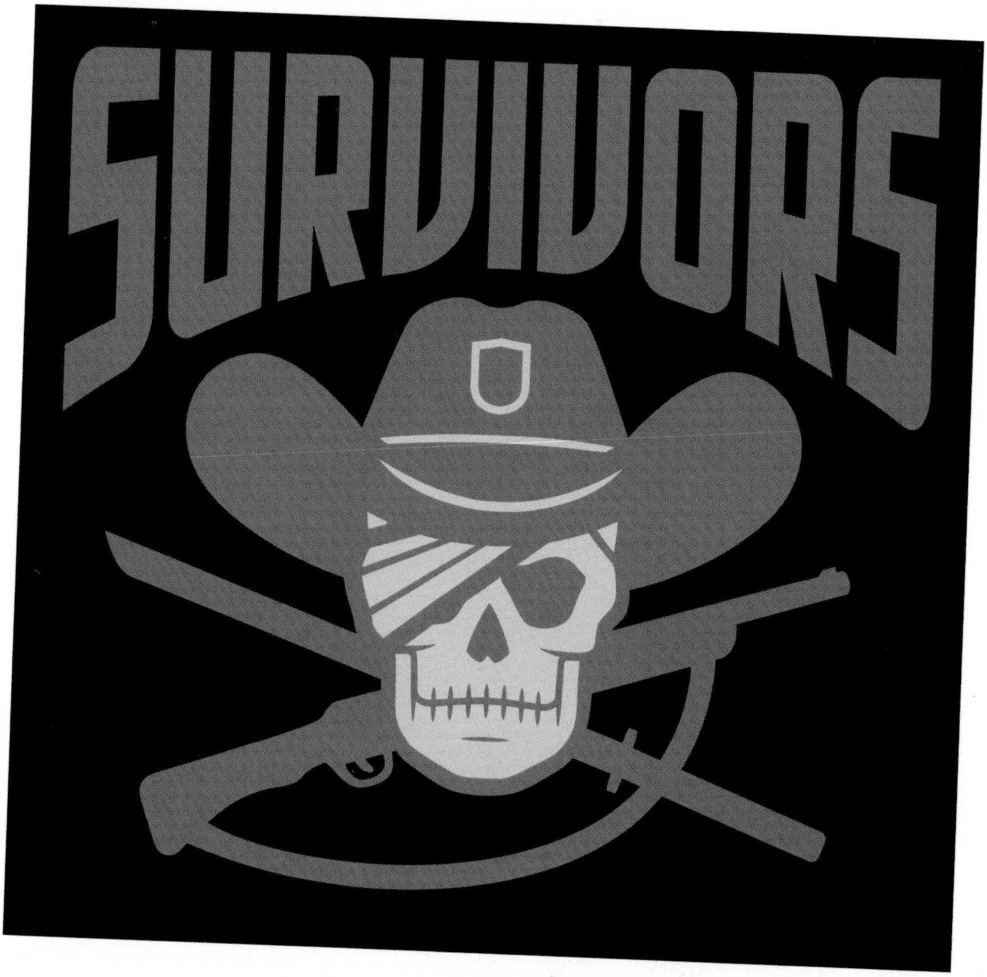
SURVIVORS

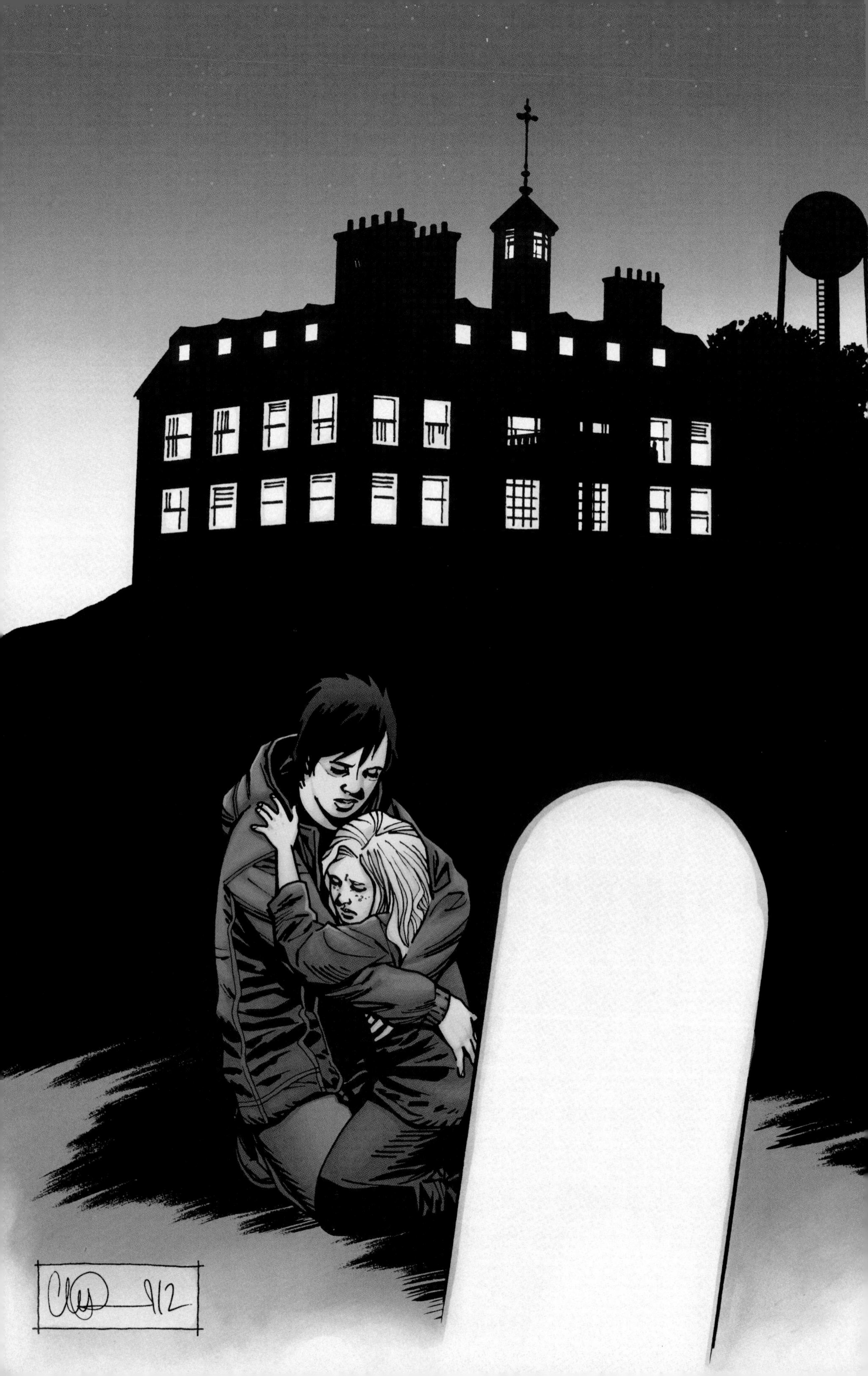

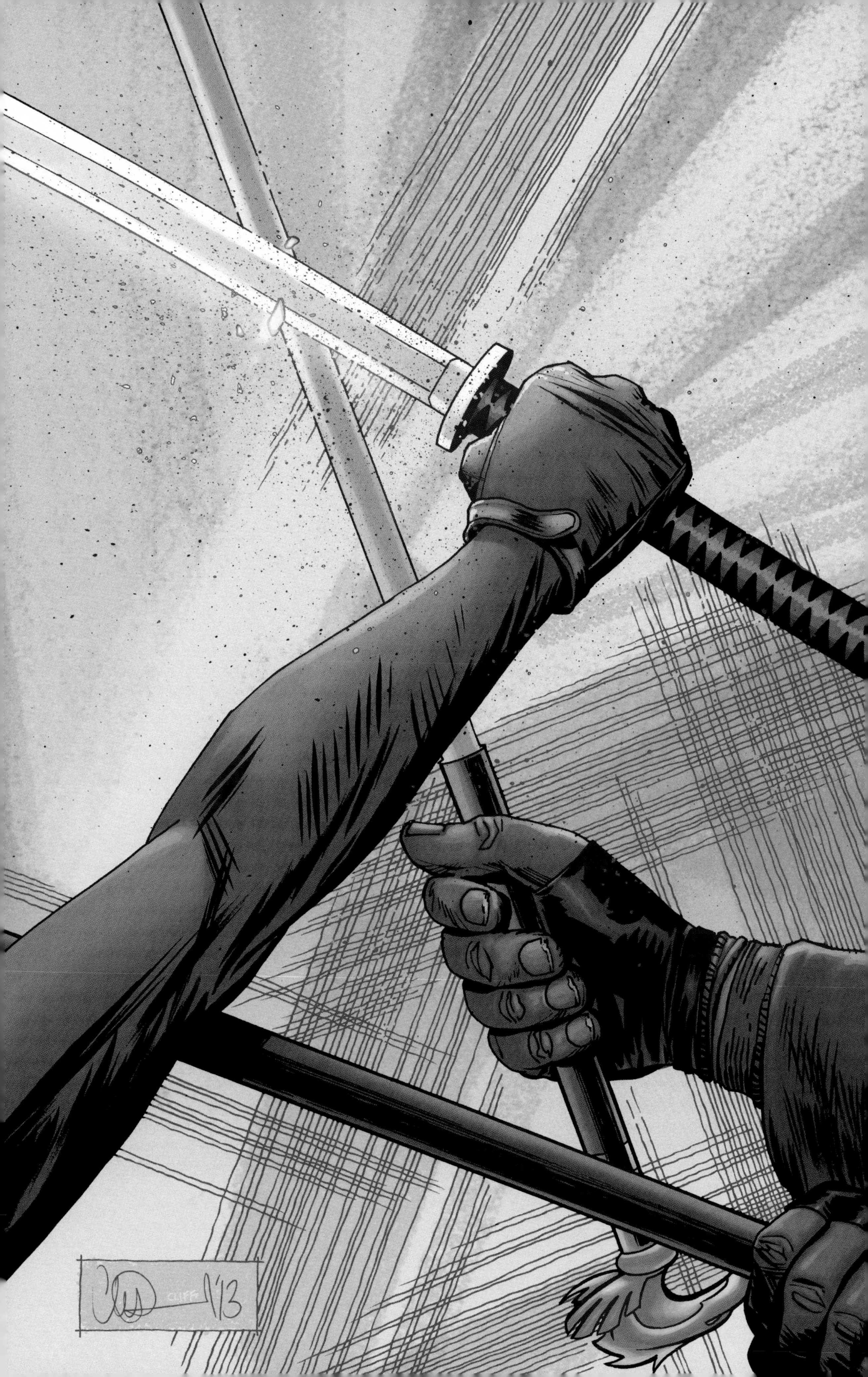
CLIFF 1'13

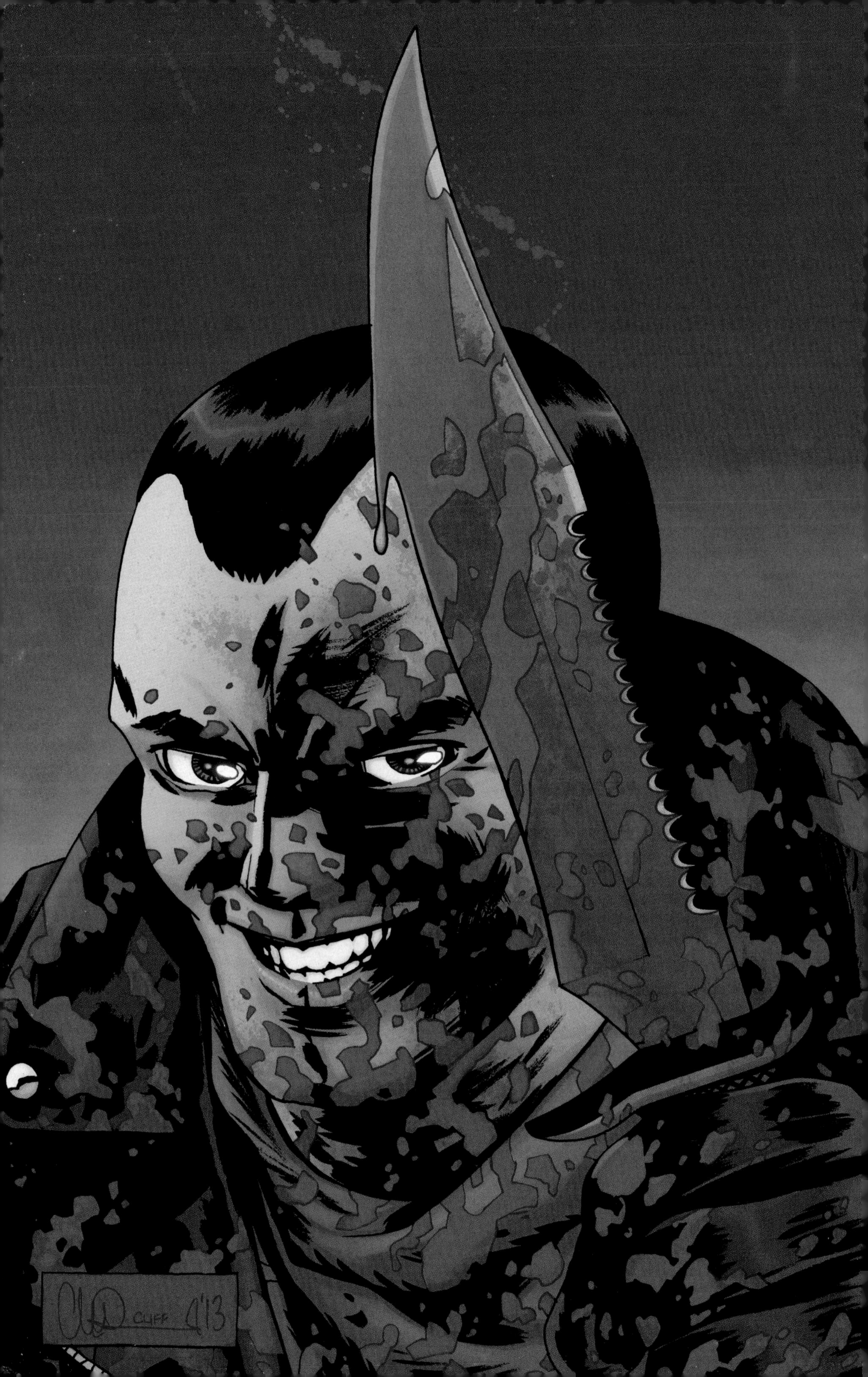
CLIFF

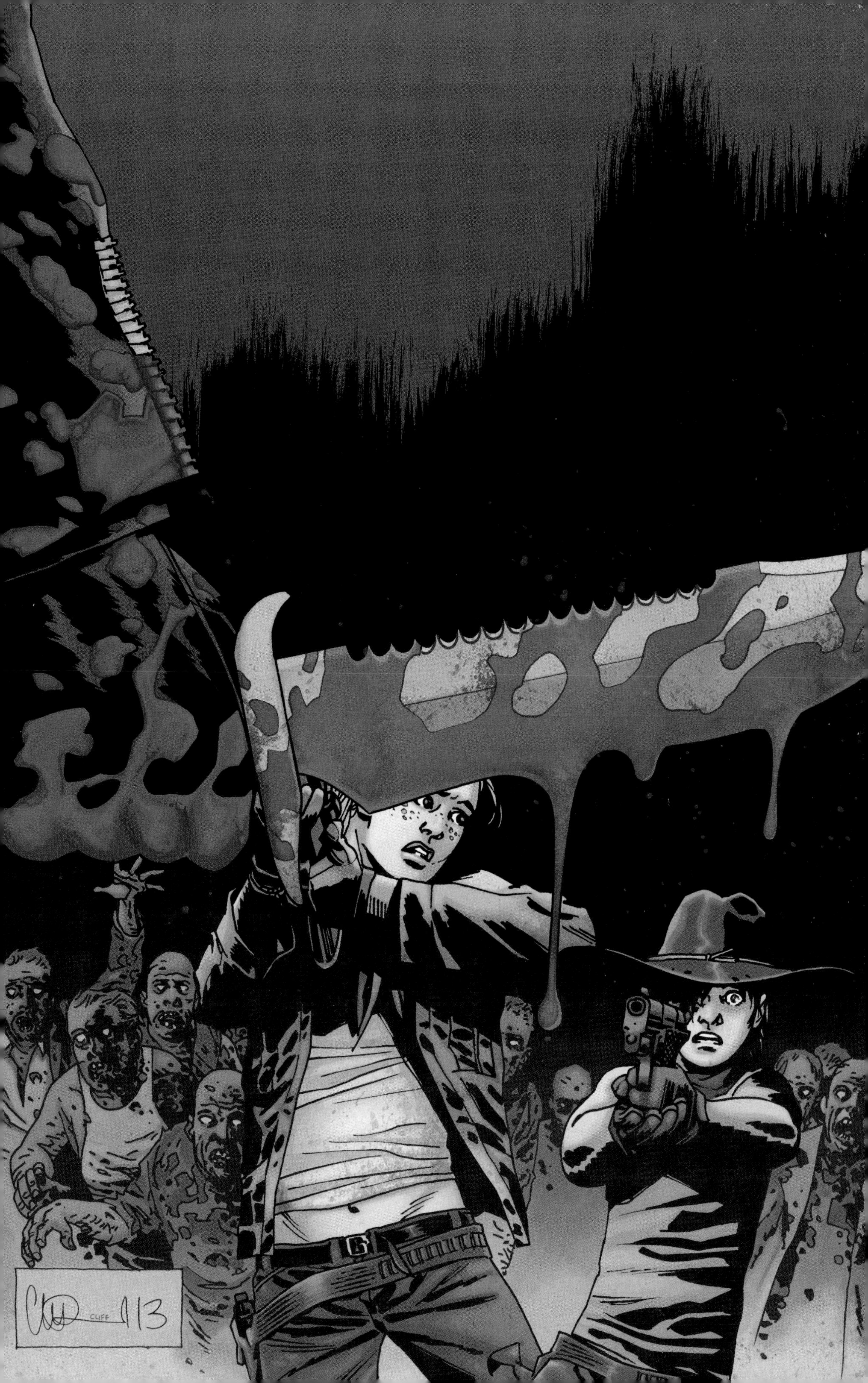

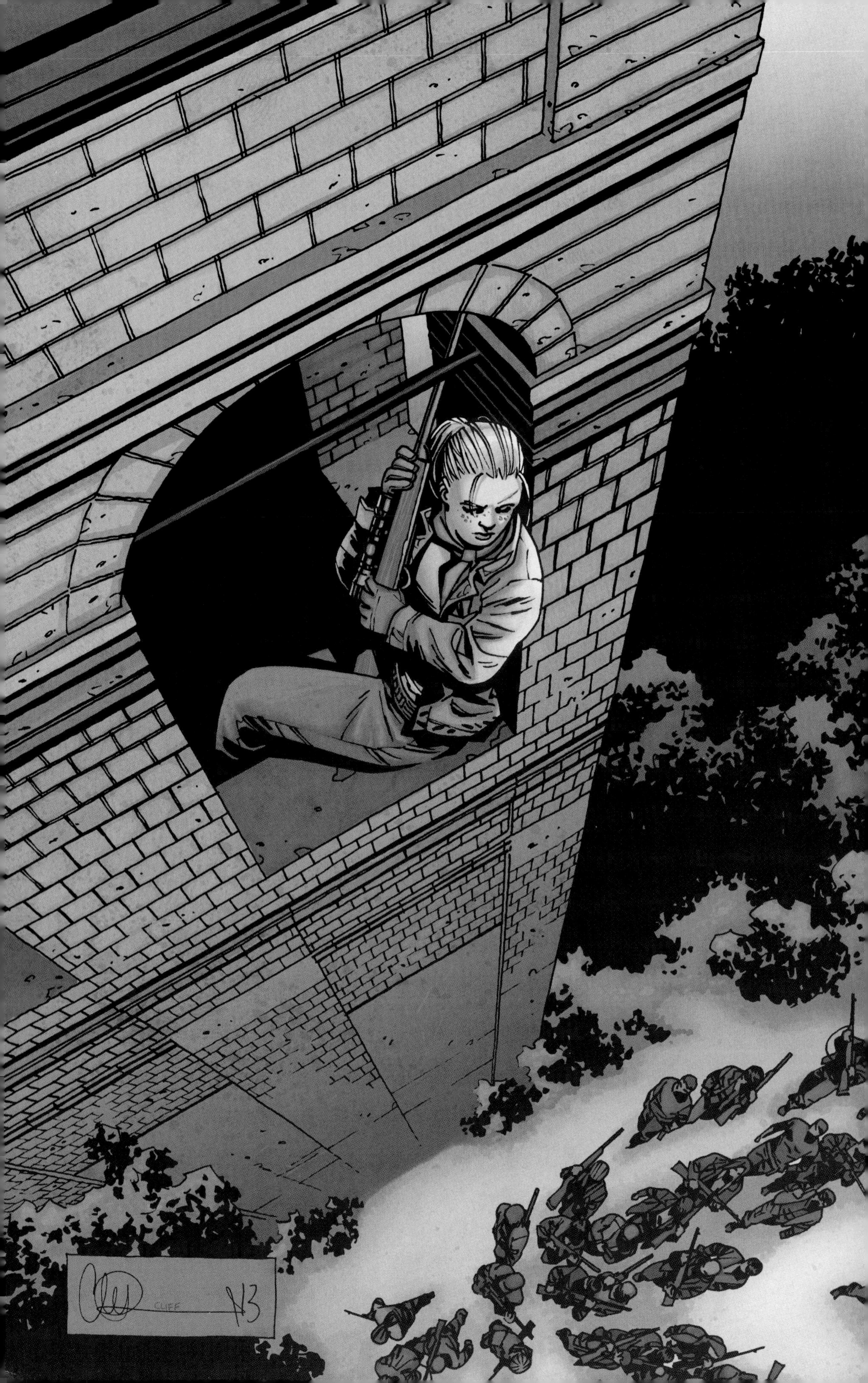

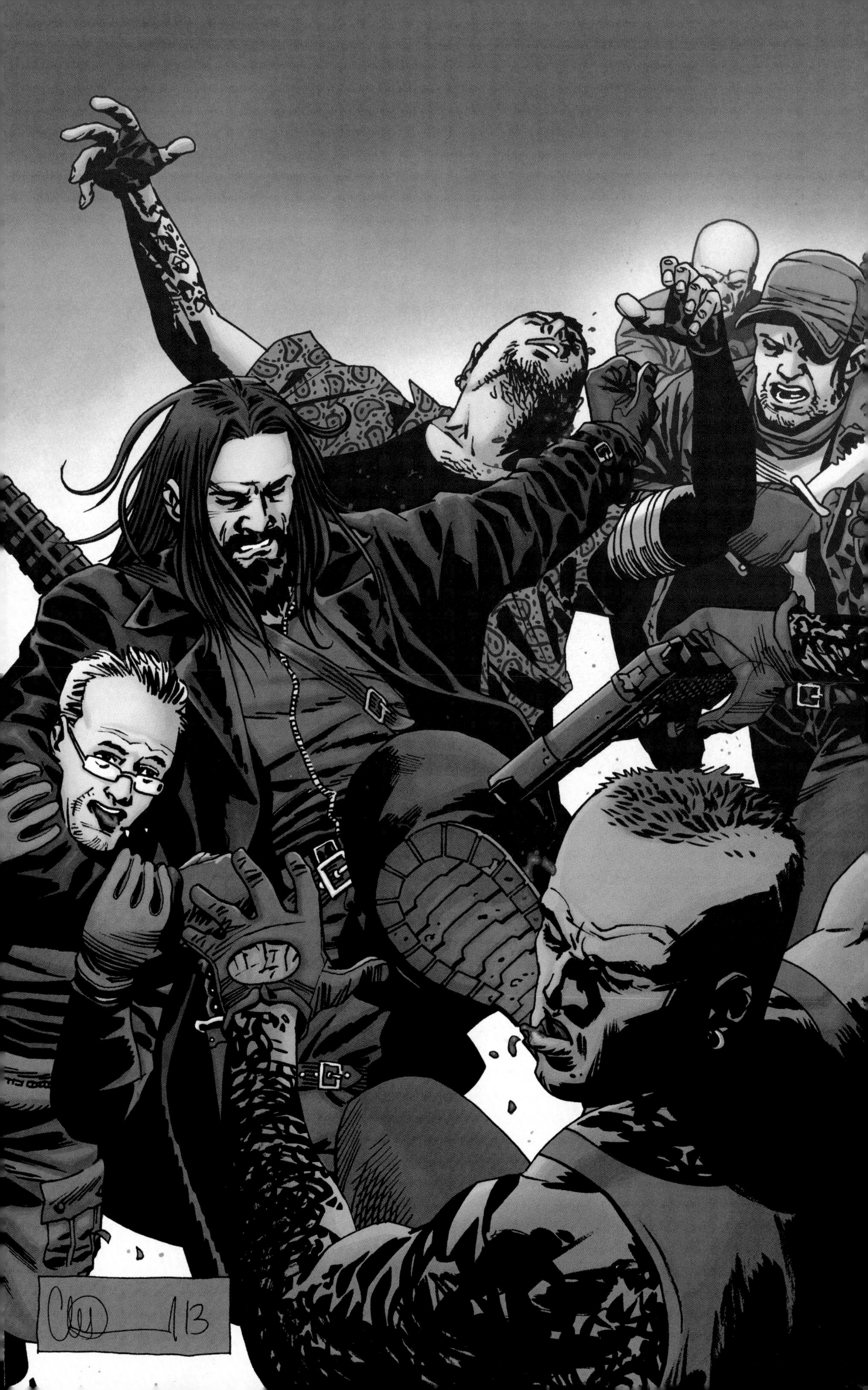

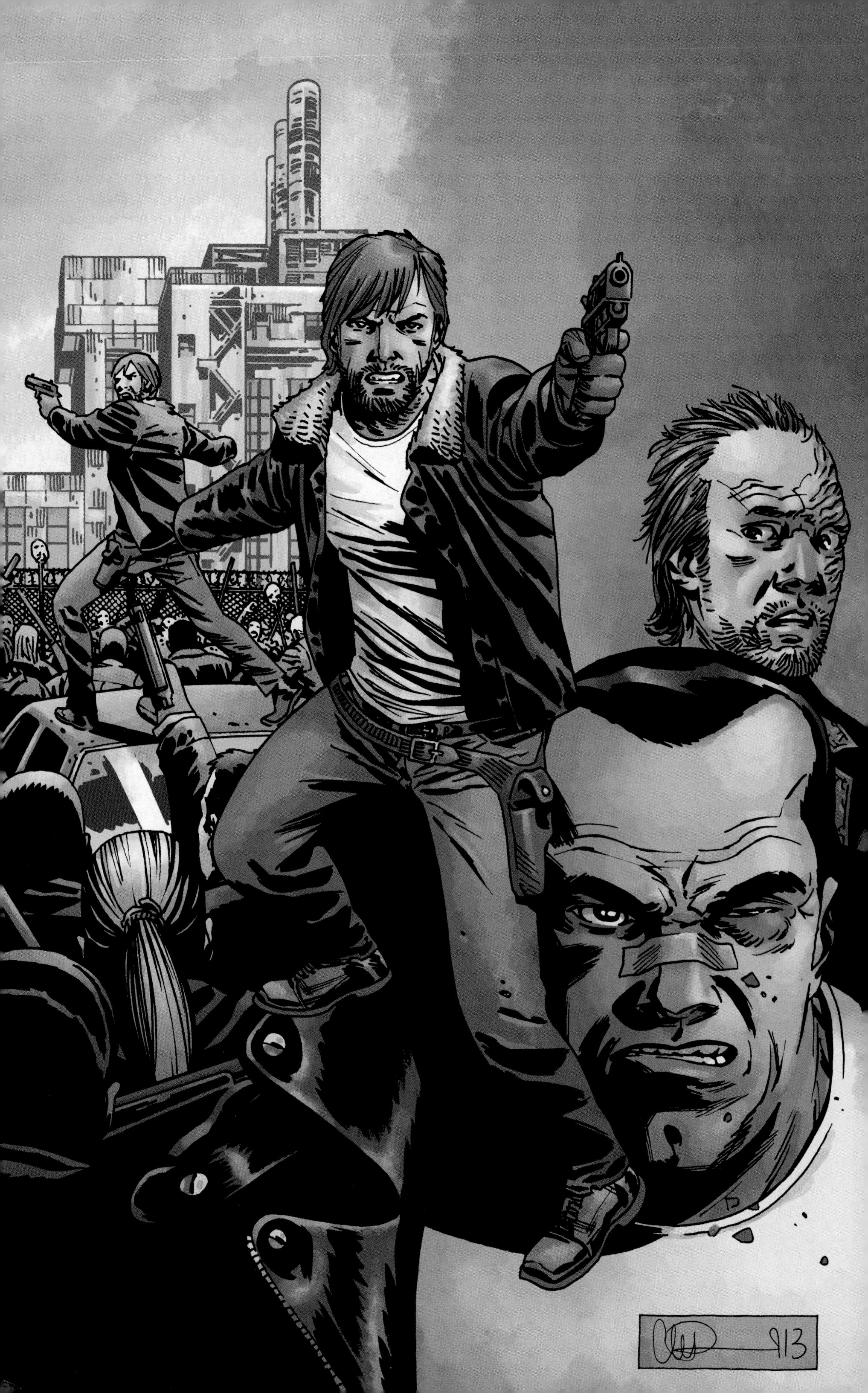

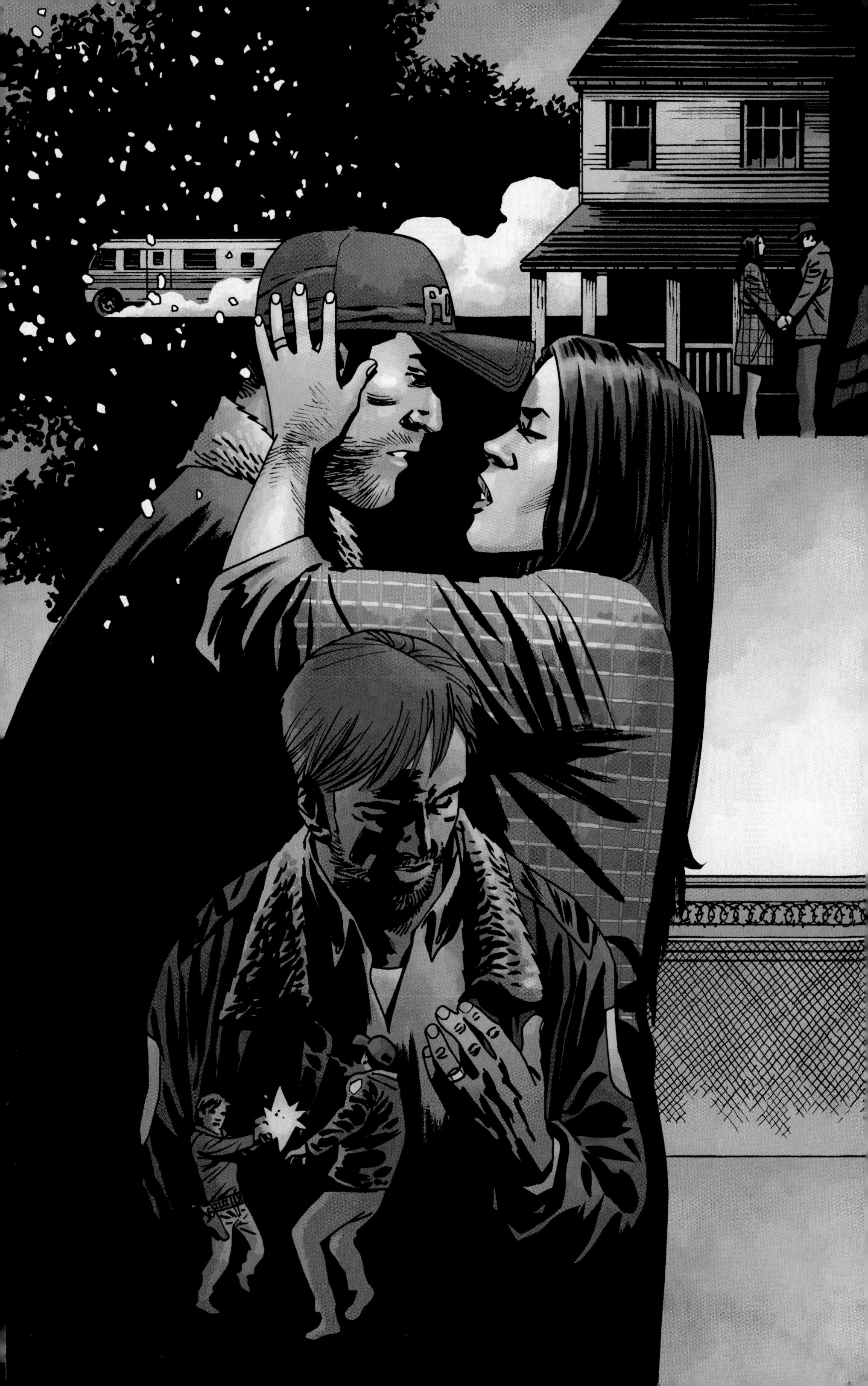

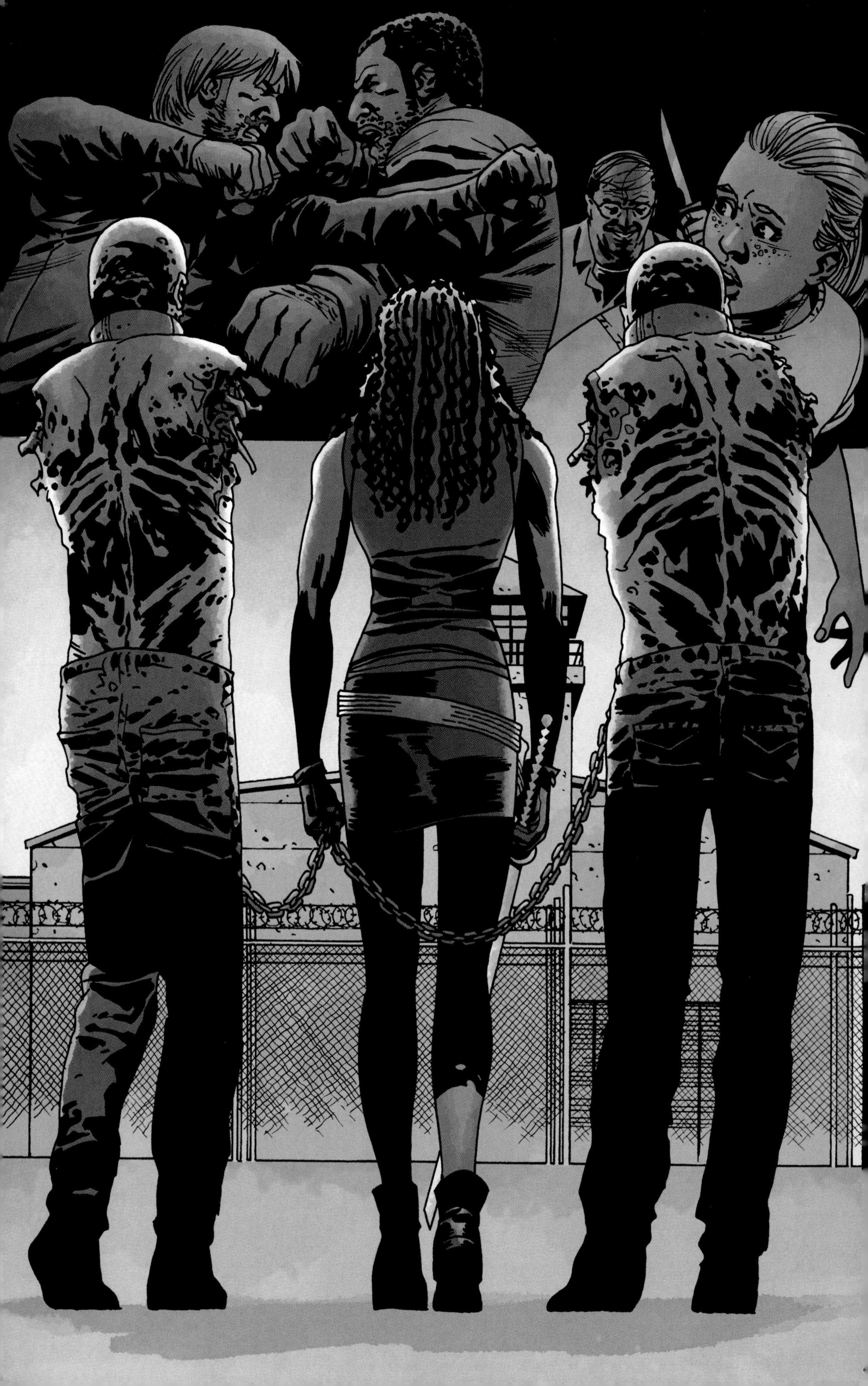

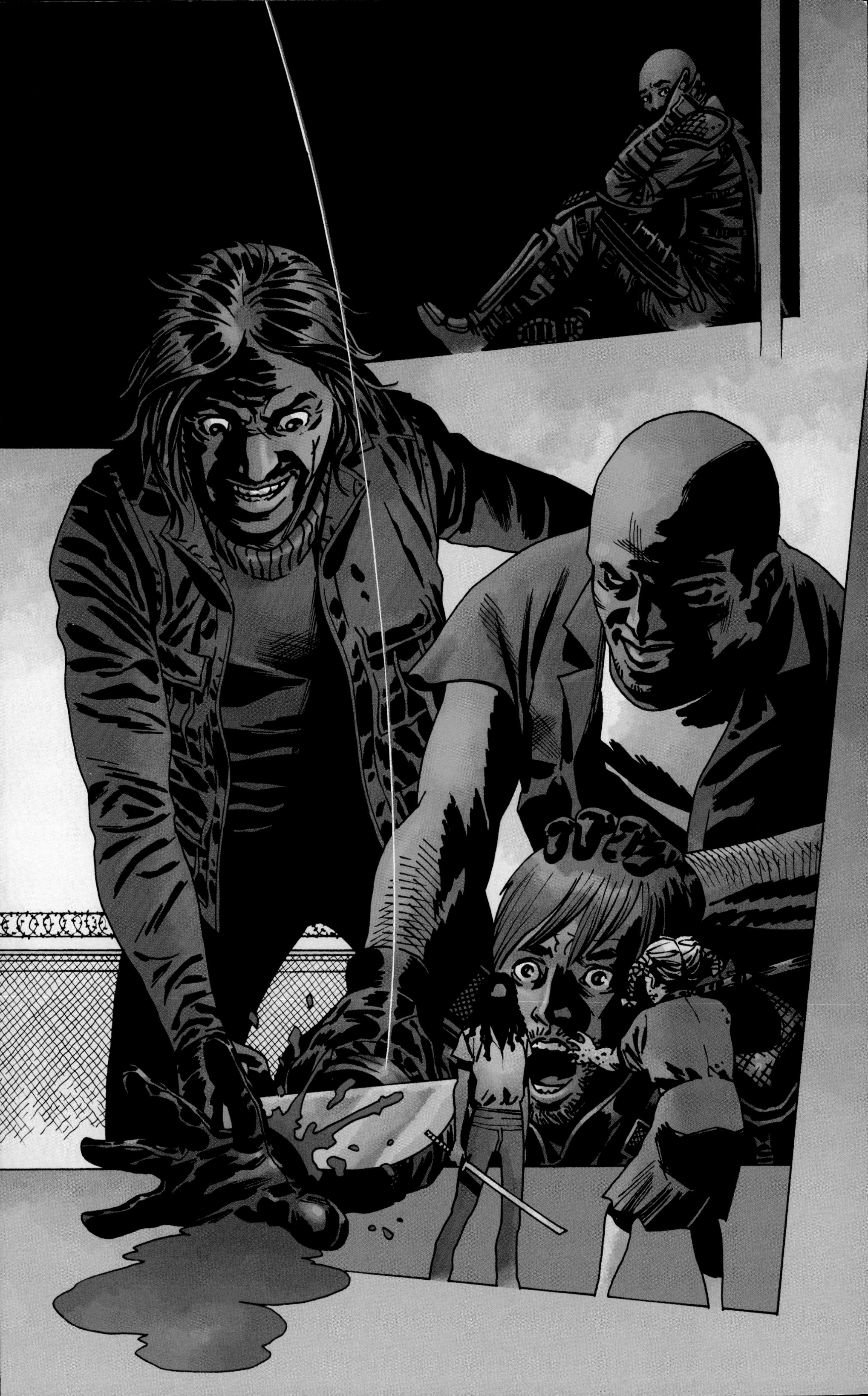

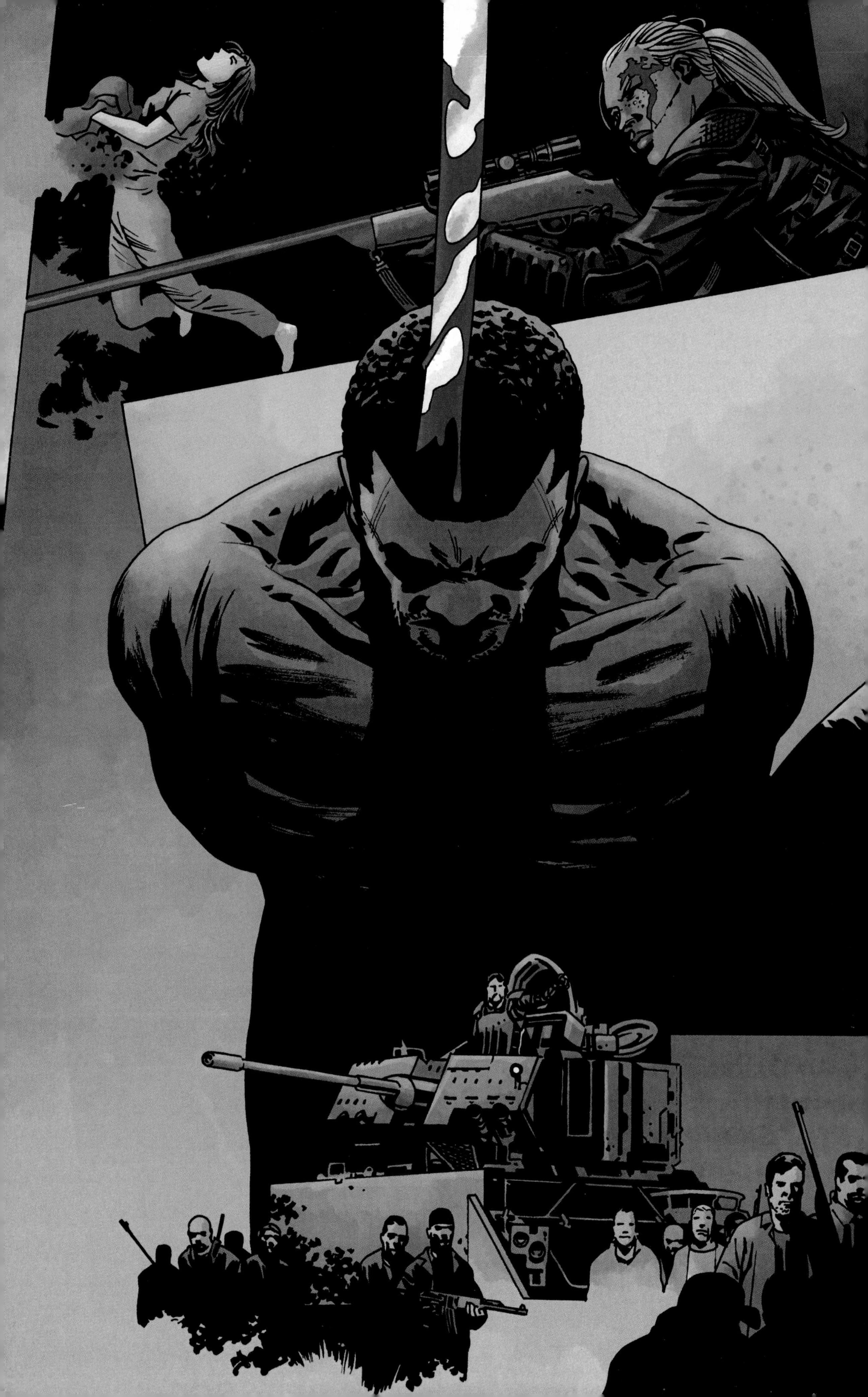

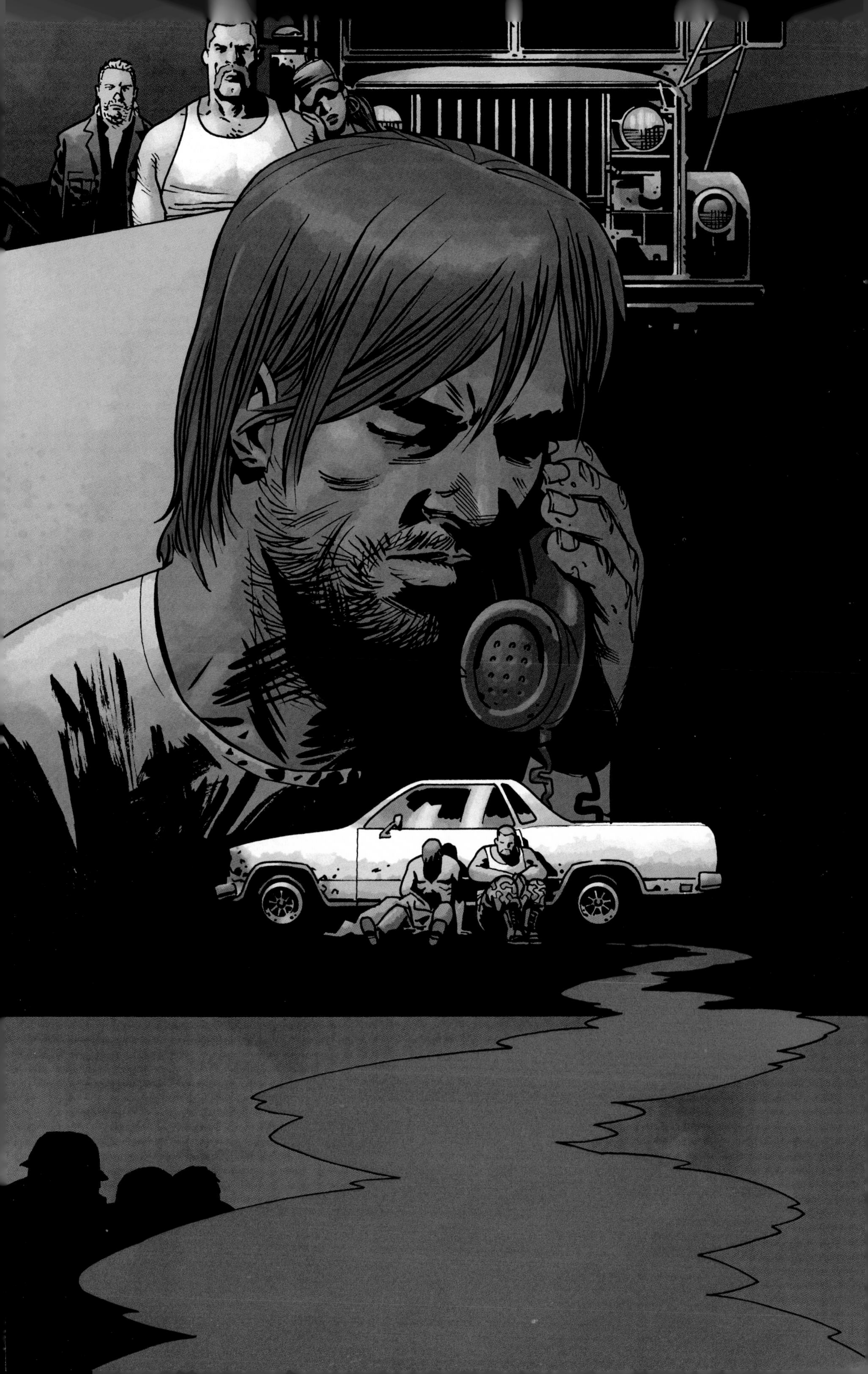

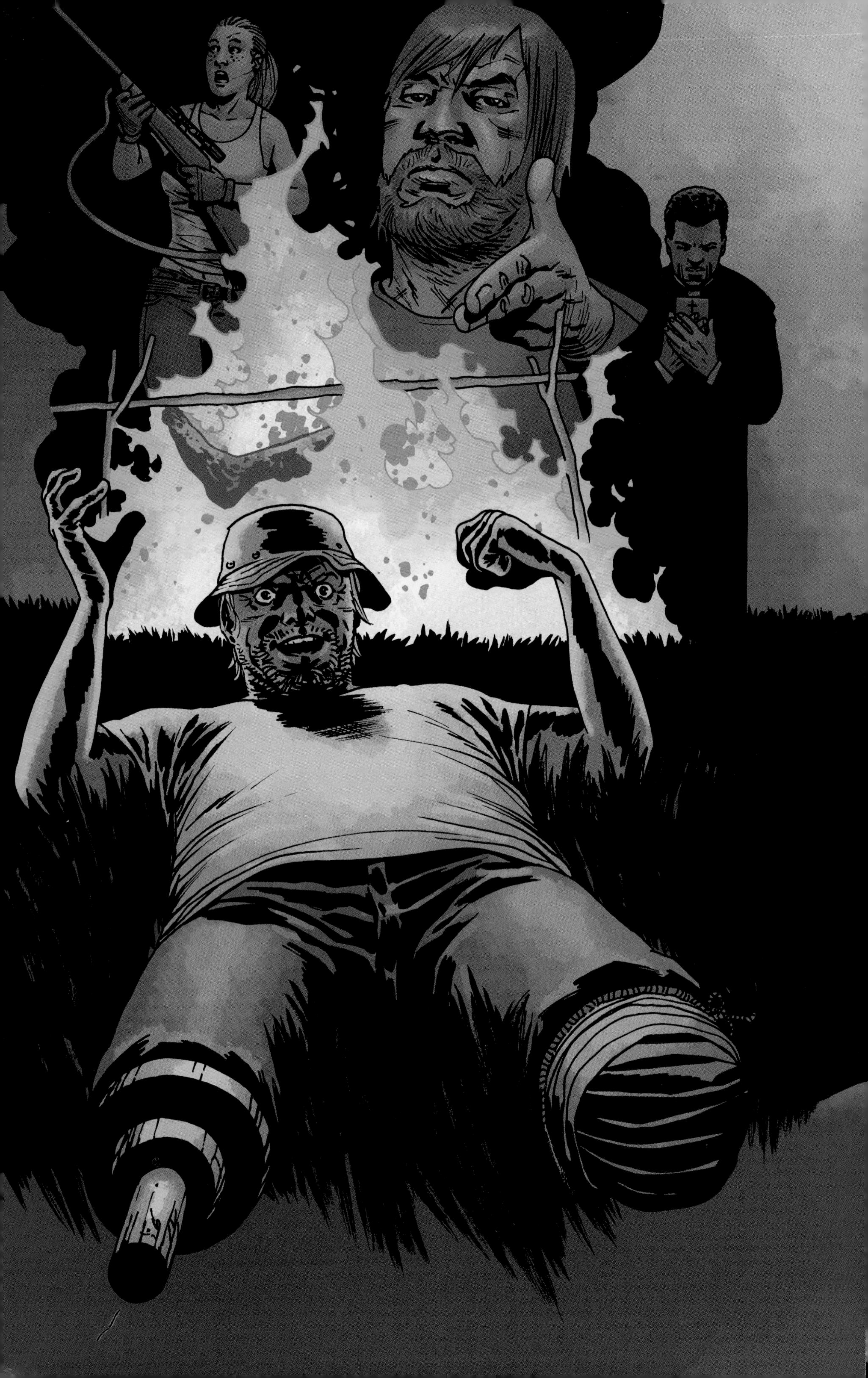

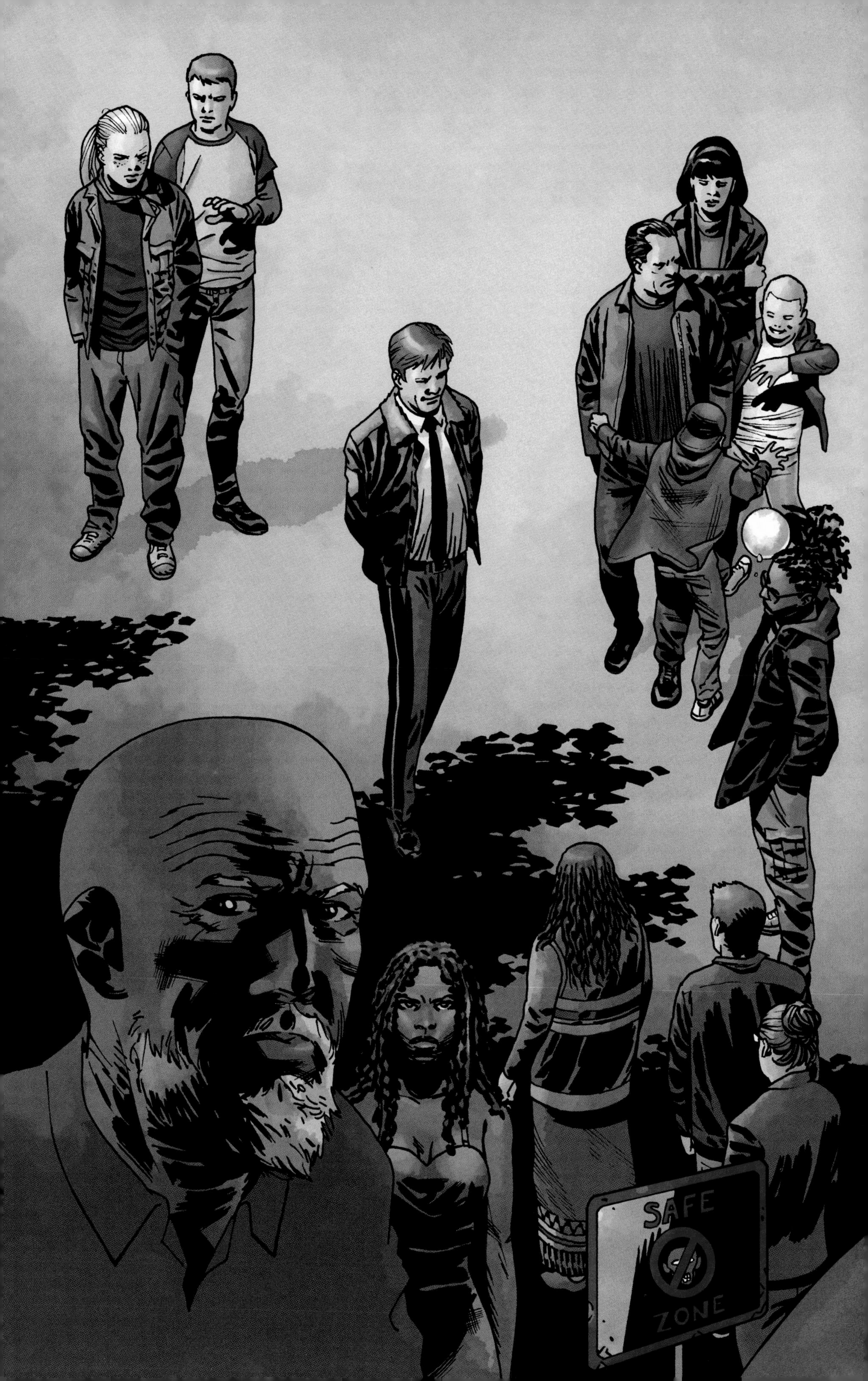
SAFE
ZONE

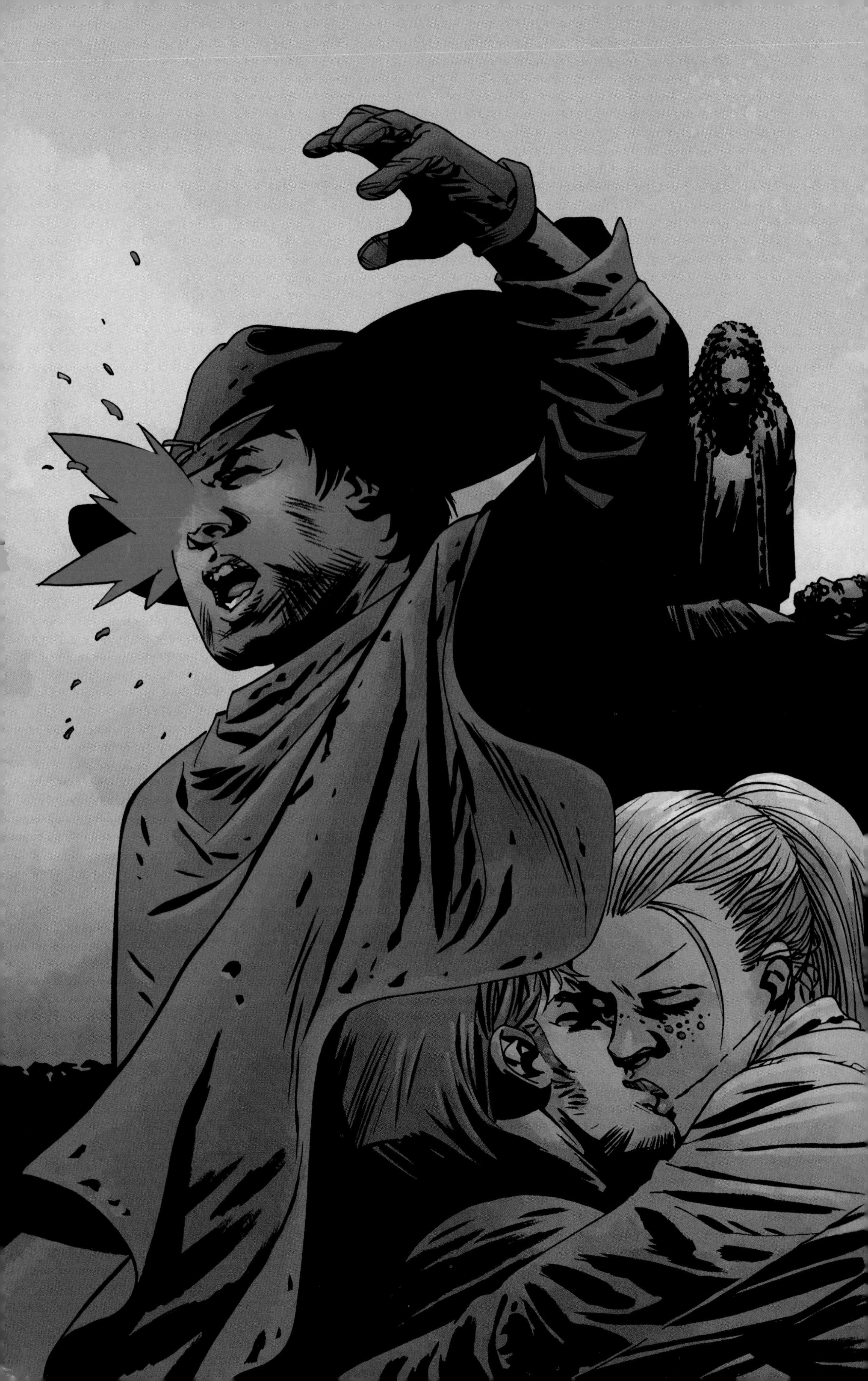

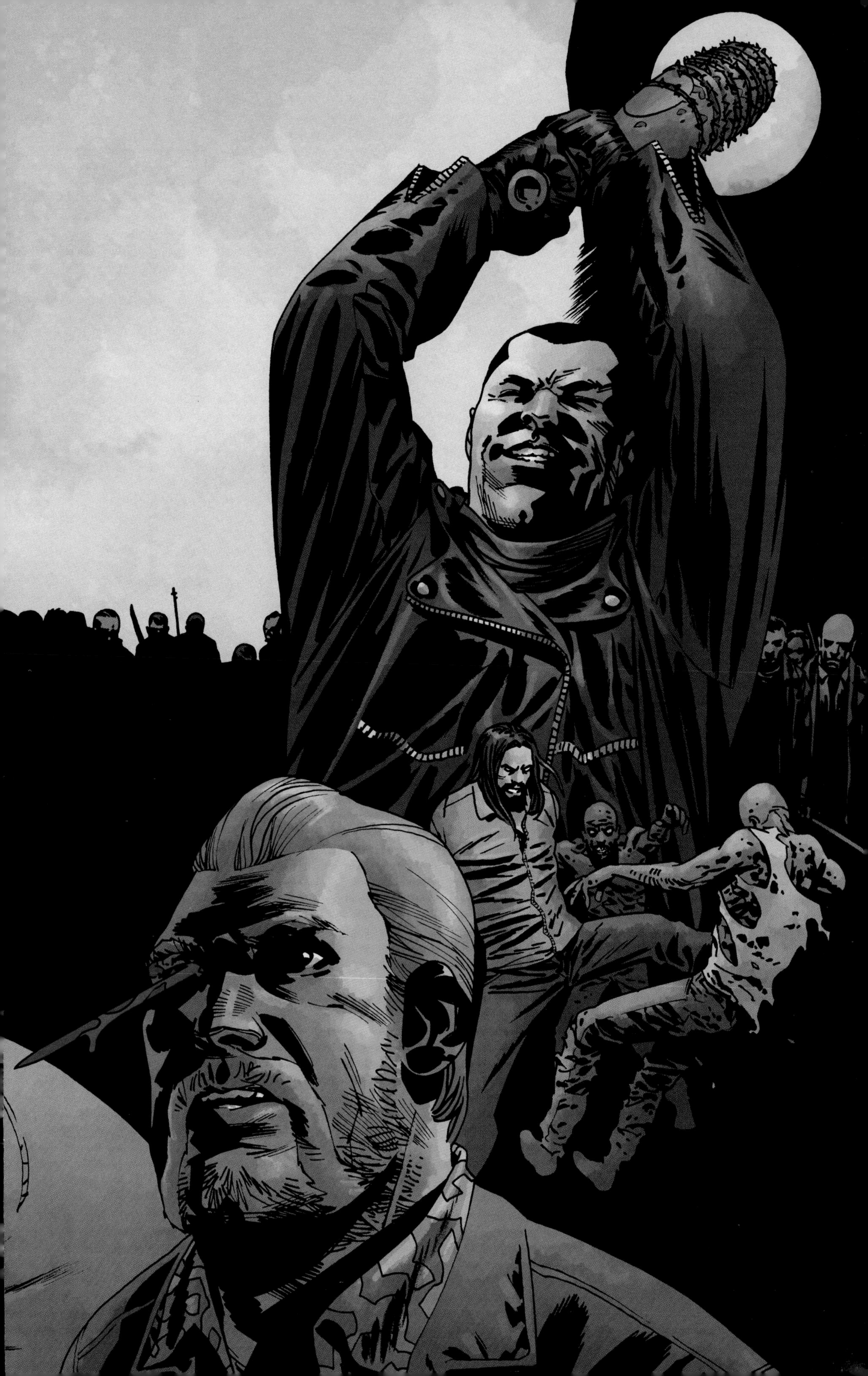

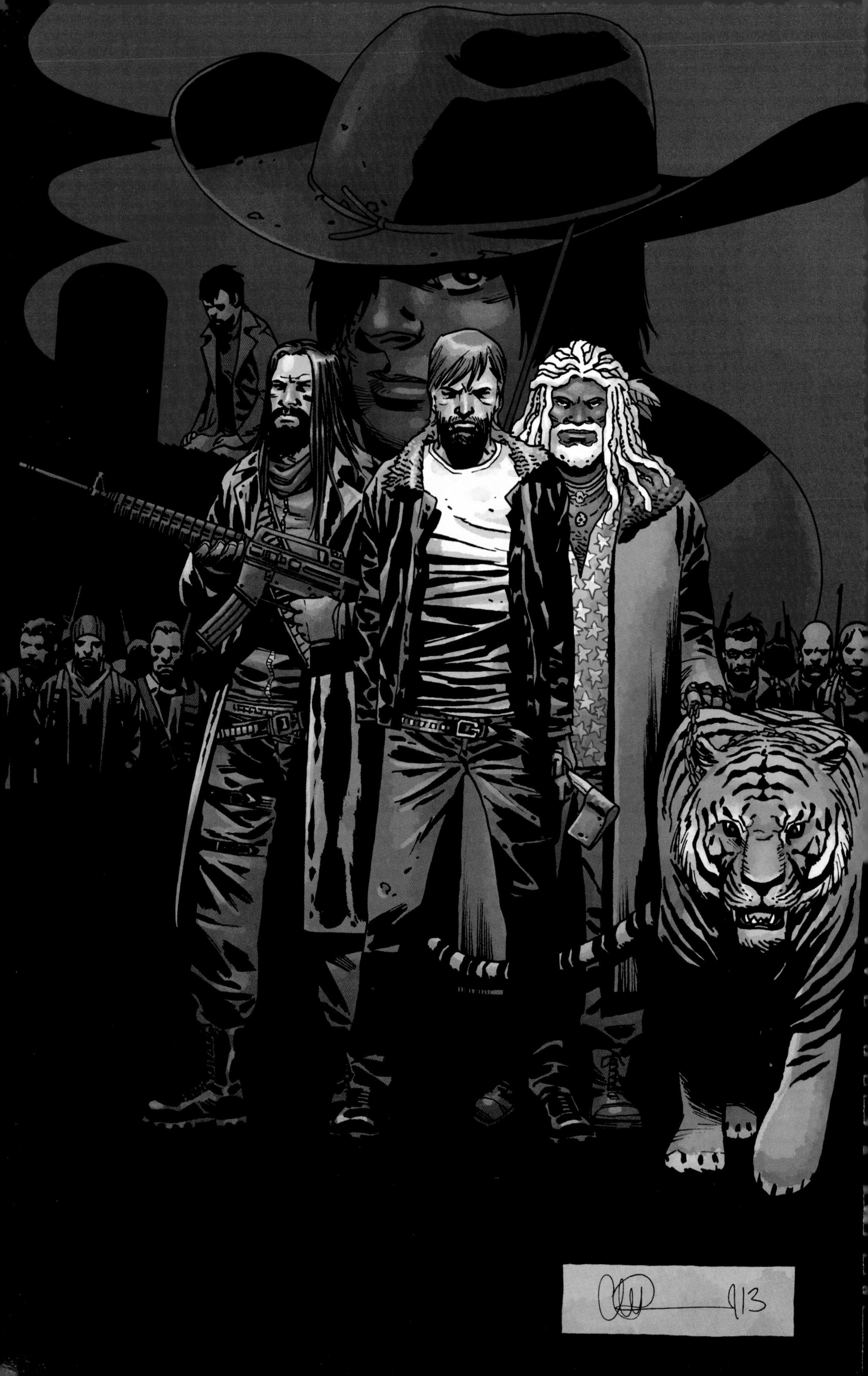

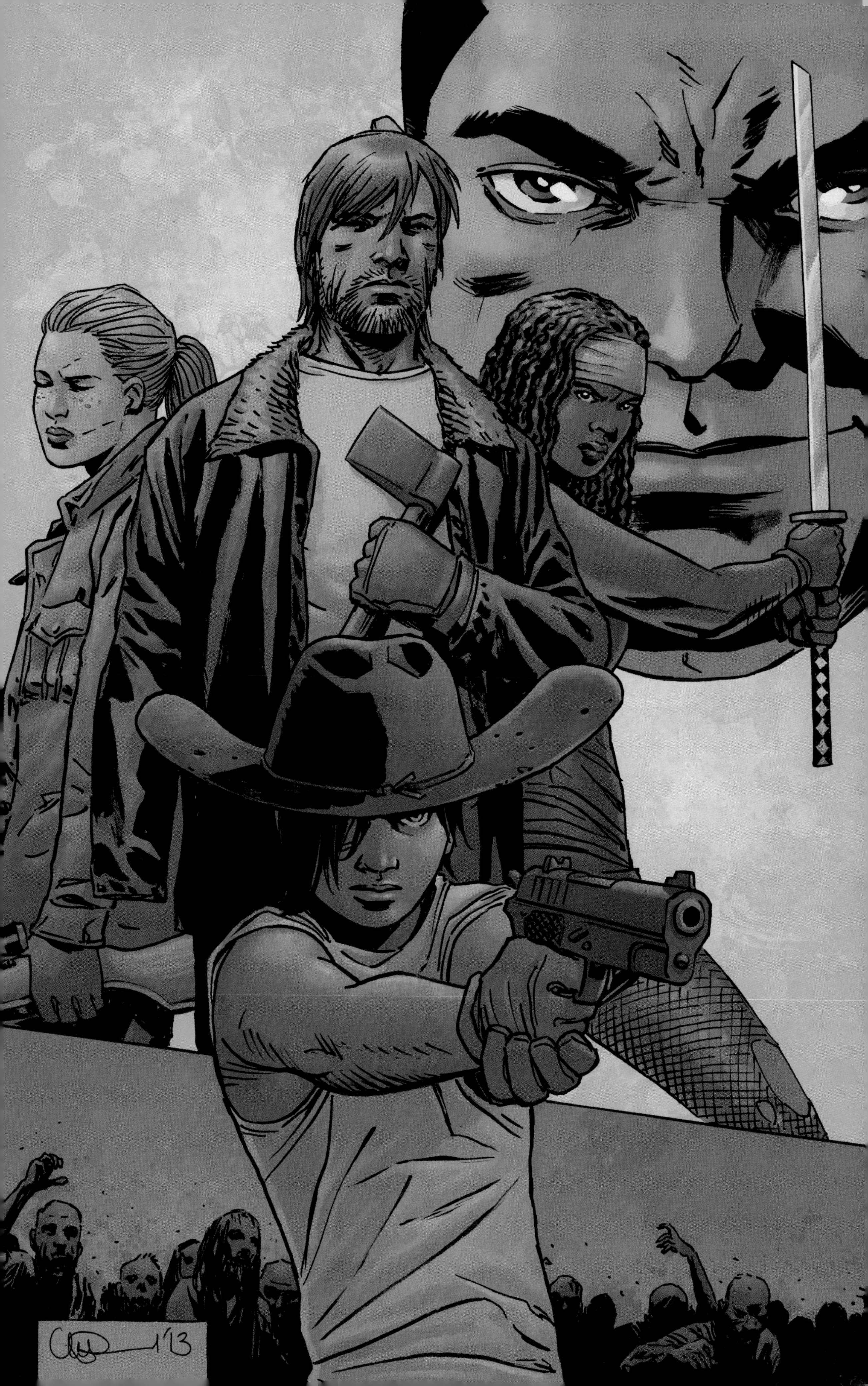

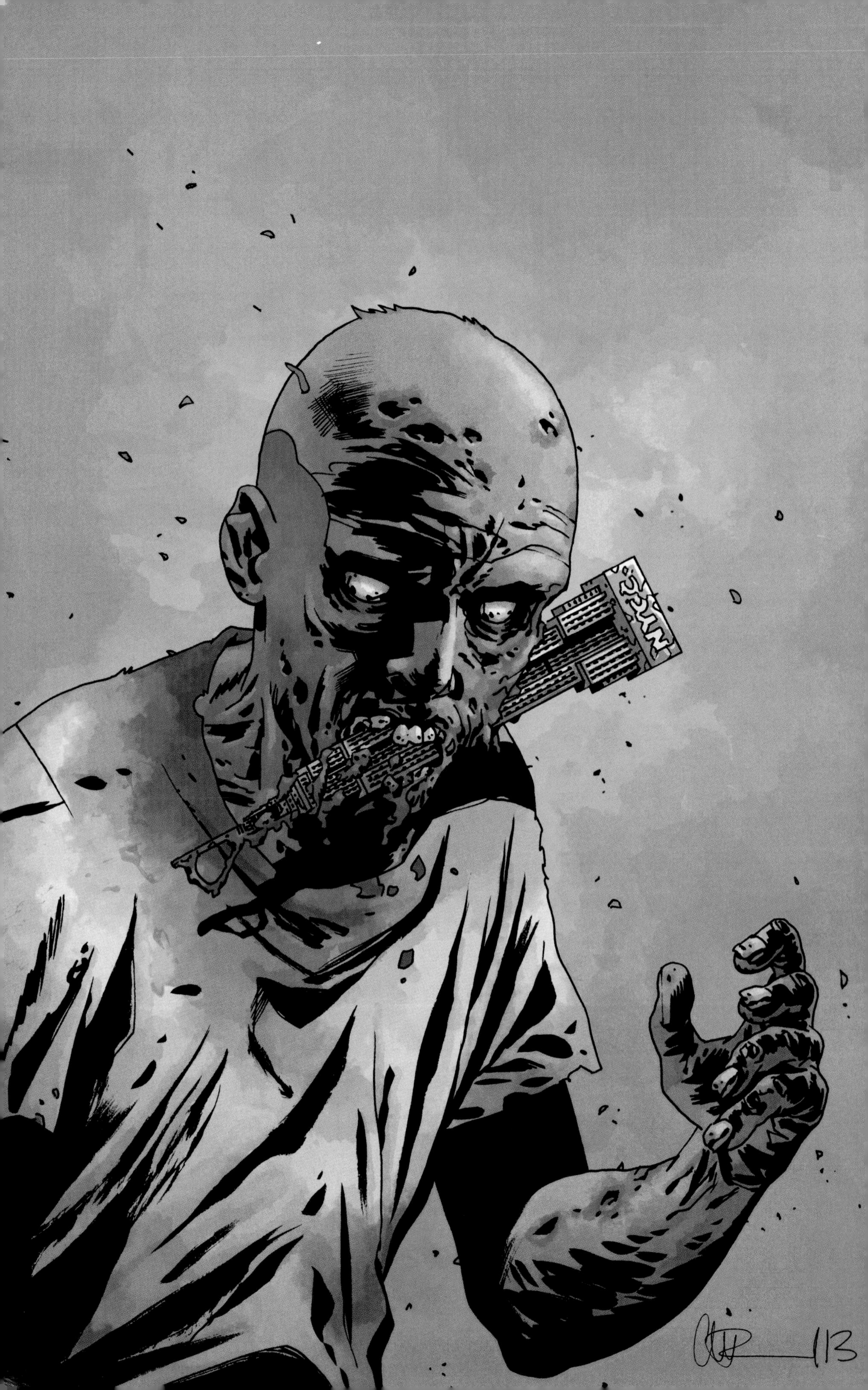
113

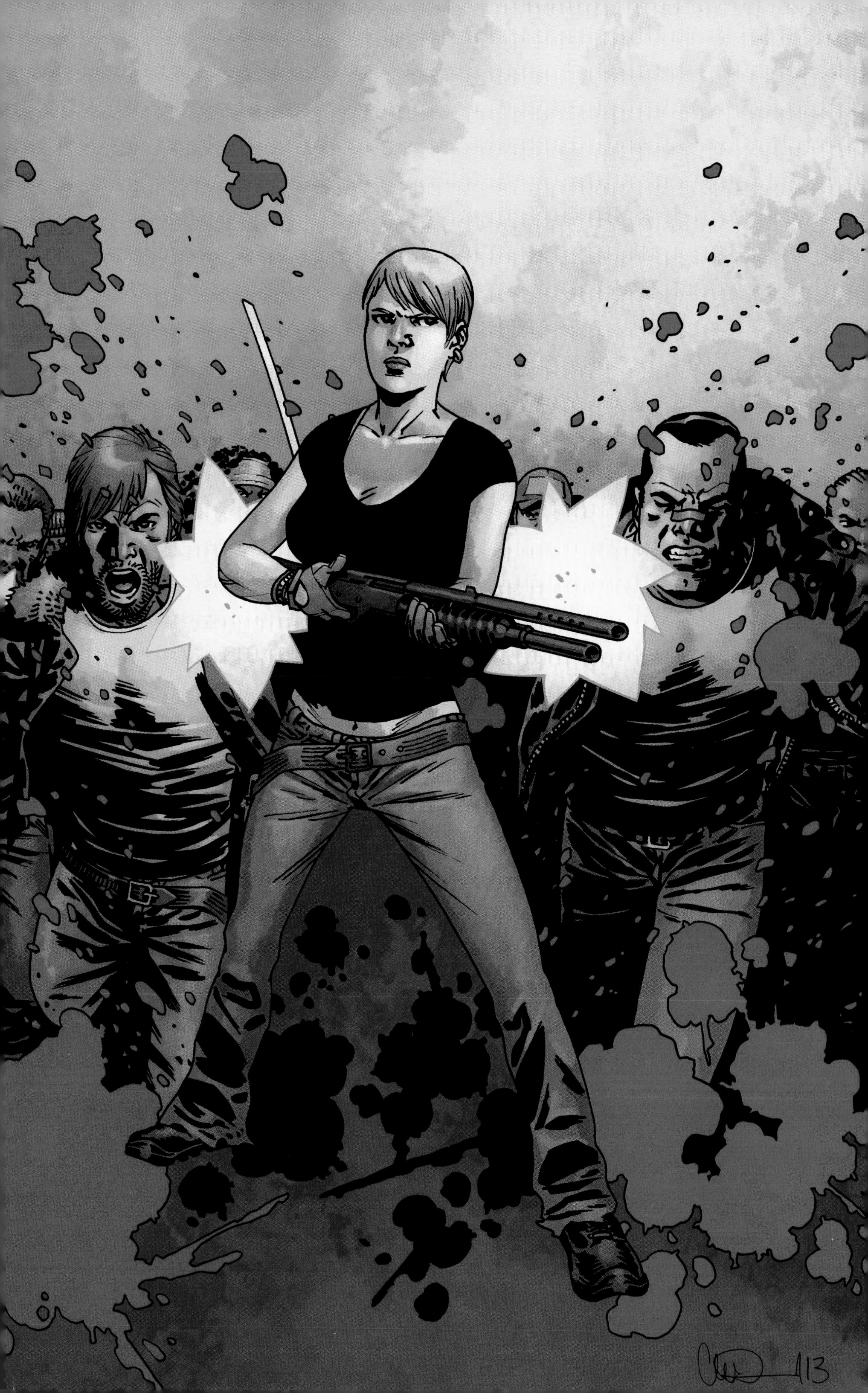

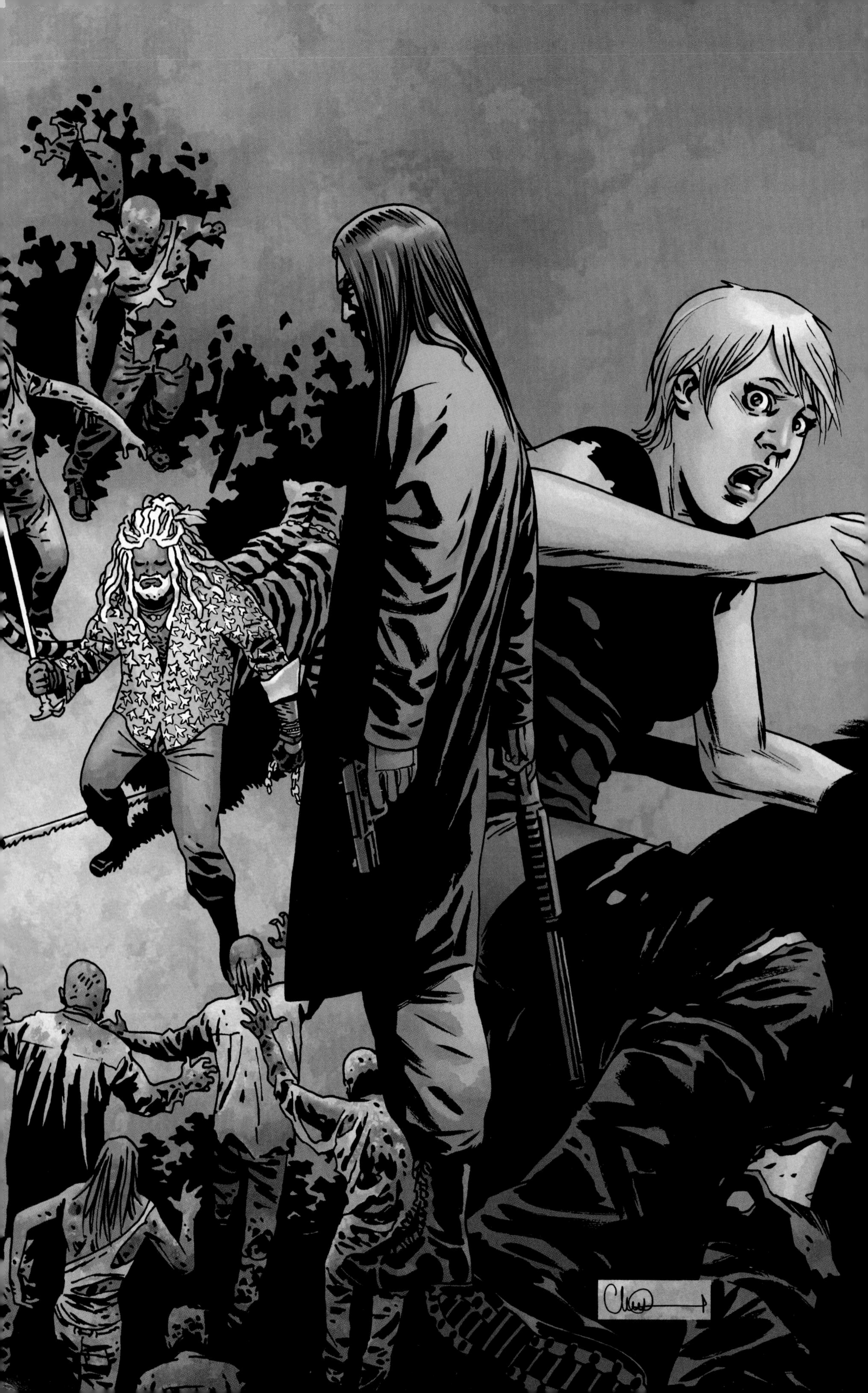

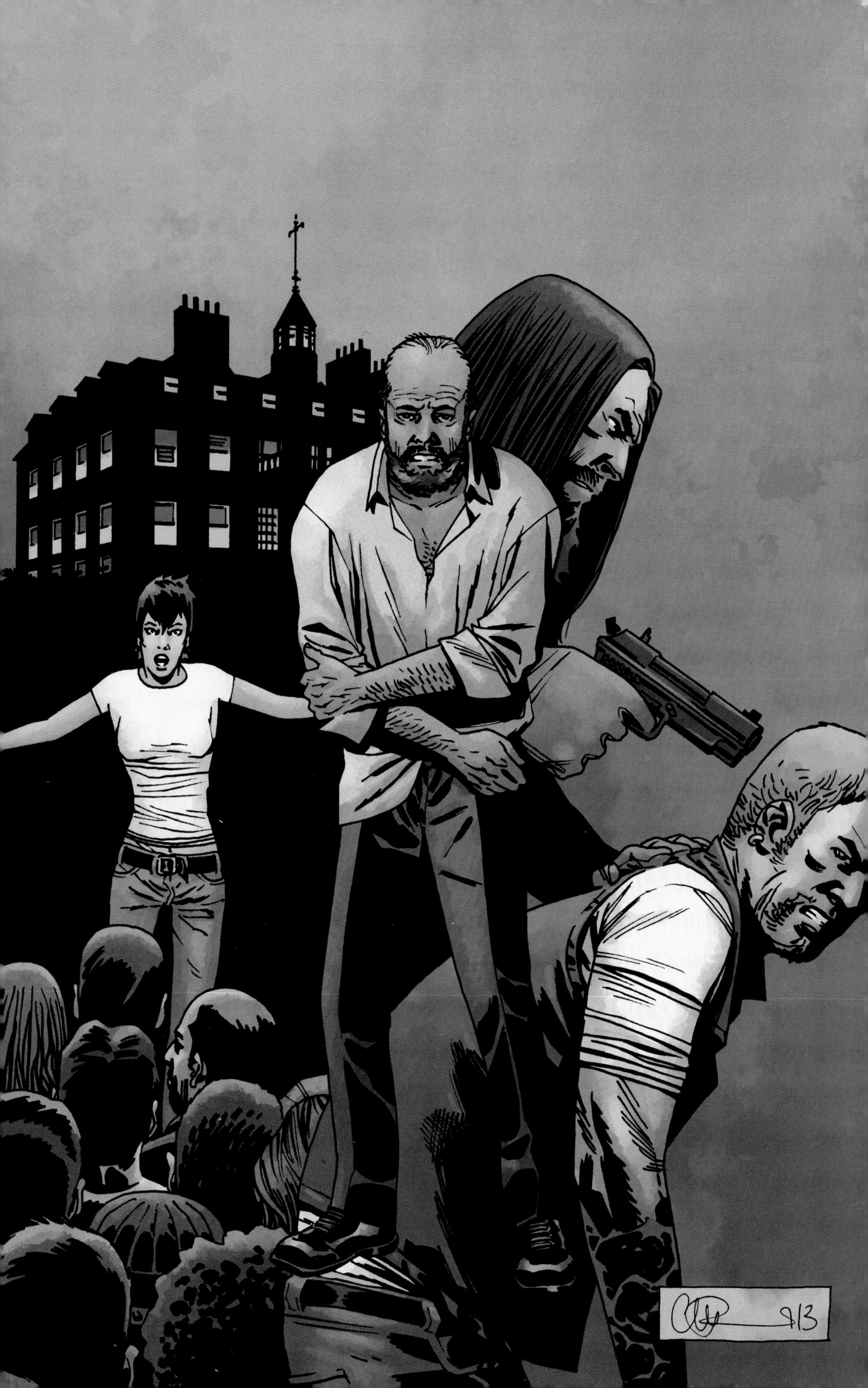

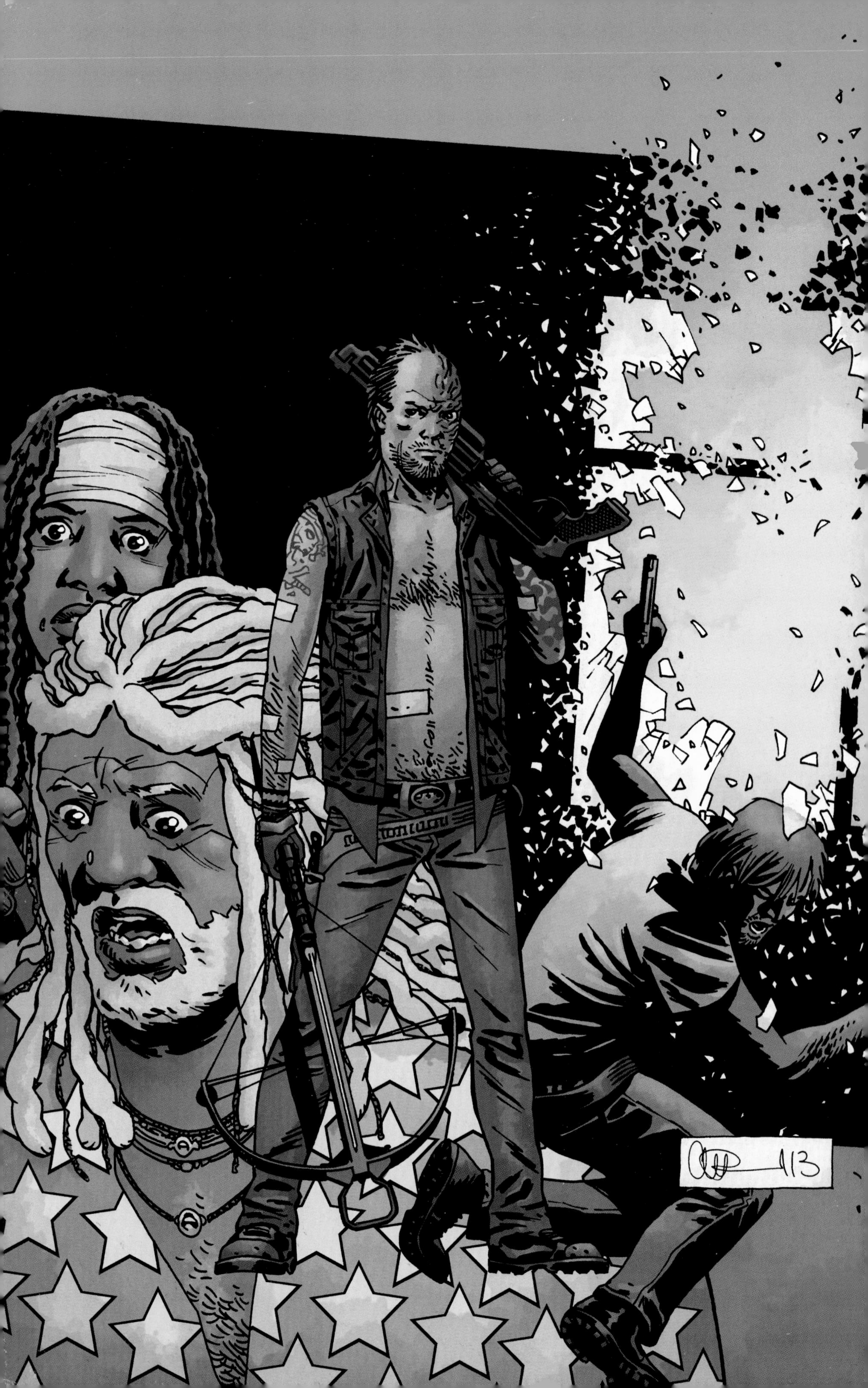